Say no More

Karen ROSE

Say no More

HEADLINE

First published in 2020 by
HEADLINE PUBLISHING GROUP

1

Cataloguing in Publication Data is available from the British Library

Hardback ISBN 978 1 4722 6570 8
Trade Paperback ISBN 978 1 4722 6569 2

Typeset in Palatino by Avon DataSet Ltd, Arden Court, Alcester, Warwickshire

Printed and bound in Great Britain by Clays Ltd, Elcograf S.p.A.

Headline's policy is to use papers that are natural, renewable and recyclable
products and made from wood grown in well-managed forests and other
controlled sources. The logging and manufacturing processes are expected to
conform to the environmental regulations of the country of origin.

HEADLINE PUBLISHING GROUP
An Hachette UK Company
Carmelite House
50 Victoria Embankment
London EC4Y 0DZ

www.headline.co.uk
www.hachette.co.uk

To Farrah. Your books warm my heart and your characters make me wish for a place at their kitchen table. Your generosity inspires and your smile lights up the room. I hope you find Mercy's Farrah to be as brave, intelligent, compassionate, and kick-ass as you are IRL.

To Deb. I won't say your bravery humbles me (even though it does), because I know you're getting through each day the best way you know how. I will say that I'm so glad to know you and that I can't wait for us to have that tea together.

And to Martin, as always, I love you.

Acknowledgements

Sarah Hafer and Beth Miller for all the editing. Thank you for keeping track of all the cars, weapons, injuries, etc. You allow me to create accurate mayhem.

The Starfish for the plotting. Thank you!

Claire Zion, Jen Doyle, and Robin Rue for all your support, every step of the way. Thank you for loving my books and believing in me.

Martin Hafer for making sure I remember to eat and sleep while my brain is busily churning out the words, and for always reminding me that I 'freak out every time, yet still manage to finish the book,' so I should 'stop freaking out now.'

All mistakes are my own.

Prologue

Redding, California
Thirteen years ago
Tuesday, 22 May, 4.30 A.M.

She was going to die. Rhoda knew it was true. There was no way Brother DJ would take her back to Eden, and, even if he would, the result would be the same. She didn't want to go back. Ever.

She cursed the day she'd first climbed into the bed of this truck, all those years ago. How many? She struggled to remember. DJ's father, Waylon, had been behind the wheel that night that she'd gathered her children in her lap, promising them that everything would be okay. That they were going to a new home where everything would be wonderful and they'd have toys and food and a warm bed to sleep in.

How stupid was I? Naive and stupid.

Mercy had only been a year old, so she'd never known the scary time before when they didn't always have dinner because Rhoda hadn't turned enough tricks the previous night. But Gideon had seen her come home from a night on the streets of San Francisco with bruises on her face and no breakfast for them because a john had refused to pay. When she'd promised her son a better life, he'd believed her, willingly – eagerly – climbing into the bed of the truck that would take them to paradise. To Eden.

To Eden. She'd spit, but her mouth was too dry. Eden had been no paradise. It had been hell.

Gideon had only been five years old that day, so precious and

1

smart. Wise before his time. *My beautiful boy.* He'd be seventeen now. Well on his way to becoming a man. She hoped. Prayed.

Gideon. My beautiful son. She'd never see him again in this lifetime. She hoped he was well, that he'd survived. She'd cursed herself every night for the past four years for leaving him alone on his thirteenth birthday, injured, maybe even dying. Watching Waylon dump his limp body behind a dumpster, trying to catch one last glimpse of her son as Waylon tied her hands behind her, pushing her face-first into the truck bed, then taking his payment for Gideon's escape from Eden, leaving her torn and bleeding . . . It had been the worst day of her life.

Until she'd climbed into the bed of this truck a third time, her daughter in her arms. This time it was being driven by Waylon's son, DJ, who'd inherited it when Waylon died. DJ's price for the ride out of Eden had been the same as when Waylon had driven her to this same bus station while she clutched at an injured Gideon.

And even though she'd been married to other men both times, she'd complied. She'd sold her body before Eden for a lot less. What was food and shelter when the lives of your children were in danger? Nothing. So she'd paid without complaint.

The day she'd gotten Gideon out, Brother Waylon had taken her back to Eden to pay for her crimes. She had a sick feeling that today's outcome with DJ would not be the same.

She looked down at the trembling body she held too closely. Mercy was burning up. Eden's healer hadn't been able to help, but that hadn't been too big a surprise. Sister Coleen dealt with colds and minor cuts.

Mercy had an infection. It was bad. Very bad. So progressed that it could be detected by scent alone. Coleen simply wasn't equipped to deal with such things.

Which was why Rhoda had taken this drastic step. Why she'd bartered her own life to get Mercy out. To get her away. Hopefully to safety, although anywhere was better than the place they'd left behind.

Eden. Rhoda quelled what would have been a bitter laugh. She'd welcome death were it not for the small body she held. Lovingly, she brushed a lock of black hair from Mercy's sweat-covered forehead. *How I wanted to see you grow up!*

Although Mercy was already grown up. She'd had her twelfth birthday nearly a year ago. Rhoda remembered turning twelve. Remembered playing games with her friends. Mercy's birthday had been nothing like that.

Mercy's birthday had been filled with tears and pain. And fear. So much fear. *It's all my fault. I agreed to go to Eden. To blindly take my children with me. I believed a stranger.* He'd promised her food and shelter and a safe place to raise her children. And Rhoda had believed him, her children paying the price for her stupidity.

'I'm so sorry,' Rhoda whispered. 'So very sorry.'

Mercy's eyelids fluttered, her lashes lifting to reveal bright green eyes so like those of her brother. 'Mama?' Her murmur was hoarse and harsh. 'It hurts.'

'I know, baby. It'll be better soon.' Rhoda had no idea if that was true or not. But the words seemed to soothe her precious daughter, who closed her eyes again. Hopefully she was asleep.

Or unconscious.

Rhoda hoped it was the latter, actually. She hoped that Mercy had been unaware when DJ Belmont had stopped the truck an hour into their trip, and then another hour after that. And yet another hour after that, taking his payment from Rhoda's body.

But getting Mercy out of Eden would be worth anything Rhoda had to endure.

They were almost there. Almost to the bus stop where she'd left Gideon four years before. She leaned down to whisper in Mercy's ear. 'Mercy, honey. Are you awake?' Mercy's chin dipped in a silent nod. 'I need you to listen to me. This is important. Find Gideon. He'll help you.'

Mercy's eyes opened wide, her shock apparent. 'He can't. He's dead.'

'No, baby. He's not.' *Please let that be true.* 'He escaped. I smuggled him out that night, just like I'm getting you out now. He is alive and you need to find him.'

3

Emotion flashed in her daughter's green eyes. 'He is alive? But you said—'

'I know what I said,' Rhoda hissed, prepared for Mercy's disbelief. *I played the part of a grieving mother too well.* Except that she hadn't been grieving his death. She'd grieved the fact that her actions had put both of her children in danger. She'd grieved that she'd left him alone, here, at this bus stop, while he bled and suffered. 'But you need to believe me now. He is alive. And he will help you. Find him, Mercy.'

Mercy's nostrils flared, her eyes narrowing in anger. 'No.'

Rhoda blinked, stunned to hear the venom in her daughter's voice. 'What? Why not?'

'He's selfish and I never want to see him again. He escaped. He *lived*. While we . . .' Tears welled in Mercy's eyes. 'We *suffered*, Mama. We suffered because he was selfish.'

'No, Mercy. He wasn't selfish. Never that.'

'*No.* I'll be fine without him. We'll be fine, you and me.'

Rhoda's eyes filled with tears. *Not we, my sweet girl. Just you.* She wouldn't be allowed to go with her daughter, she was certain. 'Mercy, baby. There's something you need to know about Gideon.'

Mercy turned her face away, clenching her eyes closed. 'No.'

'There was a reason he left.' A good reason. Good enough that she'd chosen to part with her child. Her only son. Leaving him here, hoping that someone would find him. Help him.

'I know. He didn't want to be apprenticed. He didn't want to work. He was lazy and selfish.' Mercy spat the words she'd been fed by the community. By Mercy's own 'husband'.

Words that Rhoda had been too terrified to call what they were: evil lies. Now she was going to lose both of her children, because she was never going to be allowed to live after this latest show of defiance.

How had she let this happen? How had it come to this?

'No, Mercy.' Rhoda shook her head. 'He wasn't lazy. He wasn't selfish.' *He was attacked. He was beaten. He was all but dead.* 'He was—'

4

The truck abruptly stopped, and Rhoda cursed herself for putting the truth off too long. It was too late. She had so much to tell her daughter and only seconds to do so.

'Mercedes,' she whispered hoarsely. 'You are Mercedes Reynolds.'

Mercy's eyes widened in confusion. 'What?'

The driver's door opened. DJ was coming. *Seconds. You have only seconds. Choose your words wisely.*

'You are Mercedes Reynolds. Not Terrill.'

Mercy's brow furrowed. 'I don't understand.'

'My parents are Derrick and Ronnie Reynolds in Houston. Find them. They'll take care of you.'

'Mama?' Mercy's fingers clenched Rhoda's handmade coat. 'You're not making sense.'

But she *was* making sense. For the first time since believing a stranger's lies about paradise, she was making sense. She was making it right. No, she could never make it right. She could only tell the truth.

'Your brother is Gideon Reynolds. You need to find him. Tell him I'm sorry. Tell him that I love him.' Her eyes filled with tears and she blinked them away, not caring where they fell. 'I love you. Always and forever.'

Mercy's lips trembled. 'Mama?'

'Selena. My name is Selena Reynolds.' Then she hissed when the back of Brother DJ's hand connected with her jaw.

'Silence!' DJ thundered.

Mercy recoiled, clenching her eyes closed as she stiffened, waiting for the next blow, but DJ didn't have a problem with Mercy so the blow never came.

Touching the tip of her tongue to her bleeding lip, Rhoda met DJ's dark eyes and said nothing. As she'd been taught.

DJ shot her a warning glare. 'No more of your lies, Rhoda. You've caused enough trouble for one day.'

Rhoda dropped her eyes to the terrified child in her arms. *She's a child.* The community held that Mercy was a woman grown, but she was not. Rhoda's daughter was an almost-thirteen-year-old girl, scared out of her mind, but too beaten down to fight back.

Emotionally and physically. Mercy's husband had beaten her, had taken her so roughly that she'd bled. Again and again.

My fault. All my fault. I should have stopped him.

But that was an impossibility. Rhoda had been unable to stop the man's harsh treatment of her own body, much less Mercy's.

They'd been possessions. Nothing more.

'You'll keep your end of the bargain?' she asked.

DJ nodded once, his expression grim as he held out his arms.

Rhoda tightened her hold on Mercy. 'I'll carry her,' she insisted, then swallowed a yelp when DJ hit her again.

'Stop making trouble, Rhoda,' he growled, then grabbed Mercy from her arms.

Rhoda scrambled to the edge of the truck bed, managing to get one foot on the ground before DJ returned to shove her backward.

'Stay here,' he barked.

She crawled to one side of the truck so that she could look over the side. Mercy lay on the asphalt parking lot, curled into the fetal position, her body visibly trembling. What had he done to her?

'Mercy?' she called, hearing the fear in her own voice. 'Mercy—'

But Rhoda's cry was abruptly muted when DJ grabbed the chain around her neck and yanked it, cutting off her air supply. On reflex, she grabbed the locket at the base of the chain and pulled it away from her throat, trying to give herself room to breathe. But DJ yanked harder and she opened her mouth, gasping for breath.

She hated the chain. Hated the locket it held. Hated how the man who'd owned her had used it just as DJ did now. To control her. To show her who owned the very breaths she took. *Not me.* She hadn't owned the breaths she took for twelve long years.

The chain wasn't jewelry. It was a slave's collar and she'd borne it for far too long.

Something sharp punctured her skin before sliding up the back of her neck, beneath the dreaded chain that dug deeper into her throat as black circles began to dance in front of her eyes.

She wondered if this was it. *Is this how he'll kill me?*

But then a loud crunch filled her ears, and the chain went slack around her neck. She gasped in air that burned, one hand

6

circling her throat protectively. The other still clutched the hated locket.

Until it was snatched from her hand.

'Stay here,' DJ growled. 'I mean it, Rhoda.'

But Rhoda wasn't listening anymore. She crawled to the truck's open tailgate and slid to the ground. Grabbing the edge of the truck's bed, she made her way to her daughter on unsteady legs.

DJ was crouched beside Mercy, one of his big hands yanking at her chain. In his other hand he held a pair of bolt cutters, and he proceeded to cut the chain from Mercy's neck. But Mercy wasn't fighting to breathe. She was as limp as a rag doll, pliant in DJ's harsh grip.

DJ rose, holding both chains now. Rhoda thought he'd put them in the truck, but he strode toward a grassy area and used the bolt cutters to dig a shallow hole into which he threw the lockets. He covered them up, patting at the grass he'd cut away until the area looked undisturbed.

Rhoda stumbled to Mercy's side, dropping to her knees beside her daughter. 'Mercy? Say something. Please.'

But Mercy remained frozen where she lay, still in the fetal position. Wildly Rhoda searched the area, but the parking lot was deserted. There was no one to hear her. No one to help.

DJ was returning, his face dark and furious.

'What did you do to her?' Rhoda demanded, beyond caring what he'd do to silence her. All thoughts were for the daughter she'd failed in every possible way.

DJ smiled and the sight sent a cold shiver across her skin. 'I told her that Brother Ephraim was on his way.'

The cold shiver became paralyzing dread. 'Is he?'

DJ just smiled bigger. And drew a gun from beneath his jacket.

Rhoda's heart stopped. This was it, then. The moment he killed her. 'No. Not in front of her. Please.'

DJ laughed. 'You made your bargain, Rhoda. I kept my end. You're both here. Out of Eden.' He lifted the gun, but to Rhoda's horror, he pointed it at Mercy.

Rhoda threw herself over her child. 'No! You promised!'

7

'I promised to get you out. I never promised to let you live.' Leaning over, he pulled Rhoda away from Mercy as if she weighed nothing.

She expected a loud blast, but all she heard was a little pop.

Silencer, she thought dully. *He planned this. He never intended to let either of us go.*

Mercy's body jerked and a bright red stain began to spread on the front of her dress.

'No.' *No, no, no.* Rhoda was sobbing, reaching for her daughter, but DJ held her just far enough away. 'Mercy? Mercy. Please. Open your eyes. Please.'

Mercy's eyelids fluttered open. *Mama.* She mouthed the word, no sound emerging.

'Say goodbye to Mama,' DJ said mockingly as he pressed the gun to Rhoda's abdomen.

Rhoda's body jolted, a searing pain exploding in her gut. She screamed, unable to contain the excruciating pain. How was Mercy not screaming?

But she wasn't. Her daughter lay on the ground, staring up at her. She was still breathing, though. *She's still alive.*

'Mercedes,' Rhoda ground out. 'Find Gideon. Gideon Reynolds.'

Mercy didn't respond, continuing to stare, her eyes filled with confusion, pain, and terror.

'Shut up, Rhoda,' DJ snarled. 'She's not going to find anyone. She's going to die here. Just like Gideon did. Just like you are.'

Rhoda shook her head hard. 'Selena. I'm Selena. Not Rhoda. Never again.'

DJ shrugged. 'Whatever.' He tried to yank her to her feet, but her knees buckled.

'Ephraim will kill you for this,' she rasped.

DJ just laughed. 'No, he won't. He never does. He can't.'

That made no sense, but Rhoda's mind was spinning out of control and not much made sense. 'Why are you doing this?'

'Because I can.' He tightened his hold on Rhoda's arm and dragged her to the truck, hefting her to her feet, leaning her against its side. 'Watch, Mercy.'

He pressed the barrel of the gun to Rhoda's temple. This was it, then.

'Say bye-bye, Rhoda,' he said, humor in his voice.

'Selena,' she gritted out. 'If you're going to kill me, at least have the guts to say my name. *Selena Reynolds.*'

He chuckled. 'Goodbye, *Rhoda.*'

Watch, Mercy. Brother DJ had commanded it, so Mercy obeyed as she'd been taught to do. She watched, a scream frozen in her throat. *Mama!* But her mother didn't answer because her mother was gone.

Dead.

Her mother had collapsed against the side of the truck, a hole in the side of her head. For a moment she stared at Mercy, her eyes wide.

Dead.

And then Brother DJ lifted her mother's body, his arm under her legs, and tossed her over the side of the truck into the bed. The bed where he'd taken her mother three times since they'd left Eden.

The only home Mercy had ever known.

Her mother hadn't even protested. It had been the payment for getting them out. Mercy knew that. Her mother had told her so after each time. Mercy had wanted to answer, had wanted to tell her mother that it wasn't worth it, that *she* – Mercy – wasn't worth it, but she'd been unable to speak.

DJ hadn't been gentle, but it was still better than . . . *him.* Brother Ephraim.

My husband. Just thinking the word made her shudder. And he was on his way. Brother DJ had told her so. Ephraim would find her here. He probably wouldn't kill her. Although she'd wish he would.

She always wished he'd just kill her, but he never did.

Brother DJ rubbed his bloody hands on his pants and began walking her way. 'Come on, Mercy.'

She just stared up at him, unable to say a word.

He leaned down, grabbed her arm, and forced her to stand, but her legs were like limp noodles. She hurt, everywhere. Her abdomen burned. She pressed her palm to her body, then stared at it dully.

Her palm was covered in blood. *I'm bleeding. Because he shot me.* It was like a dream. Not real. Except it was. Her mother was dead. *And I'm bleeding.*

'Oh, for fuck's sake,' he grunted. 'Not you, too.'

She continued to stare. She'd heard Ephraim use that 'F'-word, but only when he was really angry. Never in as casual a tone as Brother DJ's.

He began to drag her toward the truck and she suddenly understood what he planned to do.

He's going to kill me, too. He never intended to let either of us go.

But why had he driven them all the way here? Wherever here was. The sign said *Redding Bus Terminal.* She knew what a bus was, but despite being able to read the other two words, she didn't understand them.

They'd driven for hours. *Why come all this way only to kill us both?* He could have stopped at any time and killed them on the side of the road.

He was toying with us, she realized. Making her mother believe that Mercy would be free. Her mother had been so hopeful . . . Now she was dead.

Mercy squinted when bright lights abruptly blinded her. A car. Another car had appeared and was pointing its lights at them.

'Fuck!' Brother DJ cursed again. He lifted his gun, pointing it at the bright lights. He fired once, then dropped her arm when blue lights began flashing above the bright white lights. 'Cops.'

He ran to the truck, firing at Mercy again. Every nerve ending in her leg sparked, the shot hitting her midcalf. She opened her mouth to scream, but no sound would come.

Brother DJ got in his truck and sped away, firing a final time, but the bullet missed her, hitting the asphalt near her head. Shards of stone exploded from the road, and little pricks of pain licked at the side of her face.

And then it was quiet, the only sound the soft motor of the car that had spurred Brother DJ to run.

Cops. That meant police officers.

Who were bad. They'd hurt her. Beat her. Take her to prison.

Make sure she never saw daylight again. *If they ever catch you, say nothing. Admit nothing. Never tell about the community. Never say 'Eden'.*

The threats she'd heard a thousand times from her teachers in the community spun in her mind like a tornado, giving her a rush of energy. *Get away.* She had to get away.

She pushed herself to her hands and knees and began to crawl away from the lights. Toward the grass. Toward the lockets Brother DJ had buried.

She hated her locket. But she needed it. Felt . . . wrong without it. She hated that she needed it.

Mama. Her mother's locket was there, too.

Her mother, who was dead. Whose body was in the back of Brother DJ's truck.

Her mother, who'd tried to save her.

The car behind her never moved. No people emerged. No one shouted a threat. No one tried to stop her. So she kept crawling.

Finally her knees touched grass and she wanted to cry. She hurt. So bad. The world began to spin, but she kept pushing her body forward.

Just a little more. A little farther. And then she saw it. The patch of earth Brother DJ had disturbed when he'd buried the lockets. She collapsed next to it and clawed at the dirt until her hand closed around the chain that Ephraim had used as a weapon against her so many times.

She dragged it from the ground, then clawed until she found a second chain. The lockets were covered with dirt, hiding the two children kneeling in prayer under an olive tree, all under the spread wings of the archangel Uriel. But Mercy didn't need to see the engraved image. It was permanently etched in her mind. Just as were the names engraved into the backs of each locket.

Miriam. Rhoda. The names they'd been given in Eden. Miriam was so common a name, her mother had always called her Mercy for short. The past year Mercy had thought it a cruel joke, because there had been no mercy for her or her mother. But the nickname made sense now. *Because my name is Mercedes.*

11

She wasn't Miriam. She was Mercedes. And her mother was Selena.

Except that her mother was dead.

Tears filled her eyes. *Mama.*

She didn't know how long she lay on the ground, tears running down her face. But when the screech of sirens filled the air, she was too tired to move.

The police were coming and she was too tired to move.

'Miss?'

Curled on her side, Mercy struggled to open her eyes. But she was too tired. So tired. *Need to sleep.*

Hands were on her, turning her to her back, and her mind screamed at her to run. But she couldn't move. *So tired. Leave me alone. Need to sleep.*

'Shit,' a man said. 'She's been shot. Gunshot wound to the lower abdomen. Another midcalf.'

'Pulse is thready,' a woman said. 'BP falling. Let's get her loaded.' A hand stroked her face. 'It'll be okay, honey. We're going to help you.'

Mercy wanted to believe her. Wanted it so badly. But people didn't help you out here. They lied and got you to lower your guard. Then they hurt you.

But Ephraim hurt you. Brother DJ hurt you, too. And they were *inside.* They were community. They were supposed to have taken care of her.

Whatever these people did to her, it couldn't be worse than what her own husband had done.

And if they killed her?

She almost hoped they would. It would be a relief.

One

I'm back. Oh God, I'm back. Mercy Callahan inhaled deeply, hoping yoga breathing would calm her racing heart. *Why did I think this was a good idea? This is a terrible idea. I'm just going to make things even worse.*

'Mercy, did you sleep at *all* on the flight?'

Mercy startled at the voice in her ear, glancing at her best friend as they emerged from the Jetway into the terminal, which teemed with people. *Too many people.* Mercy had to steel her spine against the urge to run away. To run back to New Orleans. *Again.*

'No. I'm too . . .' Anxious. Terrified. Wound tighter than a coiled spring. 'Too everything.'

Farrah made a sympathetic noise. 'I know, honey. But it *will* be okay. And if it's not, I'm here. I won't leave you, and if you need me to, I'll take you home.'

Home. New Orleans truly had become home. People loved her there. People respected her there. People didn't pity her there. Or they hadn't until six weeks ago. There was something about having your face spread all over the front page of newspapers all over the country that kind of put a person in the public eye. When the picture was under a headline that read *RESCUED FROM A SERIAL KILLER*, the public eyes were filled with speculation and horror and a physical distance that Mercy rationally knew was a fear of saying the wrong thing. But it was still distance.

But she'd still been okay. Until that damn CNN interview five

13

days ago. One of the other two survivors had talked at length about her experience, making sure to mention all the victims so that no one forgot their names. *As if I could.* Of course the woman being interviewed had mentioned Mercy and of course Mercy had tortured herself by watching it.

The content hadn't been awful. It had been respectfully delivered, but seeing her own face on the TV screen, how pale she'd been, how absolutely terrified . . . Mercy hadn't slept that night or any of the nights thereafter. It was like having a house dropped on her head. Everything changed.

And every one of her co-workers had seen the broadcast. Every single one. They didn't have to tell her so. Mercy had seen the truth on their faces and it had rattled her to her core.

It made her feel like a stranger in the first place that had ever truly felt like home. But New Orleans was home thanks to Farrah, and that her friend was sticking close by her side was better than any gift Mercy had ever received. If Mercy did run back to New Orleans, Farrah would never blame her.

'Thank you,' she whispered.

Farrah nudged her shoulder into Mercy's. 'One step at a time, girl. You know the drill.'

Yes, Mercy knew the drill. One whole day at a time had been too terrifying to contemplate, back when she'd first met Farrah, back when she'd been eighteen and trying so hard to make a life for herself. She'd managed a step at a time. A breath at a time. She still needed the mantra to keep her sanity, especially at night when the memories encroached like prowling wolves scenting helpless prey.

Or on flights back to Sacramento. Mercy preferred the wolves, quite honestly. This city, *this state,* they were frequent stars in her nightmares.

'I know. One step at a time.' Mercy made herself smile. 'You showed me. You and Mama Ro.'

Farrah Romero's mama was priceless, a woman with a warm smile who took no shit from anyone. Mercy wished her own mother had been more like Mama Ro, the wish shaming her more than words could say.

Mercy's mother had been brave in her own way, sacrificing her life – quite literally – there at the end. Those were the worst nightmares of all.

'Let's get your luggage,' Farrah said. 'Then the rental car. We'll find somewhere to eat and let you pull yourself together before we see your brother.'

Mercy had to swallow back the bile that rose to burn her from the inside out every time she thought about her brother. Gideon. How she'd hated him, for so many years.

How wrong she'd been. *God, I am a horrible person.* He was going to hate her, and if he didn't, he should. Him and his best friend, Rafe.

She'd done both of them wrong. A wave of dizziness had her sucking in air as she realized too late that she'd been holding her breath. And that she'd stopped walking in the middle of the terminal, forcing disgruntled travelers to go around her. *I'm rude, too.* 'God,' she gasped as little black dots flickered all around her. This was such utter bullshit, but she couldn't seem to make it all stop.

'You're all right.' Farrah's hand was on her back, rubbing small circles as they stood there. Farrah ignored the frowns on the faces of the travelers, focusing only on Mercy. 'That's my girl. It's a panic attack. You know what to do. Breathing's good. In and out.'

Mercy blinked hard and readjusted the strap cutting into her shoulder. The cat carrier was heavy, but that was good because the biting pain was helping to center her. Not that she'd admit that to anyone ever again. The last time she'd admitted that pain helped her focus, she'd ended up in the psychiatric ward on a seventy-two-hour hold. That had . . . sucked. 'I'm okay. I'm fine.'

Farrah smiled, bright as sunshine. Her best friend had the very best smile. Just seeing it made Mercy want to smile back. It was Farrah's superpower. 'Of course you're okay,' she said, giving her back a final pat. 'Let's get moving, so we can get something to eat.'

Mercy told her feet to move. *One step at a time.* Thankfully her feet listened and she and Farrah were headed toward baggage claim. 'We have to get the cats settled first. I'll find a pet store to get litter boxes. And food.' Hearing the word 'food', Rory yowled pitifully

15

from his carrier, and Mercy patted the side. 'Hush, beast. You'll survive a little longer.'

Farrah made a derisive noise. 'I think your cats could miss a meal or two, Merce. Or ten.' She lifted the cat carrier she held in one clenched fist. 'Jack-Jack weighs sixty-two pounds.'

Mercy laughed, the sound foreign but welcome. Farrah could always make her laugh. 'Not quite sixty-two pounds.' Her Ragdoll kitties topped the scales at nineteen pounds each. 'Besides, the vet said they're both healthy. Not fat, just sturdy.'

Farrah's brows lifted. 'Sturdy. I like that. I think I'll start using that word for myself.'

Mercy frowned. 'Stop that. You're curvy and gorgeous. I wish I had your curves.' Farrah was soft, her whole demeanor inviting hugs, and the bright, bold colors she wore glowed like jewels against her dark skin. Today's outfit was bright yellow and had heads turning with smiles and appreciation.

Farrah sighed, a put-upon sound that she'd drama'd up for Mercy's benefit. 'No, you don't. It's hard to find clothes for curves. I wish I were stick-slender.'

But Mercy saw the twinkle in Farrah's eye and knew the truth. 'No, you don't. You like the way Captain Holmes stares at your curves.'

Farrah grinned. 'That I do, and I make no apologies. My man is *fine*.'

'Yes, he definitely is.' Even though Captain Holmes could be intimidating in cop mode, he was kind and funny and he'd always treated Farrah like she was the sweetest of treasures. That made the man more than fine in Mercy's book, even if he did make her feel small whenever he was in the room. 'But not my type,' she added when Farrah gave her an amused look. 'He's very . . . big, isn't he?'

Farrah threw back her head and laughed. 'He most certainly is, in *all* the right places. One in particular.'

Mercy's cheeks heated. She hadn't meant that, but Farrah had a bawdy streak. 'Was he okay with you just dropping everything to come with me?' she asked, changing the subject.

Farrah sobered, nodding. 'He was perfectly okay with it. You said you needed me and that was good enough for him. That we're staying in a house owned by a cop made him feel better about it, though.' She shrugged. 'He worries.'

A house owned by a cop. Mercy winced, thinking about the cop in question. Homicide detective Raphael Sokolov, Gideon's best friend. The brother of his heart in the way that Farrah was the sister of hers.

Rafe probably hated her, too. If he didn't, he should. Or would, given enough time. She selfishly hoped that he wouldn't, though. Her memories of Rafe as she'd sat at his bedside for two weeks – his golden hair, his slow smile, and his unfettered happiness despite his pain – were the only bright spots in the nights she'd spent tossing and turning and fearing to sleep in the six weeks since returning to New Orleans. 'The cop is on disability leave.' Because he'd taken a bullet. *For me.* 'Did you tell your captain that?'

Farrah made a face. 'Well, no. But a cop's a cop, Mercy. Just because the man is recuperating from injuries doesn't mean squat. He's still a cop deep down. Instincts don't go on sabbatical, you know.' She narrowed her eyes abruptly. 'He knows we're coming, doesn't he?'

Mercy opened her mouth, then closed it again.

Farrah's frown deepened. *'Mercy?* He knows we're coming, *doesn't he?'*

'No, but his sister does. I called her to ask if we could stay with her for a little while.'

'Okay.' Farrah's frown receded, but her wariness remained. 'The sister is Sasha, right?'

'Right. Rafe's house has three apartments. Rafe was staying on the bottom floor because he couldn't do the stairs, at least when I was last there.' *Before I ran away like the coward I am.* 'The bullet tore the muscles in his thigh.' Mercy shuddered at the memory of the pain he'd suffered, but she couldn't dwell on that now or she'd never make it to baggage claim. *Breathe in and out. Nice and easy.* She swallowed hard and pushed on. 'The bottom-floor apartment actually belongs to Daisy.'

17

'Your brother's girlfriend,' Farrah said conversationally, but every mention of Gideon was said with care, like she expected Mercy to bolt. Or faint dead away.

Neither was out of the realm of possibility at the moment.

'Yes. I like Daisy. She's artsy and fun.' But the woman had experienced her own share of heartache and Mercy felt a kinship that she wished she could have further explored. *Now's your chance, Callahan. You're back. You can do all the things you wish you'd done when you were here six weeks ago.*

Things like having a heart-to-heart with Gideon. Like begging for his forgiveness.

Gideon loves you. You know that. But it was a lot for anyone to forgive. She wouldn't blame Gideon if he couldn't. Still, she needed to make that right, too.

'Daisy's such a cute name. I can't wait to meet her,' Farrah was saying warmly. 'So if Rafe has taken Daisy's apartment, where does she live?'

'On the top floor. They just switched. Rafe's sister Sasha rents the middle floor.'

'And that's where we're going to stay?'

'For a few days.' She patted Rory's carrier. 'Until I find an extended-stay hotel that takes cats.'

Farrah studied her as they walked. 'Extended? Exactly how long is "extended"?'

Mercy bit at her lip. 'I don't know. I have . . . some time off.'

'How much time off?'

Mercy braced herself for Farrah's reaction. 'Two months.'

Farrah stopped walking, staring at Mercy in stunned disbelief. *'Two months?* How?' She pulled Mercy's arm so that they were against the wall, out of the traffic flow. 'How did you get *two months* of vacation?'

Breathe in and out. Nice and easy. 'It's not vacation. I'm on leave. Personal leave.' *And I'm lucky to have it,* she told herself for the hundredth time.

Worry clouded her friend's brown eyes. 'You never mentioned requesting leave.'

'Because I didn't.' Mercy leaned against the wall, closing her eyes. 'I effed up. At work.'

'Oh, honey,' Farrah murmured. 'What happened?'

'It was after that CNN special interview on Monday night. I got distracted. Mixed up some test samples.'

Farrah's indrawn breath said all that she didn't. Mixing up samples in Mercy's line of work was a big deal. A *very* big deal. She held people's futures in her hands. Their innocence or guilt often rested on the results of the DNA analysis she ran for the New Orleans PD. *I could have ruined an innocent man.*

'I figured it out, though,' Mercy added, 'after I'd run both samples. I was able to correct the first report before the DA could use it to file charges. I told my supervisor, and he and *his* supervisor called me into a meeting Thursday afternoon. I thought I was getting fired.' Mercy opened her eyes to find Farrah's full of compassion and concern. 'I'm lucky that I 'fessed up and that it was my first mistake. They said that they knew I'd been under a lot of pressure and that they wished they'd encouraged me to take leave when I first came back from Sacramento.' When she'd first run away from Gideon – and Rafe – only to hide her head in the sand. 'But they couldn't.'

'Not unless it affected your job.'

'Which it did.'

'Of course it did,' Farrah said, her voice so abruptly sharp that Mercy flinched. 'You were abducted by a freaking *serial killer*, Mercy. You almost *died*.'

The tears of anguish in Farrah's eyes kept Mercy from taking offense at her tone. 'But I didn't. I'm okay.'

'No, you're not okay, you stubborn thing.' Farrah brushed a trembling hand back over her hair, the close-cut natural style that framed her face so well. 'Just because you weren't physically injured doesn't mean you're okay. Plus, Detective Sokolov was injured and he did almost die. It was a *trauma*.' She pressed her fingers to her lips as she visibly fought for composure. 'I almost lost you,' she added in a devastated whisper.

Mercy didn't want to think about it. Not now. If she allowed herself to remember the ordeal, she might turn around and run for the nearest plane out of Sacramento. 'I thought if I just worked and kept to my routine, that I'd get through it. It's worked before.'

Farrah's voice was back to quiet. Soothing. 'It worked before because you were also seeing a therapist.'

'And I have to do that, too,' Mercy admitted. 'My supervisors said that no one blamed me for my mistake, and that they wanted me back, but that a therapist would have to sign off on my state of mind.'

Farrah squeezed her arm. 'Are you okay with this?'

Mercy shrugged. 'I have to be. It's a reasonable requirement. Plus, I love my job and they were actually really nice about it all. I think I was harder on myself.'

'No,' Farrah drawled dryly. 'Say it ain't so.'

Mercy's lips curved. 'It ain't so.'

'And you are a lying McLiarface who lies.'

Mercy snorted. 'You've been babysitting your nephews recently, haven't you?'

'I have.' Farrah set the cat carrier on the floor, enveloping Mercy in a hard hug. 'It was like a wake-up call for you, huh?'

And how. Mercy nodded miserably against Farrah's shoulder. 'Yeah. I realized that I could have sent an innocent man to prison and . . . I kind of fell apart. I had to come clean.'

'Of course you did. You are a good person, Mercy Callahan.'

Mercy wasn't so sure about that. She'd done some pretty awful things. *But you're here to make amends*, she thought, and therefore didn't argue. 'When the bosses gave me two months of leave, I decided I had to face what happened in California.'

Farrah pulled away, her expression wary. 'In California? You mean in Sacramento? Or . . .'

Farrah knew of Mercy's history in California – her most recent brush with danger in Sacramento back in February, but also the childhood she'd spent in fear in the northernmost part of the state. Farrah was the only one who did know all the details, except for the new piece of information that had left Mercy reeling, adrift, and fleeing for home. Mercy hadn't shared it with anyone. She hadn't completely processed it herself yet.

say no more

There's something you need to know about Gideon.

Oh, Mama. Why didn't you talk faster? Why didn't you tell me long before it was too late? Because now Mercy knew the truth and it had upended everything she'd thought she'd known before.

'Or,' Mercy whispered, unwilling – unable – to say the word that haunted her waking thoughts and worst nightmares.

Eden. The cult that had fostered DJ Belmont, who'd killed her mother. The cult that had glorified Ephraim Burton, who'd . . . *Hurt me. Over and over and over.*

Farrah's shoulders sagged because she understood all the implications of what Mercy hadn't said aloud. 'Oh, honey. Why now, after all these years? What changed?'

That was the question, wasn't it? She'd escaped Eden thirteen years before, had undergone years of therapy to forget what she'd experienced. Well, not to forget. No one ever truly forgot sexual assault. But she was able to live with the memories, to relegate them to the proper places in her mind. She'd been doing so well.

Until Sacramento. Until Gideon. Until she'd learned the truth.

'Gideon,' she murmured. 'He changed everything. I have to see him. To tell him that I'm sorry.'

Farrah frowned. 'Sorry for what?'

'For hating him all this time.'

'Mercy, honey, we've had this conversation. He left you in that awful place. He killed his boss and ran away because he didn't want to work. Left you and your mama to bear the consequences, which were brutal. Resentment is natural.'

Except that none of that was true. It was a filthy lie, concocted by the men who'd owned them back then. *Why didn't I question? Why did I believe that ridiculous story? Why did Mama let me believe it?* A sob started to take root in her throat, and Mercy fought it back. 'He was only thirteen.'

Farrah cupped her cheek. 'I know. He was young and scared. He probably didn't know what you and your mother were suffering after he left.'

Mercy shook her head. 'No, you don't understand. I found out

21

something when I was here before. I found out *why* Gideon escaped. He didn't just run away.'

Farrah's eyes widened. 'What? How did he escape, then?'

Mercy thought about her mama, about those final minutes of her life. 'Mama told me to find him. Right before she was . . .' *Murdered.* Mercy couldn't say that word, either. *Because it was my fault.* Her mother had sacrificed her life. *For me.* 'At first I was shocked, because I'd thought he'd been dead all that time. But Mama said that he'd escaped, that he was alive, and that he'd help me. But then I got so angry. I said no, that he was selfish. Mama said, "There's something you need to know about Gideon." And now I know what that was.'

Farrah waited patiently, as if they weren't standing against the wall of a crowded airport terminal.

Mercy swallowed again. 'They hurt him. They beat him. Almost killed him.'

'Oh my God,' Farrah whispered, horrified. 'Why? Because he killed his boss?'

'He did that, but only because he fought back when one of the men tried to . . .' *Say it. Stop being a coward. Say. It.* 'Tried to rape him. He killed the man by accident and the other men from the community beat him so bad that he almost died. He couldn't walk, couldn't see, was barely conscious.'

Farrah stared in shock. Then she gave herself a little shake and asked, 'How did he get out?'

'Mama.'

'Oh.' The word escaped Farrah on a quiet rush of breath. 'I get it now. Your mama smuggled him out, didn't she? Just like she smuggled you out.'

Mercy nodded. 'But she left him at a bus stop, all alone, hoping someone would find him. She *had* to leave him. She *had* to go back . . . *there.*' To Eden. 'Because of me.'

'To protect you. Oh, Mercy. I'm so sorry.'

Mercy blinked rapidly. She would not cry. Not here. 'I didn't know. I hated him all those years. I hated him for something he didn't do.'

'He'll forgive you. I know it.'

'He already has.' For that, anyway. 'I guess I haven't forgiven myself.'

'No,' Farrah drawled again. 'Say it ain't so.'

Mercy was amazed to hear herself chuckle. 'It's so. It's *so* so.'

Farrah hugged her again, hard. 'We'll get through this. You and me. I won't leave you.'

Mercy couldn't quite breathe from being squeezed but didn't want to move out of Farrah's embrace. This was love, safety. Acceptance. 'You're staying for two whole months?' she asked lightly, even as she clung.

'I'll stay until I know you're okay. I got time coming from the university and if I get lonely for my captain, he can get himself on a damn plane. You're worth it, Mercy.'

'I love you, Ro.' Mercy blurted the words, shocking herself. Farrah had often said the words to her, but Mercy had never been able to say them back. 'I should have said it years ago. You're the sister I never had. Your family is my family.'

Farrah reared back, blinking in surprise, and then her eyes filled with tears again, but this time they were tears of happiness and affection. 'Oh, baby girl. I love you, too.' She straightened her spine and grabbed the cat carrier. 'Let's get our suitcases before my mascara starts to run.'

Mercy forced her feet to move. One step at a time. One breath at a time. *You can do this. Be brave.* At least she had a few hours to center herself before coming face-to-face with her brother or any of the Sokolovs.

'Would you look at that?' Farrah said, pointing down the escalator to where people waited at baggage claim. People holding signs.

Specifically, people like Sasha Sokolov holding a sign that said *CALLAHAN*, each letter in a different color. Because that was the way Sasha rolled.

She was tall, like her brother. Blond, like her brother, with the same dark brown eyes that lit up with an inner joy that Mercy envied. Just like her brother.

'That's Sasha, I take it?' Farrah drawled.

Nervously Mercy scanned the waiting crowd for Rafe, but he wasn't with his sister. Relief left her a little dizzy, even as disappointment sat like lead in her gut. Why would he come to meet her? She'd left him without a single word. 'Yeah. I, um, didn't know she'd be meeting us. I didn't even tell her which flight we were on.'

Because she hadn't wanted Sasha to meet them. She hadn't wanted anyone to meet them. She needed time to prepare herself for the hard conversations that lay ahead.

'Mercy!' Sasha shouted, waving her rainbow sign. 'Over here!' Not willing to wait – for much of anything – Sasha charged, side-stepping several travelers like a running back dancing upfield.

Farrah laughed. 'I think this is gonna be fun.'

Mercy had just braced herself for impact when Sasha grabbed her in a fierce hug, lifting her to her toes. 'I'm so glad to see you,' Sasha whispered, then pulled away, holding her hand out to Farrah. 'I'm Sasha.'

Farrah bypassed Sasha's hand, going for the hug, and Sasha made a happy sound. 'I'm Farrah. Thank you for meeting us.'

Sasha stepped back with a mock glare for Mercy. 'It wasn't easy. I've been here for hours, waiting on every flight that could possibly have started in or transferred from New Orleans.'

'I'm sorry,' Mercy mumbled.

Sasha waved her apology away. 'Introduce us properly, Mercy.'

'Sasha, this is my best friend, Dr Farrah Romero. Farrah, Sasha Sokolov.'

Sasha lifted her perfectly arched brows. 'Doctor?'

'I'm a biophysicist,' Farrah explained. 'I work for a university.'

Sasha nodded. 'Very cool. If you're willing, I'd love for you to chat with my youngest sister, Zoya. She wants to be a doctor. A medical doctor, I think, but she's only seventeen, so . . .'

Farrah smiled. 'I'd be happy to talk to her.'

'Excellent.' Sasha shook her head. 'Where are my manners?' She took a cat carrier in each hand and gave a low whistle. 'Shit, Mercy, how many cats you got in here? And are they sitting on bricks?'

Farrah nodded. 'Right? They're behemoths.'

Mercy made herself smile, because her anxiety was beginning to build again. There were too many people here. Too much noise.

'Hey,' Farrah murmured, sensing her tension. 'Go sit down. I'll get our bags.'

Mercy shook her head. 'I'll go get our rental car and meet you at the pickup curb.'

'Nope,' Sasha said. 'No renting of cars needed. I drove my father's SUV today, which you will be borrowing while you're here. He never drives it anymore, not since he got the Tesla.'

Tesla? Really? Farrah mouthed.

'Karl owns a successful marketing agency,' Mercy told her, then turned to Sasha. 'That's not necessary, really.'

Sasha gave her a long, long look. 'Yes, it is. Gideon is family. You are Gideon's sister. Therefore, you are family, and no family of ours rents a car when they visit.'

'I'll be here for a while,' Mercy said, flailing for some argument she could make stick in the face of the tsunami that was Sasha Sokolov.

'Better still,' Sasha returned. 'Also, I already stopped at the pet store this morning for cat supplies. Food, litter, a litter box. Even some toys. So once we get your suitcases, we can go straight to my place, where you can rest.' With that, she stalked off toward the baggage carousel, handling the cats as if they weighed nothing.

'Wow,' Farrah said with clear admiration. 'I'm impressed. It took me years to bulldoze you like that and she figured it out in a few weeks. Are they all like that?'

Mercy sighed. 'Yes. They have a large family.' A big, noisy, pushy, boisterous family who loved each other so much. Who loved Gideon so much. 'There are eight kids, and Mrs Sokolov is as big a force of nature as Mama Ro.'

Irina Sokolov had also bulldozed her way through Mercy's defenses, mothering Mercy as if she'd been another Sokolov. Mercy had balked at first, preferring solitude as she'd sat by Rafe's hospital bed, but Irina hadn't allowed it. They'd developed a natural rapport and by the end of her visit, Mercy had grown fond of the older woman, missing her counsel when she'd fled back to New Orleans. *It will be good to see her again.*

'And Sasha's brother?' Farrah asked slyly. 'Is he a force of nature?'

Ignoring Farrah's innuendo, Mercy honestly considered the question. 'No. There's a . . . a quietness with Rafe that the rest of the family doesn't seem to possess.' At first she'd thought it was because he'd been injured and was in pain, but she'd quickly learned that his quiet ran deep, but that he hid it from his family and she'd never asked why. She wasn't sure if she'd wanted to know, because knowing would foster the closeness that Rafe had wanted, but that had scared her to death. 'Or at least I didn't see it in the two weeks I was here.'

'I cannot wait to meet him,' Farrah said. 'I'll help Sasha find our bags. Why don't you go to the ladies' room to freshen up? It'll be quieter there. We'll wait for you by the door over there.'

Mercy nodded, grateful. 'I will. Thank you.' She paused a moment, though, watching Farrah and Sasha getting to know each other by the baggage carousel. Farrah said something that made Sasha throw back her head and laugh and in that moment, she looked so much like her brother that Mercy's heart hurt.

Rafe had laughed like that. Not often – he'd been in too much pain – but once or twice she'd say something wry and his laugh would boom out, joyful and happy. He'd been golden in those moments. Beautiful. *Untouchable by someone like me.*

And then that last time, the last day she'd been there, he'd sobered, staring at her as if he'd never seen her before. *Stay*, he'd murmured. *Let's see where this goes. Please.* And then he'd kissed her, shattering everything she'd thought she'd known about who she was and what she wanted.

That was what had made her run home, the straw that broke the camel's back. That terrifying, beautiful, amazing kiss. *He should be so angry.* Maybe he wouldn't even want to see her again. Maybe she should find a hotel, like right now.

Or maybe she should grow the hell up and stop being a frightened child. Deliberately turning her body, Mercy headed for the ladies' room, trying to calm the butterflies in her gut that had changed to angry bees.

Sacramento, California
Saturday, 15 April, 5.00 P.M.

Finally. Ephraim had been waiting for hours, his own flight from New Orleans having landed early that afternoon. Mercy had led him on quite the merry chase, with two cross-country flights in under a week.

He'd booked his flight to Louisiana as soon as he'd seen Mercy's face on the TV on Monday night. Or at least as soon as he'd recovered from his shock at seeing her alive when he'd thought her dead for thirteen years.

The CNN interview had been full of shocks. Mercy was still alive. She'd survived being abducted by a serial killer. But there was another victim – Eileen, who'd been given the name of Miriam when Ephraim had married her. Now she was dead at this serial killer's hands. And the most dangerous shock of all – Miriam's locket had been found and was now in the hands of the police. Which meant that, unless Miriam had removed their wedding photo from the locket, the cops now knew his face.

Fortunately, he no longer wore the pirate patch like he had in the photo. Not out in the world anyway. Only in Eden, because no one in the community could know that he'd gotten surgery none of them would have access to.

But the real chances of the cops knowing his face were slim. If they had his picture, they'd have it spread all over the TV. Just like Mercy's had been in that broadcast.

The CNN reporter had been so *helpful*, telling her viewing audience where Mercy now lived. Ephraim had followed Mercy around New Orleans for days, learning her routine. He'd planned his grab for last night, only to learn from her neighbor that she was flying back to Sacramento and he'd missed her.

He hadn't planned to kill Mercy's neighbor, but the woman had seen his face. He'd had no choice. His preferred method of eliminating threats was snapping his victim's neck – and he was damn good at it – but he wanted the old lady to look like she'd died of natural causes, so he'd suffocated her instead, which took more

27

effort. Tracking Mercy had been a lot more trouble than he'd expected.

But it had all worked out because there she was, walking toward the ladies' room. Mercy Callahan, or so she called herself now. When she'd been his wife, she'd been Mercy Burton. And since Eden didn't permit divorce, she was still Mercy Burton.

Slowly, he moved toward the restrooms, not wanting to attract any attention. He had no idea if Mercy or her bastard brother had told anyone about him, but there was a chance that his photo from Miriam's locket might have surfaced, and he wasn't going to be careless.

Careless men got caught. *I will not get caught.*

Not for the first time, he cursed Miriam, wishing he could have been the one who'd snapped her neck instead of the random stranger who'd killed her. If she'd stayed where she was supposed to be – *in Eden, with me* – she'd still be alive. Her locket would be safe, instead of in the hands of the police. His photo would still be secure.

He'd told Pastor that putting their wedding photos in the women's lockets was a terrible idea, but the man seriously thought he was infallible. After thirty years of being told he was God's emissary, Eden's own priest, Pastor believed his own press and had developed a serious God complex.

But Pastor was old. *And I'm next in line.* The only threat to his taking control of Eden after Pastor's death was DJ Belmont.

And I'm about to grind him into the ground like the cockroach he is. As soon as he dragged little Mercy back to Eden, he'd be able to prove that DJ had lied. DJ had sworn to Pastor that he'd killed Mercy and buried her where her body would never be found.

But DJ's lie was evidenced by the young woman walking into the ladies' room, all by herself.

That she'd separated from her companions was a bit of luck. He didn't want to have to kill the other two women, but he would if he had to. He wanted to take only Mercy back with him.

Where she belonged. And nobody was going to stop him.

TWO

Luckily the ladies' room was completely unoccupied and quiet. She could think in the quiet. Not that she really wanted to think.

She was back in California. Back to Gideon. Back to Rafe. And back to the memories of Eden that seemed so much closer to the surface here.

Eden. As much as she dreaded having to face Gideon and Rafe again, just being in California had her nearly hyperventilating. Eden was here, somewhere. Somewhere north of Sacramento, way up in the mountains where monsters could hide and continue their abuse.

Monsters like Ephraim Burton and DJ Belmont. She shuddered. DJ had killed her mother, but it was Ephraim who'd terrified her to the depths of her soul. He still did. The memory of him, big and hulking, harsh hands that hit and hit, still had the power to reduce her to the traumatized girl she'd been. His one eye, intense and so cruel. His body that had . . . hurt her.

Say the word, Mercy. He raped *you for an entire year.* Until she'd nearly died. She *would* have died, had it not been for her mother's sacrifice.

But Mama *had* sacrificed, enabling Mercy's and Gideon's escapes. Gideon had been searching for Eden ever since. He'd become a special agent with the FBI, to help people. To find Eden. To free the others who were still enslaved. Still afraid and hurting. *While I ran away to hide from him, to hide from life. To hide from everything.* All the

29

while refusing to help him find the monsters that had taken everything.

No more. Everything had changed, all because of Gideon and his passion for the truth. The FBI knew about Ephraim Burton now. They knew that he'd been Harry Franklin before robbing a bank had sent him into hiding. Had sent him to Eden. An FBI task force was looking for him.

If they found him, they'd arrest him for murder and sexual assault. *So many victims.* The FBI would want her to testify against him. She'd have to see him again. To look at the face that still haunted her nightmares.

The angry bees in her gut swarmed and she was abruptly glad she hadn't had anything to eat on the plane. Ephraim Burton was out there. And so was DJ Belmont. Walking the earth as free men when her mother was dead. *And I've been hiding all this time, afraid of my own shadow.*

No more. Because she'd returned to do the right thing. 'I may still be afraid,' she muttered quietly, 'but I'm sure as hell not hiding anymore.'

She looked up, stared at her own reflection. She was pale and there were dark circles under her eyes. But her eyes were clear and she straightened her spine, suddenly refilled with purpose. *You are not weak. You have survived. You are here. And you are not a little girl anymore, cowering in fear as he raped you. You're a grown woman, in charge of your future.*

She was here in Sacramento to make amends. To Gideon, to Rafe. But if she could make amends *and* destroy the men who'd tortured her and her mother and so many others at the same time?

That was an empowering thought. 'You can do this,' she said to the woman in the mirror.

She would make amends. She would make the men who hurt her mother pay. *One step, one breath at a time. I'm back, you sons of bitches.*

Mercy gave a hard nod to her reflection. She knew what she had to do now. She wasn't sure how to do it, but she wouldn't have to do it alone.

She had Gideon. And Rafe. They might hate her, but they'd help her take Ephraim and DJ down, because they were both good men who did the right thing.

And it wasn't like she'd have to face Ephraim today. The FBI was searching for him, but it wasn't like he was going to pop up and surrender himself. So she had a little while to bolster herself.

She turned to the mirror to give her face a light coating of foundation and to apply her lipstick. At least she didn't look like death warmed over, even if that was exactly how she felt.

Gathering her things, she squared her shoulders and walked from the ladies' room.

Only to come to an abrupt halt, her breath seizing in her lungs. *No. It's not possible. It's a dream. A nightmare. It's not real.*

But then her nightmare smiled, a glass eye glinting as it reflected the overhead lights. 'Hello, wife.'

The eye was new, but the voice was familiar. So damn familiar. *You like it, don't you. Tell me you like it. Tell me. Tell me or I'll break your fucking arm, you little whore.*

Mercy stared up at him, her mind beginning to fuzz, little black dots dancing in her vision. *Ephraim.* It couldn't be true. It couldn't be real.

'Nothing to say?' he mocked. 'No greeting for your husband?'

A *snick* seemed to echo in the silence between them and Mercy had only a split second to wonder what it was before feeling the bite of a blade against her wrist. He grabbed her other hand and yanked.

'You'll come with me,' he growled, 'and you won't say a word. Nod once if you understand.'

Her brain was telling her to run, but her feet were made of stone. She stood there, able only to stare at him, her heart beating like a wild thing in her chest.

He yanked again, pulling her hand through his arm. The knife now pressed against her side, through her blouse.

He's going to ruin it, she thought numbly. *He's going to make me bleed on it.*

Her feet still didn't move, even when he yanked her again.

'Move your ass, bitch,' he whispered in her ear.

And then another voice, one that made her shiver. 'Mercy?'

Oh God. Rafe. He spoke in her best daydreams, deep and musical. But she didn't respond. Couldn't respond. She was . . . not there.

'Mercy!' He was shouting now, from behind them.

Her feet were finally moving. She was walking to the door. With Ephraim.

I'm not going to get the chance to be brave. I'm sorry, Mama. I'm sorry, Gideon.

And then there was a loud *crack* and the arm holding hers was gone.

Eden, California
Saturday, 15 April, 5.05 P.M.

Amos Terrill rubbed his thumb over the lines of the script he'd just carved into the lid of the hope chest. He was almost finished with it, this special project on which he'd been laboring for the past five months, mostly in secret. He'd made countless hope chests, coffee tables, kitchen cabinets, armoires, and jewelry boxes over the thirty years he'd lived in Eden. All of them had been gifts for the membership or items to be sold to bring money into the community coffers.

This was the first time he'd ever made something for himself. Something he didn't intend to share with anyone.

No one except his Abigail. His heart.

A splinter caught at his thumb and he pulled it out, sucking at the small wound before returning to his task. He could sand the hope chest later. He didn't have much more time to himself. Everyone knew he stopped working at suppertime, and then people would start dropping by.

Amos, can you fix this? Amos, a minute of your time? Amos, need a pair of strong hands to help with . . . It didn't matter what. It was all the same after thirty years.

He picked up the detail blade, his favorite of all of his carving tools. He'd brought it with him to Eden, when he was young and full of hope, ready to change the world.

Now he knew the truth and every day had become a struggle, each harder than the day before.

He had to stay positive. Had to keep smiling. Had to stay patient. Had to nod and pleasantly reply that all was well when he was greeted in passing.

In other words, he had to lie.

He finished carving the last word and took a look at his work. It had become something of a trademark, a personal signature he'd added to all the larger pieces of cabinetry he created.

The words were carved in a scrolling, old-fashioned script: *Surely Goodness And Mercy Shall Follow Me All The Days Of My Life. Psalms 23:6.* Anyone in the community would think it simply a beautiful Bible verse, one that matched the song that used to be in his heart.

But it wasn't. It was a tribute. Penance, even. His way of trying to make it up to a beautiful little girl whom he'd failed. So utterly.

Mercy. He thought of her often, especially after the birth of his Abigail, whose name meant *father's joy.* As with most things in his life, Abigail's birth had been bittersweet, losing her mother just minutes after they'd held their baby for the first time.

He'd thought he'd lose them both. Like he'd lost his first family. Mercy. Gideon. Rhoda. *Dammit, Rhoda, I'm so sorry. You tried to tell me, but I wouldn't listen.*

He hadn't wanted to listen.

But now he knew the truth and he needed to get Abigail out. To safety. To freedom.

He wouldn't fail her like he'd failed Mercy, Rhoda, and Gideon.

He picked up the hope chest and turned it over effortlessly, a lifetime of woodworking giving him more strength than most men. He began to carve his true signature into the base of the chest, no larger than a dime. A small olive tree with twelve branches. It was exacting, but, at the same time, something he could do with his eyes closed, he'd done it so many times.

'Papa!'

Amos startled, the knife in his hand skipping over the wood, and pain ripped into his finger. 'Ugh!' he cried, unable to stifle the sound.

'Papa?' Abigail bounded into his workshop, with the same energy with which she tackled everything else in her life. 'Tackled'

33

being the operative term. Abigail never walked when she could run, never sat when she could stand. Never whispered. Ever.

His lips curved up into a smile even as he grabbed a clean rag to press to his finger.

'Abi-girl,' he said with genuine warmth. Abigail was the only one who could summon anything close to happiness for him. She was the only thing that was real and had been for the past six months. Ever since Amos had witnessed Brother Ephraim calmly breaking the necks of Sister Dorcas, her husband, and their sixteen-year-old son, three of the dearest people in the world. Amos's throat burned every time he remembered Brother Ephraim so carelessly tossing their bodies into an unmarked grave.

After which Ephraim had returned to tell the membership that Dorcas and her family had chosen to return to the world after the untimely death of their dear Miriam.

Miriam, who'd walked around with shadows in her eyes. Who, the last time Amos had seen her, had been bruised and bloody and begging to die.

Sister Dorcas had begged Amos for his help. *Please help us get her out of here. Please.*

Amos had done his best, or he'd thought so at the time, working through the night to fashion a hope chest similar to the one he was now building for Abigail. It wasn't ornate and hadn't had a false bottom, but it had been large enough that Miriam had been able to hide inside. Her father and brother had hoisted the hope chest into the bed of Brother DJ's truck when no one was around to see their muscles strain under the added weight. Miriam was supposed to have climbed from the back of the truck and run for freedom the moment that Brother DJ had slowed enough to make it possible.

But it had all been for naught. Miriam must have been attacked by an animal because her body had been returned to them, too damaged to be identified. And, as punishment for their part in her escape, Sister Dorcas, Brother Stephen, and their son, Ezra, had been murdered in cold blood.

I failed them, too.

But he would not fail again. He would not fail his Abigail.

34

'Are you all right, Papa?' she asked, leaning in to peer at his bleeding finger.

'I'll be fine,' he assured her. 'What brings you skipping into my workshop, Abi-girl?'

She giggled. 'Abi*gail*, Papa. How many times must I tell you?'

It's Mercy, Papa. Not Mercy-girl. How many times must I tell you?

He swallowed hard, shaking off the memory of his daughter, dead for thirteen years. He tapped the end of Abigail's adorable nose, so like her mother's. 'Until I get it right, obviously.'

Abigail sighed dramatically, then stared again at his finger. 'That's bleeding a lot, Papa. You should go to the healer.'

He glanced at his finger, grimacing at the sight of the rag, already heavy with blood. 'You're right. Why don't you go to Deborah's house and play? Tell her mother that I'll be by to get you as soon as I get my finger taken care of.'

He tossed a tarp over the almost-finished hope chest, hiding it from view. He didn't want anyone to see it. He didn't want anyone getting close enough to realize that its interior wasn't nearly as deep as it should be. He didn't want anyone spying the false bottom that hid a crawl space just large enough for a seven-year-old girl.

For Abigail.

The chest clearly hadn't worked for Miriam. If it had, she'd be free instead of dead, so Amos was saving it as a last resort to get Abigail out. He first had to convince Pastor and Brother DJ to allow him to go into town when DJ took items to be traded, because there was no way Amos would leave his little girl hidden in the back of the man's truck all alone. *Move carefully. Take your time.* He didn't want Brother Ephraim to become suspicious of him or he might end up in an unmarked grave like Sister Dorcas and her family. And then who would take care of his Abigail?

Abigail grabbed his uninjured hand. 'I came to tell you that I have supper.'

He looked down at her, unable and unwilling to hide his affection. 'You do? Butter sandwiches again?'

She rolled her eyes. 'No, Papa. It's roast chicken with pumpkin. Deborah's mother made extra by mistake. She said we should eat it or it would go bad.' She cocked her head, her pigtails swaying to one side. 'I think she makes extra by mistake on purpose.'

Amos smothered a chuckle. 'You do?'

Of course Deborah's mother did. She was a good woman who hated to think of anyone going hungry. Her husband was a good man, always available to help.

Amos would miss them when he and Abigail were gone from this place.

'Yes,' Abigail said with a sharp nod. 'She does it all the time, Papa. If it was truly an accident, I think she should have learned better by now. I think she likes to feed us.'

This time his chuckle escaped. 'Well, we shouldn't let on that we know her secret. We will accept her delicious gift and be thankful, yes?' He closed the door, not bothering to lock it.

The door had no lock. None of the homes in Eden did. Except the Founding Elders' homes. And the clinic.

Which was where he needed to go. He bent over and kissed Abigail's soft hair. 'Go play. I'll be by to pick you up very soon.'

He watched her bolt across the compound's open courtyard, narrowly avoiding Sister Joan, who only chuckled and shook her head.

There were good people here.

And bad people.

Amos wondered which of the membership were evil like Brother Ephraim, hiding behind a nice smile and a friendly hello. He wondered which of the people he'd lived among for thirty years were aware that Brother Ephraim knew how to kill with his bare hands, or which, like himself, had simply been oblivious.

Amos had been so blind. So willingly blind, because there had been signs. Signs he'd been too happy to ignore.

No more.

Drawing a breath, he descended the steps into the clinic. It was housed in an earth home, partially underground, like all the dwellings in Eden. He glanced around, finding the room empty. He didn't bother searching – there really wasn't anywhere the healer could be hiding. The patient treatment area was one big room, with a curtain that could be pulled for patient privacy.

36

He avoided looking at the bed in the corner, pristinely made. That was where Abigail's mother had died in childbirth. Afterward it had been especially hard to remember why he was here, living separate from the world. In a proper hospital, women didn't usually die in childbirth.

Not like here, in Eden.

There was only one other place the healer could be. He approached the door to the healer's office, where she kept supplies and medicines, intending to knock, but his fist froze midair. The door was slightly ajar, a faint whirring sound catching his ear. He frowned, having not heard anything like that before.

He approached carefully, afraid of what he'd see. The last time he'd investigated an odd noise, he'd witnessed Ephraim murdering three good people.

He stared, his mouth falling open. He could only see a portion of the healer's desk, but what he did see jarred a distant memory. A thirty-year-old memory. An upright box. A keyboard. A . . .

He wasn't sure what the last thing was. A screen of some kind, but thinner than anything Amos knew existed. Sister Coleen, the healer, was staring at it.

It was a . . . Was that a *computer*? Here? In Eden? It couldn't be. It simply couldn't be. He'd used computers in high school, but the screens had been large and nearly square.

She leaned to one side, briefly disappearing from view. When she straightened, she held a sheaf of papers, which she paged through, then stood.

Oh no. Amos stepped back, nearly tripping over his own feet as he crossed the room to the door, where he stood, still holding the rag around his bleeding finger. *Think fast.* 'Sister Coleen?' he called.

She appeared at the door, looking slightly alarmed. 'Brother Amos. When did you get here?'

'Just now,' he lied. He held up his finger. 'Need some help with this.'

She pulled the door shut, locking it with a key she wore on a string around her neck along with her locket, the same style that every woman in Eden wore. Even the healer wasn't exempt from the marriage laws, having been given to a new husband after her first husband died from old age.

Amos had thought her like every woman in Eden, but clearly she was not. She had a . . . computer. It was too hard to believe. Where was she even getting the power to run it?

The compound had a generator, but it was used for things like Amos's power tools. Not for *computers*. He was stunned.

She no longer held the papers she'd been reading. She must have left them in the office, because now she met him at the door, ushering him to the table next to the bed where Abigail's mother had died.

Amos's mind was reeling. The healer had a *computer*.

How long had she had it? How had she hidden it? He'd been in that office. He'd built that desk.

His breath stuttered as he realized that he'd built it to very exacting specifications – including a small locked cabinet that would have been the perfect size for the tall . . .

He couldn't even remember the word.

'How much blood have you lost?' Sister Coleen asked. 'You're so pale, you might be going into shock.'

No, he thought. *I'm already in shock. I've been in shock since I saw Ephraim kill three of my best friends.* 'A lot,' he said weakly. 'I'm a little dizzy.'

Sister Coleen gently peeled the bloody rag away. 'Oh my, this is a deep one. I keep telling you to wear gloves when you're working with your knives.'

He nodded numbly. 'I will.'

She tsked. 'That's what you always say, Brother Amos. If you slice your finger off, I can't fix it. Then how will you take care of that pretty little girl of yours?'

He mumbled something in response that seemed to please her, but he couldn't hear himself speak over the pounding in his head.

They had a computer. *Here. In Eden.*

They also had a killer here in Eden.

And Amos had no doubt that if anyone found out what he knew, he'd be killed, too. *God, please help me get my baby girl out of this place before they do.*

Sacramento, California
Saturday, 15 April, 5.10 P.M.

'Mercy!' Rafe Sokolov lifted his cane to strike the man a second time, but his legs were unsteady. The man toppled him to the floor with one hard sweep of his arm, glaring, his face one that Rafe knew all too well.

Ephraim Burton, the devil himself.

Rafe had seen the photo of Burton, found two months before in a locket – silver, engraved with two children kneeling under an olive tree, all under the spread wings of an angel with a flaming sword. The symbol of Eden. Of evil. He'd memorized every line of the man's face, hating him with every fiber of his existence. This man had hurt Rafe's best friend, Gideon. And even though she'd never said so, Rafe was certain that he'd also hurt Mercy.

That he was the man who had raped Mercy when she was only twelve years old.

'Mercy!' Rafe shouted again, but she didn't turn around. Didn't move.

Burton scrambled to his feet, kicking Rafe hard in the hip. 'You're insane. Stay away from me!' he said and moved to grab Mercy again. 'Come along, dear. You're okay. Let's just leave.'

'No!' Rafe thundered. Lurching forward, he hooked the curve of his cane around Burton's leg and yanked with all his strength.

Burton stumbled and cursed, but Rafe was already on his knees, yelling at the top of his lungs as he pulled his gun from his holster. 'Police! Stop or I'll shoot.'

Burton spun around to look at him, dragging Mercy around with him.

Rafe sucked in a breath that burned. He'd dreamed about Mercy throughout the long weeks since she'd run from Sacramento. *From me.* And from her brother. But she hadn't looked like this, so lost. Remote.

Rafe had seen her like this one other time – on the security video that had captured her abduction by a killer two months ago. She'd gone blank then, like a zombie. She looked like that now. Standing there, in the clutches of a man who aimed to hurt her. Again. She wasn't fighting.

She wasn't even . . . there. She'd checked out of her current reality. The realization made Rafe's blood run cold.

'Who the hell are you?' Burton snarled, shattering Rafe's panic. Restoring his focus.

'The man who's going to kill you if you don't let her go right now,' he snarled back, aiming his gun at Burton's fucking head. Then, raising his voice again, Rafe shouted, 'Someone call 911. I need police assistance!'

Burton looked at his gun, took a quick, frantic look at the crowd gathering around him, then pushed Mercy so that she fell into Rafe and took off, pulling people to block the path he'd taken. He was out the door before Rafe could catch his breath.

Shouts of 'Gun, he has a gun!' rang out, sending people screaming and falling to the floor, hands over their heads. Parents threw themselves on top of their children. It was chaos.

But Mercy didn't move.

'Mercy?' Rafe moved her so that she sat beside him. She just . . . stared.

'Put down the gun!' a man ordered, running up to them, his own gun drawn. He was young, maybe twenty-five, and the gun in his hand trembled.

Rafe carefully laid his weapon on the floor, his hands in the air.

'I'm an off-duty cop,' he said. 'ID's in my inside pocket.'

Visibly shaken, the airport officer patted his pocket and pulled out the ID. 'Detective Raphael Sokolov,' he said, panting slightly. 'What the hell is this about?'

'That man.' Rafe pointed at the door. 'He left through there. He's wanted by the FBI for bank robbery and murder. I need to get my phone, okay?'

The cop nodded warily. 'Go ahead.'

Rafe held up his phone, then called 911 himself. While it rang, he tilted Mercy's chin up as gently as he could. She was catatonic. Her gaze blank, she sat up on her own, but she was motionless. Like a robot whose battery had run down.

And . . . 'Oh shit, she's bleeding.' Blood had seeped through her white blouse and was spreading from her side to her back.

'This is the operator. What is your emergency?'

'This is Detective Raphael Sokolov.' He told the woman his badge number. 'I need a BOLO for a fugitive escaping from the American terminal at the Sac airport. He assaulted a woman and ran when I tried to stop him. He's about six one, two hundred fifty pounds, muscular, dark hair, black eyes. He was on foot, but he might have a vehicle. His name is Harry Franklin, but he goes by Ephraim Burton as well.' Harry Franklin was Burton's real name. The name on the FBI's most wanted list. 'I also need an ambulance. The victim is bleeding and unresponsive. Conscious, but not cognizant.'

The airport cop had flagged down two other officers, who were now exiting the airport, weapons drawn. Rafe didn't have too much confidence that they'd catch him, but at least they were in pursuit.

'Rafe? Rafe?' Sasha pushed through the crowd that had once again begun to gather now that the airport police had arrived. She carried two small carriers, one in each hand, and was followed by a tall African American woman who looked terrified. She must have been the friend that Mercy had told Sasha she was bringing. The brief relief that her friend wasn't male was quickly shoved aside as Sasha dropped to her knees, carefully setting the two carriers aside. 'Oh my God, Rafe. Are you okay? What happened?'

In his ear, the operator was speaking. 'Are you there, Detective?'

Rafe held his hand up to Sasha, silently asking for her patience. 'I am.'

'I have an ambulance en route and I've notified the airport security to send any medical personnel they have on duty. I've also put out a BOLO on Harry Franklin, aka Ephraim Burton. Is he armed?'

'He must have been. His victim is bleeding from a wound in her side.' He looked around and saw a blade on the floor, having skittered up against the wall when he'd taken Burton down. He pointed it out to the officer, who'd returned and was doing a good job with crowd control. 'Make sure no one touches it. Please.' To the operator he said, 'He had a switchblade. He dropped it. It's here and needs to be taken into evidence.'

41

'I'll inform the first responders. Can you stay on the line?'

Rafe had to focus, a difficult task with Mercy sitting beside him like a doll, staring at nothing. 'I need to contact the FBI. They've been searching for him. But I can use my sister's phone for that.' He held out his hand and Sasha dropped her phone into his palm. He almost called Gideon but decided against it. Gideon would be too frantic to think clearly if Rafe blurted out that Mercy was here and had been hurt. Rafe had known that Mercy was coming because Sasha had told him, but they'd agreed not to tell Gideon, as Mercy had specifically asked that she be allowed to contact him herself when she arrived.

She hadn't told Sasha anything about informing Rafe, and he wasn't sure if that was a good thing or a bad thing. All of his anxiety had been wrapped around seeing her again – would she be glad to see him or would his presence cause her to run back to New Orleans again?

Six weeks ago he'd pushed her for more than she'd been comfortable giving him, kissing her when he'd known he needed to give her more time. More space. She was a survivor of rape, for God's sake. But he hadn't been able to resist her lips when she'd smiled at him on that last day. But then she'd run, leaving him to curse himself for his clumsiness.

Why she'd returned was still a mystery, but Mercy wasn't saying anything right now, even though her friend from New Orleans was pleading with her to speak.

I can't do this to Gideon. Not right now. He found the contact information for Special Agent in Charge Molina, Gideon's boss.

He handed Sasha his phone. 'Stay with the 911 operator, please.'

Sasha swallowed hard. 'What's going on, Rafe?'

'Just wait. I need to make another call.'

The woman who'd followed Sasha dropped to her knees on Mercy's other side, gently lifting the hem of her blouse. 'It doesn't look deep. I don't think it's bleeding anymore.'

Rafe exhaled, too relieved to speak for a moment. 'Good. Just . . . I don't know. Watch her for a minute.'

He dialed Molina's number and a crisp male voice answered.

'Special Agent in Charge Molina's office, this is Jerry Fowler speaking. How can I help you?'

'This is Detective Sokolov, SacPD. I just saw Ephraim Burton in the airport, aka Harry Franklin. He's a fugitive, wanted for—'

'I know the name, Detective,' the man interrupted. 'Where are you, exactly?'

'In Sac airport, at baggage claim. He was trying to abduct Mercy Callahan, who just arrived from New Orleans.'

'I see,' the man said. There were clacking keyboard noises on the other end. 'Have you notified SacPD?'

'Yes. They're en route. Miss Callahan was injured, but it doesn't appear to be life-threatening.'

'May I speak to her?'

Rafe studied Mercy, who still stared sightlessly. 'No. She's conscious, but appears to have disassociated.'

There was a long pause with more keyboard clacking. 'I see,' the assistant finally repeated. 'I've notified SAC Molina and our dispatch. Will you be available for interview?'

'Of course. Whatever you need. But I'll be at the hospital with Mercy. I'm leaving as soon as SacPD gets here and cordons off the crime scene.'

'I'll send whatever agents SAC Molina assigns to the hospital. Do you need me to know anything else?'

Rafe made himself think. 'I don't think so.' But his mind was coming off the adrenaline rush and he began to remember the things he'd forgotten to tell the 911 operator. 'Oh wait, he didn't have an eye patch, like in his photo from the locket. He had a glass eye. It reflected the light. But his face had tan lines. The area around his eye was lighter, like he still wears the patch sometimes. He also has a little gray at the temples.'

'Noted. Thank you, Detective. Can we reach you at this number?'

'No, this is my sister's phone. My phone's still tied up with 911 dispatch.' He gave Molina's assistant his cell phone number.

'Thank you. We'll be in touch very soon.'

The call ended and Rafe handed Sasha her phone before holstering his weapon and turning to the woman still kneeling at

Mercy's side. She was sheltering Mercy from the barrage of clicking camera phones, and for that Rafe was grateful. Mercy had just been assaulted. She'd hate having her privacy violated as well.

'I'm Rafe Sokolov,' he said.

'Farrah Romero. I'm Mercy's friend from New Orleans.' Quiet tears were running down her face, and the woman's Southern drawl was currently thin with fear and panic. 'What happened?'

Sasha had crouched in front of him, sheltering him from the camera phones as well. 'Why isn't she responding?'

'I don't know.' He gently pushed Mercy's hair away from her face and cupped her cheek. 'Mercy, honey, you're safe. It's okay.'

'What *happened*?' Farrah asked again, more forcefully this time.

'She was coming out of the ladies' room and . . .' Rafe hesitated, not knowing how much Mercy had told her friend. He opted for discretion. 'Someone from her past was there. He tried to drag her away. He had a knife, but it looks like we were lucky and she's not hurt badly.'

Farrah met his eyes and somehow he knew that she knew about Eden. About Burton.

'You told the FBI that he had a glass eye,' Farrah whispered. 'He didn't when Mercy knew him. You're sure it was Burton?'

He nodded. 'Absolutely positive. Sasha, can you get my wheelchair?'

'Of course.' Sasha stood, then laid a hand on his shoulder. 'Are you all right, Rafe?'

'Yeah. Just . . . get my chair, please.'

Sasha nodded and went to fetch his wheelchair, which had rolled away when he'd launched himself out of it to strike Burton with his cane. *Wish I'd shot him in the back when I had the chance.* But he hadn't, and it pissed him off. He'd grabbed his cane instead. His fucking cane.

He'd been on disability for six weeks, but as soon as he'd been able to stand, he'd gone to the range every damn week to keep his skills sharp, his reflexes sharper. And to feel like a cop again, just for a little while, even though he wasn't sure he ever would be one again.

Why hadn't he drawn his weapon? Why had that damn cane been his first reflex?

He'd have to worry about it later. For now, he needed to focus on Mercy. At least he'd kept her from Burton's clutches. For now.

The man had come for her *thirteen years* after her escape. Rafe had never believed he'd given up. But *how* had Burton found her? How had he known she'd be at the airport today? He started to ask Farrah who else had known they'd be on that flight, when the woman exhaled in audible relief.

'I think she's coming around,' Farrah said in a low voice.

Mercy was blinking now, slowly. With purpose, unlike the robotic way she'd blinked before. She looked to the right, then left, then closed her eyes. 'I'm sorry,' she murmured.

'For what, baby girl?' Farrah whispered in a kind of crooning singsong tone.

Mercy shook her head slightly. 'I don't know. Is he gone?'

'Yeah,' Rafe answered. 'He's gone. You're safe. Are you hurt anywhere other than your side, anywhere that we can't see?'

She touched her side, opening her eyes to see her blood-covered fingers. 'Oh.' Then she turned to Rafe, her head tilted in the exact way that Gideon's did when he was puzzling something out. 'You're here.'

He wasn't sure if it was a yay-you're-here, or a why-the-hell-are-you-here, or simple surprise to see him. It was impossible to determine from her flat expression and tone. 'I came to meet you. But I didn't want to overwhelm you in case you didn't want to see me, so I stayed out of the way until Sasha could tell you that I'd come along.'

But he wasn't giving Mercy the option to tell him to leave. There was no way he was letting her out of his sight. Not now.

Sasha crouched beside them again, having retrieved his wheelchair. 'I was going to ask you if you were okay with him being here when you came out of the ladies' room, but then . . .' She shrugged.

'Yeah,' Mercy said in a monotone. 'Then.' She was talking now, responding to conversation, but her expression was completely closed off, her eyes unreadable.

But at least she wasn't blankly staring. That had been damn creepy.

A team of medics made their way through the crowd and one of them went down on one knee in front of Mercy. 'Hi. I'm Rick. I understand you had a bit of excitement here. How can I help you?'

'She needs stitches,' Farrah said.

'I'm fine,' Mercy said in that same flat tone.

'You're *not* fine,' Farrah said sharply. 'Goddammit, woman, will you let someone take care of you for once?'

Mercy didn't react. Didn't flinch. Just sat there as calmly as if she'd been meditating. 'I am fine.' She looked at the medic. 'I'm so sorry to have bothered you, but as you can see, I don't need medical attention. A few Band-Aids will be sufficient for the cut on my side.'

'Mercy,' Farrah whispered brokenly. Tears were slipping down her cheeks. 'Please.'

Mercy patted Farrah's hand absently. 'I've had a lot worse, Ro. I'm okay. I promise.'

That did not make Rafe feel even a little better. Or Farrah, from the way her face crumpled.

Sasha met Rafe's gaze helplessly. 'We can't force her to get medical attention.'

Rafe sighed. 'Let's take her to Mom and Dad's.' He glanced at Farrah. 'Mom's a retired nurse. She'll know what to do.'

Farrah's nod was shaky. 'Okay. Thank you.'

'Are you okay with that, Mercy?' Sasha asked.

'I have to get the cats settled,' Mercy replied, not answering the question. But she hadn't said no and Rafe wasn't going to ask again.

'I can get the cats settled for you,' Sasha said. 'Will you allow me to do that for you, at least?'

'I need Rory.'

Rafe frowned, the sudden spurt of jealousy both irrational and real. 'Who is Rory?' Then he remembered. 'The cat. Right. Jack-Jack and Rory, right?'

Mercy looked at him then, her expression so serene it was terrifying in its own right. 'Right.' She drew a breath. 'Thank you. I . . .' She looked away. 'Just, thank you.'

He didn't dare touch her. She was so incredibly fragile. He wasn't sure what to say, but he did know that *I was doing my job* or *Anytime* were bad responses. He decided on, 'You're welcome.'

Sasha handed Rafe his phone. 'The operator came back. She said the ambulance is here.'

'No,' Mercy said loudly, and then she did flinch, having startled herself. 'No hospital. No ambulance.'

'I'll take care of it,' Rafe said, making his voice as gentle as he could, then relayed the information to the operator, but it was too late.

Another pair of medics rushed in, pushing a stretcher. Rafe ended the call with 911 dispatch, then reached for his cane. Grimacing, he pushed up, his good leg bearing his weight as he lowered himself into the wheelchair. He only used the chair when there was a lot of walking involved, like at an airport. He hated the chair, but he found his legs were weak and rubbery. It was his adrenaline crashing, but knowing that didn't make him any happier about having to use the chair. Hooking his cane over the back, he propelled himself to meet the medics halfway.

'Do you need help, sir?' one of them asked.

'Not me.' Rafe showed them his police ID. 'The injured woman is over there.' He pointed to where Sasha and Farrah were helping Mercy to her feet. 'She doesn't want medical attention.'

'Now that we're here, we have to have her sign the form.'

'I'm sure she will. Be easy with her. She's had a shock.'

'Of course.'

Rafe watched as the medics approached Mercy as one might an animal caught in a trap. Mercy's expression remained unchanged as she reiterated that she didn't want transport and signed the medic's form. Her hand didn't even tremble.

Rafe was trembling, though. Now that it was over, all he could see was Ephraim Burton's snarling face. All he could hear was the way he'd called Mercy 'wife'.

The man would try again, but there was no way that asshole was laying a finger on Mercy. *He'll touch her again over my dead body.*

Rafe knew that Mercy wasn't his. She might never be his, no

matter how much he'd wished for it, for her to return to him. But he would make sure that she lived whatever life she wanted, with whomever she wished to live it, wherever she wished.

Even if it's not with me.

Life had dealt her far more than any one person should have to bear. She deserved peace.

Eden, California
Saturday, 15 April, 5.25 P.M.

Amos left the healer's clinic, still reeling from seeing a computer in Eden, but stopped short when he saw the crowd gathered around Pastor in the central courtyard. Amos scanned the group for Abigail, quickly making his way to her side, then kept his expression concerned, mirroring the rest of the community as Pastor gravely announced that Brother Ephraim was missing. The man had gone out to the mountain to fast and pray, as he did several times a year. And now he couldn't be found.

Which, given that Ephraim was a killer, was also probably a lie.

A killer and abuser, Amos thought grimly. *I knew. I knew, but I didn't want to admit it. Didn't want to admit that Ephraim Burton destroyed my family.*

That he'd beaten Gideon. That he'd destroyed Rhoda.

That he'd been so cruel to Mercy that Rhoda had died saving her.

I should have been at Rhoda's side. I should have been the one to save my daughter.

Because Mercy had been his daughter. Not of his blood, but of his heart.

And I failed her the most. He'd allowed her to be given to a brute, even though she'd cried and begged him, her father, to help her.

Amos swallowed hard, willing himself not to cry. *Not here. Not now. Not again.*

He had failed Mercy, but he would not fail Abigail. He held his daughter's hand gently, feeling her dismay. Her fear.

He was afraid too, but not for the same reason. Abigail was only responding to the tension of the adults around her. Amos was afraid

48

because he now knew that Eden was no paradise. The healer had a computer. Pastor had to know about it. Nothing happened in Eden that Pastor didn't know about. Amos wondered who else knew. He wondered who he could trust.

He doubted everything and everyone. For the first time in more than thirty years, he doubted his pastor.

He'd stood behind the man thirty years ago, when Pastor had been accused of embezzlement and fraud. Of stealing from their church. Amos had been young and impressionable and more than a little in awe of the man. So when Pastor let it be known among his trusted flock that he was moving to start a new kind of church, Amos had followed him.

To Eden. And for thirty years, he'd been a faithful servant – to God, to Pastor, and to the community.

But no more. He would get them out, him and Abigail, and then he'd tell the world about the marriage laws that forced twelve-year-old girls to marry brutes like Brother Ephraim. He'd tell the world about the apprentice laws that forced thirteen-year-old boys to serve masters who tried to rape them.

He hadn't believed Gideon when he'd run to them seventeen years before, pale and trembling and crying. He hadn't believed that Brother Edward had touched his son inappropriately. He'd believed the Elders, who'd claimed Gideon had killed Brother Edward, that he'd maimed Brother Ephraim. That Gideon was lazy and hadn't wanted to work. Even though Amos had known that Gideon wasn't lazy. He'd been a good boy. A good son.

He'd told himself there was nothing he could do when Brother Ephraim took Rhoda, claiming she was compensation for Gideon's sin of murder and for stabbing Ephraim's eye out. He'd told himself that there was nothing he could do to keep his Mercy from sharing Ephraim's bed. He'd believed Pastor and the Founding Elders at every turn.

But no more. He'd get his Abigail out, and then he'd tell the world what Ephraim had done.

49

Three

W*hat a clusterfuck.* Crouched behind the driver's seat of a beat-up family minivan, Ephraim held his breath as the woman pulled up to the booth to pay for the time she'd parked. Her name was June Lindstrom, and she was shaking like a leaf in a hurricane. If she didn't give him up on purpose, her fear just might.

'Remember,' he said quietly, 'I'm here and there is a gun pointed right at you.' Which was mostly true. It would take a second for him to move from his hiding place to take her out, but he could manage it.

If there was one good thing about Eden, it was that manual labor kept him in shape. He was as flexible and strong as he'd been when they'd started the community thirty years ago. Stronger, actually. He'd been a scrawny seventeen-year-old. Now he could lift a weaned calf. He could certainly take out a scared woman, even if he hadn't been armed.

'I r-remember,' she stammered. 'Don't hurt me, please.'

'I won't, if you keep our bargain. Act naturally when you pay at the parking kiosk. Use the automated lane. Do not get in the lane with the attendant.'

'I've never paid that way before.'

'Well, today you learn something new.'

The car rolled to a stop and June fumbled with her ticket and then her credit card, mumbling prayers under her breath as she paid.

At least she'd obeyed and hadn't stopped at an attended lane. He didn't want to kill an attendant, too.

Finally they were moving again. 'I did what you said,' June said pitifully. 'You said you'd let me go. You promised.'

Like that meant anything. Ephraim had made millions of promises in his life, none of which he'd ever intended to keep.

'Just drive,' he ordered, risking a peek through the middle window. She'd mounted a shade over the window, which had been a godsend. It kept anyone from seeing into the minivan's interior and allowed him to peer out, also without being seen.

June obeyed, then said, 'Where do I go? We need to go north or south on I-5.'

'Go north.' Once they went far enough, he'd have her pull over and dispose of her. The van was old enough that it might not have GPS, but he wasn't going to take any chances. He'd dump the van as soon as possible and steal another car. He needed to get away so he could think.

Ephraim was rattled and he didn't like it at all. Everything had been going so well. He'd had Mercy in his hands. *In my fucking hands.* He unfolded his body from the floor and sat in the seat behind June. *Much more comfortable.*

Until a car came from the other direction. He blinked hard, the oncoming headlights making his headache worse. *Fucking asshole, hitting me with a goddamn cane.*

He'd seen the blond man sitting in a wheelchair all by himself, but he hadn't given the guy a second thought. He was in a wheelchair, for fuck's sake. He had not anticipated that the guy was going to have freaking ninja skills.

The whole evening had been a clusterfuck. *I should have pulled my gun.* That crack on the head had jostled his brain for a few seconds, and before he knew it the blond bastard had pulled his own gun. By the time Ephraim could have pulled his, there were too many people surrounding them. He would have had to shoot his way out and he didn't have that many bullets.

His gun was old – thirty years old. He'd procured it shortly after they'd started Eden and had kept the gun a secret all this time. It didn't make sense to advertise that he owned a weapon, even to his fellow Founding Elders. Especially to the Founding Elders, because they were all lying bastards. *Takes one to know one, after all.* Hell, the others probably had secret guns, too.

Unfortunately his gun wasn't a model kept in Eden's gun locker. Those were all hunting rifles, their use closely monitored by Brother DJ. Ephraim had only a few rounds of ammo left, all as old as the gun itself. He'd have to get more.

Because next time I'll be prepared. Except that he'd lost the element of surprise. Now Mercy would know he was coming, and she and that Fed brother of hers would make plans.

They'll be ready next time.

So will I. Because there had to be a next time. He needed Mercy, preferably alive. He needed to prove to Pastor that DJ was a lying sack of shit and needed to be dealt with.

Hopefully by meeting his fate with 'wolves'. It was Eden-speak for someone who'd questioned authority and had been quietly killed in the middle of the night. It might be one person, or a couple, or even a whole family. It depended on how widespread the rebellion ran.

It was Ephraim's job to deal with the rebellions and it was one of his favorite Eden responsibilities. Mauling the body postmortem to make it look like 'wolves' was just icing on an already fun cake. It was also an important job because it kept the innocents from wandering at night. It convinced those who were considering questioning them not to do so.

'You can pull off at this exit,' Ephraim said and June obeyed. If she weren't so old, he'd take her back to Eden, but she was nearly as old as Pastor. She wouldn't be able to pull her weight and they already had too many elderly members who sponged off the rest of them.

When he was in charge of Eden, he'd help their elderly meet their Maker expeditiously. That way, he'd get rid of the dead weight and the few who remembered the community's beginning at the same time. Win–win.

June took the exit, slowing as they approached the end of the ramp. 'Where—' She faltered, letting loose a loud hiccuping sob.

'Turn right,' he said, irritated with her.

She did and he was pleased to see that it was a farm road. Nobody around.

'Pull into that little road on the left.' It was an orchard. Lots of cover in the trees. It wasn't picking time yet, so it could be a while before her body was found.

June did as she was told, crying in earnest now. 'Don't. Please don't.'

'Be quiet.' He opened the side door and got out, then opened her door and shoved the pistol into her ribs. 'Put the car in park and get out.'

'You promised!' she wailed. 'I did what you said!'

'And I said be quiet!' he barked, yanking her from the driver's seat. 'Walk. When we've gotten far enough, I want you to face one of the trees and count to five hundred. I'm taking your car, but you can flag down help on the road.'

She stumbled, her body shaking with her sobs. Wheezing in breaths, she finally made it into the orchard.

'This one,' Ephraim said. He'd make it quick. No reason to torture her further. 'Face the tree.'

She did and he shot her in the head, then once again as her body hit the ground to be sure she wouldn't survive to report him to the police. The shots echoed in the quiet of the early evening, and Ephraim ran back to her minivan to get away quickly in case the sounds of gunfire drew attention. He hadn't fired a gun in a while and had forgotten how loud they were. *Should have just broken her neck. Would have been quieter.* He'd remember that in the future.

Once he'd driven back to the main road, he took the next side street and pulled over again. There he raided her purse, taking her cash and credit cards. The cards he'd drop in a dumpster somewhere, along with her phone. It would make an adequate motive for her death.

She didn't have much cash – under fifty dollars. But every little bit helped.

Ephraim had money of his own – a lot of money. The problem was, it was in offshore accounts managed by Pastor, and Ephraim could only get funds through the old man. That would also change once the old man died.

He would have killed Pastor years ago if the wily old bastard hadn't kept the bank codes for the offshore accounts safely tucked in his own mind. To Ephraim's knowledge, nobody knew the codes except for Pastor. He alone dabbled in the accounts. In the old days, Pastor would slip away to the city, where there were bankers on his payroll. Nowadays he did it online with Eden's one computer.

The money had continued to grow, as had their percentages of the pie because half of the original Founders were dead. Ephraim's brother, Edward, had been murdered by that little bastard Gideon, and DJ's father, Waylon, had had a heart attack, the two dying within days of each other, seventeen years before. Doc had died twenty years ago, but he'd been ancient when they'd set up their first camp. Now the only two left of the original Founding Elders were Pastor and Ephraim. And DJ, who'd unfairly been given Waylon's share. Given that DJ was younger than all of them, he could control all the money once Pastor and Ephraim were gone.

And there was no way Ephraim was going to let that happen. He'd lived in the middle of fucking nowhere for thirty fucking years and some of that money had been his before coming to Eden. Edward had earned it and Ephraim was his brother's only living heir. DJ would not touch a penny of that money. Especially given that he'd lied about having found and killed Mercy after her escape.

So Ephraim needed to get Mercy and drag her back to Eden. He'd botched tonight's attempt, but he'd be successful the next time. He'd considered showing Pastor a video clip of Mercy from that CNN interview, but Pastor still believed that the Apollo moon landing was a Hollywood trick. DJ had shown him what was possible with Photoshop and now Pastor didn't believe anything unless he saw it with his own eyes.

So I need Mercy. I want Gideon, but only so I can kill him. The man held no value other than to satisfy Ephraim's need for vengeance.

Buckling up – no reason to give a cop cause to pull him over – he headed back toward the interstate, just as his phone rang. It was a basic smartphone, provided by Pastor, but Ephraim didn't use it often. The sole person he had left on the outside was his mother and her dementia was so progressed that she didn't know him anymore, and he only left Eden a few times every year.

'Yeah?' he answered. If it was DJ, he couldn't let on that he knew Mercy was alive. Ephraim wondered if DJ even knew. He had to assume that he did, otherwise he wouldn't have gone to so much trouble not to bring back any current newspapers that covered Miriam's murder and Mercy's abduction by a serial killer. And that covered the locket.

Fucking hell. That stupid locket. Stupid wedding photo. The man with the cane had recognized him. That photo had to be in the hands of the authorities. That severely limited Ephraim's options for moving around freely. *Fucking hell.*

'Ephraim?' It was Pastor, and Ephraim straightened in his seat out of habit. It pissed him off.

'Yes, Pastor?'

'When are you returning? You were supposed to be back this morning.'

I'll come back when I feel like it, you old fucker. But Ephraim didn't say that out loud. He wouldn't cross Pastor until he had the bank account information. 'I ran into some difficulties. I need another few days.'

'Difficulties?'

Shit. It was Pastor's mild tone. Nothing good ever came from Pastor's mild tone.

'I hit my head,' Ephraim said. Which was technically true. That blond asshole's cane had clocked him but good. 'I have a possible concussion and I'm laying low until I can drive safely.'

It was a ridiculous lie, but the best he could conjure on the spur of the moment.

'Oh, good heavens,' Pastor said, abruptly concerned. 'I knew you had to have a good reason. DJ thought you might have decided not to come back.'

The little prick. He'd like it if I never came back. Then he'd get control of Eden and the money. It wasn't like DJ wasn't already skimming off the top of whatever payment he brought back to the community. Pastor was insane to have given DJ sole responsibility over transporting their products to the buyers and taking the payments. The prick was stealing from them. It was obvious to Ephraim. Unfortunately not to Pastor, and the old man ruled with an iron grip.

'Of course I'll be back,' Ephraim said, injecting a little aw-shucks into his words. 'When have I ever not come back?'

'That's what I told DJ. He has so little faith.'

Ephraim rolled his eyes. Pastor had been drinking his own Kool-Aid for too long. All the praise and worship had blown his sense of reality. No one in the know had any faith, except in sex, drugs, and cold hard cash.

'I'll be back, Pastor. I just need to take it easy for a few days. Is there anything wrong? Did you need me back for anything special?'

'No. Just checking on you, like a good shepherd cares for his flock.'

Oh please. 'I have a splitting headache, Pastor.' Very true. 'Is it all right if I call you back tomorrow?'

'Yes, I'd like that. Call me every day, so that I know you're okay. Where are you staying?'

'In Santa Rosa. With Regina.'

The madam operated the only place of business that Ephraim frequented. She kept a stable of young faces, replenishing them with fresh talent whenever Ephraim was due to visit. He paid her well, and she protected his privacy. Win–win.

'I see,' Pastor said. 'Should we target more of the younger girls for Eden? I hate that you have to go elsewhere for your needs.'

My needs. Pastor sounded so Victorian sometimes. 'That would be amazing. I can ask Regina if she knows of any runaways that would suit.'

'You do that,' Pastor said warmly. 'I'll talk to you tomorrow. Go take some aspirin.'

'I will,' Ephraim promised. 'Gotta go.'

He really wanted to check into one of the hotels close to the airport, but he didn't dare now. He had no doubt that his fuckup this afternoon had put Mercy's Fed brother on alert. If the authorities put his photo on the news, a hotel clerk could recognize him and turn him in.

So he headed toward Santa Rosa. He'd be safe at Regina's place. He had some research to do and she always let him use her Wi-Fi. His first task would be to identify who that blond guy with the cane was. That asshole was going down, and Ephraim was going to make it hurt. With the blond guy out of the picture, and Gideon gone, Mercy would be unprotected.

She'd walked away with him in a daze, her eyes blank. It would have creeped him out except that he remembered her having done that during the year they were married, every time he visited her bed. She'd just tune out.

It was still a little creepy, actually, but at least he knew she wouldn't put up a fight.

Eden, California
Saturday, 15 April, 5.35 P.M.

Pastor was on the move. He'd sent out a search party of most of the compound's men, including Amos, to look for Brother Ephraim. But he'd sent them as the daylight was waning, when they'd be less likely to see anything – a trail, any markers Ephraim had left behind. A body.

Amos didn't care if they found Ephraim or not, alive or dead. He wanted to know what Pastor knew. He *needed* to know.

Because some small part of him still wanted to believe that Pastor loved them all, that he was the shepherd he'd always claimed to be. That Amos and all of Eden's residents were safe in Pastor's care.

A larger part of him knew that such blind faith was folly, and that was what had gotten him into this mess to begin with.

Amos fell behind to the back of the pack and waited for them to walk far enough ahead that he was left in the encroaching shadows. That was all right. He didn't need light to see. He knew these woods. He always knew the woods, familiarizing himself with the terrain whenever Eden moved to a new location. He was the carpenter, the woodworker. He spent hours examining the trees, picking out the best specimens for his work.

Now he crept quietly through the forest in the direction that Pastor had gone. And, sure enough, after a few minutes, he heard the man's voice, full and rich, with its 'preacher cadence'.

'Well, where is he?' Pastor demanded.

Amos frowned and went still.

Who was he talking to? Pastor had walked off by himself.

'You said that last time,' Pastor snapped, although no one else had spoken. 'Fetch him. Now.'

Amos crept closer and blinked. Held tightly in Pastor's hand was a slender . . . box. It looked like a deck of cards. Except it was lit up, illuminating Pastor's scowling face as he spoke.

'I see. When he is no longer indisposed, can you have him call me?'

Call him? *Call him?* That thing . . . that *tiny* thing was a . . . a *phone?*

No way. Wow. He remembered car phones, and Eden newcomers had whispered about how small the devices had become, but this . . . *Wow.*

Pastor must have ended the call, because he looked up to the sky and murmured, 'Dammit, Ephraim, what have you done now?'

Amos held his breath, listening for the next words, but Pastor tapped the thing in his hand and held it to his ear. 'Ephraim?'

Amos stiffened. Ephraim had a phone too, obviously, and was not lost in the wilderness. Which was a shame.

'When are you returning?' Pastor asked. 'You were supposed to be back this morning.' Then he frowned. 'Difficulties?'

Oh. Amos knew that tone. When Pastor spoke gently like that, it was never a good thing.

'Oh, good heavens,' Pastor said, sounding abruptly concerned. 'I knew you had to have a good reason. DJ thought you might have decided not to come back.' Then he rolled his eyes heavenward again. 'That's what I told DJ. He has so little faith.'

Brother DJ was involved, too. Of course he was. Amos had never liked the young man, especially after Brother Waylon died. Amos had loved Waylon Belmont like a brother, but the man's son had been coddled to the point of ruination.

'No,' Pastor said. 'Just checking on you, like a good shepherd cares for his flock.' Another eye roll. 'Yes, I'd like that. Call me every day, so that I know you're okay. Where are you staying?' A pause. 'I see. Should we target more of the younger girls for Eden? I hate that you have to go elsewhere for your needs.'

Target. His needs. Amos leaned against a tree, his knees suddenly weak. *Younger girls.* They'd brought in younger girls *for Ephraim.*

They gave him my daughter. Mercy. Bile rose in Amos's throat and he had to focus on not throwing up.

'You do that,' Pastor was saying warmly. 'I'll talk to you tomorrow. Go take some aspirin.'

Pastor tapped the screen again, then slipped the phone – which was still blowing Amos's mind – into his pocket. Exhaling impatiently, he turned for the compound.

Amos held himself as still as stone, not risking a single breath, a single twitch.

Pastor walked by within about twenty feet of him, muttering, 'Damn the day I let you in. Should have kicked you to the curb years ago. Would have if it hadn't been for Edward.'

Amos waited until he could no longer hear Pastor's footsteps and made his way to where the man had been standing. There were some large boulders on the ground that Pastor had been sitting on – and it appeared that one of them had rocked a little when he stood up.

Crouching low, Amos looked around to make sure he was alone before tentatively pushing at the boulder. Which really did move. Way too easily.

He pushed a little more and the boulder rolled back, revealing that it was hollow. And that it was hiding a small satellite dish. Amos had seen these back in the 1980s, before he'd come to Eden. His neighbor had been the first on their block to get a satellite dish for cable TV. But here?

He stared for a long moment, trying to make sense of it all. Then remembered where he was supposed to be. He returned the boulder to where it had been, then backed carefully away, into the forest. Retracing his steps, he caught up to the search party, still looking for signs of Brother Ephraim.

'Brother Amos,' one of the others called. 'We were worried. We thought we'd have to send a search party for you, too.'

Amos made himself smile apologetically, hoping that no one could hear the nervous pounding of his heart. 'Sorry. I thought I saw a movement in the woods, but it was only a fox.'

The group of men, most of whom Amos would have called friends, gave him a good-natured ribbing about getting lost in the woods and the difference in size between Ephraim Burton and a fox.

Should have said that I saw a snake, Amos thought. *Would have been closer to the truth.*

Sacramento, California
Saturday, 15 April, 6.55 P.M.

Jeff Bunker ignored the ringing of his phone, focusing instead on his laptop screen. He still had five minutes to make this deadline, dammit, and he wasn't going to let his editor rush him into making a mistake. He'd been working this Mercy Callahan story for the past six weeks, ever since a brutal serial killer had been brought down practically in his own backyard.

He frowned at the words on the screen, his fingers slowing to a random *tap-tap-tap* on the keyboard. *Stop. Just stop. Admit the truth.*

Which was that he wasn't proud of this story. It wasn't his best work and he wasn't finished with it. He couldn't help the feeling that he'd only exposed the tip of the iceberg. With just a little more time . . .

No, that wasn't the truth. Not the whole truth, anyway. Yes, he wanted more time. But he'd *had* time today. He'd had nearly seven hours to finish the story, between airports and the flight from New Orleans. But he hadn't even started until he'd gotten home from the airport, his heart still racing to beat all hell.

His knew he'd worried his mom, ignoring her demands to know where he'd been for the past three days. *You may be in college, Jeffrey*

Bunker, but you're still only sixteen years old. You can't just disappear for three days!

She was right, of course. But he hadn't been able to talk about it. It wasn't just that he didn't want to talk about it. He physically couldn't. His tongue was still as frozen as it had been ever since last night. Ever since he'd come upon that old woman's body.

And had seen her killer's face.

So as soon as he'd gotten home, he'd fled up the stairs to his bedroom, where it was safe. Where the killer couldn't find him.

He hoped. *Please don't let him find me. I really am too young to die.*

He'd stared at his laptop for a long time that afternoon, trying to think of what to write about Mercy Callahan, but only able to think about the man he'd seen leaving the apartment of Mercy's next-door neighbor.

After the man had killed her. He'd *killed* her.

And then, as if seeing the man's face in Mercy's apartment building hadn't been bad enough, the guy had been on Jeff's flight. The man had been several rows behind him, but Jeff had sat frozen in fear for the entire flight. *Did he see me? Did he recognize me? Will he kill me, too?*

He'd finally thrown himself into writing this piece on Mercy Callahan to keep from thinking. To keep from remembering the body of the old lady lying on her floor amid the wreckage of her apartment. Mercy's neighbor had been dead. He'd checked.

And had he called the cops? He huffed bitterly. And have them think he'd killed her? *Hell, no.* He'd backed out of the apartment, hoping he hadn't touched anything but too freaked out to remember.

Not my business. Not my business. But he didn't believe the mantra now any more than he had the night before as he'd chanted it endlessly as he'd tried to sleep. 'Tried' being the operative word.

Focus on your work. Get this story done. Then you can figure out what to do about the old lady.

But now he simply stared at the screen, only able to see the old woman's body, crumpled on her apartment floor. He hadn't been able to help himself – he'd lifted her to the sofa. Yes, he'd even disturbed a fucking crime scene, but he hadn't been able to stand the thought of her lying in the middle of the trash the intruder had left behind.

The intruder he'd seen leaving the woman's apartment.

When his phone rang again, Jeff picked up. 'I'm not finished yet,' he snapped.

'Yeah, kid, you are.'

Jeff had to bite his tongue to keep the *I'm not a kid* from escaping his mouth. Because as much as he hated it, he was a kid. *Let it go*, he told himself. *Stay calm and employed.*

He'd been lucky to get this job with the *Gabber*. Not many of the students in his classes had actual real-life jobs in journalism. That this one was with a less-than-classy gossip blog wasn't amazing, but he was getting paid. And everybody had to start somewhere. *I mean, TMZ was a rag when it first started out.*

It's still a rag. His mother's voice was like a buzzing gnat. *You could do so much better, Jeffy.*

Probably, but this was what he had right now.

'It's not finished, Nolan. I'm not finished.'

'And I say you are. You've been working this story for six weeks, Jeff. It's time to let it out into the world.' Nolan Albanesi spoke in levels of oil. There was the sleazy, greasy Nolan and the icky, too-much-fried-food Nolan. This was the WD-40 Nolan, easy, slick, and hard to elude.

'Why?' Jeff asked, suspicious.

Nolan laughed. 'Haven't you seen the news?'

'Not yet. I've been working on the story write-up pretty much nonstop.' Which was a lie, but there was no way he was telling Nolan about the old lady's body.

'So industrious,' Nolan mocked. 'Send me what you've got, kid. I'll polish it and post.'

Alarm bells were dinging. 'Why?' he repeated.

'Because your subject was nearly abducted from the airport an hour ago. It's all over the net.'

Jeff inhaled sharply. 'What?'

'You heard me. Some dude tried to grab her and take her right out of the airport. The fact that she's the same Mercy Callahan who got snatched back in February hasn't been connected by a lot of the news agencies.'

Think, Jeff. Think, for fuck's sake. 'You said that some dude tried. He didn't succeed?'

'No. But Callahan's news again and we're ahead of the power curve. We've got your article. So send it to me,' Nolan finished, carefully enunciating every word. 'Or I'll give the story to someone else.'

'No!' Jeff exploded. *Over my dead body.* He winced. Bad choice of words, because the image of the old lady's body barreled back into his mind. 'It's just not finished. There's more to this story, Nolan. I know it.'

'Then write a sequel,' Nolan snarled. 'But for now, send me the fucking story or you're fired.'

Jeff's stomach was sick. He couldn't be fired. It wasn't much money, but he needed every penny of it. His scholarship didn't cover even half of his college expenses. 'Fine. But give me a minute to delete a few paragraphs. There's stuff there that I'm not comfortable including.'

'Send it to me,' Nolan said, back to his slightly sleazy self, but at least he wasn't yelling anymore. 'I'll decide what gets deleted, but I want to read it in its entirety first.'

Yeah, right, Jeff thought. He might have been a little young and a little naive, but he wasn't stupid. 'Fine, will do.'

Ending the call, he scanned the story and deleted the paragraphs that had seemed titillating before last night. Before that dead lady's body. So Mercy had been a party girl in college. So what? So were thousands of other women. The asshole who'd been all too ready to dish dirt for a price wasn't relevant to her story now. He gave it one last read-through, then uploaded it to the *Gabber*'s server.

He closed his eyes. And now he had to figure out what to do about the dead lady. And Mercy Callahan. Because he'd be so very surprised if the man who'd tried to abduct Mercy from the airport wasn't the same man he'd seen leaving her neighbor's apartment. After killing her.

Jeff stood abruptly, pushing the chair back. He paced the length of his bedroom, trying hard not to spiral into panic again. He wanted to talk to his mother. Get her advice. But he knew what she'd say. He had to tell the police what he'd seen.

Shit. Reaching into his desk drawer, he pulled out the bottle of scotch that he'd taken from his mother's stash. The bottle was still nearly full, because he'd found out that he hated scotch. But it was the only liquor he had, except for the Kahlúa he'd also swiped from his mother, and that had ended poorly last time.

He grimaced as he knocked back a small swallow of the scotch, then two.

By the time he'd had a half-dozen swallows, he'd finally slowed his pacing. He sank onto his bed because the room was spinning now.

I'm scum. 'I'm a terrible person,' he slurred, covering his eyes with his hands.

But at least he'd cut the most damaging parts of the story. That was something, right?

No, that's basic human decency, his mother's voice said. *That's the very least I expect from you, Jeffy. Don't disappoint me.*

'Okay, Mom,' he said slowly. 'I'll call the police.'

When I'm not so drunk, because who'd believe me like this?

Four

It was humiliating. Mercy stared out the window of the SUV she was to borrow from the Sokolovs for the duration of her stay. Going all zombie like that. She hated when that happened. But the worst had finally happened. Ephraim had found her.

She drew a breath, forcing the memory of Ephraim's cruel eye from her mind. *Push it in the box. Push hard. Now nail it closed.* It was a visual that usually worked. Some days she had to mentally hammer a lot more nails into the box to keep it closed. Today was one of those days.

She'd been braced for a rough road, but she'd been ready to try. Now, after staring into that one eye of his? *I'm still ready.* Which was kind of a shock, if she was being honest with herself.

He'd found her. After all these years, Ephraim had found her. And she wondered why she hadn't been afraid before that he would. She had wondered what the Founding Elders had told the people of Eden after her disappearance. Probably that she'd been torn apart by wolves. It was what they'd said when Gideon had run away.

And I believed them. She imagined the people of Eden had believed the lie about her 'sad demise' as well. But DJ had known the truth. No wolves tearing her limb from limb, just a monster wearing the pretty face of a young man with white-blond hair. Who shot girls and their mothers with his gun.

And . . . she wasn't going to think about that right now. *In the box. Hammer the lid.* She visualized her hand gripping the hammer, each

65

strike confident and sure. Each nail entering squarely, with finality. The lid staying closed. The bad things trapped inside the box.

A soft meow came from the ball of fur in her arms. The first thing she'd done when the SUV doors were closed was to let Rory out of his carrier. She'd asked no one's permission and no one had said a word in protest.

'He's very pretty,' Rafe said from beside her, startling her even though his deep voice was purposefully quiet. Nonthreatening. She truly appreciated his effort.

'Thank you,' she murmured. 'He's a good cat. They both are.'

Rafe had climbed into the backseat with her after Sasha had loaded their luggage and his wheelchair into the back of the SUV. Farrah was up front with Sasha, who was driving a little faster than she probably should have, but she was nervous. As she should be.

I've brought trouble to their door. And that wasn't okay. Mercy would have to find another place to stay, but she hadn't even tried to suggest it tonight. She was too tired to argue with all of them.

Fortunately, Sasha wouldn't be getting a ticket. They had a police escort, but it hadn't lessened their fear. Everyone had been silent up until the moment Rafe had spoken. The atmosphere was so tense, it could have been sliced with a knife.

'How old is he?' Rafe asked.

'They're six years old. Littermates.'

Rafe was quiet for a long moment. 'Rory brings you comfort?'

'He does.'

Another silence, then Rafe sighed. 'We need to tell Gideon. It's not fair for him to hear about this from the news or another Fed.'

Mercy's first reflex was to say no. Firmly. But Rafe was right. 'Can . . . can you do it? I'm still . . .'

'I understand.' He reached out and she thought he'd touch her, but he gave Rory a stroke instead.

'Soft,' he commented.

She wasn't sure if she was disappointed or relieved that he'd touched the cat and not her. But she supposed it was okay to be unsure. She had, after all, just endured what Farrah would call a 'trauma'.

Mercy glanced at Rafe from the corner of her eye. He was as handsome as she'd remembered, blond and somehow tanned in April, although he had dark circles under his eyes, too. She wondered why he hadn't slept well. Wondered if it was because his injuries still pained him or if he'd been worried about seeing her.

Retrieving his phone, he caught her staring. One side of his mouth lifted, but he made no comment. Instead, he hit a contact on his phone and Mercy closed her eyes.

Gideon.

She'd hoped to have a little more time to prepare herself, but it didn't matter. She'd had plenty enough time. Weeks since learning why her brother had escaped Eden. Years since they'd been reunited after her escape.

She didn't remember the day of their reunion very well. She'd been out of it, still. Thirteen years old and traumatized. In pain from the surgeries she'd endured after being discovered nearly dead at the Redding bus station by a well-meaning bystander. She'd been placed in foster care after her release from the hospital, but she'd had no idea how much time had passed, having rocked herself for hours at a time.

And then Gideon had walked through the door of the foster home, looking handsome and healthy and strong and so excited to see her. But she hadn't wanted to see him. She'd wanted to scream at him and claw her hatred into his skin. She'd wanted her brother to pay for every time Ephraim had hurt her. For every time the monster had hurt Mama. She'd wanted Gideon to pay for Mama's death at DJ's hand. She'd wanted Gideon to drop to his knees and beg her forgiveness, but he hadn't and she'd hated him for that, too. Everything in her life that was bad was because Gideon had run from Eden. Abandoning them. *Abandoning me.*

Or so she'd thought. Now she'd be begging *his* forgiveness.

'Hey, it's me,' Rafe said softly when his call had connected.

With Gideon. *God. He should hate me. He still might before all this is over.*

'Well . . .' Rafe cleared his throat. 'Yes, something's happened. First, I need you not to freak out. Everyone is okay.' Rafe winced and Mercy could hear Gideon's voice from where she sat, even though Rafe had not put his phone on speaker. 'Mercy is here.' Another wince. 'Yes, here in Sacramento. Here with me and Sasha. Plus a friend who came with her.' A pause and more wincing. 'I don't know exactly why she's come back or how long she's going to stay, but, Gid, I need you to listen.' He blew out a breath and continued. 'I'm not sure how to say it, so I'll just say it. Ephraim Burton was in the airport, waiting for her.' A pause, then, 'You still there?'

Apparently Gideon was still there, because for the next two minutes Rafe nodded, listening. 'I understand,' he finally said. 'I was shocked, too.' Rafe glanced at Mercy with a slight grimace. 'She's physically okay. Burton sliced her side, a cut about two inches long.' He massaged his temples. 'He tried to drag her away. I . . . stopped him, but he got away.' He rolled his eyes. 'Of *course* I reported it. I called it in to SacPD dispatch and I called your boss, too. They've got airport police pulling surveillance tapes to figure out where he went. Then I called you because I didn't want you to hear about it from someone else.' He listened again, his expression softening. 'No apologies necessary. I knew you'd be upset. You have every right to be. But she really is okay. We're just on our way to Mom and Dad's house for a little bit of first aid.' He offered the phone to Mercy, then mouthed, *He wants to talk to you.*

It's time. Mercy swallowed hard and forced her hand to reach for the phone. 'Hello?' she said, barely able to hear her own voice over her beating heart. The phone was warm and it smelled like Rafe. She drew the scent in, letting it calm her as she'd done weeks ago when she'd sat by his bedside after he'd saved her life. He smelled like citrus and clean wood smoke and it was the best scent ever.

'Mercy?' Gideon's voice broke, drawing her mind away from Rafe's scent. 'Tell me you're all right.'

'I'm fine. I promise. I'm not bleeding anymore.'

'Where are you, exactly?'

'In an SUV. The backseat. Right side.'

There was a huff, then a shaky laugh. 'Right. I forgot. Miss Literal. I guess you must not be too hurt or you couldn't make jokes.'

Mercy wasn't joking. She'd simply answered his question, but after giving it a few seconds' thought, she could see where he might have thought she was joking. She'd never quite gotten the hang of humor.

'Right. I'm only a little hurt, like I said.' She hesitated, then pushed forward. 'I came back to see you. To . . . explain some things. Can we schedule a time to meet? I know you must be busy—'

'Mercy, stop. There is nothing that is more important to me than seeing you. I'm already in my car.'

'With me, Mercy!' a female voice called out. Daisy. 'Hi!'

The memory of Gideon's fearless girlfriend made Mercy smile. The woman bubbled joy. 'Hi, Daisy.'

'We're on our way to the Sokolovs' house,' Gideon went on. 'If that's okay.'

Her smile faded. *No, no, no.* It was not okay. *I'm not ready. I'll never be ready.* But Rory was purring in her arms and Rafe was smiling at her encouragingly. 'Yes, of course. I mean, if it's okay with the Sokolovs.'

'It is,' Gideon said with the assurance of someone who knew he was always welcome.

Mercy had that with the Romeros. And with her brother. Her other brother, anyway. The half brother whose green eyes matched her own.

And Gideon's. It was time she told her brother that she'd found their father's family. And admitted that she'd hidden the information because . . . *I'm selfish.*

'Then I guess I'll see you soon. Bye.' She handed the phone back to Rafe, cuddling Rory closer, nuzzling his soft fur. His purr was a relaxing sound on a good day.

This wasn't a good day. Dread hung heavy, weighing her down like a lead apron.

'Yep,' Rafe was saying. 'Plan on staying for dinner. Mom will be happy to have a full house.' He ended the call and reached out again, stroking Rory with tentative fingers. 'It *will* be okay, Mercy.'

She forced a smile. 'Of course it will.' She drew a deep breath. *Be brave.* 'And for you,' she murmured, because she needed him to know.

He leaned in closer, his scent a balm to her frayed senses. 'For me?' he whispered.

She nodded. 'I came back for Gideon. But also for you.' *To tell you that this will never work out.* She needed to say those words, too. But the look on his face had her mouth closing, blocking the grim pronouncement.

It was a wonder that he didn't light up the entire vehicle, his grin was so bright. He was . . . golden.

But his voice was still barely audible when he replied, 'I hoped so. I missed you.'

She hadn't cried during the whole airport fiasco, not while the police were asking her questions, not while the crowd of people craned their necks to see who she was and why she was causing such a stir. But those three little words had her eyes burning. *I missed you.*

She'd missed him, too. His smile, his quiet happiness, his laughter. The way he made her feel like she was . . . enough. She turned her head before he could see her tears, but she was too late.

Or he was simply too observant, because a soft handkerchief was pushed into her hand. 'It's clean.'

She choked on a laugh. 'Thank you.'

He leaned back in his seat, looking like the cat that got the cream. On other men it would look conceited and smug. On Rafe, it looked happy.

He missed me.

She wasn't sure what it meant. Wasn't sure that she should even allow him to feel such things. But she didn't want him to stop. She wanted to lean into him, to draw from his strength, to warm herself with the heat that he put out. He was like a furnace.

But she didn't.

She wasn't made to give effortless affection like he did. *Maybe I never will.* Maybe after Ephraim's abuse, she'd never be normal. Fury at Ephraim Burton suddenly bubbled and boiled over. She wished she'd killed him.

He touched me. Cut me. Was going to take me back to Eden. And I was going to let him. She'd allowed him to lead her away, a lamb to slaughter, and she hadn't even tried to fight.

That made her angrier, but the anger was at herself, and she deflated. *I'm so tired.*

And then something warm brushed her elbow and she looked down to see that Rafe had placed his hand on the bench seat, palm up, about three inches from her hip. Just there, no pressure.

Hers to take. If she wanted.

And she wanted. Loneliness swelled, taking her by surprise.

Be brave. Be a different Mercy. It doesn't have to mean anything more than comfort. Just like Rory gives.

Which actually *was* humorous. *How ridiculous.* The comfort she got from her cat was nothing like what she could get from Rafe Sokolov. *But at least I can do humor.* Her lips curled upward and she readjusted the cat so that her hand was free. Carefully she placed her palm on his, her shoulders sagging when he twined their fingers together. It was real. And secure.

He never said a word. Never even indicated that they were touching. Except for the tiny squeezes that he gave her every few minutes or so, until Sasha pulled the SUV into the Sokolovs' driveway.

'We're home,' Sasha announced. 'The kitties can chill in my old bedroom unless you need to hold one when Gideon comes.'

Ah. Sasha had figured out that Mercy's cats helped reduce her anxiety, much like Daisy's service dog, Brutus, a tiny papillon mix. That wasn't a big surprise, though. Sasha was a social worker. Empathy was her stock-in-trade.

'I think I'll be okay without them,' Mercy said, and Rafe gave her hand another little squeeze before letting her go to open his car door.

'I hope you're hungry,' he said. 'I texted Mom that we were coming with guests. She's cooking.'

'I'm starving,' Farrah said lightly. 'What is she cooking?'

Sasha shrugged. 'Something Russian. Whatever it is, it'll be amazing. Farrah, can you take the other cat? I'll get the litter boxes and food. You need your chair, Rafe?'

'No. I'm good.' He swung his legs from the SUV, leaning on his cane as his feet hit the pavement. 'Better hustle, Mercy. Dinner is waiting and we are not very polite. You snooze, you lose around here.'

Holding Rory as tightly as the cat would allow, Mercy followed them in. Maybe it would be okay after all. And then the police cruiser pulled up behind them, blocking the driveway, reminding Mercy of the bitter truth.

Ephraim Burton was still out there and he would be back. Picking up her pace, she all but fled into the Sokolovs' house. Where it was safe. For now.

Granite Bay, California
Saturday, 15 April, 7.50 P.M.

'Welcome, welcome!' Irina Sokolov ushered them all into their family home, a smile on her face. 'My goodness, you two girls must be exhausted after your trip.'

And your ordeal went unsaid. Diplomacy and hospitality were Rafe's mother's gifts and he loved her for them, especially at the moment when Mercy rushed into the house, looking over her shoulder at the cruiser parked across the driveway.

Her smile was gone and Rafe wanted it back. He'd managed to eke one out, there at the end, but he'd been watching her over his shoulder as she'd given the cruiser a long, hard stare, the pale haunted look returning to her face.

'Mercy. It is so good to see you again.' Irina started to give Mercy a hug, then hung back. 'You're bleeding.' She shot Rafe an outraged glare. 'Why did you not tell me that she was injured?'

Rafe frowned at the red stain spreading on Mercy's blouse. She'd changed in the restroom at the airport, giving the bloody blouse that Ephraim had sliced to the police for evidence. But this new blouse was now bloody as well. 'She said she'd stopped bleeding.'

'And I didn't want him to tell you, Mrs Sokolov,' Mercy said. 'I'm really okay. I must have bumped it when I was getting out of the SUV. I'll just change again. Please start dinner without me. I don't want to make everyone wait.'

'Nonsense,' Irina tutted. 'I will have a quick look and bandage you myself.' She turned to Farrah, her smile wide. 'You are Mercy's friend from New Orleans, yes?'

'Yes. I'm Farrah Romero. Thank you for inviting us to dinner. I hope we haven't intruded.'

'*Dr* Farrah Romero,' Sasha inserted. 'Mom, I'm going to set Mercy's cats up in my room. Don't let Rafe eat all the *kavardak*!' she called as she charged up the stairs, cat supplies in hand.

Irina shook her head. 'There will be plenty. I made extra. Come with me, Mercy. We'll go to my powder room on this floor. I have a first-aid kit there. Farrah, we have other bathrooms if you'd like to freshen up before dinner. Karl!'

Rafe's father appeared in the kitchen doorway, a *Kiss the Chef* apron covering his suit. Rafe realized he must have a meeting downtown later that night.

Or . . . *Crap*. Rafe blew out a breath. He'd forgotten that his parents had tickets to a play tonight. His mother did look awfully nice. They should have been in their seats at the theater by now.

Oh. Dammit. They skipped the play, he thought, feeling relief mixed with guilt. He'd needed his parents tonight and they'd dropped everything to help, just as they always did.

'Yes, my love?' Karl said sweetly, perking up when he saw Mercy and Farrah. 'Welcome, ladies. I hope you're hungry.'

'They will eat,' Irina said firmly, and Rafe watched his father bite back a grin. 'I need you to go to the SUV and get their luggage.' She made a shooing motion to Mercy. 'The powder room is at the end of the hall. Let's get you bandaged up. Farrah, my husband can show you around when he comes back with your bags.'

'What about me?' Rafe asked, feeling extremely useless, which seemed to be his norm these days. *Hold on, there. You kept Mercy safe tonight. That's not useless.* 'What can I do?'

'Go stir the stew,' his father said as he passed Rafe in the foyer. 'That's what I was doing. Don't let it burn.' But he stopped, hand on the doorknob. 'What's that?'

Rafe looked to where Karl was pointing. 'My new cane.' Unlike the wooden cane that his father had hand-made for him when Rafe had left the hospital, this new cane was a cheap aluminum model that Sasha had picked up at a drugstore near the airport. 'I had to surrender the one you gave me to the Feds as evidence, because I used it to hit that bastard Burton. They say I'll get it back.'

Karl frowned. 'But that one's not tall enough for you and you're hurting. I'll make you another one. Go, give the stew a stir, then sit down.' And then he was gone to do Irina's bidding. That was Rafe's dad. He saw opportunities to help, so he helped. No questions, no looking for credit. Karl Sokolov was the best man Rafe had ever known.

And Karl was right about the cane. It wasn't a good fit at all. Rafe made his way into the kitchen, wincing at the pain shooting up his thigh.

'Did you reinjure your leg?' Farrah asked quietly as she followed him. 'You must have hit it hard when you took Burton down in the airport.'

'I may have,' Rafe admitted dolefully, because it hurt like hell. 'It didn't bother me until we got out of the SUV, but that was mostly adrenaline, I think. I'll make an appointment with the doctor to check it out.'

'Thank you,' Farrah murmured, meeting his eyes. She was a tall woman, taller even than Mercy, who was about five feet eight.

'For what?' he asked, genuinely puzzled.

Her brows lifted. 'For saving Mercy's life, both tonight and six weeks ago. She's like a sister to me and we all love her. The thought that she might have been killed . . .' She swallowed hard. 'I can't even consider it.'

Rafe shuddered at both memories, but Mercy's lack of affect was what disturbed him most. He dropped his voice to a barely audible whisper. 'She walked away with him, Farrah. It was like she wasn't even there.'

She nodded, moving to the stove, her gaze troubled. 'I know.' Picking up the spoon Rafe's father had been using, she took over the stirring. 'Sit, Rafe. Elevate that leg. I'll get you an ice pack and I have some ibuprofen in my purse.'

'There's an ice pack in the freezer,' he said, grunting his discomfort as he obeyed her orders. 'I'll take a couple ibuprofen, thanks. Can you get me a glass of water? Glasses are in the cupboard next to the fridge. Have you seen her like that before?'

'You mean all zombielike?' She gave him the ice pack, painkillers, and a glass of water, then took the chair beside him, her attention split between him and the simmering pot. 'Once. But it wasn't as bad as it was today.' She hesitated, then firmed her lips, as if not wanting to share more.

Rafe understood. 'I want you to keep her secrets,' he said quietly. 'She's lost control of so many of them. We know what happened to her in that cult, whether she wanted us to or not. Same with her abduction back in February. She wasn't allowed any privacy during either of those situations. If she's shared things with you in confidence, I don't want to intrude. I won't intrude.'

Farrah's smile was quick and bright. 'I think I like you, Detective.'

He had to smile back. There was no other alternative in the presence of such unfettered optimism. 'Likewise, Doctor.' He downed a few painkillers, hoping they worked. When the pain was this bad, they weren't as effective. 'So how did you two meet?'

'She was my roommate at Tulane,' Farrah said fondly. 'I got back to my room after an orientation and there was this pasty white girl sitting on the other bed with this lost look on her face. She was overwhelmed that day – too much activity, too much noise, too many people. My sister gets like that sometimes, overstimulated, y'know. So I sat down next to her and put my arm around her shoulders and said, "Hi, I'm Farrah and I'm a hugger. I come from a family of huggers and you're stuck with me for the next few months. Live with it, girl".'

Rafe chuckled. 'And how did that go over?'

'About like you'd think. She got all stiff and proper with "I'm Mercy and I'm *not* a hugger." She moved about a foot away, with that look on her face – the one that says she's not amused. But then I gave her a cookie and she kind of melted.' Farrah returned to the stove to stir the stew. 'She was just . . . hurting and touch-shy. But Mercy has a good heart.'

'I know.' He did know. She'd sat with him for hours after he was shot, reading to him, watching whatever he wanted on the TV. Encouraging him when he was down. Little touches that he'd quickly realized were a big deal for her. 'But now she hugs you back?'

'Yes, but it took a long time. Not until I took her home for Sunday dinner and my mama got hold of her. Mama cuddled her and fed her and fussed over her and Mercy hadn't ever had that before.'

'She'd been in foster care up until that point,' Rafe said carefully, not sure how to get the information he wanted without violating Mercy's confidences.

'Yes, she had. They weren't bad people, her foster-parents. They wanted to give her love and affection. They wanted to adopt her, but Mercy wasn't ready for that. I guess she finally was by the time our paths crossed.'

That Mercy's foster family had been good to her was a relief. That they'd wanted to adopt her was a surprise. He was almost certain that Gideon hadn't been aware of it. But another question rose in his mind, because Mercy's path *had* crossed Farrah's. 'Why New Orleans? What brought Mercy there?'

Farrah focused on stirring the stew. 'That's a question you'll have to ask Mercy.'

'I will.' He steered the conversation away from Mercy because that creak of the floorboard meant that someone was coming. 'But you're a New Orleans native?'

Farrah grinned. 'Born and raised. Probably'll stay there till I'm old and pruney.'

Rafe was charmed. 'Why?'

'Because my family is there.'

'And her captain,' Mercy said, entering the kitchen. She took a deep, appreciative breath before gingerly sitting at the table next to Rafe. 'That stew smells really good.'

He tried not to get too excited by her seating choice, but it was hard when she was so near. She smelled like flowers, and the emerald green sweater she'd changed into hugged every one of her lush curves. *Don't rush her. Do* not *rush her.* 'Did Mom get you fixed up?'

Mercy nodded. 'It needed a few butterfly bandages, just like I said. What smells so good?'

So her injury was not a topic of conversation. Rafe could work around it. For now. 'It's *kavardak*, which is really just a homestyle beef stew. The word means "mess", so you basically throw whatever you want into it. Mom's is the best.' He pointed to Farrah. 'Who is her captain?'

'Captain André Holmes,' Mercy said with a fond smile. 'Farrah's . . . intended.'

Farrah snorted a laugh. 'That's what he calls himself. My "intended".' She wiggled the fingers on her left hand, showing off a diamond that sparkled. 'But he put a ring on it, so he can call it whatever he likes, even if he's old-fashioned about it.'

'*Pozdravlayu c pomolvkoy!*' Rafe told her. 'Congratulations on your engagement. May you have a happy home, blessed with laughter.'

'Who is to have a happy home?' his mother asked, shooing Farrah away from the stove after entering the room. 'I'll take over here. You are a guest. You sit and relax. I'll make tea.'

'Farrah is engaged,' Mercy said, patting her friend's hand when she sat at the table with them. 'Her fiancé is a captain with New Orleans PD.'

Irina sighed. 'More police officers. I am surrounded by them – three of my eight children are police officers. The fiancé, he is a good man?'

'A very good man,' Mercy assured her. 'He's been my friend for years. I introduced them.'

Farrah rolled her eyes. 'Only because we were at a party and Mercy wanted to escape. She'd promised me that she'd stay for a while, but figured she could get out if I was distracted by a tall hunk of gorgeous man.'

Irina winked at her. 'Was she right?'

'Yes, I was,' Mercy said. 'They couldn't take their eyes off each other. And I only agreed to go to the party to get Farrah to go because I knew André would be there,' she added smugly. 'I knew they'd be perfect for each other and they are.'

Irina put a loaf of bread in the oven, then put on a kettle to heat. 'It was that way with Gideon and Daisy. I knew they'd be perfect together and they are, but they stubbornly resisted being introduced by me. Gideon actually denied himself my cooking for several months because Daisy attended our Sunday dinners.'

Farrah glanced at Mercy, whose smile had disappeared at the mention of Gideon. 'How did they finally meet, then, if they rebuffed your matchmaking attempts?' Farrah asked.

'I introduced them,' Rafe said. 'I'd known Daisy since she was a little girl and she'd recently come back to town, but she was attacked and nearly abducted.'

'Oh.' Farrah's gaze settled on Mercy, who'd grown a little pale. 'The same one who took you, Merce?'

Mercy nodded soberly. 'The same. Daisy pulled a necklace from her attacker's throat when she was fighting for her life. A locket. Rafe had seen the design before, because Gideon used to have a nearly identical tattoo. Rafe called Gideon for help on the case.'

'And then Gideon and Daisy realized I was right all along,' Irina finished, then cocked her head as a car door slammed outside. 'And here they are, just in time for dinner.'

Beside him, Mercy tensed.

Beside her, Farrah soothed. 'It'll be okay, Merce.'

'I know.' But she sounded uncertain. Trembling, she stood as the front door was flung open and footsteps thundered across the foyer floor. She looked like she was facing a firing squad, and Rafe didn't know how to help her.

'Rafe?' Gideon called out. 'Where is she?'

'In here, Gideon,' Irina called. 'In the kitchen.'

Hesitantly, Rafe stood and offered his hand, genuinely surprised when Mercy took it, squeezing hard. 'He loves you so much,' he murmured into her ear. 'It *will* be okay.'

Her nod was shaky, her grip becoming punishing as Gideon appeared in the doorway.

Her brother came to an abrupt halt, staring at her from haggard eyes. 'Mercy,' he whispered hoarsely. 'You came back.'

Five

Santa Rosa, California
Saturday, 15 April, 8.20 P.M.

'Coffee?'

Ephraim looked up from his laptop to see Regina Jewel standing in the doorway to his room, a steaming cup in her hand. 'Please.'

She entered without the slink in her step that she showed the rest of her customers. Ephraim had known her too long for her wiles to have any effect on him – plus, at forty-five, she was about thirty years too old for him. But she knew what he liked, from the girls she kept to the coffee she prepared.

'Thank you. I needed a hit of caffeine.' His head pounded and he felt a little sick.

Regina eyed him with concern. 'You don't look so good, my friend.'

Except that they weren't friends. But they weren't enemies either, and Ephraim aimed to keep it that way. Powerful in her own right, Regina owned enough cops to run her business smoothly. She was first and foremost a businesswoman, and she respected the financial relationship they'd built over the past decade.

'Got a headache,' Ephraim muttered.

Regina stroked her fingers up his neck, then began to massage his shoulders, which felt so damn good. Until she brushed a lock of his hair at the back of his skull aside and probed, making him hiss.

'Bad bump,' she said. 'Your headache from getting hit in the head by any chance?'

79

'Yes.' Ephraim had to hold back a snarl. 'The massage felt good. More of that.'

'I'll do more later. I need to get some ice for your head.'

'No, it's not that bad. I popped some Tylenol,' he said, then looked back at his laptop. He stored the device here, in Regina's house. She allowed him to keep a locker in her bedroom, and only Ephraim had the key. He didn't think she'd try to snoop, and she knew far worse things about him. Besides, his laptop was password protected, so even if she got curious, she couldn't snoop.

He didn't dare use his laptop when he was in Eden. DJ Belmont was damn handy with technology, and Ephraim would bet his last dollar that DJ had rigged their system so that he could view all computer searches. There was only one computer in Eden, anyway, kept locked up in the clinic. They had a satellite hookup that enabled them to access the Internet, and that was how Pastor managed their funds. It was also how DJ communicated with the customers who purchased whatever illegal substance they happened to be making at the time. Nearly thirty years earlier, it had been pot, but the Feds had gotten good at sniffing out large pot farms. They'd dabbled in opioids, but that had required too much labor for too little profit. Now they grew and sold psilocybin, but that market was becoming iffy as well, what with cities decriminalizing it.

They were good for now, because the market was still strong. It could be decades before shrooms were legal everywhere. Ephraim had no doubt that DJ had a plan for their next illegal venture, and it was all on that one computer. One that Ephraim wouldn't touch with a ten-foot pole.

'Who is Raphael Sokolov?' Regina asked, looking at the screen as she resumed massaging his shoulders. Damn, the woman had good hands.

'A cop. He's the one who hit me tonight.'

'Then he's a bastard,' Regina said soothingly.

'That's for sure.' Ephraim dropped his head, stretching his stiff neck.

'Why did he hit you?'

'I really don't know,' Ephraim lied smoothly.

She chuckled. 'He didn't hit you *that* hard, E. Not enough to scramble your brains. But it's okay. I heard the news reports. I know there are BOLOs out on you all over the state. The reporters say that you tried to abduct a woman from the airport. I saw her photo. She's a little old for your tastes, isn't she?'

'She wasn't when I married her,' he muttered.

Regina stopped the massage. 'You're *married*?'

'Unfortunately, yes.' Because all of his wives were too old now. He wished he could just get rid of them like he did his very first ball and chain, but Pastor frowned on open murder. He'd been able to pass off the first wife's early demise as an accident to the Eden community, but Pastor knew the truth. Ephraim had been officially punished, which for him required taking on another wife who was also too old for his liking. At least most of his wives behaved themselves.

Unlike Mercy, Rhoda, and then Miriam, who'd all run away.

'That's all you're going to tell me? "Unfortunately, yes"?'

'Yes.' Because Regina didn't know about Eden, and he never intended for her to. It was enough that she knew about his predilection for young girls, but at least there they each had equally damaging information on the other. Yes, Ephraim liked to fuck fourteen-year-olds, but Regina sold them, so they were at a stalemate.

'So you married Mercy Callahan?' Regina prodded. 'Did she leave you?'

'Something like that.'

'Huh. And this Raphael Sokolov. Is he her new man?'

'I don't know.' And that pissed him off. He'd been digging into Sokolov for nearly an hour and all he knew was that the man was a homicide detective on leave because he'd been injured saving Mercy Callahan from a deranged killer.

The same deranged killer who'd murdered another of his wives. It was a CNN report about Miriam's murder that had alerted him to the fact that Mercy was still alive.

'I see. What *do* you know, Ephraim?'

'That I'm tired of answering your questions.'

With a thin smile, she pulled up a chair. 'Too bad, because I have

81

quite a few more. I'd heard Mercy Callahan's name before tonight, but I couldn't remember where, so I looked her up. She was one of the three women who escaped that serial killer who was taken down back in February.'

Ephraim tamped his temper down. It wasn't a good idea to make Regina annoyed. 'Yes, she was.'

'And before then, she was living a private life all the way in New Orleans. Where she just happened to be coming from today, according to the news reports. She'd just flown into Sacramento when you tried to grab her.'

Damn reporters. That was more information than Ephraim had expected them to know. 'So?'

'So, you knew she was going to be there. I'm wondering how? Especially since I fielded three phone calls from a guy named Pastor, trying to find you. Apparently you left my number as your emergency contact.'

Ephraim's heart stuttered in his chest, but he managed to meet her shrewd gaze. He'd forgotten that he'd given Regina's number in case of an emergency, but he remembered it now. One of his wives had been about to give birth and Pastor had insisted on a contact number. He couldn't believe he'd been so stupid as to give the man the actual number or that Pastor had remembered it. It had been at least ten years ago. 'Pastor called here?'

'Three times. I told him that you were busy the first two times. The third time he demanded that I "fetch" you. I told him that you'd gone out to the store. I don't think he believed me.'

'When was the third time?'

'Tonight. A few hours before you showed up. I knew something was wrong. You were supposed to be here all week, but you left after one night. The same night that CNN aired a special report on that serial killer, the report that listed Mercy Callahan as one of the women who'd gotten away – aided, I should add, by Detective Raphael Sokolov, who helped to save her life.'

Ephraim grabbed his thighs, digging his fingers deep to keep from reaching for her skinny throat. 'If you knew who they were, why did you ask me?'

'I got curious. You see, I'd expected you to stay longer than you did. I had two young lovelies all ready for you. Turned away other clients because I thought you'd be staying your normal time, but you walked out on me – without paying me. And then I find out that some guy named Pastor is asking about you, because you were obviously not where you were supposed to be. Where were you?'

He made himself smile, even though he wanted to wring her damn neck. 'I don't think that's your business, Regina.'

'When I lie to cover for you, it is. Did you have beignets when you were in New Orleans?'

He gritted his teeth. She was too damn smart for her own good. 'Back off, Regina.'

'Or what?' She seemed genuinely confused.

'Or you'll wish you'd listened.'

Regina laughed. She actually laughed.

Ephraim was holding on to control by a thin thread. But he remained silent, already visualizing how he'd snap her neck. It was his preferred method of disposal – quiet and easily explained away. It was how he'd killed his first wife, which hadn't exactly been planned. More like he'd lost his temper and grabbed her. He guessed she'd been more delicate than he'd thought. Regina was not a delicate woman, but he'd had a lot of practice since then, most recently with Miriam's family. Snapping the necks of Miriam's parents and brother had been incredibly satisfying, and justified. They shouldn't have helped his wife run away from Eden.

But he needed to be more careful with Regina. She was armed. He saw the slight bulge of a pistol in the pocket of her housecoat.

When he said nothing, she smiled sweetly. 'I watched that news report again after I heard that you'd tried to grab Mercy Callahan tonight,' she said. 'They interviewed a woman who'd also escaped the killer's clutches after being held and tortured. She wanted the viewing audience to remember the women who didn't survive. She read all their names and mentioned that Mercy had also escaped, along with another woman. She said that Mercy had been childhood friends with one of the dead women – an Eileen Danton. Name ring a bell?'

Ephraim took a steadying breath. 'Nope.' *Because her name wasn't Eileen. It was Miriam. Miriam Burton. And she was my damn wife.*

And she'd run. He wasn't exactly sure how she'd gotten away, but her family had had a hand in it, of that he was certain. For their crime, he'd killed them and buried them in an unmarked grave. And then, because he hadn't been able to find Miriam, they'd had to consider that she'd gone to law enforcement for help. Which meant they'd had to move Eden. Again.

That had been a pain in the ass, especially in November, with winter approaching. 'Never heard of her.'

Regina smiled again, way too sweetly. 'That's really interesting. Because, you see, the killer apparently took trinkets from his victims.'

Ephraim shrugged. 'So? That's normally what they do, right?'

'Right. But he took a locket from Eileen. They showed it on the news. Said that the third lady who'd escaped him – a Sacramento radio personality named Daisy Dawson – had ripped it from his throat while fighting for her life. It was an important clue, apparently.'

Stay calm. Just breathe. He'd seen the telecast, just as Regina had. He'd seen the locket on the screen. And he'd been afraid that his face would be recognized, that he'd be identified. The newscast had made no mention of finding any photos inside the locket, so he'd assumed Miriam had removed them. But now he knew better. That damn cop in the airport had recognized him, so clearly the police had the wedding photo.

Goddamn wedding photos. I'm going to murder Pastor as soon as I get back to Eden.

With Mercy in tow. There was no way he was going back without Mercy now.

'And?' he managed in a smooth voice that didn't tremble at all.

'And there was a design on the locket. Two children kneeling in prayer under a tree, all under the wings of an angel holding a fiery sword.'

'Sounds pretty.'

'Oh, it is. Just like the tattoo on your right pectoral.'

Ephraim stiffened. *What the fuck?* 'What makes you think I have a tattoo?' He never removed his shirt. Never. *Except . . . motherfucking bitch.* Except when he showered.

Her lips curved smugly. 'Yes, I can see that you understand. Of course I keep cameras in the showers, Ephraim. It's for your protection, you see.' She tapped a manicured fingernail on the edge of his laptop. 'So this is what I think happened.'

My protection, my ass. He tensed his fingers, readying himself to break her fucking neck. 'Please, enlighten me,' Ephraim said, hoping he sounded bored. And not rattled. Because he *was* rattled. And he suspected he knew exactly where this was going.

'Oh, I will. I think you saw the telecast, saw Mercy and Eileen. Saw that Eileen was dead. She was tied to you somehow. I don't know how yet. Hell, maybe she was your wife, after Mercy left you. But they said that Mercy had returned to New Orleans after her rescue from the killer, so that's where you went.'

'You should be a writer. Such intriguing fiction.' Except she'd figured it out. Every fucking detail.

She simply smiled. 'And I checked your laptop. You purchased a one-way ticket to New Orleans in the name of Eustace Carmelo – less than five minutes after the news report ended.'

He stared at her. 'You *checked* my *laptop*?' *How?* How had she gotten past his password? 'What the actual *fuck*? This is my property.'

'My house, my rules.'

'My locker. My fucking property.'

She shrugged. 'You're missing the point here, Ephraim.'

He was seething. So damn furious. 'What *is* your fucking point, Regina?'

'That you booked a flight to New Orleans with a fake ID as soon as that CNN special was over. But something must have gone wrong *there*, because you followed her back *here*.'

Something *had* gone wrong. He'd followed Mercy for days, trying to figure out when he could safely grab her. Determining her schedule had been easy enough – she went to work, her apartment, and her half brother's house – but the woman always had too many people around her, leaving Ephraim frustrated. She worked at the

New Orleans police department, so grabbing her outside work was not going to happen. Each time she'd returned home for the evening she'd pulled into her parking place and was immediately met by one of the other residents of the apartment house, usually gathered on the stoop. She was a popular person, his Mercy, clearly liked by her neighbors.

The discovery of the half brother had been lucky, actually. That information had come from the man's daughter, a chatty little thing, about nine years old. *A little too young, unfortunately.* Give the girl another few years and she'd have been perfect. Ephraim had followed Mercy from her office to the man's home Thursday night and had almost had her in his hands when she'd left after dinner, but her brother had accompanied her home, walking her to her door then driving away with her car. Ephraim had wondered why her brother had taken her car as he'd ventured into the apartment building, but she hadn't answered her door, and he'd been unable to break in.

So Ephraim returned to the half brother's house yesterday, learning all about Mercy's reunion with her half brother's family from the little girl. She'd shared that her mother had borrowed Mercy's car because the family car was in the shop, which explained why the brother had taken her car the night before.

All of that information had come in handy when he'd knocked on the door of Mercy's next-door neighbor, introducing himself as Mercy's brother, John, and asking if the woman had seen her. The neighbor had invited him right in, telling him that she wasn't home because she was spending the night with her best friend and returning to Sacramento the following day. Her neighbor had been so happy to meet Mercy's 'brother' that she'd given him freshly baked cookies and told him everything he needed to know about Mercy Callahan. Everything except that she'd have some big blond surfer boy detective meeting her at the airport. *Bastard.*

So yeah. Something had gone horribly wrong.

'Well?' Regina asked coyly. 'How did I do?'

She'd gotten everything perfect. He drew a breath. 'What do you want?'

'What I always want, Ephraim. Or should I call you Harry Franklin? Both names are on the BOLO.'

He ground his teeth. *Fucking hell. Goddamn motherfucking hell.* 'I don't know that name.'

'Well, maybe not. It has been thirty years since you disappeared after robbing a bank and killing three people. I'm assuming Ephraim is your alias, although it's a truly horrid name.'

She was right about his name. It was horrible. 'Ephraim' had been Pastor's choice, not his own. Just as 'Eustace Carmelo' had been. And the names weren't just Pastor's choice. They were Pastor's punishment, a constant reminder that Pastor held him in contempt.

But Regina wasn't right about the robbery. He hadn't been involved, not that anyone would believe it. He'd been an innocent bystander that day. And the only other people who knew the true story were now dead. 'How much?'

'The Feds never recovered the money you stole. I imagine you've got it squirreled away somewhere. I'll take that.'

He kept his outer expression tense, but relaxed inside, knowing exactly what he needed to do. 'I don't have it. My brother gave it to Pastor for safekeeping.'

'Then you'll get it from this Pastor guy.'

Fat chance. But all he said was, 'I'll need some time. Plus, you should know that all that cash is marked.'

'That's okay. I can change it.'

He'd known she had money-laundering networks – she had to, because running a house of prostitution wasn't legal in Santa Rosa, California. At least not in the past hundred years.

'Then I'll get it. In exchange, what assurances do I get that you won't turn me in?' Not that he was going to give her the chance, of course.

'You don't, dear. You'll have to trust me.'

Like there was any way in hell that he'd ever trust her again. 'I guess I have to, don't I?'

She smiled. 'I guess you do. I'm so glad we had this chat, Ephraim.' She rose, put the chair back where she'd found it, and turned to leave. She didn't see Ephraim come up behind her. She didn't make a sound, because he'd covered her mouth with his hand before snapping her neck like a dry twig.

Dropping her body on the bed, he took the gun and her keys from her pocket, then covered her up. Made it look like she was sleeping. Someone would find her in the morning, but he'd be long gone by then.

Hiding her gun in the bag with his laptop, he grabbed his suitcase, left her house, and drove away in her car, wondering where he'd now spend the night.

Granite Bay, California
Saturday, 15 April, 8.25 P.M.

Mercy couldn't take her eyes off her brother, even as a quiet *oof* came from behind him as Daisy slammed into his back. A sharp bark followed the *oof*, which meant that she had brought her service dog, Brutus.

Of course Daisy had brought Brutus. The dog went everywhere that Daisy went.

And Daisy went where Gideon went. *As it should be.*

Mercy wanted to say hello. Wanted to say something. But even though she opened her mouth, no words came out. She stood there, staring stupidly, as if she hadn't a brain in her head.

And maybe she didn't. She'd walked away, after all. From Gideon. From Rafe. From this family that her brother had made for himself when she'd sent him away with no explanation all those years ago.

Tell him that you missed him. Tell him that you're sorry. But the words would not come. *Then just say hello, dammit. That's all you need to say.*

'Yes. I came back.' It wasn't what she wanted to say. Not even close.

Gideon took a hesitant step toward her, and Mercy tightened her grip on Rafe's hand. She was holding Rafe's hand. She hadn't even realized that he'd offered or that she'd taken him up on it.

Next to her, Farrah rose and gently gripped her shoulders,

pointing her toward Gideon. 'Let go of Rafe, honey,' she whispered. 'You're about to break his poor hand.'

Mercy immediately drew her hand away. 'I'm sorry. So sorry, Rafe.'

'You're fine, Mercy,' Rafe said in a low voice that soothed her frayed nerves. 'Maybe you and Gideon want to take this into Dad's office, where you'll have some privacy?'

Mercy nodded numbly. She'd come all this way to talk to her brother, but her feet suddenly felt like lead. Part of her wanted to stay with Farrah and Rafe, because they were safe. But she owed Gideon the courtesy of a private explanation. 'Privacy would be good.' She drew a breath, straightening her spine. 'Gideon? Would you show me to the office? I don't know where it is.'

Gideon looked around the kitchen, seeming surprised to see the others. 'Of course.' He smiled, but it was clearly forced. 'But first, I'd like to meet your friend. I'm Gideon Reynolds.'

Embarrassed, Mercy's cheeks heated. 'This is my best friend, Farrah Romero. She came with me from New Orleans.'

Farrah's smile was gentle as she shook Gideon's hand. 'I'm so glad to finally meet you.'

Gideon swallowed hard. 'Do you work with Mercy?'

Because Mercy had told him nothing of her personal life. She'd hoarded the details, at first still nursing her anger over what she had thought had been Gideon's role in her torture at Ephraim's hands. Then, once she'd known the truth, she'd been too overwhelmed and ashamed to tell him anything.

Not that Gideon understood that, because she hadn't told him anything. *I am a very bad person.*

'No,' Farrah said. 'I met her in college. We've been friends for many years. I work at the university. I'm in research.'

'She is a doctor,' Irina said. 'And engaged to be married to a police captain.'

Gideon's smile became warmer, less forced. 'Irina should be a detective. She finds out all the good details before the rest of us do.' Then he turned back to his sister. 'Mercy?'

Farrah returned to Mercy's side and gave her a small nudge. 'I'll be here. Call if you need me.'

'Thank you.' Mercy commanded her feet to move, and then she was following her brother out of the kitchen and into the hall, where Daisy stood, wearing her Brutus bag cross-body.

Daisy reached up to give Mercy a hug. 'Welcome back,' she said softly. 'I missed you.'

Mercy sucked in a harsh breath as her eyes began to burn. 'Thank you. I . . . I missed you, too.' And it was true. Daisy's buoyant optimism was so much like Farrah's, and Mercy had wanted to drown herself in it when she'd been here before.

Daisy's grin looked a bit forced. 'Of course you did,' she said lightly, and then she went into the kitchen to wait with the others, leaving Mercy and Gideon alone.

'This way,' Gideon said, leading her down the hall and through a great room with cathedral ceilings and carved wood everywhere. He finally knocked on a door, opening it when someone inside called to come in.

'Gideon, my boy.' Karl was seated at his desk, Sasha leaning against his chair. They were looking at something on his laptop, which Karl closed quickly. Then he stood. 'It's always good to see you.' He rounded the desk to give Gideon a hug while Sasha watched, her expression smoothing from upset to unreadable. Just as her father's had.

Which made Mercy wonder what they'd been looking at on that laptop.

'I was wondering if we could use your study,' Gideon said. 'But if you were doing something important, we can find another—'

'Hush.' Karl gathered his laptop under his arm and motioned to Sasha. 'Let's go check on dinner. Your mother will have something for us to do.'

Gideon sat in one of Karl's guest chairs and pointed to the other, indicating that Mercy should sit. She complied, biting back a wince when the bandage pulled.

Gideon frowned. 'Are you in pain? Should you see a doctor?'

'I saw a nurse. Irina cleaned the wound and bandaged me up quite capably. I'm fine.'

'Okay.' Gideon sat back, his eyes full of worry. 'If I'd known

90

you were coming, I'd have had the FBI there at the airport.'

'*I* didn't know I was coming,' she admitted. 'Not until I got off the plane. I kept thinking I'd turn tail and run again. I'm sorry I did that before.'

'You don't have to apologize. You did what you needed to do to protect yourself. I understand that.' He hesitated, swallowing hard as the worry in his eyes gave way to hurt. 'I guess I don't understand why you needed to protect yourself from me. What—' His voice faltered and he had to clear his throat. 'What did I do wrong?'

Mercy's eyes stung again. *No, you will not cry*. That wouldn't be fair to Gideon. 'Nothing,' she whispered, her voice breaking. 'It was me. All me. I didn't know, Gideon. I didn't know why you'd left Eden.'

Gideon's expression flashed from surprise to sadness to resignation. 'I figured that you didn't know the day we Skyped with that kid from San Diego.'

The young man who'd known an Eden escapee, who'd loved him, and who'd grieved him when he'd committed suicide out of misplaced guilt. During that Skype session, the young man had raged that Eden had preached against homosexuality while their leaders raped young men. It was at that moment that Mercy had understood the truth.

'Did you ever . . .' Mercy had trouble even saying the words. 'Did you ever want to, you know, end it?'

Gideon's eyebrows shot up. 'You mean end my life? No.' Then he sighed. 'Yes. Back in high school. But it was fleeting and Rafe got me through it. Did you?'

She nodded. 'Farrah got me through it. Got me into therapy. Her family is a lot like the Sokolovs.'

Relief shone in Gideon's eyes, so like her own. So like their brothers' and sisters'. *Tell him*.

'So you did have a family?' he said, oblivious to the fact that he had one, too. A biological family. *And that's my fault*. 'I'm so happy to hear that. I was worried that you had no one.'

Because she'd allowed him to believe that. She drew a breath and

91

slowly let it out. 'I have a family. The Romeros, sure. But I also have another family.'

He frowned, confused. 'How? Who? Are you *married*?' He asked the last question with a kind of horror.

Which wasn't too difficult to understand. His best friend had a thing for Mercy, and Gideon didn't want Rafe to get hurt.

'No, I'm not married. I've never had an actual relationship. Not one that's lasted more than a few weeks.' Which had made her attachment to Rafe so much scarier than it should have been. She'd fallen hard into 'like'. It wouldn't have taken much more time to fall into an even deeper, more binding emotion.

'Then how do you have another family?'

'I aged out of the system when I was eighteen,' she said, noting Gideon's surprise at her abrupt subject change.

'I know. I tried to find you for a long time, but you'd vanished without a word and your old foster family had moved to another state.'

She smiled at the memory of the family who'd loved her. 'The Callahans wanted to adopt me, but I wasn't ready for a family, not then.'

'Callahan,' Gideon repeated. 'You took their name.'

'After I left, yes. We still keep in touch. They're a good memory during a time when I had nothing good.'

Gideon's face fell. 'You had me.' But then he sucked in a harsh breath and she could see the moment that he truly understood. The hurt on his face gave way to horror. 'But you didn't know why I'd run. You didn't know the truth. You must have thought I'd left you to rot in Eden.'

She nodded, both relieved and devastated all at once. 'Mama tried to tell me, the day she got me out. But I didn't want to listen. I'd been indoctrinated with the lie that you'd murdered Edward McPhearson because you didn't want to work, because you were lazy.'

'Oh, Mercy,' he breathed. 'I'm so sorry.'

'You have nothing to be sorry for. We were both victims of Eden.'

'It was hard afterward?' he asked tentatively. 'After I left?'

92

'Yes,' she said simply. She wasn't going to get into any of that right now. She had things that she needed to say first. 'For Mama and for me. And I blamed you.'

'I understand.'

Mercy shook her head. 'No, you really don't. I have something to tell you and I need to get it out, so just let me talk, okay?'

Gideon nodded, his concern unabated. But he remained silent, just as she'd asked.

'I aged out at eighteen. I considered coming to find you, but . . . well, I didn't want to. I knew where you were, of course. I've always known where you were.' Her lips curved, just a little. 'I followed your career, even though I thought I hated you at the time. And I both lived for and hated the days you'd call me – my birthday and Christmas, like clockwork. I knew I should let my anger go. My therapist told me that it was eating me from the inside out, but I couldn't. My hate was the only thing that kept me going sometimes.'

Gideon's eyes filled and he opened his mouth to speak, then snapped it shut.

He's going to hate me. I know it. 'Anyway, after my eighteenth birthday, I found our grandparents. Or one of them, anyway. Mama's father had passed away a few years before, and her mother was in a hospice. Cancer.' Abruptly on edge, Mercy rose and began to pace around Karl's office. 'She knew I was Mama's daughter at first sight. Actually, for a minute she thought I was Mama.'

'You look just like her,' Gideon murmured, then clamped his lips closed again.

Mercy remembered the moment she'd laid eyes on her maternal grandmother, the absolute joy in the old woman's eyes. Like Mercy had been the prodigal daughter, returning home. But mostly she remembered how the old woman had wept when she realized that her daughter was dead and that she'd missed all of Mercy's life.

Mercy hadn't felt a lot of sympathy for her. The woman had thrown her daughter out of their home for having two illegitimate children.

'I know. Sometimes I'm happy that I look like her and sometimes I hate looking in the mirror at myself.' She returned to her chair and sat, forcing herself to meet her brother's worried eyes. 'Mama's mother changed her will. Left everything to the two of us. I'm the executor. I told her that I'd find you and tell you, but . . . I didn't. Yours is still in trust.' She closed her eyes. 'I found a good financial advisor. Your share has grown a lot.'

She fell silent, unable to make the necessary words come.

Gideon exhaled heavily. 'Is that what you're worried about? That you didn't tell me about the money? I don't care about money, Mercy. I care about *you*.'

Tears burned and Mercy could no longer hold them back. They felt hot on her cold cheeks. 'No, it's not just the money. I took my share and went to New Orleans.'

Gideon was silent so long that she opened her eyes. He was staring at her, his cheeks wet with his own tears. 'Why New Orleans? Were you trying to get away from me? To go as far away as you could?'

'Yes and no. See, our grandmother had searched for us, but we were already in Eden by then.'

Gideon's swallow was audible. 'Why did she search for us?'

'Because our father's parents came looking for Mama. Looking for you. They didn't know that I'd been born, too.'

Gideon started to speak then shook his head. 'Go on. I'm listening.'

'They went looking for her right after they found out that their son had fathered a child with a fourteen-year-old.'

'That was Mama.'

'No, another fourteen-year-old. He'd been in sales and traveled a lot, basically impregnating young girls all over the southern US. His parents – our grandparents – were appalled. One of the girls had him charged with statutory rape and he went to jail for a little while. His parents found out that there had been other girls.' She shrugged. 'Our father kept pictures of all of his families. Like trophies. His parents wanted to make sure their grandchildren were being taken care of. They had money.'

Gideon was very calm and that was very unnerving. 'Had? Then they're dead.'

'Yes. They died several years before I got to New Orleans.'

'What about him?'

'Our father? He's dead, too. Overdosed. The same year you escaped Eden, ironically enough.'

'Good. I hated him. He made Mama cry, every time he drove away.'

'You remember him?' Somehow that surprised her.

'Vaguely. I was three the last time he came sniffing after Mama. You were born nine months later.' He tilted his head, studying her. Still calm. 'If this isn't about money and everyone is dead, what are you so afraid to tell me?'

Here we go. 'Not everyone's dead. We have siblings. Half siblings, to be technically accurate. His parents hired PIs to track down all the grandchildren. We were the only two they didn't find.'

He blinked at her, his eyes hardening before he carefully schooled his features into an expression that was far too calm. 'I . . . see. Are any of these half siblings legitimate? To be technically accurate,' he added coldly.

She winced. He was mad. *He has every right to be.* 'Yes. Two are legal heirs, another four are like us.'

'You've met them all.' A statement, not a question. And still unnervingly calm.

'Yes. They're all . . . close. They have family dinners. Reunions. Holidays. They're nice people. All of them live in or around New Orleans. And they've welcomed me.'

His calm expression was morphing into one of betrayal, and it was like a knife in her gut. Because she deserved it. She deserved every ounce of resentment and rage he could muster.

'How long have you been welcomed by them?' he asked, the question barely audible.

'I didn't meet them right away. I was afraid to. I wasn't in a great place emotionally when I first arrived in New Orleans.'

'But you settled there. Near them.'

'Yes. I used the money from Grandma's will to go to college. Met Farrah. Met her family. Started therapy. I eventually got a car and found John's house. That was after my first year at Tulane.'

95

'John.'

'He's the oldest. He's thirty-five and is the glue, I guess. He and his wife do all the organizing, but everyone hosts at different times. Adele is the youngest. She's twenty-three. All together there are seven nieces and five nephews.'

'You met them *seven years ago*?' Gideon asked, stricken.

She flinched. 'No, not then. For a year I drove to John's house and sat outside, watching them come and go. All the holidays and parties. I watched them living their lives, trying to get the courage to talk to them.'

'And then?' Gideon asked gruffly.

She studied his face, but she couldn't tell if he was feeling anger, regret, or what else. He'd wiped his expression clean. But she knew he was feeling something, because his jaw was so tight, it was a wonder he hadn't cracked a few teeth.

'And then, after about a year and a half of what I thought was stealth, John came out to the car and asked if I wanted to come in. Turns out they'd all been watching me while I watched them, almost from the beginning.'

Gideon was silent for a long, long moment. 'So you have relationships with our siblings, is that what you're saying?'

It was almost a relief. Almost. Because Gideon hadn't asked the truly hard question yet. *Why didn't you tell me?* She still didn't have a good answer. 'Yes.'

'And you didn't tell me.' Another statement, not a question. Of course it wasn't a question. Because she *hadn't* told him.

'No, I didn't.' She drew a breath and hoped this would end okay. 'They asked me to tell you, to reach out to you.' She exhaled and it hurt. 'To tell you that they wanted to meet you. To know you.'

'To have a relationship with me,' Gideon said, his voice gone deep and gravelly.

Mercy fought the urge to shiver. She wasn't afraid of Gideon. Not physically. But she was afraid of what he'd say.

Because she wanted him to keep loving her. It was a hard thing to admit after so many years of pent-up rage. Wrongly placed rage.

Why hadn't her mother told her earlier why Gideon had fled? Why hadn't she told Mercy privately where he'd really gone?

Because I might have corrected one of the Eden leaders when they continued repeating the vicious lie. She'd been an impulsive child, quick to speak her mind.

Ephraim Burton had changed that. Now she was ultra careful to the point of obsession.

And none of this was Gideon's fault.

'You kept them to yourself,' he said, accusation now clear as a bell.

'Yes,' she said, forcing herself to meet his hard gaze. 'I kept them to myself.'

'Because you hated me.'

She nodded once, because that was also true. 'When I got out of Eden and saw you so happy and healthy and living your life as if Mama hadn't sacrificed for you . . .' *As if I hadn't sacrificed for you*, she left unsaid, because it felt petty and wrong. Because it *was* petty and wrong. 'I hated you. You had a life and I was this wraith, just . . . existing. So I hated you. And once I found the others, I kept them to myself.'

'For six years.'

She swallowed hard. 'Yes. For six years. I'm sorry, Gideon.'

He smiled, but it was devoid of any warmth. 'For which thing, Mercy?'

'For all of it. For hating you. For pushing you away all this time. For keeping you from knowing our brothers and sisters and nieces and nephews. They really want to know you.'

Gideon's stare became a glare before he looked away. 'Which two are legit?'

'John and Angela. I'm closest to John. I think most of us are.'

'And their last name?'

Because neither she nor Gideon had known their father's name. Mama had clearly known, but she'd never mentioned it. 'Benz. Our father was John Benz Sr.'

Gideon's gaze jerked to meet hers, his eyes wide. 'Mama named you Mercedes when our father's name was Benz?'

97

Mercy could only nod, hoping her brother was seeing the humor in that and not the treachery of her betrayal.

He looked away again, his gaze fixed on Karl's desk. 'What did you tell him?'

'Who?'

'John.' A muscle in his cheek bulged as he ground his teeth. 'John and Angela and the others. If they asked you to tell me about them for six *fucking* years and you obviously didn't, what did you tell them about me? About why I wasn't meeting them?'

Mercy kept her chin level, not giving in to the urge to run. 'I told them that you weren't interested in meeting them.'

Gideon's throat worked as he struggled to speak. 'You lied to them, too? To *all* of them?'

'Yes,' she whispered. 'But I'll make it right. I wanted to come clean with you before I told them.'

His shoulders drooped, his head falling forward. He looked so defeated that Mercy wanted to comfort him, but when she leaned in to touch him, he jerked away.

He looked at her then, his anger directed squarely at her. 'Don't,' he said quietly.

'All right.' She settled herself in the chair, her hands folded in her lap. Just as she'd been taught to do in Eden. *Be a good girl. Be obedient. Be seen and not heard. Or else.*

Standing, Gideon shoved his hands in his pockets. 'I need time to work through this,' he said evenly. 'You've been through a lot, most of which you haven't begun to tell me, I'm sure. I don't want to be angry with you, but right now I am. Give me some time to vent some steam.'

Tears burned once again and she dropped her chin so that he wouldn't see. 'I understand.'

'No, I don't think you do.' He took a step toward her, then stopped. 'I want a relationship with you, Mercy. I want to know our family. But right now, I can't.' He hooked a finger under her chin, tugging until she looked up at him, his touch gentle. 'Give me some time. How long will you be here?'

'I have two months.'

His brows rose. 'You took leave?'

'Something like that,' she murmured.

'All right. Send me John's contact info. Tell him what you need to tell him to make things right between you. I'll call him in the next day or two, when I've decided what to say.'

'And me?' she whispered. 'What have you decided about me?'

His eyes softened. 'You are my sister. I've loved you since the day I first held you when you were only a day old. I will always love you. Me needing time doesn't mean my feelings have changed. This is me needing to stay calm. You've experienced enough anger for a thousand lifetimes. You won't get it from me, too.'

She swallowed a sob, but it came out anyway. 'I'm sorry, Gideon. I'm so sorry.'

He pushed the hair away from her face before giving her a box of tissues from Karl's desk. 'I know. I also know how hard it is to break old emotional habits. That's why I need time. You have my cell number, right?'

She jerked a nod, drying her cheeks. 'Of course.'

'Then call me if you need to. I'll always answer. Stay close to Rafe and the Sokolovs until we locate Burton. He won't put his hands on you again.'

'Okay. That's fair.' It was more than okay, more than fair.

Gideon had made it to the door before turning back to meet her eyes, his expression now very grim. 'It was Burton, wasn't it? If I opened your locket, would I find a wedding picture of you and Ephraim Burton inside?'

'Yes.'

Gideon's eyes closed and his whole body sagged, his grip on the doorknob seeming like the only thing keeping him upright. 'I hoped not, but I knew. Somehow, I knew.' He leaned into the door, resting his forehead on the wood. 'If you hadn't hated me, I'd have been shocked.'

'I don't hate you now.'

He looked up, his eyes full of pain. He understood, and it was like a weight rolled off her shoulders. Unfortunately, it seemed to have rolled onto his. 'I'm glad for that, at least. We'll be all right,

Mercy, you and I. We've come too far not to be. I'll call you tomorrow, okay? I have to check in with my boss and see who they've assigned to find Burton. She won't let me work on it, so I'll take some leave to protect you.'

'You don't have to—'

'I do,' he interrupted. 'Let me do this. I didn't keep you safe when you were twelve years old and that has haunted me for years. Let me protect you now. Please.'

She couldn't resist his hoarse plea. 'Thank you.'

'I'll tell Rafe. He'll keep you safe until I'm in the right headspace to do it myself. He's a good cop, even if he's got a bum leg right now.'

'He saved me tonight.'

A ghost of a smile curved his lips. 'I owe him once again. He's saved you twice now.'

Once from an armed serial killer and then again tonight.

'You saved me that night, too.' She stood, gripping her hands so tightly that they hurt. 'So thank you.'

'We'll be all right, Mercy,' he repeated, but this time with the warmth that she'd feared she'd lost forever.

And then he was gone, leaving her to sink back into the chair and cry.

Six

Granite Bay, California
Saturday, 15 April, 8.40 P.M.

Sasha and their dad came into the kitchen, expressions grim. Sasha slid into the seat that Mercy had vacated and slumped, arms crossed. 'What's going on with Gideon and Mercy?' she asked bluntly.

Karl began to set the table, nodding in agreement. 'The tension between them was so thick we could have cut it with a knife. Speaking of knives, Sasha, please get the silverware.'

She complied instantly, springing into motion, her movements graceful and fluid.

Just like mine used to be, Rafe thought, then shook the thought from his mind. There were far more important concerns. 'I'm not sure. Mercy came back to talk to him. I'm not sure what about.'

'All I know is that Gideon was a wreck the whole way over here,' Daisy offered. 'He's afraid to say the wrong thing, afraid he'll drive her away again.' She glanced at Farrah, who sat very quietly. 'Do you know?'

Farrah lifted one shoulder. 'It's hard to say with Mercy. She keeps her feelings pretty close to the vest.'

'Translated,' Sasha said, 'she knows but Mercy trusts her not to blab.' She gave Farrah a look of respect. 'Good on you.'

Daisy's normally happy expression dimmed. 'It's a big responsibility to carry secrets like hers must be. Weighs on one's shoulders.'

Rafe wondered whether Daisy was talking about Mercy's secrets or Gideon's. Both siblings had experienced horrors that no child ever should. He wasn't sure he was ready to bear Gideon's secrets, but Mercy's? Yeah, he'd been ready since he'd first laid eyes on her.

Farrah's smile was sad. 'I worry about her all the time.'

'So do I,' Rafe murmured, then wished he hadn't said the words aloud when his parents gave him knowing looks. He hadn't told anyone how much he'd missed Mercy, but he figured they all knew.

Daisy sighed. 'Gideon hasn't slept well since she went back to New Orleans. He wakes up with nightmares, saying her name. I hope she tells him what he needs to know eventually, because not knowing is killing him.'

No one had an answer to that, and their silence hung heavy over the table.

'So,' Irina finally said, 'how goes your physical therapy, Raphael?'

He might have been grateful for the topic change, but the subject of his PT was only slightly more welcome than a discussion of his feelings for Mercy Callahan. 'Not bad.'

Sasha finished her part of setting the table and returned to sit beside him. '"Not bad" doesn't sound good. Is Cash beating you up again?'

Farrah looked relieved at the topic change as well. 'Who's Cash and why is he beating you up?'

Irina chuckled. 'Cash is Cassius, my youngest son, Sasha's twin. He's a physical therapist,' she added proudly. 'He works with all the professional basketball players.'

'Not all of them, Mom,' Sasha said with a chuckle of her own. 'Just our team.'

'Wow.' Farrah had perked up. 'Like who?'

Sasha pouted. 'He won't say. He's got ethics.'

'No, not ethics,' Farrah teased. 'Say it ain't so.'

'But it is so,' Irina said. 'He would never talk about his clients.' She made a face. 'Not even to me. And not even about my own son.'

Rafe had to laugh at that. 'He told me that you keep bugging him. Give the kid a break, Ma.'

Irina lifted her brows. 'I would give him a break, as you say, if my *older* son gave me information when I requested it.'

'Ooh,' Farrah whispered loudly. 'Burn.'

Rafe knew that they were making light conversation to take the focus away from whatever Mercy and Gideon were saying to each other. He guessed he'd have to sacrifice his own privacy to play along. 'It's not going as well as I'd hoped, to be honest.' He hesitated. 'I'm not sure how much better I'm going to get and even though Cash keeps a positive attitude, he's not sure, either.'

Sasha's face fell. 'That sucks, brother.'

Karl's brow scrunched in concern. 'Perhaps another opinion?'

Irina sat up straighter, indignant. 'Why? Our Cash is the best!'

'He's doing all he can, Dad,' Rafe agreed glumly. 'I keep doing what he says to do – or trying to. It's all I *can* do right now.'

Irina pulled a pan of bread from the oven. 'How much longer does he think you need to keep trying?'

'Until I can walk and be a cop again?' Rafe snapped, then sighed. 'I'm sorry, Mom. It's a touchy subject.'

She put the pan on the table then squeezed his shoulder. 'Is okay, Raphael. I know you are frustrated.'

Rafe glanced at Farrah. 'Sorry our conversation got so intense. We're normally more fun when guests come.'

Farrah smiled sadly. 'I can't imagine how hard it is. You owe me no apologies. My fiancé lives for his work. If he thought he could no longer be a cop . . .'

'Yeah.' Again he hesitated, then decided to let his family in. Just a little. 'I'm not sure what else I could even do. All I've ever wanted was to be a cop.' He craned his neck to look around the doorway, to be certain Mercy wasn't on her way back. 'I don't want Mercy to know. She has enough to worry about right now and I know she feels guilty about me getting shot.'

Farrah mimed zipping her lips. 'She won't hear a thing from me.'

Sasha had become uncharacteristically quiet, and Rafe turned to her with a lifted eyebrow. 'What?'

She shrugged uncomfortably. 'We can talk later.'

'Oh, heavens,' Farrah said, searching her handbag. 'I've left some medication in my suitcase. Karl, where did you put it, please? I just got over bronchitis and need to finish all my antibiotics. You know how it is.'

'Of course.' Karl rose and went to the doorway. 'I'll show you where I put your things.'

Sasha frowned when they were gone. 'What was that about?'

Rafe had already decided that he liked Mercy's best friend very much. She'd just cemented his good opinion. 'She wanted to give us time alone. I saw the bottle of antibiotics in her purse when she gave me ibuprofen earlier. So what has you so upset, kid?'

Sasha rolled her eyes. 'You're only five years older than me.' Then she sighed. 'We've all been a little worried about you, that's all. I mean, we're all hoping you regain full use of your leg, but what if you don't? Have you considered . . . y'know, talking to someone?'

Rafe fought his own sigh. They meant well, his family, but this was why he kept his feelings to himself. His laid-back 'nothing bothers me' surfer persona had taken years to perfect. It was a most effective shield. *That I obviously have misplaced somewhere.* This was what happened when he gave his family an iota of information. They always pushed for more. 'You mean like a shrink?'

His mother narrowed her eyes at him. 'A mental health therapist, Raphael. Don't minimize their importance with denigrating sobriquets.'

Rafe bit back a smile. 'Wow, Mom. Those are some five-dollar words there.' Her scowl had him sobering. She was serious. Very. 'I know they are useful, and yes, Cash did recommend someone.'

Sasha looked relieved. 'Who?'

'Some therapist that his athlete friend used when he got hurt and had to leave the game. I have the therapist's name, I just haven't called yet. But he only gave it to me today,' he added when his mother opened her mouth to no doubt nag him to call now. 'Give me a day or two, okay? Things just got hairy.'

Irina nodded reluctantly. 'I will wait. But no more than two days.'

'And then the nagging will commence?' Rafe asked with an affectionate smile.

'Yes.' Irina gave the stew in the pot a final stir. 'Karl! Farrah! Dinner is ready.' She put the pot on the table. 'We'll start now. Mercy and Gideon can join us when they are finished talking.'

'I'm good with that.' Daisy ladled stew onto her plate. 'I'm starving and this is one of my favorite meals.'

Karl and Farrah returned, Farrah making a show of shaking the pills in her medicine bottle. 'Silly me. I had them in my purse all along.'

Karl patted her shoulder. 'I think my daughter has spoken her piece, so now we can eat.'

'Oh, this is good,' Farrah said when they'd all been served. 'I'd love the recipe for this, Irina.'

'Of course. It's very simple, a bit of everything . . .' Irina trailed off as Gideon appeared in the doorway.

Alone. His eyes were red and he was visibly trembling. 'Daisy . . .' He cleared his throat. 'We need to go.'

Daisy's eyes widened. 'But I'm not finished yet and you haven't eaten at all.'

'Wrap it up to take with you, then. Please.' His gaze landed on Rafe. 'She's not okay. You might want to talk to her. I need some time. Just a little time.'

Rafe was already pushing to his feet, gripping his cane hard. 'What happened?'

'I can't. Not right now.' Gideon's expression was just short of begging. 'Just don't leave her alone, not for a minute.'

'You know I won't.'

Gideon looked at Farrah, his mouth tightening in irritation. 'Did you know? About our family?'

What family? Stunned, Rafe looked around the table, noting everyone looked as confused as he felt.

Farrah nodded, also shocked. 'I knew. I didn't know that *you* didn't know, though. Her stress levels make sense now.' She rubbed her forehead wearily. 'I thought she was dealing with PTSD from the abduction six weeks ago. I didn't think to ask her about John and the others. I'm so sorry. Some best friend I am. I hope you didn't get too angry with her,' she added. 'She was so afraid that you'd hate her.'

'Why would you think to ask her if she'd told me that I have family in New Orleans?' Gideon asked, much more kindly, although his eyes still held devastation. 'And I didn't yell at her, I promise. But I wanted to, so that's why I need some time.'

'I'm good to go,' Daisy said. With Irina's help, she'd wrapped two plates of food, and Rafe hoped Gideon would actually eat his. His friend looked too thin.

'I'm going to take some time off,' Gideon announced. 'I'll be able to guard her soon.'

That really pissed Rafe off. 'I can do it,' he growled.

Gideon stretched out his hand as if to calm him. 'I know you can. I know you will. But I need to. We can figure out a strategy later. I promise. For now, I need to know she's safe from Burton.' He swallowed hard, his eyes becoming suspiciously shiny. 'I'll call you tomorrow.'

And then he was gone, Daisy in his wake.

Rafe glanced at Farrah, who looked like she was about to cry. 'What is this about family in New Orleans?' he asked gently. 'Tell me what you can, so I can help her.'

Farrah closed her eyes briefly, then looked up at him. 'They have a bunch of half siblings who live in New Orleans. That's why she landed there. Her maternal grandmother told her that her paternal grandparents had come searching for them years ago, and left their address. Mercy didn't actually meet any of the sibs for almost two years, even though she knew where they were. She was so afraid that they'd reject her. I think that she needed to know that our family had unconditionally accepted her before she had the courage to confront her blood.'

'But they did not reject her?' Irina asked cautiously.

'No. They all love her. Their family is almost as big as mine. Four half brothers and two half sisters, plus seven nieces and five nephews. Mercy has loved being their auntie. She babysits them and takes care of them. Tutors them.' Her smile was wistful. 'Spoils them rotten.'

God. Six half siblings and all their families. *No wonder Gideon needs time.* That news was quite the bombshell.

Rafe put the remaining pieces together. 'She didn't tell Gideon about them because she was angry with him, because she didn't know that he'd run from Eden after he'd been abused, too.'

106

'I guess so. I thought he knew about John and the sibs. I really did. I just figured that Gideon didn't want to see them, like Mercy hasn't wanted to see him.'

'She told you that she'd told Gideon about them?' Irina asked. 'She . . . lied?'

Farrah sighed. 'Not actually, now that I go back over our conversations in my mind. But she let me believe it. I should go to her now. This is why I'm here – to put her back together again.'

Rafe stood, grabbing his cane. 'I'll go in first. Maybe you can fix her a plate?'

Farrah studied him for a moment, then nodded. 'That I can do.'

Granite Bay, California
Saturday, 15 April, 9.20 P.M.

Mercy's head jerked up at the light knock on the door. She didn't know how long she'd been sitting there, crying like a foolish child. Dinner had to be over and Karl probably wanted his office back. Drawing a breath, she swiped at her wet cheeks with the back of her hand. 'I'll be out in just a second,' she called.

'Mercy, it's me,' a deep voice said.

Rafe. *Fucking hell.* She did not want him to see her like this. She did have a little pride, after all.

No, you have too much pride. Which was to blame for this whole mess. She could have told Gideon about their half siblings at any time – any time over the last six weeks, any one of the birthdays or Christmases that he'd called her since she'd met them, or simply any other time. She'd always had his phone number.

But she hadn't, and now she had to bear the consequences.

She forced herself to stand and greet Rafe with her chin up. 'Come in,' she said, trying to sound . . . well, not as dejected as she felt. *I've fucked it all up.*

Not all of it. Gideon said you'd be all right. He doesn't lie.

No, he didn't lie. He never had. Everyone else back then had lied to her, but Gideon had always told her the truth. He'd always been there for her, taking her punishments, making sure she had enough to eat even if it meant he'd gone hungry. She never would have believed what Eden had said about him if her mother had refuted it, but Rhoda hadn't. Mercy had begged her mother to tell her that it wasn't so, that Gideon hadn't left them to suffer, but her mother had allowed her to continue believing it until that night in the bed of DJ's truck.

She now understood her mother's reasons, even though she remained a little bitter. Her mother had known that if Mercy knew the truth about Gideon when she was nine years old, she would have openly defied the lies of the Eden leadership, causing her own punishment and endangering Gideon's safety. Rhoda had ensured Gideon's escape through perpetuating the lie, but none of any of this was Gideon's fault.

The door opened and Rafe appeared, his face somber, his eyes soft. No judgments. His mouth lifted in a rueful half smile as he closed the door behind him and she was suddenly frozen in place, caught between the desperate need to flee and . . .

An even more desperate need to stay. To feel safe again. To feel accepted. Wanted.

It was selfish, so damn selfish, but she wanted Rafe Sokolov to hold her. Even if she was going to have to tell him it would never work out. They had different lives. They lived in different parts of the country. But none of that seemed to matter at the moment.

He hadn't said a word since entering the room, leaning heavily on his cane as he slowly made his way toward her. *Giving me time to run.* But she didn't run, the understanding in his gaze making her chest tight. New tears clogged her throat again and she didn't have the energy to hold them back.

'Hell, Mercy,' he murmured when he reached her. He propped his cane against the chair in which she'd been sitting and opened his arms.

Without hesitation, she walked into them, shuddering when his arms closed around her, holding her as she cried. She wasn't sure how long they stood there, but she felt the tensing of his body as he leaned his hip into the chair. He was hurting.

I'm hurting him. She tried to pull away, but his arms tightened their grip. 'You need to sit.'

'Don't go,' he murmured into her ear, making her shudder again as he shuffled them sideways and lowered them into the chair. Together. She was sitting on his lap, her weight resting on his good leg, the injured one stretched out straight.

She shouldn't be doing this. She should get up, sit in the other chair. But he was warm, his arms strong, and she allowed herself to admit that she needed this. Craved the feel of him. But she shouldn't be selfish. 'I'm hurting you,' she protested, even as she rested her head against his shoulder. 'I don't want to hurt you.' *Not your leg. Not your heart.*

'No,' he said softly. 'We're fine, Mercy. You're fine. Don't go. Not yet.'

Exhaling a sigh, she burrowed closer, letting him hold her, so grateful not to be alone. 'I'm sorry.'

'For what?' he asked lazily, stroking her hair in a way that made her want to close her eyes and sleep.

'Um, for falling apart in your father's office?'

His chuckle rumbled under her ear. 'You aren't the first. Won't be the last. I think all of us kids have fallen apart in this office at one time or another. I don't think Dad gets much work done in here, to be honest.'

His warm voice was making her even sleepier. 'You've fallen apart in here?' She covered her mouth when she yawned. 'Really? When?'

'Really,' he said lightly, still stroking her hair. 'I'm a good listener, if you want to talk. If not, we can sit here as long as you like.'

She didn't miss that he hadn't answered her question, but that was okay. She was also a good listener and understood the value of patience. 'If it's okay, I'd rather be quiet for a while. I'm not used to talking so much.'

He chuckled again. 'Hopefully you can get used to everyone else talking around you, or you're going to tire of us Sokolovs pretty quickly.' He abruptly stilled. 'Do we bother you?'

'No. Absolutely not. You're the kind of family I always dreamed of. Like Farrah's family.'

'And . . .' He hesitated. 'Your brothers and sisters?'

109

She sighed. She hadn't doubted that Gideon had shared the bombshell she'd dropped on him. 'Yes.' She was quiet again, and he let her be. But finally she said, 'Gideon was so upset and he had a right to be.'

'He'll come around,' Rafe promised. 'I've known him for sixteen years. He loves you. He has dreamed of your acceptance for so long.'

'He shouldn't,' Mercy whispered, 'but I hope you're right.'

'Tell me about your brothers and sisters,' he murmured quietly.

He was changing the subject, distracting her from her fears without chiding her or diminishing her. Mercy liked that a lot. 'The oldest's name is John Benz. He and Angela were our father's legal children.' She hesitated, then sighed. 'My mother named me Mercedes.'

Rafe went still for a moment, then snorted a laugh. 'She was young?'

'Eighteen, give or take a few months. All the sibs winced when I told them and then they died laughing.'

Rafe continued to stroke her hair with the perfect amount of pressure. 'How often do you see them?'

'Every week. Brunch with John and his wife and kids. The kids think I'm like *CSI*, so I'm cool for the moment. When they meet Gideon, they'll be so impressed that he's FBI.'

'I'm glad you have them, and once Gideon's temper cools, he will be, too.'

His strokes had become slower as she relaxed against him. 'You need to let me go, or I'll fall asleep right here. It would be awful for your leg if that happened.'

His hand slid from her hair to her back, his touch a little more intense now, fingers massaging the muscles that were the tightest. 'Where do you want to go, Mercy? Mom's going to insist that you eat, but after that, you need to decide if you want to stay here at Mom and Dad's, or come back to my house and stay with Sasha. Either way is fine with me. I'll make sure you have someone guarding you, wherever you sleep.'

'Thank you.' She thought about it for a moment. 'Will your mother be offended if we don't stay here?'

'Not at all.'

He sounded confident, but Mercy would check for herself when she saw Irina again. 'If she's really okay with it, I'd like to get to your place. I love Farrah's family, and John and the others are the best, but I get overwhelmed with all the talking and the noise. I think your family would be similar.'

'They can be . . . friendly,' he said, affection clear in his tone. 'That's why I left home when I was eighteen. My grandmother left a house to all of us kids, but it needed work. I lived there while I went to college, fixed the house up whenever I had free time, then bought the others out when I'd saved enough money. It's always been my oasis. I can always come here anytime if I need a little drama. I'll let Mom know that you're going home with me.' He kissed her temple, then met her gaze. 'I want to make all of this better for you, but I don't know what to do.'

'You're doing it,' she said, pressing her cheek to the hard wall of his chest. 'Thank you.'

'You're welcome.'

For a long, long moment they sat there in the quiet, the steady thumping of his heart beneath her ear the only sound that mattered. 'I need to help,' she finally said wearily.

'Need to help with what, specifically?'

'Finding Ephraim Burton.' Somehow saying both of his names together made him feel more like a stranger, less like her own personal nightmare. A little bit, anyway.

His hand rubbed big circles on her back. 'All right.' His reply wasn't condescending. It was simple acceptance, like it made perfect sense that she'd help.

'But I don't know where to start,' she confessed.

'Let's start tomorrow,' he said softly. 'Tonight, you need to take care of you.'

She wanted to argue but didn't have the energy. 'All right,' she said, intentionally mimicking his words and tone, making him chuckle.

'Good,' was all he said before falling silent once more. He rubbed her back, occasionally stroking her hair, his constant touches more than mere comfort. His hands anchored her. His arms made her feel safe.

Safe enough to sleep.

Sacramento, California
Saturday, 15 April, 10.05 P.M.

In hindsight, Ephraim should have waited until morning to kill Regina, so that he could have gotten a decent night's sleep. His head still pounded and he was exhausted, but hotels were not an option. He didn't want to risk even a shitty motel because Regina had been right about the BOLOs. Cops and Feds all over the state were looking for him. The airports would be alerted, as would the borders if he tried to hang out in Mexico.

But he didn't want to be in Mexico. He wanted to be wherever Mercy Callahan was, so he'd headed back to Sacramento. He hadn't been able to find Raphael Sokolov's address online, no matter what search engine he'd used, so he'd have to track Mercy another way. He didn't know what that way would be, but he'd figure it out in the morning.

Now, he just needed to find a place to sleep.

He stopped in a northern suburb of Sacramento, a community in which every house was dark. Slowly he drove through the streets, checking for any place that looked unoccupied, but the houses were close together and he didn't want to risk surprising someone inside who might yell loudly enough to be heard. He followed the main street out of town, finding himself on a farm road, not unlike the one where he'd dumped the woman's body earlier this evening.

What was her name again? *Right, June Lindstrom.* He needed to remember the details, needed to listen to the news for word of her discovery. Her death couldn't directly be traced to him, but eventually the cops would figure out that she'd left the airport at the same time that he'd fled.

He turned off his headlights as he approached the old farmhouse at the end of the lane. It had definitely seen better days. Even in the darkness, he could see that the paint was peeling and the weeds grew high all around the property. Quietly, he got out of the car that he'd stolen after ditching Regina's sleek Lexus. This car was an older model, a real clunker. It still had a cassette tape deck, for God's sake, so it was unlikely to have GPS. Which was exactly what he needed right now to stay off the grid.

He walked toward the farmhouse, keeping to the shadows. Checking all the windows, he found only one occupant – an old woman sitting in her recliner, watching TV.

Drawing Regina's gun from his pocket, he made sure the suppressor was on tight and crept to the back door, ready to break one of the small window panels so that he could reach in and unlock it. But to his surprise, it was already unlocked.

He opened the door and slipped in, checking for any kind of home alarm system, but he saw nothing. He crossed an old kitchen into a drab hallway, stopping cold when a floorboard squeaked.

'James?' a frail voice called from the living room. 'What are you doing home?'

He had no idea who James was, but this was a bad idea if the guy would be returning soon. Ephraim wanted to sleep and not worry about anyone else coming in.

He continued walking toward the living room, wincing when more floorboards creaked.

'James?' the old woman called again, a thread of fear in her voice. 'Is that you?'

He wondered what would happen if he said yes, then froze when the lights abruptly came on. The old woman stood at the end of the hall, one hand on the light switch.

The other cradling a rifle like a baby. And not just any rifle. It was an AR-15 with an extended magazine. Ephraim blinked in surprise. The rifle she held wasn't legal in California configured as it was, so the old woman wasn't afraid of breaking the law. He had to admit to being reluctantly impressed.

She stiffened. 'Who are you?'

'Who is James?'

'My grandson,' she said, lifting the rifle to her shoulder with a speed and grace that surprised him.

Granny may have been badass, but she wasn't as fast as Ephraim. He shot her in the chest, both the gun and the suppressor doing their jobs. All he heard was a slight pop and she dropped like a rock.

'I'm sorry,' he murmured as he crouched next to her body. He really was. It was a shame that such a feisty old lady should meet her end so anticlimactically. He moved the rifle from her arms and took her pulse. She was still alive, dammit. With regret, he shot her again, then put her body in the chair, making it look like she was still watching TV.

Then he locked all the doors, placing chairs under each of the doorknobs. If James the grandson came home early, he'd have to break a window and Ephraim would hear that.

Climbing the stairs, he found a nice bedroom decorated with paisley and lace. A second bedroom looked like a tornado had struck, dirty clothes on the floor and posters of basketball players on the walls. *Must be James's room*, he thought. He found a laptop on an old desk and, figuring it couldn't hurt to try, tapped the keyboard with one finger.

To his utter shock, the laptop turned on – with no password protector.

Granny must trust James a lot. Or James must not think Granny is very smart.

A quick search of his email revealed that James, a fourteen-year-old, was camping with his Boy Scout troop this weekend. Ephraim grimaced, the very sappiness of the situation leaving a bad taste in his mouth. Boy Scouts? Really? He didn't know kids still did that shit. Maybe out in the country they did.

At least he'd get some uninterrupted sleep. James wasn't due home until tomorrow afternoon.

By then Ephraim would be gone, on his way to wherever Mercy was.

Seven

Granite Bay, California
Saturday, 15 April, 10.30 P.M.

Rafe had lost track of time. Sitting in the quiet of his father's office, which smelled of old leather and the sweet pipe smoke that took him back to his childhood, he held Mercy tight in his arms, satisfied on a primal level by the soft, slow breaths she took. He'd done this. He'd made her feel safe enough to finally get some rest.

From the dark circles under her eyes, he knew she hadn't slept well for far too long. His good leg had fallen asleep long before she had, but his discomfort was a minor thing. He'd been more uncomfortable on stakeouts, and tonight he had an armful of beautiful woman, so he called the situation a win.

He brushed a kiss over her temple, wishing he had a magic wand that would make all of this go away. But he didn't, so he'd support her in whatever she needed to do. Her wanting to help find Burton was a big deal. Six weeks before, she'd been adamant that she'd wanted no part in the search for Burton and Eden. That was the same day that Gideon's boss had finally identified Burton as Harry Franklin, a man wanted by the FBI for a thirty-year-old bank robbery and triple murder.

Molina had made an assumption that had reared back to bite her in the ass. So had Gideon. Both had assumed that Mercy would be happy to help.

But she hadn't been then and she wasn't now. Now she needed to, and that was a far different thing. Either way, he knew where to start, even if she didn't.

Because he already had started. He'd been searching for Ephraim Burton and Eden for the past month, ever since she'd run back to New Orleans. He hadn't told anyone, even Gideon, because he wasn't working in any official capacity.

He knew the FBI and SacPD had been vigorously searching for Burton, but they clearly hadn't been successful. He wanted to growl at the thought of the man's hands on Mercy, wishing he'd shot the bastard at the airport when he'd had the chance.

He could still help her, though. He could help her find Ephraim and take back the part of her life the monster had stolen. Yes, she would probably return to New Orleans sometime too soon, to the life she had there – her job, her friends, her newly found family – but for the moment she was here, with him. Letting him hold her. Sleeping peacefully in his arms.

A light knock had him sighing. Of course this was too good to last. The door popped open and Sasha stuck her head in, her eyes going soft when she saw Mercy asleep in his lap.

She turned to whoever stood behind her and put her finger over her lips before tiptoeing into the office. Farrah was behind Sasha and his dad behind Farrah, who carried a covered plate. Whatever it contained smelled really good. Rafe hadn't had a chance to finish his dinner, and his stomach growled loudly.

Sasha took the covered plate from Farrah, gesturing that their guest take the extra chair. Sasha put the plate on their father's desk, then perched on the corner. 'We waited for over an hour,' she whispered.

No wonder his leg had gone to sleep. Still, holding Mercy had been totally worth it.

Farrah's gaze was on her friend, her face a picture of worry. 'Is she okay?'

'She will be,' Rafe murmured. 'She'd be better if you all didn't come in here to wake her up.'

Karl dragged his chair around his desk, so that he could sit at Rafe's side. He propped his laptop on the arm of Rafe's chair. 'We need to talk.'

Granite Bay, California
Saturday, 15 April, 10.35 P.M.

Mercy slowly woke to whispered voices. She recognized Farrah's soft drawl and Rafe's rumbling replies, but seeing Sasha and Karl was a bit of a surprise. She jerked upright, not missing the wince on Rafe's face.

I hurt him. Dammit, but . . . God. She was sitting on his lap. In front of everyone. 'I'm sorry,' she said hastily. 'Let me up.'

But Rafe held her tighter. 'No other chairs,' he said, which, although true, was utter bullshit and everyone knew it. Still, Mercy found herself relaxing just a bit. She sat up straighter, blinking hard. 'What happened?' She glanced at the desk, at a covered dish that smelled amazing. 'Is that mine?'

Sasha handed it to her. 'Give Rafe some. His stomach is growling.'

'Shut up,' Rafe said, unperturbed. 'Is that Mom's stew?'

Mercy removed the foil covering. 'It's here. Along with . . .' Her gaze shot to Farrah.

Farrah was smiling wryly. 'Comfort food.'

Mercy took a bite of the creamy mac and cheese. 'Your mama's recipe? You made this for me?'

'Yep. And don't you be telling my mama that I shared the recipe with Irina.'

Mercy chuckled, touched at the thoughtful gesture. Farrah's mother's macaroni and cheese was Mercy's go-to comfort meal. 'Mama Ro will make you cut your own switch.'

Farrah grinned. 'Except Irina traded her bird's milk cake recipe, which is freaking delicious, so I think I'll be safe.' She sobered. 'We need to talk to you, Mercy.'

Mercy's stomach tumbled, her hunger abruptly gone. 'What happened?' she asked again, looking at the equally sober faces. Even Rafe looked subdued.

'Eat,' Farrah insisted, giving her a look that said she meant business.

Too tired and worried to argue, Mercy gave Rafe one of the forks and moved the plate so that they could share. 'We'll eat. You guys talk,' she said.

Karl opened his laptop and Mercy remembered that Sasha and Karl had been looking at something when she and Gideon had first entered the office. She tensed, because the two hadn't wanted anyone to see what they'd been reading. Or maybe they just hadn't wanted her to know. Which meant it was probably very bad.

'Your name hit the Internet,' Karl said carefully. 'It was already out there, after that interview with the other survivor of . . . you know.' He winced. 'That man who took you. Who shot my son.'

'Serial killer,' Mercy said quietly, already wondering what was so bad that Karl was dancing around it. 'You can say it, Karl. I'm not made of glass. I don't think Rafe is, either.'

Rafe's hand came to rest on her back, a warm, comforting presence. 'Just tell us.'

Karl sighed. 'Someone's looked you up. There's an exposé. It's not exactly complimentary.'

Mercy felt the blood drain from her face, the smell of the food suddenly making her feel ill. 'Tell me.'

'The reporter talked to your neighbors,' Sasha said gently. 'They were very supportive. Said you were "the best" and made treats for the kids in the building and did chores for the old folks.'

'But?' Mercy's gaze locked on Farrah's, cold dread spreading from her gut to her extremities, and she put the fork down before her hands became too numb to hold it. 'Who did they find?' She'd wanted the question to come out in a strong voice, but she only managed a whisper.

'Peter Firmin,' Farrah murmured. 'And Stan Prescott. The reporter had . . . the video.'

No. Please, no. Mercy didn't want to believe it, but she knew Farrah would never lie. Not about this. She closed her eyes, more tears burning her eyelids. 'Goddammit.'

'What?' Rafe asked, his voice considerably louder and filled with anger. 'Who are those guys and what did they say? What vid—'

Mercy swallowed hard and shoved the plate toward Rafe. 'I need

say no more

to—' Pushing off Rafe's lap, she ran for the office door, barely conscious of Rafe calling her name.

'Dammit,' she heard Farrah say as she yanked the door open. 'I knew I should have told her alone.'

Why didn't you? Mercy wanted to cry, but she didn't, intent on finding the bathroom before it was too late.

Granite Bay, California
Saturday, 15 April, 10.55 P.M.

Farrah got up to go after Mercy, but Sasha gently restrained her. 'Mom's waiting in the hallway,' Sasha said. 'We agreed to let Mom help her if she needed it. Mom's trained to deal with situations like this and she can tell Mercy what we're doing to make it right.'

Farrah sank back in the chair, looking miserable. 'Dammit,' she swore again.

Rafe turned to stare at his father. 'What the hell is this about, Dad?'

Karl ran a hand over his face, shattered. 'Fuck,' he muttered, then looked at the door Mercy had slammed as she'd fled. 'I'm sorry. I need her to know that I'm so fucking sorry.'

Rafe blinked. His father didn't swear often. He gentled his voice. 'What's happened?'

'Mercy had . . . encounters with two men while she was in college,' Farrah answered for him. 'Neither were good guys and . . .' She swallowed, wiping tears from her eyes. 'Mercy was not okay back then. She was on her own for the first time and trying to deal with her past, with what Ephraim Burton did to her. I didn't know about Eden then. I only knew that my friend was not okay. I tried to get her to come out of her shell, so I took her to a few parties with me, keeping her close. She started to open up, so I stopped hovering. Which was my mistake. Usually I knew all the attendees, but one night we went to a party off-campus and . . .' She sighed. 'Stan Prescott was there and he . . .' Her voice broke. 'He put something in her drink and took video. It wasn't good video, thankfully, and Mercy's face wasn't recognizable, but . . . I realized she was gone

119

and found her before anything really bad happened, but it was bad enough.'

Rage boiled over, scalding Rafe from the inside out. 'What did she do when she found out?'

'It tipped her over the edge and she spiraled into a depression I couldn't pull her out of.'

Rafe waited for Farrah to say more, frowning when it became clear that she didn't plan to. *Fucking hell.* 'What about the video?'

Farrah's body sagged. 'Prescott was arrested for attempted rape, but he made a plea deal with the DA. Got the charge reduced to harassment, on the condition that he relinquish the video. He got a suspended jail sentence and Mercy didn't have to go through a court trial. We thought it had gone away.' She swallowed. 'But he must have kept a copy.'

'Sonofabitch.' Rafe lurched to his feet, only to crash back into the chair when his bad leg buckled.

Sasha moved from her perch on the desk to the arm of his chair, her arm sliding around his shoulders. 'Dad called his lawyer to get the story taken down. They're working on it.'

That was something, at least. Karl Sokolov had started his career in radio but had long ago branched out into marketing. Between the marketing agency and his media outlets, he and his lawyers knew more than a thing or two about managing negative press.

'I called André to get a message to the DA who filed the bastard's plea deal,' Farrah said. 'I'll let you know as soon as I hear something. I can only guess that someone paid Prescott enough for the video that he thought it was worth the risk.'

Rafe drew a breath, needing the facts before he lost his fucking mind. That someone would do that to Mercy – to anyone – but especially with all Mercy had already been through . . . 'What about the second *encounter*?' he bit out, because there was no way he was going to be able to read that trash. Even if he could, he didn't think Mercy would get over it if he did.

Farrah's jaw was tight. 'Peter Firmin is just an opportunistic jerk. They went on a few dates after she'd started at the NOPD lab, but he broke it off, saying that she was the coldest fish he'd ever tried to kiss. He was pretty vocal about it at the time, telling everyone they knew. Mercy was so embarrassed. André stepped in and paid the asshole a visit.' Her lips firmed. 'André convinced him that it would be detrimental to his health if he talked anymore, so he stopped.'

Rafe was surprised. 'Your fiancé, a cop, threatened him?' Although that was fine by him.

Farrah's chin lifted. 'Firmin is a cop, too.'

'Well, shit,' Rafe muttered, and Farrah nodded.

'That's the reason Mercy felt safe going out alone with him to begin with after the video nightmare, but the bastard rushed her and then humiliated her when she said no. After that little chat with André, Firmin left her alone. We hadn't heard a peep out of him until this article.' Farrah's eye twitched. 'He said that if he'd known roofies were what "turned her crank," he'd have tried that. Then he laughed and said he was just kidding, of course.'

'Of course,' Rafe bit out. 'How did a reporter get this story so fast? I've googled Mercy and I never saw anything like this.' He stopped abruptly when he realized what he'd revealed. 'I googled her to find ways to help her,' he said weakly.

Sasha squeezed his shoulder. 'I did, too. I needed to know if she was okay after she left here. I was afraid she'd try to . . . you know.'

'Hurt herself?' Karl asked. 'That worried me, too. That's why I wanted to tell her as a group, to make sure she knew she had us on her side. I didn't think that through. You tried to tell me, Farrah. I should have listened.'

Farrah reached over and patted his knee. 'Probably you should have, but that you all have her back is something she'll appreciate when she's able.'

Rafe hoped so. 'Back to my question. How did this reporter get the story so fast?'

Karl opened his eyes on a sigh. 'The reporter said he'd been working the story for six weeks, since her name came up as having escaped the serial killer. He figured there was more to the story, especially after he got his hands on the hospital surveillance video that showed Mercy leaving with the killer and not fighting back.'

'Like she did tonight,' Sasha said grimly. 'Someone at the airport got the whole thing with Burton on video and posted it. She's as expressionless as a statue, docile as a lamb. If you didn't know the truth, you'd think she wanted to go with him.'

Rafe's churning stomach turned inside out and he had to swallow the bile that rose to burn his throat. 'Fucking hell.' He leaned into Sasha wearily. 'Has anyone connected her to Eden?'

Both the FBI and SacPD had kept the existence of the Eden cult from the press, and it hadn't been mentioned in the interview with the killer's other escapee. They'd released a photo of the locket as a lure to other Eden survivors, hoping to get more information before making their investigation public. Eden moved its location whenever someone escaped its walls, in case the victim told law enforcement where to find them. Making the investigation public would only prompt the cult leadership to hide yet again, so it was still a secret. Or at least Rafe prayed it was.

Mercy had been through enough without that spotlight. It would be a media frenzy for sure.

'Not as far as we could see,' Karl said. 'The one good thing about that idiot Prescott's video is that it can be used to explain her lack of affect when she faces stress. If she wants to make any statement at all, she can speak of the lingering effects of the roofie incident. She doesn't need to mention Eden at all.'

Rafe hoped his father was right. Addressing the facts in a practical fashion might smooth Mercy's way. At least a little. But his gut thought differently. 'This is going to devastate her.'

'Yes, it will,' Farrah said evenly, '*if* you treat her like a victim. Mercy is strong. She's had to be. She's survived things that we can never understand. I've known her for eight years and Karl has the right approach. We need to be strong for her. Do not pity her.'

Rafe remembered the way her body had shaken with the force of her sobs. 'She's not that strong,' he murmured. 'Nobody is.' He grabbed his cane and eased his body to standing. 'I'm going to check on her. Does Gideon know?'

Karl nodded. 'I called him. He . . . didn't take it well.'

'We'll help them through this, Dad,' Sasha declared. 'Tell her we love her, Rafe. She's family.'

'I will.'

Granite Bay, California
Saturday, 15 April, 11.00 P.M.

'Here, *doragaya maya*.' Irina placed a cup of hot tea in Mercy's clammy hands. 'Sip it. Slowly.'

Sitting on the bathroom floor, Mercy obeyed. 'Thank you. You're very kind and I'm very sorry.'

'Bah.' Irina waved her apology away. 'I'd be sick too, if I heard that kind of news.'

Irina's direct approach was almost identical to Mama Romero's – and just what Mercy needed at the moment. 'How bad is the article?'

Irina shrugged. 'It's not good. The reporter quoted your neighbors, who said nice things, but those were overshadowed by the quotes from the two men. And the video, of course. Which none of us viewed, nor will we.'

Mercy sighed as she sipped the tea. 'Thank you for not sugarcoating it.'

'I was a nurse for almost thirty years. I do not sugarcoat. Unless it is dessert.' Irina sat on the edge of the tub, studying Mercy as she pulled a package of crackers from her pocket. 'You look better. Try to eat these.'

'I'm sorry I missed your dinner.'

Irina pushed Mercy's hair from her damp forehead. 'Shush, Mercy. We are family here. You do what you must to take care of yourself. Not to worry about hurting our feelings.'

The woman's accent became thicker when she was in caregiver mode. Just like Mama Romero's did. 'Gideon is lucky to have you.'

Again, a shrug. 'I do not know about that. But we have loved and supported him through his trials. You are now lucky as well. You have us, too.'

'Thank you. Mama Romero has loved me through many trials, so I'm doubly lucky.'

'I'm glad. Gideon worried that you were alone.' Irina cupped Mercy's cheek in her palm, her expression tender. 'You are a good girl, Mercy. We will find a way to make you shine like a new penny by the end of this. These men who hurt you will be sorry.'

Mercy wasn't so sure about any of those statements. 'The police took my case seriously back then. I hope they'll be supportive now as well. I was never wild in college, which helped me then. That shouldn't have been a factor, but it was.'

Irina scowled. 'It should not have been a factor, as you say. You could have been a naked dancer and you still would have been a victim, wronged by this . . . *kazyoel*.' She spat the final word in a way that needed no translation. 'How do you say . . . ?'

'*Asshole*, Mom,' Rafe said from the doorway.

Mercy stiffened and reflexively tried to straighten her hair. 'Rafe. I'm—'

'If you say you're sorry, we will have words,' Rafe said mildly. 'Is everything okay in here?'

'Oh, sure,' Mercy said lightly. 'I'm just having a minor nervous breakdown. But the tea seems to help.'

Rafe gave the mug in her hands a sharp glance. 'Mom?'

Irina rolled her eyes. 'It is peppermint tea, Raphael. I am not so careless as to give Mercy my special tea without asking her first.'

Mercy looked from Irina to Rafe. 'Special tea? Do I want to know?'

'It's THC-infused tea,' Rafe said. 'Legal here.'

'But not in New Orleans,' Irina said sharply. 'Do I look like *duraska* to you, *dorogoy moy*?'

'No, Mama,' Rafe said dutifully, dipping his head in apology. 'You know I could never think you an idiot. But if Mercy gets drug tested when she goes back to work, that stuff sticks around.'

'Which is why I did not give it to her.' Irina nudged Mercy's shoulder playfully. 'But if you want some, you need only to ask.'

Mercy found herself laughing in earnest. 'I'll remember that. Thank you.' She glanced up at Rafe. 'Don't worry about me. I know what pot smells – and tastes – like. I was five years old the first time I tried it.'

Irina blinked, clearly shocked. 'You were given it? By whom?'

'The community grew pot back then. I didn't realize it when I was a kid, but I figured it out later, once I'd gotten out. It was their cash crop. The fields were huge. Pastor told us that it was for our own consumption and the healer used it for basic pain relief since we didn't have access to pharmacies. But looking back, the yield was far more than the community could have used in a decade.'

'Did your mother give it to you?'

'Oh, no. The adults must have known what it was, but it was never discussed, at least not where the kids could hear. Mama got some from the healer for Amos's arthritis. He was her husband until . . .' Her stomach took a nasty dip at the memory, and she sipped on the non-special tea, waiting until the wave had passed. 'Until Gideon escaped. Amos was a good man. I think he truly believed in the community's precepts. He was always good to me, anyway. But he had arthritis and his hands hurt when it got cold. He was a carpenter, so he needed his hands. Mama would make him the tea before he went to sleep and one night I tasted it when he wasn't looking. That's a taste I will never forget.'

Rafe was watching her thoughtfully. 'I wonder if the Feds have checked for marijuana crops in their search for Eden.'

Mercy shrugged. 'I don't know, but I doubt that Eden grows it anymore. We moved after Gideon's escape and left the fields behind. Someone might have gone back to harvest it later, but that wasn't something that the regular members knew much about.'

'They might have a new cash crop now, though.' Rafe had his phone out and was texting. 'I'm letting Gideon know that you're okay and asking if he knows anything about the ways the community made money. It might give us a lead to their location.'

Mercy sipped the tea, watching him, waiting until he'd put his phone away. 'Or you could ask me.'

Rafe looked uncomfortable. 'Is that okay? I mean, to ask you to remember?'

'It will have to be okay,' Mercy said firmly. 'I want to help find them.'

'Then we'll start there,' Rafe said, his mouth curving into the smile that warmed her heart. 'I'm proud of you, Mercedes.'

She shot him a glare. 'I wish I hadn't told you my name.'

Irina's brows lifted. 'Why? What is wrong with Mercedes? It's a lovely name.'

Mercy huffed her displeasure, but Rafe's smile only grew. 'My bio-dad's last name was Benz,' she explained.

Irina snorted. 'That will remain our secret, yes?'

'No,' Sasha said from behind Rafe. 'Because it's comedy gold.' She pushed Rafe over so that she could see into the bathroom. 'That's not special tea, is it, Mom?'

Mercy laughed. 'No. We've already been down that road.'

'And I missed it.' Sasha exhaled a put-upon sigh. 'We were worried about you, kiddo. You want to come back and talk about this now?'

No. 'Okay,' Mercy murmured and took the hand Irina offered, rising from the floor, which had been blessedly cool against her heated skin.

'Nobody in our family saw the video,' Rafe said soberly. 'We won't do that to you.'

'Thank you,' she murmured.

Irina gripped her chin, staring hard into her eyes. 'You did nothing wrong. Repeat that, Mercy Callahan.'

'I did nothing wrong,' she said quietly.

'Again,' Irina demanded. '*I* believe you. I want to know that *you* believe you.'

She's right, Mercy thought. Borrowing some of the older woman's strength, she straightened to her full height. 'I didn't do anything wrong,' she said firmly.

'Better,' Irina said with a sniff. 'Still not what I want to hear, but better.' She dropped Mercy's chin, set the mug on the sink vanity, and grasped both of her hands. 'You are not alone, Mercy, even if you might feel that way.'

Mercy's smile was rueful. 'I know I'm not alone. But it's different when it's you. Me, I mean.'

Irina tilted her head, going silent for such a long moment that Mercy began to fidget. The older woman turned her gaze to her children. 'I know,' she finally murmured.

There was a moment of absolute silence as the full meaning of her words sank in. Then Sasha gasped audibly. 'What?'

Rafe had grown abruptly pale. 'Mom?' he whispered.

Mercy could only stand there, gaping in shock. 'You?'

Irina squeezed Mercy's hands, but her gaze remained fixed on Rafe and Sasha. 'It was long ago, *dorogieyie*. Before I left Russia. It was why I left Russia. Why *my* mother got me out, just like Mercy's mother did for her.'

Sasha's eyes had filled with tears. 'You never told us.'

Irina's smile was sad. 'Why would I? *When* would I? When you were children? It's not something that one tells their babies and even after you started growing up, one of you was still too young. And now that Zoya is seventeen . . .' She trailed off. 'It was such a long time ago that it didn't seem positive to bring it up. I don't like to speak of it, but your father knows and has long accepted it. We cannot punish the man who assaulted me, but we can help others. It's one of the reasons we are so active with the rape counseling charities and why we encouraged public service.' Her lips turned up, a small smile but a real one. 'You all have made us proud – Rafe, you and Meg and Damien are police officers, Sasha a social worker who helps children, Jude is a prosecutor, Cash a physical therapist, and Patrick fights fires. I may even get a doctor in the family if Zoya continues in her path. My children right wrongs, protect the community, save lives, heal bodies, and nurture spirits. No mother could ask for more.'

'It's also why you were so upset when you thought Gideon had been . . .' Sasha pursed her trembling lips. 'Assaulted.' She wiped her eyes. 'I work with victims every day – children, even – and I can't say the word.'

'It is harder when it is family, I think,' Irina said gently. 'And yes, knowing that Gideon was almost assaulted was very difficult for me.' She stroked her thumbs over Mercy's knuckles. 'Knowing how you suffered as a girl, and then once you'd believed yourself safe, had to endure the second *kasyoel* who recorded his crime with his phone . . . This is much harder. The men who hurt you must be punished – the man in Eden and the man in New Orleans – and if we can help make that happen, then that is what we will do.'

Mercy swallowed hard because Ephraim had forced her for an entire year. But she'd managed to lose at least some of those memories. Her twelve-year-old mind had often shut down to spare her the full horror. The clear memories she shoved into her mental box and nailed it closed.

Wishing for a fraction of Irina's strength, Mercy turned her focus to Rafe, who looked broken.

Rafe's throat worked as tears ran down his face, unchecked. 'I'm sorry, Mom. I'm so sorry. I don't . . . I don't know what to say.'

Irina released Mercy and wrapped her arms around her son. 'Thank you for your sorrow on my behalf, *sin rodnoy moy*. As I said, it was long ago. I haven't "gotten over it," nor have I forgotten. But there are whole blocks of time when I do not think of it. That is the best I can expect and I'm grateful for those times, but when I hear of other victims, I remember.'

'So do I,' Mercy said quietly. But she hadn't volunteered to help other victims like Irina and Karl did.

'Stop it,' Irina chided. 'I can see your thoughts on your face, Mercy. We each have our path to healing. We each must decide what we are able to do for ourselves and for others. What is it that the airline attendants say? Put the mask on yourself first? If you want to help others in the future, I will be there to guide you, if you wish. But you will not berate yourself for the way you've sought healing. Am I clear?'

Mercy managed a smile. 'Yes, ma'am. Someday I'd like to hear how you escaped your situation.'

Irina's smile was genuine and serene. 'Someday I will tell you. Now, let us leave this bathroom. It is not a sanitary place to have a family meeting.'

Rafe's laugh was shaky. 'I love you, Mom.'

Irina took his cheeks in her hands and pulled him down, placing a kiss on his forehead. 'And I love you, Raphael.' She did the same to Sasha. 'And I love you as well, Anastasia.'

'Boo,' Mercy said, forcing a lightness into her voice that she didn't feel. Not yet anyway. '*Your* real name is nice, Sasha.'

'Yours is expensive,' Sasha fired back, then hugged her mother again. 'Do the others know?'

'No. I suppose I must tell them now, but it can wait, yes?' She lifted her brows at her children. 'Yes?' she repeated.

'Yes, Mama,' they said in unison.

'Your secret is safe with us,' Rafe said, then cleared his throat roughly, still visibly shaken. 'Can you be around food, Mercy? Because I never got to eat dinner and I'm starving.'

'I can,' Mercy said. She hoped. Keeping food down when she was this stressed was never an easy task. 'I never got to finish the mac and cheese that you made me, Irina.'

'Farrah said it was your comfort food. We thought you deserved some comfort this night. Come.' Irina took Mercy's empty mug and led them out of the bathroom.

Mercy and Rafe were the last to file out, Rafe looking so shattered it made Mercy's heart hurt. She took his hand and threaded their fingers together. 'Will you be okay?'

Rafe stared at his mother's retreating back. 'Yes. Eventually. I . . . we didn't know.'

'She shared it for me, to help me,' Mercy murmured, overwhelmed by Irina's generosity. 'You have an amazing mother, Raphael Sokolov.'

'I know.'

Eight

Granite Bay, California
Sunday, 16 April, 12.00 A.M.

Rafe had questions. *So many questions.* For his mother, for his dad, for Gideon, and for Mercy herself. The only thing he knew for certain was that he needed to get Mercy somewhere quieter. The two of them sat at the Sokolov family table while his mother, his father, Sasha, and Farrah made plans with Daisy over the speakerphone. His father's attorney was working to get the video removed from the website that published the foul article on Mercy, thank goodness. Fortunately, money talked, and his father had contacts in powerful places.

Daisy had used her media connections to get an interview set up for Mercy with a reporter who'd been sympathetic and fair during and after the February fiasco. Now they were all speaking animatedly about what Mercy should and should not say to the reporter. All while Mercy sat with them, pale and hunched, and very alone despite the crowd.

He slid his arm across the back of the chair, wincing as she flinched. 'I'm sorry,' he whispered in her ear. 'I didn't mean to startle you.'

She turned to meet his eyes, hers filled with fear, sadness, and utter exhaustion. 'I know. I'm just . . .'

'You're tired, and my family can be a lot,' he murmured quietly. 'I'm aware of this.'

She smiled in earnest at that, understanding flickering amid the pain. 'I guess so. They're helping. I appreciate it. It's . . . I'm tired.'

'Which is why we're blowing this joint,' he said lightly, holding up his phone. 'I texted my brother Damien. He's coming to escort us back to my house. You'll get some quiet and some sleep.'

Her brow crinkled a little, then smoothed. 'Oh, right. Damien is another police officer.'

'Yep. He works in the Russian division, out in West Sac.' He patted her shoulder when her frown returned. 'He's a good guy. You can trust him.'

'Oh, I'm sure I can. I was just wondering why West Sac has a Russian division? Do they investigate Russian organized crime?'

He chuckled. 'No. West Sacramento has a large Russian community. Damien's group serves them. Damien's fluent in Russian, so he was a natural for the division.'

'Do you speak Russian?'

'Some. Mom spoke it at home when we were little, but mainly when she got . . . emotional. That translates to upset because one of us was misbehaving. Or when she was driving and someone cut her off in traffic.' He was encouraged by the humor in her eyes. So much better than the numb despair that had dominated a moment before. 'That's why I know the word for "asshole".'

Her lips twitched. '*Kaz* . . . What was it?'

'*Kazyoel*.' The word his mother had used to describe the piece of shit who'd drugged Mercy. New rage bubbled up inside him and he wanted to throttle the *kazyoel* with his own hands. But his rage wasn't what Mercy needed at the moment. She needed his support. His comfort. His protection.

'I'll have to remember that word,' she said, and then her shoulders seemed to relax a fraction. 'Thank you, Rafe. You all have made a really sucky evening a little bit better.'

It was all Rafe could do not to lean in and kiss her. But it wasn't the time. She'd already fallen asleep in his arms. That was more than he'd expected. Still not enough, but more than he'd dreamed.

A throat clearing had him looking at the rest of the table, which had gone silent. 'Yes?' he asked, falling back behind the wall he'd built over the course of his life, pulling his nonchalant persona around his shoulders like a cloak in winter.

131

'Are you listening to anything we're saying, Rafe?' Sasha demanded.

'Yes. And no,' Rafe answered honestly. 'You guys can talk all night, but I think Mercy needs to get some sleep. I'm taking her back to our house. Farrah, you too, if you're ready to go.'

'I'm so sorry, Mercy,' Daisy said, dismay in her tone. 'I didn't realize how late it was. You must be exhausted.'

Irina and Karl looked equally dismayed as they really looked at Mercy. 'Oh, *izvini doragaya maya,*' Irina sighed, zapping back from savvy media planner into mama bear in the blink of her eyes. 'We are sorry, too. You can sleep here, of course.'

Mercy's gaze flicked to Rafe's. 'Thank you, but . . .'

Rafe jumped in to save her from needing to decline. 'It's quiet at my place, Mom. Sometimes some folks need a little quiet to rejuvenate.'

Sasha's eyes turned shrewd as she tilted her head, studying him for a moment, then giving him a brisk nod. It was like she saw that he needed the quiet as much as Mercy did. 'I'll get the cats ready to go.'

Farrah was smiling at him. 'I'll get our bags.'

Karl harrumphed. 'I'll get the bags. You and Irina can wrap up some supper to take back for leftovers.'

Irina was already on her feet. 'But it's secure here, and—'

Just then the front door opened and closed loudly. 'Rafe?' Damien called.

'In the kitchen!' Rafe called back. 'Damien's going to escort us home,' he told his mother. 'He'll stay up on the third floor since Daisy's with Gideon tonight.' As she should be, because Gideon needed her. Rafe hadn't seen his friend that devastated in a long, long time.

Irina's smile was rueful. 'I should have known you would have prepared, Raphael. But tomorrow is Sunday. You will come back for dinner, yes?'

Rafe gave her a nod. 'Of course, Mom. We wouldn't miss it. Thank you.'

Irina winked at him. 'Is nothing,' she said, waving her hand and layering her accent on thickly. 'You're a good boy, Raphael.'

Mercy snorted quietly. 'Suck-up,' she whispered to him, but she was smiling and that was all that mattered. She turned to the rest of the group. 'Tomorrow I'll be able to think more clearly and I'll do whatever we agree is best. Rafe is right. I need a little quiet time to recharge. I don't want you to think I'm unappreciative—'

Karl patted her hand. 'We get it, Mercy. Rafe thinks we don't know that he fixed up that house to give himself quiet time, too.' He arched a brow at Rafe. 'You really didn't think you'd fooled your mother and me all these years, did you?'

Rafe opened his mouth in surprise, then closed it again when he realized he had no idea what to say.

Mercy snickered. 'Busted.'

He had to smile back at her. Mercy was beautiful, but smiling? Her face simply glowed. And reassured him that she was going to be strong enough to weather this storm.

Rafe turned to his brother, who now waited in the doorway. 'Damien, you remember Mercy, right?'

Damien, still in uniform, crossed the room to shake her hand. 'Gideon's sister, of course. I understand that you've had an eventful evening. We'll get you back to Rafe's place safely, don't worry.'

'Hey, everyone?' Daisy asked from the speakerphone. 'Gideon's here. He has an update.'

'I just got off the phone with Molina,' Gideon said. 'SacPD informed her that they got a call from the spouse of June Lindstrom, who never came home from the airport. She texted her husband that she was on her way home after her flight, right about the same time that Burton attacked Mercy. The airport provided surveillance video from the parking garage and the parking payment lanes. A man fitting Burton's description was seen forcing Mrs Lindstrom into her minivan. The parking booth camera captured her mouthing *Help me.* There's no audio, but there's little doubt that her vehicle was how Burton escaped the airport.'

'And Mrs Lindstrom?' Mercy asked, her chin trembling.

Gideon's voice gentled. 'No word on her yet, Mercy. The minivan was found in downtown Santa Rosa, of all places, through its GPS. Surveillance videos near where the van was found show the same man leaving it behind. He disappeared into an alleyway, carrying a small suitcase.'

'I think Mrs Lindstrom is probably dead,' Mercy said quietly.

'I think you're right,' Gideon replied. 'I'm so sorry, Mercy.'

Rafe wasn't sure what Gideon was apologizing for – that the woman might be dead or for what he had said to his sister before leaving the house.

Mercy swallowed. 'Thank you. But I still don't understand how he knew I'd be at the airport?'

Gideon sighed. 'He was on an earlier flight from New Orleans. Airport video shows him coming into the Sacramento airport this morning. Well, yesterday morning now.'

Mercy had grown even paler, which Rafe hadn't thought possible. 'He was in New Orleans? With me?'

Farrah stiffened. 'Shit.'

'It appears so,' Gideon replied with surprising calm. He sounded like the pre-Daisy Gideon, all buttoned up and unnervingly composed. 'He boarded using the ID of Eustace Carmelo.'

Mercy startled in surprise, then huffed out a bitter chuckle. 'Of course he did.'

Rafe turned to her, confused. 'Why "of course"?'

She rubbed her temples wearily. 'Ephraim Burton isn't his actual name.'

'His real name is Harry Franklin,' Rafe said, wondering where she was going with this. 'He changed it after going on the run for bank robbery and murder thirty years ago. We knew that.'

'Yes, but he took the name "Ephraim Burton" when he joined Eden,' Mercy corrected. 'I don't know how much time passed between the robbery and his arrival in Eden, but the name change was *because* of Eden.'

'How do you know that, Mercy?' Gideon asked.

'I heard him grumbling once, after his son Carmelo was born. I was almost thirteen. He was muttering, "Fucking Ephraim. Fucking fruitful. Fucking Pastor. Fuck him and his names." At that moment, he was glaring at a card that he was putting in his wallet. Later, when he was asleep, I peeked.'

Almost thirteen, Rafe thought. Which meant she'd been abused by that monster for a whole year by then.

Gideon's gasp was audible. 'Mercy. If he'd caught you . . .'

'I know, I know.' She waved it off. 'I was in hell, Gideon. I didn't think he could do anything worse than he'd already done if he caught me.' A shudder shook her, but she soldiered on. 'I hoped it was something I could use against him. Something I could use to get me and Mama free. But all it was was a driver's license in the name of Eustace Carmelo.'

Rafe wanted to ask her about that shudder, because he had the sinking suspicion that Ephraim *had* caught her. But he tucked the question away for until the two of them were alone. Mercy had been forced to confront enough shit for one night.

'So Pastor gave him another alias?' Daisy asked. 'After Ephraim's son, Carmelo?'

Another bitter chuckle from Mercy. 'Ephraim Burton has several sons. One is Eustace. One is Carmelo. Eustace, Carmelo, and Ephraim all mean "fruitful." I asked Eustace's mother why she'd chosen that name and she looked surprised. Told me that Pastor had suggested it and that Ephraim hadn't wanted it, but Pastor's word was law. Carmelo's mother said the same thing.'

'Several sons?' Karl asked. 'By different mothers?'

Mercy shrugged. 'I was Ephraim's sixth wife. We all lived together in his house.'

Karl exhaled. 'He had six wives at the same time?'

'One big happy family,' she said bitterly. 'One of the wives had died before we came to the compound, so I guess I was number seven.' Her lips twisted. 'Lucky me. Another wife died a few months after I . . . after our marriage. And then, of course, there was Mama. I don't know how many he had after I left and she was killed.'

The table fell silent until Irina said through gritted teeth, 'You were *not* his wife. You were a *child*. You know that, yes?'

Mercy smiled at her, a genuine smile that softened her face. 'Yes, ma'am. I know that.'

'How many children did he have at that point?' Gideon asked, troubled.

135

'Nine,' Mercy said flatly. 'Five sons. He did his part to populate the community.'

Sasha was biting her lip. 'But not you . . . You never had any . . .'

Mercy shook her head hard. 'No. Not me.'

Everyone kind of slumped in relief at that. Except for Rafe. He could see that there was far more that Mercy had left unsaid, and none of it was good. 'Anything else, Gideon?' he asked. 'I was going to take Mercy and Farrah back to Daisy's place.'

'And I'm here, Gid,' Damien added. 'Rafe and I'll make sure that the bastard doesn't touch her.'

'Thank you,' Gideon said. 'There is one more thing. Airline records show that Eustace Carmelo took the red-eye from San Francisco into New Orleans on Monday evening.'

Mercy shuddered again. 'After that damned newscast.'

Farrah looked sick. 'He was in New Orleans watching her? For almost a week?'

'I think so,' Gideon said reluctantly. 'Molina's got calls in to the New Orleans field office as well as the police department and sheriff's office. We're trying to trace his steps.'

Mercy was frantically trying to do the same, counting on her fingers and mouthing, *Work, grocery store, gym* . . . Then she went completely still. 'Gideon, I visited John this week. If Ephraim was watching me all week, he knows where they live. John's got kids. Three under ten years old. What if Ephraim can't get to me and goes after them? He does that. He'll use the people you love to hurt you.'

'Text me his phone number and address,' Gideon said. 'We can warn them to take precautions.'

'Contact my fiancé, Captain André Holmes,' Farrah instructed. 'He knows Mercy, plus he knows all the players in that awful article. He can help. I'll text you his contact info, and I'll let him know you'll be calling.'

'Thank you,' Gideon said gratefully. 'Molina and I appreciate it.'

'I never heard from Molina after I called her at the airport,' Rafe said. 'Does she need my statement?'

'Officially, yes. She ran with what you told her already, though. She told me to tell you that she can send someone by tomorrow to get a formal statement. So if a Fed-in-Black shows up, let them in,' he added, trying for a lightness that fell a little flat.

Irina spoke up. 'If they come by at two, they can have some of my bird's milk cake.'

'If there's any left,' Gideon bantered. 'I might not leave any for anyone else.'

'Then I make two,' Irina declared. 'Now we are finished. Mercy and Farrah are falling asleep in their chairs. They are still on central time, after all.'

And it was after midnight, Pacific time. Rafe was more exhausted than he'd been in a long time.

Rafe used his cane to push himself to his feet and held out a hand to Mercy, his heart thumping harder when she took it, squeezing hard, holding on like he was a lifeline. 'Come on. Let's go home.'

Sacramento, California
Sunday, 16 April, 12.50 A.M.

Jeff Bunker groaned, pulling the pillow over his head to block out the incessant pounding on his bedroom door. 'Go away!' he shouted.

Or he'd meant to shout. It came out as a whimper instead. He felt too awful to care.

'Shut up,' he mumbled, praying this whole thing was simply a nightmare, his penance for drinking way too much scotch.

'Are you telling me to shut up, Jeffy?'

God, this nightmare was getting worse. It sounded like his mother was standing over him, yelling at him.

'Yes. Please,' he moaned.

'Oh, for heaven's sake.' A bottle clinked hard, glass hitting his metal trash can. 'Jeffrey Alan Bunker, are you *drunk*? *Where* did you get this alcohol? You're only sixteen. Dammit. Wait. Was this the scotch I got for Christmas from my boss? You *stole* from me?'

He peeked out from under the pillow, instantly regretting his life choices. All of them. The light burned his retinas and the yelling kept getting louder. 'Mom?'

'So you *are* alive,' she mocked. She was standing at the foot of his bed, hands on her hips, arms akimbo. 'What the actual heck is going on here, Jeffy? I knew I should never have agreed to you graduating high school early. You are not ready for college.'

Jeff wanted to cry. 'Mom, why are you here?' he whispered. 'Can you stop shouting?'

She laughed. 'If you think this is shouting . . . We haven't even started, Jeffy. Sit up. Now.'

Shit. Her soldier voice. She'd left the military twenty years ago, but the intensity of her soldier voice hadn't diminished. His body tried to comply with her order, but his stomach protested. 'Fucking hell, Mom.'

She gasped. 'Jeffy! Language.'

'Mom!' he gasped back. 'Trash can. Please.'

With an impatient, angry sigh she dumped the contents of his trash can on his desk, then handed him the empty bin. 'You deserve to be sick. How could you, Jeff? How *could* you?'

He blinked, trying to focus through the haze. 'Huh? How could I what?'

'Get drunk? Disappear for days without a word?' She shoved her phone in his face and he recoiled, all the letters out of focus. 'Write this . . . trash?'

'What?' he asked dumbly. 'What is it? 'Cause I can't see.'

'Serves you right. Your poor father's turning in his grave. I am so ashamed of you, I could cry.'

'Join the club,' he muttered, but knew it had to be bad. She never brought up his dead father unless it was. His father had died of cancer when Jeff was eight years old, but his mother maintained what was basically a shrine to him in the spare bedroom. 'What time is it?'

'One a.m.'

He stared at her. 'What? Why are you even awake at one a.m.?'

'Why am I awake? Why do you smell like a brewery?'

'Distillery,' he corrected absently. 'What are you talking about?'

'This.' She jabbed her finger at the phone screen. 'This piece of trash that is so far beneath you that I . . .' Her voice broke on a genuine sob. 'I don't even know what to say.'

That got his attention. His mom being speechless didn't happen often. Her crying was even rarer.

He squinted at the phone screen. 'Let me see it. Can you maybe . . . I don't know. Make me some coffee?'

She tossed the phone in his lap, making him wince again. 'Shi— oot, Mom. Be careful.'

'*Be careful*, he says. *Make me coffee*, he says. I should turn you over my knee, is what I should do,' she grumbled. 'You want to be so goddamn independent, get your own coffee.'

He blinked a few times, grateful when her phone screen came into focus. It was his story on Mercy Callahan. 'What's wrong with it?'

'What's wrong with it?' she whispered, tears still tracking down her face. 'You admit that you wrote that?'

'Yeah, of course,' he said, scrolling through the article. 'It's not my best work, I admit, but—' He broke off, staring in horror. There were quotes that he'd deleted and – 'Oh my God.' It was the video. *The* video. The one he'd decided not to send to his editor the night before. 'Oh no. Oh no, oh no, oh no.'

His mother came back to the bed, lowering herself to perch on the edge. 'You . . . didn't write that, then?' Her relief was evident.

His gaze flew up to hers. 'I did, but I took a lot of it out before I sent it in. I never sent this video to the *Gabber*. *Never*, Mom. I never even uploaded it to the *Gabber* server. I never copied it to my own laptop. It was on a thumb drive and I viewed the video from that.'

She closed her eyes, exhaling slowly. 'Thank the good Lord for that, at least.'

He scrolled further, his stomach hurting more with each word he read. 'I didn't write this part either, Mom. I swear it. I took out the reference to this Prescott guy because he was a sleazebag.'

Just like my editor.

Oh my God. How had Nolan gotten this? 'I don't know how this happened.'

'Well, you'd better figure it out quickly because it's had over a million views since it was put up.'

Jeff backed out of the article to see the time stamp. 'It was posted last night at eight p.m. I sent in my edited version at seven.'

'Then drank yourself stupid?'

'Yeah. Because . . .'

'Because?' she prompted. At least she was no longer yelling.

'Because . . . reasons.'

She looked away, her lips still trembling. 'Grow up, Jeff. You posted a video of a woman being assaulted. And you make it all better by getting drunk.'

'No, Mom. Yes, I'm drunk. No, I didn't post that video. *I did not.*'

'Then how is it under your name?'

'I don't know. Let me think.'

She wiped her face with her fingertips. 'Where did you get the video?' she asked, a little more calmly.

'From this real douchebag in New Orleans named Stan Prescott. He sold me the thumb drive.'

'*Wait,*' she interrupted. 'You were in *New Orleans*? Are you *serious*? How the *hell* did you get to New Orleans? You are sixteen years old. You don't even have a car.'

'I flew.' He dug his knuckles into his temples. 'You can yell at me about that later.'

'Trust me, I will.' She drew a deep breath and let it out. 'So, back to the video.'

'Fine. I was doing an article on one of the women who escaped that serial killer back in February. Mercy Callahan. She lives in New Orleans. One of her college friends there pointed me to this guy. Said he had some information.'

'This is not "information," Jeff.' She crooked her fingers in air quotes. 'This is evidence of a criminal act.'

'What? How?'

'He drugged her, Jeff. He drugged her, then recorded her . . .' She pinched her lips. 'He tried to rape her.'

Oh God. 'I didn't know that, Mom. I didn't watch it all. I couldn't. How . . .' He shook his head, trying to think, for God's sake. And then he knew. 'Oh. The payment.'

'What payment?'

'The guy said he had good dirt, but it was going to cost, you know? I told Nolan and he approved the payment.'

'Nolan is your boss?'

'My editor, yes.' Jeff rubbed his aching forehead. 'When I talked to him last night, I told him that I was deleting something I wasn't comfortable with and he said to leave it in, that he'd delete it. I knew better than that, but I wasn't expecting him to contact the guy who gave me the video.' The guy who'd drugged and sexually assaulted a college girl. 'He had Prescott's name for the payment and he must have called him. Oh my God, this is awful.' He looked up to find his mother still crying. 'What am I going to do about this, Mom?'

'You're going to do the right thing. You're going to quit that awful job. You're going to get that video taken down. And then you're going to contact this woman and make it right, no matter what you have to do.'

'Okay, Mom. I just don't know where to start.'

'Start by getting that video taken down. *Now.*'

'But I can't do that. I don't have access to the server. Only Nolan does.'

She bit her lower lip. 'Then call him and tell him that you'll sue his ass for publishing that video under your name if he doesn't take it down. I know a judge. I'll call him for some advice.'

'You're going to call a judge at one in the morning?'

She took her phone from her pocket. 'He'll still be awake. He's a night owl.'

Jeff didn't want to know how his mother knew this. He remembered her dating a judge when he was a senior in high school. She'd met the man when he'd brought his bulldog into the veterinary clinic where she was the receptionist. Dinners with the guy had been awkward as fuck.

'Okay,' was all he could think to say. 'I'll figure out where she's staying.'

'In Granite Bay,' his mother said as she searched her contact list. 'Oh, here he is.'

'How do you know she's in Granite Bay?'

'Google her and you'll see what your article has done to her,' his mother snapped. 'The media has surrounded the house where she's staying.' Then she turned on the charm. The judge had answered his phone. 'Bellsie, this is Geri Bunker. I hope I didn't wake you.' She tittered. 'Oh, I remember. Listen, I need some advice. Are you alone?' Her smile was a little too satisfied for the situation. 'Oh good. So it's like this . . .'

Bellsie? Jeff grimaced, then googled Mercy Callahan and groaned again. Shit. There were hundreds of results, the most recent an article about her near abduction from the airport. It also had a video, grainy because it was from the airport security cameras. It showed a zombielike Mercy being walked toward the door by . . . *him*. The man he'd seen leaving the dead woman's New Orleans apartment next door to Mercy's.

He was not shocked, but he was horrified, even more horrified than he already had been.

She wore a blank expression, like a doll. Even when the big man was struck down by some blond guy's cane. A cane? Seriously? But Jeff's disbelief turned into admiration when the blond yanked at the killer's leg with the cane's hook after both men crashed to the floor. The blond guy had serious ninja skills with that cane.

He was also in a wheelchair. And looked damned familiar.

Jeff scanned the article and remembered who the blond was. Detective Raphael Sokolov. He'd been involved in taking the serial killer down. And, according to this article from tonight, he'd taken Mercy Callahan to his family's home on Medallion Avenue in Granite Bay.

At least he knew where she'd be, he thought grimly. At the house on Medallion Avenue surrounded by news vans.

'Okay, we'll do that,' his mother said after a series of hums, nods, and *uh-huh*s. 'Thank you, Bellsie. And I'd love to go out with you next week. Text me a place and time and I'll be there.' She ended the call. 'He says we need to formally file a cease-and-desist with the website. Once that's filed, either they have to take it down, or we can report them to the FBI. This is considered "revenge porn".'

'I'm going to report Nolan anyway,' Jeff muttered. 'This woman is fragile. Something like this could push anyone over the edge, but . . . Damn, Mom. Did you see her walking through the airport?'

She nodded, her expression pained. 'Poor girl. How are you going to make this right to her?'

'I have no idea,' he admitted. 'Hey, Mom, how did you even know about this?'

'Your aunt Patricia called. She had an alert set up for anything with your name in it. Trying to be supportive. She called and woke me up. She was screaming. She'll be glad to know that you didn't do this. Not voluntarily, anyway.' She patted his arm. 'Get on your laptop and issue the takedown order.'

Now? was on the tip of his tongue, but he bit it back. She was right. 'Okay. Thanks, Mom.'

She met his eyes soberly. 'You're welcome. Find a better job, Jeffy. There isn't enough money in the world worth your soul.'

'I will. I promise.' He had to. This was not the way his career was supposed to be. He wanted to help people and only hurt the bad guys. *Now I'm a bad guy.*

Nine

Mercy crept down the stairs of Rafe's house, hoping she didn't make any floorboards creak. She needed room to pace. To meditate. Because Ephraim had been in New Orleans. He'd been watching her for almost a week.

She knew she should have been asleep, but even though she was completely exhausted, sleep had eluded her. Farrah had climbed under the covers in Sasha's guest room still fully dressed, dropping off into a deep slumber before Sasha had finished readying the bedding. Mercy had managed to doze for what might have been an hour, but *that* nightmare had shocked her into full alertness.

Mercy hated *that* nightmare, the one where she saw her mother gunned down by DJ Belmont. She hated all the nightmares, but that one was the worst. If she'd been in her own apartment, she would have been in her kitchen, baking cookies for her brothers' and sisters' kids. Snickerdoodles were the overall favorite.

They'd made her family and she'd betrayed them. Stolen time they could have had with Gideon. And now she'd probably brought danger to their doorstep.

The nightmare had woken her, but it had been dread at the thought of facing John and all the brothers and sisters that had her staring at the ceiling. That and the knowledge that Ephraim had stalked her in New Orleans for a whole week and she hadn't even known he was there.

He'd been in the same city as her family. Who at least by now

144

knew to be careful, to watch the children more carefully. Gideon had called Farrah's captain, who'd called John, who'd called Mercy a few minutes after two a.m. California time, frantically urging her to come home where he and all the sibs could keep her safe.

She'd broken down again, sobbing into the phone, confessing what she'd done. John, to his credit, had been stunned, but kind. He still didn't know about Eden, but Mercy had told him enough that he understood her childhood had been traumatic. Finally John had told her that they loved her and to sleep, that they'd figure it out.

And through all the sobbing and confessing, Farrah had slept like a log, making Mercy envious. Farrah always slept like a log, while Mercy rarely slept at all. Especially recently.

She'd made the trip to John's this past week on the pretense of delivering the dozens of cookies that she'd made when she couldn't sleep. She hadn't even been able to stay to watch his kids eat a single cookie, simply shoving the plastic container into John's arms and running from the raw pity in his eyes. He'd seen the CNN newscast too, but she hadn't been able to talk to him about it.

She couldn't make cookies in someone else's apartment, especially while they were sleeping, so she was punting to the next nervous-energy-burning activity in her repertoire.

I could have paced upstairs, Mercy thought, rolling her eyes at herself as she descended the last step into Rafe's foyer. Farrah wouldn't have woken up. Sasha claimed to also sleep like the dead, so it wasn't like Mercy's footsteps would have woken her, either.

Or you could just admit the truth, to yourself if no one else. Because she now stood in the little foyer of Rafe's house, staring at his apartment door. She wanted to knock. She wanted to sit next to him, to breathe in his scent, to feel his arms around her. She wanted to sleep, and he made her feel safe enough to do so. That hour she'd slept in his arms had been more precious than gold.

She'd actually lifted her fist to knock when she realized what she was doing. He was asleep. Waking him up so that she could sleep would be wrong and selfish, and she'd been both of those things enough tonight. Lowering her fist, she surveyed the square footage of the landing, determining it large enough for her needs.

She needed to do more than pace. One of the most valuable takeaways from years of therapy was that pacing burned off energy, but meditation could actually silence the voices. Which, at the moment, were legion.

Ephraim at the airport. *Hello, wife.*

DJ from her nightmare. *Watch, Mercy.* Right before he shot her mother in the head.

Her mother, pleading. *Find Gideon. There's something you need to know about Gideon.*

They all talked and talked until she wanted to rip her hair out, so she assumed the starting position for the tai chi routine that was her favorite. It aided in meditation, calming her mind when it was going full throttle, giving her the focus to shove the voices into the box and nail down the lid.

She sank into the movements, one flowing into the next, timing becoming irrelevant. When she finished her routine, she did it again. And again. Until her body began to relax and her churning mind was suspended.

Lowering her arms to her sides, she filled her lungs with air, expelling it on a quiet rush. And in the quiet, she could finally think past the panic that had kept her frozen in its grip since she'd stepped onto that airplane in New Orleans.

'It'll be okay,' she whispered, then became aware of someone breathing behind her. She spun, pressing her palm to her racing heart when she saw Rafe leaning in his doorway, dressed only in sweats, his chest bare.

'It'll be okay,' he repeated quietly.

'How—' Clearing her throat, she tried to project calm. 'How long were you standing there?'

'Long enough to watch you go through your routine a few times,' he said with a smile. 'You're very pretty when you do that.'

'Do what? Tai chi?'

He nodded. 'Elegant and graceful.'

'It's my meditation,' she said, flustered at the compliment. 'One of the ways, anyway.'

'Does it help?'

She nodded. 'Except when the life gets scared out of me afterward.'

He chuckled. 'Sorry. I was afraid to say anything. I didn't want to scare you. I should have gone back inside, but . . .' His smile turned a little bashful and it was an endearing sight. 'I didn't want to stop watching you.'

She felt her cheeks heat in pleasure at the compliment. 'Did I wake you?'

'No. I should be sacked out solid, but I couldn't sleep.'

'Me either,' she admitted. 'Farrah falls asleep as soon as her head hits the pillow. I envy her that skill.'

'My brain was racing.'

'Mine too.' She wanted to say more but had no idea what she should say. Instead, she gestured lamely to the stairs. 'I should let you try to sleep.'

'Or you could come in for a cup of tea,' he said, and her heart began to race again, but not in fear.

It was anticipation and it was more than a little heady. 'If you really don't mind.'

Gripping his cane, he stepped backward into his apartment, beckoning her in. 'I don't mind at all.'

She looked around as he closed the door behind them, partly out of curiosity and partly to avoid staring at the chest he was making no move to cover up. 'You didn't change anything from when Daisy lived here.' The walls were still covered in vibrant, colorful murals, the open closet door revealed a jumble of sports equipment, and the corners were still stacked high with fabric of every imaginable color. It was like a hobby shop had exploded. Mercy had loved it at first sight.

'It's only temporary,' he said with a shrug. 'Daisy'll want her place back eventually. Once my PT is done and I can take the stairs again. If she's not married to Gideon and raising their five children by then.'

The PT was not going well, then. Mercy was glad she hadn't asked. Not sure how to respond, she pointed to the whiteboard against the living-room wall. 'That's new.'

It was a free-standing model, the kind that flipped to reveal another board on the other side. The whiteboard was filled with his PT schedule. He went three times a week and he was clearly discouraged by his lack of progress, real or perceived.

She could identify with that. Her own mental health therapy had been a similar struggle. Two steps forward, one step back. It still was.

'Ah, my board,' Rafe said, walking into the kitchen, leaning heavily on his cane. 'It helps me keep my schedule straight.'

This surprised her, because the schedule hadn't looked complicated. Every Monday, Wednesday, and Friday, same time, same place.

'What kind of tea?' he asked. 'I have a whole drawerful. Well, Daisy does. Come take a look.'

Mercy picked a packet of chamomile from the drawer. 'It helps me wind down.'

He nodded once. 'Have a seat on the sofa. I'll bring it to you.'

She cast a doubtful gaze from the two cups on the counter to the cane in his hand, but made no protest. He was a grown man. He knew what he was capable of doing.

She'd settled on the sofa when she spied the edge of a canvas leaning against the far wall, behind several other paintings. It was a painting she'd recognized when she'd been here six weeks before, a painting that had shattered her heart at first sight. She was on her feet and pulling the painting free before realizing that she'd even planned to move. Placing it in front of the others, she stood and stared at the crudely painted field of daisies, a young girl sitting in their midst. A smiling young girl with black hair and green eyes.

The girl was Mercy and she remembered the day she'd sat in the field of flowers. But they hadn't been daisies. Most had been light purple, a few others had been red and—

Oh. Details clicked together in her mind. *Oh my God.* 'Poppies,' she murmured.

'I think they're daisies,' Rafe said. 'Poppies are red.'

She looked over her shoulder to see him placing two steaming mugs on the coffee table. He'd brought them in on a tray, which made complete sense – and made her glad she hadn't said anything about his being able to carry both mugs one-handed.

'At least they're supposed to be daisies,' Rafe added. 'Gideon is good at many things. Painting . . .' He waggled his hand in a so-so gesture.

'These are daisies because Daisy made him paint,' Mercy said. 'He changed the flowers because he had Daisy on his mind. The flowers were actually purple and red.' She pointed to the young girl sitting in the field of flowers. 'That's me.'

He approached her warily, as if worried she'd bolt. Which was probably fair. 'I thought so. I moved it out of sight when you left. I was a little . . .' He shrugged. 'I missed you.'

'I'm sorry.'

'It's okay. You did what you needed to do. I understand.'

'I was still unkind to have run away.'

'Well, maybe a little,' he allowed.

Her lips twitched. 'All right, then.' She returned her gaze to the painting, sobering. 'This day actually happened. I was nine years old. It was a week before Gideon's thirteenth birthday.' She rubbed the heel of her hand against her heart again because the memory hurt. 'There was a field of flowers beyond the gates of Eden. We were expressly forbidden to go there, but we could see it when the teachers took us on field trips outside the gates. The purpose of the trip that day was to gather roots for the healer. We kids were cheap labor, I guess.'

'But you got tempted by the flowers,' Rafe said and she shot him a startled look.

'How did you know?'

He pointed to the painting. 'Because you're sitting in them.' His voice held more than a note of 'duh'.

'Good point. Well, I got caught. I was good at avoiding harsh punishments as a kid because my stepfather, Amos, was a gentle man.'

'Sounds like you cared about him.'

'I did. He never laid a hand on me. He was a good man.' She frowned, troubled. 'I hope he wasn't punished because Mama and I escaped. Although we were part of Ephraim's household by then.' She shook her head, dislodging the notion for now. 'Anyway, I got caught and the punishment for going to the flower field was severe and out of Amos's hands. A week in the box.'

'What was the box?' Rafe asked grimly.

'What it sounds like. It was a little outbuilding, an outhouse actually. But its only use was for punishment. They'd lock the person in with no light for a week. Twice a day you'd get food and water.'

'Mother of God,' he whispered. 'They put you in there? At nine years old?'

'No, but only because Gideon stepped up when they were about to throw me in. He took my punishment. Spent a week in that goddamned box.' She swallowed hard. She really didn't want to cry any more, but the tears were pushing against her throat. 'It was freezing cold at night and blistering during the day. And because the punishment was meant for me, he was only given the food and water rations that I was supposed to have gotten.'

'They starved him.' Rafe's voice was hoarse.

Guilt grabbed at her, and she had to fight it back. Yes, Gideon had taken her punishment, but none of them had deserved it. Not ever. Years of therapy had taught her this. If only she could truly believe it. 'Yes, they starved him. They let him out on his thirteenth birthday. I remember him coming into the light, how he shielded his eyes. How gaunt he was. My mother cried. So did I.' She ran her fingertip along the top of the painting. 'That night, he had his fight with Edward McPhearson.'

'The man who tried to rape him.'

She nodded. 'He was the blacksmith and Gideon was to have been his apprentice. He fought the man off, even as weak as he was, coming off a week of malnutrition and dehydration.'

'McPhearson hit his head on his anvil and died.'

'Right. And then Ephraim led some of the community's men in a mob, intending to beat Gideon to death. That's when Gideon fought back. Stabbed Ephraim's eye. That's why he wore a patch.' She remembered his face in the airport with a shudder. 'I don't know when he got the glass eye. I only remember him wearing a patch.'

'That was the night your mother broke Gideon out of Eden.'

'Yes. The last time I saw him, he was being led out of the box.'

'Not your fault, Mercy. You were only nine years old. Plus Ephraim took your mother right after that, didn't he? It was a traumatic time. I'm not surprised you blocked things out.'

'Head knows, heart still feels guilty.'

He said nothing for a long moment, then sighed. 'I get that, too. Do you want the painting?'

She shook her head, hard. That day still haunted her. 'No, thank you. But the field was not daisies, that's what I was trying to tell you. It was poppies. Mostly purple poppies. Purple *opium* poppies.'

He stared for a moment, before his eyes flooded with understanding. 'Oh. They'd moved from a cash crop of marijuana to opium.'

'I think so. That was why we kids weren't allowed in the field. Not many of the adults, either. Only the highest-ranking wives were allowed. I think they were the harvesters.'

Rafe stared at the painting before turning his gaze on her. 'Did you mean what you said last night? That you want to help catch Burton?'

She blinked at him. 'Yes, of course I did. Why?'

He backed away from her until he reached the whiteboard. 'I've been keeping myself occupied since you left.' Abruptly he flipped the board, revealing a bulletin board on the other side.

Mercy froze, her legs wobbling beneath her. The bulletin board was filled with photos, maps, and documents. Front and center was Ephraim Burton, glaring out of Eileen's wedding photo with his one good eye, his other patched because Gideon had stabbed him.

Haltingly she took a step forward, then another, until she was a foot away, silently studying each photo in turn. There was a mug shot of Ephraim's brother Edward from thirty years before. Ephraim's senior class yearbook photo, in which he'd worn a bow tie. He was barely recognizable, he was so young. But there had been cold calculation in his eyes even then.

There were satellite maps of the wilderness around Mt. Shasta. Somewhere in those woods was the location of the compound when she and Gideon were children. There was a map of Santa Rosa, with an X marking a spot, a photo of a run-down house thumbtacked beside it. Next to that was a photo of an old woman, labeled *Belinda Franklin, mother*, then another photo of a nursing-home sign. *Sacred Heart Palliative Care.*

She turned to the man standing silently beside her. 'Rafe. My God. What is all this?'

'Everything I've been able to find in the last few weeks.'

'Does Gideon know?'

'No. I haven't found a solid lead yet, but I've been looking.' He met her gaze, his piercing. 'I can't turn back time for you, Mercy. I can't undo what Burton did to you, even though I'd do anything in my power to try. But I *can* help you find him. Help you get justice.'

Mercy could barely breathe. Emotion flooded her. Appreciation, gratitude. Respect. Affection, pure and unadulterated. He'd done this. *For me.* She opened her mouth, but no words would come out.

The expression on her face must have been enough, because he smiled grimly. 'Do you want to work with me? Will you help me find him?'

Finally a few words came in a rough whisper. 'Yes. Thank you.'

He gestured to the sofa. 'Then let's get started. It won't be pleasant, but I need you to tell me everything that you remember about Eden.'

Sacramento, California
Sunday, 16 April, 5.15 A.M.

To Rafe's relief, Mercy sat on the sofa, her focus back on his bulletin board. The look she'd shot him before saying she still wanted to help had gripped him hard, making his heart pound and his eyes sting. It was raw gratitude, relief, and something more. Something that made him shove his hands in the pockets of his sweats because in that moment he'd needed to touch her. Needed to hold her.

But she was fragile and he wasn't going to push.

'What do you want me to remember?' she asked, her voice soft. But not weak. There wasn't a weak bone in that woman's body.

He turned away, pretending to hunt for a notebook, but really just needing the time to pull himself together. Surreptitiously he swiped at his eyes with the shirt he'd tossed on Daisy's overstuffed armchair, then pulled the shirt over his head.

When he turned back, she was no longer staring at the board. She was staring at him, the 'something else' in her eyes having shifted to . . . Need? Want? Old-fashioned lust? He wasn't sure which it was, but he felt it too and was suddenly aware that the sweats he wore would conceal nothing. *Do not push. Do not scare her away.*

Swallowing hard, he sat on the other end of the sofa, pulling his notebook over his lap, her gaze becoming a little glazed as she followed his every little movement. Nervously he tapped his pen on the notebook, and the sound jerked her out of the trancelike stare.

But not a trancelike stare like the one at the airport. She was with him this time, he could tell. She'd been fully engaged, and rather than being pale and drawn, her cheeks were a shade of pink that tempted him to get up and put that glazed look back in her eyes.

But not now.

Her green eyes shot up to his, guilty at being caught looking. Rafe forced a wry smile. 'You okay?'

She pushed her hair away from her face with an embarrassed chuckle. 'Yeah.' Clearing her throat, she turned back to the board. 'What exactly do you know so far?'

The sexual tension ratcheted down a fraction, enough that Rafe could actually draw a comfortable breath. Enough that he had to wonder what it would be like with her, if he'd actually burst into flames if she ever truly let him in. Because merely sitting on the same sofa had given him a painful hard-on.

That was completely inappropriate at the moment.

He manhandled his thoughts back into some semblance of coherence. 'Well, Harry and his brother, Aubrey, were born in Santa Rosa. Harry is forty-seven and Aubrey would have been fifty-nine.'

'If he hadn't gotten his just deserts the night he tried to rape Gideon,' she said matter-of-factly.

'Correct. Belinda Franklin, their mother, is now seventy-six. She lives in a nursing home in Santa Rosa.'

Mercy got up to inspect the photo of the care facility. 'Looks like a nice place.'

'It is. It's an expensive place.'

She turned, one brow lifted. 'Who pays for it?'

He smiled at her. 'Follow the money, right? I don't know yet.'

'Does the FBI know where she is?'

'I'm sure they do. I haven't asked. They'll know I'm working on my own and they'll tell me to stop.'

'Better to ask forgiveness than permission?' she asked.

'It's a good motto for a reason,' he replied, and she laughed.

'I guess so.' She turned back to the photo. 'Have you been to this nursing home?'

'Once. I posed as a family friend, but the staff was suspicious. She has dementia, and I don't think she gets many visitors.'

She turned, wide-eyed. 'Did you see her?'

'Kind of. I got to the doorway of her room.'

'What did she say to you?'

He grimaced. 'To get the hell out. I thought she sounded damn lucid at that moment, but that doesn't mean that she doesn't have bad and good days. I was escorted out – politely – by her aide.' He remembered Belinda's cold eyes, her sneer. Having now met Ephraim Burton in person, he could see the resemblance.

'Were Harry and Aubrey her only children?' Mercy asked.

'Yes. As far as I know, anyway.'

She frowned. 'Can anyone trace the visit back to you? I don't want Ephraim gunning for you, too.'

'Oh, I think that's a given after the airport last night. He was decidedly unhappy with me.' He fell silent then, waiting until she'd once again met his gaze. 'I want him to come gunning for me, Mercy. I'm ready.'

She exhaled on a sigh. 'I can't even go there right now, Rafe. I know you're some big bad cop, but—'

'But a crippled one?' Rafe interrupted bitterly.

Her eyes flashed. 'Do *not* put words in my mouth, Detective

Sokolov. I was going to say that you might be a big bad cop, but he's a sociopathic monster who'd kill everyone in your family to bring you to your knees.'

Rafe blinked at that. 'Excuse me? What does that even mean?'

Mercy began to pace. 'It means exactly that. I remember several moves during the time I was in Eden. We'd always move after someone was either devoured by wolves because they got caught too far from the main gates after sunset or deliberately cast out into the forest to be devoured by wolves because they'd "betrayed" their faith.'

'Devoured by wolves?' Rafe repeated. 'Really?'

Mercy stopped pacing to level him a glare. 'Yes, really. It's a genuine concern in the mountains. If not wolves, then bears. Their remains were sometimes brought back for burial – if there was enough left over. It's what they claimed happened to Gideon after he "ran away".' She used finger quotes.

'But they didn't have a body. Because he actually escaped.'

'True, except that they had remains. Whose remains, I don't know.' She sucked in a breath in alarm. 'God, Rafe, that means they killed someone. Someone *else*, outside Eden.'

'Let's table that for later. For now, let's focus on Eden. Did you ever see the remains of other escapees?'

She pursed her lips. 'Yes. Not something my mind can ever completely lock away. It was meant to keep us afraid. To keep us in line.'

'And it worked?'

'Yes, it worked,' she snapped, exasperated. 'Of course it worked. It was horrific.' She drew in a breath, let it out, visibly calming herself. 'My point is, the family of whoever was "devoured" or whatever was punished for their relative's sin. Or their foolishness, if they claimed it was an accidental devouring. I remember three moves – one when I was four, one when I was seven, and the one after Gideon left when I was nine. The first two times, the families didn't move with us. They were outcast.'

Rafe grimaced. 'They killed the escapees' families?'

She shrugged. 'I don't know if they killed them with their own

155

hands or let the animals have them, but they wouldn't have just let them go.'

'No, I suppose not,' Rafe said, thinking as he noted everything she said in his notebook. 'And so when Gideon disappeared? Did you think they'd kill you and your mother, too?'

She nodded grimly. 'I did. I was so damn scared. Amos was scared, too. He thought we'd all be cast out. But then they took us with them. Mama was immediately taken from Amos and put in isolation. As soon as we were settled, Mama was given to Ephraim, compensation for Gideon killing Edward and stabbing Ephraim's eye.'

Rafe's gut roiled. She spoke of her mother's fate so clinically, but he knew it was her coping mechanism and he wouldn't deny her comfort in whatever form she chose to take it.

'And you?' he asked softly.

Her chin lifted, as if she was bracing herself. 'I was allowed to stay with Amos until I was twelve.'

'When you were given to Ephraim,' Rafe finished heavily. 'Why do you think they let you live?'

Another shrug. 'They probably spared Amos because he was the community's carpenter. But me and Mama? Maybe to make an example of us? To give Ephraim endless revenge? Because Ephraim was waiting until I was twelve? Everyone knew that Ephraim was "rough on his wives". That was the euphemism for sadistic brutalization.'

Rafe closed his eyes for a long moment, fighting back bile that burned his throat. 'I'm sorry,' he whispered. He knew she'd returned to the sofa when it rocked slightly.

'I know,' she whispered back. After a few seconds, she said in a normal voice, 'We should ask Gideon what he remembers. He was five when we arrived and I was barely a year old.'

He opened his eyes, startled to see she'd chosen the middle cushion, sitting much closer, but still not touching him. 'We'll do that,' he promised.

'What other kinds of things do you want to know?'

'Were any of the people who supposedly got devoured making

waves in the community? Did any of them get cast out for questioning the rules?'

'Like marrying off twelve-year-old girls? I don't know.' Her gaze went far away, her eyes narrowing in thought. 'Maybe. After Gideon left, I was ostracized from the women and girls. I wasn't allowed in school any longer and I wasn't allowed to go on any more field trips to the forest or hang out with anyone.'

'That had to have been difficult,' Rafe murmured, earning him a surprised laugh.

'It was at first. But it was paradise compared to what happened after I turned twelve.'

His stomach twisted harder. At some point she might want to tell him what happened, and when she did, he'd listen. *But not today*, he thought, knowing he was being selfish. *I'm not ready today*. He still hadn't processed the bombshell his mother had dropped on them the night before.

And none of this is about you, Prince Charming. Get off the pity train.

'Maybe Gideon will remember something,' he said, his words coming out strangled.

Mercy shot him a glance so full of compassion that it stole his breath. 'It's not easy,' she said, as if reading his mind. 'Not easy to go through. Not easy to hear if it's someone you care about. Like your mom.'

'And you, Mercy.' He needed her to understand. 'Wherever we end up, even if it's just friends, I do care about you. And not because you're my best friend's sister. Well, not just because of that, anyway.'

'Thank you,' she said gently. 'I only meant that this is a difficult topic, no matter which way you approach it. And just because you weren't the victim of the actual crime doesn't mean your feelings don't matter.'

'That's very wise advice,' he said warily.

'That's very expensive advice,' she corrected. 'Took me years of therapy before I could even hear the words, much less internalize them. Still can't quite adopt them, but that's the journey.'

He didn't want to think about how difficult those therapy sessions must have been for her. 'When Eden moved after Gideon's

157

escape, where did it go? I mean, did the compound stay around Mt. Shasta? Gideon said he could see the mountain in the distance the whole time he was in Eden, even though they moved around.'

She tilted her head, thinking. 'Not near Shasta,' she finally answered. 'I don't remember seeing the mountain after that. And it wasn't as cold. Maybe a lower elevation? Maybe we went a little farther south.'

'And the poppy field?'

'They never replanted it, not in the new place. They may have gone back to harvest the existing poppies, but I don't know.'

He tapped his pen against the notebook some more, thinking. 'You said the move before Gideon left was when you were seven. Were there poppies in the location before that?'

She curled her legs, tucking her feet beneath her. 'No, I don't think so. Gideon might remember better, but I think there were pot fields before that.'

'Were the members aware of the illegal drugs? Did the leaders use the money for the community?'

'If the adults knew, they never spoke of it, not around us kids, anyway. As for using the cash to make our lives even a little better? No, that was not the case. We lived very simply. Made our own clothes, canned vegetables for the winter, raised a few cows and goats for milk. Kept chickens for eggs, pigs for bacon, and sheep for wool, that kind of thing. They brought a few things in from outside, like flour. But nothing to make our life less simple.'

'So there had to be actual money spent. Where did you get the fabric to make the clothes?'

'Some of the women had looms, but occasionally we had store-bought fabric on bolts. They told us they traded for it. There was one man who went into town once a week or so to trade and get supplies, like tools and certain medicines. The things we couldn't make on our own.'

'Okay,' Rafe said, writing that down. 'Who was the man who was allowed out of the compound?'

'Before Gideon left, it was a man named Waylon Belmont. After Gideon left, Waylon died. It was just a few days later.' Her gaze hardened. 'His son, DJ, took over his route.'

It took him only seconds to realize what she was saying. He knew the basic elements of her story. He knew her mother had smuggled both Gideon and Mercy out, four years apart. He knew that whoever had driven them had let Gideon go, but had shot Mercy and killed their mother.

Waylon had let Gideon go, but Waylon's son, DJ, had shot Mercy, leaving her for dead. Rage exploded inside Rafe, but he shoved it back. He had a name now. He'd get more later. And he'd find DJ Belmont eventually, and make the man sorry he'd ever been born. But not today. Not now.

Now she needed him to help her dredge up her worst memories. So he made himself nod levelly, addressing a less obvious element of her statement. 'Waylon helped your mother get Gideon out. And then he died a few days later.'

She blinked at that. 'I guess so. I never made that cause-and-effect connection before.'

'How did he die?'

She looked troubled. 'I don't know. It was sudden and I remember Amos being devastated. Well, mostly because Mama was gone because Gideon had "betrayed" us, but also because he and Waylon had been friends for years. Amos wasn't a Founding Elder at Eden, but he was among the first to join up. Waylon would sell the . . .' She trailed away, her gaze suddenly gone somewhere else.

Rafe perked up. 'Would sell what?'

'Furniture,' she said thoughtfully. 'Amos was a carpenter. He built the houses and made furniture for new families in Eden, but he also made furniture to sell. He had a very specific style – and he marked each piece with a little olive tree. Y'know, for Eden.' She abruptly focused. 'Can I use your laptop?'

'Of course.' He grabbed it from the little end table, typed in his password, then handed it to Mercy.

She typed quickly, frowned, then typed some more while Rafe watched her intently. After more than twenty minutes, she looked up with satisfied triumph. 'Like this.' She turned the laptop and he leaned in close to see. 'Found this on Pinterest.'

159

'Oh wow.' There were three photos, one of an amazing wood table, a second photo showing the intricate carvings on each leg, and the third, the stylized mark of a tree carved into a corner of the table's underside. 'Just like Gideon's tattoo and the locket.'

She nodded. 'Amos told me once that he'd designed the symbol and had carved the model for the mold that Edward McPhearson used to use to produce the lockets. But it was our secret. He told me a few days before my wedding. Told me never to mention it, especially to Ephraim, but that every time I would look at my new locket, I could remember my father. Amos always considered himself my dad.' She smiled sadly. 'I called him Papa.'

'Did he try to make it so that you didn't have to marry Ephraim?'

'He did. He was supposed to get a new wife after I was married, because I'd done the cooking and cleaning after Mama went to Ephraim's. But he didn't get one, at least not for the year I was with Ephraim. I think they punished him by giving the woman to someone else. I'd forgotten about that.'

'I think you blocked a lot of things out. Probably kept you sane.'

'My shrink says the same thing.' She began typing again. 'We also made dolls.'

He frowned, trying to keep up. 'Dolls?'

'Yes, the girls made them. Dolls and some ceramics. Some quilts, too. A lot of them had a tree or an angel hidden somewhere.'

Rafe sat up straighter. Dolls, quilts, and furniture were things they could track. 'Did the leaders know you all were hiding Eden symbols in your crafts?'

'I don't think so. It was always done with a wink, you know? And we had our own signatures. Nobody spoke of it, because it would have been considered vanity and that was a sin. So we just did it and planned to claim ignorance if we got caught.' She typed more, paging through catalogs and Pinterest boards, her expression growing more intense as the minutes passed. And then she blanched, the color in her cheeks draining away.

'What?' Rafe asked, unable to maintain his silence a moment longer. 'What do you see?'

Again she turned the laptop and again Rafe was impressed by

the quality of the workmanship. The quilt was a starburst design, with Mt. Shasta front and center, the sun either rising or setting behind it. 'That's incredible,' he said.

'I know.' She traced a fingertip over the photo of the quilt. 'I remember this one, actually. It was made by one of Mama's friends.' She sighed. 'Eileen's mother.'

Eileen, who'd escaped back in November only to be kidnapped by a serial killer the following month. Abruptly he wondered if Eileen's family had been killed by Eden as well, or if they were being tortured like Mercy and her mother had been.

'Where is it?' he asked, wanting to comfort her, but having no clue how to do so.

'The quilt?' She scanned the screen. 'Here's the user who tagged it.' She looked up, her eyes suddenly bright. 'We could contact them and ask where they bought it. Same with Amos's furniture.'

He grinned at her, in perfect accord. 'Let's make up a dummy account and send out a few emails.'

She grinned back. 'Let's.'

Sacramento, California
Sunday, 16 April, 6.30 A.M.

Ephraim lounged against the pillows on Granny's bed with a satisfied grin. 'Yes,' he hissed to the article on his laptop screen. It was titled *10 Things to Know About Mercy Callahan*, and had, at least for a little while, included a damning video showcasing Mercy's inner slut.

He'd banished his fury at the thought of Mercy willingly submitting to another man's sexual demands when she'd been so unresponsive with him, but then felt vindicated when he read her more recent boyfriend's 'colder than a fish' statement.

A retraction at the end of the article denied any responsibility of the site's management regarding the uploading of videos portraying sexual assault and stated that they were against it.

Part of him wished he'd seen the video himself, but he mostly was glad he hadn't. Then he'd have to go back to New Orleans and kill the bastard who'd taken the video in the first place. He did not want to go back there, because Louisiana was too damn muggy and it was only spring.

Plus he'd have to drive to New Orleans and the only way he'd do that was if Mercy ran home before he could grab her here. No more flying until Pastor made him a new driver's license. It wouldn't take the FBI long to track down the name he'd used to buy the tickets to and from New Orleans.

Luckily, he wasn't going to have to return to New Orleans. He knew exactly where Mercy was, thanks to the articles by other reporters. She'd holed up in the Sokolovs' house in Granite Bay, east of Sacramento. He just had to bide his time until her guard was down and she went somewhere alone. Or at least somewhere without a cop. Although he wasn't afraid to take out a cop or two if it meant returning to Eden with Mercy in tow.

He wanted to prove DJ's lies. He wanted to show that Mercy still lived, even though DJ had sworn that he'd killed her. He wanted DJ cast out.

He wanted all the money that Pastor had been quietly accumulating for the past thirty years.

He could be patient a little while longer, but he needed a better place to crash in the meantime. Granny's little Boy Scout would be back from his camping trip by that afternoon, and Ephraim didn't intend to still be here.

Opening a new tab in his browser, Ephraim searched for empty homes for sale in the Granite Bay area, quickly discarding his search when he saw the relative wealth of the community. Rich people alarmed their homes, even hiring security guards sometimes. He didn't want a poor neighborhood, because he liked his creature comforts, so he searched for a middle-class area where nicer houses sat abandoned, preferably in a secluded location where nobody could either sneak up on him, surround him, or report him as a squatter.

He settled on three possible homes, copied their addresses, then gathered his belongings, taking great care to wipe off anything that he'd touched, wishing he'd had the presence of mind to do the same at Regina's. He'd left his prints everywhere in Regina's house, especially in the room where he'd killed her. That had been his room, every time he'd stayed with her. There was no easy way to erase his presence. Not that he was overly worried about that.

Because who are Regina's people gonna tell? Quickly he clicked back to the first tab he'd opened that morning and refreshed the page, checking again for any reports on a murder at Regina's address.

Just as before, nothing. He wasn't surprised. Regina ran a prostitution ring. She kept underage girls, selling them to men who liked them young. *Men like me.* Her staff would find her body and dispose of it, and her second-in-command would take over, likely thrilled with the promotion.

In fact, the new boss of Regina's place would probably be very grateful. Not that Ephraim was going to chance it. He wasn't ever going back there.

Satisfied that he'd considered every potential issue, he made himself breakfast in Granny's kitchen, appreciating the preserves she'd stored in her pantry. He cleaned out the old woman's pantry, storing the canned goods in the trunk of his car. Who knew when he'd get hungry on the road, and canned garden veggies were better than no food at all.

He'd also take her rifle and search her house for any items he might need. Ammo, rope to tie Mercy, duct tape to keep her quiet . . . all of the normal tools of the trade.

He would need a disguise, though, before he could come anywhere close to the Sokolovs again, especially the cop. He could wear a wig. A fake beard. Anything that would disguise his features, since the asshole knew his face. Law enforcement across the whole damn state knew his face now, thanks to that fucker with a cane.

Ephraim did one more Google search, looking for costume stores in the area.

Ten

The costume store's alarm hadn't sounded, but Ephraim was taking no chances. He kept an eye on the big picture window in front, just in case the alarm was a silent one.

He had most of what he needed. A few wigs that weren't too cartoony, a mustache/beard set, some theatrical makeup that he had no idea how to use. He could google it later. He grabbed a bottle of spirit gum and a package of scars. He'd started for the back entrance where he'd left his car when he heard a soft *click*.

'Ah, fuck,' he muttered. *Not again.*

'Don't move,' a woman said, her voice trembling. 'I will shoot you.'

Slowly he turned to find her to be about twenty years old. Cute, if not a bit coltish. In one hand she held what looked like a .22. In the other, her cell phone. Both hands shook like leaves in a hurricane.

Behind her was an open door, probably to a storeroom. He'd checked it when he'd come in, but it had been locked.

'I said don't move!' But she backed up a step, her terror clear on her face. 'I called the police, so don't make any sudden moves.'

She really needed to stop watching bad movies, he thought. 'I don't want to kill you,' he said quietly. And he didn't. Especially since he hadn't pulled the bullets out of Granny. If he shot this girl with Regina's gun, they'd be able to connect the crimes. If he shot her with his own gun, the neighbors would hear the gunshot.

Which didn't really matter, because he'd left his own gun in the car. *Fucking hell.* It didn't matter and he couldn't just stand there waffling. He didn't have any time to waste.

Her laugh was shrill. 'I don't want to kill you either, but I will. Drop the stuff and put your hands up.'

He shoved the stolen items beneath his shirt and tucked its hem into his pants so the disguises wouldn't fall out. Then he calmly pulled Regina's gun from his pocket and pointed it at her. 'Drop the gun.' He began walking toward her, shaking his head when she clutched the gun tighter and backed up, matching him step for step.

'Hurry!' she cried into her phone. 'Please hurry. He's got a gun!'

When he reached her, he took the gun from her shaking hand, pocketed it, then grabbed her head in both hands and gave a quick twist. Dropping her to the floor, he turned and ran.

He'd parked his car a few feet from the back door and, luckily, had left the engine running because his hot-wiring skills were a bit rusty. It had taken him a few tries to steal the thing to begin with. At least now he didn't need to fumble with it.

He slid behind the wheel and was around the next block when he heard sirens. Hands gripping the steering wheel until they hurt, he kept driving, obeying the speed limit, until he was in the next town, his heart still beating so hard that he was dizzy.

He pulled onto a side street and leaned against the headrest until his heartbeat returned to normal.

Too close. Too fucking close. Another thirty seconds and his ass would have been toast. *I should have just shot her and run.* But he hadn't wanted to leave a bullet behind and there was no way he'd have had time to dig a bullet out of the wall, much less out of her body if the wound wasn't a through-and-through.

At least he had a disguise now. And he had a few addresses for empty houses.

But he needed to find another car without GPS before he went house hunting, in case there had been security cameras behind the store. Last thing he needed was to have this piece-of-shit clunker

165

added to the BOLO. 'Pain in the fucking ass,' he muttered.

But it could have been much worse. He could have gotten caught. And then he'd never be able to show Mercy the error of her ways, and that wouldn't do at all.

He rubbed his hands over his face, then checked the abandoned-house addresses he'd noted. He'd just put the address into Maps when his phone vibrated in his hand, making him yelp.

And then swear. *It's Pastor. Again.* He considered letting the call go to voice mail, but reconsidered. He wouldn't tell Pastor what he was up to, because he didn't want to give DJ Belmont any opportunity to cause trouble for him – or to come up with an explanation for why he'd lied about Mercy's death. He wanted Pastor to see the shock and the guilt on DJ's face when he hauled Mercy through the gates of Eden by her hair.

But he wasn't sure how to buy himself a little more time.

Clearing his throat, he answered. 'Hello?'

'Ephraim.' Pastor sounded annoyed. 'Where *are* you?'

'I told you that I'm sick.'

'That wasn't what I asked.'

Shit. Pastor had gone all cool and snobby. 'I went to Regina's. I told you that.'

'Yes, I know. I also know that I called this morning and was told that Regina could not come to the phone. It's been a while since I've talked to a police officer.'

'It must have been Dusty, Regina's assistant. She has that way about her.'

Pastor's chuckle sent an unpleasant shiver down Ephraim's spine. 'I might have believed you had the speaker not identified herself as Officer Wong from Santa Rosa PD. She asked who I was and I hung up.'

New dread sat like lead in Ephraim's gut. What if the cops could trace the call? What if they found Eden? 'I'm sure that DJ's set up your phone to be untraceable.' He hoped.

'He assures me that he has. I'm going to ask you one more time. Where are you, Ephraim?'

'San Francisco.' The lie came out smoothly. 'Regina's place was closed when I got there last night. Now I know why. I went to a place in San Fran that stocks my type.'

'Right,' Pastor said, and for once Ephraim couldn't read his tone. 'When will you return? Your sabbatical has run its course.'

'Considering I've been sick as a dog for part of it, that's not really fair. I'm going to take a few days to get my body better, and then I'll be back.'

'Bring me back some Frankenwaffle,' Pastor said, very mildly, then hung up.

'Shit, shit, shit.' That last part had sounded downright menacing. Ephraim's hands had finally stopped shaking, but now they were shaking again as he typed Frankenwaffle into a Google search.

Sacramento. The waffle place was in Sacramento and there were no other locations.

He knows. He knows where I am. How did he know? *Motherfucking hell.*

He stared at his phone, realization dawning, and the dread in his gut grew even heavier. 'Fucking hell.' He tried to pop the little SIM card from his phone, but his hands were shaking too hard – with fear and dread and cold fury. How *dare* they? How dare they keep tabs on him like this?

I am going to kill DJ Belmont.

He managed to yank the SIM card free, then got out of the car and placed the phone beneath his tire. A few passes under the tire left the phone crushed and useless. He snapped the SIM card in half, then dropped the pieces in the leftover travel mug he'd taken from Granny's house. There wasn't a lot of coffee left, but enough to damage the card eventually. He'd toss the mug and the card into the first dumpster he passed.

Motherfucking little prick. DJ had gone too far. Again. But this time he wouldn't let him win.

Ephraim needed to get back to Eden, to stop the greedy bastard before he completely poisoned Pastor against him. DJ wanted it all. He wanted the power, the money. He wanted control of everyone and everything around Eden, and he'd toss Ephraim to the fucking wolves without a blink.

Except that DJ wouldn't get the chance, because now Ephraim had ammunition. He knew where Mercy Callahan was and he was going to bring her back.

Dead or alive. Either would serve his purpose.

Sacramento, California
Sunday, 16 April, 10.15 A.M.

The knocking on Rafe's door woke him from what had been a very comfortable sleep. He blinked hard to try to make sense of where he was and . . .

Oh. He breathed deeply, taking in the lingering clean scent of Mercy's shampoo. She slept up against him, her head on his shoulder. His laptop had slid off her lap to the sofa and his notebook was on the floor. They'd drifted off together while searching the Internet for more furniture with Amos's olive tree and more dolls and quilts with their hidden Eden symbols.

The knocking resumed, a little louder this time, and Rafe carefully pulled away from Mercy, gently easing her down to the soft arm of the sofa. Grabbing his cane, he made it to the door, just as the knocking started again. He yanked the door open, hoping the noise hadn't woken Mercy. She desperately needed to sleep.

It took him a second to reconcile the sight of the Korean American woman on his doorstep, her fist still raised. 'Rhee?' he whispered.

His Homicide partner for the past two years gave him an incredulous look. 'It hasn't been that long since we saw each other, Sokolov. You okay?'

'Yes, sorry. I was . . .' He shook his head and stepped from the apartment, forcing her to back up a few feet. He pulled the door shut. 'I was asleep. Still a few cobwebs up there.'

Eyeing him curiously, she held up a coffee cup and the aroma had him nearly moaning. The logo on the cup told him it was from the shop the two of them stopped at every time they had a chance. A block from SacPD, it was a favorite hangout for a lot of the cops.

'I came bearing gifts,' she said. 'Aren't you going to let me in?'

168

He swallowed a mouthful of coffee, uncaring that it was still a little too hot and scalded his tongue. 'Mercy's here. She's asleep.'

Erin Rhee was a very smart woman, her entire demeanor sharp and sometimes cutting. She rarely missed a thing, and this morning was no different. 'Asleep. With you?'

'Kind of. We'd been . . . talking.' He'd almost said searching, but there was no way he was letting Erin know about his completely off-the-record and under-the-radar investigation. He was on disability leave and wasn't supposed to be working on anything. 'We had a long evening and ended up falling asleep on the sofa.'

'Okay.' She lifted her brows. 'By long evening, you mean stopping an assault in progress, getting yourself on the news, and getting a very offensive video pulled down from a trashy website?'

He stared down at her. She was barely five-two, although she swore she was five-four in her boots. Either way, he towered over her, but Erin was not a woman to be intimidated. 'You're remarkably well-informed.'

She snorted. 'Come on, let's sit on the stairs. I'm afraid you're going to fall over.'

It was then he realized he'd been leaning dangerously off-kilter, the aluminum replacement cane too damn short. Joining her on the stairs, he sipped at the coffee, wondering why the hell she was here, but way too polite – and intelligent – to ask her outright. His partner was fierce. But also kind, deep down. He didn't like making her angry, but mostly because he really liked her and didn't want to hurt her feelings.

'That's your I-don't-know-what's-happening face,' she remarked, her lips quirking up in a grin.

He chuckled. 'So put me out of my misery?'

'I will. First, how are you?'

'Tired. We didn't get here till almost two this morning. Otherwise . . .' He let the thought trail off with a shrug. 'Same old, same old. Going to PT, wishing my leg would hurry up and heal.'

She gave him a brisk nod, sparing him the niceties. That was Erin, to the point, cutting out all of the bullshit that they both knew wouldn't help. 'I wanted to give you a heads-up on a few things.'

169

Leaning against the wall from her perch on the stair above him, she tilted her head meaningfully. 'I am not here.'

'You are not here,' Rafe agreed, fighting a smile. 'I'm dreaming and this coffee is really just a metaphysical symbol of a crutch. A dream-cane.'

She snorted again. 'Shut up. Look, I know you haven't been idle these past weeks. Maybe the first few, because you were hurt pretty damn bad.'

Her eyes flickered with sadness and not a small amount of guilt. Erin had been with him at the scene when they'd rescued Mercy from the killer. She'd suffered a few broken ribs and one 'slightly punctured lung,' as she'd put it. She'd only returned to work the week before.

'You kept me from getting hurt even worse than I did,' Rafe told her soberly. No jokes now. 'You have nothing to feel guilty about.'

She shot him an impatient look, but her cheeks tinged pink with embarrassment and her gaze dropped to her hands for the briefest of moments. 'I said, shut up. I heard some stuff that I think you should know.'

He sat up a little straighter. 'Okay. I'm awake now.'

She laughed quietly. 'And shutting up? Never mind, you're a Sokolov. Full shut-up mode is impossible for you guys. Anyway, there was a robbery about two hours ago. Costume store in Orangevale. No alarm went off because the assistant manager on duty fell asleep in the storeroom last night while taking inventory and forgot to set it.' She shrugged. 'College kid, working full-time and taking a full load of classes.'

'Industrious,' Rafe said cautiously.

Sadness flickered in Erin's dark eyes once again. 'Not anymore. Now she's dead. Guy broke her neck with his bare hands.'

'Oh my God. Poor kid.' His eyes narrowed. 'What did he steal?'

'Disguises. Kid had 911 on her cell, but her killer was gone before they got there. Must have just missed him. Store cameras got a good angle.' Erin held out her phone and Rafe bit back a gasp.

'Fucking hell.' It was a still photo of Ephraim Burton, a gun pointed at the young woman, who looked absolutely terrified. She'd also had a gun but clearly was too afraid to use it. 'Wait. If he has a gun – with a silencer – why didn't he just shoot her? Why use precious seconds to break her neck?'

Erin gave him an impressed nod. 'You *are* awake. Good boy. I wondered the same thing. And after seeing your ugly mug on the news last night, I figured you needed to know what this asshole is capable of doing. And that he'd be disguised.'

Rafe grimaced. 'I'm on the news?'

She shook her head. '*That's* what you took away from all this?'

He shot her an irritated glance. 'Fuck off,' he said, but it was completely without heat. He and Erin had a very comfortable working relationship and he was afraid she'd get teamed up with someone else before he could get back on the job. 'What I meant was that if I'm on the news, that's probably how the reporters figured out where Mercy was last night.'

'Not a huge stretch. Why aren't they outside your place? I was surprised that I didn't have to run the media gauntlet.'

'Mom and Dad's address is in the white pages, but this place isn't because when I bought out my brothers and sisters, I planned to rent it out. The deed's in the name of my rental corporation.'

'That was smart.' She lifted a brow. 'I assume you lost them when you came back here last night, because they would have followed you.'

'I did. My mom wore Mercy's coat and a big hat and my Dad called her Mercy as he helped her into his car. The news van that was still there took the bait and followed them around while Damien got us home. Mercy and Farrah hid in the back under a blanket.'

'How is Mercy, by the way?'

'Confused and scared. And pissed off.' He sighed. 'And ashamed that the video was posted, even though she knows she didn't do anything wrong.'

But his mother had smoothed some of Mercy's anxiety about the video the night before by sharing some of her own story. Which Rafe still couldn't think about without wanting to throw up. Well, both their stories made him want to throw up. But mostly they'd made him want to kill some rapists.

Which isn't helping.

'I'm sorry,' Erin murmured. 'I only met Mercy a few times when she was here before, but I liked her. She's a strong woman.'

'That she is,' Rafe said, and even he could hear the pride in his voice.

Erin chuckled. 'So it's like that, huh? Well, good luck, big guy. I'll get you a vest from tactical storage just in case Gideon goes all caveman protective on your ass.'

Rafe was not even going there. 'Why did Burton snap the woman's neck if he had a gun?' He squinted at the photo, using thumb and forefinger to enlarge it, studying the weapon, inwardly sneering at its flashy gold color. 'That's an FNX-45. It would have killed her and anyone standing behind her. So why not just shoot her?'

'I don't know. If I hear anything about that, I'll let you know.'

Rafe relaxed against the railing and considered his question. 'The gun might not have been loaded, but I think that's unlikely. Ephraim Burton doesn't strike me as someone who'd wave an unloaded gun around. It's definitely not the same gun he had at the airport last night.'

'How do you know?'

'I got a glimpse of it on the airport's security footage, and, for starters, the grip is all wrong. Second, his was a revolver, and third' – he made a face at the suppressed weapon's exterior – 'it wasn't gold, for God's sake.'

She bit back a smile. 'Fair enough.'

'Who carries an actual golden gun?' he grumbled, then winced. 'You're going to get mad at me, but in my experience, it's mostly women who go for the flashy guns.'

She nodded with distaste. 'It's true.'

'Plus, last night's gun didn't have a silencer. It was a Smith and Wesson .38 Special. Snub-nosed. So . . . not the same gun.'

She smiled at him with genuine affection. 'I've missed you, partner.'

'Same goes. You get yourself a new partner yet?'

'Nope. I'm on desk duty still. Which totally sucks but does allow me to eavesdrop on other conversations. Which is how I heard about this robbery.'

He felt a frisson of relief that he hadn't lost her yet. 'Why wasn't he carrying this gun' – he pointed to the photo on her phone – 'last night at the airport? It's bigger, flashier, and less easy to conceal, but more powerful than the .38 Special.'

'Maybe he didn't have it with him.'

'Maybe. Maybe he stole it. It's *gold*, for God's sake. I can't see him buying a flashy gun like that.'

'Possible. Still doesn't explain why he used precious seconds to snap the vic's neck.'

They sat in silence for a full minute, each of them thinking. Rafe ran various scenarios through his mind, chucking the ones that seemed most unlikely. 'He got away from the airport last night in some lady's minivan. June. Can't remember her last name.'

'Lindstrom,' Erin supplied.

'Oh, right. Have they located her yet?'

Her brows lifted. 'You think the gun was hers?'

'I don't know. But both Gideon and Mercy believed that Burton would kill the woman.'

Erin raised her forefinger. 'Hold on a minute.' She scrolled through her contacts, then dialed one of them. 'Hey, Tiff, got a minute?'

Should have thought of that myself. Tiffany Snow was their lieutenant's right arm. Not much happened that the clerk didn't know about.

Erin laughed quietly. 'Sorry. I *was* rude to swan in with coffee and not bring you anything. I'll bring you a latte tomorrow morning.' She rolled her eyes. 'Yes, of course it's a bribe. Can you tell me if they found the Lindstrom woman yet? She's the—' Erin exhaled, shooting Rafe a grim look. 'Damn, I kind of knew she was dead, but I didn't want her to be. Do you know what kind of weapon?' Again she listened, then nodded. 'Got it, thanks. Any other bodies turn up? With either gunshot wounds or snapped necks?' She pulled the phone from her ear and muted her end. 'She's checking.'

'What caliber gun was used to kill June Lindstrom?'

'Thirty-eight. Bullet was still in her. It's on its way to Ballistics.'

'Maybe he didn't want to use that gun again,' he mused. 'Maybe he didn't want to leave a trail.'

'Maybe. Lots of maybes, partner. Hold on, Tiff's back.' She unmuted her phone. 'What do you have?' She listened, her eyes growing wide. 'Really? Well, that's a helluva mess. Thanks for this. You'll let me know if anything else comes up?' She disconnected and met Rafe's gaze. 'A Santa Rosa woman was found dead this morning. Broken neck. Cops are at the scene right now.'

'June Lindstrom's minivan was found in Santa Rosa last night,' Rafe said quietly. 'Burton was seen getting out of it, but the security cameras lost him when he ducked into an alley.'

She blinked at him. 'Where did you hear that?'

'Gideon,' he said grimly. 'I'd almost forgotten that, with all the other shit going on.'

Erin lightly banged her head on the wall behind them. 'Why can't we share information with the FBI?'

Rafe's grin was razor sharp. 'We are.'

Her lips curved. 'Yes, we are.'

'Mom's making a huge dinner this afternoon. Gideon'll be there. We may or may not talk more about this, if you want to join us.'

'I just might. What does all of this mean for Mercy?'

'I don't know. I've asked her to remember stuff about Eden, anything we can use to track their movements.'

'And?'

'We might have something. Furniture and other crafts, made there and sold or traded outside.'

She drew herself straighter, then faked a few coughs. 'Oh my, I may have had a relapse. I might have to take a few days off. Whatever shall I do with all that spare time?'

He snorted, despite the gravity of the situation. 'I really do miss you. When we find a lead, I'll let you know. Until then, you might be able to help more in the office.'

Her frown came as close to a pout as he'd ever seen, surprising him. 'You're no fun.'

'And you're Miss By-the-Book.' He narrowed his eyes. 'Which makes me wonder, what gives?'

She lifted one shoulder, uncharacteristically vulnerable. 'I want to help you. I . . .' She shook her head. 'Never mind.'

'No, what? Talk to me, Rhee.'

She blew out a frustrated sigh. 'Shit, I wish I hadn't said anything now.'

'But you did. So say more.'

'It's just that . . . You've always been a friend, Rafe. I value that, and that whole near-death thing made me reconsider my priorities.'

'I know about that,' he murmured, thinking of the woman asleep on his sofa.

Erin made an uncomfortable sound. 'You know I mean *friend*, right? Like nothing . . .' Her lips twisted before making little kisses.

He smirked. 'Yeah, I figured that out myself, thanks.' The last time she'd come to Sunday dinner, she and Sasha had seemed to connect. 'If you come to dinner, Sasha will be there.'

Erin's cheeks pinked up, confirming his suspicions. 'Please say you're not matchmaking.'

He obeyed, even though it was mostly a lie. 'I'm not matchmaking.'

She rolled her eyes. 'What's your mom making for dessert?'

'Bird's milk cake.'

Erin hummed in a decent rendition of orgasmic bliss. 'My favorite of all her desserts. I'm in.'

They were interrupted by an anxious voice from somewhere upstairs. 'Rafe?'

'Farrah is Mercy's friend,' he explained to Erin. 'Down here, Farrah. My partner's here. Come meet her.'

Footsteps sped down the stairs and Farrah appeared on the landing. 'Where's Mercy?'

Rafe thumbed over his shoulder, pointing to his apartment door. 'Asleep. She's fine, Farrah. She couldn't sleep and didn't want to wake you.'

Farrah gave him a knowing look, then smiled at Erin as she descended, stopping to sit two stairs above them. 'I feel like I'm on my mama's stoop in the old neighborhood,' she said, her drawl like a soft blanket. 'I'm Farrah Romero.'

The two women shook hands. 'Erin Rhee. My job was keeping this one here out of trouble.'

'I hope they gave you hazard pay,' Farrah said lightly. 'Mercy told me about you. How you helped save her. Thank you.'

'My job,' Erin said simply. 'But also my honor.'

Farrah only flashed her a bright smile. 'I'll make breakfast if someone has eggs and bacon.'

'I do,' Sasha called from the second floor. 'Farrah, come help me whip something up. Rafe, I heard that Mercy's asleep, but you can't do the stairs. We'll bring you something, okay?'

'Think Mercy slept through all that?' Erin whispered.

'Given how tired she was, I'm betting she did.' Farrah got up. 'Coming, Sasha! Y'all sit tight. We'll be back in a jiff.'

Rafe watched her go, then turned back to Erin. 'Did Tiff say who the body in Santa Rosa was?'

'Oh, that was the most important part,' Erin said. 'It was the home of Regina Jewel. From which she ran a brothel. One of the girls found her dead and used the dead woman's cell phone to call 911. Police found twenty women in the house. Three were staff, the others were her "merchandise." Three of them were under fourteen. They told police that they were there for "Mr Ephraim." Several of the older girls said they'd been forced to service him over the years, when they were thirteen and fourteen. Once they grew up, Regina placed them with other clients. They didn't know Ephraim's last name, but he'd show up three or four times a year.'

Rafe sat back, stunned. 'Holy shit.'

'I know, right? What a fucker. He likes them young. And the golden gun?'

Rafe's mind was reeling. 'It must be Regina's.'

She tapped her nose. 'Right in one.'

'Holy shit,' Rafe breathed. 'This could change everything.'

She looked at him warily. 'How?'

'Ephraim is *from* Santa Rosa. That's where he grew up as Harry Franklin. That he wound up frequenting prostitutes in Santa Rosa *can't* be a coincidence. He could have found prostitutes in Redding or San Francisco or even here in Sacramento.'

'What do you think that means?'

He hesitated in saying what he really thought, because with a single call to their boss, Erin could have him ripped off this case, and Rafe needed to see this through. But she'd put herself at risk coming to see him today, giving him this information she'd overheard. He'd always trusted her to have his back, so he blurted it out before he could change his mind. 'His mother is in a nursing home in Santa Rosa.'

'Ohhh,' she breathed. 'Maybe he's been visiting her, too. Maybe we could lure him there.'

'Or maybe she knows where else he might hide. I need to tell Gideon.' Definitely about this development. Probably not that he'd already tried visiting Burton's mother.

Erin frowned. 'Remember, I am not—'

'Here. Got it. You are not here. He's gonna figure it out anyway, you know.'

She shrugged. 'I know. I'm okay with it. Just keep it off the record, okay?'

Rafe dialed and Gideon answered on the first ring. 'What's wrong?' he demanded. 'Is she okay?'

'Mercy's fine, but we need to talk. I'm at my place. It's important.'

'I'm on my way.'

Eleven

Mercy sat at the farthest corner of the Sokolovs' dinner table, trying to take up the least space possible. It was slightly less overwhelming now, at least. Thirty minutes earlier, the kitchen, dining room, living room, hell, the whole house, had been filled wall-to-wall with Sokolovs. Six of Irina's eight children had shown up, along with nine grandchildren. Missing were only Jude the prosecutor, who'd moved to LA – much to everyone's dismay – and Patrick the firefighter, who was on shift that day.

They'd come to meet Mercy, to welcome her, and it had warmed her heart – until the noise had grown so loud that escape was all she could think of. But she couldn't take a walk outside because Ephraim was out there somewhere.

Thankfully all the Sokolov children except Rafe and Sasha had gone to their own homes. Zoya, the youngest, who still lived at home, had been 'banished' to her room, in the teenager's words. She hadn't voluntarily vacated the kitchen, having immediately hit it off with Farrah. The high school senior wanted to be a doctor and had spent the meal asking Farrah a hundred questions about her research position at the university.

Mercy wouldn't have minded if Zoya had stayed, because the discussion of ways to 'help Mercy' had begun immediately after the mass exodus. Mercy, however, was finding it hard to listen, still reeling from everything Rafe had told her on the drive over.

At least she'd gotten some sleep. He hadn't woken her until

178

twenty minutes before they'd needed to leave for his parents' home, just enough time to splash her face with some water and change into a proper outfit. Which had surprised him. He'd actually thought she'd show up to his family's dinner table in yoga pants and a Hello Kitty sweatshirt. She'd never truly understand men.

Except she did understand that Rafe was trying his best to keep her safe. Gideon had ridden shotgun while Sasha drove. Farrah and Daisy had driven over with Erin Rhee, who'd been obviously armed.

Because, Rafe had explained, Ephraim was armed and had killed at least three people in the hours since his attempted airport abduction. *Three people, two of whom were completely innocent.* The poor woman from the airport, an innocent college girl in a costume store, and a woman who ran a prostitution ring. *My God.*

She knew Ephraim Burton was a monster, but three people . . .

She wanted to run away, but nowhere was safe. Ephraim was out there somewhere, wielding at least two handguns, snapping necks and killing anyone who got in his way. She wouldn't put any of the people in this room in danger by running off by herself.

There was impetuous, and there was stupid. *I may be impetuous, but I'm not stupid.*

'Mercy?' Gideon asked, his voice cutting through her thoughts. 'What do you think?'

She sighed. 'Sorry. I wasn't listening.'

'It's loud in here,' Rafe murmured. 'Do you need to leave?'

She shook her head. Everyone had gathered here to help her. She was going to focus, even if it made her sick. At least she now knew where the nearest bathroom was.

'Can you repeat it, please?' she asked.

Gideon's smile was gentle. 'Sure. Daisy has an interview set up for you with a reporter at one of the TV stations in the city. It's tonight, if that's all right.'

Mercy nodded. 'Better to get it over with. Maybe it will make all the other news vans leave us alone if they see there's no story.'

'From your mouth to God's ears,' Karl said. 'And the video is no longer on any website that we could find.'

Mercy's face heated. Seeing that video for the first time had been one of the top five lowest points in her life. Hearing it discussed so clinically was . . . rough. 'Thank you,' she whispered.

'We'll go with you to the station,' Karl said steadily. 'We won't let you be alone.'

Mercy opened her mouth to protest, but closed it again. Denying this family's support would be too rude.

'But if Mercy needs quiet time afterward, we'll let her have it, right, Dad?' Rafe said.

Karl nodded. 'Of course.'

Mercy nodded. 'Thank you.' Then, following her instincts, she leaned over to kiss the older man's stubbled cheek. 'You're all very wonderful. I can see why Gideon loves you so much.'

Karl actually blushed.

'Let's move on to the notion of using Eden's trading practices to track them,' Gideon went on. 'I've let my boss at the Bureau know about the furniture and crafts. They've got a team working to find all the possible examples of Eden products. Thank you for bringing us this lead.'

Mercy kept her smile mild. 'Anytime.'

Beside her, Rafe snorted. 'I'll remember that tone. If you ever direct it at me, I'm gonna run.'

Gideon shook his head. 'Come on, Rafe, stop joking around.'

'I'm not,' Rafe protested. 'You're being all lord of the manor, Gid.'

'You *are* a little heavy-handed, Gideon,' Sasha agreed.

Gideon shot a questioning glance at Daisy, who cuddled her little dog, Brutus, to her chest. 'I'm Switzerland,' Daisy declared. 'Don't look at me for help.'

Gideon sighed. 'You did good work, Mercy. Thank you. But please leave this for law enforcement.'

Mercy nodded, keeping the same smile on her face. She and Rafe had done their parts – they'd informed the FBI of their suspicions. But she didn't want to drop it in anyone else's lap. She wanted to be involved. Now she knew what Rafe had been going through, keeping the work he'd been doing to himself for fear it would be taken from him.

'Of course,' she promised. 'I'll be a virtual sieve to the FBI.'

Gideon's frown said that he did not believe her. 'See that you are.'

'Do we know any more about where Ephraim went when he left the costume store?' Rafe asked, and Mercy was grateful for the subject change.

'No, not yet,' Gideon admitted. 'But that doesn't mean anything. I'm as much on the outside of this case looking in as you guys.'

Because he'd recused himself, taking vacation time to keep her safe. Again, she wanted to run away, far from everyone who hovered over her. Everyone but Rafe, who seemed to truly get her.

'What about the locket?' Daisy asked. 'The Feds released a photo to the CNN interviewer last week. Has anyone said they've seen the design?'

Because that had been Molina's hope – that other escapees would see the Eden symbol and come forward.

'So far, no,' Gideon said. 'At least nobody's contacted the FBI. Erin, has SacPD heard anything?'

Erin shook her head. 'Maybe we should post only a picture of the locket and ask if anyone's seen it. It got lost in the news report. It was just a one-sentence mention among a whole lot of details.'

Gideon shook his head. 'That's too direct at this point. We don't want Eden to know we're looking for them.'

Daisy bit her lip, hesitating. 'What if Mercy wore Eileen's locket during her interview tonight? We can direct the reporter not to mention it, but if someone sees it on her . . .'

No. Mercy wanted to scream it. *No!* But she didn't say a word, drawing into herself.

'I'm sorry, Mercy,' Daisy said quickly. 'It was a bad idea. Forget it.'

There was silence at the table then, everyone looking at her, as if expecting to see her disagree that it was a bad idea. They thought it was a good idea, Mercy could tell. *But I just can't.*

Rafe covered her hand with his. 'The interview itself will be difficult enough. Mercy needs to project confidence and she can't do that if she's having PTSD episodes over the locket around her throat.'

Rafe's words hit home. PTSD was exactly what she was experiencing. It was real. But it wasn't a good reason to reject what really was a good idea. *It's just a locket. Just silver. Just jewelry.*

'You're right,' Daisy agreed. 'It was a dumb idea.'

'No, it's not dumb.' Mercy was startled to hear her own voice. 'It's smart. It's also a way to taunt Ephraim Burton if he's watching. Maybe make him so angry that it lures him out, makes him do something rash.'

Rafe was shaking his head. 'I don't like that idea. At all.'

'Neither do I,' Mercy said, grateful that her voice didn't tremble. 'But he's killed three people in the last twenty-four hours. Three people. At least two of them – the minivan lady at the airport and the college kid at the costume store – were killed as a direct result of his obsession with me.' About the brothel madam, she had no idea. 'I don't know why he's obsessed, other than I got away and he can't handle it, but if this continues, more people could die. It costs me nothing to wear the locket.'

'It costs you peace of mind,' Rafe protested.

'My peace of mind isn't more important than the lives of innocent people who get in Ephraim's way.'

Sniffling got her attention and she turned away from Rafe to see his mother wiping her eyes. 'You're a good person, Mercy.'

Mercy managed a small smile for the woman who'd given her comfort the night before. 'Thank you.' She drew a breath and exhaled carefully. 'But I don't need to wear Eileen's locket. I brought mine with me.' She met Gideon's eyes. 'And Mama's.'

Gideon went very still. 'You what?'

She nodded. 'The locket was the only thing I had left of Mama and I didn't think you deserved to have it, but I was wrong. So I brought it to give you.'

'You didn't have to bring them, Mercy,' Gideon said quietly.

She sighed. 'I know, but I'm tired of keeping things from you.'

He leaned across the table and gripped her hands. 'Thank you. I was going to call John later today. Will you stay with me when I do?'

More sniffling from Irina had Mercy smiling again. 'Of course.'

The table fell silent until Erin cleared her throat. 'I have a question,' she started, then stopped when her phone began to vibrate on the table. She checked the screen, then looked up at Rafe, troubled. 'It's Tiff.'

'Please, take it,' Rafe said.

With a nod, Erin excused herself and stepped into the hallway off the kitchen.

'Who is Tiff?' Mercy asked.

'Our lieutenant's clerk,' Rafe said. 'She's the one who passed on the information about the murdered madam in Santa Rosa and the discovery of June Lindstrom's body this morning. She promised to let us know if any more bodies were discovered.'

'So more than three,' Mercy murmured, and no one said a word to dispute her. No one said anything at all until Erin came back in, her expression drawn.

'An elderly woman was found dead in her home north of the city, discovered by her grandson. She'd been shot in the chest twice. Bullet appears to be a .45, but we won't know for certain until the ME does an autopsy and sends the bullet to Ballistics. Rigor had set in, so she'd been dead at least eight hours or so.'

'She was the reason Burton didn't want to use the golden gun on the college kid,' Rafe said bitterly. 'That's why he broke her neck. Burton was carrying a gold-colored gun with a suppressor when he killed the young woman in the costume store – a gun he took from the Santa Rosa madam. He didn't want to shoot the college kid and have the bullet match with the old woman.'

But the death didn't make sense. None of them did, and tears burned at Mercy's throat. 'Why did he kill an old woman?'

'It appears he slept there,' Erin said gently. 'The bed was unmade and the shower had been used. They'll dust for prints and screen the drains for any hair he might have lost. It's being handled by the sheriff's department right now. I'm assuming the FBI will take over at some point.'

Gideon had slumped in his chair. 'We need to find this bastard, and soon.'

Mercy squared her shoulders. This was the reason she'd come back. 'I can be bait. Use me.'

Two loud nos had her flinching. Gideon was halfway out of his chair, leaning on the table to get closer to her. Rafe had lurched to his feet, standing taller with a white-knuckled grip around the handle of the brand-new cane that his father had made for him that morning.

'I won't let you be bait,' Rafe gritted through clenched teeth.

'No way in hell,' Gideon added.

Farrah looked stunned. 'Mercy, please. Let's think this through.'

Mercy ignored Rafe and Gideon, turning to Farrah with a tired smile. 'I have. I knew when I came back that I'd have some role in finding Eden. This is it. Erin? What do you think?'

Erin hesitated, then nodded. 'I think we can make it work, but only if my boss and Gideon's boss agree and only if they provide a lot of backup.'

'Erin,' Rafe growled.

Erin didn't drop her gaze, meeting Rafe's eyes directly. 'Rafe. This can't go on. He's murdering innocent people all over the damn place.'

'No.' Gideon was shaking his head vehemently. 'I won't have it.'

Mercy felt surprisingly calm. 'I didn't ask your permission. Erin, what do you need me to do?'

'Nothing for now. Get a little rest?' Erin glanced up at Gideon, who was glowering. 'If we do nothing, he'll get her, Gideon. He's obsessed. He won't give up. And we can't maintain this level of security forever, short of WITSEC. Sooner or later something's gonna slip, and she'll be unprotected. That's when he'll strike, if we don't take care of him first. If the powers that be agree, we will set this up so that Mercy has complete coverage.'

'I'm still here,' Mercy said, ignoring the glares coming from her brother and her . . . She faltered, not sure what Rafe was. Her friend, she decided. That word was perfect for now. 'Gideon, this isn't your call. Nor yours, Rafe. It's my decision and I'm deciding to say yes.'

The doorbell rang at that moment and Irina rushed away to answer it, but paused in the doorway to give Mercy a thumbs-up. 'Brave,' she said.

I hope so. I sure hope so.

A minute later, during which Rafe and Gideon continued to glare at her, Irina returned, followed by a very tall man with bright blond hair. He looked familiar, somehow.

Mercy recalled his face seconds before he introduced himself. He was the FBI agent who'd helped Gideon find the killer the night she'd been abducted. She wasn't sure what exactly the man had done to help, but Gideon said they owed him a great deal.

'I'm Special Agent Hunter,' the man said. 'I'm here to take your official statement, Detective.'

'Mine?' Erin asked, confused.

'No,' Rafe said. 'Mine. Hi, Tom.'

Tom looked around the table, clearly sensing the tension. 'Is this a bad time?'

'No, it's fine,' Rafe told him. 'We can use my father's study.'

But Karl had risen to his feet, still looking confused. 'Wait. You're Tom Hunter?'

Tom's lips quirked up in an almost-smile. 'Yes, sir.'

'*The* Tom Hunter?' Karl pressed.

'Well, it's a fairly common name,' Tom said, amusement in his eyes. 'I can't be the only one.'

Karl shook his head. '*The* Tom Hunter who led Boston to the finals three years running?'

Tom looked a bit bashful now. 'Yes, sir. But that was a lifetime ago.'

'It was a year ago,' Karl protested. 'I was sorry when I heard you'd left the game. You were a pleasure to watch on the court.'

Mercy was now confused. 'Court?'

'He's an NBA player,' Karl explained.

'Was,' Tom corrected. 'Now I'm with the Bureau.'

Rafe's mouth had fallen open. 'Holy shit. I didn't make the connection before. Holy fucking shit.' He darted an apologetic glance at Irina. 'Sorry, Mom.'

'Is okay,' she said, chuckling. 'Raphael, take the nice agent to your father's office. I will bring tea.'

'That's not necessary, Mrs Sokolov,' Tom protested.

'Nonsense. You go. Now.' She shooed both Rafe and Tom with a flick of her hands.

'That was . . . weird,' Mercy said, when the two were gone.

'The last twenty-four hours have been weird,' Farrah agreed.

Daisy turned on Gideon with an indignant frown. 'Did you know who he was?'

Gideon shook his head. 'I don't follow basketball. I thought he was a rookie agent with impressive computer skills.'

'Well, we'll have to get him on my radio show,' Daisy declared.

Gideon looked displeased. 'You'll do no such thing. He has a different job now and he might not want to receive that kind of attention. It could negatively affect his work.'

Daisy pouted. 'Dammit. But I know you're right.' She jabbed his arm with her finger when he smiled, a little smugly. '*This* time, you're right. This *one* time. Don't go getting a fat head.'

'Too late for that,' Mercy muttered, and Sasha choked out a laugh.

'He's your brother. I got five of them, so I feel your pain. They treat us like we're useless.'

'I do not,' Gideon insisted. 'I just got her back. I don't want to lose her again.'

'Still right here,' Mercy called. 'Still can hear you. And you won't lose me.'

Which she genuinely hoped was true. But dammit. Ephraim had already killed four people, three of them innocents. *I have to do something, right now.*

Granite Bay, California
Sunday, 16 April, 3.50 P.M.

Nothing was happening at the Sokolov house. Ephraim had been here most of the day after his search for an unoccupied house had been a failure. Both unoccupied houses were actually occupied – one with about two dozen addicts and the other by two guys making meth.

Ephraim hadn't wanted to tangle with any of them, so he'd

headed over to the Sokolov house, and was glad he had. He'd arrived in time to see two SUVs filled with people pulling into what had to be a six-car garage, at least. Through his binoculars he'd spied Mercy sitting in the backseat of the lead SUV, a gray Chevy Suburban. The second vehicle was a blue Range Rover, with a small woman behind the wheel.

At least the windows weren't tinted and the vehicles didn't look like official law enforcement. Mercy had a personal guard, but no formal protection. That would make things a little easier.

The detective – Raphael Sokolov – had been sitting in the Suburban's passenger seat, Gideon Reynolds behind the wheel. The sight of Reynolds made Ephraim want to charge and shoot him dead.

But the garage door had been quickly lowered, and Ephraim had been left to brood and seethe. He needed Mercy to prove to Pastor that DJ had lied about her death. But he wanted Gideon in a choke hold. Wanted to watch the fucker take his last breath, but not before he cut out the man's eyes.

It was justice, after all.

He didn't care about anyone in the house. He wanted Mercy alive, Gideon stone-cold dead, and the Sokolov cop to be permanently in that wheelchair, in pain for the rest of his miserable life.

So he'd sat and watched, growing more bored by the moment. A horde of additional people had arrived – more Sokolovs, Ephraim figured by the overabundance of blonds who carried covered dishes and wrangled noisy children. All of them had left in the last hour, but Mercy, Gideon, and the Sokolov cop remained. So Ephraim had stayed put.

He wanted to get closer to the house, but he didn't dare. He'd seen Mercy arrive and now knew that she wasn't actually staying in this house, which meant that he couldn't leave. He needed to follow them when they left. He needed to know where Mercy was sleeping. He needed to catch her unawares.

He blinked hard when his view of the house grew fuzzy. He shouldn't be tired. He'd gotten an excellent night's sleep in Granny's bed. He gave his head a shake, slapping his cheeks lightly to stay awake. *Need to think. Need to plan.* He might be AWOL from Eden for a while, depending on how long Mercy was going to stay. He would wait her out, but that could take days at a minimum.

He needed cash and was abruptly struck with a fresh worry. Grabbing his new prepaid smartphone from his pocket, he went to open his banking app, then realized he hadn't downloaded it. He started the process, resigned to the fact that he'd have to add data sooner than he'd anticipated since he wasn't connected to Wi-Fi.

Ephraim scowled at the phone as the app slowly downloaded. At least the phone had been easier to obtain than he'd thought, only requiring the bribe of beer and cigarettes to one of the kids sitting outside the store. The kid had bought him one flip phone, one smartphone, a pair of cheap binoculars, and several prepaid cards carrying data and minutes.

He could have gone into the store himself, but he hadn't wanted to risk it, despite wearing one of the disguises he'd stolen that morning. He was certain that his own mother wouldn't recognize him.

Of course, his mother didn't recognize anyone anymore. She hadn't known who he was the last three times he'd visited. He hadn't been back in a long while.

And he wasn't going to think about his mother right now. It was bad enough that she was dying alone with strangers. *Should have taken her to Eden years ago. Should have been taking care of her myself all this time.*

But he hadn't. His brother hadn't wanted her involved in their crimes, but his brother was long dead. Murdered by Gideon. Ephraim still remembered his mother's tortured sobs when he'd come to give her the news. He'd offered to take her with him then, but she'd refused. Said she couldn't abide the sight of the men who'd taken her son.

But, Ma, the boy who killed him is gone. Killed by Waylon Belmont, DJ's father, when the boy's mother stowed the two of them away in the bed of Waylon's truck. When Waylon discovered them, he'd killed Gideon and brought Rhoda back for punishment. *Or so he'd claimed.* Clearly Waylon had lied to him too, because Gideon was alive and well. Enjoying his life while Ephraim's brother rotted in the ground.

'You don't understand,' his mother had cried. 'I'm not talking about the boy who killed him, although I hope you're right and that he's dead, because if I ever found him, I'd kill him myself. I'm talking about the people who lured him there to begin with, who made him a prisoner for all these years. You both should be here, with me. Stay with me, son. Stay with me and don't go back.'

But Ephraim had gone back, because the money that Pastor had been 'managing for them' all these years was his, and he wasn't leaving Eden until he got it. At least he'd been smart enough to safeguard the stipend Pastor gave him, moving as much as he could from his 'Eden account' into a private bank account that neither Pastor nor DJ had access to.

The bank app had finally finished downloading and he quickly logged in to his Eden account. And blew out a breath that was part dismay, part frustration, but mostly fury.

Zero. Zero dollars and zero cents. Pastor had cleaned him out.

He was relieved that he'd moved a substantial amount of money over before he'd left for New Orleans the week before, but the relief was overshadowed by pure rage.

'Sons of bitches,' he snarled, closing the banking app on his new phone and reopening it, hoping for a different result. Of course it still read zero. That account had held fifty thousand dollars just days ago. He wished he'd cleaned it out himself, but he always kept his withdrawals low enough to avoid attention. He primarily used his Eden account to pay for his mother's nursing home and Pastor knew that. Pastor always made sure the account had enough to cover the exorbitant fees.

But no longer. Ephraim stared at the screen, wondering what had tipped them off. Wondering when they'd realized he wasn't where he was supposed to have been. He thought about the three calls Pastor had made to Regina's while he'd been in New Orleans.

Fuck. The tickets. That was what had tipped them off. He'd bought the tickets with his Eden account.

God. I was so stupid. But he'd been rattled, seeing Mercy's face on

189

the screen, realizing that she was still alive. Seeing that his Miriam was dead, her locket taken into police custody. He'd been too rattled to think clearly and it was now biting him in the ass.

He'd figured that because he'd bought the tickets on his secure laptop – at least he'd thought it was secure at the time – nobody would know, but of course they were watching his Eden account. Or DJ was, the fucker. Ephraim could see him running to Pastor, whispering trash in his ear. They'd still be tracking him if he hadn't smashed his old phone.

He froze, then turned the new phone off. They probably knew he was trying to access the account right now. They might even be able to track his location through the bank account. He had no idea if that was even possible, but if it was, DJ would have learned how to do it.

Ephraim knew he was probably being paranoid, but he was spooked and he hated it. Hated DJ for being a miserable worm with no sense of gratitude. Hated Pastor for taking DJ under his wing, for treating him like a son.

Their father–son relationship had started years before DJ's actual father died. Waylon had dropped dead from a heart attack just days after Ephraim's brother had been murdered, leaving DJ an orphan at seventeen years old. Pastor had swooped in then, taking DJ to live in his home, virtually adopting the little prick. *Poor little orphan boy.*

Ephraim snorted. Seventeen had been plenty old enough for DJ to take care of himself, but no one had the courage to tell Pastor that, Ephraim included. Because Pastor had declared that DJ would be his heir apparent when DJ had been only nine.

Right after Marcia had disappeared with Pastor's real kids. Twins, a boy and a girl. Ephraim's heart kicked in his chest. He hadn't thought of Pastor's first wife and kids in years. Marcia had been kind of a mom to him too, when Ephraim had been eighteen and scared and thrust into the role of a Founding Elder when Pastor had first conjured Eden.

'It wasn't supposed to be forever,' Ephraim murmured. That was what Marcia had said to the Founding Elder council the night before she disappeared with her two children. Later, Waylon had publicly claimed that she'd escaped through the gate but had fallen down a ravine, taking the children with her, probably trying to escape a wild animal. But the animals had found her anyway, Waylon had claimed. He'd found their remains at the bottom of a ravine more than a week later.

Ephraim had been more than suspicious at the time, but Waylon didn't lie. Or so he'd thought. *I should have known better.* Both when Waylon claimed Marcia and the kids were dead and when he'd claimed Gideon was dead. And then later, when DJ had claimed Mercy was dead.

I should have known they were all lying.

Because it was a farce. Nobody in the history of Eden had actually been devoured by an animal of any kind. It was simply a way to strike enough fear into the hearts of the membership that they wouldn't try to escape. They killed dissidents themselves and mauled the bodies to look like they'd been 'devoured'. Waylon had even produced three bodies that might have been Marcia and the kids.

But the remains had been too scavenged to tell for sure.

Ephraim had believed it at the time, even though he'd killed and mauled enough troublemakers himself to know the score. But he'd wanted to believe that Marcia had run. He hadn't wanted to accept that her own husband could order her death – and the deaths of his two children.

Marcia and Pastor's own daughter had been about to turn twelve and would have been given to one of the men in marriage. She hadn't been able to bear her own daughter being 'abused', and had tried to get Pastor to make an exception, but he'd refused. It would cause anarchy, Pastor had said, and he was right.

Looking back, Ephraim wondered if Pastor had known the truth. Now that Ephraim knew that Waylon had lied about finding Gideon's body, he assumed that Waylon had lied about Marcia's kids, too. But if Pastor had known, he hadn't let on. Instead he'd appeared truly grief-stricken, taking Waylon's son under his wing.

Ephraim wondered if Marcia was still alive, and if so, if she would hide him if things got hot with the Feds. It had been twenty-four years. Bernice and Bo would be thirty-seven years old by now.

He'd been angry at the time that she'd taken Bernice away. He'd been angling to be the one who got her for his own wife.

Whatever. The truth remained that Pastor treated DJ as a son, and even knowing that DJ had lied about Mercy might not change Pastor's mind. *If that happens, I'll change the mind of the entire community.* Ephraim would be the wronged party and he'd convince the membership to attack both Pastor and DJ and he'd sit back and laugh as he watched the membership take their revenge.

But he wouldn't let them cast Pastor out of Eden. Not until the old bastard gave him the passwords for the offshore accounts. Then the membership could do as they pleased. He'd be on his way to a private island where he'd sit on a beach and drink rum for the rest of his life, the rightful steward of Eden's millions.

He'd lifted his binoculars to take another look at the Sokolov house when he heard the quiet rumble of an approaching vehicle. He ducked low just as a black SUV passed without stopping.

He peeked above the steering wheel in time to see the vehicle parking in front of the Sokolovs' house. *Fuck.* That was an official law enforcement vehicle. It wasn't the first. There had been a black sedan parked in front of the house all afternoon, but it hadn't moved.

Now a tall blond guy in a black suit got out of the SUV, flashed some kind of ID at the guy in the sedan, then was admitted into the house.

This was what Ephraim had been afraid of. Feds and cops coming by. Any of them could get in his business just for sitting too close in a junky car that didn't fit the neighborhood, and if they searched his car, they'd find Granny's rifle, Regina's golden gun, his own revolver, and the college kid's .22. A search of the trunk would reveal Granny's preserved and canned veggies as well as the rope and duct tape that he'd stolen. He suspected that the Feds wouldn't care about the preserves. The guns, however, would get him into a lot of trouble.

He needed to find somewhere else to wait, and quickly. Mercy wasn't staying here and if he wanted to follow her to wherever she was staying, he'd need to be able to see the front door.

Time to take a ride around the neighborhood and check out the real estate.

Granite Bay, California
Sunday, 16 April, 4.20 P.M.

Rafe led Tom Hunter through his parents' house and into his father's office. Motioning to the chairs in front of Karl's desk, he took one and waited until Tom had done the same.

'The last time I saw you was the night Mercy was abducted,' Rafe said. That had been the only time, actually. 'I'm sorry that I didn't recognize you.'

Tom's smile was rueful. 'I'm glad you didn't. It gets a little awkward sometimes, especially when I'm trying to do my job. Besides, we were all focused on getting Mercy back that night.'

'Thank you,' Rafe said quietly. 'I'm not sure what you did that night to help, and I don't need to know. But thank you.'

'You're welcome.' Tom pointed to the cane. 'Injuries are a bitch, right?'

Rafe nodded, racking his brain for what he could remember about this man and his former career. 'You got hurt, too.'

'Torn ACL,' Tom said with an eye roll. 'Benched me for the rest of the season.'

Rafe studied him carefully. 'NBA to FBI is a pretty big leap. Can I ask what prompted it?'

Something moved in Tom's eyes, something a little bitter and a lot sad. 'I . . . well, I lost someone around the same time. I needed a new start.'

Rafe nodded. He knew what that felt like. He thought of Bella, of what life had been like with her. What his life had been like after she'd been murdered. The utter and debilitating grief. It wasn't something he'd allowed himself to think about often. It hurt a lot less now that he'd met Mercy Callahan. 'Been there, too. My leap was more like a hop, though. I went from Gangs to Homicide.'

Tom held his gaze, his nod understanding. 'I was recruited by the Feds at DEF CON, back when I was still in college, but I put them off at the time. My contact kept trying over the years. I heard from him a few months before my injury, asking if I was still interested in the Bureau. I was ready to leave the game anyway, so I told him yes, that I'd be available after the season was over. But then . . .' He gestured at his leg. 'I was lucky. I'd recovered enough to pass basic training at Quantico by the time the next class started.'

Rafe's brows shot up. 'DEF CON? The hacker convention?' He'd heard of it but hadn't met anyone who'd ever attended. At least not that he knew of. Most hackers were very closemouthed about their craft.

'One and the same. I wanted to play basketball, but I knew it wasn't going to be something I retired from as an old man. My father played for LA until he got hurt. He became a college professor, so I guess I grew up knowing there should be options after sports.' Tom hesitated. 'I, uh, well, I asked for this interview. With you.'

Rafe's eyes widened abruptly. 'What? Why?'

'I should tell you up front that I know your brother Cash. We went to college together.'

Rafe nodded warily. He remembered that, now that Tom mentioned it. 'And?'

'Well, I saw him a few weeks ago. Wrenched my knee running and I knew he was Sac's team PT, so I made an appointment.' He shrugged uncomfortably. 'I knew Cash wouldn't out me to the Bureau. I didn't want to be put on . . . y'know. Disability.'

Rafe made a face. 'Yeah, I know.' He narrowed his eyes. 'You're the one who recommended the therapist.'

'Yes, I did. I didn't tell him specifically I was mentioning it for you, but I knew you were still out on DB. I . . . well, Gideon has been a good mentor and he talks about you sometimes. That wasn't the reason I made the appointment with Cash, you understand. That was purely selfish on my part.'

'But once you were there, you couldn't resist.' Rafe fought the urge to get up and walk away. Or limp, anyway. Tom Hunter had a sincerity that made it difficult to really be angry with him.

'Kind of. I know where you are right now. The uncertainty is the hardest part. Where will you go from here, what can you still do? You want to be useful and . . . involved. You wanna be a cop. Am I close?'

Rafe nodded. 'Pretty much.' Tom wasn't just close, he was right on the money.

'I saw the therapist I recommended while he was in Boston, but he's moved to San Francisco, started a practice there. I bet he'd drive to Sacramento to talk to you if you bribe him with that cake I saw on the table.'

Rafe found he could still smile. 'Thank you. You got a business card for him?'

'I can shoot you his contact info.' Tom waved his phone. 'AirDrop okay?'

'Yes, please. And thank you,' he repeated, because Tom hadn't needed to do this, hadn't needed to be so honest. Or helpful.

He put his phone away after accepting the contact exchange and drew a breath. 'Do you still need my statement?'

'Yes, if you would.' Tom produced a tablet and perched it on his knee, his fingers poised to type. 'Ready when you are.'

Rafe told him everything that had happened in the airport the night before, down to seeing Burton's revolver on the security footage.

'Got it,' Tom said when Rafe wound down. 'Tell me, did you notice anything else about Burton? Anything that surprised you?'

'Well, first off, he was there,' Rafe said sourly, and Tom chuckled. 'Besides that.'

Rafe considered it, went through every moment of the altercation. 'He had an eye. I assume it was glass, because Mercy said he didn't have a prosthetic when she was—' He cut himself off, unable to say the word 'married'. It had been rape, pure and simple. 'When she knew him. He must have had some kind of surgery . . .'

Tom smiled encouragingly. 'Go on.'

'Well, if he had surgery, someone has to have done it, and probably outside Eden. I don't think they had an actual doctor there, just "healers".' His heart started racing, in sync with his mind. 'Maybe we can find out who did it.'

'Maybe, maybe not. That's kind of a needle in a haystack.'

Rafe looked at his foot, tapping a rhythm that matched his quickened pulse. 'He grew up in Santa Rosa, and you know about the brothel madam, right?'

'You're suggesting that his surgeon might also be located in the same area?'

'Yes. His mother's nursing home is there, too. What if we started there? Asked if there were any surgeons who worked with Mrs Franklin?'

'We could try. It's unlikely they'll tell us. HIPAA regs and all.'

Rafe blew out a frustrated sigh. 'Dammit.' But Tom was right. 'It was just an idea.'

'It was a good idea,' Tom said thoughtfully. 'But we might have to try unconventional methods to get that information.'

He had Rafe's attention. 'Like?'

'Like finding someone on the inside. Or someone who can get on the inside.'

'I can go undercover.'

'Probably not the best plan. You're not supposed to be working this case and, besides, your face is all over the TV and Internet right now.'

And I actually tried to get inside and failed. Which, now that his face was all over the TV and the Internet, might make someone at the nursing home remember him anyway. *Dammit.*

Feeling helpless, Rafe met Tom's gaze. 'Mercy is my friend. So is Gideon. I'd do anything to keep them safe, and finding Burton will keep Mercy safe.'

'Then help me.' Tom lifted his tablet. 'What else did you notice about Burton last night?'

Rafe scowled, then reconsidered. Tom hadn't told him specifically not to get involved. Only that he wasn't supposed to. *I can work with that.* 'He didn't really seem shocked when I called him by name. More . . . angry and a little resigned. Like he'd been afraid of it happening.'

'The locket,' Tom murmured. 'We allowed CNN to show Eileen's locket in the hopes that other Eden escapees would see it and come forward. But if Burton saw the locket . . .'

'He'd be worried that we know what's inside it.'

Tom shrugged. 'It's the most likely scenario. Anything else?'

'Just that I'm still wondering how he knew she was flying to Sacramento yesterday. I know he was in New Orleans for almost a week, but that doesn't account for how he knew she was leaving – and he took the flight before hers, so he couldn't have followed her to the airport.'

Tom sighed softly. 'I didn't think anyone had called Dr Romero yet.'

Rafe stiffened. 'What do you mean?'

'I figured her family would call her, but when I saw her sitting at your mother's table I could tell that no one had. Her aunt, actually her great-aunt, I think, was found dead in her apartment sometime during the night. Whoever did it tried to make it look like a robbery, but the timing is very suspicious.'

'Oh no,' Rafe breathed. 'Poor Farrah. But what does this have to do with Mercy?'

'Mercy and Quill Romero were next-door neighbors.'

'Oh God.' Rafe's stomach began churning all over again. 'Why has no one told Farrah?'

'I don't know.'

Rafe surged to his feet, grabbing his cane to pace the length of the office, then stopped when a thought occurred. He dialed his next-door neighbor, Ned, who answered on the first ring.

'Rafe, what's wrong?'

'Why would you think something's wrong?'

'Because men in black visited your place about an hour ago.'

They had tried to tell Farrah, then. 'Are they still there?'

'Hold on. I don't think so, but I'll look.'

Rafe looked over at Tom. 'I think the Feds came by my house. Hold on, Ned's back.'

'The black suits are gone, but there's another guy outside, sitting on the hood of his car, watching your house. Big guy, like a football player. African American. Looks kind of sad, actually. He's not a cop, at least he's not wearing a uniform. Or a suit. He's wearing jeans and a sweatshirt. Looks like . . . Oh, it's one of those golden fleur-de-lis things. New Orleans Saints, I guess.'

'I think I know who he is – probably the fiancé of one of my houseguests. Can you do me a favor? Take your phone down to the guy and let me talk to him or at least give him my number?'

'Sure thing, Rafe. Hold on. Gotta find my shoes.'

Rafe rubbed his hand over his face while he waited for Ned to go outside. Finally, he heard Ned say, 'Excuse me. Are you looking for the homeowner?'

A deep voice rumbled, 'Yes. Do you know how I can get in touch with him?'

'He's here, on the phone,' Ned said. 'Wants to talk to you.'

A second later that deep voice was talking to him. 'Where's Farrah?'

'She's safe. This is Rafe Sokolov. Are you her captain?'

The man huffed a gruff chuckle. 'Yeah. Captain André Holmes. You're Mercy's guy?'

Rafe sucked in a breath. 'Not yet, but I hope to be. Listen, I have a Fed here telling me that Farrah's aunt's body was found. She doesn't know.'

'I know. I came to tell her in person. She loved Quill.' He cleared his throat. 'So did I.'

'Give me your number and I'll text you the address. She's here with us at my folks' house. It's about forty-five minutes from where you are with traffic.' He put Holmes on speaker, typing André's phone number into a new text as the man recited it, then adding his parents' address before hitting SEND. 'Did you get it?'

'I did. Thank you. Can you keep her away from TVs and computers for the next forty-five? And her phone. I've been calling her for the past two hours. I don't want her to see all my messages and freak out. Not till I get there.'

'Will do. See you soon.'

Rafe pocketed his phone and limped back to Tom. 'Thanks for letting me know. Farrah is a really nice person. I hate for her to get bad news like this.'

'Her fiancé is coming?'

'On his way. So, I guess that explains how Burton knew Mercy's

198

plans. I get the impression that the Romeros are like us – nothing stays a secret for very long. The aunt must have known and told Burton before he killed her.'

'My family is the same way. My mom was disappointed that I didn't get assigned to the Chicago field office for my first post, but I was a little glad. I love my family, I really do, but they can be . . .'

'Suffocating?' Rafe suggested, and Tom made a face.

'Exactly.' He stood up and adjusted the knot of his tie. 'I'll get out of your hair now. You take it easy, okay? No chasing after Burton?'

'I will take it very easy,' Rafe promised. *And I will chase Burton as soon as the opportunity presents. And I won't clock him with my fucking cane next time. Next time, I'm pulling my gun.*

'I, uh, noticed that you didn't promise part two.'

Rafe shrugged. 'I make it a practice not to promise things I can't deliver.'

Tom gave him a long, hard look. 'Molina will be very displeased if you go after Burton on your own.'

'I really don't care how much she's displeased,' Rafe said mildly.

Tom sighed. 'Look, I'm just the junior G-man here. Don't be getting me into trouble, okay? I've got a few ideas about how to get someone into that nursing home, but Molina has to okay it.'

'And maybe she'll even think it was her idea?'

Tom shrugged. 'I'm pretty good at suggesting things to higher-ups in ways that don't piss them off and boot me off the case. Give me a little time to present my ideas to Molina before you go off on your own, okay?'

Rafe nodded grudgingly. 'Okay. Thank you.'

Tom started to leave, but stopped a foot away from where Rafe stood, leaning against his cane. 'I would have done anything to keep my fiancée safe, so I know what you're feeling right now. But Mercy needs you alive. Please don't do anything she'll regret.'

'All right. And thanks for the straight talk on the therapist. I'll make an appointment tomorrow.'

Tom shook his head. 'You didn't distract me about you hunting down Ephraim, Rafe. But I'm glad you're going to make the call to the doc. You won't be sorry.'

'Hey, Tom? My mom made extra cake. You want a slice for the road?'

He grinned. 'I never say no to cake.'

Rafe opened the door to see his mother edging away from the door guiltily, her hands filled with the tea tray. 'Mom,' he groaned.

'I didn't listen,' Irina claimed. 'Much. I'm on my way back to the kitchen.'

'Allow me, ma'am.' Tom took the tray and followed Rafe's mother.

Rafe brought up the rear, hoping that his mother hadn't heard them talking about Farrah's great-aunt. He was going to ask her to keep it to herself, but she was already interrogating Hunter.

'Do you have any family here, Agent Hunter?'

'Um, no, ma'am. A dear friend, but no family.'

'Then next week you will join us for dinner. And you will bring your "dear friend" as well. Yes?'

Tom smiled down at her. The guy was taller than any of the Sokolovs, which now made sense considering he'd been in the NBA. 'Yes, ma'am. If it's not any trouble. I miss Sunday dinners with my family, and my friend just came back from the Middle East. She served four years and now she'll be going to nursing school at UC Davis.'

'That is a good nursing program,' Irina declared. 'My alma mater.' He'd put the tray down in the kitchen and she slipped her arm through Hunter's. 'You will tell me about your family. Please.'

Rafe smirked when Tom gave him a *Help me* look. 'You're on your own, pal.' But his smirk became a smile when he saw Mercy at the table. She was smiling back, which settled some of the worry swirling in his mind.

But then he saw Farrah chatting with Sasha, and remembered what was coming. He flicked a glance at his mother and saw she was giving Farrah a sad look of her own. *Dammit.* Rafe hoped she wasn't going to let the cat out of the bag before Captain Holmes arrived, but his fears were put to rest when she met his eyes and gave him a brisk nod before cutting a generous slice of bird's milk cake for Tom.

Rafe came up behind her and pressed a kiss to her temple. 'Love you, Mom.'

Her smile was tremulous. 'Of course you do. I am awesome.'

'Yes, you are.' He dipped to peck her cheek. 'Save me some cake, okay?'

She laughed now, shooing him away with her apron, a sweet blush staining her cheeks. 'Go. Make your goo-goo eyes at Mercy,' she whispered, making him blush.

'Yes, ma'am.' He straightened, pasted a *Nothing wrong here* expression on his face, and, obeying his mother, sat next to Mercy while his mother invited Tom to sit.

It looked like Tom would agree, but he checked his phone and sighed. 'I can't. I have to get back to the office.'

'Please, take the cake,' Irina said firmly. 'I will wrap for you.'

'Your mother is a force of nature,' Mercy whispered. She looked perfectly normal, perfectly calm. Except her voice became worried when she leaned in, her lips brushing his ear. 'What's wrong?'

Shit. He was pretty good at his *Nothing wrong here* face. He'd spent a lifetime perfecting it, in fact. But she saw right through him. 'I'll tell you later. Trust me for now?'

She pulled back enough to study his eyes. 'Yes, I trust you. Not just for now.'

Leaving him speechless. Trust was a rare commodity for Mercy Callahan. He'd known that from the moment he'd first heard her name. He'd been comforting seventeen-year-old Gideon when he couldn't break through his sister's shields. Rafe had known it every one of the minutes she'd sat by his side after he'd been shot. She was instinctively wary. *But she trusts me.*

He wasn't ever going to make her regret it.

Twelve

Granite Bay, California
Sunday, 16 April, 5.15 P.M.

Rafe kept an eye on the clock, glancing at Mercy and Farrah every few minutes. Neither woman had her phone and he'd already pulled Gideon aside, giving him the heads-up on Farrah's aunt.

'I'm glad you told me,' Gideon had murmured. 'I was about to call John with Mercy. He's probably heard already, if it's on the local news, and he'd tell her. I don't want Mercy to have to put on a brave face until Farrah's fiancé arrives. She's had to fake being okay enough for a lifetime.' He looked torn. 'She and Farrah were talking about the Romeros while you were in with Hunter, and Mercy mentioned how much she loved the old lady. They had dinner a few times a week and Mercy would take her to her doctor's appointments. She was kind of like Mercy's grandmother. I hate to keep this from her, even though I know we have to.'

'You can plead ignorance. In case she's too angry with me to let me help her, she'll still have you.'

Gideon had given him a slightly chastising look. 'I think we should stick to the truth, don't you? I don't want to give her a reason to distrust either of us. She's been told enough lies in her life.'

Rafe closed his eyes, ashamed. 'You're right. That was stupid of me.'

'No. That was generous of you. You were willing to be the bad guy to keep the door open for me, even though you clearly want her for yourself.'

'I . . .' The denial had trailed away. Because it would have been a lie, too.

Gideon had rolled his eyes. 'I've seen this coming for weeks. And, for the record, I hope it works out. She's good for you and vice versa. So let's not underestimate her, okay? Now we should get back or we'll have to answer questions and I don't want to break my own no-lying rule.'

Now, back at the family table, Rafe was glad that Gideon had kept his head straight. But it had been forty minutes since Captain Holmes had called and Rafe knew he needed to tell Mercy now, away from the group. If she was going to fall apart, he could at least give her the privacy to do so.

He nudged her shoulder with his. 'I need to talk to you about something,' he said softly. 'Come with me.'

Sasha let out a low whistle. 'Is that what you're calling it now? Talk?'

Irina leveled Sasha with a glare. 'Show your brother some respect.'

Sasha huffed, looking a little hurt at the rebuke. 'Okay, Mom. I'll rein it in.'

'Thank you,' Irina said, but Karl looked concerned.

'Is everything all right, *maya lubimaya*?' he asked, sliding his arm around her shoulders.

Irina's smile was brittle. 'I'm just tired. I didn't sleep well last night.'

Sasha's face fell. 'I'm sorry, Mom. I didn't think . . .' She got up and, standing behind her mother's chair, wrapped her arms around her. 'After all that talk of the past, I should have been more considerate.'

'You're fine, *Sahinka*. I'm a little on edge.'

Farrah began to gather the dessert plates and cups. 'Then you sit and relax. I'll clean up.'

'Thank you, Farrah,' Irina said faintly.

Rafe hoped Captain Holmes would get there soon. He didn't think his mother could hold her composure much longer. He tugged on Mercy's hand, leading her down the hall to the first-floor guest bedroom.

'Um, Rafe?' she asked, and he looked back when she stopped walking. 'Where are we going?'

203

'Trust me?' he asked, and she sighed.

'You're pushing it, pal,' she said lightly.

He might have smiled at any other time, but his heart hurt for what he had to tell her. 'I'm sorry.'

She immediately sobered, stopping outside the guest-room door. 'What's wrong?'

He pressed a finger to her lips. 'Please.'

She gripped his hand so hard he winced. But she said nothing more, hesitantly sitting on the edge of the bed while he closed the door.

He joined her on the bed, threading their fingers together. 'Hunter gave me some bad news.' He wanted to kick himself, phrasing it that way. It wasn't bad news. It was horrific. 'I . . .'

She squeezed his hand. 'Just say it, Rafe.'

'Quill Romero is dead.'

She jerked back like she'd been slapped, the color draining from her face. 'What?'

'Her body was discovered sometime during the night.'

Mercy's eyes were filling with tears, her breaths shallow and too fast. 'How?' But he could see she already understood. She covered her mouth to muffle a sob. 'Because of me.'

'No, honey. No.' Rafe gathered her close until she was halfway on his lap. 'We don't know that yet. It appears to have been a robbery.'

Mercy's body shook as she tried to quietly cry. 'Why? Why would someone rob her?' She clung to him, both arms around his neck, and he pulled her fully to his lap. One of these days he wanted to hold her like this when her heart wasn't breaking, but that wouldn't be today.

'Did she know that you were leaving for Sacramento yesterday morning?'

Mercy could only nod against his neck. 'And now she's dead because of me.'

'No, it's because a sonofabitch is obsessed with you, baby. You can't blame—'

She shoved away, glaring at him. 'Don't you dare tell me not to blame myself. I *loved* her. I *loved* her, Rafe. And she's dead and it's because of me.'

'You aren't responsible for anything Ephraim Burton has done.'

'Aren't I? If I'd cooperated six weeks ago and helped Gideon's boss find him, then he couldn't have killed her. And if I hadn't fought him in Eden, he wouldn't have hurt me so bad and Mama wouldn't have tried to smuggle me out and she'd still be alive, too.'

He stared at her. 'Mercy. Listen to yourself.'

'*I am*,' she hissed. '*I am* listening to myself and maybe I don't make sense to you, but this is how I feel, so don't you dare tell me it's wrong.'

'You're right. I don't have the right. I might have the right to my opinion, but not to force it on you.'

Mercy's gaze lingered on his for a long moment, so full of pain that Rafe felt his own eyes sting. 'I have to tell Farrah,' she whispered.

'No. Her captain is on his way. He flew out first thing after Miss Romero's body was found. He wants to be here for her.'

'How much longer will we need to wait? I don't think I can keep this from her.' Then her eyes narrowed. 'Your mother knows. That's why she snapped at Sasha.'

He nodded once. 'Mom overheard Tom and me talking in the office. I didn't want you to hear it in front of everyone. I thought you might need some quiet to process things, and that's hard to do with an audience.'

She pursed her lips as the tears began to flow again. Clearly, her anger was gone, and it looked like it had been replaced by a sadness that was bone deep. But there was something else there, something soft and grateful. 'Thank you. I appreciate it. That can't have been an easy secret to keep.'

When he opened his arms, she leaned into him, returning her arms to his neck. 'I'm sorry I yelled at you.'

He stroked her hair, wishing there were more he could do for her. 'It's okay. I get it. It's a shock and you need to process your grief the best way you know how.'

She went still. 'You sound like you know what you're talking about.'

'I do. I lost someone I loved and it almost killed me.' He remembered the day he'd found Bella's body. That was twice that he'd thought of her in the last hour, after burying her memory so deep that he'd gone whole months without feeling the crushing grief. He thought about hiding it now, but Mercy deserved his honesty. 'And I blamed myself, too. It wasn't logical or reasonable, but it was my truth.'

One of her hands let go of his neck, sliding down to cup his cheek. 'What was her name?'

He flinched, not expecting the question. But he should have. Mercy had seen more than he'd wanted her to in those weeks after the shooting, those weeks that she'd barely left his side. 'Bella.'

'I'm sorry. I'm so sorry, Rafe.'

'Thank you. It was about three years ago. I manage not to think about her when I'm awake.' He had no control over his nightmares. They were more frequent than he wanted to admit, even to himself.

'But not when you're asleep,' she said quietly, with an understanding that broke his heart all over again. He didn't want to know Mercy's nightmares, but he'd listen if that was what she needed. 'How did she die?'

He hesitated. 'She was murdered.'

'Rafe. Oh my God.' She started to say more, then shook her head. 'You don't have to tell me. Unless you need to talk to someone. Then I'm here.'

He pulled her closer, kissing the top of her head. 'Not today. Today is about Farrah.'

She shuddered against him. 'When is André getting here?'

'Any minute now.' And as if on cue, the doorbell rang. 'That's probably him.'

'Do you need to greet him?' she asked.

'No. Mom knows he's coming to see Farrah. She knows he needs to give her the news alone. She'll probably put them in Dad's office.'

'Maybe you can go anyway,' she murmured. 'Tell him that whenever she needs me, I'll go to her.'

He gave her a light squeeze, then tilted her chin so that he could see her face. 'Do you really want time alone for yourself? I can go if you need me to.'

She nodded, wincing guiltily. 'Just a little time. I need to pull myself together. Farrah doesn't need me to be a weepy mess. She needs me strong.'

'Maybe. Or maybe she'll want to cry it out with someone else who loved her aunt.'

Mercy considered it, then dropped her eyes. But not before he saw her shame. 'You're right. This is one of those moments I wish I had a primer for social situations. I always pick the wrong thing to do or say.'

'Hey.' He waited until she looked at him. 'You haven't said the wrong thing to me. In fact, most of what you've said has been pretty damn perfect.'

'No, it hasn't been, but thanks for saying so.'

'Mercy, don't tell me what I think. I told you the truth.' *Thank you, Gideon. Thank you for reminding me to tell her the truth.* 'I will *always* tell you the truth.'

She clamped a hand over her mouth again, but the whimper escaped. He grabbed the tissue box from the nightstand. 'I'll go down to talk to Holmes, but he probably has Farrah in the office already. You got your phone?'

She shook her head. 'I left it in the kitchen.'

'I'll send Gideon back with it. He'll need to see that you're okay with his own eyes.'

Her mouth bent in a watery smile. 'He will.'

Hoping he wasn't pushing too hard, Rafe dropped a quick, chaste kiss on her mouth. 'Once you get your phone, text me if you need anything, okay? I'll text you when Farrah needs you.'

She was staring up at him, her eyes wide, her lips parted, looking a little kiss-drunk. He smiled down at her because the look on her face was kind of adorable and much easier to witness than the agonized guilt. 'Rest. Sleep if you need to.'

'Wait.' She rose gracefully. 'Thank you,' she whispered. Then she pulled his head down for another kiss, this one deeper, longer.

Better. *So much better.* 'Thank you,' she repeated huskily. 'I'll see you later.'

It was Rafe's turn to be kiss-drunk and he backed out of the bedroom, stumbling and nearly falling on his ass. Luckily Gideon was there to keep him upright.

'You okay, Rafe?' he asked.

Rafe nodded, licking his lips and finding that her taste had lingered. 'Yeah. What's up?'

'Holmes is here,' he said. 'And Mercy's phone was ringing so I brought it to her. I think it was John.'

'I told Mercy that I'd text her when Farrah was ready to see her. Go on now. She's expecting you.'

Rafe made his way back to the kitchen, still dazed by that kiss. Sasha, Daisy, Erin, and his father wore matching looks of devastation and his mother's face was set firmly as she put together a tea tray. Strangely the sight of his mother's capable hands arranging teacups soothed his aching heart. He didn't know how many times in his life he'd watched her doing the same thing when one of them had received bad news. Teen breakups, lost sports tournaments, failing grades, skinned knees. Irina's answer was always a cup of tea and cake.

Another wave of love bubbled up, making his chest so tight he could barely breathe. She looked up and smiled sadly. 'I already made a tray for Farrah and her captain. This one is for Mercy.'

'She . . . she asked for a little quiet time. Gid's in there with her now.'

Irina lifted a brow. 'Thus a tray, Raphael. She can drink all the tea she wants *alone*, because I am taking her a *tray*.'

Unbelievably he smiled. 'I love you, Mom.'

She sniffed. 'So you have said.' Then she blinked, sending fresh tears down her cheeks. 'I love you too, *sinok rodnoy moi*. You have a good heart. But terrible table-waiting skills, yes? I remember the job you lost because you spilled an entire tray of drinks on that poor woman. So I will carry this tray myself.'

Rafe's laugh was more like a hiccuped sob. 'You're not wrong, Mom. Thank you.' He wanted to say so much more, but he didn't even know where to start. But he didn't think he needed to when she kissed his cheek on her way out.

Rafe sat between his father and sister with a sigh.

'This day sucks,' Sasha said sullenly.

'We need to cancel the interview,' Daisy said, stroking Brutus like her life depended on it.

'Let's let Mercy decide that,' Karl said. 'I made the mistake of assuming I knew her mind yesterday. Let's not do that again.'

Personally, Rafe wanted to cancel the interview as well. He wanted to protect Mercy from the prying eyes that would, no doubt, translate to disgusting comments on social media, no matter what she said. But his father was right. Mercy had the right to make decisions for herself.

She was strong enough to hold her head high and deal with anything life threw at her. *Stronger than me.*

So he nodded to his father. 'You're right. We have a few hours before the interview. Let her make up her own mind.'

Sacramento, California
Sunday, 16 April, 5.35 P.M.

'Thank you for coming in, Mr Bunker. I am Special Agent in Charge Molina.' The stern woman at the head of the interrogation table pointed to the man sitting beside her. 'This is Special Agent Hunter. I understand you have information for us.'

Stomach quaking, Jeff nodded at Molina and Hunter. *I'm sitting at an interrogation table. I'm being interrogated. By the fucking FBI. This nightmare keeps going from bad to worse.* He startled when his mother nudged him. 'Oh, um, yes. Yes, ma'am.'

Molina didn't smile. She studied him closely, making him wish that he hadn't eaten before he'd come. And making him grateful that his mother had come with him, even though he was sixteen years old and should have been able to do this alone. No matter what the law said.

'Tell me your story,' Molina said briskly, almost as though she thought he was lying before he even got started.

He wiped his damp palms on his jeans. 'Okay.' He looked away, trying to slow his pulse. 'Sorry, I'm nervous.'

Molina said nothing, but his mother squeezed his knee. 'Try to relax,' his mother murmured. 'The worst is over.'

Jeff wasn't sure about that. 'Okay, um . . . okay. I'm a communications major at Sac State, concentrating in journalism. I got a job with *Gabber*. It's a . . .' Piece of trash? Shit? 'A gossip blog.'

'When was this?' Molina asked.

'About three months ago. I mostly did stupid little stories, like parades or New Year's resolutions of sorority girls, that kind of thing. But then that serial killer was caught back in February, you know?'

'Yes,' Molina said mildly. 'I know.'

Jeff knew that she did. She'd been on the scene the night it all went down. 'I read about the three women who escaped and I figured that was the story no one was really telling. Well, until CNN told it last week. But at first, nobody was really talking about the women who lived, just the killer himself and the women who died. And I wanted to know more, especially about Mercy Callahan.'

Molina tilted her head to one side. 'Why Miss Callahan?'

'Because she intrigued me. I saw the footage taken at the hospital when she was abducted. It was like she'd gone catatonic and I wanted to know why.' He'd seen that same look when she'd nearly been abducted the night before and for some reason, it made his chest hurt. Now, he knew why. Now he knew that she was a victim of sexual assault. *And I'm the scum of the earth.*

Because of him, Mercy was having to relive her assault again. *I am the worst.*

But he was trying to make it better. *That counts, right?*

'So what did you do?' Hunter asked, even though the man had to have known the answer.

'I started researching her. I found out where she lived, where she went to school, and that she'd grown up in the foster system here in California, but moved when she aged out.'

Agent Hunter narrowed his eyes. 'How did you know that she was in the foster system?'

Because it hadn't been in any of the newspapers or online rags. 'I, um, talked to her next-door neighbor. In New Orleans.'

Molina's expression never changed. 'You followed Miss Callahan all the way to New Orleans.'

'Um, yes, ma'am. *Gabber* said they'd reimburse me for my travel, so I took a few days and went out east. My mother didn't know. She's not involved in any of this. I told her I was with my study group on campus.'

Molina was scarily silent, not even an encouraging nod. So he focused on Agent Hunter, bothered by the knowledge that he'd seen this man before, but couldn't remember where or when. 'I started out at the university in New Orleans, asking people in her department if they remembered her. I thought it was worth a try because it had only been four years since she graduated. Most of the staff did, but nobody would talk about her. They all scowled at me and told me to leave, that they didn't talk to gossip magazines. I was about to leave when this woman called me over. She said that she'd taken classes with Mercy and that she was a "stuck-up bitch".' His glance flitted to Molina. 'Sorry, ma'am. That's a quote.'

Molina lifted one eyebrow, making her look like a female Spock. 'Continue, Mr Bunker.'

'Oh, okay. She said that if I really wanted the true story of Mercy Callahan to talk to Stan Prescott, that he'd been her boyfriend in college. She even gave me the guy's address.'

'And that didn't strike you as odd?' Agent Hunter asked.

Jeff shrugged. 'Not really. I know lots of girls like her. You keep your back to the wall, if you know what I mean.' He mimed a stabbing motion, then remembered where he was and dropped his hands into his lap. 'I wouldn't date one and I wouldn't trust one with my secrets, but they tend to be good sources of information. So I took the address and went to visit the ex. He had a lot to say and none of it was good. He painted Miss Callahan as a party girl who liked to put out. He even had a video.' Jeff shifted in his chair, his cheeks heating with shame. 'It was only a clip, like maybe ten seconds.' He closed his eyes. 'She was naked and on a bed, but nothing else happened in the clip.'

Molina rapped her knuckles on the table. 'Look at me, please, Mr Bunker. Thank you,' she said when he obeyed. 'The video posted online was four minutes long. How did you get from a ten-second clip to a four-minute video?'

'He said that if I wanted it, I'd need to pay for it. I asked how much and he said five thousand. I laughed at him, told him no way my boss would allow that. He kind of shrugged and said he'd take three thousand. I asked my boss, expecting him to say hell no, but he agreed. I was shocked.'

'And did you pay him?' Molina asked.

'Yes. Well, half. It was half up front, then the other half on publication of my article. He was cool with that and gave me the video after I gave him fifteen hundred. He also told me to look up Peter Firmin, another of Miss Callahan's exes, so I did. He told the opposite story, that she was frigid and cold and he'd kicked her to the curb. I told him that I had a video of her partying and he kind of laughed and said that if he'd known she'd needed a roofie to put out that he would have kept trying, but then quickly said he was joking. I put all that into the article, but I removed that comment and Stan Prescott's story entirely before I sent it in to my editor. And I never sent him the video. I swear it.'

'Why did you delete Prescott's story?' Molina asked.

Jeff frowned. 'It didn't feel right. I saw that catatonic look on her face in the hospital surveillance video from February and it didn't match with Prescott's description. I told my editor, Nolan Albanesi, that I was removing some content before I sent it in. I have all my files, ma'am. I can prove to you that I didn't send what got printed under my name.'

Molina nodded coolly. 'And we will look at those files, Mr Bunker. If you didn't give Mr Albanesi the video, where do you think he got it?'

'From Stan Prescott, I think. He knew my source's name because he'd needed a name and a phone number for accounting purposes. Or so he said. I think he called him and got the video straight from the source.'

Molina nodded once. 'All right. Apparently you also visited Miss Callahan's apartment.'

'I never went in,' Jeff protested.

'How did you get her address?' Agent Hunter asked. 'She's gone to great pains to protect her privacy.'

Because of the roofie guy, Jeff thought glumly. 'I asked the second ex – Peter Firmin – if he knew where she worked and he told me to check out the NOPD lab, so I went there and waited until she came out. Then I followed her home. The next day, I got into her building and figured out which apartment was hers and started knocking on her neighbors' doors. That's how I met Miss Romero.'

'The deceased,' Agent Hunter clarified.

'Right. I pretended to be selling magazines and talked to Miss Romero for about twenty minutes. She gave me some cookies and told me that Mercy was a good person. That she took Miss Romero to the doctor and made her dinner and baked cookies for all the people in the building. That just left me with more questions, because Miss Romero's description was nothing like the others. I thanked her and left. That was Thursday afternoon. The next day, this past Friday, I went to the NOPD lab and asked to see Miss Callahan, but I was told she'd taken some personal leave for a family emergency. That was one more thing that didn't fit, because Miss Romero didn't mention it at all. So I went back to see the nice old lady.' He swallowed hard. 'I was about to knock on her door when I heard a noise inside the apartment. I guess I must have been twitchy, because I ducked around a corner into a hallway. A second later, a man came out of it. He was smiling, but it wasn't a nice smile. Kind of like the Grinch before his heart grew, y'know?'

Molina still didn't react. 'Would you characterize the man's smile as evil?'

'At that moment, more creepy. After I saw Miss Romero dead on the floor, definitely.'

'You went into her apartment?' Hunter asked.

'Yeah. Stupid of me. I thought maybe she'd gotten robbed, but the guy who left didn't look like he was carrying anything. He might have had jewelry stashed in his pockets, but nothing that I saw.'

'What did you do then?'

'For a minute I just stood in the hallway and stared. Then I got worried about the old lady and knocked on the door, but it swung open. He hadn't pulled it closed. I went in and saw her on the floor, just crumpled in a heap. And I . . .' He looked up at his mother for courage and she gave him a supportive nod. 'I picked her up. I thought maybe she'd passed out, so I put her on the sofa and tried to find her pulse. I started to call 911, then realized she was dead.' He dropped his gaze, ashamed once again. 'I panicked, plain and simple. I thought the police would blame it on me.'

'So you ran home,' Hunter said.

Jeff lifted his gaze to Hunter's, surprised to see compassion in the man's expression. 'I did. All I wanted was to get away from New Orleans, so I got a ticket on the first flight out the next morning.' He shuddered. 'And I saw the man on the plane with me. I was so scared that he'd recognize me. I didn't move the whole flight. Just kept my head down and pretended to sleep. But I couldn't sleep. All I could see was poor Miss Romero on the floor.'

'And when you landed?' Molina prompted when he went silent.

'I went straight home and worked on my article. I worked up until seven last night, and then Nolan Albanesi called and demanded that I send in whatever I had written, because Miss Callahan was in the news again, because of the attempted abduction. That's when I edited out the parts from the exes and sent it in. I never had the video on my laptop or put it on the *Gabber* server.'

'And then?' Molina asked.

Jeff took a swallow from the water bottle they'd provided, because his mouth was suddenly dry as dust. 'Then I had to figure out what to do about Miss Romero. The, um, the deceased. I didn't know how long it would take for someone to find her . . .' His gulp was audible, but he was beyond caring now. 'You know, her body. And then when I checked the news and saw that the man I'd seen coming out of Miss Romero's place was the same guy that tried to take Miss Callahan? I was too scared to do anything. Except get drunk.'

'And then?' Hunter asked.

'I fell asleep and my mom woke me up at about one a.m. I knew I had to make this right, so I called the NOPD and reported Miss Romero's body.'

Molina did the one-raised-brow thing again. 'Anonymously?'

Like she didn't already know the answer. He barely kept from rolling his eyes, but that would have been a knee-jerk panicked response. 'Yes, ma'am. I was still afraid that I'd be blamed for the old lady's death.'

'But he did call,' his mother said.

'I need to make this right for Miss Callahan and Miss Romero,' Jeff said. 'As soon as possible. That's why I'm here. Making amends.'

Molina pulled two laminated sheets from her briefcase. She slid the first across the table and Jeff was startled to see a photo array. 'Do you see the man who left Miss Romero's apartment?'

'Yes, ma'am.' He pointed to the man the press was calling Ephraim Burton, aka Harry Franklin.

'And this one?' She passed him the second sheet. 'Do you see the man who sold you the video?'

Jeff searched each face carefully. 'No, ma'am. None of these men are Stan Prescott. I have a photo of him, if that would be helpful.' He pulled out his phone and swiped until he found the photo he was looking for. 'This one. I took it for my own records. He didn't know I took it.'

Molina blinked, seeming surprised for the first time since they'd sat down. 'I see. Thank you, Mr Bunker.'

Jeff frowned. 'What's wrong?'

'Can you send us that photo?' Hunter asked.

'Why?' Jeff pressed. 'What's wrong?'

Hunter and Molina shared a look, Molina giving Hunter a slight nod. 'The man in that photo is not Stan Prescott,' Hunter said. 'We don't know who he is yet.'

'I still have the flash drive he saved the video to. I brought it with me. You want it?'

'Yes, we do,' Molina said with a brisk nod. She rose and gathered her things. 'Agent Hunter will take it into evidence, then see you out. Thank you for your cooperation, Mr Bunker.'

Jeff drew a breath. 'Are you . . . are you going to arrest me?'

Molina's mouth quirked up in the barest hint of a smile, shocking him. 'Not today. We may ask you to come back in if we need further clarification. Mrs Bunker, thank you for bringing him in. We appreciate how hard this was for both of you.'

Jeff's mother said nothing until Molina was gone. Then she pressed the heel of her hand to her heart. 'I thought you were done for, Jeffy.'

He was so relieved that he didn't correct her, even though it was humiliating to be called 'Jeffy' in front of a Fed. 'Me too. Let's go, please?'

She nodded hard. 'Absolutely. Agent Hunter, we're ready now.'

'Just a moment.' Hunter held out an evidence bag like he was trick-or-treating. 'Flash drive?'

'Oh.' Jeff dug it from his pocket and dropped it in the bag. 'I don't want anything to do with it.'

'That's smart, kid. It should go without saying, but I'll say it anyway: Do not approach the press or respond if they ask you questions.' Hunter wrote up a receipt for the flash drive, then sealed the bag. 'Look, I'm not trying to scare you or anything, but you really should retain an attorney.'

Jeff's eyes nearly popped from his head. Beside him, his mother was nearly vibrating in a combination of fear and outrage. 'But I didn't do anything wrong!' he cried.

'But you're involved. Do yourself a favor and protect yourself, okay? Come on. I'll walk you out.' Hunter led them through a warren of hallways until they were at the main doors. 'Here's my card,' he said. 'If you think of anything else, please let me know.'

Jeff took it and followed his mother out into the afternoon sun. His knees were still a little shaky. He'd honestly thought they'd keep him and knew Hunter was right about getting an attorney. 'Mom, Agent Hunter was right. I need an attorney. Do you think your judge friend would have a recommendation?'

Her mouth firmed, determined. 'If he doesn't, I'll find you a lawyer myself.'

'Thank you. I'll pay you back, some day. I promise.'

Her laugh was shaky. 'You might have to do that, Jeffy. Right now, all I want to do is go home and take a nap for a week.'

'Me too. But first, I've got one more stop to make, if that's okay with you.'

She looked at him with pride. 'Granite Bay?'

'Yes. I need to apologize to Mercy Callahan.'

Thirteen

Granite Bay, California
Sunday, 16 April, 5.35 P.M.

Ephraim had watched the house with the blue shutters for the past thirty minutes while the old man puttered in his garden. He hadn't seen anyone else coming or going, but that didn't mean there weren't more people in the house. However, he needed a place to hide and this house had a view of the Sokolovs' driveway. It would have to do.

He'd parked the beat-up car that he'd stolen after leaving the costume store. He could go back for it if he had to, because it was only about a mile away. He'd left it in the parking area for Folsom Lake, the lot overrun by people out enjoying the beautiful spring day. The hard part had been filling the duffel bag with the rifle, handguns, rope, and duct tape without anyone noticing.

But he must have been successful, because no one had looked twice when he'd set off toward the lake. After that, it had been easy to cut through the woods to get to this mansion with a view.

Most people would choose the view of the lake, of course. Ephraim wanted the view of the house across the street.

The man in the garden was about seventy, his back stooped as he pruned the roses. He wore white knee socks, a plain white T-shirt, and a pair of khaki shorts. Ephraim might have mistaken him for a gardener had it not been for the man's shoes. They were leather and expensive-looking, so he was probably the homeowner. Which didn't really matter that much.

Ephraim only cared that the man didn't look like he'd put up much of a fight. As long as he wasn't armed, taking over this house shouldn't be too hard.

Ephraim waited until the old man had lowered himself into a lawn chair, gaze fixed on his roses. He heard the man sigh as he approached, the sound one more of melancholy than physical weariness.

Giving one last look around, Ephraim drew Regina's gun from his jacket pocket and clapped his hand over the man's mouth. 'If you fight me,' he whispered, 'you will die. If you scream, you will die. Nod once if you understand.'

The man nodded once, strangely calm. Instincts on high alert, Ephraim looked around again, expecting to see security jumping from the bushes, but no one appeared. Yanking the man to his feet, Ephraim dragged him into the house. He'd watched the man come and go and hadn't noticed him fooling with anything that could have been an alarm system. Once he got inside, he saw that there was an alarm panel, but it was currently green-lit. Unarmed.

Excellent.

Covering the man's mouth with duct tape, Ephraim tied his hands behind his back with a length of Granny's rope and shoved him into a chair. A heavy one that the man couldn't move on his own. It was made of mahogany. Nice. Amos back in Eden could make better, but Amos was also a master carpenter. Ephraim couldn't help but wonder what Amos could make with wood like this, though.

He filed the thought away for later. He could decorate his new quarters any way he wanted once he had Pastor's passwords for the offshore accounts.

He'd already observed that the man didn't have a wallet in his pocket, but a quick look around the kitchen revealed a wallet and a set of keys. He was happy to find that the wallet contained about five hundred dollars in twenties and several credit cards. He left the cards alone and pulled out the man's driver's license.

'Sean MacGuire,' he murmured. The photo matched the old man's face, still suspiciously calm. 'What's with you?' he asked. 'Why aren't you afraid?'

MacGuire merely watched him with rheumy eyes.

'You are a freaky bastard,' Ephraim muttered, then, Regina's golden silenced gun in hand, went room to room checking for other occupants. After a thorough search through closets and under beds, he was satisfied that he and Sean MacGuire were alone.

The old man's bedroom held a few clues. There was a framed photo on the nightstand of MacGuire with an older woman, both smiling broadly, the Eiffel Tower in the background. Another showed them smiling in front of the Taj Mahal, and yet another had them wearing parkas and standing next to a signpost that read *Antarctica*. The couple appeared to be intrepid travelers.

Or they had been. The man's bed was unmade, but only half was used. The other half looked as if it hadn't been touched. There were no women's things on the dresser and only a few female outfits in the closet. They were the ones in the photos, Ephraim noticed.

He got an odd lump in his throat as he realized that the old woman had probably passed away, leaving the man alone.

Hopefully alone. It would suck if someone else lived here or visited.

But still. It made him not want to kill the guy. *Maybe I won't.* It would depend on the man's attitude and behavior. After all, once he grabbed Mercy, he was headed back to Eden. Nobody could find him there, so it wouldn't hurt to let the old man live.

But if MacGuire tried something, Ephraim would kill him without a second thought.

He chose the room with the best view of the Sokolovs' front door and pulled a chair in front of the window. For now, the driveway was filled with the same vehicles that had been there when he'd arrived, in the same places, which was a relief. The black FBI SUV was gone, but unless the tall Fed had taken Mercy and Gideon with him, Ephraim was still in luck.

He went back to the kitchen to find the man still sitting, the expression on his face unchanged. 'Your old lady's dead?' he asked.

The old man flinched. *So it's probably new.*

'Sorry to hear that. Look, Sean, I don't want to have to kill you, but I will. Just leave me be and I'll be out of your hair before you know it.' He opened the commercial-sized refrigerator. 'I'm starving. You want me to make you something, too? Nod once for yes.'

A single nod.

'Okey-dokey then,' Ephraim said cheerfully. 'Is it just you, wandering around this big old house?'

No nod. Nothing but a fleeting glimpse toward the far wall. Where there was a photo of a woman who appeared to be about forty, her arms around a little girl with red pigtails and Mickey Mouse ears. Sleeping Beauty Castle was in the distance. A man stood next to the woman, with a baby in one of those papoose things, or whatever the hell people called them these days.

'Your daughter?' Ephraim asked.

No response once again, but now the man's eyes flickered in fear.

'Yeah, your daughter.' Ephraim constructed two sandwiches. He ate one, then the other before making a third for MacGuire. He pulled the tape from the man's mouth, taking more care than he normally would. 'If you try to scream or bite me—'

'You'll kill me,' MacGuire said with a faint Irish accent. 'Got it.'

Ephraim held the sandwich to the man's lips, waiting until he took a bite. 'Why aren't you afraid of me?' he asked.

'Because I don't care. As you've so noted, my "old lady" is dead. We were married forty-nine years. I'm ready to go.'

At least he was honest. 'All right, then. I'm quite willing to send you to her, just remember that.' He gave MacGuire another bite of the sandwich, then put it in the fridge. 'You can finish it later.' Maybe. 'I've got things to do.' Once MacGuire had swallowed, he applied another piece of duct tape to his mouth and went to find the router so that he could get the Wi-Fi password. He had some purchases to make, and then he'd post himself at the window until the party across the street broke up and Mercy went home.

Granite Bay, California
Sunday, 16 April, 6.00 P.M.

'You can call John back if you want to,' Gideon said, breaking the tense silence as Mercy stared at her phone. She'd been willing herself to do that very thing from the moment he'd brought her phone from the kitchen. It gave her something else to obsess about, she supposed. Something to help take her mind off Farrah, who was still in Karl's office with André. *I'm so sorry, Ro. So damn sorry.* But there wasn't anything she could do for Farrah right now, so she was trying to gather the courage to call her half brother and at least make *that* situation right.

They sat sideways on the edge of the guest-room bed, hip to hip, silent until Gideon had suggested she return her brother's call. *No, our brother's call.* Mercy really wanted to be by herself for this, but she sensed that Gideon needed her. Or he needed her to need him.

Which I do. She could be honest with herself about that, at least. Finally.

'He's got to be worried sick about me,' she murmured. John had called twice in the past ten minutes, had left two voice mails and ten texts imploring her to call him.

'Mercy, you don't need to tell him about me. Not until you're ready.'

'I *am* ready,' she insisted. 'I'm just scared.'

Gideon stroked a gentle hand down her back. 'Do you want me to leave?'

Yes. And no. 'No,' she said. 'I told him that I'd lied to him.'

Gideon blinked. 'Really? When?'

'When he called me at two a.m. after André had called him. After you called André. He didn't understand, but he was kind. Said we'd all get together and figure it out.'

'And we will.' Gideon looked away for a moment, then locked his gaze with hers. 'I was hurt. Partly because you were so angry that you kept them from me, but mostly because you chose him to be your brother.'

Mercy's eyes filled with new tears. She couldn't deny Gideon's words, because they were true. 'I'm sorry.'

His smile was sad. 'But I get it and we *will* figure it all out. Now, do you want me to go or stay?'

She braved a smile, the tension in her chest loosening when he smiled back. 'Stay.'

'Then I'll stay,' he said simply. 'Want me to call?'

'No, I can do it.' She unlocked her phone, her finger hovering over the number for John Benz.

'I still can't believe Mama named you Mercedes,' Gideon said.

'Her mother said that we were both breech and had to be delivered by C-section. Apparently "Mercedes" was the result of postsurgery painkillers.'

'Mama never did drugs,' Gideon said thoughtfully. 'Not even when we were desperate and things were horrible.'

'I don't remember any of that.'

'Why would you? You were barely a year old when we arrived in Eden. I have spotty memories of the time before and I was almost five. But we usually had food and you were always clean. She wasn't a good mother in some ways, but she did her best.'

'She saved our lives,' Mercy said simply.

Gideon swallowed hard. 'Yeah, she did. Let's do this call before my allergies make my eyes water.'

'Allergies suck, don't they?' she asked as she hit John's name on her phone screen. 'Time for you to meet your brother.'

Gideon stiffened, taking in a huge lungful of air. 'I'm nervous,' he confessed.

Mercy patted his knee. 'You're going to love each other. Don't worry.'

John answered on the first ring. 'Mercy? Is that you?'

'It is. I'm sorry I missed your calls. We've had a . . . situation here. Have you seen the news about Farrah's great-aunt?'

'Yes. That's why I was trying to call you. Are you all right?'

'I will be. Listen, John . . .' *Just say it.* 'I'm with Gideon. Can I switch to FaceTime?'

A long moment of silence. 'Does he really want to talk to me?'

'Yes, he really does. He would have been talking to you all along, if I'd told him about you.'

Gideon squeezed her shoulder. 'If he's not comfortable talking to me, it's okay. We have time, Mercy.'

'Do we?' They didn't know what life was going to throw their way. They didn't know if they'd survive this latest fracas. *I don't know that I'll survive Ephraim Burton.*

Gideon blinked at her, startled. 'Of course we do.'

'Is that him?' John asked in a choked whisper.

Oh God. John was crying. Which made Mercy's tears start all over again. *Dammit.* 'Don't cry, John. Please don't cry.'

'I'm not,' John claimed, then laughed weakly. 'Okay, I am. Put us on FaceTime, Mercy.'

She did and grabbed a few tissues to wipe her face. God, her face hurt. Why did crying hurt so much? 'John, this is Gideon Reynolds. Gideon, John Benz.'

Gideon stared at the screen, a look of wonder on his face. 'Hi.'

John chuckled awkwardly. 'Hi yourself. I'm . . . Well, this is un-expected. I'm . . . I don't know what to say. It's so nice to finally meet you, Gideon.'

'Same here,' Gideon said, then pulled Mercy closer and kissed her temple. 'Mercy and I cleared up a few . . . misunderstandings and she told me about you.'

'What kind of misunderstandings?' John asked, a little suspi-ciously.

Mercy threw up a prayer that John would be as forgiving as Gideon had been. 'Do you remember when I told you that the man my mother married after she left Texas was abusive?'

John was silent for a long moment. 'Yes,' he finally said. 'There was a lot you didn't say, but you did tell me that.'

'I told you that she was killed while getting me away.'

'Yes, you did.' He hesitated. 'But the PI who Grandpa Benz hired to find you could find no police reports about her death.'

'It wasn't reported to the police,' Mercy said, unsure what she was allowed to say about Eden. She didn't want to jeopardize the FBI's ongoing investigation by revealing too much.

224

'John,' Gideon cut in. 'This is a very long story that we should tell you in person, but I can give you the abridged version. Our mother took us to what she thought was a commune where we'd be safe and happy, but that didn't turn out to be the case. She smuggled me out when I was thirteen. She smuggled Mercy out four years later, when she was almost thirteen. It was dangerous both times she did it. She . . . didn't survive the second time.'

'Oh my God,' John whispered. 'Mercy, why didn't you tell me?'

'Because I didn't want to think about it,' Mercy whispered back. 'I'm sorry, John.'

'I didn't talk about it, either,' Gideon said, half hugging Mercy again. 'Not until a few months ago. It was traumatic. For both of us.'

Solidarity, she realized. *Thank you, Gideon.*

'All right,' John said slowly. 'Hopefully one day you can tell me the unabridged version of that story. But can you tell me what was the misunderstanding that kept us all apart all this time?'

And this is the part where I admit to being a selfish person. 'I was told that Gideon had tried to run away because he was lazy and didn't want to work. I was told he'd died in his attempt. There were . . . consequences to his escape. Life was harder for my mother and me after that.'

John made a strangled sound, his eyes growing haunted. 'More abuse?'

'Yes,' Mercy said levelly. 'And I hated Gideon, because I blamed it on his laziness. But that was a lie. He escaped because he was abused, too.' She tried to smile, but it fell flat. 'I was angry at Gideon because he'd found this awesome family in Sacramento and at the time I didn't have anyone. Then I met you and Angela and all the others and . . .' She closed her eyes. 'I wanted to keep you for myself. I never gave Gideon any of the messages you sent. I'm so sorry, John. So damn sorry. I cheated you out of six years with Gideon. I'll understand if this changes things between us.'

No one said anything as the seconds ticked by, then John's voice pierced her misery, and she nearly started crying again at the warmth in his tone. 'Mercy, open your eyes.'

Preparing herself, she did, only to see John smiling at her sadly.

'Nothing changes. I promise. I said this morning that we'd figure it all out, and I meant it.'

She pressed her hand to her mouth to stifle the sob that rose to choke her. 'Thank you.'

Gideon pulled her close. 'It's okay, Mercy. Cry if you need to.'

'I'll mess up your suit.'

Gideon chuckled. 'Wouldn't be the first time. Besides, Daisy hates this suit. She says it's scratchy.'

Mercy rubbed her cheek on his lapel. 'She's right.'

John blew his nose noisily. 'How much of this can I share with the sibs?'

'Anything I've told you,' Gideon said. 'When this is all settled and Mercy is safe, we'll come out to see you. Together. And then we can all sit down and hash this out once and for all.'

John frowned, then shook his head hard. 'I forgot why I was calling you, Mercy. I saw the video. The one from the airport,' he added quickly, and Mercy figured her face had shown her horror. 'The one of that man trying to take you away.'

'His name is Harry Franklin,' Gideon said, 'but we knew him as Ephraim Burton.'

John's jaw tightened, his eyes flickering with sudden rage. 'He's the one, isn't he? The one that hurt you both?'

Gideon and Mercy exchanged a look. 'Yes and no,' Mercy said. 'Yes for me, but for Gideon it was Ephraim and his brother, Edward.'

'Mercy, that man in the video was here.'

Mercy jerked upright. 'What?'

'When?' Gideon barked.

'Friday,' John said grimly. 'My wife and I weren't home from work yet. Our nine-year-old daughter opened the door.'

'Oh my God,' Mercy breathed. 'Did he hurt her, John?'

'No, she's safe. After that policeman called us this morning, we weren't sure what to tell the kids. We didn't want to scare them, but decided it was better to be scared but safe. When we showed the kids his picture from that airport video, Michaela pointed him out. Said he'd been by looking for you, Mercy. She was going to tell you, but you left town before she could.'

'What exactly did he say to her?' Gideon asked tensely.

'Just asked if Mercy lived there. Michaela told him no. But she gave him your address.' John's jaw clenched. 'That's how he found your neighbor. The one he killed.'

Mercy felt sick. 'You have to go somewhere safe, John. Please.'

John looked from her to Gideon. 'Do you agree, Gideon?'

Gideon nodded. 'Yeah, I do. I hate to say it, but we don't know if Ephraim has helpers outside the community.'

John frowned again. 'Community? You mean the commune your mother joined?'

Gideon hesitated. 'Yes.'

John pinned them with a cold stare. 'In other words, it was a cult.'

Gideon sighed. 'It was, and the FBI is investigating. We don't want to give them a heads-up that we're looking for them, so please keep that to yourself for a while?'

John's nod was harsh. 'I will. But I wish I'd been home when he came.'

'No, you don't.' Mercy could hear the hysteria creeping into her voice and she made a conscious effort to dial it back. 'He's killed people. Please find a place to hide. Please.'

'The kids are in school,' John protested, then snapped his mouth shut. 'They're vulnerable there, aren't they?'

'If he comes back, yes,' Gideon said. 'At the moment we have no idea where he is.'

'He hurts people you love to keep you in line,' Mercy blurted. 'He knows you could be leverage to hurt Gideon and me, to make us do what he wants.'

'All right. We'll make plans to go away for a week or so. I hope that's long enough.'

Me too, Mercy thought. 'If not, we can figure out the next steps together. I don't want you guys touched by this. By any of this.'

'Same goes, Mercy. You two be careful, okay?'

'We will.' Mercy hesitated, then sighed. 'You knew I thought you'd seen the other video.'

John's jaw tightened again. 'Yeah. I read the article. The video was gone by then. I have attorneys at my disposal. I can ruin that asshole.' His lips twisted. 'Jeff Bunker. If that's even his real name.'

'It is,' Gideon said, surprising her. 'Trust me, I already looked him up. He's a college kid. Communications major in Sacramento.'

'Punk,' John growled.

Gideon's chuckle was harsh. 'You're not wrong. We're going after him for posting that video. It was part of someone else's plea deal in New Orleans, so by posting it, it linked him to the original crime. We'll take him down. Don't even worry about it. You just keep yourselves safe.' He paused, then said, 'We need to go, John. We need to inform the investigators about Ephraim coming to your house. They may want to talk to you.'

'They'll have to follow us to Florida, then,' John said. 'We're taking the kids to Disney World. That far enough away, Gideon?'

'Just make sure you keep your family in sight the whole time and call me if you see anything that makes you feel unsafe.' Gideon ended the call and Mercy drew a deep breath.

'She's just a little girl, Gideon. What if he'd grabbed her?'

'He didn't,' Gideon said firmly. 'And we're going to make sure he doesn't. I have a few friends in Florida. They might like a little side pay.'

'Bodyguards? You trust them?'

'With my life. They've had my back over the years when it's counted. I'll call John later for more information about their plans, and then I'll make the calls to Florida. You worry about you and Farrah.'

All the good feelings were swept away by despair. 'Poor Aunt Quill. I know in my head that it's not my fault, but . . .'

'I get it. But you can't let the guilt take over. Farrah needs your strength, not apologies for something you didn't cause.'

He was right. So was Rafe. 'Got it. I'll be who she needs.'

Gideon pulled her to her feet and dropped a kiss on her head. 'I know you will.'

Granite Bay, California
Sunday, 16 April, 6.30 P.M.

Rafe could count on one hand how many times in his life he'd felt so helpless. He stood in the doorway of his father's office, watching as Mercy held Farrah close, rocking them where they stood.

'I'm sorry,' Mercy whispered. 'I'm so damn sorry.'

Farrah shuddered. 'This isn't your fault, Mercy. It isn't anyone's fault except the bastard who did this to her.'

'I hate this,' Captain Holmes hissed so that only Rafe would hear.

'I know,' Rafe murmured, his breath hitching when Mercy looked at him over Farrah's shoulder. Her sad smile broke his heart and he wanted to go to her, but he respected her wishes when she mouthed, *Give us a minute.*

'Come on,' Rafe told Holmes. 'You've got to be starving. My mother wants to feed you.'

Holmes reluctantly followed him from the office and into the kitchen, where Gideon sat with Sasha and Daisy. Irina buzzed around the stove, stirring something.

Some people drank when they were upset. Some people picked fights. Others cleaned obsessively. His mother cooked. Obsessively.

Luckily, they were all big eaters. Holmes looked like he could hold his own with any and all of the Sokolovs when it came to chowing down. Holmes was a big guy, tall and broad.

'Captain Holmes, have you met these guys?' Rafe asked, gesturing for him to sit.

'I met Agent Reynolds and your mother when I first got here.' Holmes dipped his head in a respectful nod as he sat between Gideon and Rafe. 'Ma'am. Thank you for the tea. I don't know how much of it Farrah drank, but I know she appreciated the thought.'

'She is a good person, your Farrah,' Irina answered, already dishing up a plate of the lamb she'd served for Sunday dinner. 'You are hungry, yes?'

Holmes's lips twitched up into a small smile. 'Yes, ma'am.' And he must have been, because he cleaned his plate before Rafe had blinked twice.

Irina gave him seconds before he could ask or refuse, patting his arm as she took her own seat. 'So, is Farrah—' She sighed, cutting herself off. 'She can't be okay. That is a foolish question.'

'She will be,' Holmes said, digging into his second plate. 'Thank you for this. I haven't eaten anything since last night. Except airline peanuts.'

'Pah.' Irina shook her head. 'Traveling is hard enough without the airlines starving the passengers.'

'Sitting in economy is worse. I'm still sore from having my knees in my chin for seven hours.' He ate the second helping more slowly, looking around the table. 'Hey. I'm André.'

Rafe did the introductions. 'This is Gideon's girlfriend, Daisy Dawson; my father, Karl; and my sister, Sasha. Where is Erin?'

'She went outside to check with the agents,' Irina told him. 'She wants to know when they're changing shifts so that she can supervise.'

That made sense, Rafe thought gratefully. Erin paid attention to details like that. 'Erin's my partner on the force. You can meet her later.'

'André, we were hoping to ask you some questions, when you're finished eating,' Gideon said.

'Go ahead and ask now. I'm used to eating around conversations.' André's chuckle was subdued. 'I'm marrying into Farrah's family. They . . . well, they talk a lot.'

'I knew she and I were sisters of different misters,' Sasha said lightly, and then her shoulders sagged. 'I'm so sorry about her aunt. Can you tell us what happened?'

'I'm surprised that it took us so long to find her, honestly.' André nodded his thanks to Irina when she placed a plate of freshly baked bread at his elbow. The kitchen counters were filled with baked goods, marinating meats, and finished casseroles. It smelled like home should smell. 'The Romeros are very close. That she didn't show up for Mercy's going-away breakfast should have raised red flags with all of us, but she'd texted the night before that she had already invited a friend over and didn't want to be rude. She said she'd forgotten about having plans. None of her friends showed up, or they would have found her sooner. Her killer might have sent the text himself. We didn't think a thing about it because Quill was getting forgetful and she'd said her goodbyes to Mercy on Friday afternoon. Mercy stayed with Farrah at the Romeros' overnight on Friday,' he explained. 'That way they could have breakfast with the family before heading out to the airport.'

'How did you discover her?' Rafe asked.

'Anonymous phone call,' André said, then raised a brow. 'Made from a phone here in Sacramento.'

Everyone at the table stared at him in surprise. 'Where in Sacramento?' Gideon asked.

'Near a place called Carmichael. Probably a burner phone.'

Rafe and Gideon shared a puzzled glance. 'Burton wouldn't have called to report a murder he did,' Rafe said, as sure of that as he was of his own name. 'Can we listen to the 911 call?'

'Yep. Thought you might want to hear it. The call came in at about three thirty central time this morning, so one thirty a.m. here.' André pulled his phone from his pocket and tapped the screen, and a high-pitched, nervous voice began to speak. The caller was young. Male. And he sounded nothing like Ephraim Burton's growl.

'Hi, um, I need to report a death. Probably a murder. Maybe a murder? The lady's name is Miss Romero.' The young man blurted out the address. 'I, uh, I found her. It was Friday evening, maybe seven thirty? And . . . well, I might have touched her body. Okay, yes, I did touch her, but only to lift her off the floor and onto the sofa. I thought I was gonna need to do CPR, but she was already dead. She was a really nice lady. So, please go get her and tell her family. Um, thanks, bye.'

The 911 operator tried to get the man to wait, but he'd already hung up.

André shrugged. 'Lots of fingerprints in her apartment, but ninety-nine percent are going to be family and friends. Quill loved to entertain,' he finished wistfully. 'She was a sweet lady.'

Rafe asked him to play the recording again, listening for anything that might give him insight into the caller, but all he got was scared kid. 'That is not Ephraim Burton, aka Satan.'

'No,' Gideon murmured. 'It's definitely not. Who else was in New Orleans on Friday?'

'I don't know.' André accepted a slice of bird's milk cake with a grateful smile. 'I was hoping you guys might know. Quill was found on the sofa and the place was just wrecked, but nothing major was missing. NOPD found ten grand hidden in various places in the house – under the mattress, in the freezer, at the bottom of her unmentionables drawer. It wasn't hard to find, but her killer didn't take it.'

'You're sure it was homicide?' Irina asked. 'If she was elderly, it's possible she died of natural causes.'

'Unlikely.' André hesitated, then blew out a sigh. 'I'm not supposed to even know this, but I've got friends in all kinds of places and I know you all want this solved as much as we do. Quill showed signs of suffocation. Rigor was starting to fade, so the time the guy says he found her sounds right.'

'Cameras in the building?' Gideon asked. 'Please say my sister picked a building with security cameras.'

'I'd like to, but no. It's not a bad building, and it had a working camera at some point, but it was broken. The residents NOPD talked to were surprised to hear there was a camera at all.'

Rafe drummed his fingers on the table, then, following his gut, did a search on his phone. 'What about this guy?' He turned the phone to show the YouTube video he'd pulled up. 'The asshole who wrote that damn article about Mercy.'

Gideon's jaw tightened so hard that his teeth should have been dust. 'Jeff Bunker,' he hissed, fury in every line of his body.

Rafe shared the sentiment. 'Let's have a listen to Mr Bunker.'

'Who looks like he's sixteen,' Sasha said, 'because he is. Dad and I looked him up. Kid's some kind of genius, already in his second year at Sac State.'

'I don't care if he's a fucking Einstein,' Gideon gritted out. 'If I get my hands on him, he'll wish he'd picked on someone else's sister.'

Daisy laid her hand on Gideon's arm. 'Hey,' she said soothingly. 'I want to disembowel him with a rusty grapefruit spoon, but maybe we shouldn't say that out loud with other cops in the room?'

Gideon huffed a laugh, then scrubbed his face with his palms. 'Play it, Rafe. Please.'

Rafe did, and within seconds it was obvious that it was the same voice as the 911 call. The recorded Jeff Bunker was talking about the recent serial killer 'situation' in Sacramento, saying he wanted to focus on the survivors since other journalists were talking about the killer's dead victims.

'Hell of a way to focus,' Rafe snarled, stopping the video. 'Jesus, I want to fucking kill him.'

'I think we all have received that message,' Irina said, putting teacups on the table. She poured a cup for everyone, then returned to her seat to sip her tea. 'But I'd like to hear where he was going with his story. If you boys can't listen to him without dreaming up ways to commit homicide in ever-increasingly clever ways, then send me the link, Raphael, and I'll listen on my own.'

Rafe slouched in his chair, chastised as she'd intended him to be. 'You're right, Mom. Sorry.'

'Drink your tea. It's calming.'

Rafe sniffed at the brew suspiciously. 'How calming?'

She swatted at him. 'Not that calming. I wish I'd never told you all that I drink my special tea for my arthritis. Now be quiet – if you can – and play the video.'

'Busted,' Sasha whispered loudly, making him snort out a laugh. Which his bratty but very sweet sister had also intended. 'Take a breath, Rafe,' she said, sobering. 'You're no good to Mercy going all He-Man and the Masters of the Universe on this kid's ass.'

Rafe did as both women recommended, taking a breath and sipping his tea before hitting PLAY.

The video turned out to be a vlog of sorts with more than ten thousand views. Rafe figured that most of them had happened since the article was posted the night before. Jeff Bunker wanted to 'know the survivors' and to follow their 'healing process'.

'Sonofabitch,' Rafe muttered. 'He's not interested in healing. He's only interested in himself.'

'Shh,' his mother admonished. 'Listen, son.'

Rafe and Gideon scowled at each other before turning back to his phone like they could summon Bunker or something. He had to hand it to the kid – he talked a good talk. Anyone who hadn't actually read the hateful trash he'd written might see him as a stand-up, earnest college kid who wanted to change the world.

Rafe didn't care what BS the little bastard was spewing. If he got his hands on Bunker, he'd tear him limb from limb.

He was saved from listening to any more when the doorbell rang. 'I'll get it,' Rafe all but snarled, shoving away from the table, giving his phone one last look that he wished could kill. At least he was doing better than Gideon, who sat with his fists clenched, desperate rage stiffening his body.

Trying to calm himself, Rafe opened the door to find Erin. And a kid.

The kid. Jeffrey Fucking Bunker.

Fourteen

Granite Bay, California
Sunday, 16 April, 6.50 P.M.

Jeffrey Bunker, that sonofabitch. Rafe's vision hazed with red and he'd fisted Bunker's shirt before he could stop himself, lifting the kid to his toes. 'You little fucking *shit*,' he hissed through clenched teeth. 'You *dare* show your face here? Are you *insane*?' He gave Bunker a shake.

Then reality began to seep into the fog of his fury. Bunker was gasping for air and an older woman behind him was shouting for him to take his hands off her son.

But it was Erin's calm voice that finally got through. 'Put him down, Rafe. Now.'

He released Bunker, pushing him away with another snarl. 'What. The. Fuck, Erin?'

Erin exhaled heavily. 'Fucking hell, Rafe. What's gotten into you?'

'It's him,' Rafe spat. 'Bunker. The guy who ruined Mercy's life for a fucking story.'

Bunker was panting, running trembling hands through his hair. His face was ghost white. 'I'm sorry. I just came to say I was sorry.'

Erin handed Rafe an envelope. 'It's for Mercy.'

'I expected better from you of all people, Erin,' he spat. 'You *saw* what this did to her. I don't want to hear his sorries and I don't want Mercy to have to see his fucking face.' Rafe snatched the envelope and tossed it back at Bunker. 'Get out or I'll tell her brother that you're here. He might not be as controlled as I am.'

235

'He didn't do it!' the older woman shouted. 'Dammit, could you just listen for a minute?'

'Didn't do what? Didn't interview a sex offender and publish his video? Didn't violate Mercy again? Next he'll be claiming he didn't kill Quill Romero.' Rafe took a step back, ready to slam the door in all their faces until he realized that this guy would be wanted by NOPD as well. 'André! You need to see this.' He was furious at Bunker, but Erin . . . *My God*. She'd betrayed him.

And then he met his partner's dark eyes. And her mostly patient expression. Which morphed to sympathetic as they stared each other down.

'He's just come from Molina's office,' Erin said quietly. 'He came clean and his story matches up. The Feds are piecing the rest of it together as we speak.'

Rafe's gaze flicked to the red-faced, angry woman standing behind Bunker, hands protectively clutching his shoulders. Then he looked – really looked – at Bunker, who was crying, his body a trembling, shaking mess.

'I'm so sorry,' Bunker whispered. 'I didn't do this. Not the video part anyway. The rest of it . . . I did the article. Most of it. But I didn't kill Miss Romero!'

'You just made the anonymous call to NOPD,' Rafe said flatly. 'From Sacramento.'

Heavy footsteps fell behind him, and then André Holmes was shoving past him, going for Bunker, just as Rafe had. But Erin stepped in front of him, staring up defiantly.

'Hold on there,' she said, her voice still calm. It was the same voice she used to defuse hostile situations. The same voice she'd used to talk a jumper from the Foresthill Bridge. The same voice she'd used to calm Rafe whenever he'd lost his temper over the past year.

André's chest was pumping, his rage palpable. 'What the fuck is this, Sokolov?'

Rafe glanced behind Erin at the Bunker kid, who was cowering in fear. 'I'm not sure,' he said, feeling some of his reason return. 'It seems we have a new complication.'

André stepped closer to Erin, glaring down at Bunker. 'Start talking, asswipe.'

Erin placed a palm on André's chest. 'Back off, sir.'

André started to snarl at Erin, but she whipped out her badge at the same time Rafe said, 'She's my partner. Detective Erin Rhee, SacPD Homicide.' He frowned at Erin. 'You should have called first. Given us a heads-up.'

'I can see that now,' Erin said wryly. She looked over her shoulder. 'You okay, kid?'

'No, he is not okay!' the older woman shouted.

'Mom, chill,' Bunker said stiffly. 'I'm not hurt.'

'He would have killed you,' the woman said hoarsely. Now that the situation was cycling down, tears gathered in the woman's eyes.

'No, I wouldn't have,' Rafe said, still angry, but no longer out of his head with it. 'What the hell were you thinking, coming up to knock on my door? And what were you thinking, Erin, escorting them?'

Erin lifted a brow, her whole demeanor going frosty. 'I was thinking that my smart, *rational* partner might like to hear the truth.'

'What's going on here?' Gideon said, joining the welcoming committee. He didn't shout, though, so maybe he'd heard what Erin had been saying.

Erin exhaled again. 'Okay, let's start over again. I should have called first. I didn't know you'd figured out that Mr Bunker here had made the anonymous call to NOPD, or I would have handled this differently. Mr Bunker, Mrs Bunker, you have my sincere apologies.'

'It's okay,' Bunker said, his voice like gravel. High-pitched, squeaky gravel. Rafe wasn't sure how the guy managed it. 'If I was in their place, I would have done the same thing. Well, maybe not the same thing, because I'm not a million feet tall and can't bench-press a draft horse.'

'Yep,' Gideon said dryly. 'This is the anonymous caller, all right.'

Twin flags of color stained Bunker's pale cheeks. 'I told Special Agent Molina what happened. She didn't arrest me.'

'Congratulations,' Rafe drawled. 'Now tell the rest of us what the fuck is going on here.'

237

'Language, Raphael,' Irina tutted. She pushed them out of the doorway and onto the front porch, pulling the door closed behind her. It opened right back up, Sasha and Daisy following her. Daisy grabbed Gideon's arm and hugged him to her side. Sasha stood next to Rafe, arms crossed over her chest, glaring daggers, first at Bunker, then at Erin.

Irina sighed loudly. 'First of all, my seventeen-year-old daughter is upstairs studying. I know she hears the F-bomb at school, but I'd prefer she not hear it at home.'

Rafe almost rolled his eyes, but caught himself in time. 'Yes, Mom.'

Irina shot him a glare that said he'd be in deep shit later. 'Second, we have two grieving women here who have had enough stress in the past day to last the rest of their – hopefully – very long lives.' She turned her gaze on Erin. 'You really should have given Raphael fair warning.'

Erin dropped her eyes. 'I know. I'm sorry, Irina.'

'I hope so.' Irina extended her hand to Bunker's mother. 'I am Irina Sokolov. You are Jeff's mother?'

The woman shook Irina's hand warily. 'Geri Bunker. We didn't know that any of Miss Romero's family would be here. We are very sorry to disturb them in their grief. But my son wanted to make things right with Miss Callahan.'

Irina tilted her head toward Bunker. 'You are all right, yes?'

Bunker nodded shakily. 'Yes. Ma'am,' he added when his mother nudged him.

'Good. I would like to invite you in for tea, but I think we should hear what Mr Bunker has to say first. Quickly, young man. This détente is fragile.'

Bunker shot her a grateful look. 'Okay. I started this article, then found out that Miss Callahan lived in New Orleans. I went there – on my own. My mother had nothing to do with it. I kind of lied about where I'd gone.'

'Because you are only sixteen and she would have said no,' Irina said logically.

'Exactly. Ma'am. I talked to Miss Callahan's exes, and one of them sold me the video, but I did not put it in the article. My boss did.'

'You gave it to your boss,' Rafe said coldly. 'What did you think would happen?'

'I *didn't* give it to my boss,' Bunker insisted. 'He called the guy who gave it to me and got his own copy. I gave my copy to the FBI. I didn't use it.'

'Why not?' Rafe asked, still unconvinced. Until Bunker's eyes filled with tears.

'I couldn't. I saw how she looked when that killer was dragging her from the hospital in February. How . . . empty her eyes were. I didn't think the video was consensual, so I didn't use it. I didn't know that I didn't think it was consensual yesterday, but I knew it was wrong.'

Rafe stared at Bunker, trying to parse that last sentence. Bunker stared back, tears now streaking down his face. Rafe sighed. 'Okay. Assuming we believe you, why didn't you turn the video over to the cops right away?'

The kid's gulp was audible, but he straightened his spine. 'I went back to Miss Callahan's apartment to ask more questions of her neighbor, because she'd said nice things, but the accounts of the others were so contradictory that I needed more information. And I found her dead. Miss Romero, I mean.'

'And didn't call the NOPD until this morning,' André snapped. 'She'd been dead for thirty-six hours.'

'I'm sorry,' Bunker whispered. 'I'm so sorry. I was scared and I freaked out and did the wrong thing.'

'What made you call it in?' Irina asked gently.

Bunker looked at his mother. 'My mom. She found me passed out drunk and talked sense into my head. So I called the cops and reported the video. It got taken down right after.'

A harrumph came from the ground next to the front porch. Karl stood there, arms crossed. 'I wondered why it was so easy to have it taken down. I thought my attorney had developed the voice of God or something.'

Rafe studied Bunker carefully. Now that he wasn't crazy with anger, he could see that the kid appeared sincere. 'Why were you so scared?' he asked, his own tone softer.

Bunker visibly relaxed. 'Because I saw the guy coming out of Miss Romero's apartment. He looked . . . like, crazy happy. Emphasis on crazy. He scared the shit out of me.'

Erin cleared her throat. 'Mr Bunker positively ID'd Ephraim Burton from a photo array.' Her gaze rose to meet André's. 'And, according to Agent Hunter, he ID'd the roommate of Mercy's ex-boyfriend.'

Bunker whipped around to stare at her. 'The *roommate*?'

Erin nodded. 'When you asked about Mercy, he figured he might make a dollar or two from the video he'd copied from Stan Prescott, the video that was surrendered as part of Prescott's plea bargain.'

'And Prescott was *not* Mercy's ex,' André growled. 'Prescott is a slimy scumbag who roofied her at a party. She'd never seen him before or after.'

Bunker closed his eyes. 'I'm sorry. I didn't know.'

André appeared unmoved. 'You should have. You should have cross-checked.'

Bunker looked even more devastated. 'That's why I went to see Miss Romero. To cross-check.'

André started to speak, but Irina hooked her arm through his, patting him. 'You cross-check *before* you publish,' she said, her tone severe but controlled. 'I hope this is a mistake you will never make again.'

'No, ma'am,' Bunker whispered. 'I won't.'

Rafe frowned. 'So the guy who made the video, who assaulted Mercy, did not sell it to Bunker?'

Erin shook her head. 'Nope. Prescott has been in Europe for the past three weeks. He might have had contact with Mr Bunker, but it doesn't appear so.'

'All my conversations were one-on-one, in person,' Bunker said, looking disgusted with himself. 'Dammit. I believed him. And it wasn't a dollar or two. I gave him fifteen hundred.'

André whistled. 'Where'd you get fifteen bills, kid?'

'From my editor. He wired it to me. And when I held the video back, I guess he decided to take matters in his own hands. I'm sure he figured since he'd paid for it, he was going to use it.'

'Do you still work for this . . . online trash magazine?' Irina asked, her description of the gossip blog dripping with contempt.

'No, ma'am. I quit. I . . . I just wanted to tell the story. I thought other survivors might get inspiration. But I fu— messed it all up.'

'Yeah, you did,' Rafe said with a sigh. 'Why are you here now, though?'

Bunker bent over to retrieve the envelope that Rafe had thrown back at him. 'I just wanted someone to give this to Miss Callahan.'

'I caught him trying to come up the front walk,' Erin said quietly. 'I called Tom Hunter to verify what he said, and Tom did. I should have called you too, Rafe. I'm sorry.'

Rafe took the envelope from Bunker. 'I'll see that she gets this. And I'll tell her what happened before I do. If she wants to see you, how should she contact you?'

Bunker patted his pockets. 'Mom, you got a pen?'

His mother rolled her eyes. 'Yes, Jeff. I have a pen. I have paper, too.' She found the items in an enormous handbag and gave them to her son.

Bunker scrawled his name, email address, and cell phone number on the paper and handed it to Rafe. 'I really am sorry. When I saw that the guy trying to take her at the airport was the same guy I saw coming out of Miss Romero's apartment, I . . . well, I guess I froze.'

'He's a dangerous, terrifying man,' Gideon said quietly. 'It's best that you didn't confront him. Did he see you?'

The color that Bunker had regained in his face drained once again. 'I don't think so.'

'Is my son in danger?' his mother asked, her face also growing very pale.

Rafe wanted to shake them both. *Duh. Burton's only killed five people in the last two days.* That they knew of. 'It's possible. It depends on if he knows that you're the one who turned him in for Quill Romero's murder. If he figures out you saw him, then yes.'

'Can you give him protection?' his mother asked, fear in her eyes.

241

There was quiet for a long, long moment. 'I can talk to my lieutenant,' Erin finally said. 'It would be best if you found a place where you could lay low for a little while.'

'I have to work,' Mrs Bunker protested. 'I can't just leave town.'

'Don't panic until I have some more information,' Erin soothed. She turned to Rafe. 'We square, partner?'

Rafe nodded. 'Yeah,' he said, relieved that it was true. 'Thank you.'

Irina tipped Bunker's chin up and to the side, studying his throat. 'Are you all right, son?'

Fucking hell, Rafe wanted to groan. What had he nearly done?

'I'm okay,' Bunker said again. 'And I'm not going to sue, so don't worry about that. If Miss Callahan were my sister or my . . .' He searched Rafe's face. 'Whatever she is to you. Girlfriend? And if I were Miss Romero's family? I'd do the same thing.' He waved his hands airily. 'Again, if I were the Incredible Hulk. Otherwise, I'd just pen a letter to the editor.'

If the kid had been being sarcastic, Rafe would have been able to hold on to his anger, but Bunker was so damn sincere. 'Thank you,' Rafe murmured. 'I'm sorry.'

Bunker tentatively smiled. 'It's okay. You'll explain to Miss Callahan?'

'I will. I promise.'

Granite Bay, California
Sunday, 16 April, 7.10 P.M.

'What the hell?' Ephraim muttered from Sean MacGuire's upstairs window as he watched the scene unfold on the Sokolovs' front porch. Rafe Sokolov had lifted that kid by the shirt collar – right off the ground – with one hand. Only to shove him away when a small woman stopped him. The kid looked shaken and terrified.

Ephraim felt kinship with the kid. He'd experienced Sokolov's strength and the back of his head still ached from it. *Fucking cane. If I ever get that man alone, I'm going to beat his head in with it.*

His attention was diverted when more people tromped out of the house, holding court on the porch. Sokolov was joined by Gideon Reynolds and a woman that Ephraim recognized from his Google searches as Irina Sokolov, the detective's mother. Then two more women – a tall blonde with a high ponytail who'd been at the airport the night before and a small blonde who clung to Reynolds like a limpet.

Her, Ephraim also recognized. She'd been featured in that CNN special about the serial killer. She was the third survivor, Daisy Dawson. And she was clearly with Gideon.

That was interesting. He tucked the knowledge away for later. If he wanted to make Gideon pay, basic garden-variety torture of his girlfriend would do nicely.

A black man had also come from the house to stand glaring at the kid who'd been mauled by Sokolov, and Ephraim was irritated that he couldn't ID him. The man had arrived about an hour before in a red rental car and had been let straight into the house, so he'd been expected and welcomed.

Unlike the kid, who was now hiding behind another woman, who looked related to him. The woman was glaring back at Sokolov, her body vibrating with . . . something. Fear, maybe? Or rage? Or both. She had the look of a mother bear.

Like his own mother. Before she'd stopped recognizing him.

He shoved the distraction aside, waiting for Mercy to appear. But she never did and after what seemed like an eternity of talking, the kid wrote something on a sheet of paper and handed it to Sokolov.

Seemed like the crisis had been averted, and Ephraim was a little disappointed. If Sokolov had managed to hurt the kid, he'd be in trouble. Maybe even spend a few hours behind bars – hours during which Mercy would be more vulnerable.

Unfortunately, when the kid left, everything went back to the way it was before. Ephraim focused his binoculars on the license plate of the kid's car as he and his mommy left, noting it for a further look. Something important had just happened there. He'd figure it out.

He put the binoculars down and sat in the comfy recliner, his gaze still glued to the Sokolov house. He'd figure it *all* out. Now that he knew DJ's secrets, Ephraim held the real power.

He told himself that again as he pulled his second phone from his pocket. He hadn't made a single call on it and wouldn't use it for anything but talking to Pastor.

He dialed the man's cell phone number from memory, relieved when he got Pastor's voice mail. He wasn't sure he could pull this off without losing his cool if he heard Pastor's voice.

'Hi, it's Ephraim.' He made his tone both raspy and self-deprecating. 'I dropped my phone and it broke. Had to buy a new one. You can reach me at this number.' He faked a cough and cleared his throat before reciting his new digits. 'I'm in Sacramento now, by the way.' Best to 'fess up, since Pastor knew he was there. 'I . . . well, I met an old friend from my high school days when I was in San Francisco. An old girlfriend, actually. She's a pediatrician now and said it looked like I might have strep throat. She invited me home and she has a kid. A daughter. I'm going to stay here for a few days and she's getting me some antibiotics for the strep. No good bringing it back to the compound, right? Gotta go. Call if you need to.'

He hung up and rolled his eyes. He'd sounded like he was lying. Pastor would know it. But then, so would DJ, if Pastor mentioned it. Which Ephraim was pretty sure he would. DJ would know something was up, and maybe it would make him nervous.

Of course it might make DJ strike out and further defame him, but Ephraim was beyond caring. When he brought Mercy back to Eden, he'd make sure the whole compound knew that both Pastor and DJ had been lying to them.

The thought made him smile as he got comfortable, his gaze still fixed on the Sokolov house. He'd bought himself some time, at least.

Granite Bay, California
Sunday, 16 April, 7.30 P.M.

Mercy rubbed at her sore eyes. Her head hurt and the ibuprofen Irina had given her wasn't working nearly fast enough. Her face felt like hamburger from crying so much, and Farrah didn't look any better. They were surrounded by friends and family, of course. André was at Farrah's side, Daisy at Gideon's. Rafe was a solid presence next to her. Sasha sat with Karl at the head of the table, Karl looking . . . a little older than he had when she'd first arrived the day before. He still felt bad about how he'd told her about the damn article last night, but Mercy was completely past that. Now she grappled with what seemed to be the actual truth about the kid who'd posted the video evidence of another violation of her body, of her soul. Of whatever innocence she'd thought she'd had left at the time.

Tom Hunter was also at the table, having arrived a few minutes before. He'd come to ask her questions about Eden, but also to tell her about Jeff Bunker, the sixteen-year-old journalism student who'd dragged her past through the mud. He'd been surprised to learn that Bunker had already been there, to apologize and deliver a letter to Mercy. As far as Mercy knew, no one had told him the small detail about Rafe's near-throttling of the idiotic boy. Hearing that part of the story from Rafe had made her a little happy, she had to admit.

'Let me get this straight,' Mercy said to the table in general and to Tom and Erin in particular. 'This . . . kid, Jeff Bunker, was duped by Stan Prescott's roommate?'

She'd read the letter the young man had written with an initial skepticism that she was rethinking now that Hunter had confirmed the story Rafe had relayed to her in private before this family meeting. The letter was sincere, to the point, and very apologetic.

She didn't want to let the anger at the kid go, but . . . hell. She'd held on to her anger at Gideon for all these years and it had nearly ruined whatever relationship they might have had.

Gideon had forgiven her freely. Maybe she should pay it forward.

'Yes,' Tom said simply. 'His story checks out. He kept all the emails from his editor and all of the drafts of the article. He didn't set you up on purpose, Mercy.'

Farrah wasn't quite in the forgiveness phase and Mercy couldn't blame her. 'Could he have killed Aunt Quill?' Farrah asked.

'Maybe,' André said, 'but his story checks out there too, from a timing standpoint, anyway. The apartment building didn't have any

245

cameras, but the home across the street did and we got a view of the front entrance. Ephraim Burton entered twenty minutes before Jeff Bunker walked up. Burton left and got in a rental car. Five minutes later, Bunker runs from the house looking like he'd seen a damn ghost. He hightailed it to the bus stop.' André rolled his eyes. 'The kid was using the city buses because he's too young to rent a car and he doesn't actually have a driver's license yet.'

'He's some kind of whiz kid genius,' Rafe added. 'But he's still sixteen. Sounds like his editor used that to manipulate him.'

'I don't want to feel sorry for him,' Farrah said stubbornly.

Mercy covered her friend's hand with hers. 'You don't have to. Even if he didn't kill Quill, he knew who did. Yes, he's young. Yes, he was scared and, having been on the receiving end of Ephraim's rage, I know he had a right to be. But he waited too long to do the right thing.' She bit her lip. 'I actually can relate to that.'

'Not the same,' Gideon murmured.

'Yeah, it kind of is,' Mercy murmured back. 'But my point is, your feelings are your feelings and you don't have to harbor kind thoughts about this kid. If he had come forward, we . . .' She trailed off.

'We what?' Farrah pressed.

'We wouldn't have gotten on that plane. I wouldn't be here right now, in this kitchen.' A thought struck her and she shivered. 'I might not be here on the planet anymore, because Ephraim would have killed me there and no one would have known it was him.'

Silence descended over the table, heavy and thick.

Farrah let out a watery sigh that was half sob. 'God, Mercy. Now I feel like I should thank that fool kid.'

Mercy's lips tipped up. 'I wouldn't go that far.' She patted Farrah's hand, then passed her the box of tissues they'd been sharing for the last hour. 'But I know how scared he must have been. And to have been on the plane with him? For hours? I don't think my heart would have survived that.'

'He did get the video taken down,' Farrah muttered grudgingly.

Mercy shrugged. 'He's a kid, Ro. Not perfect. Hell, it took me all these years to decide to take Ephraim down.' Lifting her chin, she caught Rafe's gaze. 'So maybe we can talk about that now.'

Farrah's nod was firm. Defiant. 'Yeah. Let's take that motherfucker down.'

There was a small gasp from behind them and they turned to find Zoya, the youngest Sokolov, staring at them. But it was admiration in her eyes, not shock. 'Can I help?'

Irina frowned from where she was kneading yet another loaf of bread. Baking was Irina's tell, Mercy had discovered. The place looked like a restaurant, food covering every available flat surface. 'What are you doing here, Zoya?' Irina demanded.

Zoya pouted. 'I'm hungry. I've been banished to my room all afternoon. And I'm bored,' she added in a whine.

'Does not matter.' Irina pointed a dough-covered finger to the door. 'You are re-banished. Go.'

Zoya sidled up to her mother and kissed her on the cheek. 'I could at least help with the bread. Besides, I've heard just about everything that's been said in this house today, including what the boy on the porch said.' She unrepentantly met her mother's glare. 'I have windows, Mom. I opened one and listened. At least I didn't let down my hair and beg to be rescued.'

Irina snorted a small laugh before shaking her head. 'You are no Rapunzel.'

'And he is no Flynn Rider,' Zoya shot back, then grinned, her dimples appearing. 'But he is kind of cute. You know, for a kid.'

Mercy rolled her eyes. 'He's only a year younger than you.'

Zoya left her mother's side and pulled a chair to the corner of the table, plunking herself down between Mercy and Farrah. 'A year is like five at my age, Mercy. You know that girls mature faster than boys.'

Mercy bit back a smile. 'I have heard this, yes.' Then she became serious. 'But we're about to talk about things you shouldn't hear. Not because you're not old enough,' she said before Zoya could object. 'But because . . .' She glanced at Rafe. 'I may have to talk about things that make all of us uncomfortable. I'd prefer you not have to carry my memories. And that's the real reason.'

Zoya's expression softened and she looked so much like Rafe in

247

that moment that Mercy couldn't look away. The real Rafe was this vulnerable. The real Rafe wasn't a frat-boy surfer. The real Rafe felt more deeply than he wanted to admit, and Mercy wished he didn't think he needed to hide that part of himself. *Although I'm a fine one to talk about hiding parts of myself.*

'Mercy,' Zoya said quietly. 'You are family now. I know all about what happened to Gideon. I can connect the dots to know what happened to you.'

Gideon's eyes had widened. 'How? How did you know?'

The young woman shook her head. 'Everyone thinks I just go to my room or go to a friend's house because I'm told to. If I did that, I'd never learn anything about anyone in this house. So if I'm also a member of this family – and I am, because we did DNA testing in my biology class and I am fully your kid – then I want to be here. I want to help.'

Mercy shrugged. 'It's up to you, Irina.'

Irina dropped her chin, her shoulders sagging. Then she turned to face them, wiping her hands with a dishcloth. 'When did my baby grow up?'

'Six weeks ago,' Zoya said without a trace of sarcasm.

Six weeks ago, when all the Eden shit had been resurrected after Daisy tore a locket from the throat of a serial killer.

'Fair enough, *dochka maya.*' Irina sat next to Karl. 'So, what steps are required to . . .' She lifted her brows. 'Take the motherfucker down?'

'Love you, Mom,' Zoya said, her cheeks dimpling again. 'You are badass.'

'Don't push your luck, Zoya,' Irina warned, her own cheeks growing rosy with undisguised pleasure at her daughter's compliment.

Mercy dabbed at her eyes. 'My mother was badass, too. She was . . . brave. I mean, even to pick up and go to Eden at the beginning was brave. She was nineteen and scared with two kids to feed. She made a choice that should have been a good one, but it wasn't and she did her best to save us.'

Gideon had gone dangerously still, his eyes glittering with tears of his own. 'I want Ephraim to pay,' he growled. 'If that's life behind bars, so be it, but I want his life over. And then, we go after that prick DJ Belmont.'

'He killed our mother,' Mercy told the rest of the family. 'And I guess I need to tell you about how that happened.'

'You don't have to tell us anything,' Karl said gruffly, one arm around Irina's shoulders, holding her to him as if she were the most precious thing in his life. Which she was, and that made Mercy so damn happy.

It also made Mercy want the same. And that nearly had her freezing with fear, but she breathed through it. *Someday.* Someday she'd have a lover, know that she had his unconditional support. It might even be Rafe. But for now she just let herself . . . belong.

Farrah caught her eye and gave her a knowing smile. 'Took you long enough,' she muttered.

Zoya bumped shoulders with Mercy. 'You're stuck with us, Mercy. Like it or not.'

Mercy liked it. She liked it a lot. There was strength here, free, easy, and available for the taking. The sharing. *It was there with the Romeros, too. Just as free and easy.* And she'd taken strength from them, from all of them. But this was different. And the reason why was like a bolt of lightning.

The difference was Rafe. And that was something she'd need to consider a lot further.

For now she took some of their strength. 'So. Let's start with the main characters in this tale of the dark side.'

Fifteen

Rafe slid his hand over Mercy's thigh under the table, giving her a supportive squeeze. 'You don't need to do this.'

Mercy slipped her hand into his, holding on for dear life. 'Yes, I do. It's time.' She squared her shoulders because this wasn't going to be easy. 'I don't remember anything before Eden,' she started. 'Gideon does, a little, but from my earliest memories my mama was called Rhoda. Her real name was Selena. Selena Reynolds. She told me that right before she died.'

'Then we will get justice for Selena Reynolds,' Rafe said softly. 'And for you and for all the others that they abused. I promise.'

'Thank you.' She closed her eyes for a moment, then opened them to see the same determination on each of the faces around the table. 'My mother was married to a man named Amos when we first arrived.'

'Married the very next day,' Gideon said. 'She was told that it was against the laws of Eden that a woman be unmarried. It presented too much temptation to the men of the compound. But she got lucky, because Amos was a good man.'

Mercy nodded. 'I think he honestly believed in the Eden principles – you know, purity of living, back to the basics, nature's way, and all that. He believed in God and the Bible. Sometimes he didn't agree with the Founding Elders, but he was never disrespectful. He told me once that no one place and no one person or group was perfect. That what we did when no one was watching was the true

250

mark of a person. Amos was kind. Even after Gideon left and Amos was punished by Ephraim taking Mama for his own wife, he was kind. He missed her, of course, but he promised her that he'd take care of me and he did. He woke me up in the morning, traded furniture with the ladies for chores like making my clothes, darning our socks, things he couldn't do himself.' She found herself smiling. 'Although he tried. He was really bad at it.' She sighed. 'When I was almost twelve, he came home after building houses all day, so angry. Angrier than I'd ever seen him.' She looked at Gideon. 'He cried that day, because he'd just been told that Ephraim was going to marry me.'

André blinked. 'When you were twelve?'

Mercy had forgotten that he didn't know about Eden. 'Yes. Girls married at twelve. A lot of the men waited until the girls were older to . . . you know.' She aimed a sideways glance at Zoya, who patted her shoulder, sympathy in her brown eyes.

'They waited to consummate the marriage,' Zoya said. 'I get it. But Ephraim didn't wait.'

It wasn't a question, and was phrased so matter-of-factly that it helped Mercy go on. 'No. He didn't. He had a number of other wives, so it could have been worse for me, but it was bad enough. And that everyone knew that he was a brute and did nothing to stop him made it worse. They were all complicit.'

'Even Amos,' Gideon gritted.

'Even Amos,' Mercy agreed. 'Anyway, I'd made Ephraim angry one day and he . . . well, it was enough to spur Mama to action. She was desperate and made a deal with DJ Belmont. He went into town every week or so to trade for supplies.' She didn't have to elaborate on the nature of the deal. She could see that everyone understood. 'DJ was twenty-one at the time. He'd inherited the responsibility for supply runs when his father died.'

Gideon looked down at the table with a sigh. 'When our mother smuggled me out, it was with DJ's father, Waylon. I don't know why Waylon let me live. It's . . . haunted me for years.'

Daisy sucked in a harsh breath. 'You will not feel guilty that he spared you,' she hissed. 'Whatever the reason.'

Gideon's smile was sad. 'Yeah. I'll send the memo to my conscience.' He half turned in his chair, pulling Daisy to him. 'But thank you.' He kissed her hair, then looked around the table. 'The night my mother smuggled me out, I'd just accidentally killed Ephraim's brother, Edward. We didn't know they were brothers at the time. We thought they were friends. Ephraim came after me with a small mob.' He swallowed hard. 'They attacked me and I stabbed Ephraim's eye out in self-defense. That was what pushed Mama to get me out. I didn't know that Waylon died soon after I left.'

'It wasn't even two days later,' Mercy remembered. 'We were in shock, Amos and I. I thought Mama was too, but now I can see it was grief. She'd left Gideon at the Redding bus station, clinging to life. The Founding Elders said that Gideon had run away after killing Edward because he was lazy – Gideon, I mean. They said he'd died. Waylon brought back remains.' She had to take a second to rebuild her composure because the image was still crystal clear in her mind. 'They made us look. It was a person, but I couldn't identify him as Gideon.'

Gideon gasped quietly. 'They made you look?'

She nodded, her cheeks wet. She made no move to dry her eyes. There didn't seem to be much point when her tears were running like a damn river. 'Mama and me. I . . .' She exhaled, trying to calm her churning stomach through sheer will. 'Mama said it was Gideon.'

Farrah made a pained noise. 'She lied?'

Mercy nodded. 'Looking back, I think it was so that Ephraim would believe that Gideon was dead so he didn't go searching for him. The body . . . the remains . . . there was a tattoo. An Eden tattoo. Or part of one. He'd been torn apart, whoever he was.' She turned to Rafe. 'Let's add that person to our list of people who need justice. He wasn't from Eden. Gideon was the only one missing from the compound. I never even considered it before now. Never could make myself remember it. But somebody died that night. I can only assume that Waylon kidnapped someone and made it look like he'd been "devoured by wolves".' She crooked her fingers, then explained to the others. 'That's what happened to dissenters. They were cast out of Eden, to be "devoured by wolves" or bears or whatever.'

'How often did that happen?' Tom asked. He was taking notes on a tablet that looked like a tiny Post-it note in his big hands. Somehow him taking notes made this easier. Like it was someone else's life story.

No, it isn't. It's my story. And Gideon's. They hadn't asked for this. They hadn't done anything wrong. A thought struck her and she narrowed her eyes. 'Did you write down the part about Gideon accidentally killing Edward McPhearson?'

Tom met her gaze directly. 'No. Although if I had, no one would come after Gideon. It was self-defense. But I'll let you read my notes when I'm finished if that will help.'

Mercy nodded once. 'It would. Three times that I remember, to answer your question. Members of Eden turned up either as remains – usually recognizable – or were buried outside the compound if there weren't enough remains to bring back. Gideon was the only one I remember of the three whose supposed body was not recognizable.'

'I also remember three. Two of them might be the same as Mercy remembers, but one was when I was only five years old. We'd only just arrived then, so I'm sure you don't remember that one, Merce.'

'No. The first I remember was when I was four years old.'

Gideon nodded. 'So, during our total time in Eden, four times, including me.'

Daisy growled and Brutus popped her little head up out of the bag Daisy always wore. 'It's okay, girl,' Daisy murmured, petting the animal.

Mercy wished desperately that she had Rory in her own lap. Her cat always knew when she needed comfort. But Rafe still held her hand and that was definitely helping.

'So Waylon died two days after Gideon supposedly ran away and was found dead,' Tom said. 'When in reality, he'd facilitated Gideon's escape.'

'Yes,' Mercy confirmed. 'I don't know what DJ told people about me.'

Tom tilted his head. 'And your mother?'

Mercy drew a shuddering breath, the words freezing on her

tongue. 'I . . .' Rafe put his arm around her and drew her close. She pressed her forehead to his upper arm, suddenly struggling to breathe. 'Give me a minute.'

'Want me to say it?' Rafe whispered. 'No one will think less of you if you can't say it.'

I would, she thought. *Mama deserves to have this story told.* Again she braced herself and told Tom, 'DJ killed my mother. In front of me.'

'Oh.' It was a small cry from Zoya, full of hurt. 'I'm so sorry.'

She patted Zoya's hand, the young woman's guileless concern like a balm. 'Thanks, hon.' She turned back to Tom. 'He took us to the Redding bus station, grabbed me from the back of his truck, and dumped me on the parking lot. I couldn't move. I was . . . hurt. And sick with fever. I had an infection.'

'Because of Ephraim,' Gideon gritted out, his hands clenched into fists. 'Sonofabitch.'

Mercy didn't have the emotional energy to comfort him at the moment, but luckily Daisy's small dog did, licking the knuckles of his fist. Gideon choked back what had probably been a sob, taking Brutus from Daisy to cuddle against his own chest.

The sight made Mercy smile. And gave her the push to finish the story. 'DJ told me Brother Ephraim was coming and that just . . . froze me. He'd told Mama to stay in the back of the truck, but she ran to me, just as DJ pulled out his gun.' She focused on Gideon as if he were the only one in the room, because he should have been. She should have told him this story when they were alone. When he could cry if he wanted. But then she understood that here, with his family and people he trusted, was the perfect place to tell him. They'd comfort him, even if she didn't have any comfort left to give by the time she was finished.

'Mama threw herself on top of me,' she told her brother. 'Tried to protect me. Said, "You promised!" But DJ laughed. He said, "I promised to get you out. I never promised to let you live." Then he pulled her off me and shot me.' She touched her abdomen, where she still had an ugly scar. 'Mama was screaming, but no one was there to hear us. He shot her next, in the same place. She fell, telling

DJ that Ephraim would kill him for this, but he just laughed again.' She closed her eyes, for the first time allowing her conscious mind to replay the moment without interruption. She knew it by heart, because her sleeping mind replayed it all the time. 'He said, "No, he won't. He never does. He can't".'

Tom was typing on his tablet, his eyes never leaving her face. 'And then?'

She pressed her lips together. *Just a little bit more.* 'He told me to watch. And he shot her in the head.' She touched her temple. 'Here. Then he threw her back into the truck bed.' She became aware of wetness on her neck and realized it was Rafe. He'd buried his face there and he was crying too, and suddenly she needed this to be over. 'And then he left.'

Everyone was silent until Tom cleared his throat. 'He . . . left you there?' he finally asked.

'Well, not right then. After he put Mama in the back of the truck, he came back for me, to finish me off, I suppose. But someone drove into the parking lot. A cop.' She frowned, the memory fuzzy. 'Maybe? There were flashing lights and DJ thought they were cops. The car turned its headlights on us and it was so bright.' She could remember the brightness, how it hurt her eyes. The fear. The empty pit of despair. 'DJ ran back to his truck and drove away. Eventually paramedics came. One was a woman. I remember her saying that I'd be okay, that they'd help me. And after that I woke up in a hospital bed.'

'They were not cops,' Irina said, her voice thick, her eyes red. 'I know this part, because I was working in the hospital when you were admitted, Mercy. Not in your ward, but I heard about the girl who'd been left for dead in Redding and airlifted to us. The girl who had two lockets that had the decoration that my Gideon wore on his chest.'

Mercy blinked at the woman. 'I didn't know that.'

'You were catatonic,' Irina said. 'You sat and rocked when you were healed enough. Before then, you just stared at the ceiling. For hours. It broke our hearts, the nurses.'

'Who were the people, if they weren't cops?' Tom asked.

Irina shook her head. 'I don't know their names, but they would be listed in the police report. The driver was a security guard, a private one. I can't remember his employer, but he did come in the day after you were admitted to see how you were doing. That was according to your nurse at the time, who was a friend of mine. She's the one who told me about you. The security guard told her that he'd come to pick up his wife at the bus station, but that he was really early. He'd been sleeping in his car, out of sight of the shooter's truck, when he heard the screams. He didn't know what to do, so he figured he'd turn on his lights and maybe scare the shooter away. He felt bad that he didn't get out of his car, that he'd "only" called 911, but he had no medical training, so he wouldn't have known what to do. The paramedics were there in minutes.'

'That was still brave of him,' Mercy murmured, resolving to find the man's name and thank him. 'He saved my life that night.'

Rafe's hand tightened on hers and he lifted his head. 'We need to thank him.'

Mercy nodded. 'I was thinking that. Can you get his name, Rafe?'

Tom was still frowning. 'I'll dig into the records for you. But I'm confused. You had two lockets when you were brought into the hospital – yours and your mother's, I assume.'

'Yes,' Mercy said, not sure what his question was.

'Well, I thought that the lockets were on heavy chains. Welded on. Impossible to break. How did you get both lockets?'

Mercy blinked again. She'd never wondered about that, but Tom was right. 'He cut them off us.' Another memory surfaced, this one not normally part of her nightmares. 'He had bolt cutters and he cut them off us and buried them in the dirt. When he drove away, all I could think of was that I needed the lockets, so I crawled to where he'd buried them and dug them up.'

Gideon stared at her. 'Why would he do that? Why bury the lockets?'

Mercy stared back. 'I have no idea. Maybe he was trying to hide any evidence that would connect to Eden? I didn't even remember that till just now. I just remember needing to get to the lockets.'

'Because they were the last you had of your mother?' Sasha asked.

'Maybe. Or . . .' It was a hard truth to admit, even now. 'Or maybe the lockets were such a critical part of our lives, I felt wrong without mine even though I hated it. It was like an identity or part of our spirituality. It's difficult to explain. Kind of like a talisman. Even though it was really a display of ownership.' She shrugged.

'Can you remember anything else about that night, Mercy?' Tom asked.

She closed her eyes and let the scene play a final time. For now, anyway. She was certain she'd pay for opening the floodgates of her memories when she closed her eyes to sleep later. 'He thought Gideon was dead. He said that we'd die there, like Gideon did.'

Rafe stiffened. 'So he knew that Gideon had escaped to the bus station?'

'Oh.' Mercy's eyes widened. 'Oh yeah, you're right. I don't know if all the leadership knew Gideon had escaped, but I kind of don't think so, because they would have hunted him down.'

Daisy grimaced, but Gideon's face was scrunched in thought. 'So if DJ knew I'd at least made it to the bus station,' he said thoughtfully, 'but thought I'd died there, does that mean he heard that from Waylon?'

'Maybe?' Mercy hadn't considered that. 'I mean, at the time we were reeling over the fact that you were dead. We didn't know that Waylon had helped you escape, so it wasn't anything we thought about. Later, when DJ said that you'd died at the bus station . . . well, I was in shock. I wasn't thinking clearly about anything other than that Mama was dead. I didn't give much thought to what Mama had said about you not being dead until you walked into my foster home a few months after I'd been released from the hospital.'

'I've noted that DJ also thought you were dead and that his father might have told him,' Tom said. 'And that Waylon died not too long after. Understanding the culture and power structure of the cult could be key in finding them and bringing them down. Let's go back to the people who were supposedly "devoured." Of the four incidents you both remember, we know one was a lie. I mean, someone died, but it wasn't Gideon. Is it possible that the others escaped as well?'

Mercy shook her head. 'The other two that I remember, the people were identifiable. Now, their families? I don't know.' When Tom looked confused she sighed. 'We moved the whole compound after each person was discovered. Their families did not come with us. Nobody ever spoke of them again. It was widely believed that they returned to the "world." The "world" being not Eden.'

'We know a few people escaped,' Daisy said. 'Eileen escaped back in November. Also Levi Hull, the young man who later killed himself and whose boyfriend got an Eden-style tattoo. He got out about seven years ago. There's one other that we've been looking for. His tat is on Instagram, but you know about him, Tom.'

Tom nodded. 'We still don't know who that person is or was, but the search is still active. Gideon, what about the people you remember that Mercy doesn't because she was too young?'

'Oh.' Gideon was still stroking Brutus, who occasionally licked at his chin. He frowned, thinking. 'Marcia,' he finally said. 'Her name was Marcia. She had two kids, Bernice and Boaz. They were twins, but older than me, so we didn't play together or anything.' Then he inhaled sharply. 'Shit, how could I have forgotten that? Marcia was Pastor's wife. It was a horrible day when their bodies were brought back. Not recognizable. They were gone almost a week when they were discovered in a ravine. Their bodies had been heavily scavenged. I remember that church was canceled for a long time – days and days – because Pastor went off by himself to search for them, then later to mourn when they buried them. Nobody was allowed to play or smile or even talk. People walked around on tiptoes. It was awful. Mama drilled into my head that there were animals out there and we were not supposed to go outside the gates alone, ever.'

Mercy closed her open mouth with a snap. 'Pastor had kids before he adopted DJ?'

Gideon's brows rose. 'Pastor adopted DJ after Waylon died? In-teresting. I mean, Pastor had always spoiled DJ, but DJ was Waylon's son. That's what DJ stood for, he told me once. He was Waylon Jr.'

Sasha tilted her head, puzzled. 'How do you get "DJ" from "Waylon Jr."?'

Gideon waved a hand impatiently. 'Double-you-jay was too hard to say, so they called him DJ.'

Sasha shook her head. 'Okay.'

Gideon reached around Daisy to tug on Sasha's ponytail fondly. 'Don't think too much. Most of the names in Eden were strange. Point is, DJ was not Pastor's biological son.'

'Yeah,' Mercy said, 'but after Waylon died, Pastor adopted him. He moved in with Pastor and everything.'

'What was Pastor's name?' Tom asked.

Mercy and Gideon stared at each other. 'I have no idea,' Mercy said. 'He was always just Pastor.'

Gideon dropped his gaze to Brutus, petting her batlike ears. 'I don't remember, but I heard it. DJ might even have told me. He was four years older than me, but he'd play with me sometimes. Teach me stuff.' His expression shifted, then paled. 'Oh,' he breathed. 'Until I was nine. After that, he'd shove me away and bully me. Gave me a black eye once. I thought it was because I was a little kid and he was finally a teenager, but . . . he changed. He got . . . mean.'

Mercy immediately understood. 'When he turned thirteen.'

Rafe slumped in his chair. 'Maybe he was also abused.'

'He was Edward's apprentice,' Gideon murmured. 'Same as me. So yes. It's likely.'

'But no excuse,' Irina said harshly. 'We can pity the boy who was abused, but we cannot excuse the man that boy became.'

'No. We can't.' Mercy suddenly felt so tired she thought she'd fall over. 'I hope we're done, Tom. I can't think anymore and Farrah's already asleep.'

It was true. Farrah had fallen asleep, her head on André's shoulder.

Tom checked the time and winced. 'I'm sure I'll have more questions for you later, but this is enough for me to get started. Thank you both. I know this wasn't easy for either of you.'

She and Gideon just nodded, both of them having hit the wall.

'I'll take you back to our place,' Rafe said. 'Daisy, can Farrah and

André have the top floor?' At Daisy's nod, he turned to Mercy, looking as exhausted as she felt. 'You can bunk with Sasha.'

Irina sprang to her feet, pulling Karl up to his. 'We will pack up this food. You will all take some.' She pointed to Tom. 'Even you.'

He smiled up at her. 'Thank you, Irina. I'd love that.'

Mercy stood, then groaned. 'Dammit.'

Farrah blinked up at her sleepily. 'What?' She looked around, abruptly alert, then socked André in the shoulder. 'You let me fall asleep?'

'You needed it,' André said affectionately. 'And no, you didn't snore. This time.'

She gave him the evil eye, then focused on Mercy. 'Dammit, what?'

'I forgot about that interview. The one you set up, Daisy.'

'We moved it to tomorrow evening,' Daisy said uncertainly. 'That way you can figure out what you want to say. Today was too emotional in every way. I hope I didn't overstep.'

Mercy's knees wobbled as relief swamped her. 'No, you didn't. Thank you, Daisy. I don't think I could have managed that tonight.' After the day's sorrow and fear and the walk down the haunted lane of Eden, the sexual assault video felt oddly . . . surreal. Like it hadn't happened to her at all. Which was ridiculous, of course. It *had* happened to her, but the memory felt numb, like when an ER doctor had numbed her finger with novocaine before stitching up a bad cut. Kind of a distant throbbing. She'd been able to watch her finger tap the table and not feel it at all. That was how the memory seemed.

Which was all wrong for what she now knew she wanted to say. 'I want to do the interview, but with the video being treated as only one part of a whole.'

Daisy tilted her head. 'I don't follow you.'

Mercy's lips tipped up sadly. 'The video represents less than five minutes of my life. Devastating and humiliating and damaging minutes, but not the worst I've experienced by far. I won't talk about Eden, not if the FBI is still hoping to keep Pastor and the others unaware while they investigate. But I will say that the assault on that video wasn't the first in my life. And that I wouldn't have survived any of it without a therapist and the support of good people, whether I welcomed them at the time or not. There are other victims out there, other people who've been hurt who don't have anyone. People who might be so alone that they give up. I don't want this to simply be me clearing my name or turning public opinion in my favor. I want anyone hurting to know where to get help, and I need time to gather some resources to share. I assume you all can help me with this?' She glanced around the table, realizing she had cops, a retired nurse in Irina, a social worker in Sasha, a marketing mogul in Karl, and a radio personality in Daisy, who could give the message even more reach. If they couldn't help her, they'd know who could.

Gideon looked up at her from where he still sat, his eyes wet. 'You don't have to do this,' he whispered, but there was pride mixed with the tears.

She walked to his chair and stroked a hand over his hair. 'Yeah, I kind of do. Mama died so that I could be free. So, I'm going to be free. That can't happen if I let this video or fear of Ephraim Burton keep me chained. She wouldn't want that. It's my turn to be brave, brother.'

In a fluid movement that stole her breath, Gideon was on his feet and she was in his arms. He was sobbing – silently, but so hard that his body shook with it. Mercy closed her eyes and clung, vaguely aware of scraping chairs and fading footsteps as the kitchen cleared, leaving them alone to weep and mourn the loss of their mother, of their childhoods, of the time together that they'd lost.

'I missed you,' he finally said, brokenly. 'God, Mercy, I missed you.'

She squeezed hard. 'I missed you, too. But I'm here now.'

He lifted his head, his face wrecked, but smiling. 'You are. Because you're already brave. Don't ever think otherwise.'

It was exactly what she'd needed to hear. 'Thank you.'

Granite Bay, California
Sunday, 16 April, 8.45 P.M.

Well. That's interesting. Ephraim stared at his laptop screen, at the results that had come up from his search on the license plate he'd noted as the scrawny kid and his mother had driven away from the Sokolov house.

The old car was registered to Geri Bunker, according to the database he'd used Sean MacGuire's credit card to access. And a background check, also funded with MacGuire's card, showed her only relative to be Jeffrey Bunker.

Jeffrey Bunker, who was the author of the extremely unflattering exposé he'd read at Granny's house that morning. The one with the video that had been taken down before Ephraim could view it.

At least it explained Detective Sokolov's near assault on the kid, who was some kind of prodigy, already halfway through his college degree at age sixteen. Ephraim tucked the knowledge away for future use. If Sokolov had that kind of temper, Ephraim could use it to his own advantage.

His attention was diverted from his screen by activity at the Sokolov house. The tall blond guy in a dark suit emerged from the front door, receiving a hug from Mrs Sokolov before he jogged to a black SUV, parked on the curb. It was the same Fed whose earlier arrival had prompted Ephraim to seek safer shelter. He'd left, then come back, and Ephraim wasn't sure if that was good or bad.

The small Asian woman who'd been involved in the scuffle with Jeff Bunker got into a Range Rover, but sat waiting while the black SUV drove away.

The garage door opened, revealing the gray Chevy Suburban that had brought Gideon, Detective Sokolov, and Mercy to the Sokolovs' house earlier that day. Ephraim got busy, packing his computer into the backpack he'd had delivered earlier that day.

Thank you, Amazon. He'd ordered the backpack and a few other trinkets, using MacGuire's credit card to pay for one-hour delivery. It had taken an hour and a half, but that was still impressive, especially on a Sunday. He'd miss the little conveniences of the world when he headed back to Eden.

He peered into the backpack, ensuring that he had everything he needed, especially if he wasn't able to come back here. If he got Mercy tonight, he'd be long gone.

He mentally checked off his laptop and the new high-powered binoculars and GPS trackers he'd also purchased from Amazon, along with the revolver he'd brought from Eden and the pistol he'd taken from the costume store college kid. He tucked Regina's golden gun into his jacket pocket. The silencer made it his gun of choice. He'd need to get some ammo soon, though. The magazine held fifteen rounds, so it was technically illegal in California, but Ephraim wasn't going to tell and Regina no longer could.

He didn't know how he'd manage it, but he wanted to hide a GPS tracker on Sokolov's vehicle so that he didn't have to risk following them so closely. Plus, not having to watch every move they made would let him actually sleep tonight, a definite plus. There was no way he'd get a tracker on any of the cars while they sat in front of the house in Granite Bay, but he might be able to get close enough once they all dispersed.

He hurried down the stairs, double-checking MacGuire's restraints before heading for the door. It would be easier to simply kill the guy, but something held him back. Maybe the calm acceptance in the man's eyes. If MacGuire was trying to use reverse psychology to stay alive, it was working.

Plus, this guy had access to a lot of money. Money that Ephraim might need, and certainly wanted. Grabbing MacGuire's car keys from the hook on the wall, he waved. 'See you later.'

There were three cars in the garage – a classic Corvette, a Mercedes convertible, and a newer Cadillac, which somehow managed to look boring. He took the Caddy and backed out of MacGuire's driveway just in time to see the convoy of cars from the Sokolovs' house passing by.

At the front of the line was the rental car that had arrived that afternoon, carrying the black man whose identity Ephraim still didn't know. That bugged him, because the guy was a wild card and

Ephraim didn't like not knowing what to expect.

Second in line was the gray Suburban in which Sokolov and Mercy had arrived along with Gideon. The Asian lady brought up the rear in a blue Range Rover.

Ephraim had run those plates too, and they belonged to Erin Rhee. According to the Internet, she was Sokolov's SacPD partner and had also been injured along with Sokolov the night they and Gideon had taken down that serial killer, rescuing Mercy. He'd found a number of articles on the case, once he'd known what to look for.

Ephraim followed the caravan as it got on I-80, making sure there were always at least four cars between Rhee's Range Rover and Sean MacGuire's Cadillac. He almost lost them when they exited the highway, but it wasn't too hard to find three cars in a slow-moving line.

They came to a stop in front of an old Victorian that appeared to be fully restored and well kept. Three mailboxes were mounted near the curb, so the house had probably been subdivided. A hot pink Mini Cooper was parked on the street in front of the house.

At least the Cadillac fit this neighborhood better than the rusted piece of junk he'd left parked near Folsom Lake. He'd have stood out like a sore thumb if he still drove that piece of shit.

The garage door on the Victorian lifted, revealing a red Subaru in one of the two bays and a tan Tahoe in the other. Gideon parked the gray Suburban in the driveway behind the Subaru, and the rental car stopped directly beside it. Erin Rhee's blue Range Rover parked on the street, partially obscuring Ephraim's view. He could no longer see into the garage, but he could still see part of the driveway, and he could see the Asian woman jumping down from the Range Rover and rushing into the garage, her gun drawn.

The driver's door of the rental opened and the unidentified black man got out. He went around to open the passenger door, extending his hand to help pull a woman to her feet. *Dammit.* That was the woman who'd come with Mercy from New Orleans. Dr Farrah Romero.

Mercy's old-lady neighbor had talked a lot about Farrah during

264

Ephraim's visit. Dr Romero was her great-niece, and Mercy's very best friend, the two of them inseparable since college. Ephraim grabbed the binoculars from the seat beside him and focused on the man, committing his face to memory. He'd check him out, because he had a bad feeling about the guy's sudden appearance, and an even worse feeling that he recognized him from somewhere.

He replayed his conversation with the old lady before he'd killed her. She'd talked about every member of her huge family, and several times he'd had to steer her back toward Farrah and Mercy or he'd have been there all night long. Farrah wasn't a medical doctor, he remembered that. She worked in a lab at the university, which made the old woman both proud and a little sad, because it meant that Farrah and her fiancé were putting off starting their family and she couldn't wait to see what pretty babies they'd make together.

Fucking hell. Now he remembered where he'd seen the guy – in a photograph on the old lady's coffee table. He was Farrah's fiancé. Quickly he opened Farrah Romero's Facebook page on his phone and scrolled through her photos. He never got used to seeing how very free people were with their information online. After living off the grid for thirty years, the thought of anyone having information on Ephraim made his skin itch.

There he is. It was a photo of Farrah and her fiancé. André Holmes, NOPD.

Fucking hell. Another damn cop?

But his focus on the now-identified newcomer fractured, his breath catching in his throat when Gideon Reynolds emerged from the gray Suburban. A petite blonde at his side rushed around the SUV to wrap her arm around Gideon's waist. Daisy Dawson, he remembered. She hugged Farrah and the New Orleans cop, then Gideon hugged Farrah and shook hands with André Holmes.

Mercy and Sokolov emerged from the backseat of the Suburban, but the asshole detective ushered her into the garage before Ephraim could get a good look at her. His attention returned to Gideon, who was helping Daisy back into his SUV, and Ephraim realized he'd shoved his hand in his pocket and was gripping Regina's golden gun.

Not here. Not now. There were too many people – too many damn cops – and Ephraim wasn't sure he'd get cleanly away. When Reynolds and Dawson drove away, Ephraim had to force himself not to follow. Yes, he wanted Gideon, but he *needed* Mercy. Either dead or alive.

Yes, Waylon had lied about killing Gideon, but Waylon was dead. His influence on the community and his claim to the millions under Pastor's control were no more. DJ was still alive and the biggest threat. And DJ had lied about Mercy's death.

Mercy is key, he told himself. Once he got her, he could come back for Gideon.

And revenge would be so damn sweet. Gideon would be sorry that he hadn't died that night all those years ago. Ephraim would hear the bastard scream as he carved out his eyes. The first eye would be payment for Ephraim's own eye. The second would be the down payment for killing Edward. Then he'd take his time carving up the rest of him, making him look like the raw meat that Waylon had brought back to Eden, claiming it was Gideon's body.

Ephraim laughed bitterly. Waylon had fooled them all. Except for Rhoda, of course. Gideon's mother had to have known that the remains Waylon had returned hadn't been her son, even though she'd positively identified his body.

She should have been mine to kill, he thought, fists clenched. DJ would pay for that too, the prick.

The garage door came down, cutting off Ephraim's view. For the moment, no one was outside. The blue Range Rover and the hot pink Mini Cooper were unattended.

He ran a hand over his face and patted his head, making sure his beard and wig were in place. It wasn't going to fool them if he got up in their faces, but from a distance, in the dark? It would do.

Grabbing two of the GPS trackers, he drove slowly next to the empty vehicles, opening his door just enough to squeeze his hand through. He glanced up at the house. Lights were going on in the upstairs apartments, but no one was looking out the windows.

Slowing to a crawl, he paused long enough to slip the first tracker into the Range Rover's left rear hubcap. He did the same to the Mini

Cooper, then pulled his door closed and kept going until he reached the end of the block, where he pulled over.

He opened the tracking app on his smartphone and grunted in satisfaction. There they were, two blinking dots right next to each other.

He'd be able to follow those cars at least. Unfortunately, they didn't belong to Rafe Sokolov or Mercy. He rounded the block, stopping on the street behind Sokolov's.

He couldn't see into the house, but he could see headlights if anyone left. That would have to be good enough for now. Plus, no one could leave except for the pink Mini Cooper, not with the Range Rover parked across the driveway. Rhee would need to move her vehicle first, which would send an alarm to his phone.

Ephraim settled down into his seat, watching as windows in the Victorian began to go dark. They were settling in for the night. He could close his eyes for a little while.

Just a little while.

Sixteen

Rafe didn't think he'd ever been so drained. The single step from his garage into the foyer might as well have been a steep mountain climb.

'Need a hand?'

He turned to see André giving him a sympathetic grimace. 'I broke my leg a few years back. Took me months to get back to normal.'

The women had already gone into the house, Erin at the forefront, clearing every room before declaring his house safe. His partner had made herself their personal bodyguard and Rafe was grateful. He certainly wasn't up to the task at the moment.

'But you obviously recovered,' Rafe said, André's words giving him hope.

'Eh.' André waggled his hand back and forth. 'Mostly. I'm not as fast as I used to be, and a lot of days start and end in the whirlpool. You got a good PT?'

'The best. My brother Cash.' Who'd gone the extra mile, concerned for his mental health in addition to the rehabilitation of his leg.

'Good. Plan on using him for a long, long time. It's been eight years, and I still have to go in for tune-ups occasionally. Not just my leg, y'understand. Now it's my knees and hips, too. Turns out you distribute your weight differently. Have to compensate. So, not to be all doom and gloom, but you're in this for the long haul.'

'But you came back to the job.' It was a glimmer of hope and he held on to it.

268

'Yep. You okay if I help you up the stairs?'

Rafe nodded, stifling the embarrassment and irritation at having to accept it. André put his arm around his shoulders, practically hefting Rafe up the single step.

Ouch. Now his shoulders hurt too, but he nodded, thankful. He pressed a set of keys into André's hand. 'I think Sasha's already let Farrah in, but here's a key to the third-floor apartment in case you need to come and go. Feel free to drive the Tahoe if you don't want to keep paying for the rental.'

'What about you? Don't you need it?'

Rafe pointed to his Subaru, on the other side of the garage. 'That's mine. The bullet hit my left leg, so I can drive myself.' And he was grateful for that stroke of luck. 'The Tahoe is my dad's, but he got a midlife-crisis Tesla, so the Tahoe sits in his garage. We borrowed it for Mercy, but I don't think she'll be driving anywhere alone until we get Burton, so you might as well use it. Sasha's the hot pink Mini outside, so she's good, too.'

André chuckled. 'That's a car no one can miss.'

Rafe smiled with affection for his sister. 'Sasha likes to make a splash wherever she goes. The garage door code is programmed into the Tahoe, in case you drive it. You'll find extra blankets and pillows in the closet, and the deli down the street delivers. There's a magnet with their number on the fridge and a shit ton of take-out menus in the kitchen drawer.'

'I don't think food is going to be an issue. Your mother gave us enough for a week.'

Rafe smiled at that, too. 'Mom cooks when she's anxious, but I think you guessed that for yourself. Let me or Sasha know if you need anything else. And get some rest, okay?'

'I don't think that's going to be an issue, either. Thanks, Rafe.'

'You got it. Do you know what Farrah's plans are? I assume she'll go back to New Orleans as soon as possible. Her family must need her.' He'd been wondering that all the way back to the house.

'I don't know. She's pretty attached to Mercy and she's torn. Her mama told her to stay for a few more days at least, for Mercy. Besides, it'll take another few days to get her aunt's body to be released by the ME's office, so at this point they're mostly planning Quill's celebration.' He smiled sadly. 'That'll be something to see. Quill lived an amazing life and never met a stranger. I think the street's gonna overflow with her parade, and Quill would want Mercy there for it, so they'll hold off as long as they can if Mercy can come back.'

Rafe felt a stab of regret as André's words sank in. The Romeros loved Mercy, it was clear, and she loved them. Plus, there was John Benz, her half brother, and all the 'sibs', as she'd called them. Mercy had family in New Orleans, as well as a job. She wouldn't be staying in California.

Not forever, anyway.

André's eyes narrowed and then he sighed. 'Well, fuck,' he muttered. 'Mercy's going to be torn too, won't she? And you want her to stay.'

Rafe wasn't going to deny it. 'Good night, André. See you tomorrow, okay?'

'Tomorrow, man.' André waved and started up the stairs, his tread slow and heavy.

Rafe entered the bottom-floor studio as Erin was coming out.

'All clear,' she pronounced. 'Everything's clean.'

'Wait,' he said when she reached for the house's front door. 'Where are you going?'

'Out to stand watch until your backup gets here.' She frowned. 'The Feds sent a car, which was supposed to be here when we arrived, but they hit a traffic snarl. They'll be here soon. I told them I'd stay until they arrive.'

'You've got to be tired. Don't you have work tomorrow?'

'Just warming my chair,' she grumbled. 'No fun without you there. But yes, I do have work and my backup arrives in a half hour. Then I'll go home and get my beauty sleep. Lock up behind me.' She didn't wait for a response, leaving through the front door.

He locked the door and set the alarm, shaking his head. Like he needed her to remind him.

But that was Erin, showing that she cared. Because she did, of that he was certain.

270

He dragged his tired ass into the apartment, locked that door, and collapsed onto the sofa. His laptop sat on the table where Mercy had left it before they'd left for his mother's Sunday dinner, a stack of printouts of Eden-made furniture and crafts ready for the bulletin board.

He was too tired to get up and tack them to the board. He was too tired to get off the sofa and go to bed. But apparently not too tired for his mind to keep buzzing around Mercy.

God, she'd broken his heart tonight. *So damn brave.* And when Gideon had broken down at the end? Rafe hadn't been able to hold himself together. Luckily, he wasn't alone – figuratively or literally. His family had clung to one another in the hall outside the kitchen, wrapping Farrah and André into their group hug. Until Mercy and Gideon had reappeared, both looking awful with red eyes and noses. But both looked equally at peace – and suddenly Rafe had felt at peace, too.

Until just now. Because Mercy didn't live here. He might believe she belonged here, but she had another life. That she'd stay in Sacramento for Gideon's sake was a nice wish, but not very likely, no matter how close they got over the upcoming weeks.

In fact, it was highly likely that she'd return to New Orleans with Farrah for her aunt's funeral and decide to stay there.

His heart was seriously at risk, but he wasn't sure how he could protect himself. He could walk away now. Let Mercy and Gideon find Burton and put the bastard down. But that would be wrong. He'd promised to help.

He could simply make sure there was always distance between Mercy and himself. But the thought hurt.

Or, he could just be with her and enjoy what time they had, then deal with the fallout when it happened. He'd keep her safer than he'd kept Bella, that was for damn sure. Images of Bella's body filled his head and he pushed them away, refusing to allow his mind to see Mercy in the same way.

A knock on his door jerked him from the dour thoughts. *Fucking hell.* He did not want to get up. 'Who is it?'

'It's Mercy.'

Mercy. A tiny pulse of energy spread to his arms and legs, and he pulled himself to the edge of the sofa. 'Give me a minute,' he called. 'I'm coming.' *Don't go. Please don't go.*

'I have a key, if that's okay,' she called. 'Sasha gave it to me, but I didn't want to barge in.'

Rafe exhaled heavily, angry with his body. But it had been an eventful two days and he hadn't gotten much sleep the night before. Better not to push himself any further, he thought, resigned. 'Come in.'

Opening the door, Mercy peeked her head around it. 'Decent?'

He laughed. 'Not remotely.'

She smiled at him, her green eyes twinkling as she closed and locked the door and then crossed to the sofa. 'Liar. You're too tired to get ready for bed, aren't you?'

'Guilty as charged.' He patted the cushion next to him. 'What's wrong, Mercy?'

She sat beside him, curling her legs beneath her, her smile fading. 'Brain's racing.'

'You want to talk about it?'

'No, you should go to sleep,' she said, but her eyes said differently, telegraphing a silent plea.

'If I do, then just cover me up with a blanket and leave me here. Wouldn't be the first time I fell asleep on this sofa.' He lifted a brow. 'You, too.'

'I did that, didn't I? Just this morning. This day has been surreal. I hope Farrah at least can sleep.'

Rafe carefully rested his arm across the sofa back, not touching her, but issuing the invitation to come closer. To his relief, she did, snuggling into his side, her head on his chest. 'You did good tonight, Mercy,' he murmured, kissing her hair. 'You were so brave.'

'Thank you.' She sounded grimly determined. 'That's the plan.'

'Plan for what?'

'Being brave. Taking my life back. I'm tired of being afraid, of hiding. Of being alone because I don't think anyone will want me.'

His heart played a staccato rhythm in his chest. *I want you.* He

272

drew a breath, fighting the words back down. It wasn't time. 'You don't have to be alone,' he finally said.

That clearly wasn't the right thing to say, because she tensed.

Well, shit. He wasn't sure if he should apologize, and if so, what for exactly. 'I'm *umf*—' Whatever he was going to say was cut off when she grabbed his face and pulled him down, sealing her mouth over his. He grunted in surprise, then groaned, his body perking right up. Everywhere.

So much for exhaustion.

She was humming against his mouth, up on her knees now, so that she hovered over him, her mouth eating at his. She swung one leg over him, never breaking the kiss as she straddled him.

He groaned again, his hands full of her, all hot and incredibly energetic. Undulating against him until he could barely think. *God.* He shuddered, his hands sliding up and down her back, coming to rest on the perfect curve of her ass.

This was perfect.

She was perfect. *And desperate*, his mind whispered. *She's too desperate.*

And she *was* desperate, he realized. Not in a good way. *Stop this. Now.*

With a resolve he never knew he possessed, he yanked away. 'Wait,' he panted. 'Stop.' Leaning his head into the cushion, he craned his neck to see her face.

Desperate was indeed an accurate description. Her eyes were wild. Unfocused.

Until she blinked, going from sixty to zero in that single blink. Her face flooded with color and she tried to get away.

He let go immediately and she backed off his lap and onto her feet. Which brought the backs of her legs against the coffee table. She stumbled, knocking all the Eden printouts to the floor, her butt hitting the hard wood.

Hard wood, Sokolov? Really? He wanted to groan again, from frustration, confusion, irritation with himself. Because he was harder than any wood on the planet.

'Mercy.' His voice was low and gruff. Aroused as hell.

She dropped her chin to her chest, sending her hair flowing over her face like a curtain. She didn't answer him. Didn't look up.

His heart sank. 'Mercy, please. Look at me.' He was afraid to touch her, afraid he'd do the wrong thing. 'Please.'

She shook her head, her expression hidden behind the fall of hair. 'I'll go now. I'm . . . sorry.'

'No.' The single word cracked in the air between them, the command more desperate than she had been. 'Please. Mercy, you have to know that I want you. You have to know that.'

She huffed a bitter little laugh. 'It's not your job to make me feel better, Rafe. I was too pushy. I get it.' She stood, spinning on her heel to head for the door. 'I'll see you tomorrow.'

'Mercy.' He softened his voice. 'Don't go. Please.'

She stopped walking but didn't turn to look at him. 'This was stupid. I was stupid. I'm sorry.'

'You are not stupid. You're—' He cut himself off, because he was about to make things worse.

She turned slowly. 'I'm what?'

He swallowed hard. *Go big or go home.* 'Everything I want.'

She lifted her chin, a frown creasing her brow. 'Then why did you stop?'

He patted the sofa cushion. 'Come back. Please.' He tried to smile, but he was pretty sure he didn't pull it off. 'Don't make me drop to my knees. I might never get up.'

Her mouth quirked so briefly that he might have missed it if he hadn't been staring at her, willing her to return to him. He held his breath until she retraced her steps, dropping onto the sofa, but at the far end, not next to him.

But she was still here.

'I stopped because . . . it felt like you were afraid.'

'I was,' she said sarcastically. 'That I'd get rejected. I'll live, Rafe.'

Wow. He wasn't sure how to fix this. 'You think I'm rejecting you? That I'm not interested?'

She shrugged. 'You're the one who stopped.'

'You think I'm lying? That I don't want you? That's the most ridiculous thing.' He leaned sideways until he caught her gaze. 'Touch me. Know that I'm telling the truth.'

Her chin dipped again, but this time because she was studying his body. Closely. He pressed the flat of his hand against his cock to give himself some relief.

She exhaled quietly. 'Then why?'

'Because . . .' He shook his head. 'Was this why you came down here? You wanted to make out? I don't know what you want, Mercy, and I got the definite impression that you didn't, either.'

Green eyes skewered him, flashing fury. 'You think I don't know my mind?'

'Shit. No. That's not what I think. Well, maybe a little. It's just . . . sudden. And it makes me wonder what you wanted me to do.'

Her eyes widened at that. 'You don't know what to do?' she asked, still sarcastic. He actually remembered this Mercy. She'd been snarky when they'd first met, when she sat by his bedside for hours at a time. He'd never expected to be so captivated by such a sharp tongue.

'Oh, I know what to do. Trust me on that.' He could imagine it all too clearly, sinking into her body, hot and wet and tight. He shivered and cleared his throat. 'Jesus, Mercy, I'm hanging on to my control by a thread. But I don't want to be that man, just another person who takes advantage of you. You had a bad day and maybe you just want to be held. Maybe feel . . . I don't know. Desired?' He saw a flicker of need in her eyes and knew he'd guessed right. 'Maybe even show yourself that you could be with someone that way?'

Her cheeks flamed anew and she looked away. 'Yes.'

Compassion filled his heart till it ached, but he also felt a smidge of resentment. 'As much as I'd like that guy to be me, I want to know you want *me*. Not a convenient, warm body.'

Her mouth fell open. 'Are you saying I'm a slut?'

He sighed. 'No. God. Just . . . no. That's the furthest thing from what I was saying.' He took a moment to figure out exactly what he wanted to tell her, then went with honest. Even if it left him open to future pain. Which it would, he was pretty certain.

'I have feelings for you. Feelings I haven't felt for anyone in a very long time. I don't want this to be a one-and-done, and I suspect that it might be that for you. For tonight,' he added before she could object. 'This is not me slut-shaming you. I want you to want *me*. For *me*. Because you have feelings for me, too. At least because you want me, too. But not because you're challenging yourself to "take your life back".'

She flinched. 'I'm sorry,' she whispered. 'I didn't realize . . .' She closed her eyes. 'I'm sorry, Rafe. I didn't mean to make you feel unimportant.'

He wanted to sigh again, but bit it back. He wasn't about to make her feel worse. 'Come sit with me again,' he said gently. 'I liked that, a lot.' He held out his hand, holding his breath once again until she took it. He pulled her close, letting the breath go in a silent, relieved sigh when she tucked herself into his side. 'That's better. So much better.'

'I feel like an idiot,' she muttered. 'Can I just go back to my room?'

He chuckled. 'You're asking my permission?'

She smacked his gut lightly. 'Not ever.'

'Good,' he said with satisfaction. He kissed her temple and felt her relax the tiniest bit. He was gentling her and he knew that she was aware of this. He shifted with a wince. 'I wasn't kidding about wanting you, Mercy Callahan. I feel like I'm a teenager again, and not in a good way.'

'Good,' she echoed with satisfaction. 'That's something, at least.'

He tipped her chin up so that she met his eyes. 'What do you want?'

She swallowed hard, her expression abruptly vulnerable. 'I don't want to feel afraid anymore. I don't want to feel like I'm missing out on what normal women do with men they're attracted to.'

That was honest. Not exactly what he'd hoped to hear, but it was a start. 'And you want that with me.'

Another swallow followed by the slightest of nods. 'I wanted it when I was here before. You make me want things that I never thought I would.'

Okay, that was much better. His ego puffed up and he had to fight the urge to preen. But she'd been honest and he could be no less. 'Thank you for telling me. I thought I'd destroyed everything when I kissed you and you ran back to New Orleans. I thought I'd never see you again and I only had myself to blame.'

'I was scared,' she admitted. 'You made me feel safe and I don't think I'd ever felt that before. You still do, by the way. Make me feel safe, I mean.'

He closed his eyes at that, relief making him dizzy. 'I'm glad,' he said gruffly. 'You have no idea how happy that makes me. I don't ever want you to feel like I've taken your choices. I don't ever want you to run from me again. I couldn't handle it, Mercy.'

She brushed the back of her fingers against the scruff of his jaw. 'I didn't mean to hurt you when I left before. I didn't mean to hurt you tonight. It was just . . .' She sighed. 'I sat at your family's table tonight and felt all that love and strength and knew that I could have some of it. That I could take it freely.'

'But?'

'No "but". Not really. I thought to myself, "You have this with the Romeros. They love you and support you." But it *felt* different and I realized the difference was you. So instead of spending the drive back here thinking about everything I'd just unloaded at your parents' kitchen table, I thought about you. But I didn't stop to consider what you might be feeling, and I'm sorry for that.'

The difference was you. He was terrified to speak. Terrified he'd say the wrong thing and she'd run away again. But then she stroked his face, her touch butterfly light, and the words spilled out. 'I feel more than you're ready for.'

He opened his eyes when she tapped his chin, a little harder than was truly necessary. Her face was set in a scowl, her mouth pinched on one side. 'Are you even *listening* to me, Rafe Sokolov?'

He nodded, unable to take his eyes off her face. She was stunning like this, her eyes snapping with irritation.

'You might want to reconsider that last sentence,' she said. 'You feel more than I'm ready for? You know what? That might even be true, but you don't get to say that to me. *I* get to decide what I'm ready for. *I* get to decide if I'm afraid of what you feel.'

He wanted to kiss her breathless, but he reined it in. 'Yes, you do.

But when your decision impacts my heart, then I get to weigh in. I think that's fair, don't you?'

She scowled another second more, then looked away. 'Yeah,' she grumbled.

He had to laugh at that. 'You sound so put-upon.'

Her lips twitched and he was hit with another dizzying wave of relief. He might have actually pulled this out of the fire. 'I am,' she said. 'But you're right.' The smile fell from her face and she suddenly looked unbearably sad. Defeated. 'I don't know how to do this, Rafe. I don't know how to be a sister to Gideon or . . . whatever it is that you need me to be.'

His heart was hurting again. 'Mercy. You know how to be a friend to Farrah, right?'

A bitter huff. 'Yeah, but she didn't give me any choice. She kind of barged into my life and took over, from the moment she walked into our dorm room that first day.'

'We all owe her a debt, then,' he said seriously. 'She was there for you when you didn't have anyone else. When you weren't *ready* for anything else, she was your friend.'

'Okay,' she said with a halfhearted shrug. 'I wasn't ready then. So what?'

'So you know how to be a friend, right?' He smiled, encouraged when she nodded warily. 'So you can be my friend, right?'

She pursed her lips in a scowl, but he could see the hurt flicker in her eyes. 'That's what you want? To be just friends?'

'No!' he barked, and she flinched. 'No,' he said more quietly, and she relaxed, but still frowned. 'No,' he whispered, gripping her chin and lowering his mouth to hers, slowly enough that she could pull away if she wished. But she didn't pull away. Her eyes fluttered closed and she waited, lips parted a hairsbreadth. Waiting.

This was what he'd wanted. Her. Willing. Open. Wanting him. He kissed her softly, intending to keep it chaste, but she whimpered and it broke his resolve. He turned in to her, threading his fingers through her hair, and the kiss turned hot and lush and . . . sultry. Because she was humming now, her hands on the collar of his shirt, pulling him closer.

He pulled back enough to whisper against her mouth. 'Touch me anytime you want to. Anywhere you want to. Please.' Then he dived back in, wanting to live forever in this one moment when he felt her melt against him, her tentative fingers pulling at the buttons of his shirt. Slipping one hand beneath the fabric to stroke his skin.

'Like this?' Her words were barely audible over the pounding of his own heart, but he heard.

'Exactly like this.' He wanted to do the same, to touch her soft skin, to cup her generous breasts in his hands, to feel their weight. To make her sigh in pleasure. But this was her show, so he settled for running a hand down her side, gripping her waist. Otherwise, he remained still as a statue. Letting her explore.

Her fingers skimmed over him, making him shiver. Her kisses made him feel drunk, but they weren't enough.

Nothing would be enough, not with this woman.

He relaxed his hold when she finally pulled away, her lips red, plumped, and wet. She was breathing hard.

And there wasn't a trace of wariness in her eyes. Just heat. And want.

And I need to stop now. 'Just so we're clear,' he said, his voice gravelly and rough. 'That was exactly right. And we need to stop, because I don't have that much self-control. Not around you.' She looked very pleased with herself and it made him grin. 'You like that, do you?'

'Yes, I do.' She eased her thumb over his lower lip. 'What now?'

He laughed helplessly. 'Fucking hell, Mercy. Don't ask me that. Not right now.'

Her gaze dropped deliberately to the erection that there was no way he could hide. Her lips curled up, like a satisfied cat. 'Oh.'

He laughed again, joy bubbling up and warming him from the inside out. 'Yeah. Oh.' He pulled her against him, settling her against his chest, pressing his cheek into her hair. 'I meant it when I said I have feelings for you. I'm not sure what comes next, either. I'm rusty at . . .' He hesitated, then parroted her words back to her. 'Being whatever it is that you need me to be.'

'Just be you.' She sounded sleepy already. 'I like you.'

'I like you, too.'

She was quiet for so long that he thought she'd fallen asleep, but she surprised him. 'Tell me about Bella. If you want to.'

His heart stuttered. 'Oh. Okay.'

'You don't have to.'

'I'll tell you. But why do you want to know?' he asked. 'I'm curious.'

She made a noise in her throat, part huff, part sigh. 'I don't know. Maybe because you know everything there is to know about me now. You don't need to tell me about Bella, but maybe share one thing that nobody else knows about you?'

It was emotional quid pro quo and he was okay with that, because she was right. She'd opened her personal life like a book tonight and he knew it hadn't been easy. Hell, he wasn't sure how he'd managed to listen. He couldn't fathom how hard it had been for her to reveal.

'That would be Bella, then,' he said. 'Nobody knows about her. About our relationship. Well, almost nobody. She was the prosecutor assigned to my task force when I was in Gangs. I'd been undercover for nearly a year, trying to break into one of the bigger drug cartels in the county. She and I weren't supposed to be together. Bad for our careers.'

'And your safety,' she murmured.

'That too.' He hadn't cared about that so much back then. He'd just wanted to be with Bella in any way he could. 'She knew my brother Jude first. They worked together in the prosecutor's office here in Sacramento, and they'd been friends since college.'

'Did he know about you and Bella?'

'Not while we were together. While she was alive,' he added, unable to keep the bitterness from his voice. 'My partner and I were picking off the minor characters in the cartel. The foot soldiers. Bella was getting them to flip on their superiors, one layer of the cartel at a time. She'd give the information to us, so that we'd know how to function in the organization, who to focus on. Then one of the midlevel dealers double-crossed her. She'd offered him a deal, but he was loyal and directed his attorney to warn the bosses that she was getting too close, that it was just a matter of time before she had enough proof to bring charges against the upper echelon. That's when my partner and I were *supposed* to close in and make arrests.'

He felt Mercy stiffen at his bitter tone. 'What happened?' she asked. 'Were you compromised?'

'No. But they got to Bella.' He rubbed his jaw against the top of Mercy's head, needing the contact. 'They followed her one night when she left the office. And they killed her.'

She slid her hand inside his shirt, over his pounding heart. And left it there. Not stroking, not stimulating. Just . . . connecting.

His eyes burned. 'And you thought you didn't know how to do this,' he whispered.

She pulled away just enough to look up at him. 'Do what?'

He looked her straight in the eye. 'Be who I need you to be. You're doing it right now.'

Her expression softened, pleased. 'Thank you. For telling me that. For telling me about her.' She kissed his jaw, then settled back against his chest. 'I'm sorry you lost her. But glad you loved her.'

It was so simple a statement, yet so very perfect. 'I am, too. She was smart and funny. Stubborn as hell. Strong in ways I could never imagine. But she was compassionate, too. She made me a better person, you know?'

'Then we owe her a debt.'

He smiled at that. She'd parroted his words back at him as well. 'It was hard keeping our relationship a secret. I wanted her sitting next to me at Sunday dinner. I wanted the world to know that I was hers. But we couldn't be public. Not until the case was over. We had plans. I'd asked her to marry me and she'd said yes.'

'And after she was gone? Why did you continue to keep her secret?'

It was a valid question, a little harder to answer. 'At first it was because I didn't want to be transferred out of the task force, and I would have been had our relationship been known. I would have been "too close" to the case, and I wanted to bring the fuckers down.'

'Did you?'

'Yep.' He hesitated, then continued, figuring she needed all the information before deciding how far she wanted this thing between them to go. 'And I enjoyed it. I had to kill two of them, but the rest we took into custody. The two I killed were shooting at us and I was protecting my partner's back, but I was glad to have killed them. They were the ones who'd killed Bella. Haven't had even a second of regret.' He paused a moment, then asked a question he wasn't sure he was ready to have answered. 'Does that make a difference to you?'

'What, that you killed the men who murdered your fiancée so that your partner could go home to his family? Yes, it makes a difference. It makes me like you even more. And respect you. They wouldn't have spared you, had you hesitated.'

Peace flooded him and his tense muscles relaxed into the corner of the sofa. 'Thank you.'

'What about after? Why didn't you tell your family after?'

'I don't know. Maybe because they're so . . . them. I love them with everything that I am. But they can overwhelm me with love and I was really fragile at that point. I think I might have broken into too many pieces to put back together, if I'd let them comfort me. And then, after I'd grieved, it was kind of too late to tell them because then I would have needed to explain why I hadn't told them before. It was exhausting to even consider.'

'I understand that. But your brother Jude knows?'

'Yeah. Too much vodka one night and I blurted the story out to him. He showed up with a bottle of Absolut and a mountain of guilt. She'd taken the case over from him when the DA assigned him to another case. I think he suspected that we were together before I told him, and he felt guilty about that, too – that he'd "robbed" me of her, which was ridiculous. He ended up patting my back that night while I cried like a baby. He promised he wouldn't tell a soul because I needed to stay on that case. When I killed the two who'd murdered Bella, we got drunk again. He moved to LA shortly after I closed the case. I think he needed a clean break. Too many memories here. But we still spend her birthdays remembering her, Jude and me. We drink to her memory and tell stories that make us laugh and cry.'

Her palm against his heart was a welcome weight. 'I'm glad you have each other.'

'Me too.' He let a few beats pass. 'How long will you be here, Mercy?'

'I have two months' leave. I'll go back for Aunt Quill's funeral, of course.' A shudder ran through her body, but she didn't cry. He'd be shocked if she had any tears left after today. 'I loved her. She clucked over me like a mama hen and when I graduated from college, the apartment next to hers opened up. I moved in and had an instant dinner companion. We played cards or watched her shows.' She laughed quietly. 'She loved *Matlock* and *Murder, She Wrote*. I took her to the doctor and made sure she remembered her medicine. She loved my cats and gave them treats when she thought I wasn't looking. Like good treats. Real tuna. They loved her.'

'I bet they did.'

'I miss her,' she whispered. 'I want Ephraim to pay for what he did to her.'

'I want him to pay for what he did to you.'

'You and me both.' She yawned and snuggled closer. 'You're right. This is really nice. Simply holding each other like this.'

He smiled into her hair. 'Yep.'

'But so we're clear? I don't want to be just friends. I'd like to resume what you interrupted earlier at some point in the near future.'

His cock surged to life. 'Yeah?'

'Mm. Yeah. Do me a favor? The next time I come on to you, trust that I know what I want?'

'Yes, ma'am.'

She chuckled softly. 'Night, Rafe.'

So it seemed they were sleeping together. Rafe wasn't going to complain. He pulled the throw blanket from the back of the sofa and maneuvered them from cuddled in the corner to stretched out together, his arms tight around her all the while. 'Night, Mercy.'

Seventeen

Sacramento, California
Monday, 17 April, 6.30 A.M.

Mercy woke to a feeling of panic. Arms were holding her down, a man's arms. She stiffened, poised to flee, but then her brain became alert and she relaxed.

She wasn't being held down. She was being *held*. And the arms holding her tight weren't just any man's arms. They were Rafe's.

And he has feelings. For me.

It was . . . a lot. Especially before coffee. *Please have some.* She slipped out of his grip, tucking the blanket around him, then straightened, expecting to be stiff from sleeping on a sofa, but it had been incredibly cozy.

She couldn't wait to do it again. Or . . . She glanced at the bed, partially hidden behind a silk screen.

Go for it. Be happy. Mercy bit back a laugh when she heard Farrah's voice in her mind. But maybe her best friend was right. *Maybe not being* un*happy isn't enough. Maybe I deserve to be happy, too.*

And maybe she was still loopy from Rafe Sokolov's kisses and whispered confidences. Which had been exactly what she'd needed.

She used the bathroom, then washed her hands and face, staring at her own reflection. She still had bags under her eyes, but nothing like they'd been before last night. Her eyes were . . . bright.

And she was smiling, which was really new.

And then she remembered that Quill was dead, and that people she'd never met had seen her naked. Yes, Bunker had gotten the video taken down quickly, but it had been online long enough.

But you're going to be brave, she reminded herself. *You're going to hold your head high, because you didn't do anything wrong.*

'And you're going to turn this shitstorm into something positive,' she said out loud, just in case the woman in the mirror wasn't listening to the voices in her head.

'You sure are,' Rafe said on the other side of the door, making her jump a foot.

'Shit, Rafe. You scared me.' Her face heated, knowing that he'd heard her talking to herself.

'I'm very sorry,' he said. 'But can you talk yourself into stuff after I use the bathroom?'

She laughed, pulling the door open to see him leaning against the door frame. Shirtless. Her laughter dried up and she stared. *God.* The man was beautiful. Golden and sleek, broad shoulders and acres of muscle. And that treasure trail that made her want so much more.

His eyes warmed at her speechless scrutiny, but he broke the moment by clearing his throat. 'As much as I appreciate you drooling over me, I really need to pee.'

That startled her into another laugh and she smacked his chest as she passed him. 'I wasn't drooling.' God, she hoped she wasn't. She touched the corner of her mouth, spinning to glare at him when his laugh boomed loud and happy.

'Made you check,' he taunted, closing the door with a snap.

'You're a child,' she called through the door primly, then, ignoring his deep chuckle, went to the little kitchenette in search of coffee.

'Oh, thank the good Lord,' she murmured at the sight of a Keurig machine. This she could do. She turned it on and started a cup, then found her phone, checking for any messages from the group.

The group. She paused a moment, letting it sink in. She was part of the group now, the family, and not just because she was Gideon's sister. She was part of Farrah's family too, and part of John's and all her sibs'. She loved that she'd been folded into those families, but this felt different in a very good way.

You're going to leave. And you'll lose this.

She frowned. 'If I do leave, I'll still be a part of them. I won't let Gideon go again.'

'Or me, I hope,' Rafe said, startling her again.

She glared up at him. 'You need to wear a goddamn bell.'

He grinned, unrepentant. 'I talk to myself, too. Sometimes I even answer. What's for breakfast?'

'I don't know,' she replied sweetly. 'What were you planning to make?'

His grin softened to a smile and he dropped a kiss on the tip of her nose. 'Pancakes.' He pointed to the counter. 'Pull up a stool. I'll get your coffee.'

She obeyed and watched contentedly as he held on to the counter for balance, bending over to pull a pan from the cabinet and showcasing a very nice butt in the sweats he'd slept in. He was still shirtless, which she thought he was doing on purpose, but she wasn't about to complain. She touched the corner of her mouth again, just to make sure that she really wasn't drooling.

'I left a new toothbrush on the counter in the bathroom,' he said as he poured pancake mix into a bowl. 'And I found a hairbrush that Daisy left behind. I'd offer you her clothes, but you're a little taller than she is.'

'Like eight inches,' Mercy protested. 'That's not a "little", Rafe.'

He looked over his shoulder, waggling his brows. 'You shouldn't open doors like that, Mercy.'

She frowned at him. 'Like what?'

He chuckled. 'Never mention "eight inches" around a guy. We'll just snicker.'

She considered what she'd said, then shook her head. 'You really are a big kid, aren't you?'

He threw back his head and laughed. 'Keep 'em coming, Mercy. I am a *very* big kid.'

'Oh, for heaven's sake,' she muttered, but she laughed. 'I'll be right back.'

She returned to the bathroom and freshened up as best she could. She hoped that Sasha was a heavy sleeper, because she was going to have to slip into the apartment and pick up some clean clothes.

She slid back on the counter stool, a little disappointed to see that Rafe had put on a shirt. 'So now you're modest?' she asked, sipping the coffee he'd put next to a plate and silverware.

'No, now I'm frying bacon,' he said, pointing to a pan. 'I don't care for third-degree burns, thanks.' Then he grinned. 'But I'll take my shirt off again after I'm done cooking if you ask me nicely.'

She shook her head, charmed, as she opened her email on her phone. Then squinted at an email address that she didn't recognize. Her heart sank for a second or two, thinking that the messages were in response to that damn article, but then she smiled. 'Hey, we got two replies to all those Pinterest emails we sent yesterday.'

'All right! What do they say?'

'This one is from Kay in Maine. She bought one of Amos's tables. She said she bought it about five years ago, in a shop near Crater Lake. That might be too long ago to help us.'

Rafe flipped the pancakes. 'What about the second one?'

Mercy read it, then looked up, barely able to contain a squeal of excitement. 'This one is from Diana in Phoenix. She bought the quilt that Eileen's mother made. She bought it back in October.'

Rafe left the stove to read the email over her shoulder. 'In a shop in Snowbush. Where is that?' The bacon popped and he hurried back to the stove. 'Can you look it up on Google Maps?'

'Already doing it,' Mercy said, then exhaled slowly. 'It's just a speck on the map. The closest town is Likely, California. It's up in the northeast corner, catty-corner to where the Oregon and Nevada borders meet. Close to the Modoc National Forest.'

Rafe's eyes were sparkling. 'So, maybe a four-hour drive?'

'Four hours and forty-four minutes.' She drew a deep breath, trying to stay calm enough to think. 'Can we go and ask the shop where they got the quilt?'

He met her gaze. 'Absolutely.'

She laughed, feeling giddy. 'Do we have to tell Tom Hunter?'

'Do you want to?'

She forced herself to sober, to think. 'No. I want to check this out myself. Is that wrong?'

He leaned over the counter to brush a kiss over her mouth. 'No. We'll tell him if we find something. How's that?'

She beamed. 'Perfect. Feed me breakfast and I'll change my clothes. We can be there by lunch.'

Rafe plated the bacon. 'We should tell Gideon, though. I don't want to risk getting ambushed by Burton.'

Mercy's good mood dimmed a little bit. 'I know you're right, but dammit.'

'I know. I'd love to have ten hours alone with you in the car, but I'm also not willing to risk your life. Also, check the weather. Lassen's a little south of there and some of those mountain roads stay closed through June.'

'Oh. I forgot about snow.'

'I've got chains if I need them. I'll make sure they're in the back of my Subaru before we leave.'

She glanced at his leg. He was leaning on his cane with one hand, the plate with bacon and pancakes in the other. 'Can you drive?'

'Yep. Left leg's the problem. I'd offer to let you drive, but you forgot about snow.'

'I've lived in New Orleans for eight years and we haven't had snow in all that time. It gets chilly, but nothing a nice Irish coffee can't fix.'

He took the stool next to hers. 'I'll fill a thermos with coffee. No booze around here, though. Daisy's eight years sober, so we all abstain. Solidarity, you know.'

'Straight coffee is perfect.' She held up her coffee cup. 'To making Ephraim Burton pay.'

Rafe's expression grew grim as he touched his cup to hers. 'To bringing the motherfucker down.'

Mercy nodded once. 'I'll drink to that, too.'

Sacramento, California
Monday, 17 April, 7.30 A.M.

Rafe locked his apartment door, a backpack full of supplies at his feet. He glanced up the stairs to where Mercy was changing her clothes in Sasha's apartment, and wondered what was taking her so long.

It had been long enough since he'd been with Bella that he'd forgotten how much time women needed to dress themselves. And he'd never really had that intimacy with Bella. Their time together had been a series of stolen moments and rushed lovemaking.

When Mercy was ready, he was going to take his time.

And I'm not going to think about that now. Because he had to share a vehicle with her for the next ten hours or so and he was not doing that with a hard-on.

He busied himself in the garage, packing up the Subaru with cold-weather gear. He threw one of Sasha's parkas in the back along with a few blankets and the tire chains. If they ended up on any of the mountain roads, his Subaru would be fine.

Glancing at his phone, he frowned. Gideon must have still been asleep, because he hadn't answered any of Rafe's texts. He started to call him, when he heard voices in the foyer. Opening the door to investigate, he stopped short, surprised. 'Erin? I thought you were going home?'

Erin had her hand on the front doorknob and jumped at the sound of his voice. 'Dammit, Sokolov. Don't sneak up on me.'

'I should wear a bell,' he said placidly. 'I thought you were going home last night. Please tell me that you didn't sleep in your car all night.'

Erin winced a little. 'No, I didn't sleep in my car last night.' Then she hopped out of the way when the front door shoved open.

'I think I should use the bathroom, too,' Sasha said, then saw Rafe staring. 'Shit. Why are you awake?'

'Why are *you* awake?' Rafe shot back.

'We're going to breakfast,' Sasha said, more as a question than a statement. 'We just finished a morning run. We both drank a lot of water and . . .' She waved at nothing, but her cheeks were uncharacteristically pink.

'Breakf—' Oh. *Oh*. Rafe's lips twitched. 'Okay.'

'Smart move,' Sasha snapped. 'Especially since Mercy didn't come back last night.'

'She fell asleep on the sofa,' Rafe said. Not a lie.

Sasha wasn't buying it. 'Why *are* you awake, Rafe?'

'We're going for a drive.'

'Before eight a.m.,' Erin said dryly, not even bothering to hide her suspicion. 'Alone.'

'I'm ready,' Mercy said from the second-floor landing. 'Sorry I took so long. Needed to give Jack and Rory some love.' She stopped on the bottom step, eyes widening at the sight of both Sasha and Erin.

Rafe blinked, then blinked again. She looked so different. Her hair was up in some kind of bun-thing and a pair of thick glasses dominated her face, making her green eyes look owlish. Her cheeks were hollowed out, her cheekbones too sharp. And there was a black beauty mark above her lip. He leaned forward, squinting, to be sure it was actually Mercy. She was still stunning, but not the woman with whom he'd shared pancakes and bacon. 'What the hell did you do to your face?'

She chuckled. 'Just some makeup. I took out my contacts, so I could wear my glasses.' Her smile faded. 'It's my best attempt at a disguise. I'm not ready to deal with the fallout from that video. Not yet.'

His heart felt sore. 'I get it. And I have to say, you did an amazing job. I didn't even recognize you.'

Erin was watching them. 'That's a lot of trouble for a little drive. And is that a pair of mittens in your hand?'

Sasha pushed past Rafe, into the garage, where she stood next to the open hatch of the Subaru, hands on her hips. 'They're going into the mountains,' she told Erin. 'He's got blankets and tire chains.' She frowned. 'And my parka?'

'You guys planning a run for the Canadian border?' Erin asked, not joking.

Mercy aimed a wary glance in his direction but said nothing.

'Nope.' Rafe might have asked Erin to go with them since Gideon hadn't answered any of his texts, but her overbearing interrogation was pissing him off. 'Just a drive.'

Erin nodded. 'You can't get out of the driveway. I'm parked across it.'

Rafe ground his teeth. 'Can you move your Rover? Please?'

'Sure. Once I'm satisfied with an explanation that contains the actual truth.'

Sasha returned to the foyer, holding her fist out to bump. 'Go, girl.'

Erin bumped it, her lips curving. 'Well, Rafe?'

'She's really good,' Mercy said, sinking to sit on the stairs. 'She's got me feeling like I'm five years old and about to be sent to the corner. You might as well tell her. I'd like to get on the road.'

'To where?' Erin asked.

'Likely,' Rafe bit out.

Sasha frowned. 'Likely . . . what?'

Mercy snorted. 'So we can avoid the "Who's on First?" routine, we're going to Likely, California. It's up near the Oregon–Nevada border.'

'Why?' Erin pressed, drawing out the single syllable to at least three.

Mercy tapped at her phone, then held it out to show Erin and Sasha. 'This quilt. It was bought at a store north of Likely, back in October.'

Erin took her phone and studied the photo of the quilt, then enlarged the image. And gasped softly. 'It's the angel with the flaming sword.'

Sasha hung over Erin's shoulder so that she could see. 'Where?'

'Down at the bottom.' Erin pointed. 'Right here in the corner.'

'Oh my God. It's like the angel on the locket. And Gideon's old tattoo.' Sasha looked from Rafe to Mercy. 'Was this quilt made in Eden?'

Mercy nodded. 'By Eileen's mother. She taught me how to quilt when I was barely old enough to hold a needle. I'd know her signature anywhere.'

Erin scowled at Rafe. 'You weren't going to tell anyone?'

'I was going to tell you,' Rafe said, 'but you got in my face and that's not okay.'

'So you're going alone,' Erin muttered. 'With a fucking crazy man looking to drag you back to Eden by your hair, Mercy?'

'Hey, I was going to be with her,' Rafe protested. Yes, he'd planned to ask Gideon to go with them as backup, but Erin had crossed the line from overbearing to insulting. 'I may limp, but I can still—'

'Fucking hell, Rafe,' Erin snarled, then snapped her mouth closed when Mercy shushed her.

'Farrah's upstairs, trying to sleep. Let's use our inside voices.'

Erin drew a breath and exhaled slowly. 'Okay, this is how this will go. You can have your little drive to Likely, California. You can look like someone else, Mercy. You can shop for Eden trinkets to your heart's content. But I *will* be going with you.' She held up her hand when Rafe opened his mouth to argue. 'It has nothing to do with your ability, Rafe. It has everything to do with being smart and not becoming a goddamn statistic. I'll follow you up in my Rover. Sasha, you want in?'

Sasha shrugged. 'Sure. I have a few personal days left. I'll take one. Just give me a few minutes to clean up and call in to work.' She started up the stairs, patting Mercy's shoulder in thanks when she moved over to let Sasha by. 'You still need the bathroom, Rhee?'

'Yeah.' Erin pointed at Rafe as she passed. 'And I need to call in too, to let them know I'm not coming in. You'd better not leave before we get back or there will be hell to pay.'

He made a face at her back, which made Mercy chuckle. 'I *can't* leave, can I?' he said sarcastically. 'You've parked me in.'

'Good job, Last Night Me,' Erin hissed. 'We *will* talk about this, Rafe. Hand to God.'

Rafe watched them go up the stairs and had to fight not to pout like the five-year-old Mercy had mentioned. 'Dammit. I would have asked her to go with us since I haven't heard back from Gideon, but she's being obnoxious.'

'She cares about you,' Mercy said quietly. 'If Farrah were awake, she'd be doing the same thing. I sent her an email telling her where we're going so she doesn't worry when she wakes up.'

Rafe sighed. 'You're right. I know she cares. At least she's not riding with us. Now I'll have that ten hours in the car with you today.' One side of his mouth quirked up. 'Except I feel like I'm with a stranger.' He waggled his brows. 'Mysterious.'

She laughed at him. 'Shut up.' She came down the final few stairs, leaning up on her toes to peck his lips. 'It'll be fine. We can all shop and then do lunch. I bet Erin'll be nicer if you buy her lunch.'

'Maybe,' he grumbled. 'Let's wait in the car. Who knows how long they'll be?'

She waited until they were both in the Subaru before turning to him with a grin. 'So . . . Erin was here all night? With Sasha? That's really sweet.'

She looked so happy that his grumpy mood evaporated. '"Sweet" isn't normally the word I would use when describing Erin, but, yeah, I have to agree.'

She reached across the console to squeeze his hand. 'See? It's going to be fine.'

Sacramento, California
Monday, 17 April, 8.00 A.M.

Ephraim bolted upright, swearing when the pain in his hand woke him up. He'd fallen asleep in Sean MacGuire's Cadillac and had just smacked his hand into the steering wheel while reaching for his phone, which was making a god-awful sound. It wasn't the melodic chimes he'd set to wake him up, but a jarring clanging that sounded like someone was banging pots together. He peered at his phone and then he really was awake, his adrenaline pumping.

'Fucking hell.' It was the tracker app. Erin Rhee's Range Rover was on the move. Struggling to sit up, he turned on the ignition and put the car in gear, rolling a few feet before he figured out which direction he needed to go.

Making a beeline for Sokolov's Victorian, he slowed in time to see a red Subaru pulling out of the garage and backing out of the driveway. He shuddered out a relieved breath. *Good.* He wasn't too late.

The Subaru started up the street, away from him, and he waited to see what the Range Rover would do. He couldn't just fly by them. That would raise all kinds of suspicions.

Relax and breathe. He grabbed the binoculars and peered into Rhee's vehicle. She was behind the wheel, her head barely visible. Beside her was a tall blonde with a ponytail high on her head. That would be Sasha Sokolov.

And in the Subaru? He shifted to one side to get a better view and was finally able to relax. Rafe Sokolov was behind the wheel. A woman with black hair done up in a bun was leaning in to adjust the radio. Had to be Mercy.

Perfect.

The red Subaru had paused, waiting, as it turned out, for the blue Range Rover to follow. So wherever Sokolov and Mercy were going, Detective Rhee would have their backs. That wasn't good when it came to getting Mercy alone. Incapacitating three people would be a lot harder than just one. But, if they truly were staying together, Ephraim would know exactly where they were going, which more than balanced things out.

He had enough bullets to take all three of them down if he had to. Then he'd get Mercy and go back to Eden. Glancing at his gas gauge, he mentally thanked MacGuire for filling the tank. He wouldn't have to stop for a long while.

Snowbush, California
Monday, 17 April, 12.30 P.M.

They'd run out of conversation about half an hour back, but the silence was an easy, comfortable one. Rafe glanced over at Mercy, surprised to see her awake and alert. He'd thought she might have fallen asleep.

He now knew all about her college major (chemistry with a master's in cellular biology), her favorite color (green), her favorite band (Journey), and the ins and outs of her job at the NOPD crime lab. She'd talked a little about her job during the time she'd sat at his bedside back in February, so he'd known where she worked. But now he knew about the DNA testing she did, which was impressive.

He'd told her about a few of the undercover busts he'd done and, after some cajoling, had admitted that he'd downloaded every song Taylor Swift had ever recorded.

But one question had bugged him the entire ride and he needed to ask soon or they'd be there and no longer alone. His phone's GPS indicated that they were less than ten minutes from the general store where Diana from Phoenix had bought the Eden quilt.

'Why two months?' he blurted, and she turned to him, eyes wide behind her glasses.

'What do you mean?'

'Why did you take two months' leave?'

'Oh.' She pursed her lips. 'Well . . .'

She trailed off and said nothing more. Finally he prompted, 'Well?'

She sighed. 'It's embarrassing. And I'm ashamed. But it was the kick in the butt that I needed to come here and make things right with Gideon, so . . . I made a mistake at work. It was last week, on Tuesday, the day after that CNN special interview aired. I knew the program was coming, but I guess I didn't anticipate how seeing his face on the screen would make me feel, you know?'

His face needed no explanation. Mercy had waved off her abduction as not a big deal, seeing as she'd walked away alive and unhurt, unlike most of the serial killer's other victims. He'd personally wondered when her mind would force her to deal with what had happened.

'I think so, yeah. When I saw the man who'd murdered Bella, I just remember seeing red. I nearly botched the whole operation by going in hot and mad. Seeing that guy, knowing what he'd done . . . it fucked with my head.'

'That sounds about right,' she said ruefully. 'And as good a description as any. Seeing my face on the program, how scared I looked, and then they showed the tape of him dragging me from the hospital and how I just went all zombie on him.'

'Like at the airport.'

She winced. 'Exactly. It was like it was happening all over. And nobody asked my permission to include any of those images.'

'It was like being victimized again.'

295

'Yes. But this time it was different, because I knew my co-workers would have seen it. Nobody in the lab seemed to have read the write-ups in the West Coast papers. And those who did read about it never mentioned it to my face. I got off pretty easily when I went back to work in February, after I . . . you know. Ran away from you all.'

He held out his hand and she took it. 'I get it, Mercy. You had a lot of processing to do.'

'But I hurt you and I'm sorry.'

He pulled their joined hands to his mouth and kissed her knuckles. 'You can make it up to me later,' he said lightly. 'So you messed up at work?'

She sighed, defeat in the sound. 'Yeah. I let the stress get to me.'

'Honey, you're human. Most people would have buckled under that kind of stress long before you did.'

'Yes, but my mistake nearly sent an innocent man to prison. I got samples mixed up.'

'Shit,' he breathed, understanding better now. 'Was it caught in time?'

'Thank goodness, yes. I caught it. And, after I fixed it, I turned myself in.'

'You did? Why?'

'Because it was the right thing to do. My supervisors were good about it. They told me to take the personal time and talk to a therapist, but that they do want me to come back. It was more than fair.'

Rafe had to swallow another snarl at the thought of her going back. He wasn't going to try to influence her either way. Not now, at least. Maybe at the end of six weeks he'd have laid a sufficient foundation to their relationship so that he could ask her to stay.

'I can understand why you might feel embarrassed, but you shouldn't. You did the right thing. You showed integrity when others wouldn't have. That's something to be proud of.'

She shrugged. 'Well, maybe. But that kind of mistake has always been one of my fears, always in the back of my mind. When it happened it really threw me.'

'Hm. I hadn't thought about the stress on the lab techs.'

'You should. Detectives are always in our faces with "Where are my results? What's taking you so long? What the hell do you do in here all day?" Then they look at my computer monitor like they expect me to be playing video games or something.'

Rafe winced, because he'd done the same thing more times than he wanted to admit. 'I think I'm going to take an apology offering to the lab.'

She laughed. 'If it's anything like my lab, make it a dessert. I bet your mother would make you something delicious to take in.'

'I'll ask her the next time I see her.'

Mercy sighed. 'Can you not tell anyone about this? I mean, Farrah knows, but I don't want people to think I'm flighty or irresponsible. Especially after that video.'

Rafe couldn't hold back his scowl. 'Of course I won't, but you weren't flighty at work. You made a mistake. And that is so different from the video that I don't even know where to start. You were blameless in that. Farrah told us that she'd dragged you to that party.' He glanced over to see her lips droop sadly. 'It wasn't her fault, either. Don't think I'm blaming her. I'm blaming the asshole who put something in your drink.'

'I wasn't being careful, but it's exhausting, always being careful. I told myself before we went to the party that I was going to have fun. I was going to be . . . normal.'

'You being careful or careless is immaterial. You did nothing wrong.'

'Head knows it. Heart, not so much. But Farrah did notice I was gone.' She huffed a little chuckle. 'She went all badass superwoman, barging up the stairs and shoving people aside. I don't remember it, but it was on the original version of the video the police recovered. She busted open the door just in time and shoved him out of the way and grabbed the phone from Prescott's roommate.'

Farrah had said that she'd gotten to Mercy in time, but hearing it again made him sag with relief. 'The one who sold the video to Jeff Bunker's trashy rag.'

'Yeah. Asshole,' she muttered. 'I don't know how the roommate got a copy of the video, unless his phone automatically uploaded it to the cloud. Which is possible.'

'Very possible. This was what, six years ago? We weren't automatically looking at the cloud back then. Not like now, anyway. And speaking of now . . . we're here.'

They'd passed through the town of Likely about ten minutes before he'd asked her about her leave and were now rolling into the town of Snowbush, population one hundred sixty-two. There were the general store, a hardware store, a diner, a gas station, and a post office.

'They should have called this town Probably,' she said, but her quip fell flat because her voice trembled.

He pulled into one of the empty spaces in front of the store, put the Subaru in park, then turned to face her. 'Hey, what's wrong?'

'What if we don't learn anything?'

'Then we're no worse off than we were this morning, and we'll keep looking.'

She managed a shaky smile. 'Okay, then. Let's go quilt shopping.'

Eighteen

Snowbush, California
Monday, 17 April, 12.45 P.M.

*F**ucking hell. Holy fucking hell.* Ephraim checked the tracking app again, just to make sure. Rhee was stopping in Snowbush. In front of the general store.

Snowbush. Goddammit. How the hell did they find this place?

He'd followed them all the way from Sacramento, east on I-80, thinking they might be headed to Reno. He'd considered making his move when the area grew remote, but with both Erin Rhee and Rafe Sokolov probably armed, he didn't like the odds.

And then they'd taken a turn northwest at Reno and the landscape had become familiar.

Very familiar. Curiosity had stayed his hand at first, but dread had quickly followed.

He'd driven this road that ran parallel to the Nevada border. He'd stopped at the general stores in Likely and in Snowbush. He'd searched the roads west into the Modoc National Forest, hiking miles of trails. All in his search for Miriam, the woman the news called Eileen.

His wife who'd escaped the compound in November. He'd searched for two weeks, checking all the bus stations from Reno to Redding, north to Medford, Oregon, and as far south as Chico, but no one had seen her. Finally he'd snatched a random backpacker, killing her and mauling her body so that it appeared she'd been set upon by wild animals. Then he'd taken the remains back to Eden.

And then, as the community was packing up and moving again,

299

he'd taken Eileen's family – her parents and her younger brother – and snapped all their necks, burying them in a mass grave.

Pastor had told the community that they'd chosen to return to the world. Ephraim didn't know if the members truly believed it, and he didn't much care. He only cared about getting Mercy back to Eden, proving DJ had lied, and putting himself next in line for the money.

Cold, hard cash. Millions of dollars. That was his focus. *So focus.*

It didn't matter that Mercy and her crew were currently less than thirty miles from the previous location of Eden. It didn't matter that they were going to talk to the shopkeepers.

What mattered was separating Mercy from her bodyguards and taking her to Eden's new site.

And the best part was that they weren't too far away. They could make it in a few hours. This time tomorrow, he could be shoving DJ's body into a grave.

The thought made him smile.

But first, he had to get Mercy alone. That would be the hardest part.

He slowed as he headed into the town, noting the red Subaru and the blue Range Rover parked side by side in front of the general store, across the street from the hardware store, which advertised hunting rifles and ammunition. He would never buy ammo when he could steal it, but the sight made him take a mental inventory.

He had his own revolver, Regina's golden gun, Granny's rifle, and the handgun the college kid from the costume store had pointed at him. He'd taken three boxes of cartridges from Granny's house, and the college kid's gun still had a full magazine. Both his revolver and Regina's gun were down two rounds. So if taking the two detectives out required a firefight, he probably could manage it, but he still didn't like the odds.

Especially not here, where most people carried weapons as a matter of course. The official motto of Modoc County was 'Where the West Still Lives,' and that was the truth. If Ephraim started a gunfight with those two detectives anywhere near the town, he had no doubt that at least one resident would jump in.

So he kept driving, not stopping until he was out of Snowbush limits and out of sight of the general store. He'd wait until Rhee was on the move again to follow.

He wanted to know how they'd found this place. And what else they knew.

Snowbush, California
Monday, 17 April, 1.00 P.M.

'You're my fiancée and we're shopping for knick-knacks to decorate our new house,' Rafe whispered into Mercy's ear as they walked into the store.

She gave him an amused look, hoping he couldn't see how much she didn't object to the idea. Not now, of course. Maybe not ever, but it was a nice dream. 'Oh really?'

He grinned. 'Really.'

'Afternoon,' the young woman behind the counter greeted, her smile friendly. 'My name is Ginger. If I can be of any help, just let me know.'

Mercy smiled back. 'Thank you, Ginger. We will.' The bell above the door jingled, signaling that Erin and Sasha had followed them inside. 'And who are they supposed to be?' she murmured as the young woman called out the same greeting.

'My sister and her girlfriend,' Rafe replied. 'But if you tell them I said the G-word, I'll call you a liar.'

Mercy snickered. 'Scared of them?'

'Hell, yeah.' He looped his arm through hers and they wandered the small store, which was half groceries and half gifts, crafts, and souvenirs. 'Because I'm not stupid.'

Mercy was examining the shelves and displays, disappointed not to see any quilts. She'd just convinced herself that they'd driven all this way for nothing, when she stopped and stared. 'Oh.'

It was a jewelry box that resembled an old-fashioned chest of drawers, with curved legs and intricate carvings. She traced the inlaid bone on the lid with trembling fingers. This was Amos's work. She was certain of it.

'It's nice,' Rafe said conversationally, but she'd felt him tense beside her. 'But you don't have enough jewelry to fill it.'

She forced a chuckle, keeping up the charade. 'You can buy me some, then.'

'That's a beautiful piece.' Ginger had come from behind the counter to stand next to them. She couldn't have been more than eighteen and not an inch over five feet tall. 'It's handmade by a local artisan.'

'It's really lovely,' Mercy agreed. 'Do you know who made it?'

'I don't know the man's name, no. He doesn't sign his work, either.'

Yes, he does. You just have to know what to look for. 'No? That seems like a shame. This workmanship is exquisite. I'd want everyone to know my name if I could make something like this.'

'I know, right?' Ginger ran a fond hand over the lid. 'It has the space for a music box, if one wanted to add it. Not trying to put any pressure on you at all, but this is the last thing we have from this artist. All of our other items have sold. This one came in just as the weather turned bad and tourism dropped off for the season. Also, it's pricier than his other work. I'll be sorry to see it go – when the right person comes along, of course,' she added, her cheeks pinking with embarrassment. 'Like I said, no pressure at all.'

'No worries, I know what you meant.' Mercy scanned the store again. 'Actually, I was hoping to find a quilt. One of my friends bought one here and I admire it every time I go to her house.'

'Oh, the quilts are long gone. We didn't get that many in our last delivery.' Ginger's forehead crinkled in a slight frown. 'Which was a long time ago, come to think of it.'

'When was that?' Rafe asked casually.

'Gosh. Back around Halloween, I think. We still had our ghosts and goblins display up. I put the jack-o'-lantern I'd carved on top of one of the smaller tables by this same artist, and it sold the next day. The table.' She grinned winningly. 'Not the jack-o'-lantern, because I can't carve to save my life.'

Mercy chuckled. 'Me either. Did the artist himself deliver the tables?'

'Oh no. He's a recluse. His friend brought them by and picked up his payment. I wanted to meet the artist. I wanted a custom display case for my dad about a year back. He'd just gotten the flag from my great-grandfather's casket and I wanted to give him something nice to put it in.'

'I'm so sorry for your loss,' Mercy said quietly.

The woman shrugged. 'Papaw was almost a hundred. He had a really good life. Still miss him, though.' She visibly shook herself. 'Anyway, I never got to meet the woodworker himself.'

'Maybe they'll be back with more work now that spring is here,' Rafe suggested.

Another shrug. 'Maybe. But the guy who repped the artist brought stuff in at least once a month for the last few years, even in the dead of winter. Then as of November' – she snapped her fingers – 'nothin'. It wasn't all woodwork. There were quilts and some dolls. Knitted scarves, sweaters, and blankets. Every now and then a cross-stitched sampler. It's all gone now, except for this lovely.'

The door jingled again. 'More customers. Give me a shout if you have any other questions.'

'Will do.' Mercy waited until she was gone before tentatively lifting the jewelry box lid. And couldn't control her gasp. 'Oh my God,' she whispered. 'Rafe.'

'I see,' he said softly.

On the inside of the lid, carved in an ornate, scrolling font were the words *Surely Goodness And Mercy Shall Follow Me All The Days Of My Life*.

Her eyes burned and she blinked rapidly, not wanting to cry in this store. Her makeup would run and that would be the end of her disguise.

Sasha and Erin joined them, staring silently for a moment. Then Sasha murmured, 'It's a hymn, isn't it?'

Mercy nodded. 'He used to sing it to me. My stepfather, Amos. When I was really small, I thought the words were "Surely good Miss Mercy shall follow me all the days of my life." I thought the song was about me. He called me Miss Mercy until the day I left his

303

house.' To marry Ephraim. 'He gave me a beautiful hope chest for my twelfth birthday, but . . .' She'd had to leave it behind.

Sasha squeezed her arm. 'Sounds like he loved you.'

'He did.' She drew a breath, sliding her arm free from Rafe's. 'Can you turn it upside down, Rafe?'

He leaned his cane against a nearby shelf. 'Of course.' Gently he did so, handling the jewelry box like it was priceless crystal. 'What are you looking for?' Then he made a noise in his throat. 'Oh.'

It was a small olive tree with twelve branches.

'Do you need something?' Ginger was back.

'Yes,' Mercy answered, not taking her eyes from Amos's mark. 'How much is this?'

'Six hundred and fifty dollars.'

Mercy winced. 'Ouch.'

Ginger looked uncomfortable. 'I can't change the price. Only the store owner can.'

Mercy stared at the jewelry box, wrestling with herself. She might have told herself that she was only buying it to submit into evidence, but that would be a lie. Because she could hear Amos's delighted laughter when he called her Miss Mercy, his pure baritone singing the song the way she'd thought it went, and the memory was . . . sweet. Glancing up at Rafe, she saw understanding in his eyes. 'I really want this, but . . .'

His smile warmed her. 'Does it bring back good memories?'

She nodded, kind of hating that it was true. 'Some of the only good ones.'

He didn't break eye contact. 'Then get it.'

She turned to Ginger. 'I'll take it. Thank you.'

The woman beamed. 'Excellent. Come up to the register and we'll get it done.'

Mercy followed her, reaching for her wallet. 'I think I might know the artist,' she admitted. 'Or at least of him. I wish I could contact the man who was his representative.'

'I don't have his card. Sorry. He just came in whenever he had new items to trade.'

Mercy could feel Rafe standing behind her, the heat from his

304

body letting her know that she was safe. It gave her the courage to press forward as the woman ran her credit card. 'Was he young? The rep, I mean.'

Ginger handed Mercy the credit slip to sign. 'No. Not *young* young. Maybe thirty, thirty-five.'

Mercy forced herself to remember what DJ Belmont looked like and figured she'd deserve an Oscar if she could pull off the next round of questions without gagging. 'Looked like Matthew McConaughey with blond hair? Like white-blond? Tall and kind of rangy? Wore a cowboy hat?'

Ginger blinked, then blushed. 'Yes.'

Oh dear. This girl had a crush on DJ. Mercy was suddenly, viciously glad that he'd stopped coming by. This girl was far too nice to end up as DJ's prey.

Mercy made herself smile. 'Any idea where he came from? I'd love to find more cabinets like this. Maybe even a hope chest.'

Ginger looked down at the counter, then glanced around furtively, as if checking for anyone else who might be listening. 'Well, I did see him leave once. He drove into the forest.'

The Modoc National Forest started just a few miles west of town. Mercy leaned in, forcing a conspiratorial smile to her face. 'Can you give me any more than that?'

Ginger glanced around again, then inclined her head. 'I followed him,' she confessed. 'He was mysterious and I was young and stupid. And crushing.'

'I can see why,' Mercy agreed. 'He was something.' Something evil, vile, and utterly disgusting. 'I might have crushed on him too, when I was younger.'

Might have, but hadn't. Gideon might remember a 'nicer' DJ, but in Mercy's memory he was a spiteful, spoiled bully.

'I didn't follow him long,' the girl whispered, 'but he went south on 395 and turned onto Modoc County Road. I followed him for about twenty miles, and then he turned onto a road that wasn't paved. It was a private road, not part of the national forest. I wasn't brave enough to go any farther. It was just a crush, you know?'

Mercy smiled gently. 'I know. Thank you.'

'Ginger!' a man bellowed from the other side of the store. He wore an apron and stood behind the deli. 'Stop yakking and get back to work.'

'Sorry, Nick,' Ginger called, then dipped her head so that she could roll her eyes unseen. 'He owns the store. Sorry.'

'I don't want to get you into trouble. I'll be going now.' Mercy turned to find Rafe holding the jewelry box under one arm, leaning on his cane with the other. 'Ready, honey?'

'Whenever you are, snookums,' Rafe replied.

Sasha appeared from the snack aisle, hands filled with bags of chips. Erin walked beside her, looking amused at Sasha's gagging sounds. 'Be cute outside,' Sasha told them. 'We'll be out in a few minutes. We're stocking up on supplies.'

Leaving them to shop, Rafe loaded the jewelry box into the back of his Subaru, then opened Mercy's door. 'Matthew McConaughey?' he murmured, eyes narrowed. 'Really?'

'If Matthew had a rotted soul,' Mercy muttered. 'I hated DJ.' Her voice shook. '*Hated* him.'

Rafe had the sense to look apologetic. 'Sorry.' He closed her door, then came around to his side. 'I was being a jealous jerk and that was wrong of me.'

'It's okay.' Now that the whole charade was over, she felt a little sick. 'DJ was here, trading Amos's cabinets and Eileen's mother's quilts.'

'Yes,' Rafe said evenly. 'And the timing of the last delivery matches Eileen's disappearance from Eden.'

Mercy thought of Eileen and the family who'd found and cared for her, giving her a few good weeks before she'd been snatched by a serial killer. 'Mr Danton found her walking along the road in Macdoel, though. That's over by Mt. Shasta. Has to be at least a hundred miles from here. If DJ left here to go into the Modoc Forest, Eden might not have been far from here. How did Eileen get all the way up to Macdoel?'

And then a train went by, blowing its horn as it passed the town.

'Oh,' Mercy said softly. 'I didn't know trains ran through here. I guess that's one way.'

Rafe was already searching his phone. 'Cell signal sucks here. I barely have one bar.' He tapped his finger against the steering wheel impatiently, glaring at his phone. 'Shit. It timed out. I've got no Internet. We'll have to check on the train routes when we're in a less rural area.'

Mercy jumped when the back doors of the Subaru opened and Erin and Sasha climbed in, Sasha behind Rafe and Erin behind Mercy. Doors slammed, then Erin said, 'That man is an asshole. He was yelling at Ginger and giving her the third degree once you all left.'

'He asked Ginger to tell him exactly what you'd said,' Sasha added, then tossed one of the bags of chips to Rafe. 'He went behind the counter and then they were whispering so we couldn't hear.'

'What did she say to you at the end?' Erin asked. 'We were buying food and missed that part.'

'Basically that DJ was the man who'd repped Amos's work and that she'd followed him once into the forest.' Mercy shook her head. 'She had a crush on him. I'm so glad that didn't go anywhere. DJ was vile.'

Rafe opened the bag of chips. 'You want to see what's up that road?'

Mercy nodded. 'Yeah. I do.'

'Count us in,' Sasha said. 'I got provisions in case we get stuck.'

'You got chips and candy bars,' Erin said dryly.

Sasha grinned. 'Health food. Besides, you got deli sandwiches, because you're the grown-up.'

Erin handed out the sandwiches. 'Eat up. We'll follow you out.'

'Why not just go with them?' Sasha asked. 'If they've gotten the need for conversation out of their system,' she added with a bawdy wink. 'Snookums.'

Mercy was sure that her face was beet red, but Rafe just shook his head. 'Because Erin isn't here to keep us company,' he said. 'She's here to watch our backs.'

Sasha sighed. 'Right. Goddamn reality is such a buzzkill.'

Erin smiled, amused. 'Give me a minute to eat and we'll be ready to go. I don't want to eat while I drive. Not around here.'

Mercy craned her head around the seat to see Erin's face. 'Why not?'

'Because that man behind the deli counter was watching us the whole time we were looking at that jewelry box and now he's talking on the phone. Don't look,' Erin added in a hiss.

Mercy didn't twist to look through the store window, but she did glance at Rafe, who appeared unsurprised. 'You noticed him, too?' she asked.

Rafe nodded. 'Yep. And it gave me the same bad feeling.'

'Maybe we shouldn't go off-road,' Mercy countered. The last thing she wanted was to put these people in danger because of her.

Not because of you. Because Ephraim and DJ are monsters.

'He could have been a homophobe,' Sasha ventured. 'I don't think he liked it when I kissed Erin's cheek.'

'Which is why you did it,' Erin countered.

Sasha tossed her head, making her ponytail swing. 'Duh.'

Erin checked her watch. 'Going into the forest will be fine, Mercy. We have more backup coming.'

Rafe lifted a brow. 'You called Gideon?'

'Texted him before we left your house,' Erin replied, not one bit repentant. 'Kept calling once we got on the road until I woke him up. He was most unhappy that he had not been invited to our little party.'

'I tried to invite him,' Rafe said. 'He never replied to my texts.'

'He was asleep, and he about had a panic attack when he saw the missed texts from you. Luckily I was specific in mine. Why didn't you tell him what you wanted?' Erin asked.

Rafe gave her a withering look. 'No way was I going to put that information in writing. I'm on leave, remember?'

Erin pouted. 'So I was your second choice?'

'You were the one who pushed yourself into our trip,' Rafe pointed out. 'I would have waited for Gideon. Probably.'

Erin scowled. 'You could have told me.'

He shrugged. 'Before or after you tore me a new one, Detective High-Handed and Superior?'

Erin sighed. 'Okay. I might have deserved a little of that. Sorry.'

'It's okay,' Rafe allowed. 'But only because Mercy reminded me that you care.'

Mercy checked her own phone and sighed. She also had two texts that had downloaded when they'd rolled into town. There wasn't enough signal for Rafe to do an Internet search, but there was apparently just enough to text. 'I've got two messages from Farrah. She isn't happy with me, either. She and André woke up, found me gone, and are on their way up here as well.'

'I know,' Erin said. 'She texted me and Gideon, too. I figured I'd let her communicate her own irritation.'

Sasha was just staring at Erin. 'So that's why you bought eight sandwiches. I was wondering, since you can't even finish one. You know, being so tiny and all.'

Erin chuckled. 'Throw your worst, Amazon Girl. Tiny is not an insult.' She rewrapped the uneaten half of her sandwich in its plastic. 'I'm good to go whenever you are, Rafe.'

Rafe had wolfed down his sandwich and tucked the garbage neatly into a trash bag. 'Me too. What's Gideon's ETA?'

'About thirty minutes out. I'll text him to follow us down the county highway rather than waiting to meet him here. Then he won't have to backtrack. I'm curious to see what's back there.'

'Makes two of us,' Rafe replied.

Erin tugged on Sasha's ponytail. 'Move your tall self. We've got places to go.'

Snowbush, California
Monday, 17 April, 1.45 P.M.

Finally. Ephraim started MacGuire's Cadillac and headed back toward the five-building town that was Snowbush. Rhee's car had finally begun to move. They were going south, back the way they'd come.

At some point he'd have to get gas, but he'd be good until he got to Reno. As long as the tracker kept working, he didn't have to stay on their tails. At least he'd made good use of the time he'd spent waiting. He'd googled how to disable the Cadillac's GPS while he'd been at Sean MacGuire's house the night before, but he hadn't had an opportunity to actually do it. He felt a lot more confident, knowing that no one could track him as he tracked Erin Rhee.

He let his brain go on autopilot, watching the scenery pass by. He'd really liked this area. The weather wasn't as extreme as it had been in a lot of the places Eden had landed over the past thirty years.

Of course their original location would always be the best. Pastor owned property up there. Or he'd . . . appropriated it. His old church membership really had been a gullible group. Of course, getting away with identity theft had been a lot easier forty years ago when Pastor had started his previous flock.

Back then, a man could get out of prison, pick a new name, invent a background, and – as long as that man had the gift of earnest manipulation like Pastor had – could develop an entire network of rich, naive, generous parishioners. Parishioners who never once checked his background or résumé.

Parishioners who'd believed when their pastor promised that he hadn't embezzled from them. That he hadn't stolen their money or bedded their women.

Ephraim still couldn't understand people like that. They wanted to believe in a fairy tale, even when the facts were glaring them in the face.

Seventy-five percent of the original Eden settlers had been members of Pastor's old church who'd followed him, their loyalty and devotion utterly blind. Ephraim didn't understand them, but he could still be grateful for the money they'd brought into the coffers.

The millions that Pastor now managed in offshore accounts had started with that money plus the money his brother Edward had gotten from the bank heist that had put him and Ephraim on the FBI's most wanted list – sending them on the run. And into Pastor's fold.

And thirty years later, Ephraim was still there. Still serving the community. But really just waiting for Pastor to finally kick the bucket.

I would have helped him do it years ago if I'd known those damn bank access codes.

310

Ephraim wondered if DJ had the bank codes, and his eyes narrowed. He wouldn't be surprised. DJ had been sucking up to Pastor – literally and figuratively – ever since he'd been old enough to understand the community's true power structure.

Ephraim was so deep in thought that he nearly missed the blip on his phone's screen. He drew a breath, suddenly tense. Rhee was turning onto the county road.

Toward where Eden had existed up until the November before. *Up until Miriam ran away, forcing us to move. Fucking hell. Motherfucking hell.*

Ephraim found himself stomping on the gas pedal, then forcibly calmed himself. *Think.* It wouldn't do to get stopped by the sheriff's department, because they did patrol.

He didn't want to have to kill a cop. That got messy and was a lot harder to hide.

So he slowed to the speed limit, making sure he put on his blinker before cautiously turning onto the road that led to the home he'd left behind.

Nineteen

Amos was itchy, grateful for Monday. Grateful for work to keep his hands busy, even as his mind whirled. He'd had far too much time to think the day before, it being the Sabbath. No one worked, except those who fed the animals. And the women who cooked for their families, of course.

Amos missed that, having a woman in his household. He hadn't loved Abigail's mother, not like he'd grown to love Rhoda, but he'd liked her. Respected her. Had even waited two years to . . . well, consummate their marriage. She'd only been sixteen when her family had brought her into the community, and the thought of touching her then had made Amos physically ill. And she'd been so scared. He hadn't been able to hurt her, so they'd slept in the same bed for two years, celibate, until she'd turned eighteen. It had still been awkward, but she'd grown to care for him during those two years. He didn't think she'd loved him either – if an eighteen-year-old was even capable of such love – but she had respected him, too.

It had almost killed him to watch her die after giving birth. But when the healer had put a red-faced, squalling Abigail into his arms, it had been a balm to his soul. A reason to keep going.

One of the other women in the community had been weaning her own baby and had agreed to nurse Abigail for the first year. It had been difficult for Amos, handing his baby over, even to a woman he'd known for years. Especially in the night, when he'd had to take the baby to her and wait for Abigail to finish.

312

Luckily the healer had sent Brother DJ into town with instructions to buy a breast pump, which Amos had heard of, back in the world, but had never had cause to witness. He'd been only nineteen years old when he'd arrived in Eden.

So young. So foolishly trusting.

His heart hurt with the knowledge of truth, like having the scales ripped from his eyes. But he was no longer nineteen and foolish. He was forty-nine, with a daughter to protect. So he'd spent the Sabbath day sitting in the rocking chair that he'd made with his own hands, thinking and planning until darkness had fallen.

He was still thinking and planning. He had been all day today as he'd worked in his woodshop. He stepped back from the cabinet he'd made for their newest family – a single mother with two children. They'd recently been brought in from the city. He thought about the woman, about why she'd chosen to come to Eden. Her son was barely twelve and had already gotten involved with a dangerous gang. The daughter was fourteen, pregnant, and clearly unhappy to have been ripped away from civilization. Even unhappier to have been immediately married off to one of the compound's men.

Luckily neither of them had been given to Ephraim or DJ. The mother accepted the rules of the compound – had embraced them, even. She'd been grateful for the structure, pinning her hopes on Eden helping her children to straighten up and fly right. Her attitude was common enough.

No one was brought here against their will. Not bound and helpless, anyway. Rhoda had been lied to, she'd confided. Or at least hadn't been informed that she'd be required to wed within hours of her arrival.

She was happy with me, though. He hoped so. God, he hoped he'd at least done that right.

'Brother Amos?'

Amos spun around, startled at the sight of DJ Belmont in the doorway of his workshop. He put his hand to his racing heart and forced a smile. 'Brother DJ. What brings you here?'

What if he knew? What if DJ knew that he'd listened to Pastor's

313

call? That he'd seen Ephraim kill three people? That he'd seen the computer in the office?

He realized that he'd gripped the carving knife in his hand a little too tightly and dropped it on the worktable beside him.

DJ didn't seem to have noticed. 'I was wondering if you had any finished items to take into town.'

'Not at the moment,' Amos said. The hope chest was almost finished, but he was saving that to smuggle out Abigail, if he could find the right time. *That time is now.* 'But I will in a few days.' He tilted his head, wondering how much latitude he'd earned for his thirty years of service to Eden. 'I have a piece in mind that will be rather substantial and will require two people to move, plus some setup once it's delivered. I was wondering if I might accompany you on one of your deliveries.'

He had no such piece in mind, but he needed to know if his request would be shut down immediately. He needed to know if he'd be able to accompany Abigail once he had the hope chest finished.

There was no way he was putting his child in a chest and simply turning his back on her. She was no Moses to be hidden in the bulrushes, hoping for a good person to find her at the other end of her journey. Besides, they'd already tried to smuggle Miriam out. Amos had made the chest big enough for her to hide in, but something had gone wrong and there'd been no one to help her. Now she was dead, as was her whole family.

Surprise flickered in DJ's eyes before he smoothed his expression to one of almost condescension, as if Amos were a small boy asking for a pet pony. 'I don't know. I'll have to ask Pastor.'

Which meant no. *Well, then. That answers that.* Disappointment swirled with the panic in his gut, but Amos merely nodded, keeping his own expression smiling and mild. 'Of course. Let him know that the piece I'm considering should bring a good price from any of the shops, but if he doesn't believe it wise for me to accompany you, then I won't plan to build it.'

DJ inclined his head. 'I'll tell him. When do you think you'll have' – he startled abruptly, blinking as if something had shocked him – 'something ready for me to take to town?'

'In a few days. Thursday at the latest.'

DJ smiled absently. 'Thank you, Brother Amos.' He turned and hurried out the door.

Amos went to the window, watching as DJ crossed the common space, heading for the gate. *You need to follow him. Find out what's happening in this little corner of hell.*

As casually as he was able, Amos ambled across the yard, then, looking both ways, slipped into the trees that bordered the community.

On instinct, he headed toward the boulder that hid the satellite dish, gratified when he spied DJ perched on the same fake rock where Pastor had sat on Saturday evening. Amos had passed that boulder a hundred times over the almost six months since they'd moved here, but he'd never really *seen* it. He paid attention to trees, not rocks. He might have passed by it another hundred, maybe thousand, times without ever thinking to check beneath it.

DJ had a device similar to the one that Pastor had used, tapping it as Pastor had. Putting the phone to his ear, DJ snapped, 'What is it?'

He listened, his body growing more and more rigid as each second passed. 'What did she look like?'

Who is 'she'? Amos wondered, then stared when DJ paled.

'Are you sure? *Mercy Callahan?* Are you *sure* that's what her credit card said? *Mercy?'*

Mercy? *Mercy?* Amos covered his mouth with his hand to cover his own gasp. He didn't know the name Callahan, but how many Mercys could there be? Especially how many Mercys could make DJ this agitated?

But Mercy was dead. DJ had told them so. She'd died when Rhoda had smuggled her out.

A kernel of hope began to take root in his rapidly beating heart. *What if DJ lied?* Ephraim had lied. Pastor had lied. Why not DJ, too?

Which meant . . . Mercy might be alive. Mind reeling yet again, Amos watched as DJ lurched to his feet and began to pace.

'What did she buy?' A pause. 'Yeah, I remember it. "Surely goodness and mercy." Fucking goddamn verse. I never should have let him start carving that stupid Bible verse into the fucking wood.'

Mercy bought something I made. Oh, dear Lord. Amos felt light-headed and had to lean against a tree.

DJ went even paler. 'She did *what? Me?* She described *me?* Fucking hell, why didn't you say that first? Did you get the license plate on her car? Send it to me.' Another pause, during which DJ checked the screen of the device, before returning it to his ear. 'Yeah, I got it. Thanks.' He ran a hand through his hair as he listened again. 'No, I haven't seen the news lately, but thanks for the heads-up. I . . . owe you.'

He said the last two words like they tasted bad. 'No, I don't have any more product. We had to leave it behind when we moved. It'll be a few months before we have a new batch.' He grimaced. 'Yeah, I know. The market's shrinking, blah, blah, blah. I've heard it before. But there's still a market, right? The demand for shrooms isn't just going to disappear overnight because a few cities have decriminalized.' He stopped pacing, blowing out an impatient breath. 'No. I've told you before, I do not have facilities to make meth even if I wanted to. Look, I need to go. Thanks for the warning. I'll leave tonight as soon as I can get away. Can you keep her there? Like damage her tires or something?' He exhaled heavily. 'Right. I guess not. No, thanks anyway. I'll see you tonight.'

He jabbed the device's screen with his finger, then stood stock-still for a moment, his body still rigid. Then, using his thumbs, he began to tap the screen rapidly, tapping his foot as he stared at it, clearly waiting for something.

But what?

Amos got his answer – sort of – when DJ began to read from the screen.

'Oh shit,' DJ muttered. 'It *is* her. Oh my God. Fucking hell. This can't be happening. This *cannot* be *happening.*' He slumped on the boulder, looking out toward the mountains, his expression slack. Numb. 'You were supposed to die. Why didn't I just kill you in the woods? Goddammit.'

Amos felt the same numbness, his legs trembling so much that he feared he'd crumple to the ground. *It is her. Mercy.*

My Mercy is alive?

The kernel of hope blossomed in his chest, followed by radiant joy. *My Mercy is alive.* But the happiness was quickly swallowed up by icy fear. If she was alive, who had DJ buried?

Or had he buried anyone? Amos didn't know what to think anymore.

Except one thing was clear. DJ was leaving tonight.

And Amos would find a way to get himself and Abigail on that truck. His plan to smuggle her out in a hope chest would never have worked, not with DJ refusing to allow him to go into town even one time. *I'll figure out how to stow away in the truck bed and we can be free.*

He had to save Abigail. And he had to warn Mercy.

Modoc County, California
Monday, 17 April, 2.45 P.M.

Rafe wished they were driving through the forest under different circumstances. It was a beautiful drive. A beautiful day. A beautiful woman at his side.

But the air was thick with tension as Mercy looked side to side as if she were a spectator at a tennis match. She was searching the trees, nervous since Erin had voiced her concerns.

Which were valid. Rafe hadn't liked the way the man behind the deli counter had looked at them. He hadn't liked the way the man had talked to the young woman behind the counter. And that he'd gotten on the phone as soon as they'd left?

Yeah. None of that felt right.

But he might be able to alleviate some of Mercy's concern. 'Burton's not going to jump at you from behind a tree,' he said quietly. 'Not today, at least.'

Mercy cast him an anxious glance. 'Am I that transparent?'

He smiled at her, offering his hand, palm up. Relieved when she took it and squeezed. 'Yeah,' he said. 'Pretty transparent. About Ephraim, anyway. But I get it. He's your worst nightmare and you

317

had to literally face him just two days ago. So yeah, I get that you're unsettled. But I've been watching, and I haven't seen any sign that we were followed.'

She smiled tightly. 'Thank you. That means a lot.'

'And if you can't relax on my say-so, I get that, too.'

She brought his hand to her lips and pressed. Not a kiss. Just contact. Vital and affirming.

'You're not alone, Mercy. Whatever happens between us, I will not let you face this alone.'

She lowered his hand to the console between them. 'Gideon and Farrah are going to be pissed off.'

Rafe checked his rear-view mirror. He could see Erin's blue Rover, but Gideon hadn't caught up to them yet. Nor had Farrah and her captain. He'd been driving through the forest for nearly an hour, but the roads were twisty and even if Gideon or Farrah were behind them, they might not see them.

'I can't speak for Farrah,' he said, 'but Gideon will get over it. Besides, he'll be more pissed off with me. I should have waited for him to answer my call before I left.'

She shrugged. 'I would have pushed you to leave anyway. I was hell-bent on proving that I could contribute something important to the search.' She turned to look out the window. 'Because I feel guilty that I walked away back in February. Ran away, if we're being technical.'

He made a scoffing noise. 'Technicalities are highly overrated.' He slowed when a turnoff became visible in the trees ahead. 'We've gone about twenty miles, just like Ginger from the store said. And there's the *Private Property* sign. You want to give this one a go?'

They'd already tried two side roads, but both had been dead ends.

She made a face. 'Sure, why not?'

Activating his turn signal, he grinned over at her. 'That's the spirit!'

She laughed. 'Sorry.' Then she sighed. 'I'm afraid we'll find nothing, but also afraid we'll find something. Which sounds batshit crazy, I know.'

'No, it doesn't.' He glanced back at Erin, who had followed them onto the side road. 'And if we find nothing, we keep looking.'

Mercy drew a breath, bracing herself.

They drove in absolute silence for another twenty minutes, following the curve of the severely rutted road, still covered with snow. This deep in the forest, there wasn't enough sunshine to melt it and the temps would remain cool for at least another month or so.

'I can't believe the snow is still here,' Mercy said, reading his mind.

'Could be worse. At least the roads are drivable. Some of the roads in Lassen don't open until late June.'

They hit a deep hole and the Subaru bounced around. Rafe slipped his hand free of her hold to grip the wheel and wrestle them to the smoother part of the road.

Which still bounced them around.

'Sorry about this,' Rafe gritted out.

'It's—' Mercy gasped. 'Rafe. Look.'

He was looking. 'Holy shit,' he murmured.

It was a clearing of sorts. More like a campground. A very large campground. Two tall posts stood on either side of the entrance, a crosspiece spanning the width. It looked like the entrance to a ranch, minus the sign.

Erin pulled into the clearing behind him and Rafe rolled the Subaru to a stop, leaving the engine running as he opened his door, hand on his gun. 'Stay here until I tell you that it's safe, okay? If anything even looks weird, you drive yourself out of here.'

She nodded mutely.

Grabbing his cane, Rafe walked back to Erin's Range Rover, his senses on high alert. He didn't hear anything except the sound of their engines, but that didn't mean they were safe.

Erin jumped to the ground, her hand also on the gun holstered on her belt. 'What the actual fuck?'

Rafe just shook his head, almost afraid to hope that they'd found what was left of an old Eden settlement. 'Let's take a look.'

Karen Rose

Modoc County, California
Monday, 17 April, 2.55 P.M.

Ephraim glared at the Cadillac. It was no longer stuck in the snow, but he'd wasted precious minutes rocking it free. At least it still drove, just in case he needed it to get away if things went wrong. Wishing he'd stolen a vehicle with four-wheel drive, he shouldered his backpack and gathered his guns.

The Cadillac had fit in perfectly in Granite Bay and the neighborhood around Rafe Sokolov's Victorian, but it was woefully ill suited to this terrain. Sokolov and Rhee, on the other hand, were probably able to navigate a blizzard of biblical proportions.

Luckily, he didn't have to walk too far and he knew the area like the back of his hand. Eden had been located here for seven years, after all. He set off, taking a shortcut that would lead him to the former settlement. If he played his cards right and didn't lose his cool, he could shoot the two cops and Sokolov's sister, then take Mercy back to Eden in Sokolov's Subaru.

If he was forced to get away in the Cadillac, he'd steal a four-wheel drive as soon as possible. He'd need the extra power to get up the mountain. The community had relocated to one of their previous hideaways, necessary since they'd left in such a hurry. And in freaking November. Snow had already been deep in the mountains and digging out new earth homes simply hadn't been possible in the short time they'd had to evacuate after Miriam's escape.

At first he'd been angry that Mercy and Sokolov had found the previous Eden, but it really was perfect. He could drag the bodies of the three he didn't care about into one of the earth homes and leave them there to rot. Or be eaten. This time of year, with winter still hanging on and food in short supply, their bodies would be scavenged by hungry animals in no time.

And Mercy and I will be free.

Modoc County, California
Monday, 17 April, 3.05 P.M.

Rafe and Erin approached the clearing cautiously, but it became quickly apparent that it was abandoned. There was a central court-yard, circular in shape, about the size of an ice rink. Structures were arranged on the perimeter. 'Twenty-six,' Rafe whispered after counting them. They were vaguely domelike, with what looked like stairways leading down to open doorways.

'Earth shelters,' Erin said quietly.

Rafe brushed snow from the sloping side of the structure nearest to where they stood. 'Covered in vegetation.' Vines, mostly, but also some shrubs. 'This area would have looked green from above. Which explains why Eden was never visible from the air.' He'd pored over the satellite maps of the area around Mt. Shasta, but he'd never checked maps this far east. He didn't know if the FBI had, either. It didn't really matter, because the settlement was very efficiently camouflaged.

Erin turned in a slow circle, studying the layout. 'The fence poles are twelve feet tall, around the outside perimeter, but there's no fencing to connect them.'

'They may have taken the fencing with them. Like the doors.' Rafe's instincts were screaming that something was very wrong here, but that was understandable given the horrors that must have occurred within the compound's walls. 'We need to radio for backup.'

'But who?' Erin pushed back. 'Do we really want locals on the scene? They might be great, but at the same time, this is too big not to handle appropriately. We can't take the chance that they'll be sloppy with . . . all this.'

'The FBI is leading the search for Burton and Eden, so Gideon can call Molina. And we'll stay here until the FBI can secure the area.'

Erin nodded. 'Agreed. I want to check out one of these earth shelters. Cover me?'

Rafe wasn't so sure that was wise, but he followed her, drawing

321

his gun from his holster. 'Don't go too far in. If they're not stable, they could collapse on your head.'

Erin gave him an arch look. 'Thank you, Professor Sokolov.'

He rolled his eyes. 'I'm serious.'

'And I'm not stupid.'

'Jury's out on that,' Rafe muttered as she descended the stairs of the closest structure, her flashlight lifted over her head, angled down.

She turned to glare at him before disappearing through the doorway. Within thirty seconds she was backing out, pocketing her flashlight. 'Empty,' she said when she rejoined him. 'But extensive. There are separate rooms inside. At least three in that one – what looked like two bedrooms and an open sitting room. If we walked to the back side of these homes, we'd see the hole for what was probably a stovepipe. There were gouges in the door frames, like there used to be hinges there. I think you're right that they took the doors with them.'

'Toilet facilities?' Rafe asked.

'Not in that one, although one of the rooms might have had an outhouse-type hole. I didn't get that far. But there doesn't appear to be plumbing. Or people.'

'No tire treads in the snow, no footprints. I think it's okay for Mercy to take a look around.'

'I'll go get her,' Erin offered. 'This snow isn't easy to walk in.'

Rafe wanted to protest – *I can do it!* – but she was right. The snow was a bitch and his cane kept sliding when it hit the layer of ice beneath the most recent accumulation. 'Thank you.'

A minute later, Mercy and Sasha were at his side. 'This isn't Eden,' Mercy said. 'Or at least not the way I remember it.'

'How so?' Erin asked.

'We had houses,' she said. 'Actual houses, made of wood, with four walls and shingled roofs. The Founding Elders had really nice houses, but these all look the same. And this is smaller than I remember. There are how many structures here?'

'Twenty-six,' Erin answered.

'We had at least forty.' She went silent, turning in a circle to study the abandoned settlement, much as Erin had done, but her expression was distant, clearly lost in memory.

'So Eden is shrinking in numbers?' Rafe asked, and she blinked, her eyes refocusing.

'I guess so. The layout . . . it's familiar. This was the common area. Houses ringed the perimeter, just like these huts. Shared spaces were at two, six, and ten o'clock. Most families had cookstoves for small meals and general heating, but that hut at two o'clock would have been the shared cooking facilities for larger meals like turkey, wild boar, or deer. The hut at ten o'clock was the clinic. Six o'clock was the school.' She walked to a slight bowl-shaped depression in the ground. It measured about six feet in diameter. 'Fire pit.' She pointed to the largest structure at twelve o'clock. 'The church. Pastor's home was next door. Outhouses used to be behind each home. I don't see that here, but they could be hidden behind the huts. Can we walk beyond the ring?'

'I don't see why not,' Erin said. 'What are you looking for?'

'The outbuildings.' Mercy started walking, cutting through the huts to the land behind them, and Rafe had to lengthen his stride to keep up, careful not to slip in the snow. 'The stables. Amos's workshop. The smithy. I can't see them being belowground huts.'

The smithy. Where Gideon had been attacked and accidentally killed his attacker.

She stopped walking when she got to an area about twenty by twenty. It was flatter than the common area had been. Crouching, she brushed at the snow, then looked up.

'Concrete slab. This was either the smithy or Amos's workshop. They were a little away from the homes because of the fire hazard. The smithy always had a fire going, of course, and Amos's workshop had so much sawdust.' She moved to a similar area with level snow cover and, crouching again, revealed another concrete slab. 'This was probably Amos's place. They were always placed the same way, going clockwise.' She settled on her haunches, looking out to the trees. 'There was a generator between them that ran on gasoline. It powered Amos's tools. His saws were the only things that ran on electricity, in all the compound.'

323

She stood up, frowning. 'It doesn't look so scary like this, does it? Just kind of sad.' She continued on a clockwise path, a circle concentric to the ring of homes. 'The stable would have been here.' Her shoulders straightened. 'Behind Ephraim's house.'

'What was his job, Mercy?' Sasha asked quietly.

'He was responsible for the animals.' Her lips curved bitterly. 'He was actually good with them. Treated them with respect. Even affection. Far better than he treated his wives and children.' Her frown returned. 'How could they have lived in such cramped quarters? Ephraim had four or five wives at any given time. Plus children.'

'The houses extend out underground,' Erin explained. 'At least the one that I went into did.'

Mercy's frown deepened. 'How horrible. To be stuck in a confined space like that. With *him*.'

She looked beyond where the stable would have been, peering through the trees, growing suddenly still. Without a word she headed in the direction she'd been staring, and they followed, stopping behind her when she fell to her knees in the snow.

'It was always behind the church,' she muttered as she frantically parted the snow with her bare hands.

Revealing a cross made from wood. Painted white. Now that Rafe knew what to look for, he saw four more crosses poking up from the snow.

She'd uncovered the graveyard.

Rafe carefully lowered himself to his good knee, stretching his bad leg out sideways. Leaning on his cane for balance, he dug into his pocket for his leather gloves. 'Put these on.'

She took the gloves, looking taken aback. 'I won't touch them,' she said solemnly. 'I know better.'

She was a lab tech, working with evidence every day. He supposed she had a right to look a little insulted. He smiled at her, keeping it gentle because she looked so fragile in that moment. 'They're so your hands don't get cold.'

'Oh.' She put on the gloves, shaking her head. 'Stupid of me.'

'Hush,' he admonished, then pulled out his phone to shine his flashlight on the cross. '"Damaris Terrill, Beloved Wife of Amos and Mother of Abigail".'

Mercy looked a little shell-shocked. 'He got married again. Had another child. A daughter.'

Rafe touched her shoulder lightly. 'You okay, baby?'

She met his eyes, hers swimming with tears. 'He lost the chance at another wife after my mother got taken from him,' she whispered hoarsely. 'He tried to keep them from marrying me to Ephraim. They told him that he would be punished. That he'd never get another wife, but he kept shouting at them that it wasn't right, that I was too young.' She swallowed hard and blinked, quickly swiping her cheeks with her hands, still covered with his warm gloves. 'I thought I'd ruined his life. But he got another chance. And then she died. And he had to make her cross.' Her voice broke. 'He always had to make the crosses.'

Rafe's throat grew thick. That she'd worry about Amos, even after all she'd endured . . . 'You are a good person, Mercy Callahan. Don't ever let anyone tell you differently. Especially not yourself.'

She gave a watery chuckle. 'You're a little biased.'

'I'm right.' He looked back to the cross. 'She was so young. Not quite nineteen.'

'Already a mother.' She sighed. 'A lot of women died in child-birth. I was so afraid that I'd—' She shook her head. 'Never mind.'

She started to rise, but he stayed her with a light touch to her knee. 'Tell me. Please.'

She drew a breath and carefully exhaled, her gaze traveling to the other little crosses, their tops barely visible in the snow. 'I was afraid I'd get pregnant. I saw so many of the women constantly pregnant. Infant mortality was very high.'

'You were afraid you'd die, too?' he asked quietly.

She shook her head. 'I was afraid I'd survive. With a baby. I was scared to bring another child into his home. Part of me wished that he'd kill me and get it over with. Those were the times that I really hated Gideon,' she finished with a whisper. She cleared her throat. 'I mean, I understand now. I do. But when I thought he'd run away and left me – us, me and Mama – to suffer for his actions . . .'

A strangled sound made them both turn. Rafe muttered a curse when pain burned up his leg. Mercy went pale.

Gideon stood there, just as pale as Mercy. Nearly the color of the snow.

Behind him were Daisy, Sasha, and Erin, wearing matching looks of devastation.

That Rafe hadn't heard any of them was testament to how completely Mercy had pulled him into her memories. Into her suffering.

'I don't think that anymore, Gideon,' she said. 'I swear it.'

His mouth opened and closed, no words emerging. He stumbled forward, falling to his knees in front of her. 'I'm so sorry. God, I'm so sorry.'

She put her arms around her brother, pulling off one glove to stroke his hair as his shoulders shook. Rafe knew he should look away, that he should give them privacy, but he couldn't make his body move. He knew he was crying and couldn't care less. This whole thing was so fucked up. So many lives ruined.

And he didn't know how to fix it. So he remained motionless, powerless. And hating Ephraim Burton with every fiber of his existence.

'I looked for you,' Gideon cried. 'I searched and searched. But I couldn't find you. I'd think about what was happening to you and . . . God, Mercy, I'm so sorry. I should have looked harder.'

'I know,' she whispered. 'I'm sorry, too. But it's not your fault. Not mine, either. You couldn't have found us, because they didn't want us to be found. Don't cry. Please.' A sob choked her. 'Dammit, Gideon, you're breaking my heart.'

Gideon drew a shuddering breath. 'Sorry.' He straightened, still on his knees, then cupped Mercy's equally wrecked face. 'I'm just making it worse.'

'No,' she said sadly. 'You make it better. Now that I know the truth, it's better.'

They were quiet for a long moment, and then Gideon looked around them. 'It's different, isn't it?'

'Some things, yes. Some things are the same.' She gestured to the white crosses. 'Graveyard's in the same place.'

Gideon's gaze dropped to the cross she'd uncovered. 'Amos married again.'

'And she died. The thought of him making her cross . . . it hurts. I remember the day he made yours.' New tears streaked down her face. '"Gideon Terrill, Beloved Son".' Her voice broke again. 'They wouldn't let him put the cross on your grave. They said you'd sinned, a mortal sin, even. You'd killed. So you couldn't be buried with everyone else.' She swallowed hard. 'So one night he woke me up and we snuck out of the gate to where they'd buried you. Or the body they said was you, anyway. Amos had made a little plaque. "Beloved Son". He buried it a few inches deep, just enough that it couldn't be seen. And we both cried. For you and for Mama, because Ephraim had already taken her away.'

Rafe hadn't understood why Mercy had loved Amos so much, but he was finally beginning to. Yes, the man had allowed terrible things to happen to her. Yes, he'd remained in a cult that was so evil. But he'd cared for her. He'd loved her. He'd loved Gideon, too.

Gideon shuddered out another breath. 'Thank you.' He rose, holding out a hand, first to Mercy, then to Rafe.

Rafe eased himself to his feet, grimacing when his leg throbbed. He met Gideon's gaze with apology. 'I'm sorry. I should have tried harder to call you, Gid.'

'Yeah. You should have.' Then Gideon shocked him by pulling him into a hard hug. 'But it's okay,' he whispered. 'Thank you for bringing her here. I probably would have nixed the entire idea and she needed this. So did I.' He let Rafe go. 'But don't do it again. Please.'

'I won't,' Rafe promised.

'Oh no.' Mercy had moved to the far end of the small graveyard and was uncovering another cross. This one was natural wood, while the others were painted white. She looked over at them wearily. 'It says "Comstock".'

'They put one up for Eileen,' Gideon said. 'I wonder who they killed pretending it was her.'

Because Eileen had escaped, only to have her life stolen permanently by a serial killer.

'No. It doesn't say "Miriam". It's her family, Gideon. Dorcas, Stephen, and Ezra. The date is November first of last year.'

Gideon cursed. 'They killed them, too.' Then he frowned. 'Wait. They acknowledged their deaths?'

Daisy, Erin, and Sasha joined them at the edge of the graves. 'They didn't normally do that, did they?' Daisy asked quietly.

'No,' Mercy answered for him. 'Or if they did, they wouldn't be allowed to be buried in the community graveyard, because it was "hallowed ground" and they'd been cast out, devoured by wolves.' Her gaze returned to the cross. 'Amos didn't paint it. I wonder why.'

'He always painted them,' Gideon murmured. 'Paint was expensive, but Amos always said that it was worth the cost. That we needed to honor the dead.'

'November first would have been right about the time that Eileen escaped,' Daisy commented. 'She was found wandering by the side of the road up in Macdoel a few days later.'

'And it jibes with what Ginger in the store said,' Sasha added, then brought Gideon and Daisy up to date with what they'd learned in the Snowbush general store.

'We were discussing who to call to secure the scene,' Erin said. 'But we'd have to go back to Snowbush and ask to use one of the shops' phones. No cell service here.'

Rafe left Erin and Gideon to figure out who was best to call – who was closest and who they thought they could trust not to mess up the scene. He walked over to Mercy, who still knelt in the snow.

'You're going to get sick,' he murmured. 'Your jeans are soaking wet.' Just as his were, drenched from the knees down and getting cold very quickly. 'Hypothermia can set in quickly, even when the temps are mild like this.'

She rose, never taking her gaze from the wooden cross. 'Eileen's mother was good to me,' she murmured. 'I went to school with her brother, Ezra.'

'Amos didn't put their birth dates on the cross,' Rafe noted.

'I know. And he didn't make individual crosses, either. He always made individual crosses with birth and death dates and something special, a message of some kind. Whatever the family wanted. I don't know why he didn't this time. Maybe he was rushed or maybe they wouldn't let him, like with Gideon. The leaders would have packed everyone up and moved after Eileen escaped. That's what they always did.' She sighed. 'I know it's stupid, but I really have been hoping that the families of the dead really did get back to civilization, that they weren't "devoured by wolves".'

'Not stupid,' Rafe chided. 'It's never stupid to hope.'

She looked at him then, her mouth turning up in a sad smile. 'Thank—'

But she never got to finish. A gunshot cracked the air, followed by a shrill curse behind them, and they spun to see Erin sinking to the snow. Which was rapidly growing bright red with her blood.

'Down,' Rafe barked, shoving Mercy into the snow, just as Gideon shouted '*Gun!*' Rafe pulled his weapon, looking frantically for a shooter.

Fucking hell. Looked like Eden wasn't so deserted after all.

Twenty

Modoc County, California
Monday, 17 April, 3.45 P.M.

Mercy looked up from where Rafe had pushed her into the snow. And she saw him.

Ephraim. He'd come from the far edge of the compound, from the direction of the school, but he'd made it as far as the church before he'd started firing.

'There, behind the church!' She pointed to Ephraim, who'd taken cover behind the domed roof of the earth shelter that was the largest and tallest of all of the structures in the compound. She and her group were out in the open, only able to hide behind the trees, while he was protected by earth and stone. 'Rafe, he's right there!'

'Gideon!' Rafe shouted. 'Behind you!'

Ephraim had snuck up on them, separating them from the way out. *No way out.* The words taunted her mind, singing gleefully every time she tried to push them away. To shove them in the box in her mind. To nail the lid shut. *You're trapped. Trapped. No way out.*

She watched, unable to take her eyes off Ephraim as he appeared above the church's roofline, his rifle aimed at Gideon. Who was crouching next to Erin, cradling his hand to his chest and reaching for the weapon he'd dropped in the snow.

Mercy could see the snow tinged with red below his hand. Ephraim had shot him and was still shooting. She'd counted five shots already, all fired in rapid succession. Most magazines held ten rounds, but high-capacity magazines could hold thirty or even more.

How many rounds did Ephraim's rifle magazine hold?

Cursing, Rafe lurched to the side because Gideon was blocking his line of fire. 'Gideon, get down!'

Daisy yanked Gideon down just as Ephraim fired again, the bullet going wide to hit the tree where Gideon's head had been only seconds before. Bark flew everywhere and, beside her, Rafe cursed again. Mercy could feel the fear rolling off him and that set her own panic spiraling, dragging her down.

Down, where it was dark and numb and nothing hurt.

'*Mercy*,' Rafe hissed. 'Stay with me. We're going to be okay. I won't leave you. *Stay with me.*'

The sound of his voice was like an anchor, holding her for a moment. Just long enough to think. *No more.* She would not disappear. *Not today.* She dug her nails into her own wrist with the hand she'd bared to comfort Gideon, the small spike of pain helping her focus. Keeping her centered.

It had been a technique she'd learned in therapy. Her therapist hadn't been entirely pleased with the option, but it helped Mercy keep herself from becoming a walking zombie, so Mercy was wholly on board.

She opened her eyes, seeing Sasha lying on her side next to Erin, putting pressure on the wound in Erin's leg. Gideon was holding one of his hands with the other, his face contorted in a grimace.

They were hurt. Her family. Her friends. They were hurt.

And then Gideon was standing, holding his service weapon in his left hand as he aimed at Ephraim, who'd slipped far enough into view to point his rifle at her brother. Gideon got off a single shot before Ephraim squeezed off three in rapid succession. Gideon went down on his butt in the snow before curling onto his side.

Mercy tried to scream, but the sound stuck in her throat. Daisy was at Gideon's side, remarkably calm, as she ran her hands over his chest. Mercy started to move, but Daisy shouted that Gideon was all right.

'Kevlar vest,' Rafe muttered, shaken. 'He'll be bruised. Maybe a few fractured ribs. But he'll live.'

Mercy was glad she was on her stomach because she was certain her knees would have folded beneath her. *I need to do something. Think, Mercy. Think, dammit.*

She didn't have a gun. Didn't have any weapons at all. Not even Mace.

But she did have herself. *Me. He wants me. Stand up. Let him take you.*

But she couldn't make herself move, self-preservation holding her back. *Don't be selfish. Dammit, Mercy.* Gideon, Rafe, and Erin had sacrificed for her. It was clear that they were Ephraim's targets as well. They were the cops. They had the guns. They were in his way.

But I'm who he wants. She pushed herself up to her knees and time seemed to stand still when Ephraim froze next to the wall of the church, staring at her. For what seemed like forever, they stared at each other. And then, like it was slow motion, Ephraim raised his rifle and aimed, his lips curving in a triumphant smile.

But Mercy dropped back to her stomach as the blast that came from beside her had her covering her ears out of reflex.

Rafe had fired.

Mercy thought she heard Ephraim scream, but it had to have been in her mind, because she couldn't hear anything now. Her ears were ringing, her heart pounding, her eyes watering, and her glasses were wet with snow, but her vision was clear enough to see that Ephraim was backing up as he fired again. One, two, three shots.

Sasha pitched forward, landing across Erin's body.

Mercy's heart dropped into her stomach. 'No. Sasha!' She started to rise, but Rafe yanked at her coat, pulling her back down. She wanted to fight Rafe's hold, but she saw Sasha moving, one hand on her upper arm.

Gideon had staggered back to his feet, taking shelter behind a tree, firing at Ephraim with his other hand.

And then Daisy was moving, grabbing Erin's gun, shooting at Ephraim, but the bastard had slipped through the huts and was now running along the outer ring. He appeared for only seconds between huts, firing at them as he ran for the front gate. He was going to get away.

The air around her rang with one continuous barrage of gunfire, and Mercy was beyond deafened. But she wasn't catatonic. She hadn't become a zombie.

Gideon started running unsteadily after Ephraim, disappearing from view through the huts. Rafe used his cane to get to his own feet, and then he was half running, half limping, following Gideon.

Mercy wasn't sure if she should stay in place or join the other women, but then she decided to stay where she was. If she was with them, they were more of a target. So she didn't move.

Until, through the ringing in her ears, she heard a thin scream coming from the direction Ephraim had run. Mercy didn't stop to think, she simply ran toward the scream. Crossing the open common area, she passed Rafe at the school, ignoring his commands for her to stop, to go back. She ran faster until she'd returned to where they'd left their vehicles, then came to a dead stop, sliding in the snow a few feet as she stared in horror.

Gideon's Suburban was parked behind Erin's Range Rover. And behind that, parked perpendicular to Gideon's SUV, was Karl Sokolov's Tahoe – the one Rafe had loaned to André and Farrah.

André was on his back in the bloodstained snow, hands closed around Ephraim's throat while Ephraim straddled his chest, delivering blow after desperate blow to André's head with his fists. Farrah had leaped into the fray, yanking at the rifle strapped to Ephraim's back, screaming for help as she tried to dislodge the sonofabitch. The snow was disturbed all around them, as if the two men had rolled while trying to incapacitate each other.

Ephraim was hitting much harder with his left fist. The right sleeve of his coat was dark with blood. *At least Rafe got him*, Mercy thought with grim satisfaction.

'Hit—' *His right arm!* she'd wanted to shout, but Rafe was suddenly beside her, huffing as he shoved her behind his Subaru.

'Stay down, dammit,' he hissed. 'What are you thinking? You want to get Farrah killed?'

God, no. Please don't let him hurt her. Trembling, Mercy shifted so that she could see around Rafe.

Both Rafe and Gideon were trying to get a clear line of fire at Ephraim, but Farrah was in Rafe's way and Gideon's left hand was

333

shaking. Gideon's whole body was shaking, his lips pressed together in a harsh line. He was in pain, Mercy realized, and afraid of shooting Farrah by mistake.

Mercy saw the flash of metal a split second before Ephraim plunged a knife into André's biceps. André shouted a curse, loosening his grip just enough for Ephraim to spring backward, grabbing Farrah as he struggled to his feet. Gideon got off a single shot, but Ephraim had ducked low enough that his head was behind Farrah's.

The shot missed Ephraim, hitting one of the gateposts instead. His uninjured arm around Farrah's throat, he dragged her toward the Tahoe, both its front doors open, the motor still running. He'd deftly pulled a golden gun from his pocket, shoving the barrel against Farrah's temple.

'Back off, Gideon,' Ephraim shouted, 'or I'll kill her. I swear it.'

Unable to remain silent, Mercy stepped around Rafe. 'No!' she screamed as loudly as she could.

Ephraim swiveled his head toward Mercy, and André used the momentary distraction to leap to his feet, pulling his own weapon to aim at Ephraim. André's voice boomed as he commanded, 'Let her go.'

Shoot him now! Mercy wanted to scream. But she could see Ephraim's finger on the trigger and logically knew that even if the bastard got shot in the head, he could release the trigger on reflex in death and Farrah would die. But the logic didn't calm the frantic need to scream, so she clenched her teeth, keeping the words inside.

'Drop your guns and step back, boys,' Ephraim barked. 'Or I will pull the trigger. I'll shoot her head off. I have absolutely nothing to lose.'

Farrah's eyes had closed and her mouth moved, no sounds coming out. But Mercy could see the words on her lips. *Please, God, please.* Farrah was praying.

Mercy followed suit, afraid to draw a breath.

Gideon and André dropped their guns and stepped back, both breathing hard, fists clenched. Gideon continued to back away, inching toward his Suburban. He was going to follow them.

'You too, blondie,' Ephraim said, jutting his chin toward Rafe.

His eyes were wild. 'Then I need to see your hands. Gideon, stop moving, right now. I swear to God, I will shoot her. My finger is fucking itchy.'

André shifted, his hands visible, but curved, as if he wanted to get his hands on Ephraim's neck again. 'I will kill you if you harm one hair on her head.'

'But she'll still be dead,' Ephraim snapped. 'Blondie, drop the fucking gun.'

Rafe dropped his weapon to the snow, and Mercy wanted to pick it up. But it wouldn't make any difference. She'd only fired a weapon a few times in her life and she didn't want to get Farrah killed.

'Very smart.' Using Farrah as a shield, he backed up until he could hoist himself into the Tahoe. In one movement he put the SUV in gear and shoved Farrah away. She landed on her knees in the snow, collapsing onto her hands as Ephraim floored it, nearly hitting the gatepost when the Tahoe fishtailed as it raced away.

Both André and Rafe dove for their guns, both firing at the Tahoe as it sped out of view. André gave chase, shooting as he ran.

Rafe muttered something about his 'fucking cane' as he moved toward his Subaru, dragging his bad leg behind him.

Gideon had already jumped into his Suburban and . . . nothing. Mercy could hear him cursing as she ran to Farrah's side, dropping to her knees to draw her friend close.

'Oh my God, oh my God,' Mercy whispered, rocking Farrah, who was sobbing silently. 'Did he hurt you?'

Farrah shook her head and clung to Mercy. Rafe had joined them, looking grim as André reappeared, a scowl on his face and Ephraim's knife still embedded in his upper arm.

'Fucking sonofabitch,' Gideon swore as he got out of his SUV.

'Why didn't you follow him?' André yelled, breathing hard. 'He got away, for fuck's sake.'

Gideon lifted the hood of the Suburban, shaking his head as he stared at the engine. 'Because that bastard took my fucking spark plugs,' he shot back. 'Fucking asshole.'

Rafe popped the Subaru's hood. 'Mine too,' he muttered once he'd checked. 'I bet he disabled Erin's Rover, too.' He checked the

Range Rover's engine, his shoulders sagging. 'Motherfucker. We're stranded here.'

André was now kneeling beside Farrah, and Mercy let her go so that André could hold her. Trembling, Mercy stood, took a few steps, then sank back into the snow when her legs gave out.

'André,' Mercy croaked out. 'Your arm.' The knife sticking out of his biceps, all the blood in the snow . . . It felt like a bad horror movie. *Except it's real.* 'I'm trying to remember my first aid. Do we pull it out or not?'

Holding on to Farrah with his good arm, André gave the knife a disgusted glance. 'Depends on how far away we are from help. If more than two hours, we yank it and pray. I'm fine at the moment. It hurts like a bitch, but I can deal.' He turned his attention back to Farrah, crooning comfort into her ear. 'You're okay. I love you.'

'Gideon!' Daisy shouted.

Mercy's attention was yanked toward the hill, where Daisy and Sasha supported a pale Erin between them. Daisy waved a phone at them. 'Molina's sending backup.'

'Thank you,' Gideon called back. 'Sat phone,' he explained before making his way to Erin and taking Daisy's place when Sasha stubbornly refused to relinquish her hold.

Mercy forced herself to stand, meeting the others at the tailgate of Rafe's Subaru, which he'd opened so that Erin could be lowered into the hatch. Sasha climbed in beside her, using the blankets and parkas to elevate Erin's head and feet.

'She needs a hospital,' Sasha said quietly. 'She's lost a lot of blood and she's still bleeding.'

'I'm right here,' Erin gritted through clenched teeth. 'Not dead.'

'Hush,' Sasha admonished. 'Let me help you. Rafe, where's your damn first-aid kit?'

While Rafe got it for her, Mercy pulled the scarf from her neck and handed it to Sasha. 'Wrap her leg. It's no tourniquet, but it might help stop the bleeding.'

Sasha obeyed, her hands shaking. 'Thank you.'

'It was nothing.' *Truly nothing.* With a nod, Mercy stepped back, wrapping her arms around herself. All this pain, this . . . havoc was because of her. *Because Ephraim wants me back.* Leaning against the Subaru, she closed her eyes, feeling very helpless. Very alone.

And then Rafe was at her side, hugging her so hard that it hurt. He pulled away, giving her a head-to-toe visual assessment. 'Are you okay?'

She could hear him mostly, the ringing in her ears having sufficiently subsided. She nodded. 'You?'

'I'm fine.' And then his expression changed from worry to anger. 'What were you thinking back there? You got up. You let him try to shoot you. Made yourself a fucking target. What were you *thinking*?'

'That he wanted me, not you,' she admitted.

Fire flashed in Rafe's eyes. 'Never do that again. *Never.*'

Mercy nodded but left her true answer unsaid. She would totally do it again, if it made a difference. 'What if Ephraim comes back?' she asked. 'We're sitting ducks.' Plus they needed to get help for Erin, André, and Gideon, and somewhere warm for the rest of them. Their clothes were soaked, and everyone was shivering.

Rafe pointed to Gideon, who was talking on the satellite phone he'd taken back from Daisy. 'He's calling for help. Sat phones are the only way to get a signal out here. I should have made sure I had one, too. I won't make that mistake again. In the meantime, we'll defend ourselves if he returns. We've at least got cover now.'

Gideon joined them, still on the phone, the wound on his hand covered with gauze from the first-aid kit. He muted his end of the conversation and said, 'Molina is on her way from Sacramento. She's sending locals to pick us up and take us into town. Hunter will be here any minute to secure the scene.'

André led Farrah to the Subaru and lowered her into one of the backseats, the knife in his arm making the scene even more surreal. 'Stay here. I'll be right back,' he told her before coming to stand with the three of them. 'Gideon, tell your boss that the Tahoe is missing its back window and that both passenger windows are pebbled. Your dad must have had run-flat tires installed, because I shot the back right tire but it didn't slow him down.' He closed his eyes wearily. 'I'm out of ammo. If he comes back, we're toast.'

Gideon told Molina about the damage to the Tahoe that Ephraim

337

had stolen, then ended the call. 'The locals aren't too far out and they're sending a medic team. Until they get here, I've got more ammo for my service weapon and my backup.' He handed the backup to André, then scooped his own gun from the snow. 'The medics were told about the knife in your arm. They said the ER docs would remove it, that we shouldn't touch it.'

André turned his scowl on the knife. 'I've had worse. I can wait.'

'What happened, André?' Mercy asked.

André sat on one corner of the tailgate. His jaw was tight, perspiration beading on his forehead despite the cold temperature. 'We got here as the shooting started. Ephraim was running toward the main road and Farrah was driving so that I could be on watch, just in case, y'know? She pulled your dad's SUV sideways to block the road. She was afraid he'd killed you. She got out before I could stop her and . . .' He swallowed hard. 'Dammit. She and I will have words about this later.'

Mercy patted his uninjured arm. 'She's okay, André. He didn't hurt her.'

André's eyes flashed. 'He killed her aunt. He terrified her. He needs to be stopped.'

He needs to die, Mercy thought grimly. 'Did he come after her?'

André swallowed again. 'Yeah, so I tackled him. Fucker's stronger than he looks.'

'He raises the animals,' Mercy said. 'Daily manual labor.'

'Still.' André huffed. 'He got in a few good punches until I got my hands around his throat. I wish I'd squeezed harder.'

Mercy nodded, the tiny movement harder than it should have been. *I'm so damn tired.* 'Me too.'

Rafe turned Mercy toward the backseat of the Subaru. 'Sit with Farrah. She needs you. We're going to keep watch. If he comes back, you duck low. You do not sacrifice yourself again. Do you hear me?'

Mercy didn't even consider arguing. She was cold, her legs like rubber, and Farrah did need her. She gave Rafe a tired nod, then climbed into the seat next to her friend and put her arms around her. 'We're okay,' Mercy murmured.

Farrah shuddered out a breath. 'I heard Rafe. You shouldn't have sacrificed yourself for me like that. When Rafe pushed you out of the way, you should have stayed there.'

Sasha looked over her shoulder in irritation. 'She did it again? Dammit, Mercy, you make me want to smack you.'

Farrah's eyes widened. '*Again?* Fucking hell, Mercy.'

Mercy hesitated. 'It turned out all right. That's how Rafe shot him.'

Farrah shook her head in disbelief. 'You idiot.' She threw her arms around Mercy's neck for a rib-crushing hug before pulling back. 'Never again. Promise me, Mercy.'

Mercy gave a single nod, but it was a lie. *I'd do it again. In a heartbeat.*

Reno, Nevada
Monday, 17 April, 8.15 P.M.

Special Agent in Charge Molina settled into the hospital waiting-room chair. 'How are Miss Sokolov and Detective Rhee?'

Erin had been airlifted to the Reno hospital, and even though Sasha's injuries hadn't been urgent enough to require the helicopter ride out of Snowbush, she'd refused to allow Erin to be alone.

The rest of them had first headed to the smaller hospital in Alturas, about thirty minutes north of Snowbush. Both Gideon and André had received stitches. Luckily Mercy, Farrah, and Daisy were unhurt, physically at least. Farrah was still withdrawn, the attack piling on top of her grief over her aunt Quill. Mercy was worried about her, holding one of her friend's hands tightly while André held Farrah close with his good arm.

Mercy also worried about Rafe. He grimaced whenever he moved his leg. *He shouldn't have been doing all that running. Not any of that running,* she corrected herself. He was in pain and it was so hard not to feel guilty about that. Her mind knew it was all on Ephraim's head, but her heart kept reminding her that none of her friends would have been targeted had it not been for . . . *Me.*

But she kept the thought to herself. It wasn't true. She'd told herself so a hundred times as the six of them had been driven from

Alturas to Reno, traveling in two FBI vans as their personal vehicles had been taken into evidence. Gideon and Rafe had been extremely irritated by this, but it was necessary. Ephraim had tampered with their engines. They had to be certain that he hadn't done more than steal their spark plugs.

'Erin is out of surgery,' Rafe told Molina wearily. He looked like he'd aged twenty years in the past four hours. 'She should make a full recovery in time. Sasha only needed stitches – it was just a graze. She and my mother are with Erin now. They'll stay with her until she can be released, and they'll all go back to my parents' house.'

'That's good,' Molina said. She looked over at Gideon. 'And you? You're all right, too?'

Gideon was glaring at Mercy – really, he hadn't stopped glaring since the bullets had stopped flying – but now turned to his boss with a sigh. 'Physically, yes.' His hand had taken one of Ephraim's first shots, but there would be no lasting damage and for that, Mercy was grateful. His bruised ribs seemed to be giving him more pain at the moment. Thankfully the Kevlar had stopped the bullets, but the impact wasn't insignificant. 'I won't be boxing anytime soon, but I suppose that's a small price to pay.'

Daisy's lips twitched. 'You didn't box before, Gideon.'

He smiled down at her, a true smile. 'That's why it's a small price to pay.'

Molina shook her head, maybe even fondly, Mercy thought.

'Captain Holmes?' Molina leaned forward to look at André and Farrah, who sat at the end of the row. 'Dr Romero? You are also all right?'

'I'll be fine,' André said, his deep voice a soft rumble. 'Farrah is shaken up, but we'll both be okay.'

Farrah only nodded her agreement, her lips pressed firmly together. But she squeezed Mercy's hand encouragingly, which was exactly what Mercy needed at the moment.

'Glad to hear it.' Molina crossed her arms. 'Tell me what happened.'

They'd been put in a private waiting area at Molina's request, having informed the hospital that the shooter was still out there, his behavior unpredictable. A federal agent out of the Reno office had positioned himself outside the door to the waiting room as soon as they'd been shown in.

Mercy wondered if it was to keep Ephraim and the press out, or to keep the six of them in. Because now that the pleasantries were over, Molina looked pissed off.

Mercy cleared her throat. 'This is my responsibility. I wanted to check out a store where an Eden quilt had been purchased.'

Molina nodded. 'Agent Hunter told me that Gideon had mentioned the quilts. What happened then?'

'We drove to Snowbush and found the jewelry box in the general store.' It had also been taken into evidence, and Mercy had almost cried at the loss. 'It was made by my stepfather, in Eden. I recognized his handiwork.' She went on to explain what had happened in the store, that the young woman behind the counter had remembered DJ Belmont. 'We didn't know Ephraim was tracking us.'

'I found a tracker hidden behind Detective Rhee's hubcap,' Gideon said. 'I gave it to the agents who took over the crime scene. Burton had been following Erin.'

'When would he have had the opportunity to plant the tracker?' Molina asked.

'I've been thinking about that,' Rafe said. 'There was only a short window when her vehicle would have been completely unattended, and that was when we'd all first arrived at my house last night and Erin was clearing each room. That would have been around nine thirty, maybe nine forty-five. Gideon and Daisy had already left, and the rest of us were either in the garage or in the house. After that, she was either sitting in her own vehicle or her backup was on watch outside. She was still there when we left this morning.'

'Detective Schumacher was assigned to night watch,' Molina said. 'I handpicked her for the job. I know she's trustworthy. At least we've established the time frame. And none of you left the house until morning?'

'Sasha and Erin went for a run, but Mercy and I didn't leave.'

'And my friend Farrah and her fiancé were there for an hour or so after we left,' Mercy added.

Molina's brow went up. 'I know. Dr Romero called me after she'd read the email you left her saying where you'd gone.'

Mercy glanced at Farrah, who glared back at her. 'You scared me,' Farrah said, her vulnerable tone at odds with her glare. 'I don't apologize for snitching on you.'

Mercy squeezed her hand. 'I'm sorry I scared you.'

Farrah sniffed. 'Don't do it again. And thank you, Special Agent Molina, for acting so quickly to get us help.'

Molina acknowledged her thanks with a nod. 'As soon as you told me, I sent Agent Hunter after you.' Tom Hunter had arrived at the clearing as the local emergency personnel had been caring for Erin. He had been extremely unhappy with all of them.

Molina turned back to Gideon. 'That call you made to my office is going to save your bacon, Agent Reynolds. It's going to allow me to protect you from repercussions.'

Repercussions. Shit. 'Has your team found anything at the scene?' Mercy asked tentatively, because this clusterfuck really was her responsibility and had left her with very mixed feelings.

She was terribly sorry that Erin, Sasha, André, and Gideon had been hurt. She was sorry that Farrah had been terrorized. But she wasn't sorry that she'd gone to Snowbush herself, and she wasn't sorry she'd found the prior Eden compound.

And she still was definitely *not* sorry that she'd made herself a target to Ephraim Burton. That she'd caused her friends and family a moment of fear, yes. That she'd faced Ephraim, knocking him off guard long enough to be shot by Rafe? Not a single sorry for that.

'The scene is secured,' Molina said briskly. 'We've arranged for a team with ground-penetrating radar to scan the grounds around the graveyard at first light. If the Comstock family is buried there and you believe that they were likely killed because of Eileen's escape, we need to find their bodies.'

'And Burton?' Rafe asked.

'Still missing,' Molina said. 'We found a Cadillac parked off the county road, about a half mile from where you turned off.' She hesitated. 'It belonged to Sean MacGuire.'

Rafe's mouth fell open. 'He lives behind my parents.'

Not another death, Mercy thought. *Please*. 'Did Ephraim kill him?'

'No, but his prognosis isn't good. His daughter had already informed the local police that the car was stolen. She'd found her father bound to a chair in his home and gagged. He's a diabetic with a constant glucose monitoring system, which transmits his sugar levels to an app on his daughter's phone. When her phone informed her that his levels were dropping, she rushed over and found him. That was late this morning. The Cadillac had GPS, but it had been disabled.'

'And my dad's Tahoe?' Gideon asked.

'Found north of Alturas,' Molina said. 'He set the SUV on fire.'

'Of course he did,' Gideon muttered. 'Do we know what he's driving now?'

'An old truck he stole from a rancher. We're looking for it now.' Molina paused, studying their faces, her expression kind but firm. 'He's desperate. He's not going to give up.'

'I know,' Mercy said quietly.

'And you're not going to solve anything by offering up yourself as a sacrificial goat,' Molina added, still kindly.

Both Gideon and Rafe started to speak, but Molina held up her hand. 'I get why you did it, Miss Callahan. Please know that. But I must admit that I *don't* get why he's after you. This is the second time in a week that he's tried to abduct you. Or kill you. Why, after all these years, is he coming after you? He's gone to great lengths to find you. He went all the way to New Orleans to hunt you. It can't be ego, can it?'

'Sure it can,' Mercy said. 'But not only ego. There were always politics in Eden. I didn't understand what was going on when I was there, but I was only twelve.'

'And being abused,' Daisy murmured.

'That too,' Mercy agreed. 'All I know is that DJ Belmont started to kill me that night thirteen years ago, but was interrupted. And that when my mother told DJ that Ephraim would kill him for killing us, he just laughed and said that Ephraim couldn't.'

'I read that in Agent Hunter's report,' Molina said. 'What do you think that means?'

Mercy had been giving this a lot of thought as they'd driven from Snowbush to the Reno hospital. 'I think it means that DJ and Ephraim had some kind of feud between them. That they held damaging information over each other's heads. That makes sense, given that Ephraim was there hiding because of the bank robbery that he and his brother committed. Robbery and three murders,' she amended. 'Who knows if Pastor was also hiding? Or even Waylon, DJ's father? They were all the original Founding Elders. Maybe they were *all* hiding. And, after all these years, I imagine they know each other's business.'

Molina considered this. 'Do you think that Ephraim believed you dead all this time?'

'Yes, I do.' Mercy glanced at Gideon, relieved that he was no longer glaring at her. 'When Gideon escaped, DJ's father brought back a body and claimed it was Gideon's. The body was so damaged that I couldn't identify it, but my mother did. She knew it wasn't Gideon, though. I figure that they did something similar for me. They had to demonstrate the consequences of running away to keep up the fear. You leave, you die. It was that simple. I don't know if Ephraim knew that Gideon wasn't really dead, or that I wasn't either, but we do know that he actively searched for Eileen.'

'So you think Ephraim would have found you if he'd really looked?' Molina asked.

'I do. There was a police report about the shooting in Redding when I was left there, wasn't there?' Mercy asked. 'Hunter referred to it last night. There had to have been one when Gideon was found there, too. If Ephraim had really wanted to, he could have found us. I don't think he even tried, because he believed us dead.'

'So back to my question,' Molina said. 'Why does he want you *now*?'

Mercy shrugged. 'I don't know, and that's the truth. It could be that he saw the CNN report somehow, although I don't know how he could have. There's no TV in Eden. Although the timing makes sense considering he booked his ticket to New Orleans that night.'

Molina nodded thoughtfully. 'True. We've established that Ephraim was in Santa Rosa the night of the CNN report, at the house

344

from which Regina Jewel operated her prostitution ring. One of the underage girls who'd been forced to work for Regina said that she saw Ephraim that night. The girl had been scheduled to "service" him, but she was relieved because he canceled and left the building. She said that Regina was really annoyed, because she'd blocked out the girl's schedule for two days.'

Mercy closed her eyes, both relieved that the girls in that awful place were free and knowing that true freedom was going to require a lot of therapy. 'Are they safe now? The girls? Will they get counseling?'

'Yes,' Molina said gently. 'They're safe and will be receiving physical and mental health services. All right, I think that's enough for the moment. Where will you all be staying tonight?'

Mercy looked at the others. 'Can we go back to Sacramento? I need to feed my cats.'

André nodded, his arm tight around Farrah's shoulders. 'I second that. We all need some rest. I'd feel safer staying in a secure home than a hotel.'

'But let's stay together, okay?' Daisy said with a worried frown. 'Gideon, we can stay in Sasha's apartment, and Farrah and André can keep the top floor.'

Mercy nodded. That meant that she'd stay with Rafe in the tiny studio apartment again. And even if he *was* furious at her, just being with him sounded really, really good.

'Then I'll put someone outside to stand watch,' Molina said. 'Until we find Ephraim, none of you go anywhere without telling me or whoever is on watch, okay?'

Gideon rubbed at his temples. 'Okay.'

'I've assigned Agent Hunter to be your escort tonight. He'll drive you back to Sacramento.' Molina rose and patted Gideon on the shoulder. 'We'll find him, Gideon.'

He smiled, but it was forced. 'I know.'

Mercy wasn't so sure. Ephraim knew how to hide. He'd been doing so for thirty years. 'Agent Molina, will I be able to get the jewelry box back at some point?'

'Yes, Mercy. I'll make sure of it.'

Karen Rose

Sacramento, California
Monday, 17 April, 8.30 P.M.

'Jeffrey Bunker, if you don't stop that pacing, I'm going to glue your butt to a chair.'

Jeff turned to where his mother was cross-stitching while watching her favorite TV show. 'I'm sorry, Mom. I'm just . . . wired.'

She spared him a glance over her glasses. 'Sit down, honey, and we can talk about it. Either that, or get on my treadmill and run off some of that energy, because you are driving me crazy.'

He flopped onto the sofa beside her. 'I wish I knew what to do.'

'About what?' she asked.

He blinked at her. 'About what? About ruining Mercy Callahan's life, that's what.' It had been the only thing he could think about all day long.

'I suspect you didn't so much ruin her life as make it more complicated,' she said quietly. 'That man who's after her is ruining her life, if anyone is. Your article certainly didn't help her state of mind, but I'd say you're lower in the pecking order of villains.'

He swallowed hard, his eyes burning. He'd cried so much already. Like a kid. Like a stupid kid. *I am a stupid kid.* 'I don't want to be a villain,' he whispered. 'I want to do right.'

She bit off a thread and lifted her work to the light, examining it. 'Then do right.'

'How?'

'Jeff, you're a smart young man. Brilliant, even. A whole lot smarter than I ever was, for sure. But brains aren't everything. They aren't even half of what makes a person good.'

He blinked, then swiped at his wet face impatiently. 'What makes a person good?'

'Helping other people. Integrity. Kindness.' She turned to face him. 'Why did you want to write that article to begin with, son?'

'I wanted to explore the victims. Not the dead women. Lots of people are talking about them. I wanted to know how someone . . . I don't know. Recovered? Can a person recover from that kind of experience?'

346

'Good question. Why did you focus on Mercy Callahan?'

'Because of the three, she was the quietest. Almost like a ghost. Almost like she hadn't been abducted at all. The two other women have talked to the media. Heck, Daisy Dawson is the media. She's got a radio show and everything.'

'What does Daisy do with that radio show?'

He opened his mouth, then closed it. What did she do with it? 'She plays music in the morning. She's cheerful, I guess. But she also talks about charities and ways . . .' He closed his eyes. 'Ways that the community can help other people. You're way smarter than me, Mom.'

His mother chuckled quietly. 'Say that into my phone. I want to make it my ringtone.'

He laughed with her, feeling a little bit right for the first time in a long time. 'I listen to Daisy's program sometimes,' he said. 'She goes by Poppy, you know.'

'I know. I've been listening to her morning show for months. I recognized her yesterday when she was busy keeping that FBI agent boyfriend of hers from ripping your head off.'

He was surprised. 'You didn't say anything.'

'I didn't think it was the right time to ask for an autograph,' she said dryly. '*I* was busy keeping Detective Sokolov from ripping your head off.'

He sighed. 'I guess I deserved that.'

'Yep,' she said, popping the 'p'. 'You really did. But not all of it. You deserved for them to be furious with you. You *didn't* deserve to be knocked around. Even though I understood why that cop did it. But back to Daisy. She uses her platform for good, Jeffy. I've heard her talk about pet adoptions and raising money for homeless kids. She's brought on self-defense experts and a few weeks ago even brought on her sponsor from AA and they talked about addiction and staying sober. She uses her platform for *good*.'

'I don't have a platform. Not anymore. I mean, I quit the *Gabber*, but even if I hadn't, it's closed down.' His boss was probably even facing charges for knowingly posting a video of a sexual assault. Which was warranted, the sleazy bastard.

I am so glad I kept all my records. If he hadn't, he might have been arrested, too.

His mother chose a new color of embroidery floss and threaded her needle. 'Last I checked, that story you wrote had over a hundred thousand hits. People are even watching your YouTube channel.'

He thought his eyes might be bugging out. 'You know about my YouTube channel?'

She drew a rueful breath. 'I do now. Let's just say your aunt Patricia has explained it *all* to me.'

And likely embarrassed his mother in the process. 'I'm sorry, Mom.'

'I know you are. You got in over your head, Jeffy. But now you're on the shore and you have a chance to try swimming the river again. You know the pitfalls and the risks. You can make different choices. And, if you make good ones, you can at least help someone else, even if Mercy Callahan never forgives you.'

His gaze shot to hers. 'You knew that was what was really bothering me, didn't you?'

She gave him a knowing smile. 'Like I said, I'm not as smart as you, but I *have* raised you. I've seen you checking your messages and I know you've started to call the Sokolovs' house more than once.'

Jeff took her phone and started a voice memo. 'This is April seventeenth and Geri Bunker is way smarter than me.' He handed her phone back to her. 'For your ringtone.'

She swallowed hard, like she was trying not to cry. 'Make the call, Jeff. Talk to Mrs Sokolov. She seemed very nice. Ask her how Miss Callahan is doing. And ask her for ideas on how you can best use this platform of yours to do some good, before your fifteen minutes of fame are over and you go back to being a regular college kid who doesn't wash his socks.'

He started to get defensive about his having fifteen minutes of fame, but knew deep down she was right. He sighed dramatically. 'I bet Ronan Farrow never has days like this. You know who Ronan Farrow is, right?'

She tapped her phone and showed him her ebook app. 'I've read both his books. You told me last year that you wanted to do investigative journalism like he does, so I've familiarized myself with his work.' She pocketed her phone. 'If you ever meet him someday, you can ask him if he has days like this. And then you can get his autograph for me.'

She's been listening to me. Overcome, Jeff leaned over and pecked her cheek. 'Love you, Mom.'

Her eyes glistened. 'Love you too, son. Now make the call.'

He stared at his phone for a long moment, then shook his head. 'I'm scared to. What if she hates me? I don't want anyone to not like me, much less hate me.'

'I think a lot of people dislike Ronan Farrow,' she said lightly. 'They're probably the people whose crimes he's exposed.' She grew serious then, leveling him with the same stare she'd given when delivering the pre-punishment this-hurts-me-more-than-you speech when he was a kid. 'Not everyone is going to like you, son. And good people don't do good so that they'll win popularity contests. They do good because it's the right thing to do.'

He made a face. 'Do I get points for doing good even when I'm scared?'

She smiled. 'Don't know about points, but I will make you a pie.'

'Apple?'

'Yes. I even have ice cream to serve with it. Now call.'

Jeff dialed. And held his breath as the phone rang. At the last minute, he put it on speaker, so that his mother could hear, too. He'd lain awake all night, his mind concocting terrible images of Mercy hurting herself because of what he'd allowed to happen to her. People killed themselves over less than this, he'd thought, over and over until he'd been ready to tear his hair out.

Yes, he was dramatic, but if Mercy wasn't all right, he wasn't going to be in any shape to repeat the conversation to his mom.

'Hello?' It was a girl. She sounded young. 'Sokolov residence. How can I help you? And if you're a telemarketer, just give it up right now.'

He coughed on a surprised laugh. 'Um, hello. This is Jeff Bunker. May I speak with Mrs Sokolov?'

'She's not here right now. Can I take a message?'

349

'Oh. Okay. Yeah.' He organized his thoughts.

'Is that the message? "Oh. Okay. Yeah"?' the girl asked, her tone laced with humor.

It put him enough at ease that he could get real words out. 'I was calling to check on Miss Callahan. I know she won't want to speak with me, but I was up all night worrying and—' He cut himself off. 'I'm rambling.'

'It's okay,' the girl said gently. 'And Mercy is okay. She appreciated you getting that video taken down and she understood why you didn't call the cops about Miss Romero's body right away. The man you saw is scary. She knows that better than anyone.'

So there was history there. *I knew it!* He was about to ask, then caught his mother's challenging glare. 'Thank you,' he said instead. 'I'm glad she's okay. If you could tell your mother that I called and, if she can, to please call me back. My article has sent a lot of people to my own blog and my YouTube channel.'

'I know,' the girl said, unimpressed. 'One of them was me. You have some decent writing skills, Mr Bunker, but you're wasting your time on that gossip trash.'

Part of him preened. But most of him stayed focused. 'Thank you, and you're right that it was trash. That's why I wanted to talk to Mrs Sokolov. I read online that she and her husband do a lot of charity work. I was hoping they could give me some advice for how to use my fifteen minutes of fame to do something good.'

His mother gave him a proud smile.

'Oh,' the girl said softly. 'I'll tell her. It'll be a while before she calls you, so don't be worried. We had a family emergency and Mom had to go out of town, but I'll pass this on to her.'

He wanted to ask about the emergency, but his mother's lifted brows kept him on task. 'Thank you,' he said again. 'Maybe I should contact her by email if she's dealing with an emergency. She doesn't need to call me back. Does she have an email?'

'Uh, yes,' she said, like he'd asked if her mother had a pulse.

'I can give you my email so that you can forward it to her.'

'Oh, I can find your email. I've been on your blog and YouTube channel, remember?'

He smiled at that. 'Can I ask who I'm speaking to?'

'Zoya,' she said. 'I'm the youngest Sokolov. Listen, I saw you from my window yesterday and I thought you were pretty brave to face my brother and Gideon. They can be formidable when they're upset and they were very upset with you. But now they're not, so . . . good on you. Stay safe, okay? The man you saw is . . . well, he's really dangerous, but you knew that already.'

Something in her tone had the hairs lifting at the back of his neck. 'He's done something else?'

Zoya hesitated, then sighed. 'Yes. I can't tell you any more than to stay safe and keep your eyes open. He is not in custody. Yet.'

'Okay. Got it. Thanks again. You stay safe, too.' He ended the call and met his mother's eyes. 'Did I do good?'

His mother pulled him close to kiss his forehead. 'You did. Now I'm going to make us supper.'

'And pie!'

'And pie. Go gather your dirty socks.'

'Yes, ma'am.'

Jeff went to his room, fully intending to pick up his dirty socks, but his gaze fell on his computer and he suddenly knew what he needed to do. First he needed to write a retraction of all of the lies that had ended up in his article about Mercy Callahan. And then he'd do some real good.

Instead of focusing on the aftermath of her February abduction, he focused on the impact of the media bullying of victims of assault – of all kinds. He apologized to Mercy and all of the victims who'd been shamed publicly after already having endured an assault. He offered his platform to those victims, giving them a place to tell their stories.

If they wanted to read their own stories on his YouTube channel, he would upload them. If they wanted him to read what they'd written, he'd do that, too. He would keep their identities secret and he'd offer space for crisis counselors to publicize the services they offered.

It was the least he could do. He wanted to do this correctly, though. Rather than posting it right away, he pulled up the email

351

from Irina Sokolov, who'd contacted him less than an hour after he'd spoken with her daughter. She'd said she'd be more than happy to work with him on productive uses of his platform, and she'd copied in Daisy Dawson, who'd responded just as positively.

He hit REPLY ALL, attached the article, then typed his message.

Dear Mrs Sokolov and Miss Dawson,

Thank you for offering to help me not only make amends for the emotional damage to Miss Callahan I inflicted, but also for helping me grow as a person. I don't want to be the person who allowed that article to be written. Even though the video was uploaded without my knowledge, I accepted it from my source without consideration of the possible outcomes. As my mother says, I got in over my head. Thank you for helping me to start digging my way out.

I've attached a proposal for use of my existing platform. I won't have the spotlight for much longer, so I'd like to give it to those who can make the best use of it for as long as it lasts. If you would take a look and tell me what you think, I'd be grateful.

Best regards,

Jeffrey Bunker

He hit SEND and closed his laptop. It wasn't enough, not nearly enough. Pushing away from his desk, he stood to look in the mirror over his dresser. The face that looked back at him was tired. But determined.

'Jeffy?' his mother asked from the open doorway of his room. 'I was calling you to come to dinner, but I guess you didn't hear me. Are you okay?'

'Not yet.' He tossed her a lopsided smile. 'But I can look at myself in the mirror, so that's a start, right?'

She gave him a decisive nod. 'Right. I'm proud of you. Your father would have been too, God rest his soul.'

His shoulders sagged, like a weight rolled away. Not all of the weight, not by a long shot, but enough that he thought he could eat his mother's supper without it sitting on an anxious stomach. 'Thanks, Mom.'

Sacramento, California
Monday, 17 April, 11.30 P.M.

Rafe stopped his pacing to glare at Mercy. 'Mercy, are you even *listening* to me?'

She startled, because clearly she hadn't been. She was sitting on the sofa in Daisy's old place, her cat on her lap and a cup of tea in one hand. Her other cat had claimed the back of the sofa, lying behind her head, curled around her neck like a purring mink stole while she absently scratched its head. She'd been staring at Rafe's bulletin board, her gaze unfocused.

She blinked at him now, then smiled serenely. 'No.'

He wanted to rant at her, he really did, but he found himself laughing instead. He sat beside her, turning so that he faced her. 'At least you're honest about it.'

She sipped her tea and gave the cat in her lap a long stroke. André had brought the two cats and all their supplies downstairs to the studio apartment when they'd returned from Reno. Mercy had immediately cuddled up with Rory, and the cat's loud purrs indicated that he was on board with helping her manage her anxiety. It was working, because she seemed to be sitting in her own little bubble of calm.

'You already knew the answer, Rafe. I'm not sure why you even asked the question.' She raised a brow. 'I tuned you out an hour ago.'

He drew a breath, praying for patience. 'Dammit, Mercy. If you don't listen to me rant, how do I know you won't do it again?'

'I know, I know. I shouldn't have made myself a target. What was I thinking? Do I have no instinct for self-preservation? How would Gideon have survived if I'd been shot?' She smiled dryly. 'I heard you the first three hundred times, all the way from Reno. After that it seemed like . . . overkill.'

He snorted again. 'Stop making me laugh. I want to be mad at you.'

She stopped petting the cat to pat Rafe's knee. 'You go right ahead and be mad all you want.'

353

'Now you're patronizing me.'

She smiled. 'Yep.' Then she sighed. 'I'm sorry I scared you.'

'But not sorry that you popped up like some sacrificial Whac-A-Mole?'

He'd caught her midsip and she coughed, setting the cup aside while she got her breath. 'Sacrificial Whac-A-Mole?' she sputtered.

'Yes.' He glared at her. 'You made yourself a damn target.'

She sobered and he could see that under her nonchalance, she was deeply affected. 'Yes, I did. You did it for me. So did Gideon. And so did Erin.'

He knew what she meant. Back in February, they'd all put themselves on the line when she'd been abducted by a killer. '*We're* cops. *We* were doing our *jobs*.'

'No, you weren't. Well, Erin may have been. I think she was the only one who followed any kind of procedure. *You* took chances. And Gideon . . . he would have traded his life for mine. Do you really think that I could have watched you all be picked off by Ephraim while I did nothing? Do you think so little of me, Rafe?'

Rafe opened his mouth, then shut it again when he realized he had no comeback to that.

She reclaimed her cup of tea, never breaking their eye contact, knowing that she'd made her point.

He rubbed his hands over his face, leaving them there. Hiding behind them like a little kid. Vulnerability was not fun. 'You scared me,' he murmured. 'I thought I'd lose you.'

She tugged one of his hands from his face, threading their fingers together. 'I get it. But, Rafe, I stood up to him today. Well, I didn't stand. I knelt. But I looked him in the eye and I didn't back down. Don't take that away from me. Please.'

His heart immediately softened. 'All right. I won't. At least I'll try not to.'

Her smile lit her eyes. 'I didn't zombie out.'

He chuckled, both at her words and her delight in them. 'I noticed that. What made the difference?'

'I've been thinking about that. In the airport, I wasn't expecting him. Ephraim, you know.'

'I know.' Rafe had to tamp down his fury at the man who'd tried to take Mercy yet again. If he could have, he'd have broken Burton in two. 'But you were expecting him today?'

'Yeah, kind of. I mean, you said yourself that I was looking around like I expected him to jump out from behind a tree.'

'And then he did,' Rafe said ruefully.

She shrugged. 'It's creepy, knowing he was following us. It's creepy, knowing the store owner in Snowbush was on the phone as soon as we left. All of it's creepy, but I'm so tired of being afraid. Today I wasn't.' She made a face. 'Okay, I was totally scared, but I held it together.' She hesitated, then showed him the scratches on the inside of her left wrist. 'Sometimes a little jolt of pain is enough to derail the panic attack.'

He turned her hand, examining the deep gouges with horror. 'You did this to yourself?'

'Yes. I don't mutilate myself, Rafe. I've never done that. But I realized a while back that I could distract myself with a little . . . something. For a while I wore a snap bracelet. One of those things that smokers or cussers use when they're trying to quit. Farrah gave it to me when I was trying to quit smoking a few years ago and one day some guy on campus got in my space. He'd been asking me out for weeks and I kept politely refusing. Then one day he got tired of asking, I guess. I was so scared and I think I'd already zoned out.'

Rafe's jaw hurt, he was clenching it so hard. 'And then?'

'Then he saw the bracelet and I think he thought it was funny to snap it. It . . . snapped me out of the zombie zone and I kneed him in the nuts.'

Rafe barked out a surprised laugh. 'Good for you.'

She smiled at him. 'I don't know how to shoot like you guys, but I'm not entirely helpless. I wield a mean can of pepper spray. And I have a Taser, but I left it back in New Orleans.'

That she should have to arm herself made him angry as well, but that was more a fact of life than due to Burton. 'I'm glad you found a way to derail the panic attacks, but I hate that it hurts you.'

'To me, it's a fair trade. I think I need that moment to think. And you gave that to me today.'

He felt his cheeks heat, but not with embarrassment. It was pleasure and maybe a little pride. 'I did?'

'You did. I could feel myself falling into it, like a dark nothing, but you were there and you were warm and you were talking to me and telling me that it would be okay. That you wouldn't leave me. It gave me that little window of clear thought I needed to pull myself out of the free fall. So thank you.'

He lifted her wrist to his lips and brushed a kiss over the healing scratches. 'You're welcome. So what do we do next?'

She grinned again, her dimple appearing. 'With the case?'

He rolled his eyes. 'Yes, with the case.' But it was all he could do to keep his gaze from darting to the bed behind the painted screen.

'Boo,' she said, then squared her shoulders, almost as if she were bracing herself – but for what he wasn't sure. Until she said, 'I want to go to Santa Rosa, to the nursing home where his mother is.'

For a moment Rafe could only stare. 'You want to do what?'

She didn't repeat herself, merely sipped at her tea, her gaze still locked on his face.

He sighed. She fully expected him to argue with her, he could see it in her expression. 'Why?'

'You could call it closure. I'd like to meet the woman who spawned Ephraim Burton, even if she called him Harry Franklin. Plus, I'd like to know if she's seen him recently and knows where he's hiding.'

'Don't you think the FBI has tried to get that out of her?'

'Maybe. But they clearly weren't successful or they would have found him.'

'Unless she doesn't know.'

'She might not. I'd still like to talk to her. I am, after all, her daughter-in-law.'

He couldn't hold back his rage this time. 'No, you're not,' he snarled. 'You were never married to that monster. Not in the eye of the state of California or God or anyone with a shred of decency. There was no marriage license, for one. No license, no marriage. And he was already a bigamist. *No marriage.*'

356

'I know,' she said calmly, and he could feel his anger draining away. 'But I'll bet you that she doesn't.'

Rafe needed a minute to process this. 'What are you suggesting?'

'I have a wedding photo of her son and me. I'm very *worried* about his well-being. I haven't seen him in too long and I'm *worried* because I don't know where he'd go.' She batted her eyelashes. 'I'm very *worried*, Rafe.'

He shook his head, not sure where to even start. 'I tried to talk to her and she told me to go to hell. It'll never work. She won't talk to you.'

'Then I've only wasted a day in my life. I can assure you that I've wasted far more worrying for real about Ephraim Burton.' She dropped the facade and let him see that worry. 'He *shot* Gideon. Luckily he was wearing that Kevlar vest. Ephraim shot Erin. He shot Sasha. He stabbed André and held Farrah at gunpoint. He would have killed all of you. I can't live with that. If you don't want to go with me, I can accept that. But I *will* go. And I'll tell Agent Hunter that. Agent Molina, too. Short of arresting me or putting me in protective custody, they can't stop me from entering a nursing home to visit my own mother-in-law.'

She was terrifyingly serious. 'I can't talk you out of this, can I?' he asked wearily.

'No.'

'Then I'll go with you. Let me make a few phone calls.'

She nodded once. 'Thank you. And then maybe we can go to sleep. I'm really tired.'

He could see it now, the bone-deep fatigue she'd masked as serenity. 'Sleep sounds wonderful.'

Eden, California
Monday, 17 April, 11.55 P.M.

'Papa, I'm cold.'

Amos tightened his arms around Abigail, wishing he'd brought another blanket. The days on the mountain were cold enough, even though it was spring, but the nights . . .

Karen Rose

Temperatures had dropped below freezing and his little girl was shivering violently despite the three blankets he'd already wrapped around her. He wished he could start a fire, but that was an impossibility. All he could do was hope his body heat would be enough.

'I know, baby. It shouldn't be too much longer now. But you need to be very, very quiet, okay?'

She nodded wordlessly, her eyes huge in her small face. But she said no more, obedient and still. Maybe for the first time in her life. He'd told her that they were going away on an adventure and that she'd have to be very, very quiet. Like a mouse. He'd told her that it would be dangerous, but that he'd make sure she was safe. But that she was to obey him without question.

She'd nodded, her eyes suddenly way too old for a girl of seven. 'Are we coming back, Papa?' she'd asked.

He'd told her that he didn't know. Which was true enough. He prayed the answer was no, but . . .

She'd nodded again and asked if she could bring her stuffed bear. He'd made sure that she'd watched him pack it in his bag, along with a loaf of bread, some cheese, a jar of jam, and a canteen of water. He'd also packed the wallet he'd brought with him to Eden, which held his ID, long expired, and an envelope with two hundred dollars in twenty-dollar bills. He'd given Pastor all of his personal savings and his inheritance, but the money in the envelope had come from his grandfather, who'd told him to keep it 'just in case'. Mad money, the old man had called it.

Amos suddenly missed his grandfather so much it stole his breath. The man had been in his eighties back in 1989, and dying of cancer. He'd wanted to join Pastor in Eden, but he'd been way too sick to make the journey. Amos had stayed with him until the end, and then, after burying him, sold the house his grandfather had left him, signed the proceeds over to Eden, and made the journey all alone.

I was a fool. Such a fool. But he was fixing that. Changing it, he hoped.

Through all his packing, Abigail had watched, those eyes of hers

358

missing nothing. He'd nearly finished when she'd run from their little living area to his bedroom, returning with the Polaroid photos that he'd only shown her once.

He wasn't even aware that she'd remembered them. 'Papa,' she'd said. 'You can't forget Mercy and Gideon.' She'd put the Polaroids in his hands and he'd nearly broken down and cried. They were treasures and he wouldn't have left them behind. He'd put them out on his small dresser along with his grandfather's pocket watch, intending to carry them in his shirt pocket, close to his heart.

One of Eden's early residents had brought a Polaroid camera with them and had taken photos of Gideon, Mercy, and Rhoda in exchange for a custom wardrobe. Amos considered it one of his most satisfying transactions. Eventually the member's camera had run out of batteries and film and had been left behind after one of their moves. The Polaroids of his first family were faded, but he could still see Mercy's sweet toddler face, Gideon's always-serious expression, and Rhoda's incandescent smile.

These were among his most valued possessions. He never would have left them behind. But that Abigail had remembered them . . . *I'm so blessed. Please, God, help me get my baby girl out.*

This had to work. If they were caught, Ephraim would kill him like he'd killed the Comstocks, of that he was sure. And Abigail would be given to another family. He couldn't bear the thought of it.

But if DJ didn't pass by soon in his truck, he'd have to carry Abigail back through the gate to their house and hope no one saw them in the shadows. Amos had, hopefully, bought them a little time by going by the clinic earlier and coughing convincingly enough that Sister Coleen gave him some of the herbal tea she blended specially for coughs and colds. He'd gotten some of the tea for Abigail too, claiming that she also was coughing pitifully. Which Abigail wasn't, of course, but it was unlikely the healer would mention it to anyone who'd know differently till tomorrow.

By then they'd be on their way to freedom or they'd be back home and Abigail really would have a cough, because he'd kept her out in the cold all night.

Sister Coleen had told him to get some rest and to take the next day off. That if she saw him going into his workshop, she'd drag him back into his house herself.

Exactly what he'd wanted to hear. Nobody would think twice now if he didn't show up for work. Nobody would come to check on them for hours and hours, giving them time to get far, far away.

He knew that he couldn't make it to civilization on foot. Not with Abigail. He didn't know the way and had no idea how long he'd need to walk. Even if he carried her on his back, it was unlikely that they'd reach a town before they were discovered missing.

If that happened, it would all be over.

He needed to wait for DJ's truck to come by, and then they'd begin their journey in earnest.

He breathed out in relief when he heard the *chug-chug* of the old Ford. DJ had appropriated Waylon's truck when he'd passed on – his truck, his job, his place on the Founding Elders board, and everything else.

Amos wasn't sure if it was even the original truck or if DJ purposely bought identical replacements to maintain the illusion of continuity. Of comfort and constancy. But it didn't really matter which incarnation of Waylon's vehicle this truck was. It was, simply, his and Abigail's only way out.

Amos clutched Abigail closer to him and whispered in her ear. 'Quiet, now. Please.' She nodded against his chest and he sent up a prayer that his plan would come to fruition.

Sure enough, DJ's truck slowed to a stop. Leaving the engine running, DJ jumped out and kicked at the tree that blocked the road. The tree Amos had cut down, creating the obstacle.

Don't check it too closely, he prayed. Otherwise DJ would see that the tree had been chopped and the jig would be up. But DJ didn't look at the chopped end, too busy dragging it from the road by its limbs.

Now. Now. Now. Sweeping Abigail into his arms, he quickly lifted her over the tailgate. Then Amos swung himself over, taking care to land lightly, hoping DJ's grunts and curses covered the small sounds he had made.

DJ continued to wrestle with the downed tree and Amos used

the time to take one of the blankets he'd wrapped around Abigail to cover them both, head to toe. He'd chosen the darkest blanket they owned and DJ's truck was black. *Please let us blend in. Please, God, hear me. Help me save* this *daughter.*

DJ stopped cursing and Amos held his breath. This was the moment he'd feared the most. *Don't let him come back here for anything. Don't let him check.*

It wasn't until the truck started moving that Amos began breathing again. Abigail snuggled closer, her little hand patting his chest, right over his pounding heart. She remained silent, though, just as he'd asked.

He had no idea where they'd end up. He had no idea what he'd do when he got there. He had no idea how much two hundred dollars would buy, thirty years later.

He only knew he had to get his Abigail somewhere safe. Somewhere warm. And then he'd find Mercy and beg her forgiveness. Hopefully she remembered him kindly.

Twenty-one

Amos had no idea how long they'd been driving. He'd been doing his level best to keep Abigail warm. And to avoid puking, because the road they'd taken was bumpy and full of curves.

It wasn't the first time he'd been in the back of a moving vehicle since joining Eden. Every time they'd moved the community, they'd packed this truck with the heaviest equipment, then hitched a trailer to the back. Not a nice trailer. A bare, utilitarian trailer that had held as many people as they could fit. Waylon, and later DJ, had managed to borrow or rent trucks and trailers for every move. Only Founding Elders and the oldest of their members were allowed to drive or ride in cars. The others, which usually included Amos, had sat on the trailer floor. Some were sad to leave the place they'd called home while others were excited to see where they'd end up.

At one point, at their peak membership, they'd needed seven trucks and trailers to make the move. That time Amos had been tapped to drive. He hadn't seen much, though. Trees and more trees and a winding little road that disappeared into the darkness.

Because they always moved at night. Fear was the common emotion each time, because they'd been told that they were moving because the FBI was looking for them. Just as they'd looked for Koresh and the Branch Davidians.

Many of their members had joined after the horror in Waco, Texas, bringing tales of government atrocities. Some had brought

362

newspaper clippings and grainy photos. The images had been horrific.

Amos wondered now if those had been fake, too. Whether real or fake, they'd served their purpose, increasing the compound's fear of government control, of the loss of their rights to religious freedom.

Now, he realized, they'd simply given up their rights without a fight.

No more.

He held Abigail a little tighter, relieved that she'd made the trip as well as she had. She'd shown no fear and had, in fact, comforted him for much of the journey until her little pats to his chest had slowed and she'd fallen asleep. She was warm, her breathing even, and for a few minutes, he let himself doze.

Until he felt the truck slow. He stiffened, listening, but hearing nothing except the rumble of the engine. He swallowed hard, hoping the pounding of his heart didn't wake Abigail. Fortunately, she was a very heavy sleeper. He focused on the direction they took, for no other reason than to keep himself calm. Or at least not actively hyperventilating, because Amos didn't think he'd ever be calm again.

And then the truck stopped and all was quiet. No birds, because it was still night. And it was darker here, the moon no longer visible. That much he could see through the thin spots in the blanket that still covered them. Whether it was cloudy or they were under a thick canopy of leaves, he couldn't tell.

The truck shimmied slightly as the driver's door opened but didn't slam closed.

Amos's heart beat so hard that it hurt. *God, please don't let him look back here. Don't let him see us.*

But he heard no voices, just the light crackle of leaves as footsteps faded away. Amos held his breath, risking a peek from underneath the blanket. Nothing above. No DJ staring down at him.

And then he heard the tinkle of crashing glass. Not from the truck. It was farther away.

Should I get up? Should I grab Abigail and make our escape? Or is this a trap and DJ is waiting for us? Is he armed? That last question was most likely a yes. The truck had a gun rack in the cab and Amos had always seen DJ stow a rifle there before he'd left on his weekly supply runs.

But DJ wasn't in the truck at the moment. If Amos could get that rifle . . .

But . . . but . . . Indecision and fear left him frozen in place, huddling under the blanket with his little girl.

And then he heard a door open and close – like the door to a house, not a car – followed by a quiet curse. DJ. He was coming back.

No, no, no. I should have run when I had the chance.

But the truck door didn't open. Instead, another engine started up, a smaller sound. Not a truck. A car?

The car drove away, in the opposite direction from which they'd come, from the sound of it. The engine grew quieter until Amos could hear nothing at all.

Now. Go now.

Carefully he pulled free of Abigail's hold, settling her small body on the truck bed, making sure she was covered up, then crawled to the tailgate and rolled over it, keeping his body as close to the truck as possible.

He looked around wildly, but saw nothing but a small house, all dark inside.

DJ was gone.

Amos didn't question further. Still crouching, he rushed to the driver's-side door, slightly ajar, his knees buckling with relief when he saw the key still in the ignition. Two seconds later, he was behind the wheel and turning the key. The engine roared to life and he did a quick U-turn.

When they'd arrived they'd turned left, then right and right again once the truck had slowed, so Amos turned left, and left again.

And shuddered out a sob, because there, like a shining beacon, was a highway. He didn't know which way to go, but DJ had turned left, so Amos went right. And then he floored it, flying down the road in the dead of night until he came to a town.

Snowbush, Population 162, the sign said. The town was dark. Not a single light burning anywhere.

No sheriff's department, either. He saw a diner, a general store, a hardware store, a gas station, and a post office. Pulling in behind the hardware store, he rushed to the back and retrieved his most precious bundle. Gently settling his still-sleeping Abigail on the bench seat, he grabbed his backpack from the truck bed and placed it on the floorboard, next to his feet. A glance behind him proved that there was indeed a rifle, which Amos would not hesitate to use if DJ chased them in the car he'd taken.

Why DJ had taken that car made absolutely no sense, but Amos couldn't think about that now. His brain was racing, one thought pounding: *Go. Go. Go.*

So he got behind the wheel, cranked up the heater, and then pulled out onto the highway heading south.

Away from where they'd come.

Away from Eden.

Toward . . . ?

He had no idea. But anything had to be better than what he'd left behind.

Sacramento, California
Tuesday, 18 April, 5.50 A.M.

Blearily, Jeff lifted his head from his pillow. His phone was ringing. How could his phone be ringing? *Goddamn telemarketers.* He groped for it, intending to jab it into silence.

His finger veered away at the last moment as he blinked at the screen. It was a local number. Knowing he'd regret it, he answered. 'Hello?'

'Jeff. This is Daisy Dawson.'

'You're perky,' he mumbled, and she laughed, waking him up a bit more.

'It's my job to be perky at six a.m. Morning radio, remember?'

His mind clicked and he sat bolt upright. 'Is something wrong?'

'No, no. Relax. I read your email.'

'Oh, right.' It was coming back to him now. 'I haven't posted it. I wouldn't, not until I got the okay.'

'I can't give you that, not as it's written anyway.'

His heart sank, but then she continued. 'Mercy would need to approve it. I forwarded it to her, but I doubt she's seen it yet. However, I would like you to present your proposal to the coordinator of one of the local rape crisis centers, with no mention of Mercy. I think giving a platform to victims could be a positive thing. The coordinator was already scheduled to do an interview on my show this morning, so she'll be in the studio. I know you were told to keep a low profile, but I've informed Agent Molina and she's on board. Agent Reynolds can pick you up. Your mother, too. He'll keep you safe.'

'Wow.' He was fully awake now, his adrenaline pumping. It was better than Mountain Dew. 'Yes. I'll do it. I need to wake my mother up. What time do you want us to be ready?'

'The crisis center coordinator will be here from nine to ten, but I have to be on the air in a minute and a half, so I'm calling now. How about you be ready at eight thirty?'

'Yes. Yes, please.' He pressed the heel of his hand to his pounding heart. 'Thank you.'

'I can't promise it'll go anywhere, but she's a great resource if you really want to do some good. Gotta go. See you soon,' she said and ended the call.

Had that really happened? He hadn't been dreaming, had he? He pinched his arm, hard. 'Ow.' Yeah, he was awake. Then he checked his call log and, yes, the call had happened.

'Jeffy?' his mother called through his door. 'Are you okay? I heard you talking.'

He jumped from the bed and flung open his door, full of energy, but the good kind. 'Did I wake you up?'

She wore her housecoat and a worried frown. 'No. I haven't been able to sleep. What's going on here?'

His excitement plummeted. God, she looked exhausted. 'Why couldn't you sleep?'

'Just worried about that man still out there.' She held out her phone. 'I found out what the Sokolovs' family emergency was. There was a shooting up near the Oregon–Nevada border. Detective Rhee was hospitalized. Sasha Sokolov was also hurt, as were Agent

366

Reynolds and Captain Holmes, the police officer from New Orleans. It doesn't say that the shooter was the same guy that you saw there, but who else would it be?'

Jeff stepped backward, dropping onto his bed. 'Wow. That's awful. Poor Mrs Sokolov. She didn't mention it in her email and Daisy didn't mention it when she called just now.'

His mother frowned, confused. 'Daisy called?'

'Yes.' He relayed the call. 'She says Agent Reynolds can keep us safe.'

His mother sighed. 'I don't want to leave the house, but I suppose if that man really wanted to find you, he could. We're safer with Agent Reynolds. You want to meet with this coordinator?'

Jeff met her tired eyes. 'I do. She may say that my idea is dumb, but then again, she might not. I need to do this, Mom.'

She nodded once. 'Then you will. We have two and a half hours. That's enough time for a good breakfast and for you to iron your white shirt.'

He opened his mouth to protest because it was *radio*, for heaven's sake, but she raised her eyebrows. 'Okay, Mom. One ironed shirt, coming up.'

'Pancakes and sausage, coming up.' She clapped her hands. 'Get moving. Your shirt won't iron itself.'

Sacramento, California
Tuesday, 18 April, 6.15 A.M.

Mercy watched the sky outside the studio apartment window grow rosy. It was morning, finally. Which was a relief and . . . not. She'd lain awake for hours, feeling safe and . . . not.

Today she'd see Ephraim's mother. If things went well, they might find out where he was hiding. The worst that could happen was that she wouldn't help at all. But one thing was for certain. Mercy would come face-to-face with the woman who'd raised the man who'd tortured her for an entire year. The man she'd locked eyes with the day before. The man who was hunting her.

So while she was relieved that the day would finally begin, she was terrified. Because the worst that could happen wasn't that she'd simply meet Ephraim's mother and walk away. The worst that could happen was that Ephraim found her, because if he did he'd kill everyone around her.

And that included the man who'd slept with his arms around her all night long. He hadn't demanded anything. His hold had been frustratingly platonic. Because he knew she wasn't ready.

Rafe Sokolov was a good man. She'd known they existed. She still believed it. Her experience in Eden hadn't soured her to the possibility of good in people.

But even though Rafe Sokolov made her feel so damn safe, he scared her, too. Or, at least, what he made her feel scared her. She'd lain there for hours, afraid to move, when all she really wanted was to turn in his arms and let him show her what she'd been missing her whole life.

It wasn't just sex, although that was a huge part of it. What she really wanted was intimacy. Vulnerability.

Trust.

She trusted Rafe and that was perhaps the most terrifying thing of all. Not because she was afraid he'd betray her. He wasn't built that way. She'd known it even as she'd sat at his bedside while he recuperated from surgery. *He's a good man.*

But if she let him in, then lost him? She wasn't sure she could handle that.

'You are thinking so hard that you woke me up,' he mumbled behind her, kissing her shoulder, covered in her TARDIS pj's. They'd been a Christmas gift from Rory and Jack-Jack, but the *Doctor Who*-themed gift tag had been written in Farrah's pretty handwriting. *Because they can't write*, she'd said laughingly.

I'm so lucky. I have friends who love me. So even if this thing with Rafe crashed and burned, she wouldn't be alone. But it wouldn't be the same.

'Sorry,' she whispered. 'Didn't mean to wake you.'

Rafe lifted up on his elbow to kiss her temple. 'You're shaking, Mercy. What's wrong?'

'I don't know.'

'We don't have to go to Santa Rosa. Nobody will be angry if you change your mind about seeing Burton's mother.'

She swallowed hard. 'I guess I am transparent.'

'Maybe a little. But maybe there's more to it?' He tightened his arms around her, skirting the line between pain and comfort, but somehow managing to stay on the comfort side while giving her the little jab she needed to break the panic cycle.

She hadn't even been aware it was happening. Of course it had been, though. She'd been panicking throughout all the hours she'd lain awake. She relaxed then. A little. 'I guess I'm not used to . . . this,' she finished, suddenly awkward.

He immediately loosened his hold, but she covered his arms with hers and pulled them back. 'Don't go. I mean . . .' He was quiet behind her, giving her the time and space she needed to put words to her thoughts. 'I like it, you holding me like this. I'm not used to it, though.'

'And that scares you.'

There was no judgment in his tone. No hurt or annoyance or condescension. 'Yes.'

Another kiss to her shoulder. 'I know why it scares me, but why does it scare you?'

She half turned at that, surprised. 'It scares you?'

His brown eyes were so serious. 'Yes, of course it does. I felt something for you the moment I met you, Mercy. Something I hadn't felt for anyone in years. Not since Bella.'

The woman he'd loved and lost. *Loved.* The word mocked her, but the voice of her therapist intruded. *You are lovable. You deserve love.*

The woman had made Mercy repeat it dozens and dozens of times, which hadn't made her believe it then. But the mantra did resonate in her mind now, and maybe that was the point. To create a kind of muscle memory. Whatever its purpose, it worked now, creating that little bubble of space that gave her a moment to think before habit kicked in to deny the possibility.

He'd loved Bella. *He feels something for me.*

And he's scared, too.

369

'You lost her,' Mercy said quietly.

'I did. And I didn't think I'd survive it. But I did. I just don't want to have to survive again and right now this thing between us, whatever it is or will be, is uncertain. If I fall for you and lose you . . .'

I thought I'd lose you, he'd choked out the night before, when he'd let her glimpse his vulnerability.

I get it now. 'I won't make myself a target again,' she said quietly, willing to make the promise.

He shuddered against her, pressing his forehead to her shoulder. 'Thank you,' he whispered. 'But . . .'

She waited. And waited, but he said nothing more, just pressed tight against her back, his breathing ragged. *But what?*

Concerned, she looked over her shoulder, the movement making him lift his head to meet her gaze. She didn't mean to gasp, but the sound emerged before she knew to shove it back down. He looked . . . wrecked. Simply devastated. This, she knew immediately, was vulnerability.

This was trust. His trust. *In me.*

'But what?' she asked softly.

'But . . .' His jaw tightened, making the muscle in his cheek twitch. 'It's not just that I'm afraid to lose you. Because . . .' He closed his eyes and she wanted to force him to open them so she could see his emotion. But she didn't. She waited, allowing him to gather his composure. 'Because you're not staying.'

She opened her mouth. Closed it again, because she didn't know what to say. He was right.

He cleared his throat and barreled forward. 'As it stands right now, you're not staying. You'll go back to your life in New Orleans and I'll stay here.'

Oh. Her heart hurt, but she forced herself to say the words. 'We don't have to take this any further, Rafe. I don't want to hurt you.' *But I probably will. Dammit.*

His chuckle was mostly a huff of air. 'I don't want to be hurt, either. Been there, done that, and it sucks. But I'd rather have whatever time with you than nothing, which might make me a masochist, but . . .'

She shifted to her back, meeting his gaze directly. 'Me too.'

One corner of his mouth quirked up, making him devastatingly handsome in the morning light. Blond hair mussed, golden scruff on his strong jaw. And miles of muscles under the T-shirt he'd worn to bed. 'Which thing?'

'Huh?' she asked stupidly.

The other corner of his mouth kicked up, and he slowly grinned. 'Which thing are you agreeing with? You said, "Me too".'

'Oh. Right.' She shook her head, making him grin wider, a smug grin that looked good on him. 'Now I forgot.'

He laughed. 'You're good for my ego, Mercy Callahan.'

She stroked his jaw, loving the feel of stubble under her fingertips. It was just enough to feel good, not so thick and coarse that it hurt.

Not like *his. And I am not going to think of him. Not here. Not in Rafe's bed, which is safe and good. And right.*

'You're good for mine too, Raphael Sokolov.' She swallowed hard. 'I want things with you.'

His grin disappeared, his eyes growing dark and aroused. 'What kind of things?' he asked, his voice gruff and raspy.

'The things that scare me. Not because you scare me,' she added when he stiffened. 'I don't want to disappoint you.' She pressed a finger to his lips when he started to speak. 'Let me finish.' He kissed her finger and settled back on the pillow, waiting. 'I don't want to disappoint me, either. I've had a few relationships. They haven't been amazing. One or two weren't terrible, but it was mostly . . . platonic, you know?'

He nodded once, but still said nothing, which pleased her.

'I've been with men, not many. Two. Well, two and a half.'

He barked out a laugh. 'Do I want to know about the half?'

She laughed along with him, realizing that she'd never laughed in bed with any of the men she'd dated before. '*He* wasn't half. What we did was . . . half.' She pressed her palms to her flushed cheeks. 'Dammit. Now I'm blushing.'

'And you're so pretty that way,' he murmured, his voice dropping an octave. Or six.

She shivered and gave him a fast, awkward smile. 'My point

371

was . . . God, what was my point? Oh yeah.' She shoved him lightly when he snickered. 'Stop it. My point was that I'm not *in*experienced, but it's never been . . . glorious.'

His eyes widened briefly before returning to that sleepy, sexy look. 'Glorious. I like that word. It's a very good description of how it's supposed to be.'

'I'm glad you approve,' she said primly, then laughed again when he snorted. 'What I'm trying to say is that you're special. And if we—' She shook her head again. '*When* we do intimate things, I want them to be glorious. And I'm afraid they won't be and we'll both be disappointed.'

He was quiet for a long moment. Truly quiet, as if he was giving this real thought, not just waiting for her to finish so that he could talk.

She liked that, too.

'What do you want, Mercy?' he finally asked, completely serious. 'Do you want to wait? If so, I can do that. Do you want to dip your toe in?' He lifted one blond brow. 'Or cannonball?'

She covered her eyes with her hands. 'Oh my God. Really, Rafe?'

He nuzzled her neck, kissing up her jaw to behind her ear. 'Really, Mercy. We can do nothing or everything or something in between. Whatever it is, I am pretty sure it'll be glorious.'

He was teasing her, but only a little. And only to put her at ease. Which worked surprisingly well. 'I want to be brave. You know. Sexually.'

His voice lost its teasing, but his mouth stayed on the skin behind her ear. 'You don't have to be.'

She dropped her hands from her eyes, meeting his. 'But I *want* to be. I want to be brave with you.' She winced. 'But maybe not cannonball. Not just yet.'

His lips twitched and his hand moved over her shoulder to the top button of her pj's. He toyed with it, making her shiver again. 'But maybe dipping your toe in? The water's warm.'

She laughed again. 'God, we're like middle schoolers, aren't we?' Then she closed her eyes on a gasp when he let go of her button and covered her breast with his palm, only the thin layer of her pj's keeping them from being skin on skin.

'I'm much better at this than I was in middle school. I promise. Can I show you?'

'Yes,' she whispered. 'Please.'

He slipped the first button free, kissing the skin he'd bared. His lips were soft and warm and made her body edgy and tight as she waited for him to go on.

'You say "stop" or "no" or anything like that and I'll stop,' he said, back to serious. 'I promise.'

'I trust you.'

He shuddered, dropping his forehead to her collarbone. He was quiet, motionless for so long that she stroked a tentative hand through his hair. 'What's wrong?'

'Nothing. It's all right. All good. I was scared that you were afraid of me. I'm still afraid that if I move too fast, I'll scare you away.'

She shifted to kiss his hair. 'I'd come back.'

He looked up abruptly. 'But I would have scared you to start with. I never want you to be afraid of me.'

She traced the line of his eyebrows, the slightly crooked ridge of his nose, his lips. 'I'm not. I never have been. There's something about you that makes me feel safer than I've ever felt. But, Rafe?'

'Yes?'

'Can we go back to dipping our toes in? Because that felt really nice.'

His smile was beautiful. Glorious, even. 'Absolutely.' He returned his focus to her buttons, freeing them one by one until her top lay loosely open, but still covering everything important. He drew a breath and held it before brushing her top aside, then went still. 'You are more beautiful than I imagined.' He glanced up. 'And I imagined, Mercy. A lot.'

She could barely breathe. 'I imagined, too. Don't make me imagine anymore.'

He kissed her mouth softly. 'All right. Remember, if you want—'

She glared up at him. 'Yep. Heard you the first time. I think I got it, Rafe.'

He chuckled then and slid down to kiss the hollow of her throat, the valley between her breasts.

She sucked in a breath, holding it. Waiting. And then his lips brushed her nipple and her lungs emptied on a quiet moan.

'Good?' he murmured, giving her a tiny lick.

'Yes. Oh God. Don't stop. Please, don't stop.'

She could feel him smile against her nipple. 'Yes, ma'am.' Then he took her into his mouth and she arched, closing her eyes and letting go. Letting herself feel. Hearing herself whimper as he lightly rubbed her other nipple as he sucked and licked.

By the time he'd changed sides, her hips were moving of their own volition and he paused, lifting his head. 'Mercy. Look at me.'

She forced her eyes to open and nearly whimpered again. His eyes were dark and hot and his lips were wet. Color rode high on his cheeks and his pupils were huge. 'Do you want more?'

She swallowed hard. 'Yes.'

His hand slid down her stomach, over her pajama pants, cupping her between her legs. 'Here?'

She arched again, getting some of the friction she needed, but not nearly enough. 'Yes.'

His fingers curved, putting just the right amount of pressure on her clitoris, and she bucked up into his grip. 'You like that?' he asked slyly, his expression almost feral.

'You know I do.'

'I like to hear it.'

She clenched her teeth, wanting more, but afraid to ask for it. 'Yes. I like it. A lot.'

'Breathe, Mercy,' he teased, dropping kisses on both her breasts before kissing her mouth. 'Or you'll pass out and I'll have to give you mouth to mouth.'

She laughed breathlessly. 'Shut up.'

'Well, that's just mean.' He kissed her again, smiling against her lips. 'How much more do you want to dip in the water? Another toe or your whole foot?'

She laughed again, struck by the ease, the naturalness of all of this. Of him. 'Touch me. Please. Still no cannonball.'

He grinned and slid his hand beneath the waistband of her pj's, then toyed with the waistband of her underwear. 'Touch you like this?'

She narrowed her eyes at him. 'Do you want to ever get to cannonball?'

He pursed his lips, trying to quell his smile. 'Yes, ma'am, I do. Whenever you're ready. For now, though . . .' He sobered, all serious now. 'You're so pretty. I can't wait to see you. All of you.' He moved his fingers down and then he was touching her and it felt so damn good. 'Like that?'

Her head rolled back, pressing into the pillow. 'Yes. More. Please.'

Without a word he obeyed, sliding lower, and then into her, and she moaned.

'Looks like we both get a little wet today,' he said, his words hoarse and rough and playful all at once.

Then he set a rhythm that had her arching into his touch over and over again, her body tensing until pleasure burst, consuming her. She cried out, loud and mindless and he kissed her, stroking her as she rode out the orgasm.

Finally, she collapsed onto the mattress, panting. When she could open her eyes, she found him staring down at her, satisfaction stamped on his handsome face.

'I think I was loud,' she said. 'I should be embarrassed, but I'm really not.'

He smirked at that. 'I think you were perfect.'

'Not yet,' she said. 'You're still . . .'

'Hard as a damn rock? Yes, I am. But that was for you, Mercy. You don't owe me anything.'

'I know I don't. But I want to.' She pressed trembling hands to his shoulders and gave him a little shove. 'On your back, Detective. We're not done yet.'

He tumbled backward, pulling his hand free from her clothing and making her wish that she'd been just a little braver. But they had time.

She'd thought she was done, her arousal banked, until he lifted his fingers to his mouth and, holding her gaze, licked them clean. 'Oh,' she whispered, fiery tingles racing all over her skin. 'You're bad.'

He waggled his brows. 'Positively wicked. I deserve to be punished. Do your worst.'

She tugged at his T-shirt. 'Take this off.'

He didn't have to be asked twice, and the shirt was gone before she could even blink. She ran her hand over all that pretty, tanned skin, pausing at the puckered scar on his upper arm. That had been one of the bullets he'd taken for her that night in February. She kissed it now, tenderly, nuzzling her cheek against the soft blond hair on his chest when he sucked in a breath.

'Mercy,' he whispered.

'Mmm,' she hummed. She kissed across his chest, licking his nipples as he'd done to hers, then dipped her hand into the sweats he'd slept in, remembering how he'd made a point of the fact that he owned no sleep pants because he usually slept in the buff.

Suddenly she wished he hadn't worn the sweats and tugged at them. 'Take these off, too.'

His eyes blazed and he choked back a low moan. 'You're killing me here.'

Her heart was beating too hard to even try to think of a cute reply. 'Do it, Sokolov.'

He grinned and lifted his hips, shucking the sweats down to his knees. 'You can pull them the rest of the way.'

But she didn't. She hovered, taking in the sight of him. *All* of him. 'You are . . .' *Beautiful.* He was beautifully made. Like art. Which sounded dumb in her head. Knowing she was blushing, she gripped him, reveling in the groan that rattled in his chest.

'I'm what?' he managed. 'Tell me.'

It occurred to her that he might need the words too, and she wondered why that seemed so surprising. He had to know that he was built like a Greek god, but she'd loved it when he'd praised her body. She'd never thought to return the favor with any of those she'd been with before.

'You're beautiful, Rafe.' She gave his cock a firm stroke, pleased when he bowed up, his head thrown back, exposing his throat. She kissed him under his chin, on his throat, on his mouth, vaguely tasting herself.

'Not gonna take me long,' he gritted out.

She kissed down the column of his throat, stroking harder and faster. 'Let me see you. Let me see if you're as beautiful when you come as I imagined.'

That was all it took. He ground out a guttural cry and came all over her hand, his cock pulsing with aftershocks. He shuddered, then relaxed, his lips curving into the most smugly satisfied smile she'd ever seen.

'I think that was an unqualified success,' he murmured, his breathing unsteady.

'I think you're right.'

He reached over the side of the bed, scooping his T-shirt from the floor, and cleaned off her hand. 'You'll get all sticky.'

'I wasn't complaining,' she said, more than a little disappointed when he pulled his sweats back up. She settled her cheek against his shoulder, sighing happily when his arms came around her like a vise. 'When do we have to wake up?'

'We don't leave for Santa Rosa until ten, so we can sleep a few more hours. You wore me out.'

She wriggled closer, inordinately pleased. 'Go me. Oh, and thank you.'

He laughed quietly. 'You are most welcome. And thank you, yourself.'

Reno, Nevada
Tuesday, 18 April, 6.25 A.M.

Amos twisted his clenched hands around the steering wheel, so stressed that he thought he'd throw up. It was barely dawn, but there were cars everywhere. People everywhere. The cars were all different. The signs advertised things he'd never heard of.

He felt like Rip Van Winkle, waking after a twenty-year sleep. *Only I've been asleep for thirty.* He couldn't begin to imagine how the world had changed. He was afraid to even consider it. It was all too much.

He kept his eyes focused forward as they passed the sign proclaiming Reno only ten miles away. At least he knew where he was now. He'd only been to Reno once, with his grandfather. They'd gone 'silver mining', panning in a creek that Amos, with the awe of a five-year-old boy, had thought was real. His grandfather had found a small pebble-sized chunk of silver and with a deep, affectionate chuckle had handed it to him.

It was now snuggled at the bottom of Amos's backpack. Worthless, really, from a monetary standpoint, but priceless in memories.

His grandfather would be heartbroken to learn that Pastor had lied to them. That Eden was a fraud. His grandfather had been one of Pastor's most devoted parishioners, had defended him staunchly. Had raised Amos to respect the pulpit and the man who stood there.

Yes, his grandfather would be devastated about Pastor. Amos could only hope the old man who'd raised him would be proud of him now. *I'm trying. But I'm so scared.*

He glanced down at Abigail, startled when she blinked up at him, her large gray eyes round as saucers. She was still lying where he'd placed her, so quiet he hadn't realized she was awake.

'Hey, Abi-girl,' he said lightly, hoping she couldn't feel his fear.

She yawned. 'Can I talk now, Papa?'

He returned his attention to the road, forcing a smile. She'd been so brave, obeying every command he'd given. 'You can. But I have to drive, okay?'

She perked up at that. 'Drive? You're driving?'

'I am. But I'd appreciate if you'd stay down for now. Just a little longer.' He had no idea who was watching. He knew he was being paranoid, but it was better safe than sorry at this point.

'Okay, Papa. But I'm hungry.' She hesitated. 'And I need to use the potty.'

His panic returned. Where could they stop? And then he saw a sign he did recognize. Golden arches. His lips curved. Some things didn't change. 'I know a place.'

He took the next exit and pulled into the parking lot of the McDonald's. 'We're not in Eden anymore, Abigail.'

She stared up at him with her old-soul eyes. Her mother's eyes. 'I know that, Papa.'

Amos chuckled, a tiny piece of fear dropping away. He was so lucky to have this child. 'Of course you do. Well. This place is one my grandfather used to take me to.'

'Back in the olden days,' Abigail said sagely.

'Indeed,' Amos replied gravely. Then he smiled. 'You ready for some breakfast?'

'I can get up now?'

He turned off the engine and pocketed the key. 'Yes.' He held out his arms. 'Want a ride?'

She sat up primly. 'I'm seven, Papa. I can walk.'

'Of course you can.' He got out, shouldered his backpack, and then opened her door. 'After you, my lady.'

She giggled. 'Silly Papa.'

He held out his hand. 'Even seven-year-old princesses hold their papas' hands, okay?'

Abigail slid from the truck, landing on her feet with a bounce, then went still, staring. At everything. Cars raced by on their way to the highway. One honked and she squeaked a terrified whimper.

They were surrounded by buildings. No forests. The mountains were brown and small, not towering and snowcapped. Nothing looked familiar.

Abigail clutched at his hand, her bravado replaced with fear. 'Papa?'

'It's scary, I know,' he said softly. 'Stay with me. It'll be all right. I promise.'

He hoped. God, he hoped.

They crossed the parking lot, Abigail pressed close to his side. She was taking everything in, barely blinking. He opened the door to McDonald's and gently tugged her inside. 'The bathroom is this way.'

He took a moment to inhale. This was familiar. The aroma of breakfast. Of McDonald's breakfast. They had a little food in his backpack, but he needed this. The connection. The anchor to something he actually understood. This had been his first job, flipping burgers at Mickey D's, and this restaurant looked remarkably like the one he'd known before.

Abigail was tugging at his hand. 'Papa, I need to *go.*'

And then he realized she'd never experienced plumbing. He blew out a breath, trying to figure out what to do. She was scared enough without sending her into the ladies' room by herself. Plus, the restaurant wasn't full, but there were enough people inside. He wasn't letting her out of his sight.

'Okay. This is going to be new for you,' he said, leading her to the men's room. 'Next time, maybe you'll want to use that bathroom.' He pointed to the door with the outline of the woman. 'But for today, you can stay with me.'

She nodded, saying nothing. She was trembling. Oh God. She was afraid. She'd been so brave during the worst part – that ride in the truck. But now she was afraid. He crouched down a few feet from the men's room door so that he could meet her eyes. 'It will be okay, Abi-girl. I promise.'

Her smile was shaky. 'Okay, Papa.' Then she did the little dance that said she really needed to pee. 'I need to go,' she whispered.

He led her into the men's room, praying nobody else was there. Nobody was. He showed her the stall and she stared at the toilet. 'Sit here,' he said, making sure it was clean first. 'I'll shut the door and you tell me when you're done. When you close the door, push this little latch to lock it. There is paper on that roll, right there.'

Luckily, toilet paper was one of the few 'modern' things they hadn't been forced to give up in Eden. Amos wasn't sure the women would have stayed, otherwise.

Not that any of them had much of a choice once they'd arrived. He swallowed the sigh, listening for Abigail's progress. He heard the rip of paper and the rustle of clothing.

'I'm finished, Papa.' The door opened and she smiled up at him. 'I can do it myself.'

He couldn't stop his smile. 'I know you can, but let me show you something.' Reaching around her, he flushed the toilet, chuckling when her eyes went round as saucers again.

She leaned over, peering into the toilet bowl. 'Where does it go?'

'Into a big pipe, that goes to a . . .' How did he explain it? 'A place that fixes the water so it can be used again.'

She looked up at him. 'Can I do it?'

He laughed. *I love you, Abigail.* 'Sure, but just once. We don't waste water, even if they can fix it to use again.'

She nodded, then flushed the toilet, giggling with delight as the water rounded the bowl and disappeared. 'Can I do that every time I pee?'

He laughed again. 'Of course. Now let's wash your hands and we'll get something to eat.'

Abigail pointed to the urinal. 'What's that?'

Oh. 'That's . . . well, that's for men who don't need to sit down to pee.'

'They're lucky.'

He nodded. 'I agree. Wash your hands.'

She looked at the sink doubtfully. 'How?'

'How?'

'How do I wash my hands?'

'Oh. Well, you . . .' He stood at the sink, tilting his head one way, then the other. There were no knobs to twist or pumps to push. He vaguely ran his hand around the faucet, then startled when the water started to flow. 'Oh.' He leaned down to take a look. There was a shiny . . . something at the base of the faucet that activated the water flow every time he passed his hand in front of it. Like a photoelectric eye, he thought. Like those doors at the mall that opened automatically. The water stopped and he waved his hand over the shiny panel again. More water. 'Well, this is new.'

'You said that already, Papa.'

He had? Huh. He actually had. 'I think I'll be saying that a lot in the future.' At least he could figure out the soap. He gave the dispenser a few pumps. 'Come over here, Abi-girl.' He wet his hands and got the soap sudsy.

She cast another wary look toward the toilet stall. 'It's clean now? The water?'

He snorted. 'Yes, it's clean. Come on, I'm hungry, too. I need to eat.'

And to sit and think. He needed to find Mercy.

He had no idea where to even start. Everything was so different. He felt like he'd landed on another planet. In a way, he had.

But at least McDonald's still had Egg McMuffins, so there was that.

Twenty-two

Broken Tooth Campground, Nevada
Tuesday, 18 April, 7.00 A.M.

Ephraim pulled the breakfast burrito from the microwave in the camper he'd taken from the pair of honeymooners, inhaling as he did so. It smelled good and he was hungry and the honeymooners wouldn't be needing it anymore. He hadn't eaten a decent meal since leaving MacGuire's house in Granite Bay, and even though the camper's bed wasn't the best, it beat sleeping in MacGuire's Cadillac as he'd done Sunday night.

He checked the view from the camper's window, pleased to see that no person or animal had come sniffing around. The honeymooners' bodies were still safely hidden in the cab of the truck he'd stolen outside Alturas, California. He wouldn't have killed them if he'd had any other choice, but pickings had been slim. Theirs was the only camper in the campground, probably because it was still too cold for most people to camp.

He figured the campground was all the young lovers had been able to afford – they'd been college students, if their sweatshirts were anything to go by. He'd actually considered hitting another campground when he'd seen their Jeep with *Just Married* painted over the back window, but he'd been too tired. He'd lost a lot of blood after that asshole Sokolov had shot him. The fight with the New Orleans cop hadn't helped matters any.

Should've killed them all. But the New Orleans cop had gotten the jump on him and by the time Gideon and his posse had arrived, there were too many of them to kill. He might have taken out two or three, but he wouldn't have escaped alive. He'd gotten lucky as it was – Sokolov's shot had been a clean through-and-through and he'd dressed the wound with a first-aid kit he'd found in the truck he'd stolen. He hurt, but he'd had worse. By the time he'd driven into the campground, he'd desperately needed a safe place to sleep.

So, unwilling to continue searching for the perfect victims, he'd killed the honeymooners and claimed their camper. He *had* let the couple finish what had been a marathon session of sex. And he'd told them he was sorry as he'd stashed their bodies in the truck. *I'm not a total monster.*

He made some coffee and ate the burrito he'd found in the camper's mini fridge, while consulting his phone. According to Google Maps, he was about two and a half hours from Sacramento, which was where he assumed Mercy and Sokolov had returned.

He was certain that Gideon had returned to Sacramento as well, because his girlfriend was on the radio at the moment. A search on Daisy Dawson had revealed her to be some kind of local radio personality who did a morning show from six to ten every day.

He was listening to her at the moment, courtesy of an online site that streamed radio broadcasts from all over the country. She was abominably perky and he thought she should die for that transgression alone.

Not to mention that she'd shot at him, for fuck's sake. Somebody needed to take these modern women in hand and teach them a little respect. He laughed quietly. *And I'm just the man for that job.*

But he had to come up with a better plan first. There was no way he was going to catch any of them unaware at this point. They'd come too close to dying the day before and they'd all be on guard. Waiting for Mercy to be alone, or any of them for that matter, would take more time than he cared to spend away from Eden. Time was ticking. He needed to get Mercy back to show to Pastor before DJ managed a total coup d'état.

He needed to draw them out. He needed a weak link, the injured gazelle that would get picked off by the predator. There was Mercy's best friend. Sokolov's family. Mercy's family back in New Orleans, her half brothers and sisters. He considered them all.

The New Orleans family wasn't a viable target. He wasn't going to be able to fly back to Louisiana, because his face was probably tacked up on every TSA bulletin board across the country.

The best friend was engaged to a cop, so she would probably be protected, too.

He flexed his finger and typed into a new search screen: *Sokolov family Sacramento*. Then he shook his head. They had almost as many kids as he did, and only one child bearer. Irina Sokolov. He'd seen her face from MacGuire's window when he'd been squatting there. She seemed open and friendly. According to the article that popped up, she was a retired nurse, so probably empathetic enough to be lured by a fake injury. And she wasn't so very tall, so even with a hole in his shoulder, he could probably overpower her.

Of her eight children, three were cops – Rafe, Damien, and Meg. Ephraim wasn't touching them with a ten-foot pole. They'd all carry guns.

Sasha was the social worker, but she was also going to be on guard after getting shot yesterday afternoon. Cash was a physical therapist to basketball stars and traveled. Who even knew where he was? Patrick was a firefighter, and Jude was an LA prosecutor, both looking like they could bench-press a damn house. Ephraim was not going to risk getting into a showdown with either of them.

But . . . yes, the eighth Sokolov child would work. *Hello there, pretty girl.* Irina's youngest daughter was a sweet young thing. Still in high school. *Zoya.*

And, according to his Google search, young Zoya had an Instagram account. Whatever the hell that was. He'd heard of Instagram and figured that it was like Facebook. He clicked on the link and scrolled through her many photographs. Most of them were of her with her friends from school. He kept swiping through photos until he found one of her wearing a soccer uniform, the name of her school clearly printed on the jersey.

Zoya Sokolov went to a private school in Granite Bay. Enlarging the soccer photo, he saw that she was blond like her sister and brother. Didn't look too ferocious. She was a little old for his tastes, but he wouldn't need her for sex.

Just as bait to lure Mercy and Rafe into his crosshairs.

Not that Rafe Sokolov would know that. He'd assume his baby sister was being defiled and it would drive him *crazy*. Crazy enough to knock him off his guard.

Leaving Mercy unprotected.

Smiling, Ephraim drained his coffee. He liked this plan. A lot.

He tossed the dishes in the small sink and started to get the camper ready to go.

Reno, Nevada
Tuesday, 18 April, 7.05 A.M.

Abigail sat back, patting her tummy with a satisfied sigh. 'That was good, Papa.' She'd cleaned the disposable plate of every bite of pancakes and sausage, and would have licked off the lingering syrup if he hadn't shaken his head. 'How is yours?'

He chuckled because she was eyeing his Egg McMuffin calculatingly. She'd taken to the concept of a restaurant with surprising ease, especially once he'd described it like dinners in the common room in Eden – a few women making food for them all to enjoy. Except here in the world, the cooking wasn't just done by women. She'd been particularly interested to hear that he'd cooked in a restaurant like this, back in the olden days, as she called it. He pushed what was left of his McMuffin across the table to her. 'You want to try it?'

'Yes, please.' She wolfed it down as well, sighing again. 'When we go back home, maybe you can make these for us. Deborah would love it.'

When we go home. Right. They weren't ever going back home again. She would never see her best friend, Deborah, again. Unless someone could free everyone in the compound.

That someone could be you.

He'd considered it, of course. Many times. But it wasn't going to happen until he was sure that his Abigail was safe. Yes, it was selfish, but his daughter was his priority.

Once he found Mercy, he'd let her decide what should be done.

She'd been living in this world for the past thirteen years. She'd know the safe thing to do. She'd know which police he could trust.

Because going to the police was . . . well, it wasn't smart. Police brutality was a real thing. He'd seen the evidence before he'd gone to Eden. He'd heard horror stories from the new community members.

The police were not to be trusted. Ever. They'd arrest him and take his child. They'd take Abigail.

His gut turned to ice at the very thought. *No.* He was not letting that happen.

Of course, given all the lies he'd been told, the stories about the police might have been a lie as well, but he wasn't taking that risk. Not yet. Eventually he'd report Pastor, DJ, and Ephraim, but he needed to find Mercy first. He needed to be sure that someone he trusted would be there for Abigail, no matter what happened to him.

'Papa?'

Amos returned his attention to Abigail, who was watching him with open dismay. 'Are you all right, Papa? You look sad.'

'I'm a little overwhelmed,' he confessed. 'You know what that means?'

She nodded. 'It's when you have this much work' – she spread her arms wide – 'and this much time.' She pinched her fingers together. 'That's what Deborah's mama says when she does the washing.'

His chest flooded with emotion, so full that it hurt. And it occurred to him, not for the first time, that if DJ came looking for him, if he was caught, he wouldn't survive. He'd never told Mercy, Rhoda, and Gideon how he felt about them. He hadn't made that mistake with this child. If anything happened to him, she'd know exactly what was in his heart. 'I love you, Abi-girl.'

Visibly pleased but blessedly unsurprised, she patted his hand. 'I love you too, Papa. Where will we go next?'

'That is a good question. I need to find a phone book and make a call. On a telephone,' he added when she looked confused. 'You learned about phones in school, right?'

Another nod, this one accompanied with a frown. 'Not from Sister Mary, though. It was from Israel, one of the big boys. He's ten. He said his big brother remembers phones from before they came to Eden.'

'What did Sister Mary say?' Amos asked carefully. Mary was the schoolteacher. She was also one of Pastor's wives.

Abigail winced. 'She told Israel to stop lying. Then she put him in the corner and after school, she whipped him with a switch.' Her eyes got big. 'She made him cut it himself and everything. But he didn't cry. Not at all. Even though she made his legs bleed.'

Amos felt sick. He'd been raised by a grandfather who hadn't believed in sparing the rod, but not to the point of blood. He hadn't realized that Eden had tortured children for telling the truth. They'd been told that Israel had been punished for stealing from one of the other children. They'd always been told that the children were punished for disobedience. *Another lie.* 'What do you think about phones?'

She looked troubled. 'I don't know. *Are* they real?'

She was questioning, which made him feel better. 'Yes, they are. I used one every day before I came to Eden. It's how you talk to someone when they're far away.' He looked around the McDonald's, where at least four people had phones just like the ones he'd seen Pastor and DJ using. 'Those are phones. Those people are talking to other people who aren't here.'

She narrowed her eyes. 'Like imaginary friends?'

He laughed because she was clearly unconvinced. 'Other people who aren't here in this restaurant, but they're real people, not imaginary. I'll find a phone and show you.' He needed to locate Mercy.

And if you can't? What then? Will you contact the police? He'd have to, but he also had to think about Abigail. *Maybe I could write a letter. An anonymous letter.* He was probably being paranoid, but thirty years in Eden had left him distrustful of the law. 'Sit right here and I'll be back.'

He opened the door on their side of the restaurant and looked both ways but saw no pay phone. He hurried to the door on the other side and repeated his search, but found nothing. There was a gas station across the street, but he couldn't see a phone booth over there, either.

He stopped by the counter, trying not to be distracted by the fancy cash registers and what had turned out to be credit card machines. People used *credit cards* at McDonald's? That was ... *Wow. Just, wow.* And the cashier didn't handle the credit cards. The customers stuck their own cards into the machine. He'd been so focused on the machine when he'd first approached the counter that he'd forgotten what he'd wanted to order.

'Excuse me,' he said to the young girl at the register. 'Where is your pay phone?'

She stared at him. 'Our what?'

'Your pay phone,' he repeated.

She shrugged. 'We don't have one.'

'Where can I find one?'

She smirked. 'In the Smithsonian?'

He frowned, biting back a cutting remark of his own. It was amazing how quickly the calm in his heart had been replaced with an acerbic attitude. This was one of the reasons he'd gone to Eden. People were kinder there. Unless they were a Founding Elder, of course. Or one of their wives. Or the healer. All of them could apparently do what they pleased.

Which was not the fault of this young person, so he reined in his temper. 'I'm sorry to have troubled you.'

He returned to their table, sliding into the booth with a sigh. 'I think we need to go somewhere else to find a phone, Abi-girl.'

'Um, excuse me.' Amos looked up to find an older woman standing next to their table. She looked to be about sixty but wore the uniform of a McDonald's employee.

Which boggled his mind. Senior citizens, working at McDonald's? The average employee age used to be sixteen and a half. Amos had been the 'old man' at nineteen.

'Yes?' Amos said, remembering his manners. 'Can I help you?'

She smiled at him, then at Abigail. 'I overheard your question and I want to apologize for the rudeness of my co-worker.' She shook her head. 'Teenagers these days. I'm Edie. Do you need a phone?'

Amos couldn't hide his relief. 'Yes, ma'am. And a phone book.'

Her expression cycled from puzzled, to understanding, and back to kind. She was studying their clothing now. Both he and Abigail wore plain clothing. Homespun fabrics. No frills. Abigail's old-fashioned dress was standard for Eden but very out of place here, and Amos's full beard stood out among the mostly clean-shaven men around him. Abigail's pigtails were mussed from sleeping in the truck, but still neat enough to give her a *Little House on the Prairie* look.

'Are you Amish?' Edie asked.

Amos wasn't sure how to respond. It took his brain a few seconds to find 'Amish' in his memory. But then he nodded. It was an easier explanation than that he'd been living in a cultish commune for thirty years. 'Kind of, yes. It's been a while since I've been to a city.'

'Ah. Well. Give me a second.'

Edie disappeared from view and Abigail turned to him, eyes wide once again. He hoped she didn't pull an eye muscle, because wide-eyed had become her permanent expression.

'What's Amish, Papa?' she whispered.

'They live in small communities like Eden,' he whispered back. 'They don't drive cars, just horses, and they farm the land.'

'Like us,' she said. 'Okay.'

Edie was back, smiling big, holding two coffees stacked in one hand and a little brightly colored box in the other. 'Here you go!' she said cheerfully. She pulled up a chair. 'Can I join you? It's time for my break. If you want, I can help you find what you need.'

Amos started to rise, but she waved him back down. 'You're fine.' She sat at the end of the table and gave him one of the cups of coffee. 'On the house,' she said, then opened the box.

Abigail was watching Edie's every move. 'What is that?'

'Ma'am,' Amos corrected. 'What is that, ma'am?'

Abigail flashed him an embarrassed glance. 'Sorry, Papa. What is that, ma'am?'

'Happy Meal toys for you.' Edie emptied the toys on the table and Abigail's delighted, if a little confused, smile brought back memories of all the excited kids begging their parents for a Happy Meal toy when he'd worked the counter.

Abigail looked to him for permission. 'May I, Papa?'

'Yes, you may. But what do you say first?'

Color flooded Abigail's cheeks. 'Thank you, Sister Edie.'

Edie looked taken aback. 'Miss Edie is fine, sweetheart.' She showed Abigail how to open the plastic packaging, then gently flattened the Happy Meal box. 'And here are some pictures for you to color.' From her shirt pocket she pulled five crayons, gently used. 'I have grandchildren,' she explained.

Abigail was staring at the toys with awe. 'These are all for me?'

'Yes, sweetheart,' Edie said.

'Thank you! My papa used to work here,' Abigail added, carefully taking one of the crayons. 'Oh, this is lovely.'

Edie's lips twitched. 'I think so, too. Blue is my favorite color.' She turned to Amos. 'You worked here? In this store?'

He shook his head. 'Not here. I worked at a McDonald's outside LA. But that was many years ago. We don't have . . . a lot of restaurants where we lived.' He'd been about to say *any*, but hesitated to reveal too much information.

Because if DJ managed to find him, he didn't want this lady to know anything that would put her in danger.

Edie nodded. 'I worked at McDonald's too, back in the early seventies. Kind of tough to have to come back to it now at my age, but you do what you gotta do to pay the bills, am I right?'

'You are indeed.' He checked on Abigail, who'd picked up the art of coloring with the speed with which she did everything else, the tip of her little tongue visible as she concentrated. 'Thank you for helping us. I have to say that I was relieved to see a McDonald's. So much has changed in the time that I've been away, but the golden arches are the same.'

'When were you last in a city?' Edie asked.

He made a rueful face. 'A long, long time ago. Let's see. Bush was president and pay phones were everywhere.'

391

Edie's eyes widened just as Abigail's had. 'Which Bush?'

Which Bush? 'Um, George?'

'I mean, father or son?'

It was Amos's turn to stare. 'Son? Wow.'

Edie gave a low whistle. 'You *have* been gone awhile. This is . . . well, this is fascinating. It's like one of those movies where you fall asleep and wake up in the future, huh?'

'Very much, I'm afraid. I take it that you don't have a phone book or a pay phone here?'

'Or anywhere,' she said. 'Sorry. I mean, you *might* be able to find one somewhere, but I haven't seen one in . . . a decade at least.' She pulled her little phone device from her pocket and put it on the table. 'Everything's in here.'

Amos had to fight to control his urge to touch it. It was so sleek and shiny. That everything could fit in there was too incredible. He'd heard about the Internet from people who'd joined Eden in the last twenty years, but only in whispers. Discussions of life outside Eden's walls were prohibited. *Such that even children are punished for mentioning telephones.* 'I don't have one of those.'

'I figured not.' Edie's brow scrunched. 'Where do you come from? After LA, I mean.'

'North of here,' he said vaguely, because, in truth, he had no idea. 'If I want to get a phone like that, how would I go about it?'

She gave him a long, hard look, then turned to Abigail. 'Where's your mommy, sweetheart?'

Abigail didn't look up from her coloring. 'In heaven,' she answered, matter-of-factly. 'My papa takes care of me.'

'Her mother died in childbirth,' Amos said softly.

Edie's face fell. 'I'm sorry. I just . . . well, I need to know that she's really yours. That you didn't just grab her from the mall or something.'

He stared at her, angry for a moment, and then he remembered the stranger dangers of the mall and felt a swell of gratitude. And relief, because even though Abigail had her mother's gray eyes, she had his dark hair and one other identifying feature. 'Abi-girl, can you show Miss Edie your birthmark?'

'I have a birthmark here,' Abigail said, setting the crayon down to tug the collar of her dress aside and point to the little red dot. 'Papa has one, too.'

Amos mimicked Abigail's action, showing Edie his identical mark, then rubbed at it with his thumb to show her that it was part of his skin. 'She's my daughter.'

'I'm sorry,' Edie said. 'I needed to ask.'

'It's perfectly fine. I'm glad you're so conscientious.' He hesitated, then sighed. 'We left our home last night. The community no longer . . . held appeal.'

Edie's expression changed, wary once again. 'The community. Like a cult?'

Goodness. For a moment, Amos could only blink. How had she guessed? His shock must have shown, because Edie nodded grimly.

'I've read about this,' she said. 'People leaving when the cult endangered their children. Is that what happened to you . . . Sorry. I don't know your name.'

'He's called Brother Amos,' Abigail chirped. 'I'm Abigail.'

Amos opened his mouth to reprimand her, then sighed. 'Yes. I'm Amos, but not Brother. Not anymore.' *Never again.* 'And . . . yes, to your other question.' He glanced meaningfully at Abigail, then met Edie's eyes, hoping she'd understand. *Yes, my child is in danger.*

Edie drew a breath. 'Well, then. A phone. You can get one at Walmart. You know about Walmart?'

'I remember the store, yes, but I've never been to one.'

Edie shook her head. 'You're in for a wild adventure, Amos.'

'It's already started,' Amos said. 'How much money does a phone cost at Walmart?'

'At least fifty dollars. Plus you have to pay for a plan.'

Amos winced. Buying a phone would make a huge dent in the cash that he'd brought with him. And the truck needed gasoline. He'd nearly fainted at the prices on the gas station signs. 'That's a lot of money. And then I need to buy a . . . plan?' What did *that* mean? 'And then I can find a telephone book?'

Edie sighed. 'Look, you might want to start at the library. They

393

have computers and you can look things up there probably faster than on one of those cheap burner phones. You can use the online white pages.'

'Burner phone?' he asked, then waved the question away. 'Never mind. It's okay. I can look things up for free at the library?'

'If you have a library card. Do you?'

He shook his head. 'I did, but it expired in 1990.'

Edie dropped her gaze to her hands and tapped the screen of her phone, revealing the image of three smiling children, all about Abigail's age. The screen also displayed the time, which Amos supposed was handy for Edie, as the woman didn't wear a wristwatch.

'My break is over,' she said, 'so I have to get back. Look, I have a library card. I can't give it to you, but I have some time between this job and my shift at Smith's. If you can wait till ten, I'll meet you at the library and help get you started.'

Amos exhaled in relief. 'Thank you. Yes, we can wait. I'll meet you there. Where is it?'

'I'll look it up.'

Then, as he watched, she held the phone in front of her face, then cradled it in her left palm. Gone was the image of the smiling children, replaced by . . .

'Is that a map?' he asked, wonderingly.

'It is. Very handy for the directionally challenged like me.' At his blank look, she laughed. 'I get lost everywhere I go.' She typed in *library near me* with one finger, tapped the screen again, then nodded. 'They don't open till ten, anyway, the public libraries.' She grabbed a napkin from the table and a crayon, then quickly wrote a list of directions. 'It's only twenty minutes from here. Or you can stay here until ten if you want, and you can follow me.'

Amos looked at Abigail, who was back to coloring with a vengeance. 'She's occupied with her crayons, so waiting here sounds fine.'

Edie pushed back from the table. 'If she gets bored, they have coloring books at the Smith's across the street. It's a grocery store. Gotta get back. See you later, Amos and Abigail.'

Abigail smiled up at her. 'Thank you, Miss Edie!'

394

Amos slid from the booth to stand, bowing his head slightly. 'Yes. Thank you, Miss Edie. You can't know how much I appreciate your kindness.'

Edie gave his arm a friendly pat. 'You're welcome. I have three young grandchildren. I'd hope someone would help them if they and my daughter were stuck and alone. Sit down, hon. Drink your coffee. It'll be all right.'

Amos watched her go, hoping Edie was right. *It'll be all right.* Settling back into the booth, he sipped at his coffee and watched his little girl play.

Sacramento, California
Tuesday, 18 April, 9.15 A.M.

'Wake up, sleepyhead.' Rafe put a cup of coffee on the nightstand next to Mercy's side of the bed. 'Here you go.'

With a yawn, she opened her eyes. 'Already?'

'You're the one who wanted to go to Santa Rosa today.'

The boxes with the lockets belonging to her and to her mother were on the coffee table, next to his wallet and keys. He knew what the lockets contained. He hoped he didn't have to look at the photo of Mercy with Ephraim Burton, but he knew he probably would because they planned to show it to Ephraim's mother, in the hopes that they would spark some kind of memory.

'True.' Stretching her arms over her head, she sat up with the headboard at her back, looking sleep-tousled and gorgeous. 'You made me coffee. How long have you been awake?'

'About forty-five minutes.' He'd already done his PT exercises, showered, and checked his messages. 'I hope the coffee's okay. I added enough sugar to make your teeth hurt.'

'Just the way I like it. Thank you.'

He dropped a kiss on her smiling mouth. 'You're welcome.' He sat on the edge of the bed, content to watch her as she reached for her phone and began scrolling through her messages. She hadn't slept much the night before. Neither of them had. But they'd both slept soundly after that make-out session.

Rafe wanted to repeat the experience. The make-out session, not the sleep. He couldn't imagine any man preferring sleep to making out with Mercy Callahan. Kissing her lips, fondling her breasts. Watching her face as she came apart.

He shuddered, wondering if they had time for another go. Just to feel her hands on him again. He wouldn't even have to come.

But then thoughts of pleasure slid from his mind when she went still, her jaw going slack. Her eyes had focused on her phone, her shoulders gone rigid.

If it's that damn video, I'll . . . He'd what? Finish what he started Sunday afternoon when he'd been tempted to knock Jeff Bunker's head off his neck? Mercy had been right. It really wasn't the kid's fault. It was the fault of the editor of that slimy rag Bunker had worked for.

'What is it?' he asked. 'What's wrong?'

She looked up, seeming startled to see him there, even though she'd just spoken to him not even two minutes before. 'It's an email from Daisy. With a message from Jeff Bunker.'

So the kid *had* upset her. 'He has no right to contact you just to help his conscience.'

She shook her head. 'It's not like that. Well, not entirely, anyway. He's written a retraction.'

'Of what?'

'Of everything he wrote about me.'

'So he's sorry,' Rafe snarled quietly. 'So fucking what? That doesn't help you.'

'But that's the point. He *does* want to help me – me and all the other women who've been victimized, then ignored or worse.'

Rafe forced himself to calm down, for Mercy's sake. 'How does he want to help?'

'He's giving up his blog and his YouTube channel to survivors of sexual assault. Women and men. The first article going viral pumped up his subscription numbers, so he has an audience for the moment. Survivors can tell their stories on their own terms. And he'll read them if they don't want to be on camera themselves. All identities kept confidential.'

Rafe's ire receded. 'I wasn't expecting that.'

'Neither was I,' Mercy murmured, then met Rafe's eyes, hers troubled. 'Daisy says they won't publish his article until I approve it, because he specifically mentions me. He's already run it past Daisy and your mother.'

'My mother?'

'Yeah. Apparently Jeff called your house and talked to Zoya.' She smiled. 'She told him to use his talent to do good.'

'She's a good kid,' Rafe said affectionately. 'Being the baby, she could have ended up spoiled rotten – and she is, but not in a bad way. What do you want to do about this?'

'I want to let Jeff run with the article. Daisy forwarded Jeff's message at five thirty this morning, but she just sent an update. He's at the studio, talking to the coordinator for one of the rape crisis centers here in town.'

Rafe blinked. 'On the radio?'

'No, not yet. The crisis center coordinator is on the radio, but Daisy said she'd contacted the coordinator about the show on Sunday morning. After Jeff's article was posted.'

'That sounds like Daisy. She couldn't help you directly, but she couldn't sit still, either. That girl has too much energy.'

'And she uses it well.' Mercy handed him her phone. 'Read it. Tell me what you think.'

Rafe read Jeff's most recent article and had to admit it was really well done. 'I like this one better than his last one, that's for sure. I like this angle better than his last one, too. And that he's letting survivors tell their own stories is admirable. I suppose the downside is that it will stir things up for you. If we left it alone, the hubbub would die down and nobody would remember his first article.'

'It would die down,' she agreed quietly, 'but it wouldn't disappear. It wouldn't even be refuted. And I did want to use this situation to help in a bigger way. Jeff's idea is a good way to start. He's also enlisting therapists so that anyone watching will know where they can get help. It's what I wanted to do, but I didn't want to go on camera to do it. The thought of being in the spotlight makes me kind of sick, to be honest.'

'If you want to say yes, Mercy, then say yes.'

'I do. Daisy says she also has a few reporters lined up to talk about Jeff's channel on the TV news and in the newspaper. They're just waiting for my go-ahead. They think they can whip up some positive attention.'

'If this gets more views, the original article could get pushed down in prominence.'

She grimaced. 'I thought that too, which is self-serving, but at this point I'm okay with that.' She typed out a reply, then hit SEND. 'There. Not overthinking it. I said yes. It's done.'

He touched his forehead to hers. 'Proud of you.'

Her smile trembled at the corners. 'Thanks.' She leaned into him, resting her cheek on his shoulder, and he wrapped his arms around her. 'This is nice, being with you like this.'

'It is. But it's getting late and we're meeting the others at nine forty-five. We all leave for Santa Rosa at ten.'

She drew back, staring at him warily. 'What others? Who is "all"?'

He rolled his eyes. 'Everybody. Or just about. André told me that we'd better take Farrah with us today, because she was an utter mess yesterday, worrying about you while they were driving up to Snowbush. And if she goes, he goes.'

'All right. Who else is everybody?'

'The usual,' he said lightly. 'Agents Schumacher and Hunter are our bodyguards and Tom's bringing a plus-one.'

Her brows went up. 'A plus-one?'

'His friend who works in a nursing home similar to the one we're visiting today. She works with veterans at the moment, specifically senior vets with dementia. Since Ephraim's mother also has dementia, Tom thought Liza would be a good resource. And then Gideon and Daisy are coming, too.'

'Wow. But I guess it could be worse. Molina could be coming.'

'She wanted to,' Rafe said, 'but she's got meetings at the field office that she can't avoid.'

'Darn,' Mercy deadpanned. 'Don't get me wrong. I don't dislike her, but she makes me nervous.'

'Me too,' Rafe admitted. 'Now drink your coffee before it gets cold, then take your shower. I've already taken mine and we need to get dressed before folks come knocking on the door. André texted and said that Farrah's making breakfast and bringing it down.' He kissed her lightly before moving off the bed, but paused to take a last look. 'You look really good in my bed, Mercy Callahan.'

Her dimples appeared, even as she blushed. 'Thank you. You're not so bad yourself.'

It was his turn to deadpan. 'Wow, the compliments will go to my head.'

'I'll spend today thinking of better ones,' she promised. 'Oh hey. I got sidetracked with that email from Daisy and forgot to ask about Erin. How is she?'

Rafe took a clean shirt from his closet and shrugged into it. 'Awake and cranky, according to Sasha. Mom sat with Erin last night so that Sasha didn't have to and could sleep, but Mom's coming home today. Erin's mother got there sometime during the night and can stay today. Then Sasha will stay with Erin until she's released, at least a few more days.'

Mercy hesitated. 'And no new news on Ephraim's whereabouts?'

Not wanting to answer that question, Rafe picked two ties from the rack and held them up. 'Blue or brown?'

'The blue one. Rafe, don't keep things from me. Please.'

His fingers stilled on the blue tie and he lifted his gaze. 'Hunter messaged me. He figured you'd want to hear this in private, versus in a crowded car, but . . .' He hadn't wanted to tell her. He still didn't. But she was waiting, expression now one of dread. 'Ephraim killed two more people last night. A young couple in a camper.' He had to force himself to tell her the rest of it. 'They were on their honeymoon. He left their bodies at their campsite in the truck he stole when he ran from Snowbush. They were discovered an hour ago by the campground owner.'

Closing her eyes, Mercy pursed her lips. 'Dammit, Rafe,' she whispered.

'I know,' he whispered back. 'We'll find him, Mercy.'

'I *hate* this,' she said, fists clenched and voice breaking. 'I *hate* that innocent people are dying because of him. Because he's after me.'

'I hate that he's after you, period,' Rafe said. 'But last night you promised not to make yourself a target again. I'm going to hold you to that.'

She opened her eyes, devastated tears spilling over and running down her cheeks. 'I keep my promises.'

He exhaled, not having realized he'd been holding his breath. 'Thank you.'

Twenty-three

Reno, Nevada
Tuesday, 18 April, 10.05 A.M.

'Again, I can't tell you how much I appreciate this, Edie,' Amos said, shouldering his backpack, Abigail's small hand clutched in his. 'You've gone to a lot of trouble for us.'

'It's no trouble,' Edie assured him with a smile. She'd changed out of her McDonald's uniform and now wore a tunic that said *SMITH'S.* 'I'm happy to help.'

She pushed open the door to the public library and walked in, pausing a moment to breathe deeply. She looked at them over her shoulder. 'I love the smell of books.' Then she smiled. 'Do you like books, Abigail?'

Amos glanced down to see his daughter's eyes wide once again. Her mouth had fallen open and the expression on her face was one of awe.

'Papa,' she breathed. 'So many books.'

He squeezed her hand lightly. 'Miss Edie asked you a question, Abigail. Do you like books?'

'Oh yes. Yes, ma'am. But I've never seen so many.'

Edie looked around fondly. 'When I was your age, the library was my favorite place.' She leaned down to whisper, 'You want to know a secret? It still is.'

Abigail grinned, saying nothing at all, content to simply take it all in.

Edie straightened. 'Let's find Miss Abigail some books. Then I can show you how to use the computer.'

She strode toward the children's section, leaving Amos and Abigail to follow. Amos chuckled when Abigail took off after her, dragging him along. For all her energy, Abigail loved stories. They'd had only a few books in Eden, all well worn, well read. Amos still had a few books that had belonged to Mercy. One of his best memories was reading Mercy a story before tucking her into bed each night.

It had been an impulse to tuck one of Mercy's old books into his backpack, a slim volume of fairy tales that Amos had found in the pile of her and Rhoda's belongings that Pastor had planned to burn after their bodies had been buried. Rhoda's body, anyway. Like Gideon, only Mercy's remains had been found. Unlike Gideon, Mercy's remains had not been brought back to Eden. DJ had buried her in the woods, so as not to attract wild animals while he'd searched for Rhoda.

Or so he'd said.

Amos didn't believe anything that any of Eden's leaders had told him. Not anymore.

He'd packed the book on the off chance that Mercy really was alive and that he'd be able to find her before DJ did. Once she was safe, Amos would give her the book.

It wasn't anything close to reparation, but hopefully it represented a good memory. Either way, it was all he had to give her.

'What kind of stories do you like, Abigail?' Edie asked, snapping him out of his thoughts.

'I don't know. Papa reads to me sometimes.' Abigail was suddenly shy. 'My school has a book. It has Bible stories.'

'I'm sure we can find you one like that,' Edie said, 'but for now, how about this one? My daughter loved this one and my grand-children love it, too. I bet you will, too.' She chose a book from the shelf and put it in Abigail's hands. 'It's called *Ramona the Pest.*'

Abigail's eyes shone. 'I can have it?'

'Abigail,' Amos warned, and her little face fell.

She dropped her gaze. 'I'm sorry, Papa.'

Edie slowly dropped into a crouch, grimacing at the audible popping of her knees. 'Abigail, you may read this book as long as you're here. And once your papa gets settled, he can get you a library card of your very own. And then you can borrow whatever books you like. You can take them home, read them, then bring them back for more.'

'Oh.' Abigail's smile was back and she hugged the book to her chest. 'Thank you.'

'It's my pleasure, sweetie.' Edie straightened with a quiet groan. 'Standing up used to be easier. Come with me, Amos. Let's sign in to a computer.'

Amos watched as she went to the desk, showed her library card, and then pointed to him and Abigail, who'd already sat in one of the chairs at the computer table, *Ramona the Pest* open in front of her.

Edie came back and patted the empty chair beside the computer she'd been assigned. 'So . . . this is how you start.'

Within a minute and a half Amos's brain was already full. Edie was typing so fast that he could barely keep up and she maneuvered the mouse with terrifying ease. He remembered just enough from his high school computer lab days to not be completely overwhelmed.

'We are now online,' she said, with a ta-da gesture.

'I had a friend who had a computer when I was a teenager,' he said. 'He had a . . .' He searched for the word. 'It had these cups and you put the phone in them. I guess that's ancient history, too?'

'Oh right.' She laughed. 'A modem. I remember those days.' Lowering her voice, she mimicked the beeps and noise the device would make, bringing back a whole host of memories. 'The modems are all internal now. They plug right into the wall.'

'Wow,' he murmured.

'You'll get used to it easily,' she promised. 'If I can learn this, anyone can. And if all else fails, let Abigail try. Kids are the best at this computer jazz. All right. This is called a browser window. It gets you into the Internet. There are a lot of browsers to choose from, but I use Chrome because it's what my daughter put on my computer. Then we go to Google. See? That's the search engine I usually use.'

Amos studied the slim screen. It looked like the one he'd seen in Sister Coleen's office at the Eden clinic. Was that really only four days ago? He wondered if Sister Coleen could access the Internet, up on the mountain. Edie had explained that the computers on the table were linked into a massive network of buried cables, so Amos wasn't sure how it would work. Unless the satellite dish allowed them access.

My head hurts. 'Okay. So how do you . . . find things?'

'Depends. What do you want to find?'

'How about a phone book?' he asked.

She chuckled. 'Okay, so we're back to that. Who or what are you looking for?'

Amos glanced at Abigail, but she didn't seem to be paying any attention to them. 'It's a "who". Her name is Mercy Callahan.'

Edie frowned. 'Huh. That name sounds familiar.' She typed Mercy's name into Google and then sat back with an exhale. 'Oh wow. That's why her name sounded familiar. She's been in the news. There was a CNN special interview just last week and she was mentioned. It was an intense report.' She cast a worried glance in Abigail's direction. 'Um, you should probably read it to yourself. You can't watch videos without earphones and they don't have those here. I don't have any with me, either. Click that link for a summary of the program.'

'Link?'

Using the mouse, Edie moved the pointer to one of the lines of text. 'These are links. Use the button on the mouse to click on it and it'll open the article. Like this.' She clicked and moved to one side, tilting the screen so that he could read it.

Amos could feel the blood draining from his face. 'Dear God,' he whispered. Mercy had been mentioned in a program about a serial killer?

'They caught him,' Edie murmured. 'She got away. Only three women did. Most of his victims weren't so lucky.'

His heart was racing, his hands shaking as he read the article. The man had truly been a serial killer, just like in the movies he'd seen as a teen. Horrified, he read about the man's victims, their names accompanied by a brief description of who they'd been, along with photos of each woman and the souvenir the killer had kept of her.

So many women. So much death.

But no mention of his Mercy. He got to the bottom of the screen and turned to Edie, who was watching him with pity. 'How do I read more?' he asked hoarsely.

'Just scroll down,' she said, showing him how.

'Thank you.' He kept reading, reaching for the mouse when he reached the bottom of the screen once again. He scrolled down and gasped.

Because there she was. In the middle of the page. *Mercy. It's her. She's not dead.*

Older, of course, but still recognizable as his Mercy. She was so thin, her beautiful green eyes dull and flat.

His vision blurring, Amos touched the screen, tracing the lines of her face.

'Who is she to you?' Edie asked, so softly he almost couldn't hear the question over the pounding of his heart.

'My daughter,' he whispered, hearing her gasp. He turned to her, wiping at his eyes with his sleeve. 'She was taken from me. When she was almost thirteen. They told me she was dead.'

'Oh, Amos.' Edie's eyes filled with tears. 'I'm so sorry.'

He gave Abigail another quick look. She was engrossed in her book. Thank the good Lord for that. He wasn't sure he could answer any questions she asked right now.

'But she got away from the serial killer,' he said quietly. 'Are you sure?'

'Yes. She wasn't interviewed for the program, but the woman who was on the show talked about how Mercy was rescued by her brother.'

Her brother? Amos had to grip the side of the table for support. 'Brother?' he managed to ask.

Edie was watching him warily. 'Yes.' Turning the screen so that she could see it, she typed *Mercy Callahan brother* into another screen. Browser. Whatever.

When the picture came up, Amos covered his mouth with his hand to keep the sob in. *Gideon.* 'Oh,' he breathed. 'My son, my boy. Gideon.'

'They told you he was dead, too?'

He looked at Edie and nodded. 'They showed us a body. They said it was him. But look – he's alive.'

'And an FBI agent,' Edie added. 'With a girlfriend, according to this article. Just one in a gossip blog, but here's a photo.' She clicked again and a photo popped up, in full color.

It was him. *Gideon*. With a small blond woman who smiled up at him like he'd hung the moon.

'Daisy Dawson,' he murmured, reading the caption below the photo. Then he frowned. 'Her name was in the other article. From the program. Is that gone? Can I see that again?'

'Not gone. Nothing's ever really gone on the Internet, or so my grandchildren tell me.' Edie did something on the screen and the first article returned. 'You're right. The woman with Gideon was one of the three who escaped. She lives in Sacramento.'

But Amos was now leaning closer to the screen, squinting at the grainy photo above Daisy Dawson's.

'Let me zoom in,' Edie said, and a second later, the photo was enlarged.

It was very grainy, but it still made Amos's racing heart stumble and stutter. 'Miriam,' he whispered.

'You know her, too?' Edie sounded like she didn't believe him, but Amos didn't care.

The name next to her photo said 'Eileen', but the woman was Miriam. Miriam Comstock. 'We buried her, too. I . . . helped her escape. They said she died.'

'She did,' Edie said gently. 'She was murdered by the serial killer.'

Amos shook his head. 'No, they said she was caught outside the community's walls. That she'd died. We buried her,' he repeated.

'O . . . kay,' Edie said with a note of trepidation.

And next to her photo was the souvenir her killer had taken. Her locket. On the front was the extremely familiar symbol of Eden – two children kneeling in prayer beneath an olive tree, all under the wings of an archangel wielding a sword. A second photo showed the back of the locket. *Miriam*.

'Excuse me. Can I have the mouse?' She gave it to him and he scrolled back up through the article, looking for any mention of Eden, but there was none.

'What are you looking for?' Edie asked.

'A mention of our town,' he said. 'I thought maybe . . .' He let the thought trail off. They'd escaped, Mercy and Gideon. They'd started new lives. 'I need to find them. Either or both.'

'Hold on.' She'd somehow gotten them back to the first screen – the one that listed the other articles. 'Mercy comes up in other articles. More recent ones. Most of them are from Saturday.' She clicked one and blew out a breath. 'She's had a rough time, Amos.'

Amos found his mouth hanging open for the second time in as many minutes. *Ephraim. You sonofabitch.*

The curse, only loosed in his mind, still startled him, but he couldn't be sorry. There on the screen was a photo of Brother Ephraim, his hand on Mercy's arm, escorting her. Grimly Amos read the accompanying text. It had been an abduction attempt. Foiled, thank God. Mercy had been hurt, though. A small wound. She'd been rescued by an off-duty Sacramento detective by the name of Raphael Sokolov.

Raphael. He'd been Mercy's guardian angel. Protecting her. Because Ephraim had hurt her. Again. Rage bubbled up through Amos's veins.

Beside him, Edie cleared her throat. 'You might want to take it down a notch. People are looking at you. You look like you want to do some major violence.'

Amos blinked hard, then realized his fists were clenched and he was panting like a bull ready to charge. Purposefully, he flattened his hands on the table. 'My apologies.'

'It's all right,' Edie said. 'If someone tried to take my daughter, I'd feel the same way.'

'How can I find her? I need to find her.'

Because Ephraim had tried to kidnap her from a crowded airport and, according to the phone call that Amos had overheard in Eden, DJ would be looking for her, too.

Panic rose to close off his throat. 'I need to find her,' he repeated. *I need to warn her.*

You could call the police. But . . . He stared at the photo on the computer screen, Pastor's voice shouting in his mind. *Don't trust the police. Don't trust the government. Trust only me.*

But Pastor had lied about so many things. Desperation warred with indecision. *Anonymous letter,* he thought. *If I can't find Mercy, I'll write that letter.*

'Can you find her address or phone number?' he asked.

Edie squared her shoulders. 'I'm not really good with this stuff, but let me see what else I can find.'

'Thank you.' Amos forced himself to sit back and let Edie work her magic.

Please let me find Mercy. Please don't let me be too late.

'Oh, for heaven's sake,' Edie muttered. She gave Amos an unreadable look. 'Don't read this article. It's Internet trash. Like the *National Enquirer* back in the eighties. Lots of lies and half-truths. Don't even bother with it.'

Amos didn't have a chance to read it, because Edie made it disappear. A new article opened and the older woman relaxed a little.

'This one's better,' she pronounced. 'Some twerpy little jerk published a very unflattering exposé on your daughter. But he retracted it and now wants to help other . . . well, other people.'

Amos frowned, stuck on the first part of her statement. 'What did his unflattering exposé say?'

Edie leaned around the screen to look at Abigail, who had stopped reading and was watching them with open curiosity.

'Stuff that nobody needs to know,' Edie replied. 'Little pitchers, Amos.'

'All right,' he said. He'd find out later. 'Do you know how I can find her?'

'Well, the first article, the one about that program from last week, it said that she lives in New Orleans.'

'Which is very far,' he said, disappointed.

'True, but as of four days ago, she was in California. In Sacramento. Which happens to be where Daisy Dawson lives. I bet

408

your son Gideon lives there too, or spends a lot of time there, at the very least. The author of this retraction also lives in Sacramento. I'd say that's where you need to go.'

'All right.' Amos picked up his backpack, but Edie stayed him with a light touch to his arm.

'Hold your horses, Papa Bear,' she said mildly. 'Before you go charging out of here, maybe we can find out exactly where in Sacramento you need to go.'

Amos sagged back into his chair, feeling foolish. 'You're right, of course.'

Edie patted his arm. 'Give me a minute or two.' She turned her attention to Abigail. 'You finished that book already?'

Abigail nodded, worry in her eyes. 'I did. Papa, are you well?'

Amos made himself smile. 'I am. Maybe we can find another book.' Rising, he reached for her hand. 'Ready, Abi-girl?'

'Yes, Papa,' she said obediently, but her worry remained.

He led Abigail back to the shelf from which Edie had taken the Ramona book. 'There are more books about Ramona,' he said. 'I remember from when I was a little boy.' He pulled all the Ramona books from the shelf and took them back to the computer table. 'I'm not sure which one comes next.'

'I can help with that,' the librarian said with a smile. 'I'm Miss Millie. I'm Miss Edie's friend. What's your name, little darling?' she asked.

'Abigail,' his daughter answered very shyly.

'Well, Abigail, I love it when kids come to the library, and I love these books. Let's go sit over here in these comfy chairs, okay?'

Amos nodded gratefully when Abigail looked up for permission. 'I'll be right over there with Miss Edie,' he promised. 'I won't leave, I promise.'

'I asked her to help you,' Edie said when he'd returned to the computer table. 'I have to leave soon, but I don't want to just desert you two. Millie and I have been friends for years and she's way better at this computer stuff than I am.'

'You seem to be doing very well,' Amos said, meaning it.

Edie shrugged. 'I do my best. I asked Millie how I can get

information from Jeffrey Bunker, the guy who wrote the most recent article. It was just posted an hour ago.' She pointed to a time stamp at the top of the article. 'See?'

Amos did see. He also saw that the article's author was discussing survivors of sexual assault.

Amos had been only nineteen when he'd entered Eden, but he knew what those words meant. That Mercy had been included with 'other survivors of sexual assault' made his rage begin to bubble again. But he held it back because Edie was still talking.

'Millie suggested I open a new email account and send Bunker an email on your behalf. So can I use your name?'

Amos nodded numbly. 'An email account? What's that?'

Edie sighed. 'Oh boy. It's a way to send messages to people over the Internet.'

Amos had too many questions. But top of his list was how to find Mercy, so he nodded to Edie. 'Yes, use my name. Amos Terrill. Two r's and two l's.'

Edie began typing and Amos didn't try to follow everything she did. Finally she stopped typing. 'This is what I wrote. "Dear Ms Dawson and Mr Bunker, I'm representing a man named Amos Terrill, who claims to be the father of Mercy Callahan and Gideon Reynolds".' She looked over at him. 'Sorry to use "claims".'

'It's okay,' Amos said. 'Whatever you need to do so that I can talk to her.'

'"Please reply to this email address if you can help Mr Terrill contact either Miss Callahan or Agent Reynolds. You can also reach him through this number".' She glanced up at him. 'That's the library's main line.'

'How long will it take?'

'I don't know,' she said apologetically. 'But I have to leave for my shift at the grocery store. Millie will be able to log in to this account, and I'll leave this page open in case Bunker replies. See this circle with an arrow? You click that to refresh. That means it goes and checks for new mail. If someone replies, you just click on it to read what they wrote. Once your session time is up, Millie can log me out.'

'Thank you. Thank you so much.'

She smiled at him. 'Like I said, if my daughter or grandkids were in trouble, I'd hope someone would help them.' She gave him a piece of paper, folded in half. 'This is my phone number. I can't use my phone while I'm working, but I'll check my messages. Millie can help you get in touch with me if you have problems. Please let me know what happens.'

He smiled, even though he felt like the earth was shifting beneath his feet. This woman had been an anchor when he'd needed one most and now she was leaving. 'I will. I promise. Thank you again.'

She gave him another arm pat. 'Take care, Amos.'

And then she was gone, leaving Amos to stare at the computer screen, willing the 'twerpy little jerk' to reply.

Sacramento, California
Tuesday, 18 April, 10.10 A.M.

Mercy bit back a sigh as she got into the black FBI van dominating Rafe's driveway. There were no windows in the back and no markings identifying them as being with law enforcement. The trip to Santa Rosa was already a production, with the van and two additional FBI vehicles that would be part of their entourage. 'I don't know why I thought we could just drive up the highway.'

'Hey, don't complain. I feel like I'm a super-secret spy on a supersecret mission,' Farrah said as she climbed in to sit beside Mercy. 'Let me have my James Bond moment, okay?'

Mercy chuckled. 'Some super-secret spies we are. Everyone is armed except for us.'

'I have some pepper spray,' Farrah said seriously. 'I threw it in my luggage before we left New Orleans. My mama gave it to me.'

Mercy felt the same flare of affection every time she thought of Farrah's mother. 'How is Mama Romero?'

'Sad. Angry. My father is having a harder time,' Farrah admitted. 'Quill was his aunt. I talked to him last night. He was crying, but told me that I needed to be here. Actually forbade me to come back until you don't need me anymore.'

411

Mercy felt abruptly guilty. 'I—'

Farrah lifted a brow. 'Don't say what you were going to say. This is not your fault.'

Mercy knew that, but . . . 'He killed two more people last night. Stole their camper.' She swallowed hard, still having trouble not feeling guilty. 'They were on their honeymoon, Ro.'

Farrah drew in a shocked breath. 'Goddammit, Mercy. Somebody needs to stop him.'

And that somebody is going to be me, Mercy thought grimly.

'And that somebody is *not* going to be you,' Farrah declared, giving her a shrewd look. 'I swear to God, if you risk yourself again . . .'

Mercy wanted to sigh, but held it in. 'I promised Rafe I wouldn't. Okay?'

'Okay,' Farrah muttered. Her scowl brightened when the door opened again. 'Liza, you're riding with us?'

Liza Barkley was Tom Hunter's plus-one. She moved with the same confidence that all the cops had, except hers had come from a tour in Afghanistan versus walking a beat on the street.

'If it's okay,' Liza replied. 'I can climb to the very back. I've got some reading to do on the way.' She squeezed by them, dropping her backpack on the rear bench seat. 'I brought snacks,' she added brightly.

Farrah laughed. 'So did I. What did you bring?'

'Bars,' Liza replied promptly, then shook her head. 'Brownies, I mean.'

Tom stuck his head in the driver's door. 'She's from Minnesota. They say "bars" up there. It's weird. But her bar-brownies are delicious.'

Liza laughed. 'Too little, too late. I'll just be sharing my bars with the ladies.'

Tom shrugged. 'I control when we stop for bathroom breaks.'

Farrah whistled. 'That escalated fast. Please don't forget that there are other people in the van who didn't threaten to withhold snacks. If we need to stop, you'll stop.'

Tom grinned. 'Yes, ma'am.' Then he glanced at his phone and

sobered. 'I need to take this. Excuse me.' He jogged to the garage, where Rafe and André were coming out of the house. Tom listened to the call, and then he, Rafe, and André had a conversation during which the other two men's expressions grew equally sober.

Rafe said something to André and the two disappeared back into the house, reappearing with a cat carrier.

'Oh no,' Mercy whispered. The dread she'd felt watching the men talk had morphed into the beginnings of a panic attack.

'What is it?' Liza asked, worried.

'They're bringing Mercy's cat,' Farrah replied, then swallowed. 'Her comfort animal.'

'Oh,' Liza murmured. 'Got it.'

André got into the front passenger seat while Rafe settled into the seat beside Mercy, sandwiching her between his body and Farrah's, his mood tense. And dark.

From where she sat in the middle, Mercy could see André drawing his weapon from his holster and holding it in his lap, his gaze darting in every direction while Rafe pulled the sliding door closed and popped the latch on the carrier. Rory climbed out, immediately curling up in Mercy's lap, but her hands were clenched into fists and she couldn't manage to relax them.

She licked her suddenly dry lips. 'What's happened?'

Rafe's jaw was taut. 'It's Ginger.'

Mercy frowned at him in confusion. 'The woman who sold me the jewelry box yesterday? What's happened to her?'

Rafe met her gaze directly. 'She's dead.'

Mercy stared at him, the panic beginning to swirl in her mind. 'No.'

Farrah reached for Mercy's hand, prying her fingers loose from the fist and holding on tightly – too tightly, but the brief discomfort was what Mercy needed. 'Breathe, Merce,' she murmured. 'What happened, Rafe?'

'Ginger was found this morning. With the owner of the Snowbush general store, Nick Corwin. In bed together.' Rafe shook his head. 'They'd both been shot in the head. Corwin's wife was on the floor, also dead. It was supposed to look like a murder-suicide.'

413

'Supposed to,' Mercy said dully, wishing she hadn't taken seconds of the breakfast that Farrah had prepared.

'There was evidence of a break-in at Ginger's house,' Rafe said. 'A broken window. Her car was parked in Corwin's driveway – behind the wife's car, which was parked inside the garage. The wife couldn't have arrived home to find them in bed with each other. Plus the wife is a lefty, but was found with the pistol in her right hand. Lots of little things didn't add up. Ginger was in pajamas, and her own bed had been slept in. The sheriff's department didn't find any of Ginger's street clothes in Corwin's room, so she'd have had to leave her house wearing her pajamas with no coat.'

'So both Ginger and the store owner are dead,' Mercy murmured. 'After Ginger told us about DJ being the front man for Eden trading. And after her boss made a phone call as soon as we left the store. That's not suspicious at all.'

Rafe's nod was grim. 'That's the general consensus. Someone killed them so that they couldn't describe – or identify – DJ Belmont.'

'Ephraim?' Farrah asked. 'Did he do it?'

Rafe shrugged. 'It's possible. If so, he was really busy. He killed the couple for their camper at one twenty this morning. The bodies found in Corwin's bedroom were found at six thirty this morning by his brother-in-law, who had finished his shift at the medical center in Alturas. He and his sister have co-owned the house since their parents died ten years ago. When she married Corwin, they moved out, but had to move back after Christmas when money got tight. He said that things were tense between Corwin and his sister because of money, but that he'd never heard them fighting and his sister had never told him that she suspected her husband of having an affair, so finding the murder–suicide scene was a shock. The brother claimed to have spoken to his sister at one a.m., when she called to tell him she'd gotten home from her job safely, like she did every night. His cell phone record backs that up. The brother's been very cooperative with the local sheriff's department.'

'How do you know time of death of the honeymoon couple so exactly?' Mercy asked, trying to think like the professional she'd always prided herself on being. But it was easier to be clearheaded when you hadn't met the victim. When you hadn't asked the questions that led to her death, and the deaths of so many others.

'The bride wore an Apple Watch,' Rafe said. 'Her pulse was being constantly monitored and stored on her phone. It recorded the time that her heart rate went to zero.'

Mercy exhaled slowly. 'So Ephraim would have had to kill Ginger, Corwin, and his wife after killing the couple at the campground, because at least Corwin's wife was still alive when he was at the campground. How far is the campground from Snowbush?'

'Three hours.' Rafe nodded to Tom when he returned. 'I told them everything.'

'I figured you would.' Tom started the engine, then turned in his seat to frown at them. 'But that's not information I was supposed to tell you.'

Meaning, he could lose his job if they told anyone else.

'Then why did you?' Farrah asked.

Tom backed the van out of Rafe's driveway and headed down the street. The agent who'd been sitting out front when they'd emerged that morning was to follow them wherever they went. It had been Molina's demand and Mercy had been grateful for it.

'Whatever Ephraim does impacts the people in this vehicle,' Tom said. 'I consider you all as need-to-know. I would want to know, that's for damn sure.'

'We appreciate that,' André said. 'We would have been on alert, but now even more so.'

Mercy's mind was still churning through the information they weren't supposed to have. 'If Ephraim left the campground as soon as he killed the honeymoon couple, he'd have gotten to Snowbush at about four thirty. And if he broke into Ginger's house and took her from her bed, then staged a murder–suicide, he probably would have left Snowbush at five thirty. Or so,' she added with an awkward shrug, because everyone in the vehicle was staring at her. 'Which means he could be here by now.' Which put new terror in her heart. 'Of course, he could have been anyway if he left the campground and came straight here.' She swallowed hard. 'I guess I hoped you'd put him out of commission for a little while, Rafe.'

Because Rafe's shot had hit him. Mercy remembered the look of shock on Ephraim's face, the fury and pain immediately after.

Rafe took the other hand she still clenched in a fist and brought it to his lips, kissing her knuckles before tugging her fingers free and twining them with his own, just as Farrah had done. He placed their joined hands on Rory and started petting his fur.

'I'll aim higher the next time,' Rafe promised. 'I won't miss.'

Higher. Like between-Ephraim's-eyes higher. 'I hope it hurts him,' she whispered, but her mind went back to the situation in Snowbush. 'Ginger didn't remember Ephraim coming into the store. Only DJ. So if Ephraim did kill Ginger, Nick Corwin, and his wife, either Corwin called Ephraim directly or whoever Corwin called did. I'd assumed that was DJ, but now I don't know.'

André leaned around the front passenger seat so that he could see them. 'That was a fair assumption. But it's also true that whoever brought Ginger to that house left her car there. How did he get away afterward? It's possible that two people were involved, that one of them killed Ginger and the others and the other drove the getaway vehicle.'

'A very good point,' Tom said. 'If I pass it on to my boss, I'll have to take credit for it, though. Since . . . you know. Need-to-know and all that shit.'

André grinned. 'Take the credit, rookie. I consider it a fair trade.'

Everyone went quiet for a few minutes, and then, behind them, Liza sighed. 'Anyone want a bar? Because I eat when I'm nervous and I've already had three.'

'Pass 'em forward,' Tom said. 'But save a few for Gideon and Daisy. Agent Schumacher will pick them up from the radio station and then we'll all be on our merry way.'

Sacramento, California
Tuesday, 18 April, 10.30 A.M.

Jeff's mother dropped onto the sofa with a tired groan. 'I'm running on fumes, Jeffy. How are you still conscious?'

Jeff bounced on his toes before sitting beside her. 'I'm buzzed, Mom. That went so well.' And it had. The coordinator from the rape crisis center had really gone for his idea, and Daisy had passed it on to the local paper. They'd named it *Their Stories*, and they already had a few survivors who'd submitted videos to the coordinator.

Doing good felt . . . good. He desperately hoped that it actually helped someone.

'It did go well. I was very proud of you, son.' But his mother wasn't looking at him, her gaze instead riveted on the front window, outside of which the FBI agent was now driving away after making sure that the house was secure.

Jeff sighed. So far the FBI didn't believe that the man who'd killed Miss Romero had seen him, but they couldn't guarantee it. 'I'm sorry, Mom.'

She whipped around to frown at him. 'This is not your fault, Jeff. The article, yes. But you're making that as right as you can. This? Witnessing a murder? This is not your fault.'

'I know that. I do. But I hate that you're afraid.'

Her expression softened. 'I hate that you're involved, but here we are. How about something to eat? You want a sandwich?' She stood, covering her mouth to hide her yawn. 'Then I'm going to take a nap.'

Jeff knew he should have been tired, but he really was buzzed. 'Thanks, Mom. A sandwich sounds perfect. You want me to make them?'

She waved him off. 'I'm already up and it's better if my hands are busy.'

I'm lucky, he thought, watching as she disappeared into the kitchen. A lot of parents wouldn't have been so supportive, but his mother had always been his cheerleader.

That she was proud of him shouldn't mean so much. He was sixteen, after all. In college, even. But down deep he felt like a little kid and her pride meant everything.

He looked at his phone, clutched in his hand. He'd kept himself from checking his email after the retraction article went live. It hadn't even been an hour, after all. But he should check his blog followers and YouTube subscribers. It would suck if his numbers dropped before they could make use of them.

He opened his account, relieved to see that his retraction had been received well. Lots of comments. Most of them positive. Of course there were trolls, but there would always be trolls.

He swiped to see his email and smiled. Mrs Sokolov had sent him a message, filled with smiley face emojis. She was such a nice lady. He hoped that she and his mom could be friends. He replied to Irina Sokolov with his thanks, then noticed a new email.

The subject line read: *Mercy Callahan*. Hoping that it wasn't anything bad – anything new that was bad, anyway – he opened it, read it, then read it again.

'Mom?' he called, then got up to find her in the kitchen. 'I just got a weird email. It's from a lady in Reno who says she knows a man who claims to be Mercy's father. He wants to contact her.'

His mother frowned. 'That is weird. And suspicious. What if it's the man who tried to abduct her from the airport? The one who killed that poor old lady in New Orleans?'

Jeff read the email a third time. 'The email was written by an Edie Arthur and says the man's name is Amos Terrill. She gives a phone number that I can call to reach him.' Quickly he did a reverse lookup on his phone. 'It's a public library in Reno.'

His mother shook her head hard. She'd grown pale. 'Send it to the FBI, Jeffy. I don't want you in the middle.'

'Okay, Mom.' He forwarded the message to Special Agent in Charge Molina, then read the message again. 'I sent it to the FBI. But . . . what if it's real?'

She was still shaking her head. 'What if it is? You let that Molina woman take care of it.'

He was unsure. Something was pulling at him, the same thing that had told him there was a story in Mercy Callahan. He'd been right about that. Wrong about the story he'd told, but right to have pointed himself in her direction.

'I'm going to call Mrs Sokolov,' he said. 'Just in case. She can ask Mercy what she wants to do about it.'

His mother let out a slow breath. 'Okay. But only a phone call. You're not leaving this house.'

He kissed her cheek. 'Yes, ma'am.' He dialed the number for the Sokolov house, smiling when his call was answered by the same voice as the day before. 'Zoya? This is Jeff Bunker.'

'Hi, Jeff.' Her voice was warm and friendly. 'I read your retraction. It's good.'

He felt his cheeks heating. 'Thanks. It was the right thing to do. But I'm calling about something else. Is your mother home yet?'

'No, not yet. What's going on?'

He told her about the email. 'I sent it to Agent Molina, but thought . . . you know, what if it's real?'

'Did you say Amos?' she asked. 'And that he's in Reno?'

'Yes. Amos Terrill. And the number is the Reno library. Why?'

'Hold on. I'm going to add my mom to this call. She's in Reno right now with my sister Sasha.'

A moment later Irina Sokolov's voice was on the line. 'Read me the email, Jeff,' she said briskly, but not unkindly. 'Every single word.'

Twenty-four

Reno, Nevada
Tuesday, 18 April, 11.55 A.M.

'I really appreciate this, ma'am,' Amos said to Millie. Edie's friend had well and truly taken him under her wing.

She grinned at him over the stack of books and magazines she'd brought him to read. 'My pleasure. This is like a librarian's dream. I get to guide you through thirty years of history.'

He had to smile at her enthusiasm. 'I don't think I'll get through all these books today.' He didn't think he could get through them in a month. He'd never been the fastest reader, his limited skill even rustier after thirty years away from newspapers or even comic books. It was overwhelming indeed.

'Then come back tomorrow. I can hold them for you behind the desk, and when you get an address I can get you a library card.'

He wasn't sure which of her comments to reply to. By tomorrow he hoped to be talking to Mercy or Gideon. He could trust them. He hoped. And as for a permanent address, he had no idea where to start. 'Thank you,' was all he could think to say.

Her grin softened to a sympathetic smile. 'It's overwhelming, I know. But your little girl seems to be fitting in.'

Together they looked to the children's section, where one of the other librarians had just finished a story-time circle for pre-schoolers. Abigail had sat in the back row, her attention riveted until the librarian had closed the book with a dramatic 'The End'. Then Abigail had begged for 'One more'.

Delighted, the woman had read another story, then tasked

Abigail with reading to the children. His daughter was in her element, reading from *Ramona the Pest*, stopping to show the children the illustrations as the librarian had.

'She's taking her responsibilities very seriously,' Amos said, his chest near to bursting with pride.

'That she is,' Millie said fondly. She glanced at the computer screen, still open to the email account that Edie had set up. 'Still no reply?'

Amos shook his head. 'I'm beginning to think I won't get one. At least not today.'

Millie sighed. 'What will you do?'

'I don't know. I need to . . .' *Write that letter to the police. Tell them about DJ. Tell them to warn Mercy, to protect her.* He didn't want to write it here and he was so tired that it was becoming difficult to even think of the words that he should say. 'I guess I need to find a place to stay tonight.' *A safe place for them to sleep.* 'Can you point me to a low-cost hotel?'

'I'll run a search and print out a list of hotels in the area,' Millie said.

'Thank you, Millie. I need to provide some lunch for Abigail. When she's done reading this book, I'll take her out to the truck and let her eat, then I'll be back in to get the list.'

She hesitated. 'I have some fruit in my desk drawer. I always bring extra. Would you like an orange or an apple for you and Abigail?'

The memory of oranges tickled his taste buds, but he hated to take her food. 'It's fine. Thank you for offering.'

She gave him a look that he remembered from his grandmother, the one that said *I know what you're really thinking.* 'Come with me, Amos.'

Obediently he followed her, inhaling the delicious scent of oranges that filled the air the moment she opened the drawer. She put two oranges and two apples in his hands. 'Enjoy them.'

He brought the fruit to his nose and inhaled again, stunned when tears burned his eyes. He cleared his throat roughly. 'I'm so sorry. It's just . . . it's been a while. Apples we could get. Sometimes we

421

could grow them, but oranges . . . I haven't even smelled one in thirty years.'

Millie swallowed hard. 'I wish I'd brought more. If you'll come back tomorrow, I will.'

'You are very kind. Thank you.' He put the fruit in his pockets. 'I'll go get Abigail. I hope I can entice her from the books with an orange.'

Millie laughed, but it was shaky. 'She loves books. This is the perfect place for her to be.'

But where is the perfect place for me? Amos wondered.

Soberly, he crossed the library to where Abigail sat in a small chair, two smaller children at her feet, completely engrossed in the story she was reading aloud. She looked up at him, disappointment clouding her eyes. 'Do we need to go, Papa?'

'Just for a little while. We need to have some lunch.'

'I am hungry,' she admitted, then looked down at the smaller children. 'If you're here when I'm finished with my lunch, we can read some more.'

The mother of the children met Amos's eyes, her lips curving into a smile. 'Your daughter is a very good reader. My twins never sit still long enough for me to read to them. Girls, can you thank Abigail for reading to you?'

'Thank you,' the twins chorused.

Abigail smiled sweetly. 'You are welcome.' She skipped to a cart and set the book atop a pile. 'That's where Miss Millie said to put the books I'm finished with. I'm ready, Papa.'

He held out his hand, his heart settling when she took it without hesitation. It didn't matter what he did or where his place would be. As long as his daughter was safe and smiled at him, it would be all right. It would be perfect.

They turned for the door as it opened, two women entering. They were clearly related. Mother and daughter, probably. Both had blond hair and the same brown eyes. The older woman's hair was streaked with silver, but her step was energetic.

She and the younger woman walked straight to the desk. He wasn't intending to eavesdrop, but he heard the older woman say his name and he froze in his tracks.

Millie cast him an anxious glance. 'Amos? These ladies want to talk to you.'

The younger woman smiled, the kind of smile that was supposed to calm frayed nerves. 'We mean no harm. Did you email Jeff Bunker, sir?'

Amos stiffened. Reading his mood, Abigail stepped closer to his side, clutching his hand harder.

'Papa?' she whispered, and in that moment she was a scared seven-year-old again, the confident reader of *Ramona the Pest* gone like mist in the sunshine.

'I did.' Amos wanted to say more but had no idea which words would be the right ones.

The older woman stepped forward. 'Are you Amos Terrill?' she asked, her accent sounding vaguely familiar. Russian, maybe?

He pulled Abigail closer, so that she stood partially behind him. 'I am.'

The older woman smiled, the same smile that still brightened her daughter's face. 'My name is Irina Sokolov. This is my daughter Sasha.' She half bent, tilting her head toward Abigail. 'And who is this pretty girl?'

Abigail was trembling and Amos was tempted to swing her into his arms and bolt for the door, but then the woman's name sank in. 'Sokolov, you said?' He'd read that name an hour before. It was in the article about Ephraim's attempted abduction of Mercy from the airport. The attempt had been thwarted by an off-duty detective. Sokolov had been his name, too.

Straightening, the woman nodded. 'Irina Sokolov,' she repeated.

'Detective Raphael Sokolov. He is your son?' he pressed.

Her smile bloomed wider. 'He is. Do you know him?'

'I read about him. On the computer.' Amos gestured weakly to the computer table with the stack of books Millie had brought him to read. 'He rescued Mercy Callahan.'

Irina and her daughter shared a glance. 'He did,' Sasha said. 'I was there. It was . . . awful. Do you know Jeff Bunker?'

'I read his name as well. On the computer,' he added again. 'We thought he might be able to get a message to Mercy.'

Abigail tugged at his hand. 'Papa? Is it the same Mercy as in the picture?'

He looked down into her puzzled face. 'I hope so.'

'But Mercy died. Like my mama. You said so. You *said*.'

Oh. How was he going to explain this? 'I know I said so, because I thought so. But she might not have.' He looked to the Sokolov women. 'Did she? Is Mercy still alive?'

Please, God. Please let her say yes.

Irina's smile was radiant. 'Alive and well,' she said. 'I think we should talk.'

'I think that would be a good idea. I was about to take Abigail outside for some lunch. Perhaps you can sit with us?'

'There's a picnic table in the courtyard,' Millie offered. 'Around the back of the building.'

'Thank you, Millie,' Amos said. 'You've been so kind.'

She smiled at him, tears in her eyes again. 'I'm a sucker for a happy ending, Amos.'

He smiled back, his chest now tight with anticipation. These women knew Mercy. His Mercy. Who was not dead. Light-headed with relief, he followed the Sokolovs out of the library, Abigail clinging to his hand even harder.

When they were in the sunshine, the Sokolovs went ahead to the picnic table and Amos stopped, crouching until he was eye to eye with his child. 'You know how we hid in the woods last night?'

She nodded. 'I was scared, Papa.'

'I was too, but you were so brave. You did everything I said and made me so proud of you. What we did last night was dangerous.'

She nodded, her eyes looking old again. 'People aren't supposed to run away from home.'

He swallowed. *Because they get murdered when they try.* 'But I did and I took you with me. I had a good reason.'

Her face pinched. 'Because Mercy isn't really dead?'

'Partly, yes. Partly because I found out some things about Eden that weren't so nice. Weren't so safe. And I need for you to be safe, Abi-girl.'

She patted his cheek. 'I am. You keep me safe.'

Her utter surety weakened his knees and he fell forward, landing on those weak knees and drawing her into his arms. 'I love you, Abigail.'

She patted his back. 'I love you, Papa.' Then she patted his pockets. 'What is that?'

He laughed around the lump in his throat. 'Miss Millie gave me a treat for you. Let's find that picnic table so you can eat it.'

He rose, taking her hand. The Sokolov women had watched them and were visibly shaken. 'I think you must have a story to tell us, Mr Terrill,' Irina said. 'Come. You can tell us about your journey and we can tell you about Mercy.'

'And you can show them your pictures, Papa,' Abigail offered.

Amos's hand went to his shirt pocket where the Polaroids were safely tucked along with his grandfather's pocket watch. 'I can.'

Santa Rosa, California
Tuesday, 18 April, 1.25 P.M.

'A wire?' From her position in the van's middle seat, Mercy stared in disbelief at the microphone Tom Hunter held in his hand, the device disguised as a butterfly lapel pin. 'You want me to wear a wire? Like Ephraim's mother is John Gotti or something?'

Standing at the van's open door, Tom's mouth twitched up on one side. 'No, not like she's John Gotti. More like she might be the only one to know where Ephraim would hide. But yes, I want you to wear a wire. We can't go in there with you and we need to know what's said. This is a camera that will transmit both video and audio to my phone. I'll wait with Gideon and Rafe while Liza goes with you into Mrs Franklin's room.'

'For the record, I'm still against staying in the lobby,' Gideon grumbled. He'd left the vehicle that he and Daisy had ridden in, still visibly annoyed at being sidelined.

Rafe only scowled. He'd already made his objections known, but apparently Agent Molina was pulling the strings, even if she hadn't physically joined them.

Mercy could understand their point of view, but she also saw the extreme possible downsides. 'Sorry, Gideon, I have to agree with Molina on this one. If Ephraim – I mean Harry – told his mother that you stabbed his eye out after killing her other son? I think your presence might do more harm than good.'

Gideon nearly pouted. 'Yeah, but still.'

Mercy nearly smiled. 'Yeah, but still.' She turned to Rafe. 'And if I'm supposed to be Harry Franklin's worried wife, having you hovering over me looking all protective and alpha male won't look right, either.' She softened her words with a smile. 'But I wish you both could be there with me. I'm . . . nervous. What if I don't know what to say? What if she won't talk to me at all?'

Farrah squeezed her hand. 'You'll be fine. And if she doesn't talk to you, we're no worse off than we were before.'

It was what Mercy had been telling herself, but now that they were in the nursing home parking lot, she wasn't so sure.

She gave Rory an absent pet. 'I wish I could take you with me,' she murmured.

'Go ahead and take him,' André offered from the front passenger seat. 'Tell the staff that he's a comfort cat. Or at least that he comforts you. I'm sure they'd buy that this is a stressful visit for you.'

She looked up, amused. 'I don't think he'd go for a baby sling like Daisy wears to carry Brutus.'

'Then take him in the carrier.' Rafe picked it up from the floor and opened the latch. 'If anyone hassles you, tell them that the cat was the old lady's and you brought him to visit.'

'It's not a bad idea,' Liza said. 'Animals are often used in therapy with seniors, and this facility allows pets if they're supervised. I checked their website while we were on the road. I say go for it.'

'Does the cat get a wire?' Farrah asked with a smile. 'Because if so, it needs to be a magical medallion.'

'If the cat gets a wire, then I definitely should have one,' Liza said cheerfully. 'I think it's only fair.'

That Liza would be accompanying Mercy had been news to everyone – and neither Gideon nor Rafe had taken it well, but Mercy saw the wisdom. Liza worked with dementia patients every day. If

426

anything went sideways, hopefully Liza could pull the conversation back on course.

If there was any conversation to be had. The FBI had sent nurses in to talk to Mrs Franklin on three different occasions in the six weeks since they'd discovered Ephraim's true identity, but the woman had refused to talk to any of them. Mercy hoped the photo in her locket would be enough to spur the woman into talking with her.

Tom chuckled. 'The cat does not get a wire, but you do, Liza.' From his pocket, he drew a chain from which a pendant dangled. 'Also a camera, video and audio. I can toggle whose feed I'm watching at any given time. And you'll both wear earpieces, so I can communicate with you if needed. They're small and not visible unless someone sticks a scope in your ear. Which better not happen.'

'No scopes,' Liza repeated obediently. 'Is that a dragon camera? Because . . . cool.'

Mercy was aware that Liza was keeping it light on purpose, and she appreciated it.

Tom made a face. 'I'm glad at least one person here isn't mad at me.'

'I'm not mad,' Mercy said soberly. 'I'm just nervous. I have to remember to call him Harry, not Ephraim. And his brother is Aubrey, not Edward. What if Ephraim or DJ or even Pastor has an inside person in the home? I don't want to trip any alarms. The FBI has kept Eden out of the press until now. What if this brings it all to light and Molina loses the element of surprise? What if Ephraim feels cornered and . . .'

Rafe slid his hand around the back of her neck and pressed his lips to her temple. 'Stop. Stop borrowing trouble. You'll do your best. If we get nothing, then we'll regroup and come at it from a different angle. Finding Ephraim Burton does not rest entirely on your shoulders, Mercy.'

Gideon sighed. 'He's right. You have to let us take some of the responsibility. And Molina's prepared for whatever we do or do not find. But I doubt you talking to Mrs Franklin will expose Eden. It's not like anyone in the nursing home would know that her son's connected to a cult.'

Tom handed the butterfly lapel pin to Rafe. 'Put it on her, please? And pass this back to Liza? I need to run a quick test.' He waited until both Mercy and Liza wore their wires. 'Fine, talk among yourselves.'

'About what?' Mercy asked. 'Like "testing, one, two, three"?'

'How about we go over a few pointers about talking to patients with dementia?' Liza asked. She leaned over the seat, between Farrah and Mercy, her dragon pendant swinging a little before settling against her skin. 'First of all, call her by her name. Mrs Franklin or Belinda. Speak to her just as you would anyone else, but when she talks, you listen. She might not be able to communicate the way she wants to, and it might frustrate her. Let her speak and give her time and space to choose her words.'

'So don't finish her sentences,' Mercy said quietly.

Liza nodded. 'Exactly. I'll be there with you, and I'll step in to redirect if I need to, or if you look like you need a second to think, okay?'

Mercy was grateful. 'Yes, that's wonderful. I know that I'm Miriam.' That was the name inscribed on the locket, because that had been her given name in Eden. Fortunately there had been a lot of Miriams, so they'd allowed nicknames, like Midge or Mimi. Her own name had been an acceptable alternative. 'But who will you be?'

'I'm Beth, your friend,' Liza said. 'If she asks how we met, tell her it was in school. I'd be surprised if she pushes for more info, but if she does, I'll distract her.'

Farrah squeezed her hand again. 'You'll be wonderful, Mercy.'

Mercy just wanted it to be over. But it wouldn't be over until it got started. She straightened her shoulders and guided Rory into the cat carrier. 'I'm ready. Let's do this.'

When Mercy, Rafe, and Liza had exited the van, Tom turned to André. 'You should sit in the SUV with Agent Schumacher. She's keeping watch over the vehicles and will get you to safety if it becomes necessary.'

André patted the holster at his hip. Luckily, it was his left arm that Ephraim had stabbed, because he was right-handed. He might have still been in some pain, but he could still use his weapon. 'I'll also be keeping watch. But I am curious about something. Isn't she senior to you? Why isn't she going in with them?'

Mercy stilled, waiting for his answer, because she'd wondered the same thing.

Tom gave Gideon and Rafe a rueful look. 'She is senior, but my boss thinks that I have a good relationship with these guys and have a better chance of keeping them in line.'

Rafe snorted. 'Seriously?'

But Gideon just shook his head. 'It's fair,' he admitted. 'Thanks, Tom. I have a feeling you helped grease the skids with Molina, or we wouldn't even be here with Mercy.'

Mercy could see the hint of heat in Tom's cheeks. 'Thank you, Tom,' she said quietly.

Tom looked embarrassed. 'Your brother's helped mentor me these past months and Rafe's mom gave me cake. It was the least I could do.' He gave a final check to the cameras Mercy and Liza wore. 'It's showtime.'

Santa Rosa, California
Tuesday, 18 April, 1.45 P.M.

Rafe, Gideon, and Hunter didn't end up sitting in the lobby but were shown to an office instead. Which was a bit of a relief, because no one had seen them come in except for the woman behind the front desk, who was not the same woman Rafe had seen when he'd been here before.

The woman who'd met them at the front door now closed the office door behind them and smoothed her nurse's scrubs, briefly revealing the outline of a holster. 'Agent Hunter, Agent Reynolds, it's nice to meet you. Agent Molina speaks highly of you both.'

Hunter shook her hand. 'Thank you and likewise. You're Agent Simpson?'

'I am. The management here has been very cooperative. They've allowed us to use this office while you're here. Please have a seat, gentlemen.'

'Thank you,' Gideon said quietly as the three of them sat in the chairs in front of the large desk. He was pale and fidgety, and Rafe would have been glad that they didn't have to sit in a waiting room for that reason alone.

Gideon might have been decent at undercover work, but only if he wasn't related to someone involved. Rafe was having a similar problem. He hadn't lied to Mercy when he said he wouldn't miss the next time he got Ephraim Burton in his sights. The motherfucker was going down.

'Detective Sokolov?'

Rafe turned to Hunter, who had a concerned look on his face. 'Yes, Agent Hunter?'

'I was attempting to introduce you to Agent Simpson. She's the lead on this operation today.'

Rafe shook her hand. 'Thank you for not making us sit in the lobby.'

Simpson gave him a smile that managed to be both sharp and sympathetic. 'This is not the optimal situation, Detective. If I had my way, you'd all be outside in the van, but Agent Hunter convinced his supervisor that you'd conduct yourselves professionally. This office is my best compromise. You'll be able to monitor what's happening in the patient's room via the wire feed. In exchange, I need your word that you will stay in this room. The woman managing the front desk is also one of ours, as is one of the nursing aides in the room next to Mrs Franklin's.'

More than a little annoyed, Rafe wanted to snarl at her, but he controlled himself. A glance at Gideon showed his best friend in a similar mood. Rafe gave him a nod. 'Mercy will be all right, Gid.'

'Of course she will,' Simpson said briskly. 'There's coffee in the pot and bottled water in the mini fridge. Please help yourselves, gentlemen.' She took the seat behind the desk and folded her hands. 'We have made progress on tracking the payments for Mrs Franklin's care. The funds come from a bank here in Santa Rosa. The name on the account is Eustace Carmelo.'

'The name on the ID that Burton used to board the flight to New Orleans,' Rafe said quietly. 'The names are those of two of his sons. Mercy said that Pastor gave Burton the ID and that Burton was unhappy about it. Something about the names meaning "fruitful".'

Simpson considered this. 'Well, at least they're consistent. The funds transferred into the account come from a company called Frutuoso. That's Portuguese for "fruitful". The business has an agricultural classification. Its main products are olive oil and pomegranate juice.'

Gideon huffed. 'Olives and pomegranates? Really?'

'I'm missing something,' Hunter said. 'Explain?'

'The olive tree is part of Eden's symbol,' Gideon said. 'It's thought by some religious scholars to have been the Tree of Life in the Garden of Eden. Eden taught this to us as children. They also taught us that the fruit of the Tree of Knowledge – the forbidden fruit that Adam and Eve ate – was a pomegranate, but the original texts never specify the kind of fruit. The Hebrew just says "*pri*", which simply means "fruit". Pomegranates are still a popular theory among Jewish scholars, although I'm pretty sure that Eden's founders were neither religious scholars nor linguists.'

'Which you are,' Simpson said. 'A linguist, I mean. Molina said you're part of the chatter unit.'

'That's what I do,' Gideon confirmed. 'It's predominantly drug gang chatter these days. At any rate, that they'd list olive oil and pomegranate juice as their products is at least suggestive of a tie to Eden. Where does Frutuoso's money come from?'

'That's what we're still trying to figure out,' Simpson admitted. 'It appears to be coming from offshore accounts, so that makes it harder to track.'

Hunter held up his hand. 'They're in.' He turned up the volume on his phone and Rafe and Gideon crowded around to see his screen.

'That's Mrs Franklin,' Simpson said softly, indicating the elderly woman sitting in a chair by the window. 'She's seventy-six years old. The doctor here on staff thinks she is capable of speaking far more than she does, but her personal doctor doesn't agree. If he knew Miss Callahan was here, he'd probably object, but we don't legally have to inform him.'

'Hi, Belinda,' a woman's voice said cheerfully. 'I brought you some visitors.'

'That's the nurse's aide assigned to Belinda Franklin,' Simpson supplied. 'She's not ours, but she passes all of our background checks. No indication of being on the take.'

So the FBI also thought that Eden might have someone embedded here, Rafe thought. Mercy had been right to worry about that.

'Go away,' Belinda said flatly but clearly.

The picture jumped a bit, then lowered. Mercy had pulled up a chair. 'Hi, Mrs Franklin,' she said quietly. 'I'll go in a minute, but I was hoping you could help me. My name is Miriam. I'm married to your son Harry.'

Rafe could hear Gideon grinding his teeth. Rafe, on the other hand, was clenching his.

'She is not nor has she ever been married to that bastard,' Gideon growled.

Rafe reached over to grip Gideon's knee. 'She's doing okay, Gid. Let her do this, okay? She needs to try.'

Gideon nodded, but his throat worked convulsively as he tried to swallow.

Rafe had thought about how hard this would be for Mercy, but he hadn't considered the impact on Gideon. *I should have.* He moved his hand to the back of Gideon's neck, holding on tight. Anchoring his best friend the best way he knew how.

Belinda Franklin turned to look at Mercy, her movements slow and so deliberate that a shiver raced down Rafe's spine. The old woman's eyes were as flat as her voice. Lifeless. His instincts screamed at him to get Mercy out of there, but he stayed where he was and watched his woman at work.

His woman. *Yes. Mine.*

'You lie,' Belinda said with quiet viciousness.

'No, I don't. I can prove it to you.' The picture jumped again, and then Mercy was holding the box in which she kept her locket. She opened it, dangling the locket in front of Belinda's face, like a hypnotist. 'Your son gave this to me the day that we were married.'

Rafe exhaled carefully. The chain from which the locket dangled wasn't delicate or pretty. It was thick, like one used to lock up bicycles. Or women. All of the women in Eden wore lockets like these. The chains were welded together, so that the women could never take them off.

'You lie,' Belinda repeated, but her dead gaze was fixed on the swinging locket.

'No, I don't,' Mercy repeated. Holding the locket in her palm, she pressed the locket's engraved symbol so quickly that Rafe wouldn't have known what she was doing if he hadn't seen another locket opened the same way. The other one had belonged to Eileen, who'd also escaped Eden and Ephraim, only to die later.

Mercy held the open locket up so that the camera on her lapel caught the image of the photo inside. 'This is Harry and me. This was our wedding day.'

Gideon made a pained sound and looked away.

Rafe made himself look, though. He owed this much to Mercy. If he wanted to share her life, he needed to share this pain. Because he was certain that Mercy didn't need to look at the photo to remember. The images of her wedding to Ephraim were indelibly stamped in her memory.

God, she was young. So young. Only twelve, her face still round and sweet and childish. But her eyes were haunted. Terrified. And even though the photo was grainy and small, he could tell that she'd been crying before it had been taken.

Ephraim, on the other hand, was smiling triumphantly. He wore the same eye patch that he'd worn in his wedding photo with Eileen, but the eye that was visible gleamed with malicious delight.

Then the image blurred and Rafe blinked. And realized he was crying.

Oh God, Mercy. I'm so sorry he hurt you.

A box of tissues came sliding across the desk. Rafe gave Agent Simpson a grateful nod.

None of them said a word, because Mercy was speaking.

'This is your son, isn't he?' she asked. 'I hope so, because you're my last hope. I need to find him. He's been missing for a month now, and I'm worried sick. I can't sleep or eat or . . .'

Belinda Franklin reached for the locket. 'My son,' she said thickly.

'Yes. Your son.'

'You're his wife.'

'Yes. I am.'

Belinda looked away from Mercy's camera. 'Who's she?'

'That's Beth, one of my friends. She's helping me find Harry. Like I said, I've been worried sick. I haven't slept in weeks and she didn't think I was safe to drive. She's been nice enough to help me search. She found you here. We . . . we went to your old house, but it was sold.'

Hunter turned to them. 'How did she know that?'

Rafe met his gaze directly. 'From me. I've been working the case on my own.'

Hunter's lips quirked up. 'Of course you have. Wouldn't have expected anything different.'

Belinda looked down at Mercy's feet, drawing their attention back to the phone screen. 'And that?'

'That's Rory,' Mercy said, and there was a smile in her voice. 'My cat. Harry gave him to me. Rory's a comfort to me, especially with Harry gone missing. Beth thought I should bring him, just in case you can't help me find him. I'm . . . well, I'm at the end of my rope.'

Belinda nodded once, then turned to stare out the window. 'I don't know where he is.'

'Oh.' Mercy blew out a breath, and then the picture moved again, settling out as she lifted the cat from his carrier and onto her lap. 'I was afraid of that.'

A few beats of silence passed, and then Liza spoke up, off camera. 'It must have been hard to leave your house behind. It looked like a real nice place. But this is really nice, too. I love your view. Harry said that you seemed happy here. That he takes you for walks when he visits you.'

'What's she saying?' Gideon asked harshly.

'There's a picture of Mrs Franklin in a wheelchair sitting next to one of the benches outside,' Simpson said, a smile playing on her lips. 'There's a man on the bench. You can't see the man's face, but he has his arm around her shoulders. It's a good guess. Hunter, your lady friend is on the ball.'

'Yes, she is,' Hunter murmured.

'He's a good boy,' Belinda said sullenly. 'When he visits.'

'When was the last time you saw him?' Mercy asked, still playing her part well.

'Dunno,' was Belinda's reply.

'It's important,' Mercy pleaded softly. 'I think something awful happened to him. He's never been missing for this long.'

The old woman was quiet again, then asked, 'You got kids?'

Mercy's hands, visible from the camera angle, clenched in Rory's fur. 'No. I'm . . . we . . . No. I wasn't blessed with children.'

Rafe remembered her tortured words from the graveyard the day before. She'd been so scared he'd impregnate her, that she'd live, that she'd bring a child into Eden, a child that Ephraim would own.

I wasn't blessed with children. Rafe wondered how hard those words had been for her to say, with such sad conviction. Mercy Callahan was the strongest woman he'd ever known.

The old woman sighed. 'I have two sons. Two boys. Good boys.' It was as if Belinda had drifted a bit, and was now swaying as she spoke with an odd cadence. 'Good boys.'

'Harry and Aubrey,' Mercy said. 'They are good boys.'

'Were.' Belinda began to rock herself. 'Aubrey . . . he's gone. My boy is gone.'

'I know,' Mercy said, reaching out to touch the woman's arm. Just a light touch, brief, then she was back to stroking the cat's fur. 'It was terrible.'

Belinda stopped rocking, turning haunted eyes on Mercy. 'My Aubrey is gone.'

In a move that surprised a gasp out of Mercy, the cat jumped from her lap to Belinda's. Mercy started to reach for the animal, then curled her fingers into light fists and placed them on her own knees. The cat lightly head-butted Belinda's hands, and the old woman began petting him, still rocking.

The locket she'd been holding slipped to the floor and Mercy rescued it, sliding it into her pocket.

'My Aubrey is gone, but I didn't use the key,' Belinda said quietly.

What key? But Rafe didn't ask. None of them did. They waited for Mercy and leaned closer to Hunter's phone.

'What key?' Mercy asked, but Belinda wasn't listening any longer.

'Didn't use the key,' she muttered. 'Didn't use the key.' Her gnarled fingers petted the cat's fur. 'My Aubrey is gone, but I didn't use the key.'

'But your other son is still alive.' Mercy reached out again, her touch now firm as she squeezed the old woman's arm. 'I think he needs help. I need to find him. Tell me where to find him.'

Belinda was looking straight ahead, her eyes unfocused. 'Two leave on foot,' she mumbled.

Mercy's indrawn breath was audible. 'Two leave on foot, one strong and one bold,' she whispered.

Belinda startled, then froze before turning her head again, slowly. Her eyes were focused now, and harder than glass. 'What did you say?'

'Two leave on foot, one strong and one bold,' Mercy repeated, louder this time.

Belinda stared at her and said nothing.

Mercy cleared her throat, but instead of speaking, she began to sing, her voice shaky and slightly off-key. '*The sun on the mountain turns everything gold.*' The tune was familiar, but Rafe couldn't place it. '*But night comes too swiftly, takes one in its hold.*'

Exhaling on a shudder, Belinda sang the final line with Mercy. '*And when the sun rises, only one will grow old.*'

'What is that song?' Hunter asked Gideon.

Gideon shook his head. 'The melody is an old hymn we used to sing in Eden, but I've never heard these words.'

Belinda was watching Mercy with an odd light in her cold eyes. 'You do know him.'

'Yes, ma'am. I do. I'm his wife.'

'You know his song. He wrote it. For Aubrey.'

Hunter tapped his screen, changing to Liza's camera. Now they could see both Belinda and Mercy. Mercy had grown pale, her hands trembling.

'He sang it to me,' Mercy said softly. 'When I couldn't sleep.'

Belinda stared at Mercy for a moment that seemed to stretch forever, and then she nodded. 'My chest. Over there.'

Liza was in motion, the camera bouncing a little. 'This chest?' It was small, made of wood, and resembled a small treasure chest.

The lid was inlaid with bone. 'Amos made that,' Rafe said, and Gideon nodded his agreement.

'That's the only one,' Belinda snapped.

'It's a very pretty treasure chest,' Liza said, then swapped the cat for the chest, the camera bouncing once again as she crouched to put Rory back in his carrier. 'Was it a gift from Harry?'

'It was.' Belinda smiled faintly as she rubbed the inlaid lid with her fingertips. 'He made it for me with his own hands.' She lifted the lid and a tinny melody filled the space, sending a new shiver down Rafe's spine. It was the same melody Mercy had sung with the words of 'his song'. Belinda drew a tray from the chest, then pulled out a key and held it up to the light from the window.

Excitement bubbled up as they watched the screen of Hunter's phone. 'That looks like a safe-deposit box key,' Gideon said.

Belinda was still looking at the key in the sunlight. 'I didn't use the key.'

'Then I will,' Mercy said.

Belinda looked up sharply. 'Why?'

Mercy didn't flinch. 'Because it might help me find him.'

Belinda seemed to be thinking about that, and Rafe held his breath while the old woman made her decision. Safe-deposit box keys were often significant. 'You'll tell him to come see me when you find him?'

'Of course,' Mercy assured her. 'I promise.'

'Then I guess it's okay.' She extended the key to Mercy, who took it with a quiet thank-you, slipping it into her pocket. 'It's only to be used in an *emergency*,' Belinda added.

'Harry's been missing for several weeks,' Mercy said. 'I think this is an emergency.'

Belinda tilted her head, studying Mercy. 'Do you have any kids?'

Blinking, Mercy opened her mouth, but Liza cut in. 'Not yet,' Liza said warmly. 'But she loves children, don't you, Miriam?'

Mercy nodded. 'I do.'

'I want grandkids,' Belinda said. 'Aubrey keeps saying he'll give me some. Harry promised too, but Harry's too young. He's just a boy himself.' She shook her head. 'And Aubrey says he hasn't found the right girl, that he's not ready to settle down.' She sighed. 'They need to grow up, my boys. Maybe one will settle down with a nice girl. You'd like them. Both of you girls. Maybe I'll have you over for dinner, to introduce you.'

Mercy looked startled at the shift. It was as if the woman had shut down in the present and returned to the past. Probably where everything was more comfortable.

'We'll tell Harry that it's time to grow up,' Liza said. 'When we see him.'

'And Aubrey,' Belinda countered. 'They're good boys.'

'Yes, they are,' Mercy said, her smile forced. 'I think it's time for you to rest, Mrs Franklin.'

Belinda nodded, the movement rocking her whole body. She closed her eyes, still clutching the chest with misshapen fingers.

'I'll just put the chest away for you,' Liza said softly. 'Unless you'd like us to give it to Harry?'

Belinda smiled, her eyes closed. 'He's a good boy.'

'Yes, ma'am,' Liza said. She opened the chest, but it was empty, so she left it on Belinda's nightstand. Toying with the pendant she wore, she looked down at it briefly, one brow raised.

'Oh shoot. I forgot.' Hunter picked up a small hand radio. 'Leave it for now.'

Liza let her pendant swing back to her skin. 'Thank you, Belinda.'

But Belinda was already asleep, snoring softly.

Mercy stood, visibly shaken. Liza took the cat carrier, then looped her arm through Mercy's, turning them toward the door. Her camera showed the hall as they made their way back to the front entrance.

438

Rafe stood, eager to get to Mercy, who looked like she would topple over at any moment. They could still hear Liza's calm encouragements. 'One foot in front of the other,' Liza murmured. 'You're almost there. See? There's the front door.'

Which had just opened to reveal an older man wearing a suit and a scowl.

'Oh shit.' Agent Simpson was out of her chair, running for her door. 'Belinda Franklin's doctor just walked in. We do not want him to know that Mercy was with Belinda. He's already threatened to sue the facility if anyone else is admitted without his permission, even though he does not have the authority to approve her visitors.'

Hunter grabbed the radio. 'Liza, get her out of the hall. Pull her into a room, the first one you come to.'

To Liza's credit, she instantly did as she was told, the camera showing a door open, then close.

'Can I help you?' an old man asked, his voice quavering.

'My friend is about to faint,' Liza improvised. 'Can she sit down for a moment?'

'Of course,' the man said. 'Does she need some water? I have a pitcher right here.'

'I don't think so,' Liza said, lowering Mercy into a chair, 'but thank you.'

'Yes, thank you,' Mercy gasped. 'Thank you. Just . . . a long day, you know?'

'And seeing someone you love in here is often harder than you think it will be,' he said kindly.

'That's the truth,' Mercy said weakly. 'I'm so sorry to barge in here.'

'That's perfectly okay. I don't get much company, especially pretty girls like you two.'

Liza stood at Mercy's side, so that the camera she wore around her neck captured Mercy's profile. Mercy was smiling at the man, who wasn't visible in the frame. 'You're a charmer, aren't you?'

The man chuckled. 'A little out of practice, but I ain't dead yet.'

'Always a good day when you can say that,' Mercy said.

The door to the room opened and they could hear Agent Simpson say, 'Oh, there you are. Your friends are waiting for you. I'll show you the way out.'

'Take care,' the man called.

'You too,' Mercy called back.

Then the two women were running after Simpson. Rafe was out of the office like a shot, Gideon on his heels, while Tom radioed Agent Schumacher that they were on their way out and to prepare to leave quickly. They caught up to Mercy and Liza at the van. Liza was already in the back and André was helping a visibly shaken Mercy into the middle seat.

'What happened?' Farrah demanded from the other side of Mercy.

'We'll tell you when we're on the road,' Hunter replied, throwing himself behind the wheel and starting the van. 'Just go to the other car, Gideon. Agent Schumacher and I will coordinate a meet when we're away from here.'

Gideon ran to the other FBI vehicle, and twenty seconds later, they were headed out of the parking lot.

The van was silent for a long moment, and then Mercy laughed, the sound slightly manic. 'Oh my God. Oh my God.' She pressed the heel of her hand to her chest, then patted the cat carrier on her lap. 'Sorry, Rory. That was intense. I hope you don't throw up.'

'Same here,' Liza grumbled. 'I feel like I did when we rode the Goliath coaster six times straight at Six Flags.'

'That one ended poorly,' Tom said. 'Told you to stop after the fifth time.'

Liza fanned herself, panting. 'Holy shit. What happened in there? Everything was fine, then we were ducking into the nearest foxhole.'

'Belinda Franklin's doctor came in,' Rafe told her. 'He doesn't like her to have visitors and thinks her dementia's a lot further along than Agent Simpson does.'

'Agent Simpson was the woman who grabbed us at the end, I assume?' Liza asked.

'Yes,' Rafe said. 'But, Hunter? We need to check out that doctor. Remember we were talking about Ephraim's glass eye? How a surgeon needed to do it? What if that guy was the doctor who did it?'

'You're right,' Hunter said grimly.

'I saw him enter,' André said. 'He looked angry. I wrote down license plate numbers for every vehicle that entered the lot after you guys went inside, so we have the doctor's.'

'Thanks,' Tom said. 'Can you text it to me? Once my adrenaline crashes, I might not remember.'

'Of course,' André said, then looked over his shoulder, concerned. 'Are you okay, Mercy?'

Farrah cradled Mercy's cheek in her palm. 'You're shaking like a leaf.'

'I'm great, actually.' She lifted her chin. 'I didn't flake out. Not a single zombie moment.'

Rafe slid his arm around her shoulders and pulled her close. 'You were amazing. And when you and Belinda sang that song . . . What was that? Did Ephraim really sing it to you?'

Mercy closed her eyes tight, her trembling growing to full-body shaking. 'No. He sang it to his cows. I heard him sometimes.'

'Because your house was close to the barn,' Rafe remembered. 'He took care of the animals.'

'Right. He was so nice to those cows.' She'd sobered now, her teeth chattering. 'One time one of his wives said that she wished he was that nice to us and he threw a hammer at her head.'

Rafe knew he shouldn't be surprised, but every new revelation was like a punch to his gut.

'What happened to her?' Farrah asked, taking Mercy's hand in hers.

'She . . .' Mercy began to hyperventilate. 'She died. Oh my God, Farrah, she died. My mother and I tried to take care of her, but she died.' A sob broke loose and it was like the dam had broken. 'Ephraim told everyone she'd fallen down, then told us if we didn't lie for him that he'd do the same to us. So we did. We lied for him.' Her voice broke. 'We lied to save ourselves. What does that make me?'

'It makes you alive,' Farrah said fiercely.

Rafe had to take a moment to quell his rage so that he could be gentle. Sharing a quick glance with André, he could tell that Farrah's captain was also trying to control his fury. *I'm glad Gideon isn't hearing this.* His friend had barely made it through the minutes Mercy had forced herself to talk to Belinda Franklin. Rafe understood because he'd shared Gideon's anguish. Now, hearing her broken-hearted weeping, he was at the limit of his restraint again. But he needed to keep it together. For her.

Once he felt the return of his control, Rafe pulled Mercy onto his lap, ignoring the seat belts as he held her tight. 'Farrah's right,' he murmured. 'It makes you alive to take him down now. You're going to take him down and we're going to help you. You aren't alone.' He stroked her hair, his own eyes burning. He kissed her temple. 'You were wonderful in there, but it had to be hard to pretend like that.'

'I wanted to hurt her,' Mercy cried, curling her fingers into his shirt and digging into his skin. 'I wanted to hit her and hit her. She raised him. She said he was a good boy. *A good boy.* He wasn't. He was a brute. A monster. And he still is. He's still killing people and he's getting away with it.'

Farrah was crying now, patting Mercy's knee helplessly. 'He won't. He can't.'

Rafe's heart was breaking. 'He won't get away with it, Mercy. I promise.'

Mercy said no more, just pressed her cheek into his chest and held on. And cried herself to sleep.

Twenty-five

Granite Bay, California
Tuesday, 18 April, 4.35 P.M.

Ephraim checked the photo on his phone once again, disappointed. Zoya Sokolov hadn't exited the school along with the other students, and he'd waited for an hour after the final bell. He'd examined the faces of every student who'd walked in or out of the doors all day long, the binoculars he'd purchased with Sean MacGuire's credit card coming in handy as he'd parked far enough away to avoid detection.

Now a custodian was sweeping the front walk, keeping the exterior of the fancy school acceptably clean for all the rich kids who'd laughed their way from the school to the parking lot, which was like an advertisement for luxury cars. Some of the students had been picked up, some had driven themselves, but every one of the vehicles cost more than most people made in a year.

The Jeep he'd taken from the honeymooners didn't fit in this neighborhood. He'd detached the camper, leaving it in the state park nearby, or he would have been even more obviously out of place. At least he'd washed the *Just Married* decorations off the Jeep's windows, but the vehicle was too old for this fancy area.

He frowned, because the law would be searching for the Jeep once the honeymooners' bodies were found. They hadn't been found yet – he'd been listening to the news all day and there'd been no mention of two dead bodies turning up at a campground. Still, he'd need a replacement vehicle soon, but that wouldn't be a problem after he got access to Eden's offshore accounts. He'd be able to buy a fleet of fancy cars if he wanted.

Of course, to get the money he had to first get Mercy, and he was no closer to that goal than he'd been the day before.

He blew out a breath in frustration. The Sokolov kid hadn't come to school today, and Ephraim was pretty certain that it was because Detective Sokolov was being careful with his family. Sokolov could keep his sister out of school for the foreseeable future, so Ephraim would need to find another way to lure Mercy's detective away from her side.

He couldn't wait them all out much longer. He'd left DJ to whisper in Pastor's ear for too long already –

A knock on the window of the honeymooners' Jeep had him dropping the binoculars and twisting toward the noise, earning him a bruise when the steering wheel jabbed into his side.

Fuck. Fucking hell. It was a cop. And he'd drawn his gun.

Ephraim didn't stop to think. Didn't stop to plan. Simply drew his own gun, shot at the cop through the window, and drove away like a bat out of hell.

So much for staying under the radar, he thought grimly. He might as well take out a skywriting ad now. *Hey, Mercy, I'm back. Run and hide so that I can never find you.*

But Mercy Callahan was not his biggest worry at the moment. He'd shot a fucking cop. They'd be looking for him. He circled the fancy private school, heading around to the back. The custodian had parked his truck in the back, so that was where he headed.

Leaving the Jeep behind, he was in the truck and had it hot-wired in under a minute. Stealing so many cars recently had sharpened his skills again. The truck was old, but it started. It was a far cry from the luxury vehicles the rich kids had been driving, but it would do for now.

Granite Bay, California
Tuesday, 18 April, 6.15 P.M.

'Mercy, wake up.' Rafe jostled her shoulder. 'Time to wake up.'

Mercy didn't want to wake up. She was warm and Rafe's arms

were around her. But she immediately knew that they weren't in his bed. They were still in the FBI van and she was on his lap and . . . oh God. She'd had another meltdown, hadn't she? 'My head hurts.'

Rafe kissed her forehead. 'I'd be surprised if it didn't. I bet my mom can fix you right up, though. So get up. We can't sit in the van, even in the garage. It's too dangerous.'

Mercy slid from his lap, trying to blink away the haze left over from what had been an epic crying jag. Farrah and the others must have already gone inside, because it was just the two of them in the van.

Rafe climbed out, unable to hide a grimace of pain. 'It wasn't you,' he said when she opened her mouth to apologize. 'I would have held you for twice as long. It's not the sitting. It's the getting up.' He extended his hand. 'Come on. We need to get inside.'

Mercy hurried, getting a glimpse of the street in front of the Sokolovs' house as the garage door was rolling down. 'Who's here?' There were two more SUVs parked on the street in front of the Sokolovs' house, both of them black.

'They're bodyguards,' Farrah said from the doorway into the laundry room. She looked exhausted and held Rory's cat carrier in her arms.

Rafe urged her forward. 'We can explain inside.'

Mercy stopped once they were in the laundry room and Rafe had closed the door into the garage. 'What happened? What's Ephraim done now?'

Rafe sighed. 'Shot a cop. While he was parked a block away from Zoya's school.'

Mercy had to grab onto the washing machine to keep from crumpling to the floor. 'He was going after Zoya? Why?'

'Probably trying to lure me out,' Rafe said bitterly. 'What an asshole. I'm glad she listened when I asked her to stay home today.' He pointed an index finger at Mercy. 'And don't you think this is your fault, either.'

Mercy shook her head. Of course she thought it was her fault. *It is my fault.*

'Come have some tea, Mercy,' Farrah said.

445

Irina appeared, putting her arm around Farrah's shoulders, her smile brittle. 'I have the kettle heating. Sit down and let me feed you. Zoya is fine. She's in the office with Meg.'

Meg, another of Irina's daughters, was a deputy sheriff and had probably raced over here as soon as she'd heard that Zoya had been a target.

Poor Irina. The normally centered woman was wound as tight as a drum. And who could blame her? *Not me. Of course, Irina might blame me, and she'd be right to do so.*

How many more of Irina's family would be hurt because of Mercy's presence in their lives?

Silently, they joined Gideon, Daisy, André, and Liza, who were already sitting with Karl at the table, which was overflowing with food, a testament to Irina's level of stress. The tension was thick as Irina served them and became thicker with each moment that the eight of them ate without speaking, because even Karl was silent. There was a grim determination to the meal, like they all felt that the other shoe was poised to drop.

So it's not just me.

Mercy had noticed right away that Tom hadn't joined them, but figured he was talking with the new bodyguards. Mercy had also noticed that the sink was full of dishes. The sight almost made her smile, despite the dread curling around her gut. Irina had probably fed all of the agents outside.

Irina Sokolov was so much like Farrah's mother, Mercy felt at home. *If you stayed, you could be home.*

If I stayed? The thought tantalized, even as it terrified her. She had family in New Orleans – her half brothers and sisters and the Romeros. She had a job that she really loved.

But Rafe is here. And Gideon. And Irina had welcomed her with open arms.

Unless Ephraim continued hurting the Sokolov family. He'd already shot Sasha, tried to shoot Rafe, and tried to abduct Zoya. *Irina might be rethinking that welcome right now.*

Well, shit. Mercy dropped her eyes to her plate, unable to eat another bite. She'd brought trouble into this household. No, she hadn't done anything to cause the trouble. *Except that I survived.* She couldn't be sorry for that, no matter how much Irina might be blaming her.

My mother sacrificed her life so that I could survive. It was the thought that had kept Mercy going every time she'd wanted to give up.

Finally André broke the silence, making Mercy want to kiss him. 'Irina, that was delicious. My mother would love the recipe.' He smiled at Irina, who'd only sipped at a cup of tea while the rest of them ate their fill. 'She'd trade recipes with you, of course, and she is an excellent cook.'

Farrah gave André a look of clear appreciation, because Irina seemed to relax a fraction. 'She really is an amazing cook, Irina. She's been teaching me.' She rolled her eyes. 'You know, so her baby boy doesn't starve.'

Irina chuckled. 'We can't have that, can we?' She put down her cup and sighed. 'Mercy, we need to have a talk.'

Mercy straightened her spine and exhaled slowly, fighting the burn of tears in her eyes. She'd cried more in the last four days than she had in the last four years. 'I figured as much. I can . . .' What? Leave? To go where? 'I'll, um, find another place. As soon as I can.'

There was a beat of silence, then Rafe shoved his plate away. 'What the hell?' he snarled. 'No, you will not find another place. Mom, what's this about? You're scaring her.'

'Don't talk to your mother that way,' Karl warned. 'Everyone take a breath and relax.'

Irina was frowning at Mercy, then covered her mouth with her hand as understanding seemed to dawn. 'Oh no. No, Mercy. I'm so sorry. I never thought . . . But I should have. Of course I should have.' Muttering in Russian, she got up from her chair to crouch next to Mercy's chair. 'I am so sorry, *lubimaya.* You think I'm upset with you. I'm not.' She took Mercy's hand and squeezed. 'We have some guests. I don't want you caught unaware, but I'm not sure how to prepare you.'

Mercy shuddered, too relieved for words. *Not upset with me.* And the other words sank in and she tensed all over again. *Prepare me?*

Rafe took Mercy's other hand. 'Who's here?'

Irina seemed to brace herself. 'Jeff Bunker, for starters.'

Mercy could only stare at her. 'The kid reporter?'

Behind her, Rafe growled quietly. 'Jeff Bunker is here? Why?'

'Because he did a good thing,' Irina snapped. 'Drop your bad attitude, Raphael. I've no patience for it at the moment. It's been an eventful day.'

'That's for sure,' Mercy muttered. 'But Zoya *is* all right? You said she was fine.'

'She *is* fine,' Irina assured her. 'The officer who got shot is not so much. He will live, though, so we must be grateful. He saw a Jeep down the road from Zoya's school and recognized the license plate as the Jeep stolen from the honeymoon couple at the campground in Nevada. He called it in but ignored commands to wait for backup.'

'Young and stupid,' Rafe said with a scowl. 'It's a wonder rookies survive their first year.'

'That's the damn truth,' André agreed.

Irina sighed. 'So we have . . . protection. And company.'

'Miss Callahan?'

Mercy turned in her chair to find Agent Molina standing in the kitchen doorway. But she wasn't alone. A man stood beside her, a small girl in front of him. His hands were on the girl's shoulders, his face wary and afraid. But also alive. His eyes were alive.

And fixed on Mercy.

'Oh my God,' Mercy breathed, coming to her feet like she was in a dream. He was older. Of course he was older. His beard was streaked with silver. But his eyes were the same. Exactly the same.

Gideon rose from his chair. 'Amos?' he asked, shocked.

It was. It was Amos. Mercy ran across the kitchen, wanting to throw her arms around him, but the little girl was in the way, staring up at her with wide eyes. So Mercy took his face in her hands.

She was trembling. So was he. 'It's you,' she whispered. 'It's really you. How are you here?'

Amos closed his eyes, tears seeping down his cheeks and into his beard. His hands covered hers and he turned to kiss her palm. 'You're all right. I . . . *Oh.*' He sobbed out the single syllable. 'I was so afraid you wouldn't be all right. I thought you were dead. All this time. They told me you were dead.' He opened his eyes to look at Gideon, who now stood a few feet away, the picture of indecision. 'You too. They told me you were both dead.'

Agent Molina moved out of the way and the little girl moved to take her place at Amos's side. He started to open his arms, but hesitated. Mercy wasn't having his hesitation, though, and launched herself into his arms. 'How are you here?'

His arms closed around her, strong as they'd been when she'd been twelve years old and so afraid. 'I came to warn you. And to get Abigail out of that place.' One of his arms left her back, and Mercy realized he'd extended it to Gideon, who stood frozen in place.

Gideon took a step back and shook his head, his expression a mass of conflict that Mercy recognized all too well. He wanted to join their reunion, but he was afraid to. And his experience with Amos had been different than hers. Mercy had had the benefit of three years of one-on-one time with their stepfather, while Gideon's last memory of Amos was him taking Ephraim to the healer after Gideon had stabbed him in the eye as he'd fought for his life.

'Warn Mercy about what?' Gideon asked stonily. 'And who is Abigail?'

Amos patted Mercy's face with all the gentleness she remembered, then took the hand of the small girl who was watching them with a mix of fascination and fear. 'This is Abigail.'

'Your daughter,' Mercy whispered. 'We found the cemetery. And the cross.' For Damaris, Amos's beloved wife.

Amos sighed. 'Right. Agent Molina said that you had.'

'Let's sit down,' Molina said. 'I think Amos can answer a lot of your questions.' She gave Gideon a pointed look. 'He's been extremely helpful, as I'm sure you will see.'

Mercy looked away from her brother when Abigail tugged on Amos's coat. Mercy knew that if she touched his coat it would be rough, made of homespun wool. She'd felt the scratchiness of it against her cheek many times.

'That's her?' Abigail asked, confused. 'She's . . . old, Papa.'

Mercy laughed, the sound surprising her. 'Hello, Abigail. I'm Mercy.'

449

Abigail's eyes were wide and gray as she openly appraised Mercy. 'I know. You're my papa's other daughter. We thought you were dead.'

Gideon abruptly left them, retaking his seat next to Daisy, who promptly put Brutus in his lap. Gideon's expression softened and he whispered his thanks.

'Mercy, sit down,' Daisy commanded. 'I'm dying of curiosity over here.'

I came to warn you. Amos's words sank in and Mercy suddenly felt cold. But then she felt Rafe standing behind her, warm and solid. 'Rafe, this is Amos Terrill. Amos, this is Detective Rafe Sokolov, Irina's son. And my . . . friend,' she added weakly, not sure what she and Rafe were to each other.

Mercy didn't miss Amos's uncertain glance at Gideon before he met Rafe's gaze. 'It's nice to meet you.'

Rafe held out his hand. 'Welcome. Mercy has spoken highly of you.'

Amos shook Rafe's hand, a small shudder visibly shaking him. 'Thank you.'

Once they were all seated around the table and Irina had served them more tea, Amos folded his hands and drew a breath. 'We left Eden last night.'

'In the back of Brother DJ's truck,' Abigail added.

Amos smiled at her fondly. 'We did indeed.' Sobering, he looked at Gideon. 'You asked what I came to warn Mercy about. For the past six months, I've been . . . aware that things in Eden aren't right.'

'Six months,' Gideon said, unimpressed. 'Took you long enough.'

Amos flinched. 'You're right. It did.' He leaned down to Abigail. 'Maybe you can go sit with Miss Zoya for a little while? Maybe she can show you another movie.'

Abigail's lips firmed. 'Gideon should be kind to you. You have his picture and everything.'

Amos's mouth curved sadly. 'Gideon has suffered quite a lot. He has a right to however he feels. Don't worry about me, Abi-girl. I'll be fine. I promise. Now go find Miss Zoya.'

'I'll take her,' Karl offered. He extended his hand, smiling when

450

Abigail took it without hesitation. Mercy wasn't surprised. Karl Sokolov exuded kindness. 'Besides,' he said with a meaningful lift of his brows, 'I need to make sure Zoya and that boy are really studying.'

That boy. Jeff Bunker, the sixteen-year-old who'd splashed Mercy's private life all over his blog page. But who had, apparently, done something good enough for Irina to stand up for him.

Oh. She remembered now. The retraction he'd written, along with offering survivors his platform to tell their stories. Had that only been this morning?

It felt like it had been a hundred years ago.

When Abigail was safely out of earshot, Amos continued. 'Yes, it took me long enough. It took me seeing, with my own eyes, Ephraim murdering the Comstocks.'

Both Mercy and Gideon gasped at that. 'We saw the cross,' Mercy said.

'You didn't paint it,' Gideon murmured.

'No, I didn't have time. As soon as Ephraim brought back Miriam's body, we moved. It was very abrupt and harder than our other moves. It was November and we'd been at that location for seven years. We'd forgotten how to move quickly. I'd made a cross for Miriam—'

'Eileen,' Gideon interrupted. 'She wanted to be called Eileen. That was her name.'

Once again Amos flinched at Gideon's tone. 'Eileen. I apologize. I knew her as Miriam for too many years. I'd forgotten that you called her Eileen when the two of you played as children.'

Mercy shot Gideon a glare and Gideon had the good grace to look a little ashamed. 'I'm sorry I interrupted,' he murmured. 'Please continue.'

'I'd gone to the graveyard to place Mir— Eileen's cross and heard weeping. I thought it was Sister Dorcas. Eileen's mother,' Amos explained when many at the table looked confused. 'I saw Dorcas with her husband, Stephen, and their son, Ezra. Dorcas was weeping. Stephen was on his knees, begging Ephraim to spare Dorcas and Ezra. Ezra was standing, staring at Ephraim with hate in his eyes.'

Amos swallowed. 'Ezra was the first to die. Ephraim broke his neck with his bare hands. Snapped it like a twig. Then he did the same to Dorcas. He killed Stephen last, but first he told him how much he'd liked . . . hurting Eileen.' Amos dropped his gaze to his hands. 'I can't say the word again. I'm sorry.'

'It's all right,' Molina said. 'I have it in the record.' She nodded at Gideon when he looked at her in surprise. 'When I became aware of Mr Terrill's presence, I brought him in for an interview. He's made a full statement, including telling us where to find the Comstocks' grave. Our forensics team has already recovered two of the bodies. Broken necks, just as Mr Terrill claimed.'

'Like the madam and the college student,' Rafe said quietly.

Molina nodded. 'Exactly like them. Breaks at the same vertebrae on each victim. Mr Terrill, if you would.'

'I wanted to leave then. That day,' Amos said. 'I needed to tell someone what had happened. But I wouldn't leave Abigail. I couldn't leave her. I failed you, Gideon. I failed Mercy and your mother. I even failed Eileen. I couldn't leave Abigail.'

'Of course you couldn't,' Mercy said, covering Amos's hand with hers.

'How did you fail Eileen?' Gideon asked, his tone less acerbic, but still far from warm.

'Her parents came to me. Asked me to help smuggle her out. I made a hope chest large enough for her to hide in. But none of us could go with her. I distracted DJ while Stephen and Ezra put the chest on the truck so that DJ wouldn't know it was extra heavy. We just hoped Eileen would get out. But something bad must have happened, because I read today that she's also dead.'

Gideon looked stunned. 'You were the one who helped her escape?'

'I tried.'

'She did escape,' Mercy said. 'She escaped Ephraim only to be taken by someone even worse, if that's possible. But she did get out. She made it all the way to Macdoel, nearly a hundred miles north of Snowbush. We think she must have hopped a train, because the settlement we found was near a train track. From Macdoel she went

452

to Redding and took a bus to Portland, where she was taken by the man who killed her.'

'Who almost killed you,' Amos said, then looked at Daisy. 'And you.'

'But we got away,' Mercy said firmly. 'It brought me back to Gideon, so some good came from it.'

'It brought me to Gideon as well,' Daisy said.

Irina sniffed. 'Only because you both ignored all my matchmaking attempts.'

That brought chuckles from everyone, even Gideon, who was studying Amos with more respect. 'You risked yourself by making that hope chest for Eileen. Thank you.'

Amos sighed. 'Don't thank me. As you said, it took me long enough. But I saw Eileen one day and she was bruised and bloody. And I remembered Mercy and your mother . . . And I had to do something.'

'What prompted you to leave last night?' Daisy asked.

'I was waiting for spring. There's still snow up in the mountains. I made another hope chest, this time with a false bottom to hide Abigail. I was biding my time, hoping for an opportunity to get her out on DJ's truck, but with me accompanying her. I didn't want her to end up like Eileen. Ephraim told us that she'd fallen down a ravine. The body that he brought back was unidentifiable, just like the body that Waylon brought back after your escape, Gideon. But then I saw Ephraim kill the Comstocks with such . . . glee. He told the membership that they'd decided to return to the world, that they'd turned their backs on God because of Eileen's death.'

'You knew that was a lie,' Gideon said quietly. 'But you couldn't tell anyone.'

'Because they'd kill me, too. And then Abigail would have no one. And then, on Saturday, I cut my finger.' Amos looked at his finger, now wrapped in a fresh bandage. 'It seems like a year ago, but it was just four days. I went to the healer and got a glimpse into her office. And I saw she had a computer.'

Gideon whistled. 'That must have been a shock.'

'Oh, it was. I mean, I'd seen computers before I joined Eden. But they were certainly not the same as they are now. We knew about the Internet. We heard about it from people who joined in the last twenty years or so, but the way I pictured it was nothing like it really is. I was shocked, mainly that other people besides Ephraim were lying. Ephraim killing the Comstocks shocked me as well, but I already knew he was a brutal man. That Sister Coleen was part of any of the secrecy . . . Well, it was hard not to show how stunned I was. Luckily the cut was bad and she attributed my reaction to blood loss. Later that night, I overheard Pastor talking on the phone. A cell phone, as it turns out.'

Mercy smiled. 'You got catapulted into the twenty-first century, huh?'

Amos nodded. 'I knew about phones as well, but nobody was allowed to speak of them. Abigail told me that one of the children in her class was beaten for telling the other students about them. I didn't realize how widespread the lies were. I didn't know who to trust.'

'Who was Pastor talking to on the phone?' Gideon asked.

'He made two calls. The first, I don't know. He was looking for Ephraim. The second call was to Ephraim himself. Apparently Ephraim should have come back to Eden already. We thought he was fasting and praying on the mountain like he did four times a year, but he must have told Pastor that he'd been hurt and needed to rest, because Pastor acted like he felt relieved that there was a good reason because DJ had told him otherwise. Ephraim and DJ do not get along, but you already knew that, Mercy.'

Mercy's throat went tight. She didn't want to talk to Amos about her mother's death. It still hurt and it would hurt him, too. But keeping it secret wasn't right, either. 'DJ shot Mama. Twice. He killed her. But before he did, Mama told him that Ephraim would kill him – DJ, I mean. DJ laughed and said that he couldn't. I assumed that meant that DJ had information on him.'

'I know about that,' Amos said heavily. 'Agent Molina told me. I wish I'd known when I climbed into his truck last night. I would have killed him myself and saved us all the danger.'

Mercy squeezed his hand. 'So you left Eden after Pastor's call?'

'No. On Monday I followed DJ out of the compound and heard him make a call as well. He talked about you, Mercy. That's why I'm here.'

Folsom, California
Tuesday, 18 April, 6.20 P.M.

Ephraim collapsed onto the bed in his camper. He'd made it out of Granite Bay, but it had been close, the cops setting up roadblocks seconds after he'd passed by. He'd been able to see them in his rear-view mirror as he'd turned onto the main drag out of town.

It had been too damn close. And for nothing.

As soon as the cops made the link between the shooting, the stolen Jeep, and the honeymoon murders from Broken Tooth Campground, Mercy would go underground, of that he was certain. Rafe Sokolov and that bastard Gideon would close ranks and he'd never get her alone.

Well, I can go under, too. He'd been in hiding for thirty years. He'd go back to Eden. Wait her out. The worst that would happen would be that DJ would find himself the unfortunate victim of an 'accident', and Ephraim would bury him. Pastor would mourn the boy he'd called his own son, of course, but as long as Ephraim played it smart, Pastor couldn't blame him.

The old man still might not make Ephraim the heir. He'd skipped over Ephraim several times in the last thirty years. Pastor had only tolerated Ephraim's presence in Eden from the very first day he'd shown up, and the feeling had been mutual. Ephraim had been young, brash, and stupid – and injured. Shot during the bank robbery that had sent him and his brother, Aubrey, on the run in the first place. Aubrey wouldn't leave him to die and dragged him to Eden because it was the only place Aubrey knew they'd be safe.

Ephraim hadn't quite appreciated the gravity of their situation or how much Pastor needed their constant adulation. Ephraim had been a seventeen-year-old punk, plain and simple. And Pastor had only allowed him to stay because Aubrey had demanded it. There had been something between Aubrey and Pastor, some history, some debt that Pastor felt compelled to repay.

Ephraim had never asked. He really hadn't wanted to know back then. He really wanted to know now, but Aubrey was long dead. Ephraim might never know, because Pastor still didn't like him.

And if Pastor held on to DJ's memory, still refusing to share those damn bank access codes? *Then I'll come back for Mercy when the coast is clear and she's gone back to her normal life.* Bringing her back to Eden – dead was fine, but alive was preferable – would force Pastor to admit that DJ had betrayed them all, and that Ephraim was the injured party.

If Mercy had returned to New Orleans by then, that was okay. Ephraim could find her there. He knew where her family lived. He knew where her best friend lived. He knew where she worked. Once Mercy's guard was down, retrieval would be child's play.

That settled, he closed his eyes to grab some shut-eye. He felt safe enough in the camper, tucked away in the woods. He'd ditched the custodian's truck, stealing another Jeep.

This time, he'd planned ahead, taking the honeymooners' camper license plates with him. He'd switched them out for the plates on a rental RV, one that advertised *See America*. He figured renters of vehicles didn't memorize their plates. They wouldn't notice that he'd switched them out until they returned their unit.

By then, he'd be back in Eden. Killing DJ.

He'd almost fallen asleep with a smile on his face when his phone rang, jarring him awake. No one had called him on either of the two new phones. The one ringing was the flip phone. He considered not answering it until he saw the caller ID.

A Santa Rosa number. It was his doctor. His mother's doctor as well.

He answered cautiously. The doctor must have gotten the number from Pastor. Ephraim sat up, pulling his gun from its holster. Just in case. 'Hello?'

'Harry, it's Dr Burkett.'

He wanted to snap that it was Mr Franklin, not Harry, but Burkett had known him since he was a little kid, so it was easier to just go with it. 'Where did you get this number, Doctor?'

'From your pastor. I called your old number and it just rang.' He hesitated. 'Was I not supposed to have your number?'

'No, it's fine. What's wrong?'

Either his eyeball had been recalled, or his mother was sick. *Be the eyeball. Please be the eyeball.* Especially since he kept it covered in Eden. None of the membership could know that he'd left the compound for modern medical care when they could not.

Not even Pastor or DJ knew he had a fake eye. It would be no hardship to take it out when he returned. *Let my mother be all right.*

'It's your mother. She's fine,' Burkett assured him quickly. 'Some days are better than others. But today she had a visitor, and I thought you should know.'

Ephraim's stomach twisted. This wasn't good. 'She's not supposed to have visitors,' he growled.

'I know, but I can only make it a request. I'd have to justify an order and I can't.'

'Who visited her?' Ephraim barked, not wanting to hear the doctor's excuses.

'A woman named Miriam Smith and her friend, Beth Jones.'

Ephraim's blood ran cold. Miriam? That had been Mercy's given name in Eden. It had also been Eileen Danton's given name. Either way, this was not good. 'I don't know those women.'

'That's interesting, because Miriam claimed to be your wife.'

Shit. 'What did she look like?'

'Tall, dark hair. Green eyes.'

Fucking hell. 'She was with a woman? Not a big blond guy?'

'No, it was a woman. I talked to the nurse's aide when I got there. She called me when the women showed up. Which is what I pay her for.'

'Was my mother . . . lucid?'

'I don't know. She wasn't when I got there, but who knows? Like I said, she has good and bad days. She was rocking and saying that her baby was gone and that she hadn't used a key. Do you know what that means?'

Yes. Of course he did. The key was to their safe-deposit box. It contained a handwritten statement detailing the guilt of all the

457

Founding Elders. If any of the founders died unexpectedly, whoever they'd entrusted with a key was to give the documents to the police. They'd all prepared a similar package, and they'd all stored the documents in individual safe-deposit boxes, except for Ephraim and Edward, who shared a box.

All of the founders had given their key to someone on the outside. It was a fail-safe mechanism. A way to keep them all honest. Or at least honest with one another. It kept them from killing one another at first. But with Waylon and Edward gone? Only Ephraim and Pastor still had files. DJ might have had Waylon's, but he hadn't used it after Waylon's death, and Pastor claimed he'd taken Waylon's key.

Of course, both Pastor and DJ were liars, so who knew what the real truth was? His plan to kill DJ dimmed a little. He'd forgotten that DJ might have access to Waylon's safe-deposit box.

'No,' he lied. 'I have no idea what that means. Probably nothing. My mother hasn't made sense in years.'

Still, he relaxed. If all his mother had said to Mercy was that she hadn't used the key, there was no real harm done. His mother didn't even have a key anymore. He'd taken Aubrey's key back after his brother's murder and retrieved his own key when his mother had started to show signs of dementia.

Ephraim had made sure to tell her not to send the incriminating documents out after his brother's death because none of the other Founding Elders had done it.

That would be Gideon's sin. For which the bastard would pay.

'Well . . .' Burkett hesitated and Ephraim's stomach twisted again.

'Well, what?'

'She told me that she gave Miriam the key.'

'She doesn't have a key,' Ephraim said flatly. He had the only keys. They were in a pocket of his laptop bag. He'd kept the keys and the laptop in his locker at Regina's place until Saturday night.

His gut took a sudden plunge. Regina had broken into his locker. She'd searched his laptop. He scrambled from the camper's bed to grab the laptop bag and check the pocket. Then exhaled in relief. The keys were still there, right where he'd left them. 'There is no key,' he added with more conviction.

'She seemed to think that she had one. She showed me a small wooden chest with a false bottom. Said she'd hidden the key there for Aubrey. Sometimes she thinks he's still alive, you know. Or you would if you visited her more often.'

Shit, shit, shit. Ephraim knew the chest. It had been made by Amos, Eden's resident woodworker. Ephraim hadn't realized that it had held anything. His mother had assumed that Ephraim had made the chest himself, and he'd let her believe it. It had made her happy and he'd certainly told worse lies.

And worse truths. He thought about the contents of the safe-deposit box, swallowing hard at the sudden burn of bile in his throat. He'd written down everything he'd ever been told, everything he'd overheard or witnessed. He'd documented every sin the Founding Elders had ever committed, but those sins weren't what had him sweating right now.

He'd kept a running tally of every penny the founders shared. Pastor showed them the earnings reports twice a year, and each time Ephraim made notes of the numbers as soon as he was out of Pastor's sight. If Mercy gave that key to the cops, they'd know exactly what Eden was worth.

The money was safely hidden in offshore accounts for the moment, but if there was one thing he'd learned from DJ over the years, it was that the Feds were capable of tracking nearly anything with their fancy computers. And now the Feds knew where to look. If Mercy had gotten a key from Ephraim's mother, she'd already given it to either her detective boyfriend or her brother.

Gideon. The Fed. He was behind this, Ephraim was certain.

If they'd visited his mother, they were probably already tracking how Ephraim paid for her care. They'd find the bank accounts and would inevitably recognize Frutuoso for an Eden account once they figured out that the company dealt in 'olive oil and pomegranates'.

Stupid Pastor. The man thought he was so damn clever. Naming the company 'fruitful'. It was bad enough that Pastor had chosen his

459

name because 'Ephraim' meant 'fruitful'. Ephraim had been only seventeen years old and full of himself, it was true. And yeah, he'd fucked the fourteen-year-old granddaughter of Doc, the oldest Founding Elder, but so what? The old man was *long* dead now, the first of all of them to die, so he didn't care anymore. Plus, the girl had wanted it. And Ephraim had married her when she'd shown up pregnant.

Not like he'd had a choice. But marriage was his punishment, as was the name change to Ephraim. It was a taunt, a constant reminder that he'd gotten Doc's granddaughter preggo. Because Pastor was a prick – a prick who thought he was too damn smart to ever get caught.

But Mercy was smart and so was Gideon. They'd figure out that the bank account was important, and who knew how long it would take them to trace the money back to the offshore Eden accounts?

I need to get that cash before the Feds do.

But the money wasn't even the scariest thing. That would be the maps he'd added to the safe-deposit box every time Eden moved. He wasn't sure what the other founders had included in their 'fail-safe boxes,' but Ephraim's approach was scorched earth, all the way. If one of the fuckers had killed him, his mother would have opened his box and found every location Eden had ever settled.

She'd find the locations of their product stashes – pot, shrooms, opioids. And the cash that DJ collected every week that he took a drug shipment to his contacts. DJ would deposit it periodically into banks in either Santa Rosa, Sacramento, or San Francisco, but never often and never in the same bank. Then Pastor would move it into the main offshore account, which the man controlled with an iron fist.

But the most dangerous map in the safe-deposit box was the one he'd made showing the locations of future settlements, because they always had a few scouted out.

If Ephraim had gotten murdered, he hadn't wanted any of the others to survive, either. His mother knew that if he didn't visit her every three months she was to assume he'd met with foul play. Except that now she didn't remember one day to the next, much less how long it had been since he'd come to see her. Which was why he'd taken her keys – or thought he had.

That she'd had an actual key, one that she'd kept secret from him? This was really bad.

He'd literally given the Feds a road map to the compound and its assets. He hadn't yet added a map since their last move, after Miriam ran away, but it didn't matter. They were reusing a past location because it had been November and they'd needed shelter as snow had already begun to fall.

So the Feds would still find them. *Fuck me.*

'Harry?' Dr Burkett prompted. 'Are you all right?'

'I'm fine,' he insisted. 'You're sure that Miriam wasn't there with a man? Either blond or with dark hair like hers?'

'The aide only said that she saw the two women. She took a photo of them with her phone. I can send it to you.'

'I can't get photos with this phone. It's very basic.' And he didn't want to give the doctor the number to his smartphone, in case the doctor was too chummy with Pastor. He didn't want DJ to be able to track him with the smartphone, like he'd done with the last one.

'I can print them up for you if you want to come and get them. And you might visit your mother. She misses you.'

'I'll stop by when I can.'

If the cops got hold of that key, they'd know everything about Eden. They'd know where the compound currently existed. And if Ephraim told Pastor that they had to move again, Pastor would want to know why. If he admitted that the Feds had his maps? Ephraim might as well kiss the millions goodbye.

He needed to get to Mercy asap. His brain started to spin, trying to think of how to best lure her away from her protectors. 'Thanks,' he said brusquely. 'I need to go.'

'Not so fast,' the doctor chided. 'I'm really surprised you didn't ask more about the key that your mother gave your wife.'

Ephraim bit back a snarl at the thought of Mercy in the same room with his mother. 'I don't know what key my mother thought she had or thought she gave to Miriam Smith, but she was mistaken.

461

And if she did have a key, it has nothing to do with me. Thank you for calling, Doctor.'

'Harry, Harry, Harry. I think it has everything to do with you. And I know you took the original key from her a few years ago.'

Ephraim licked his lips nervously. 'The original?' he asked carefully.

'The original,' the doctor confirmed, his tone smug. 'I made the copy for her. Before you took the original, obviously.'

Ephraim's blood ran cold. This man knew too much. 'You're lying.'

'I think you know that I'm not.' Burkett spoke calmly. Confidently.

Ephraim wanted to break his fucking neck. 'Why did she make a copy?'

'Because she was becoming forgetful and was afraid she'd lose the original. I didn't realize at the time that the key had belonged to you.'

'Get to the fucking point,' Ephraim growled. 'What do you want?' Because if his mother had given the copy to Mercy, there was nothing the doctor could do to him that was worse than what Mercy could do.

'My goodness. No need to be so hostile. The *point* is, I made more than one copy.'

Shit. Shit, damn, and fuck. Ephraim took a deep breath, forced his voice to be as calm as Burkett's as he adjusted his plans to include silencing this doctor who knew too much. 'Still not making a point, Doc.'

'My *point* is that now I realize that the original key belonged to you, I thought you might like the other copy I made.'

A shiver of relief loosened some of Ephraim's dread. This would be about money, then. 'What do you want?'

'I think that's a conversation best had in person. When can I expect you?'

When can I expect you? Seriously? Could Burkett truly believe that Ephraim would negotiate with him? Didn't he watch the goddamn news? Was the man truly that stupid? Did he think Ephraim was that stupid?

Not that it mattered what Burkett thought. It also didn't matter if Burkett really had a key to his safe-deposit box or not. Nor did it matter if Ephraim got the damn key back. It only mattered that Burkett wasn't allowed to use it or tell anyone else about it. And, should the good doctor die tonight, Ephraim would have accomplished both goals.

Santa Rosa was only a few hours away. 'I'll be by your house by ten at the latest.' *With my gun loaded and ready to shoot your fucking head off.*

'See you then, Harry.'

Twenty-six

'DJ was talking about me?' Mercy asked. It wasn't unexpected after their trip to Snowbush, but hearing Amos confirm it was disconcerting.

'It was likely a call from the owner of the Snowbush general store,' Molina told them. 'The time frame matches up to the call you saw the man make after you all left the store on Monday.'

'He was telling DJ that I was in the store,' Mercy said. 'So it was DJ who killed Ginger and the store owner. And his wife?'

Molina shrugged. 'Maybe. We don't have direct evidence yet, but the facts line up to give us a helluva lot of circumstantial evidence. Mr Terrill has accurately described Ginger's house as their first stop after leaving the compound.'

'Abigail and I were hiding in the bed of DJ's truck, under a blanket,' Amos explained. 'That's how we got out. DJ got out of the truck and went into the house. After he came out, he drove away in another car. That's when I figured it was safe enough to poke my head out. I got a quick glimpse of the house, but I was really checking for DJ. He was gone, so I took the truck and drove away as fast as I could go. I didn't know he was going to kill anyone,' he added, looking at Gideon. 'I promise you that.'

'I believe you,' Gideon said. He turned to Molina. 'You think that DJ Belmont killed Ginger from the general store?'

'It makes sense,' Molina said. 'DJ Belmont was a wild card we weren't expecting.'

464

'That's for sure,' Gideon muttered, then returned his attention to Amos. 'You heard DJ mention Mercy's name when you were still in Eden?'

Amos nodded, his expression still a bit stunned. 'I followed him because he'd just rejected my request to accompany him into town. I was trying to find a way to smuggle Abigail out, but I couldn't do that unless I could go with her. He didn't outright reject me, but I knew that's what he meant. I'd been wondering who was in on the lies and I figured DJ had to be, too. But I still couldn't believe my ears when he said Mercy's name. Neither could DJ, I think. When the person on the other end of the call mentioned her, DJ went pale as a ghost. He was really scared. All this time I thought she was dead. I think DJ did too, based on his surprise. He didn't bring back a body for you, Mercy. He told us that he had to bury you in the forest so that he could look for your mother. He was afraid the animals would attack him if he carried your remains.'

'So at least they didn't kill anyone to pass off as me,' Mercy said quietly. 'They did that for Gideon and Eileen. Maybe others.'

'A few others,' Amos said sadly. 'I see that now. I've been wondering if anything I've been told for thirty years was truth. But all I knew when I heard DJ say your name was that I had to get out. To warn you. And to save Abigail.'

'How did you end up in the back of DJ's truck?' Rafe asked.

'I faked being sick to give an excuse not to leave my hut for the next day, so no one would look for us. Then I cut down a tree to block the road and waited with Abigail. I'd heard DJ say he'd be "there" tonight, so I knew that was my chance. When he stopped to move the tree, Abigail and I hid in the truck bed. We stopped at a house. I didn't get out of the truck bed until I heard DJ driving away in another car. So I jumped out and took the truck.' He glanced at Gideon. 'If I'd known that he'd stopped to kidnap and kill that poor young woman, I would have found a way to tell someone.'

'I know,' Gideon said softly. 'I believe you. What happened after you drove away in the truck?'

'I drove. Just . . . drove. I knew we'd come from the north, so I

465

went south and didn't stop until I got to Reno.' His lips quirked up. 'Everything looked different, except for McDonald's, so we stopped there.'

'Good old golden arches,' Rafe murmured. 'They'll be around a thousand years from now. How did you contact my mother?'

'I didn't, not right away. I met a lady at McDonald's who thought I was Amish. She took me to the public library after her shift. Her name is Edie. She was so kind. She showed me how to use the computer at the library and . . . well, it was a lot. I still don't know what to think about your Internet. I mainly focused on news stories about you, Mercy. But I read that you were alive too, Gideon, and . . .' He blew out a breath. 'It was like a gift. Of course, the other articles weren't so precious. I saw that Ephraim had tried to take you at the airport.' He leaned around Mercy to smile at Rafe. 'Thank you for rescuing her. My heart nearly stopped when I saw the film online.'

'I could have done nothing else,' Rafe said simply.

'I still owe you a great deal. Anyway, Edie wouldn't let me read one of the articles. She said it was "Internet trash." But she did let me see the second article written by Jeff Bunker. She showed me how to email him.'

Irina picked up the story. 'When Jeff saw the email, he called the house and spoke to Zoya, who contacted me. I was already in Reno, with Sasha and Erin at the hospital just a few miles away from the library. We got there before the FBI did, which was a good thing.' She gave Molina an accusing look. 'Those agents wanted to arrest him!'

'Jeff had forwarded Amos's email to me, too,' Molina said. 'I sent local field agents to check it out. Edie, the woman who wrote the email, had left a phone number for the library. I didn't tell them to arrest him,' she added, aggrieved. 'I said for them to bring him in for questioning. Which they did.'

'Irina insisted she ride with us,' Amos said with a grateful smile. 'It was less scary that way, to be sure.'

Rafe frowned. 'Where's Sasha?'

'She stayed at the hospital with Erin,' Irina said. 'She'll drive them both home tomorrow in my car. It's all fine, Raphael. Everything is fine.'

'Except that now both DJ *and* Ephraim are after Mercy,' Gideon said with a sigh. 'DJ wants to cover up his lie and Ephraim . . . Hell, he could just want her because she got away.'

'Or,' Mercy added, 'if DJ was that surprised that I was still alive, he must have thought I died in that parking lot at the Redding bus terminal. DJ is Pastor's favorite. Bringing me back to Eden would allow Ephraim to prove that DJ had lied. Ephraim could usurp DJ's place as favorite.'

'Which makes him even more determined,' Gideon said grimly.

'And dangerous,' Rafe added, very quietly.

'So, things are not so fine,' Irina acknowledged with a sigh. 'But we are all here and safe, yes?'

'Yes,' Mercy told her. 'We are all here and we are all safe.' She held on to Amos's hand, pushing her fear away for the moment. She didn't shove it into the box in her mind, but she was able to set it aside to focus on the stepfather she'd missed so much. 'I bought one of your pieces yesterday. At the general store in Snowbush.'

'The jewelry box.' Amos nodded, his smile almost bashful. 'DJ said so on that call to the store owner.'

'"Surely Goodness and Mercy",' Mercy murmured. 'I couldn't believe my eyes.'

'I carved it into all of my larger pieces,' Amos said. 'It was the only way I could think of to remember you.'

Mercy gripped Amos's hand tightly. 'I remember how you used to sing to me. I tried to get more information about you. About Eden. But all my questions got poor Ginger killed. We have to find them – DJ and Ephraim. We have to stop them.'

'Do you know where Eden is right now?' Gideon asked. 'I've been searching for it for so long.'

Amos shook his head. 'I know it's near a network of caves and tunnels. I know it's north of Snowbush by a few hours. I know we've stayed there once before. Pastor chose it because winter was upon us on the last move and it would provide us with adequate shelter. But I don't know anything else. It was a valley. No matter how high I climbed, I could never get a sense for where we were. And I tried, please believe me, I tried. But as you will remember, even leaving the compound is forbidden in Eden, so exploring is nearly impossible. I got special permission because I needed to find the best sources of wood, but I could never be gone too long or be sure I wasn't being watched.'

'I believe you,' Gideon said again.

'We do know another thing, thanks to Mr Terrill,' Molina said, her eyes brightening. 'On that call DJ made to the store owner, he told the guy that he didn't have any more "product". That they'd had to leave it behind. That was half true. We found evidence of an underground grow house at the Snowbush site. The equipment was gone, but a few spores had sprouted in the dirt they left behind. Now that we know that they're selling psilocybin, we can listen and watch for new suppliers to that geographical area.'

'Shrooms?' Mercy turned to Rafe. 'That's their new cash crop?'

'*New* cash crop?' Amos asked, stunned. 'You knew that the Elders were selling drugs? How?'

'I remembered that the healers had pot for pain,' Mercy said. 'And I remember the field of poppies that we kids weren't allowed to go to.'

Amos sat back, looking drained. 'Poppies? For opium. Dear God.'

'Heroin, most likely,' Gideon said.

'You took Mercy's punishment for going to the poppy field,' Amos whispered. 'They put you in the box for days.'

Gideon nodded. 'But you offered to take my place.'

Mercy stared. 'He did? But you took my place, Gideon.'

Gideon made a pained face at the memory. 'When Amos heard what had happened, he ran in and said he'd go in the box for us. But I think Edward McPhearson wanted me to be weak. Then I couldn't fight him when he . . . you know.'

Amos slowly raised his hand to his mouth. 'Oh dear God. You're right. I didn't know it then. I didn't have a concept of that. I was raised in the church. Nobody spoke of boys being hurt like that. But you did fight back,' he said, his jaw rigid. 'You fought back and you saved yourself. You killed McPhearson and I'm glad you did.'

He startled when Gideon laid his hand on Amos's arm. Gideon looked kind of surprised too, Mercy thought. 'You took me out to Waylon's truck, didn't you?' he asked. 'Mama begged you to help and you did.'

Amos looked away, ashamed. 'Yeah.'

Mercy's mouth fell open. 'You did? You told me that he'd run away.'

'Because I thought he had. On the truck.'

Mercy shook her head. 'No. You said he was lazy and that's why he ran away.'

Amos looked up suddenly, his eyes glassy with tears. 'Because once Waylon brought back his body, I was afraid of what they'd do to you,' he whispered. 'Ephraim took your mother away. I tried to get her out. I offered to leave with her, but she was afraid of what they'd do to you if we got caught. And then when you were twelve, he took you, too. For what it's worth, I truly thought Gideon had died. When Waylon brought his body back, I thought it was him. I didn't lie to you about that.'

'You offered to get Mama out?' She whispered it because her throat suddenly hurt too much to speak.

Amos nodded miserably. 'She said no. She was so afraid of Ephraim.'

'But you helped her get me out,' Gideon said quietly. 'I thought I'd dreamed that.'

'I should have tried harder,' Amos hissed. 'I should have dragged your mother away. *I should have tried harder.*'

'Yeah, you should have,' Gideon agreed wearily. 'But you did try. You tried to keep Mercy away from Ephraim. You tried to help Eileen. And you took a lot of risk to warn Mercy. You could have done more, but you did do something.'

'I can't ask you to forgive me,' Amos said, so quietly that even sitting next to him, Mercy could barely hear his words. 'I don't deserve it. I was weak and I believed blindly. And you both suffered.'

'I'm not going to argue whether you were weak or strong,' Gideon said. 'But, for whatever it's worth, I do forgive you.'

469

Mercy had to clear her throat before she could trust her voice not to break. 'Same here.'

'Papa?'

Everyone turned to the little girl standing in the doorway. Zoya and Jeff Bunker stood behind her. 'I tried to get her to watch a movie,' Zoya said, 'but she was afraid that Gideon was being mean to her papa. If it's all right with you, we'll go back to Dad's office. Jeff's mom is waiting and Dad's got the movie on pause. It's *Mulan*. Jeff's never seen it.' Without waiting for a reply, the two teenagers left.

Behind her, Rafe sighed. 'Can I still hate him?'

'I don't think so,' Mercy murmured. 'Abigail? You can come sit with us if you want to. We're not being mean to your papa.'

Amos smiled sadly at Abigail. 'Gideon's not mean at all. He's kinder than I deserve. Come.'

Abigail climbed into his lap, staring Gideon down until Daisy chuckled. 'Tell her you're sorry for being mean to her daddy, Gideon.'

'I am very sorry,' Gideon said obediently.

Abigail lifted her chin. 'You should be. He has your picture and everything.' She patted Amos's shirt pocket. 'In here.'

Amos drew three faded Polaroid photos from his shirt pocket and put them on the table.

It took Mercy a moment to realize what she was looking at. A little boy, about six, looking so serious. A chubby-cheeked girl, toddler age. And a woman smiling brilliantly. 'It's us.' Her gaze jerked up to meet Gideon's. 'It's us. And Mama.'

'Oh,' Daisy breathed. 'Gideon, look at you.'

'You were adorable,' Rafe said, putting his hand at the small of Mercy's back.

But Mercy and Gideon only had eyes for the picture of their mother. She wore a huge smile, like she'd been laughing. Mercy shuddered out a breath. 'I almost forgot what she looked like.'

Gideon reached for the Polaroid but jerked his hand back, afraid to touch it. 'Me too.'

Mama's so happy. 'I have her locket, but I can't look at that picture. Ephraim's in it.' *And Mama wasn't happy after that, ever again.*

470

Gideon didn't say a word, but the look they shared said enough. Then Mercy nearly cried again when Gideon reached across the table to grip her hand in his, then took Amos's hand with the other. Mercy completed the circle, taking Amos's other hand, and she hoped he could understand what they couldn't find the words to say.

Thank you. Welcome home.

Amos's eyes grew shiny and then he was crying openly, which set off Mercy's tears. Gideon didn't cry, but his lips pursed hard, the muscle twitching in his cheek as he fought to keep his composure. Others around the table weren't as successful at keeping their emotions in check. Mercy could hear their sniffles and was unsurprised to see Farrah leaning into André's shoulder, her shoulders shaking with sobs. André's eyes were also suspiciously bright, which also wasn't a surprise. Mercy had observed his tender heart many times over the years and felt her own heart flood with gratitude that her best friend had found such a good man.

Little Abigail seemed to understand that their tears were happy ones. She smiled sweetly as she patted Amos's cheeks with a tissue that Irina tucked into her small hand – after wiping her own eyes, of course.

Abigail beamed proudly. 'Aren't you glad that I didn't let you forget the pictures?'

Amos laughed. 'I am, Abi-girl. I am so glad.'

Farrah left André's embrace, coming to stand behind Mercy's chair, still sniffling. 'Oh, look at you, cutie-patootie. We need copies of these. My mama's going to want to pinch your cheeks.'

'We can scan them,' Irina offered. 'The photos will not be harmed, Amos,' she added when Amos looked alarmed.

Mercy let go of Amos's hand to touch Abigail's sleeve. 'Thank you for reminding him to bring the pictures. I haven't seen my mama's face in so long.'

Abigail shrugged. 'I've never seen mine. She died when I was being born.'

'I'm sorry,' Mercy said softly. 'Amos, do you still have her locket photo?'

He shook his head. 'I didn't think to take it after she—' He cleared his throat. 'Afterward. The healer removed the locket and it went back to the forge.'

'Who took the photos?' Rafe asked. 'For the lockets, I mean?'

'For a long time it was Waylon. He would take the film into the town to get it developed. Then DJ took it on after Waylon died. We haven't had many weddings lately, but I assume DJ still does. He got a fancy new camera a while back. Seemed a waste of money to me.'

'May have been a digital camera,' Gideon said. 'If so, the images might be on that computer you saw in Sister Coleen's office. Which means you might be able to get one printed later.'

'That would be nice,' Amos said, laying his cheek on Abigail's hair, 'wouldn't it, Abi-girl?'

Abigail snuggled closer, patting Amos's pocket. 'Yes, Papa. And you could keep it here, like you did with the other pictures.'

The sight of Abigail patting Amos's pocket sparked a memory and Mercy patted her own pocket, panicking when it was empty. 'Oh no. Belinda Franklin's key is gone. I know I had it in my pocket.' She rose from her chair. 'Maybe it fell out in the van.'

'Tom has it,' Liza said.

Mercy blinked, having forgotten the woman was still there. 'You're sure?'

'Positive,' Farrah said. 'You were sound asleep and we didn't want to wake you to ask for the key, so I got it from your pocket.'

'What does it open?' Mercy asked, light-headed with relief.

'Probably a safe-deposit box,' Farrah said, but Molina cleared her throat imperiously.

Rafe leaned in close. 'We'll talk about it later.'

Because Molina was still here. Mercy had nearly forgotten about her, too. It seemed that it was all right for them to have discovered the key, but its purpose was something they weren't supposed to know about. 'Oh. Okay.'

'Oh. Okay,' Molina said dryly, clearly understanding what hadn't been said. 'Mr Terrill has given us enough information for the time being. I'll be going to my office to begin working on it.

Agent Hunter will be returning with me. Liza, we'll drop you off on the way. Where will you be staying, Mr Terrill? We want to be sure you have a safe place.'

Because he is a valuable witness.

'He's staying here,' Irina said.

'But my presence here may be dangerous,' Amos said, a worried frown creasing his brow.

'I am leaving one of my agents to watch this house and the surrounding properties,' Molina said. 'Burton has already broken into one house in this neighborhood to use as a lookout. If he comes back, we want to catch him. Plus, I believe that Irina's daughter Meg will also be staying to make sure Zoya remains safe.'

'We want you to stay,' Irina assured him. 'You and Abigail. You are Gideon and Mercy's family. We take care of family.'

Amos drew a thick breath, overcome. 'Thank you. Where will you two go?' he asked Mercy and Gideon.

'Back to Rafe's,' Mercy said. She loved the Sokolovs, but she needed the quiet time. 'All my things are there and I need to make sure I feed my cats.'

'You could stay here,' Irina said doubtfully. 'We have enough rooms here for us, and there's no reason for Agent Molina's people to guard two houses.'

To guard me, Mercy thought. *None of this would be happening if Ephraim weren't obsessed with me. Well, Ephraim and now DJ.* And, now that she thought about it, the fact that no one had really talked about DJ's involvement was a giant red flag. *Molina knows something that she's not saying.*

Still, Irina was right. As much as she needed the quiet of Rafe's place, it really was selfish to ask the FBI to expend so many resources. She was about to say so when Molina stepped in and settled the issue.

'We have agents stationed at Detective Sokolov's house as well,' Molina said. 'Burton was able to plant trackers on Detective Rhee's vehicle, so he was clearly in that neighborhood, too.' She glanced at Rafe. 'He also put a tracker on your sister's Mini Cooper. We found it this morning, after you all had left for Santa Rosa.'

Rafe briefly closed his eyes, his fist clenching. 'Thank you for finding it. And for adding coverage to my neighborhood. I'd hate for any of my neighbors to be assaulted like Mr MacGuire was.'

Molina pushed away from the table. 'You're welcome, Detective. Thank you for your hospitality, Mrs Sokolov. Call me if anything comes up. Anything at all.'

Granite Bay, California
Tuesday, 18 April, 8.10 P.M.

'I have food for you to take with you,' Irina announced once Agents Molina and Hunter were gone, Liza going with them.

And none too soon. Rafe liked Tom and Liza a lot, and, while he appreciated Molina's protection of his family, the older woman made him antsy. She knew things that he needed to know to keep Mercy safe. Which he'd figure out, but first he'd see that his mother rested. Irina looked bone weary and Rafe didn't like it one bit.

'We still have food from the last time you sent stuff home,' Rafe said.

Irina raised a brow. 'I have food for you to take with you,' she repeated.

Joining Irina at the stove to help, Daisy snickered. 'Give it up, Rafe.'

Rafe sighed, knowing when to retreat. 'Yes, Mom. Thank you, Mom.'

'Abigail,' Irina said, 'I have a cake that you will love, but it's also Mr Karl's favorite. Will you go tell him to come to the kitchen? If the movie is almost over, you all can stay to finish it.'

Abigail looked to her father for permission and Amos nodded. 'You know where to find the office?' he asked.

'Of course, Papa,' Abigail said with an eye roll that would have made any teenager proud. 'I'm not a baby.'

'No, you're not.' Amos kissed her forehead. 'You are growing up too fast. Now go and find Mr Karl.' When Abigail had disappeared into the hallway, he immediately turned to Mercy. 'That woman, Agent Molina. There are things she didn't tell you.'

474

'I know,' Mercy said. 'She's like that. I hope she didn't make you uncomfortable.'

Amos shrugged. 'Her interview room was rather terrifying, but better than the back of DJ's truck, so I can honestly say that I've had worse.'

'What did you tell her that she's holding back?' Gideon asked.

'She seemed most interested in Pastor. She asked a lot of questions, and I gave her what little information I know.'

Rafe sat up straighter and noted Gideon doing the same. This was important. Rafe was after Ephraim – and now DJ – because they threatened Mercy, but the Feds were after Eden as a whole. 'Like what kind of information?' Rafe asked.

'I was a member of Pastor's church. Before Eden.' Amos smiled up at Irina when she refilled his cup with tea. 'Thank you. It's just what I needed.'

Mercy looked taken aback. 'Pastor was an actual pastor? For real?'

'Pastor was his name,' Amos said, completely serious. 'Of course he was a pastor.'

Mercy bit her lip. 'I guess I assumed he was hiding from the law like Ephraim and Edward.'

'They robbed a bank,' Rafe added, not sure if Amos was aware. 'Thirty years ago.'

Amos's mouth fell open. 'I didn't know that. Good heavens.' He sipped on his tea with a thoughtful frown. 'But the timing works, I suppose. I joined Eden when I was nineteen. That was thirty years ago and the Eden church was brand-new. I was raised by my grandfather, who had been an active member of Pastor's congregation before Eden. It was a nondenominational church in LA. But then, in the late eighties, Pastor was accused of embezzlement, of falsifying his résumé and stealing from the church's accounts. He'd been the pastor in the LA church for at least ten years, and was accused of taking almost a hundred thousand dollars.' His smile was wry. 'Which was a lot of money in those days.'

'It still is,' Gideon said. 'Did you not believe the accusations?'

Amos sighed. 'I didn't, no. Mostly because my grandfather

didn't. He was one of the church elders and was devoted to Pastor and his family. The church itself was divided on the accusations. About a third believed them true and pushed for Pastor's ouster. A third stood by Pastor, who maintained his innocence. The remaining third said we were all crazy and left the church. This left only the "for" and "against" groups and they fought for control. It was vicious. I remember some of the members threatening violence on their "enemies".' He finger-quoted. 'Finally, Pastor gathered his closest supporters together in secret and announced that he was starting a new church, that if he stayed in LA the government would seize his assets and make him an example.'

'The government,' Mercy repeated flatly.

Amos sighed. 'It was a paranoid time.'

'Waco was only a few years after that,' Gideon said.

'We heard a lot about Waco.' Amos shook his head. 'I don't know if half of what we heard was true, but we got an influx of new members after that. Anyway, he offered to allow his "chosen few" to come with him. They'd get freedom from the government, freedom from the growing immorality of the world, fresh air, and back to basics. Their children would grow up without temptation and would remain pure.'

'And what did they have to promise in return?' Rafe asked.

Amos briefly dropped his gaze to his hands. When he looked up, Rafe saw shame in his eyes. 'Everything,' Amos said quietly. '"If thou wilt be perfect, go and sell that thou hast, and give to the poor, and thou shalt have treasure in heaven: and come and follow me".'

'Matthew 19:21,' Mercy said. 'But you didn't give to the poor.'

'You gave it all to Pastor,' Gideon murmured. 'What did you sell?'

'My grandfather's house. All of our belongings, except for his pocket watch. I couldn't bear to sell that. He was so disappointed that he couldn't come with me. He was sick. Lung cancer. His last wish was that I would go to Eden and "thrive". So I did. Or tried to.'

'How much did you give to Eden?' Mercy asked.

'Several hundred thousand dollars. My grandfather owned a lot of land and developers had been after him to sell for a long time.'

'Wow,' Mercy whispered. 'Did everyone give him that much money?'

'Some gave him more,' Amos said. 'Some less. Some brought nothing but themselves and their children, like your mother, but looking back I can see there were more wealthy donors than poor members.'

'What was Pastor's name, back in LA?' Rafe asked.

Amos gave him an approving nod. 'That was what interested Agent Molina the most. His given name was Herbert Hampton, but now I don't know if that was true, either.'

Rafe was already entering the name into his phone browser. 'Nothing comes up on his name, but that's not surprising if he hasn't used it for thirty years.' But he wasn't discouraged at all. This was part of the hunt, his favorite part of the job.

'Tom's probably already searching,' Gideon said. 'He's some kind of hacker whiz. If it's on the Internet, or ever has been, he can find it.'

'Or we could search the newspaper archives.'

Everyone turned to see Jeffrey Bunker standing in the kitchen doorway with Zoya, Karl, and Abigail. The sight of the little bastard reporter had Rafe's temper rising fast, and from the way Gideon's jaw bulged, his friend felt the same way. But Bunker had done some good today. He was trying to undo the harm he'd caused, and Rafe resolved to give the little punk a second chance.

'This is a private conversation,' Gideon growled, having clearly *not* come to the same resolution.

Zoya lifted her chin. 'We were told to come for cake. Back off, Gideon. We didn't do anything wrong.'

Abigail crossed the kitchen to climb into Amos's lap. 'He sounds mean again, Papa,' she whispered, but so loudly that they could all hear it. 'Why is he mean?'

Amos sighed. 'He's not mean. He's frustrated. That's not the same thing.'

Mercy was studying Bunker carefully. 'Searching the newspaper archives is not a bad idea, Jeffrey. I'm Mercy, by the way.'

Bunker at least had the good grace to look ashamed. 'I know. I'm . . . I'm sorry.'

'I know,' she said quietly.

Rafe had to bite the inside of his cheek to keep from snarling. This man had seen the video of Mercy. Yes, it was grainy, according to anyone who'd seen it. Yes, he'd gotten it taken down within hours. But he'd seen it. He'd seen Mercy, naked and vulnerable, and Rafe wanted to rip his arms off for that alone.

But Mercy only smiled at the young man. 'You helped Amos reunite with us, and I'm grateful. As far as I'm concerned, we're more than even. I've missed him more than I can say. Thank you.'

'And you reported my aunt Quill's murder,' Farrah added, 'and for that I have to thank you.'

Farrah's use of 'have to' wasn't lost on anyone, especially Bunker.

'She was a nice lady,' Bunker said, dropping his gaze to his feet. 'She was so proud of both of you. I hate that she was touched by any of this. That she . . .' He glanced up at Abigail, who was watching everything with wide eyes that seemed to miss nothing. 'Anyway. I'm so sorry for your loss.' He squared his shoulders. 'I'll go to my room now. If you need me to help search archives for this Herbert Hampton guy, please ask.'

Irina rolled her eyes. 'Sit, Jeffrey. We'll have cake.'

But Rafe was too surprised by Bunker's words to stem his own. 'Wait. He's staying here? In this house? With Zoya here? Why?' He narrowed his eyes. 'You never would have let us have "special friends" spend the night.'

Zoya glared at him as she took four servings of the cake. 'He's here because he brought Amos here, and Amos has most likely been discovered missing, which means that the people in Eden will be looking for him and anyone who's helping him. Jeff's at risk because he did a good thing. To make it worse, the FBI "can't spare" anyone to watch his house to make sure he and his mother are safe. So they are here. At our invitation. Mine, Mom's, and Dad's. You don't live here anymore, Rafe, so you can sh— be quiet,' she amended, then gave Bunker two of the four plates she'd prepared. 'Jeff, let's go back to the office. We can take your mother and my sister Meg some cake, too.'

The two of them left the kitchen, Zoya with an angry flounce and Bunker with a quiet sigh.

Irina said nothing as she served cake to everyone still at the table, but Rafe thought he saw her lips twitching. 'Mom, are you going to let Zoya get away with talking like that?'

'Yes,' Irina said simply.

'Because she's right,' Karl added, taking a bite of his cake. 'This is so good, Rini. Just like always.'

'Zoya *is* right,' Mercy murmured. '"Special friend sleepover" concerns aside, Jeff did us a big favor. I mean, I'm the one who has the most right to be angry about the article, and I'm really not. I'm grateful that Jeff cared enough to alert Irina to Amos's email. He didn't have to do that, but he did, and now Amos is here with us.' She squeezed Amos's hand, then turned a serious gaze onto Rafe and Gideon. 'Abigail already thinks you're an ogre, Gideon. I think we've got enough hatred coming at us from the true bad guys. Let's not feed it with our own anger, okay? I'm tired of being angry.'

Farrah sighed. 'You're right. Why are you always right? And don't look so happy with yourself.'

Mercy smirked. 'I'm not right all that often, so I'll be happy with myself as long as I want to.'

Rafe felt like Mercy had pulled a plug on his anger, and his shoulders sagged. He stuffed a forkful of cake in his mouth to combat the bad taste of that upcoming apology. 'Dammit,' he grumbled.

Mercy patted his face lightly. 'I'm not happy about Bunker's first article. I'm not. I'm embarrassed and I might have to wear a disguise out in public for the rest of my natural life. But here, when it's just us, I'm safe enough, and I can be clearheaded enough to know that the real danger is a lot worse than a few thousand people seeing me in a less than pleasant light.' She paused and looked around. 'Nobody has really talked about the fact that DJ is out there, too. He could be anywhere. Maybe use all that energy to think about following Bunker's advice. We need to find Eden, and Pastor is the cornerstone. If he embezzled that much money, *somebody* had to have covered the story. It exists somewhere, in some newspaper archive. We just need to find it. Amos, do you remember any of the articles from back then?'

'No. We were told not to read them, that it was just Satan's way of making us doubt.'

Rafe was about to scoff but saw the acceptance on Gideon and Mercy's faces. 'That was a thing, huh?' he asked instead.

'We were separate from the world,' Gideon said. 'And anyone who came into the compound from the outside had to take an oath to forget about the world and not speak of it. The world was determined to sway us from God and the Elders, so we were not to listen.'

'Mark them,' Mercy murmured. 'Have nothing to do with them.'

The words and the eerie, detached way that she spoke them sent a chill down Rafe's spine.

'They preached that?' Farrah asked. 'Have nothing to do with anyone who didn't agree?'

Mercy nodded. 'Every Sunday. And Monday and all the days that ended in "y". Paranoia was like mother's milk. At least in Eden.'

Amos looked uncomfortable. 'In Eden and in the LA church. And in some ways, I have to agree with that teaching. I've seen a lot today that I never, ever thought I'd see.'

'Zoya showed him some television,' Irina said.

Amos shook his head. 'I'm still . . . well, it's a very different world than the one I left.'

'What will you do next, Amos?' Mercy asked, seeming to need to change the subject. 'How can we help you settle in?'

'I have no idea,' Amos confessed. 'I need a job. I need a place to live. A school for Abigail. We need documents. Abigail doesn't even have a birth certificate. It's . . .' He trailed off helplessly.

'Overwhelming, Papa?' Abigail chirped, cake all over her mouth.

'Exactly that.' Amos wiped her mouth with a napkin. 'This much to do' – he stretched his arms wide – 'and this much time to do it.' He closed his arms around her, wrapping her in a hug.

'But you don't need to figure it out tonight,' Irina said firmly.

'We've all had a long day and I'm declaring it time to rest. Daisy and I have filled boxes for each of you. Take this food home and eat it. I texted Damien and asked him to follow you home, so I know you're safe.'

'Molina left us an escort,' Rafe said. 'Damien doesn't need to come.' Although he'd feel more comfortable with his brother in the house with them. One more trained cop could only be a good thing.

'As I said,' Irina said with a raised brow, 'Damien will be escorting you home. He just texted that he's here. Call me when you're safely inside your house.' She aimed looks at Daisy, Mercy, and Farrah. 'All of you. The boys always forget.'

Damien came into the kitchen and gave Irina a hug. 'Got your text, Mom. I'm good to follow them home.'

Rafe got up, leaning heavily on his cane. He didn't want to admit it, but he was exhausted. He couldn't imagine how tired Mercy must be. This day had been a goddamn roller coaster. 'Thanks, brother. I'll owe you one.'

Farrah hesitated, then kissed Irina on the cheek. 'I'm going to have to say goodbye to you all for now. My parents texted earlier. The ME released my aunt's body this afternoon. We're going to have her funeral day after tomorrow and I need to be home for my folks.'

Mercy looked torn. 'I need to be there with you, but if I go, I'll put everyone in your family at risk.'

'They know that,' Farrah said, cupping Mercy's cheek. 'And we all know that you'd be there if you could. André and I will fly out first thing tomorrow morning. If you still need me, I can be back by the weekend.'

Mercy's smile was sad. 'You'll video Quill's second line? She always said that she'd haunt us if she didn't get a jazz funeral procession.'

Farrah hugged her hard. 'Absolutely. I'll even carry a parasol just for you. Let's go, now. I need to pack and André and I need to sleep. We have an early morning.'

481

Karen Rose

Santa Rosa, California
Tuesday, 18 April, 10.00 P.M.

'Harry, come in, come in.' Dr Burkett held his front door open, ushering Ephraim inside. He'd aged in the ten years since doing the surgery on Ephraim's eye. The man had already been retired back then, so he had to be in his late seventies by now. And more frail than Ephraim remembered. If physical force was required, he could take the old man down, regardless of the throbbing in his pectoral where that bastard detective had shot him.

Burkett gestured at the sofa. 'Please make yourself comfortable.'

Right. That wasn't happening. Every muscle in his body was tense. Looking around cautiously, he set his duffel bag at his feet as he sank to the sofa. There was no way he was leaving his weapons in the stolen vehicle he'd driven from Sacramento. All he needed was for someone to take his bag, leaving him defenseless.

He was relieved to find that nothing seemed out of place inside the house, and he'd already checked the outside. No cops. Not a trap.

'I made some coffee,' Burkett offered cordially, as if he hadn't threatened Ephraim into coming. 'Would you like a cup?'

Ephraim considered just killing him and being done with it, but found he was curious as to what the older man wanted. 'That would be nice. I've got a long drive ahead of me.'

Burkett started for the kitchen, then turned to glare at Ephraim. 'I thought you'd see your mother before you left. She misses you.'

Ephraim rolled his eyes. 'Have you seen the news, Doctor?'

Burkett grimaced. 'Yes. But I could sign her out for a day visit. You could visit her right here.'

'I'll think about it,' Ephraim promised, but there was no way he meant it. If the Feds were watching his mother, he couldn't take the chance that she wouldn't be followed wherever the doctor wanted them to meet.

Burkett looked pleased. 'All right, then.' He disappeared for a moment, returning with a silver coffee service on a silver tray.

That was a lot of silver. Ephraim found himself mentally

482

calculating its worth as Burkett poured the coffee. 'Thank you.' The caffeine would help wake him up.

Except . . . Burkett wasn't drinking it and that had alarm bells clanging in Ephraim's mind. He pretended to take a sip, using the napkin the doctor had provided to wipe his lips afterward.

'You mentioned printouts of Mercy and the woman she was with today. Can I see them?'

'Of course.' Burkett looked away to pick up a folder from the coffee table, and Ephraim took the opportunity to quickly splash some of the coffee from the cup to the carpet. He reached for the folder when Burkett handed it to him. 'The photos the nurse's aide took are inside.'

Ephraim opened the folder and . . . there she was. Mercy Callahan. He'd expected her companion to be the black woman he'd seen with her at the airport, but this person was Caucasian and, to his knowledge, wasn't a Sokolov. This was what he'd been afraid of. He'd bet money that the woman was a cop. Which meant that the cops had the key to Ephraim's safe-deposit box. And if they didn't, she'd likely handed it over to her Fed brother. *Fucking hell.* 'You say you just missed them?'

'Yes. What was the key for? The one your mother gave this woman?'

'I don't know,' Ephraim lied.

Burkett's brows lifted. 'I think you do. I think it opens a safe-deposit box in a bank. And I think you're going to tell me which one.'

'You do, do you? Why would I do that, even if I did know?'

'Because if you don't, I'll call the police and tell them that I have the man they've been looking for since Saturday evening.'

'You think I'll just wait here for them to come?'

'Yes, because in about two minutes, you're going to be out like a light. If you tell me, I'll make sure the police don't find you. If you don't, I'll be placing a call to 911.'

What an asshole. Ephraim feigned fear. 'If you call the cops, you'll just implicate yourself. You harbored a fugitive when you operated on my eye.'

Burkett shrugged. 'No records of that exist, and do you really think they'd believe anything you say?'

'Do you really believe you can get into my safe-deposit box even if I tell you where it is?' Rolling his eyes, Ephraim started to rise, but sank back into the sofa cushion when the doctor drew a pistol outfitted with a silencer.

'Where is the damn box, Harry?' Burkett snapped.

Ephraim stared at the barrel of Burkett's gun. *I should have shot him when I first walked in the door. That'll teach me to be curious.* 'It won't matter if I tell you or not. You can't get into it without me.'

'But I bet your mother still can.' Burkett smiled. 'You took her keys, but did you remove her as an authorized co-renter?'

Fuck. No, he hadn't. He'd taken her key, but he hadn't removed her as someone authorized to open the box. Ephraim pursed his lips, abruptly furious with himself and with Burkett. And with his mother, if he was being honest. It wasn't her fault that she had dementia, but it had become a fucking pain in his ass.

'What do you think is in the box?' he asked, stifling a yawn. He hadn't swallowed any of what was probably drugged coffee, but he'd also had a very long day.

'The money you and your brother stole from that bank thirty years ago. I figure that with Aubrey dead, you get to keep it all.'

Oh. Now it made sense. His mother hadn't known that they'd given all the money to Pastor to invest as payment for joining Eden. 'It's marked,' he said. Which it had been. Apparently Pastor's connections had known how to launder it before socking it away offshore.

Burkett's eyes lit up. 'So you still have it. I don't care if it's marked. My creditors don't care, either. We only care that you haven't spent it.' He tensed his jaw. 'Tell me which bank. Now.'

Ephraim yawned again, this one faked. 'Ask my mom,' he said, slurring his words for effect.

'I did. She doesn't remember. Listen to me, Harry, and listen well. Once that sedative drags you under, you'll be asleep for at least twelve hours. If you tell me where to find the safe-deposit box, you'll wake up. If not, I'll kill you and tell the cops that I shot you in self-defense because you broke into my home.'

It was what he'd expected, but rage still boiled up from Ephraim's gut. *Asshole.*

He could go for his own gun, but the doctor would shoot him before he could draw it from its holster. He swallowed hard. And pretended to be getting sleepier. *Play along until he lets his guard down.* 'What difference does it make what the key is for? She gave it to Mercy. The cops probably have it.'

'True, but they'll have to get a warrant. All that takes time.'

'And if I tell you, I'll wake up?'

Burkett nodded too eagerly. 'I promise.'

Yeah, right. He let his eyelids dip to half-mast, so that he looked affected by the sedative but could still see Burkett. 'What if she's too batshit?'

Burkett frowned. 'Your mother?'

Ephraim made a production of swallowing hard. 'Yeah. What if the bank knows she's incon . . . incomp . . .' He pretended to be frustrated. 'Incompetent?'

Burkett's frown melted into a smile. 'Then you and I will take a trip to the bank together. When you wake up, of course.'

Fuck you, asshole. But the asshole still held a gun on him, so he continued to play along. 'Won't work. Cops will catch me. Bank will call the cops.'

'No, because I'll stay with the bank teller, and if she tries anything, I'll give her the same thing I just gave you. She won't be making any phone calls.'

Ephraim snorted drunkenly. 'And she'll just drink your coffee?'

Burkett smiled. 'I have other ways to administer the drug.'

Ephraim smiled back, making himself look as goofy as he could. 'Then I can see my mother?'

'Absolutely. I'll bring her here when we're done at the bank so that you can see her with your own eyes.'

'Okay.' Ephraim dropped his head to his shoulder. 'Costa Bank,' he slurred. 'Main branch.'

'Thank you,' Burkett murmured. 'Was that so hard?'

Ephraim let out a sleepy groan and let his eyes droop closed. He was tensed, though, listening for the sound of Burkett's finger on the trigger of his silenced gun. *So far so good*, he thought when nothing happened. *I'm still here.* He played possum for at least two minutes, biding his time until he heard the shuffle of the doctor's shoes on the carpet, followed by an audible sigh of relief.

'Sleep well, Harry,' the man said softly. 'Sorry about this, really.'

Amateur, Ephraim thought with contempt, then braced himself when he heard the jangle of . . . It didn't matter. Springing from the sofa headfirst, he stayed below the line of fire to head-butt the doctor's gut. Burkett dropped like a rock with a cry of shock, discharging the gun as his back hit the floor. The bullet hit the ceiling harmlessly, sending plaster dust falling like rain.

Ephraim kicked the gun away, then shoved a knee into Burkett's chest. Grabbing his head, he snapped the doctor's neck. 'Sleep well, Doctor,' he mocked, breathing hard. 'Sorry about this. Not really.'

He glanced to one side, realizing that the jangle had come from the handcuffs that Burkett had dropped to the carpet. He shoved them into his pocket, then, threat eliminated, fell back onto the sofa. He needed to think. There was a chance that Mercy still had the safe-deposit box key, that she hadn't turned it over to the cops. At least not yet. They wouldn't have even gotten back to Sacramento until well after six. If she didn't know what she had, she might be waiting until morning to hand it over.

And you might be wishing for a miracle that's not coming.

Regardless, he needed to empty the contents of that safe-deposit box before the cops got a warrant. He had a key of his own, but he couldn't just waltz into a bank and ask to open his safe-deposit box. Because thanks to Rafe Sokolov and that damn airport video, his face was all over the news.

I could go back to Eden and not worry about it. He'd be safe in Eden. Ironically enough, Eden was the only place he could be safe right now.

Unless Mercy gave the key to the cops and they opened the damn safe-deposit box.

The Feds would raid the compound faster than they could move to a new location. And all those beautiful millions under Pastor's control would be confiscated by the motherfucking government.

Unless he got the bank codes first.

Or . . . I could just chuck it all and go to Mexico. There were ways to slip over the border undetected. He could figure it out. He'd be free. But poor.

Dammit. It was simply too much money to leave behind. With all that cash, he'd never have to work again. He could retire someplace warm where he had no responsibilities. And hopefully he'd be surrounded by beautiful girls who were exactly to his liking. *I want that money. I* earned *that money.*

So once again, it came back to Mercy. He needed her. Needed to haul her ass back to Eden. And preferably before she handed that damn key over to the cops. Once the Feds opened the safe-deposit box, it was all over.

He rubbed his temples, trying to think of what to do next. First on the list was to trade the old vehicle he'd stolen that afternoon for Burkett's ride, which would be less noticeable around Rafe Sokolov's Victorian. He searched the dead doctor's jacket pockets, staring in surprise when he pulled out four prepared syringes and a bottle.

Ephraim held the bottle to the light to read the label. *Ketamine HCl.*

'Fucker,' he snarled under his breath. This was how Burkett had planned to keep him asleep for twelve hours. The sedative in his coffee would've been only the beginning.

He pocketed the bottle and syringes and searched Burkett's pants pockets, finding his key ring. Adding Burkett's gun to his duffel, he shouldered the bag and dragged the other man's body to the garage, which held a chest freezer and an Escalade.

Perfect. The Escalade was shiny and new, and would blend into Sokolov's neighborhood. It would also haul the honeymooners' camper with no trouble at all. He opened the chest freezer, pleased to see it nearly empty. The doctor fit well enough, after Ephraim cracked a couple of his bones.

He dumped the body into the freezer, then stepped back, wincing as he rolled his shoulder. The guy was heavier than he looked. *And I'm tired.* At least he hadn't reopened his wound. The bandage was still dry. No new blood. *Time to get out of here.*

Drawing a deep breath, he took a step toward the Escalade and froze. Then inhaled again.

Cigarette smoke. *Fresh* cigarette smoke.

Someone is here. Or was here. Drawing his weapon, Ephraim turned in a tight circle, searching the shadows for the smoker. But he was alone.

He hadn't been, though. He took more deep breaths, scenting the air, following the smell of smoke, but it was already fading. Ephraim might have wondered if he'd imagined it.

Until he found the butt on the garage floor. Gingerly he picked it up and held it under his cell phone flashlight. *Marlboro.* Most of the name was visible and the butt was still warm.

His jaw tightened. *DJ.* DJ Belmont smoked Marlboros when he went off property – not many, because he managed to never smell of cigarette smoke when he returned.

But DJ couldn't be here. That was impossible. There was no way that DJ could have tracked him here. Unless . . . *Fucking hell. Fucking fucking hell.*

Burkett had gotten Ephraim's number from Pastor. Pastor could have sent DJ here to get him.

Except . . . Eden was almost six hours' drive to Santa Rosa. For DJ to have beaten him here, he would've had to have left at four that afternoon at the latest. That was possible, depending on when Burkett had called Pastor.

I could call Pastor and ask him. Of course that would tip Pastor off if he had sent DJ.

Ephraim scowled, unable to think of a better way to discover when Burkett and Pastor had their little chat. He hadn't found a phone in Burkett's pockets and he didn't want to hang around here to search. DJ was younger and Ephraim wasn't at his fighting best. If DJ was lurking outside, Ephraim didn't think he could win a face-to-face showdown. Not tonight.

Just go. If he shoots at you, shoot back. He stowed the duffel on the

Escalade's passenger seat and started the engine before hitting the button for the garage door opener.

Gun clutched in one hand, he hunkered down as the door slid up, put the SUV in reverse, then started down the driveway, expecting a bullet to pierce one of the windows at any moment. DJ was a damn good shot. *Better than me.*

But there were no bullets. No gunfire.

There was, however, a dark sedan parked down the street that followed him as he left Burkett's neighborhood. A glance in the rear-view revealed a head of white-blond hair reflecting the glow of the streetlights. Not blond like Mercy's detective, Rafe Sokolov. That would have been bad enough.

It was DJ. He was sure of it.

Fuck you, Pastor.

Stay calm. DJ might have been a better shot, but Ephraim was a much better driver. He kept an eye on the rear-view mirror, watching the dark sedan match him, move for move.

Fucker. Ephraim pulled onto the interstate going north, weaving between cars, then allowing the sedan to get a little too close before crossing three lanes of traffic and pulling off the exit in a cacophony of horns. Not prepared for the move, DJ missed the exit and kept driving.

Ephraim exhaled in relief, then started for Sacramento, using a state road instead of the interstate. It would take him longer to get there, but DJ wouldn't know where he'd gone and that was good enough for now.

Twenty-seven

Sacramento, California
Tuesday, 18 April, 10.05 P.M.

Mercy closed the apartment door and began unbuttoning her coat as she looked at the box at her feet. 'It was nice of your mother to make more food, but I'm not sure it'll fit in the fridge. It's still full from the last time. I might have to put some of it in the freezer.'

She'd shooed him straight to the sofa as soon as they'd entered the apartment, and Rafe hadn't complained. He felt like he'd been through two dozen of Cash's PT sessions. At least.

'I think the freezer is also full. Mom's always cooked when she's stressed out. If we came home from school and the kitchen was filled with food, we knew Mom was upset about something. For all her "You *vill* do this, you *vill* do that," she really hates confrontations. She's a softie, but I won't ever admit that I said that.'

He lowered himself to the sofa, ignoring the pain in his leg because Mercy was hanging her coat in the closet like she'd done it a thousand times.

He wished she would. He wished he could tell her that he wanted her to stay. But it wasn't time for that. Not yet. They had another seven and a half weeks until she went back to New Orleans.

A fact that startled a laugh out of him.

'What's so funny?' Mercy asked, on her way to the kitchen, Irina's box in her arms.

'Come sit with me and I'll tell you.'

Two minutes later, she did, sitting so close that their hips touched. So close that he could put his arm around her shoulders and pull her

490

against his chest. So he did, feeling like he could finally breathe again when she melted into him.

'I was thinking how you still had seven and a half weeks of leave left. You've only been here four days.'

'Feels like four weeks already,' she agreed wryly. 'Facing my batshit-crazy ex-mother-in-law, reuniting with my stepfather, and being shot at by my evil ex-husband is kind of a lot.' She sighed. 'Then I think of the lives DJ and Ephraim have stolen and feel selfish for worrying about myself. And don't tell me that it's not my fault. I *know* it's not. But I still feel responsible.'

He kissed her temple. 'I wouldn't respect you so much if you didn't care about the lives Ephraim and DJ have taken. And I do. Respect you, I mean. I don't think I'd be handling this nearly as well if I were in your shoes. You're stronger than you know.'

She looked at him, gratitude in her eyes. 'Thank you. I've been considered fragile by so many people for so long. It's nice to be seen as strong. It's good for my ego,' she added with a self-deprecating grimace.

He gripped her chin gently, needing to wipe that grimace from her face. 'I don't think you have much of an ego.' He kissed her the way he'd wanted to do since they'd left the apartment that morning, long and lush and full of all the emotion he was afraid to put into words. *Stay. Stay with me.*

Turning in to the kiss, she slid her arms around his neck, making a sound that was part purr, part growl, and his body woke up. He wasn't tired anymore. Not at all.

When that kiss ended, she drew his head down for another, fluidly rising to her knees to take control, and he couldn't hold back a groan. Didn't want to hold back. He wanted her to know what she did to him, exactly how much power she held over him. Restlessly he ran his hands up her sides, skimming her breasts before sliding down to her waist, tugging her closer.

He wanted more. He wanted everything. But he didn't dare take any more, tamping down on his impatience. She'd had a rough day. He wouldn't make demands.

But if *she* did, he sure as hell wasn't going to say no. And if she didn't, he was more than satisfied. He could kiss her like this all night long if that was all she wanted.

When she lifted her head, they were both panting and her green eyes had grown dark and slightly dazed. Her lips, shiny and plump, curved. 'Oh yeah. I do,' she whispered huskily.

'Do? Do what?'

She brushed her lips over his. 'Have an ego.'

He blinked up at her. 'Huh?'

Her dimples appeared and he wanted to lick them. 'You said that you didn't think I had much of an ego, but I do. And you're really good at . . . stroking it.'

His cock lurched and he grimaced because his pants were now uncomfortably tight. Closing his eyes, he groaned as his head fell backward to the soft sofa cushion. He managed not to buck his hips, but just barely. 'You're mean, Mercy. So damn mean.'

'No, I'm not,' she said smoothly. 'I'd be mean if I was only teasing. But I'm not.' With that, she stunned him by swinging one leg over him, so that she straddled his lap.

Before he could stop himself, he covered her butt with both palms, kneading her flesh as he dragged her against him. His hips punched up, needing the contact, the friction. But he didn't need to thrust too hard because she met him halfway, grinding down on him. Hard.

'Oh my God. Mercy,' he groaned. He tightened his grip on her butt, stopping her from swiveling her hips. 'You're killing me here.'

She tunneled her fingers into his hair, pulling his head upright for another scorching kiss that scrambled his brains. 'Not gonna kill you,' she muttered darkly, sending a thrill rippling over his skin. She let go of his hair, her fingers moving to his tie to pull it free of his collar. 'Not done with you. Haven't even started.'

He shook his head, trying to clear it. 'Wait. Just wait.'

Her hands immediately stilled and his brain rebelled. *No, no, what are you saying? Don't wait. No wait!*

He forced himself to breathe. 'Wait,' he said again, not sure who he was talking to, because he wanted to roll her to her back and thrust inside her over and over.

But he had to be sure. She had to be sure. He opened his eyes to

492

see her poised above him, his tie gripped in both of her fists. She said nothing, simply stared down at him. Her cheeks were pink, her eyes intense, and she delicately touched the tip of her tongue to her upper lip as if testing it.

He shuddered, wanting that tongue on his body. Those lips wrapped around his cock. 'What do you want, Mercy? You need to be very specific.'

She smiled slowly, sensing victory. 'I want everything.' She licked his lower lip. 'Everything.'

When she started to slide his tie free, he covered her fisted hands with his. 'Wait. Please.' He needed her to spell it out. 'What does everything include? I don't want to push you into anything you don't want.'

'You're not pushing me into anything.' She tugged on his tie with both hands. 'I'm pulling you, if you want to get technical.' She leaned in for a soft kiss, but not a tentative one. There wasn't a tentative bone in her body at the moment.

Or in his. Some bones were far less tentative than others. 'Okay,' he rasped, then cleared his throat, holding on to control by the barest of threads. 'Just so we're clear, I want you more than I want to breathe. But I don't want you to regret anything we do.'

'Just so we're clear, I won't. And just so we're clear?' She tugged his tie, bringing his face a breath away from hers. '*Everything* means I want to be under you and I want to feel you inside me.' She lightly nipped at his lip. 'Is that definition clear?'

Oh. My. God. Heat washed over him and he arched backward, bucking up into her, groaning when she swiveled her hips, torturing him for sure. 'Jesus.' He gasped for air, loving the sound of her satisfied chuckle. Tentative Mercy had left the building. This was powerful Mercy and he was going to trust that she knew her mind. 'Yes. Okay. Whatever you want.'

She grazed her teeth up his jaw, closing them over his earlobe. 'Smart man.'

'But . . .' He laughed breathlessly when she ripped the tie from his collar and tossed it to one side, going for the buttons on his shirt. 'Wait. Just one more second.'

She stilled again, this time with an impatient sigh. 'What?'

He took her chin, tilting her face so that he could see her eyes. 'If you don't like anything I do, or if you want me to stop for any reason, say "stop". I will. I promise. Tell me you understand.'

She nodded gravely. 'I understand. I trust you. Are you finished now?'

'Yes.' His heart was beating so hard it almost hurt. She trusted him when no one would blame her for never trusting anyone ever again. It was a gift, and while Mercy wasn't fragile, her trust was. He'd protect her trust, no matter the cost. 'All finished. Well, with the PSA portion of our evening anyway. I hope the cardio portion is just beginning.' He had no problem ceding control. Not to Mercy. 'Where do you want me?'

She grinned, sliding off his lap until she stood in front of him. But then her gaze dropped to his body and all levity fled. He sat sprawled before her, legs spread, shirt halfway open and, he was sure, eyes sex-glazed. For a horrible moment he thought she'd changed her mind, until she slowly dropped to her knees. Frozen in place but hoping like hell, he could only stare.

'Anywhere I can have you.' She finished unbuttoning his shirt, then freed the cuffs on his sleeves. And then she touched him. Really touched him, her hand gripping his cock through his pants.

He hissed, arching into her touch. 'Mercy.'

'My name or a request?' she murmured.

'Either. Both.' His body twisted, trying to get satisfaction. 'Please.'

She let him go, fumbling with the button of his pants. He moaned when she got it free and lowered his zipper, dipping her hand into his briefs to wrap her fingers around him.

'You like that?' she asked coyly.

'You know I do. Please, Mercy. Pick a place. Sofa or bed. I won't make it much longer.'

'Oh, I think you will.' She worked him with long strokes, just as she had that morning. She'd quickly learned what he liked.

He strained, thrusting into her fist, then remembered something important. Feeling blindly in the interior pocket of his jacket, he pulled out his wallet and found the condom he'd stored there.

'Boy Scout,' Mercy teased, a husky, breathy sound.

He cursed when she twisted her fist around the head of his cock. 'If you truly want to feel me inside you, you'll stop right now, or it'll be all over.'

She pulled her hand away abruptly, rolling to her feet. 'Then hurry.'

Levering himself off the couch, he ignored the sharp pain in his leg and kicked off his shoes. Grabbing his cane, he followed her to the bed, grateful for once that the studio apartment was so small. He was shrugging out of his shirt when he froze once again.

She'd pulled her sweater over her head, leaving her in her jeans and bra. It wasn't a lacy bra. It was practical. Functional. But the plain cotton cupped her breasts like a dream and he held out his hand when she went to pull down the straps.

'Let me,' he said, amazed that his voice didn't shake.

Obediently, her hands lowered to her sides, and she waited, her eyes expectant.

No fear, he thought, relieved. Just anticipation. Which was exactly as it was supposed to be.

Rafe rounded the bed, shuddering when he touched her. He buried his face in the curve of her neck, proud of the shiver that pebbled her soft skin. 'You're beautiful. Tell me that you know that.'

She tilted her head against his and he could feel her swallow. 'You're biased, I think.'

He straightened to meet her eyes. 'You'll say it eventually. I'll make you believe it.' He slid his arms around her back, unhooking her bra with only a little difficulty.

She chuckled. 'Can I say that I'm glad you're not so good at that?'

He kissed her smiling mouth. 'My reputation as a player was a sham. Kept my mother and sisters from trying to set me up with all those women who weren't you.'

He stepped back, taking her bra with him. Then taking a breath as he drank in the sight of her. 'It's been too long.'

'It's been sixteen hours.'

'Too long.' He tossed the bra and made quick work of her slacks, leaving her in a pair of equally practical panties and a pair of socks. Winding one hand in her hair, he tilted her face up for a kiss, pressing her backward until her legs hit the bed. She fell to her back, bouncing slightly before propping herself on her forearms.

'You too. I want to see you.'

The husky demand sent a new shudder through his body. He shoved his slacks and briefs down in a jingle of coins and keys, suddenly done with the dance. He yanked off his socks, then yanked off hers.

'Lie back,' he ordered, waiting until she'd complied before reaching for the waistband of her panties. And . . . something changed. She bit her lip and looked a little scared. *You promised you'd stop.*

You promised. So he would. He closed his eyes, releasing his hold on her underwear. 'It's all right, Mercy. We'll stop.'

'I'm not changing my mind,' she blurted out.

'All right.' Drawing a breath, he sat on the bed, his hip to hers, bending his knee so that he could see her face. 'Then what is it?'

'I have a scar.' She pointed to her lower abdomen, still covered by the white cotton. 'I didn't want you to freak out about it. It's not big, but it's . . . not pretty.'

His mind spun for a few seconds, trying to put together what she was telling him. Had Ephraim stabbed her? And then he remembered. The night she'd escaped, DJ had shot her in the abdomen. On top of whatever issues had caused her mother to smuggle her out, she'd had to fight a gunshot wound to survive.

But she *had* survived.

'Do you trust me?' Rafe whispered.

Swallowing hard, she nodded.

'Thank you.' He leaned in to kiss her, long enough to have her sighing. He pulled the cotton away from her body and relaxed. It wasn't that bad a scar. To her, though, it had been the culmination of a catastrophic year. A catastrophic life. And the night she'd lost her mother.

Gently, he rubbed the pad of his thumb over the puckered skin. 'You could tattoo it,' he suggested lightly, knowing that his reaction would be one she'd remember forever. 'Maybe a small fox, peeking out of the bush?' He grazed the neatly trimmed line of her pubic hair.

She stared at him for a long, long moment, eyes wide with disbelief. Then laughed, a true belly laugh that made her breasts jiggle in the most tantalizing way. 'You're ridiculous.'

He bent to kiss the scar, relieved as hell. 'So is any worry about this. I have plenty of scars, Mercy. Whenever I see yours, I'll just remember that you're still here. With me.'

She lifted her brows. 'Planning to see it again, are you?'

He settled himself between her legs, bracing himself on his forearms so that she didn't feel trapped. 'Planning to make you so addicted to me that you won't even remember it's there.'

She brushed his hair away from his brow. 'I don't think that'll be too hard. Kiss me, Rafe.'

So he did, putting everything he had into the kiss, groaning when she slid her arms around his neck again and kissed him back.

'I'm going to take my time with you,' he murmured as he kissed his way down her throat. 'Not gonna hurry. Not gonna rush.'

She did that swivel thing with her hips that made him lose his mind. 'There's a very good chance that we'll be doing this again,' she said, already breathing hard.

He kissed her collarbone. 'That's not why I'm going to take my time.' He skimmed his lips down to her breast, licking her nipple. Making her gasp.

She let out a soft moan. 'No?'

'No. Not because I'm afraid this is it. It's because you deserve to be worshipped.' He sucked her nipple into his mouth and she cried out. He'd watched her that morning. He'd use everything he'd learned to give her this, their first time together, something she'd never forget. He moved to her other breast, sucking, then returning to kiss her mouth again, before repeating the routine until she writhed beneath him and his cock was leaking all over the sheets. He was shaking with the effort of holding back, but he wanted her mindless.

He wanted it to be glorious for her. *For both of us.*

Soon. He'd be inside her soon. *Soon, soon, soon.* He chanted the words in his mind to stave off his orgasm until she shoved at his shoulders.

'Now,' she demanded. She flung her arm to the side, fingers feeling for the condom he'd left on the nightstand. 'Do it now. Please, Rafe. Please.'

Yes. Now. He reared to his knees, putting his weight on his good leg so that he could roll the condom on without falling over. Because wouldn't that be sexy as hell.

He looked down to find her staring up at him, her green eyes dark with nothing but lust. No, not only lust. There was intense affection there too, and it gripped his heart a split second before she gripped his cock.

'Now,' she repeated.

'Now,' he echoed. And then, watching her every reaction, he slid into her, exhaling on a ragged groan. 'God. Mercy.'

Her eyes fluttered closed and she hummed. 'Move. Please.'

So he did, mentally recording every expression on her face, the pleasure he saw there. He noted what made her breath hitch and what made her moan. What made her dig her nails into his skin, what made her claw at his back. What made her wrap her legs around his hips and work herself on him.

He clenched his teeth harder, trying to hold off coming until he couldn't anymore. Shifting to one arm, he slid his hand between their bodies, finding her clit and fingering her, fast and hard.

'Now,' he whispered. 'Come for me, Mercy. Now.'

He pinched her clit and she cried out, body arching, face so goddamn beautiful that he forgot to breathe. And then he was coming too, pressing his face to her neck as his body convulsed and his vision went white.

His head stopped spinning eventually. She was petting him like he was one of her cats, long strokes up his spine and into his hair. He couldn't think of a single coherent word to say. But she did.

'Glorious,' she whispered.

His lips curved against her skin, damp with perspiration. Pride filled him, but he didn't think he could preen if his life depended on it. 'Yes.'

And he'd do even better the next time.

say no more

'You didn't need to see us off,' Farrah said when Mercy met her and André coming down Rafe's stairs. But she followed it up with a hug so hard that Mercy's ribs protested. 'You need to sleep.'

'I did. A little.' And then Rafe had woken her up and they'd made love all over again and it had been more glorious than the first time. When she'd heard footsteps on the landing, she'd left him in bed, him snoring quietly and her feeling ridiculously proud of herself for wearing him out.

Farrah coughed to cover a laugh. 'Um, right.' She sniffed delicately at yesterday's sweater that Mercy had thrown on when she'd heard voices in the hall. 'I think I know what you were doing when you weren't sleeping a little.'

Mercy's cheeks flamed and she took a horrified step back. She hadn't realized that Farrah could smell what they'd been doing.

'Leave her alone, Farrah,' André said. He leaned in to kiss Mercy's cheek. 'Go back inside now. We don't want you anywhere near the door when we go out.'

Mercy frowned. 'I hate that you're going to the airport alone.'

'We're not,' André assured her. 'Rafe's brother Damien is going to drive us in his car, then he'll come back later to return the rental.'

'He was worried that the rental's been in the driveway all this time,' Farrah explained. 'Especially after Burton planted the trackers on Erin's SUV and Sasha's Mini.'

'Has Damien been sitting outside all this time?' Mercy asked, worried about him now. 'He can't have gotten any sleep.'

'More sleep than you did,' Damien said, coming down the stairs. 'The Fed Molina sent watched my car so that I could get some shut-eye. I slept on Sasha's couch.' He winced. 'Tell Rafe that the floors are really thin.'

Mercy covered her face with both hands when his meaning sank in. 'Oh my God.'

Damien chuckled. 'I'll be back later, Mercy. Tell Rafe he can make it up to me with pancakes when he finally wakes his ass up.'

499

'I'll tell him,' she managed to splutter, then hugged André and Farrah again. 'Call me when you get home, so I know you're safe.'

Farrah cupped Mercy's cheeks, her smile sweet. 'I will. Please be careful, but more than that, be happy. You've earned this, Mercy Callahan. You've earned happiness, so grab it with both hands.'

Mercy's throat grew thick. 'I was so lucky the day our paths crossed,' she whispered. 'Love you, Ro.'

Farrah's eyes filled. 'Love you, too.'

André cleared his throat. 'Ladies, I hate to cut your lovefest short, but we do have a plane to catch. Go inside, Mercy. I'll make sure Farrah gets home just fine.'

With a teary wave, Mercy obeyed, leaning against Rafe's door and listening for the front door to close before she headed to bed. But the sight of Rafe's bulletin board stopped her in her tracks. She stood for a long moment, staring at the photos of Ephraim Burton and Edward McPhearson, aka Harry and Aubrey Franklin. In her mind she added the images of Pastor, who they now knew as Herbert Hampton, plus Waylon and DJ. All of them except for DJ had been there at Eden's founding.

I was so lucky the day our paths crossed. The words she'd just said to Farrah rolled around in her mind, but now they bothered her. Like a name or a word that hovered on the edge of memory. *The day our paths crossed*, she thought again. And then it hit her. Her path had crossed Farrah's at college, that first day. Mercy was there because her half siblings were there, even though she hadn't met them yet. Farrah was there because everyone in her family had gone to that university.

How had the leaders of Eden ended up there? How had *their* paths crossed? Ephraim and Edward were brothers, so that answer was clear, but how had their paths crossed with Pastor's? When Ephraim and Edward were on the run, why did they run to Eden? DJ was Waylon's son, but exactly how did Waylon fit in?

She sat on the sofa and reached for Rafe's notebook. At the top of a blank page she wrote, *How do they connect? Where did they meet?* Below she jotted ideas as they popped into her mind. *Random? E & E just stumbled into Eden? Why was Waylon the only one allowed to leave the compound?* And then, *Edward served time.*

Aubrey Franklin's mug shot was testament to that fact. Rafe had already researched it, tacking to his bulletin board the newspaper articles about the thirty-year-old bank robbery and murder of three people. One article said that Aubrey had served time at Terminal Island, a federal correctional institution in LA, for an even older bank robbery.

Mercy tapped her pen to the paper, then wrote, *Amos said that Pastor was accused of embezzling from his former church and falsifying his résumé.*

She'd been surprised that Pastor had been an actual pastor. But what if he hadn't been? What if that had been the résumé falsification? She underlined *falsifying his résumé*, wrote *Why?*, and then closed her eyes, picturing Pastor and Waylon.

Pastor had been . . . normal looking. Average height. Brown hair, glasses that made him look smart. His was the kind of face that blended into a crowd.

But Waylon . . . he'd been different. Huge and hulking. 'Oh,' she whispered aloud. And covered in tattoos. How had she forgotten about that?

Because you didn't have much reason to be around Waylon. And she'd been only nine years old when the man had died. Just days after returning with a body he'd claimed was Gideon's. That she'd blocked it out was understandable, she supposed.

She circled the sentence *Why was Waylon the only one allowed to leave the compound?* Then around it she jotted *Covered in tattoos* and *Most memorable face of all of them.*

She sucked in a startled breath, then exhaled it slowly when Waylon's face sharpened in her memory. She wrote, *Teardrop tat under his eye.* Teardrop tats usually meant a person had been to prison. Had *killed* someone while in prison.

Waylon had been to prison. Just like Edward McPhearson, aka Aubrey Franklin.

Ephraim had also had a record, but he'd only been in juvie. He'd still been a minor when he robbed the bank with his brother, and the two had never been caught.

501

But both Aubrey Franklin and Waylon had been to prison.

She tore out that sheet and started a new one. *PRISON*, she wrote in all caps. *TERMINAL ISLAND FCI. Was Waylon there, too? Was Pastor?*

On her phone she googled the prison, finding the phone number easily. But they weren't open until eight a.m. On the second sheet of paper, she copied the phone number and *8 am*. Then tacked both pages on Rafe's bulletin board. She could sleep a little more, for now.

She set her alarm and climbed back into bed with Rafe, cuddling up against him, sighing when his arms came around her. He held her like he'd never let go. Even sound asleep, he made her feel warm and safe. And happy.

Sacramento, California
Wednesday, 19 April, 10.10 A.M.

'Yes, thank you. I'll be expecting her call.' Rafe ended the call and pocketed his phone, still staring at the new additions to his bulletin board.

Mercy had gotten up sometime during the night and done some amazing detective work. That Aubrey and Waylon had met in prison was breakthrough thinking. That Pastor might have been there, too? That could be the thing that tied it all together.

'Whose call?'

Rafe looked up with a smile. Mercy was barefoot, her hair mussed, wearing her clothes from the day before, and rubbing her eyes like a sleepy kid on Christmas morning. Thankfully, Mercy Callahan was no kid. She was cute and sexy all at the same time.

And she's mine. Once again he wanted to ask her to stay. Once again he held back. *Still too soon.*

'One of the deputy wardens at Terminal Island. I found your notes.'

Mercy grimaced. 'What time is it? I meant to wake up and call them already. I set my alarm for eight o'clock and everything.'

'It's after ten. Your alarm went off at eight, and I snoozed it.

You'd slept through about four snoozes when I finally got up, had some coffee, then found this. Mercy, this is amazing. When did you get up?'

'It's after ten already?' she asked dismayed. 'Why didn't you wake me?'

'Why didn't you wake me up when you were doing this?'

A shy smile curved her lips. 'You looked so peaceful that I didn't have the heart.'

'Same goes. Besides, you were out like a light. I don't think a bulldozer could have woken you up.'

'I guess I was tired.' She got a cup of coffee and curled up in the corner of the sofa. 'I heard Farrah and André leaving and went out in the foyer to say goodbye.' She held up her hand, staving off his apparently obvious outrage. 'Chill, Rafe. I didn't go outside. I wasn't even in the foyer when they went out. André made me come in. Damien took them to the airport.' Her cheeks abruptly flushed. 'Oh, and he says the floors are really thin.'

Rafe snorted. 'So noted.'

'The deputy warden is calling you back? I guess you called the correctional facility this morning?'

Rafe sat beside her, settling when she cuddled close. 'I did. I already requested whatever they have on Aubrey Franklin a few weeks ago, but never got anything, so I called back this morning under the pretense of following up. The person I talked to in the office said that she'd been working on the request, but that she'd gotten sidetracked, yada yada blah blah.' He waved his hand in irritation. 'She seemed really sorry and promised to get me the information, so I asked if she could include anything about Aubrey's known associates in prison. Just now she called to say that her boss, the deputy warden, would be calling me directly.'

'You touched a nerve.'

'Maybe. I hope so.' He sighed. 'And I also talked to Erika Mann.'

'Who is she?'

Rafe opened his email with a shake of his head. 'The reporter who followed the Herbert Hampton story back in the late eighties.' He showed her the email from Zoya. 'Bunker found her.'

'"I hope this shuts you up",' Mercy read. '"Jeff was up all night searching online archives from LA newspapers. Erika Mann is the reporter you need to talk to. Here is her current contact information. You're welcome very much".' She looked up with a wince. 'Ouch. Zoya is pissed with you.'

'Maybe I deserve it.' He sighed when Mercy lifted her brows. 'Fine, I deserve it.'

She patted his thigh. 'Spoken like a man who's exhausted all of his plausible defense strategies. What did Ms Mann say?'

'Mostly what Amos said. She had a few more things to add. Hampton's résumé falsifications included claims that he'd graduated from Yale's Divinity School and had a PhD from UC Berkeley. Neither school had heard of him when she investigated.'

'Who spilled the beans initially?'

'This is where it gets interesting. One of the members of the church – a college-aged kid – got suspicious because he was studying at UC Berkeley and they didn't have the program that Hampton claimed had awarded his degree. The kid asked his professor about it and the prof got curious. The professor checked with the registrar and discovered that there was no record of Hampton having ever attended. He then called Yale and found the same thing. He told the kid, who called the church elders. Specifically one Amos Terrill, who she described as an elderly man with an almost fanatical devotion to Pastor Hampton.'

'Amos's grandfather.' Mercy frowned. 'And then what happened?'

'Terrill didn't believe the college kid, according to Ms Mann. Then the church split, just like Amos described. And then the whistle-blower kid was the victim of a "random beating" outside an all-night diner near his parents' house in LA.'

Mercy gasped. 'Oh my God. Amos wouldn't do that.'

At least Rafe could give her comfort on that point. 'No, the grandfather had died and Amos had disappeared by then. So had Hampton. But even after Hampton left, the members who'd finally successfully ousted him wanted justice. The boy's family was part of this group and they were actively searching for Hampton and calling him a crook. The kid graduated from Berkeley and became a reporter. Ms Mann said she mentored him and he had a lot of promise. He was determined to see Hampton brought to justice. He'd even started looking for him. But after the beating, he retreated and left town. She doesn't know where he is, but thinks he changed his name to throw his attackers off the trail, because his parents' house was torched a few days after the beating.'

'Wow. Amos said it got vicious, but that's worse than I expected.'

'I know. Mann says that he told her he was afraid for his parents, that seeing Hampton in jail wasn't worth their lives. She got the impression that whoever beat him up had threatened his family too, but he wouldn't confirm it to her.'

Mercy was quiet for a long moment. 'I wonder what happened to all that money that members donated to Eden?'

'That's a damn good question.'

She looked up at him. 'You *have* apologized to Jeff Bunker, haven't you? And thanked him?'

'Yes to both.' He scowled. 'And it really hurt, too.'

She kissed his cheek. 'I'm sure it did. So thank you.'

'Yeah,' he said, only slightly mollified, because it had hurt. Mostly because he knew he'd been too hard on Bunker and was ashamed of himself. 'And then I told Mann about him and she said she'd seen his retraction. She said that he could contact her if he'd like a better mentor than that sleaze he used to work for.'

That earned him a sweet smile. 'You're a good man, Rafe Sokolov.'

'How good?' he asked playfully. 'Do I get any kind of reward?'

She pecked his lips, then stood up. 'Later. What time is your phone call with the deputy warden?'

'Eleven thirty. We're doing a Skype session. You should sit with me.'

'I will, but I have to shower first.' She took a step back, then stopped. 'I almost forgot. Is it okay if Amos comes over to visit with me today?'

'Of course. But we could go over to Mom and Dad's house if you want.'

She hesitated. 'I really want him to come here. I think he was

505

overwhelmed with all the people in your parents' house last night. He'd had an eventful day.'

He grasped her hand, holding on tightly. 'So did you.'

She shrugged. 'I think he wanted to catch up with me where it's just us. I mean,' she added quickly, 'you can stay, of course. It's your house. But I think he was hoping for a more low-key conversation.'

Rafe kissed her palm. 'I get it, Mercy. You two can use one of the other apartments if you really want to talk alone. Does he want to see Gideon, too?'

'Yes. He asked me to ask Gideon and I did.' Her lips quirked up. 'Amos was using a loaner phone from Karl. The texting went really slowly. I told him to ask Abigail to help him, that kids always learn this stuff faster.'

'Is Abigail coming, too?'

'No. Some of your nieces and nephews are coming over to play with her.' Her lips curved into a full smile. 'Your mom is grandmothering Abigail, and Amos says she's eating up all the attention.'

His heart squeezed with love and pride for his mother. 'Mom is awesome like that.'

'She really is. I think Mama Romero and your mother would be the very best of friends.'

The mention of Farrah's mother reminded him of the family that Mercy had back in New Orleans. Her home. And he had the feeling that seven and a half more weeks with her would never be enough. But she was smiling and he didn't want to see her unhappy, so he forced himself to smile. 'The clock's ticking. You should take your shower if you want to be ready for our call with the warden.'

'Oh, you're right.' She was halfway to the bathroom before she looked over her shoulder. 'Are you coming?'

He grinned at her, the dread at her eventual departure stepping aside as his cock took notice. 'Am I?'

'If you're *very* good and *very* quick because afterward, I want you to make me pancakes.'

He pulled himself to his feet. 'I can do that.'

'And then call Damien. He said you owe him pancakes for having to listen to us last night.'

'I'd say that's a small price to pay.'

Sacramento, California
Wednesday, 19 April, 11.28 A.M.

'Mercy!' Rafe called. 'It's time for the call with the deputy warden. Come out already.'

Mercy checked her reflection one last time. *Hair, check. Makeup, check.* No bags under her eyes, courtesy of a decent night's sleep. She tugged at the collar of her turtleneck. *Hickey hidden, check.*

She joined Rafe on the sofa, where he had his laptop set up. 'It's not my fault. I told you to be quick.'

He smirked at her. 'Like you didn't enjoy it, too. Oh, here's the warden. Right on time.' So she was blushing when Rafe answered the Skype call. 'Warden Shipley. Thank you for calling me,' he said, his smile businesslike and definitely not blushing. 'I'm Detective Sokolov, Sacramento PD. This is my friend Mercy Callahan. She's a forensic investigator with New Orleans PD but is here as a civilian.'

Okay, so he did blush a little at 'friend'. Mercy gave the woman a nod, mildly mollified. 'Warden Shipley.'

'Hello,' Shipley said. She appeared to be somewhere around sixty years of age, her silver hair pulled back in a severe bun. 'I don't have a lot of time, but your query caught my attention. Why are you asking about Aubrey Franklin and his associates, Detective?'

She already knew, Mercy thought. The warden was being cagey. And then Mercy had to bite her lip to keep from giggling at her own pun. *Cagey. Prison warden. You're just nervous. Calm down or you won't get any information. Plus, she's ignoring you. She knows who you are and that Aubrey Franklin's brother connects to what's been happening this week.*

'Because his brother has been trying to either abduct me or kill me for the last four days,' Mercy answered before Rafe could. 'He's left a trail of bodies from New Orleans to Santa Rosa, with victims in Reno and Sacramento as well. Surely you've read about them?'

507

The woman's smile was faint, but respectful. 'Yes, I have. I wondered if you were planning to lie to me, so points to you. What does Aubrey Franklin's incarceration in the eighties have to do with his brother's murder spree now?'

'We think Harry Franklin's had help,' Rafe said, squeezing Mercy's hand out of camera view. 'We were wondering if you could tell us about anyone Aubrey associated with while he was a guest at Terminal Island.'

Shipley frowned. 'Help? From whom? You mean from other inmates currently incarcerated?'

'No,' Rafe said quickly. 'From former inmates who were released after serving their time.'

Shipley visibly relaxed. 'Oh good. Current inmate involvement would be a nightmare of paperwork. I can tell you what I remember and I also have notes from my old boss, who's since passed away. He was the contact of record when the FBI investigated thirty years ago, after Aubrey Franklin robbed his second bank. My boss was old-school thorough and kept copies of everything he said or sent to the FBI. I'll send his notes when we're finished here.'

And when I'm satisfied that you're not lying to me went unsaid.

'Aubrey served fifteen years. He was barely eighteen when he was convicted of the first robbery in the early seventies. I remember his kid brother and his mother. They'd visit like clockwork, twice a month. The mother never believed her son had committed any crime, and the kid brother looked at Aubrey like he was Superman.'

'And his conduct as he served his sentence?' Rafe asked.

'At first he was a belligerent ass,' Shipley said candidly. 'I was young and female and . . . well, I suppose you can imagine the comments I got from the prisoners. It toughened me up fast. By the time Aubrey was incarcerated I'd been working on my cell block for more than six months, and I just let his comments roll off my back. Besides, I never believed he was serious. He wasn't into women my age.'

Mercy felt the edge of anger licking at her control, because Gideon's face flashed in her mind. Edward McPhearson, aka Aubrey

Franklin, would have raped her brother if Gideon hadn't fought back. 'No, Aubrey was more into young men.'

Shipley nodded. 'I got that impression. Did he hurt someone when he got out?'

'Yes,' Mercy said. 'But that's not my story to share.'

Shipley was quiet for a few seconds, studying Mercy. 'I understand,' she finally said. 'Aubrey got the reputation of a fighter. He worked out and bulked up. Anyone who laid a finger on him got their fingers broken. He broke one inmate's neck, but he didn't take credit for it and another inmate took his punishment – thirty days in solitary.'

'Who took his punishment?' Mercy asked.

'Guy by the name of Waylon Belmont.'

Mercy tried hard to contain her excitement, but inside she was jumping up and down. *Yes.*

'Did he have prison tats?' Rafe asked. 'Maybe a teardrop for that broken neck?'

Shipley nodded. 'He did.'

'Did Waylon get extra time for the murder?' Mercy asked.

'No,' Shipley said. 'Waylon was never formally charged.'

'Because your lives were safer with the asshole dead so it got covered up,' Rafe said flatly.

Shipley shrugged and said nothing.

Mercy approached from a different angle. 'Do you know why Waylon took credit for a murder he didn't do?'

'Now, that's an actual question,' Shipley said. 'Waylon was a troublemaker. He spent a lot of time in solitary. Aubrey's "alleged" murder of the other inmate happened when Waylon was in the hole. It was his final day for that infraction. He came out of the hole, found out what happened, said he did it, and went back in.'

'So the staff knew he hadn't done it because he was in solitary at the time.'

Another shrug from Shipley. 'Likely. I wasn't in a supervisory position at that time.'

Rafe drew a breath and Mercy could feel his impatience. She gave his hand a squeeze this time. 'Warden Shipley,' she said, acting

509

on a sudden hunch, 'did Aubrey break the inmate's neck to protect someone else?'

'The inmate's neck was broken, yes. I know this because I saw it. It was the first time I'd seen a murder on the job and it's stuck with me all these years. I've always believed that Aubrey did it, but you won't find any documentation on either of those things.'

Rafe glanced at Mercy, appreciation in his eyes. 'Who was the inmate trying to attack at the time that Aubrey "probably" broke his neck?' he asked, turning back to the computer.

Shipley took a full minute to check her notes. 'Okay, here it is. The subject of the attack was Benton Travis.'

Mercy fought off her disappointment. Not Herbert Hampton. 'What did he look like?'

'Not tall, not short. Average guy. Brown hair. Wore glasses. Spent a lot of time in the prison library.'

Pastor, Mercy thought, both relieved and energized. 'Did he start a church there, by chance?'

Shipley looked impressed. 'He did. His nickname was Pastor.'

Yes, yes, yes. Mercy had to fight to keep the grin from her face. *Benton Travis.* Now they had a real name.

'What was Travis in for?' Rafe asked.

'Embezzlement, bank fraud, mail fraud, and forgery,' Shipley answered, then narrowed her eyes. 'Why?'

'Do you have a photo?' Mercy asked, ignoring the question.

Shipley's eyes narrowed further. 'Quid pro quo, Miss Callahan. Why?'

'Because he changed his name, then went on to form another church when he got out,' Rafe answered. 'From whom he embezzled. Then he disappeared. That was thirty years ago.'

'Do you have a photo?' Mercy asked again.

Shipley nodded. 'It's in the packet of information I'll send to Detective Sokolov's email. It was a shot taken for propaganda purposes, basically. Benton Travis led services in the mess hall on Sunday mornings. We had a chaplain, of course, but the inmates liked "Pastor" better.' She used air quotes. 'We got a photo of them in prayer. We thought he was using those services to coordinate

510

criminal enterprise within the prison walls, but we could never catch him doing anything illegal.'

'Thank you,' Mercy said, then remembered something. 'Wait. Was Pastor married? Did he have a family who visited him in prison?'

'No, but Waylon had a girlfriend. He met her when he was incarcerated. She was some kind of do-gooder. He had all these tats and she looked like she should be a student at an Ivy League school.'

'Do you remember her name?' Mercy asked.

'Not off the top of my head. If I get a chance, I'll ask my assistant to go to the tombs and get the visitor logs from that time frame. They haven't been digitized, so it's a pain in the ass to search them.'

'That would be very helpful,' Mercy said. 'Thank you.'

'Yes, thank you,' Rafe added. 'When can I expect that email?'

'I just sent it,' Shipley said. 'I'm late for my next meeting. Signing off.'

And the screen went dark.

Rafe and Mercy sat quietly for a moment, and then Rafe kissed the knuckles of Mercy's hand, still twined with his. 'We have a name. Pastor's real name.'

Mercy smiled. 'Yes, we do. Let's see if we have a face. Can you check your email?'

Rafe logged into his email. 'She sent the photo separately. Nice of her not to bury it in that other megafile.' He clicked it open and Mercy stiffened.

There, filling Rafe's laptop screen, were Pastor, Edward McPhearson, and Waylon. 'Benton Travis, Aubrey Franklin, and Waylon Belmont,' she murmured. 'Their paths crossed in prison.'

'Just like you figured out last night.' Rafe tipped her face up and kissed her hard. 'This is huge, Mercy.'

She nodded numbly. 'They were criminals the whole time. Criminals masquerading as spiritual leaders.'

Rafe's face softened in sympathy. 'I'm sorry, honey. I got carried away. This is . . .'

'Personal,' she murmured. 'Very personal.' She gave herself a little shake. 'Are you going to pass this on to Tom Hunter?'

'Of course.' He pulled his phone from his pocket and flinched. 'Shit. I had my ringer turned off so I wouldn't wake you up earlier. I've got twenty missed calls.' He paled. 'Oh shit. They're from my mom and Damien's wife.'

Dread grabbed Mercy's gut. She found her own phone on the coffee table, the volume turned down as well. Her stomach turned upside down, bile rising to burn her throat. 'I've got six missed calls. All from Farrah's mother.'

Twenty-eight

Dunsmuir, California
Wednesday, 19 April, 11.45 A.M.

Ephraim woke up still too damn tired for words. The nap he'd taken hadn't been nearly enough, but at least his eyes felt a little less like they'd been scrubbed with fiberglass. The spot he'd chosen to stop was peaceful and pretty perfect, actually. Especially since he could rest for a while. It would take Mercy at least four hours to get here.

But she would come, because he had leverage now. He glanced to the camper behind him with a triumphant grin. He had triple leverage now – one New Orleans best friend, one New Orleans police captain, and one Sokolov cop. The Sokolov cop might not still be alive, but Mercy didn't need to know that.

Damien Sokolov had taken a hard hit to the head when Ephraim had forced his car off the road and into a tree – ironically enough, not far from where Ephraim had killed June Lindstrom after she'd smuggled him out of the airport on Saturday night.

Ephraim's luck had finally changed. Once he'd lost DJ on the interstate, the rat hadn't found him again, and he'd arrived back in Rafe Sokolov's neighborhood with perfect timing. The house behind Sokolov's didn't have a view of the Victorian, but he had been able to see the flash of headlights through the gap separating the houses.

Lucky once more, the headlights had belonged to a car that had been parked in the driveway. It was the car that belonged to one of the Sokolovs – Damien Sokolov, another cop. The car carried two other passengers – Mercy's friends from New Orleans. Ephraim had followed, keeping a decent distance the whole way to the exit for the airport.

Looked like the New Orleans folks had been going home. If Mercy had been with them, it would have been a perfect day, but he was still happy with his haul. The road from the interstate to the airport was lightly traveled that early in the morning. Not a single witness.

Truly my lucky day. The little car had been no match for Burkett's Escalade, the SUV shoving the smaller car off the road and into a tree with no trouble at all.

The trouble had been getting the three passengers out of the wrecked car and into the back of the SUV. At least the huge SUV provided adequate cover for him to work, blocking him from view of anyone who passed by on their way to the airport. It had taken a bit of time to secure the passengers, all of whom had been stunned by the impact – or worse in Sokolov's case. He had been fully unconscious when Ephraim had approached their car, his gun out, ready to shoot the men at the very least.

Ephraim had been disappointed to see that Mercy wasn't with them, but Dr Romero would serve as an irresistible lure. The Sokolov brother would ensure compliance from the blond bastard who'd become Mercy's damn shadow.

Holmes had been stunned enough by the airbag that Ephraim was able to stab the needle of one of Burkett's prepared syringes directly into his arm, through the man's shirt sleeve. Holmes had tried to fight Ephraim off, but the gun that Ephraim held in his other hand had kept the cop frozen in place. A minute later, the man's head had lolled to one side, drawing a scream from the woman in the backseat, who'd apparently just woken up.

Farrah Romero had come at him like a drunken wildcat, all hiss and no coordination. A gash on her head was bleeding and her pupils were huge. But a well-placed slap had her bouncing back against the seat. He hadn't wasted any of the sedative on Romero – he could handle her with no problem. He'd bound her hands and covered her mouth with the same roll of duct tape he'd used on Sean MacGuire. Once she'd been secured, he slapped Burkett's handcuffs on Romero's fiancé, then sedated the Sokolov cop and bound him like he had Romero.

Romero had walked to the SUV on her own power, his gun an effective motivation, but getting the two men into the SUV had not been fun. Sokolov was a big guy, but Holmes was even bigger. Both were heavy motherfuckers. Dragging them from the car to the SUV had caused Ephraim's wound to reopen.

He touched it now, the new bandage dry and free of blood. He hadn't changed it until he'd transferred his passengers once again – this time to the honeymooners' camper that he'd left parked in the state park when he'd gone to meet Burkett.

He'd wanted to sleep then, but he hadn't felt safe until four hours later. He'd driven north, past Redding and into the forest east of Dunsmuir. He knew this area. Eden had settled here once, in the early days. Mt. Shasta loomed in the distance and the sight left him feeling peaceful.

He got out of Burkett's Escalade and dragged in a lungful of the crisp air. He liked the city in small doses, but the air really was better here.

A peek into the camper revealed that the Romero woman was awake and glaring hatefully, but the two cops were still out cold. He'd given them higher doses and had stopped to repeat the injections midway to his destination because he wanted them to stay asleep, but the woman he was going to need soon. She'd be the bait to draw Mercy to him. The men he'd keep in case anything went wrong. He'd be able to use them to bargain his way to freedom. Cops protected their own.

Once Mercy learned that her friends were in danger, she'd fall into line. She'd do exactly what he said. And once she had, he'd get rid of his hostages and whisk her back to Eden in an hour and a half along roads that most people didn't even know existed. Nobody would stop him from finally delivering his prize to Pastor.

A buzzing in his pocket startled him. For a moment he panicked, but remembered he'd turned off Romero's phone and the phones of the other two were left behind. He dug for his flip phone and saw that it was Pastor.

He debated not answering, but knew it was better to know what was going on than to show up in Eden unaware. 'Hello?'

'Brother Ephraim.'

Shit. Pastor was using the mild voice and that rarely meant anything good. 'Pastor.'

'Where are you?'

'Santa Rosa,' he lied. 'My mother is ill.'

'Ah, so the doctor got in touch with you. I was hoping all was well. I'm sorry to hear your mother isn't well. When will you be back?'

Ephraim rolled his eyes. *So much empathy.* 'As soon as I can. Is something wrong?'

There was a beat of hesitation that made Ephraim straighten his spine in interest.

'Perhaps. We may need you to bring back some surrogates.'

Surrogate meant a body too mauled or decomposed to be identified. 'Who went missing?'

'Amos.'

Ephraim blinked, genuinely surprised. 'Did he get lost? He's always out there looking for new trees to use in his workshop.'

'We might have thought so, but his daughter is gone, too. We didn't miss them until this morning. Amos told Sister Coleen that he and Abigail were sick, so no one bothered them all day yesterday. But this morning he didn't show for chapel and Abigail didn't go to school. Their home is empty.'

'Shit,' Ephraim breathed. 'But if he's on foot, he can't have gotten far, even in a day.'

'And that's why I said we may need a surrogate. We're hoping we find them. DJ is out searching.'

And lying. DJ wasn't looking for Amos. *DJ is looking for me.*

'I'm stunned, Pastor.' And Ephraim truly was. 'Amos is faithful.'

'I know. I was hoping you might know why he left, seeing as how you've been gone all this time as well.'

Ah. That explains it. He thinks I helped him. Which was ludicrous. Ephraim didn't help anyone except himself. 'I didn't know he was planning to run. I would have told you.'

Unlike that prick DJ, who – either willingly or not – helped Mercy escape. Or Waylon, who let Gideon go free.

'I know.' Pastor sighed. 'I'm frustrated. I'm sure you understand that.'

'Of course,' Ephraim said, forcing sympathy into his voice, but the words left a sour taste. Pastor wouldn't have called if he didn't think Ephraim could be responsible.

Mercy would change everything. No longer would Pastor suspect him for everything that went wrong. DJ would be the odd man out, and then DJ would be dead.

And as long as Mercy still had that damn key to the safe-deposit box, Pastor would never know how close they'd come to their location being outed to the whole world.

'I need to go, Pastor. My mother needs me.'

Ephraim ended the call, mentally promising his mother that he'd visit as soon as he could, but with his face on the news and without Burkett to bring her from the nursing home on day breaks, that visit wasn't likely to happen anytime soon.

For now, he'd focus on his immediate goal. Getting Mercy back. He opened the door to the camper. 'Wake up, Dr Romero. I need you.'

Sacramento, California
Wednesday, 19 April, 12.00 P.M.

Six missed calls. Mercy dialed Mama Romero and put the call on speaker, her heart pounding so hard that she barely heard the line ringing.

'Mercy? Oh my dear Lord, Mercy. Is Farrah with you?'

'No,' Mercy whispered. 'I saw her off to the airport at about four this morning. She was with André and Damien Sokolov, Rafe's cop brother. Why?'

'She didn't get off the plane.' Mama Romero's voice was pitched high and bordered on hysteria. 'They said she never boarded, Mercy. Where is my daughter?'

Mercy's blood ran cold. 'I don't know. But we'll find her. I

517

promise. I need to go so I can find out what's going on. I'll call you back as soon as I can.'

She ended the call and stared at Rafe helplessly. He was dialing his mother, the remaining color in his face draining away.

'Mom?' he asked hoarsely as he put his phone on speaker.

'Rafe. Oh my God.' Irina was crying. 'They found your brother's car. The police. They found his car. He never came home. Never called Jemma. He's missing, Rafe. My son is missing.'

'Who found his car, Mom?' Rafe said, closing his eyes, his struggle for control visible.

'One of the patrolmen near the airport. Damien's car was crashed into a tree. They think he was run off the road.' Irina choked on a sob. 'There was blood, Raphael. So much blood.' She broke into harsh sobs. 'We need to find him. Oh God, what if he's dead?'

There was a shushing behind her, followed by Karl's voice, murmuring soft words in Russian. He must have pulled Irina into his arms, because her sobs became muffled. Heartbreaking.

Mercy closed her eyes. *This has to stop. I have to make this stop.*

'We'll find him, Mom,' Rafe promised, his words desperate and filled with pain. 'Farrah and André are missing, too.'

The silence on the other end was abrupt. 'Oh God,' Irina whispered. 'He got them all. What are we going to do?'

Mercy stood up and went to the closet for her coat. *We're not going to do anything. I'm going to give Ephraim whatever the hell he wants.*

'What the hell do you think you're doing?' Rafe demanded.

Mercy was spun around, Rafe's hand gripping her arm. His expression was both panicked and full of rage.

'Raphael?' Irina asked sharply from the phone, clutched in Rafe's other hand. He'd propelled himself from the sofa without his cane and now leaned against the wall for balance. 'What is wrong?'

Rafe stared down at Mercy, eyes flashing. 'What is *wrong* is that Mercy is putting on her *coat*. Like she thinks she's *going* somewhere.'

Even in his anger, his grip was gentle. Mercy had no problem prying his fingers from her arm. 'Let me go,' she whispered. 'Please. I have to make this stop.'

Shocked gasps came from the speaker. 'Mercy, no,' Irina cried. 'You will not sacrifice yourself. Don't even think it.'

Mercy's lips trembled. 'He's hurting everyone. And he just wants me.'

'Mercy,' Karl said, his voice breaking. 'You will solve nothing this way. Even if you knew how or where to give yourself up, that doesn't mean he'll let Damien and the others go.'

If they're still alive. The words were on her tongue, but she bit them back.

And then her phone began to buzz in her hand. The caller ID read *Ro*.

'I think we're about to find out how and where I give myself up,' Mercy said quietly.

'On speaker,' Rafe demanded. 'Everyone hush. It's Farrah's phone.'

Farrah's phone. Not Farrah. Mercy hit ACCEPT and the speaker button. 'Ro?'

'No.'

Mercy stiffened, the sly voice making her knees buckle. Ephraim Burton. Gripping the closet door, she locked her legs and drew a breath. 'What do you want?'

'Only what I've always wanted. You, my dear wife.'

Rafe swallowed hard, his jaw bulging from clenching his teeth. But he remained quiet, staring at the phone as if he could make it give up Ephraim's location.

'Where?' was all Mercy could reply. *Think. Think, goddammit. Keep him talking.* The longer she kept him talking, the better chance they had of tracing this call. *Right? Please let that be right.*

Ephraim laughed. 'No arguments? You must think I'm a fool.'

Rafe was busily texting. A glance at his screen showed he was communicating with Gideon. *Good.* The Feds might be able to track Farrah's phone quickly.

'No, I know you're a sadistic brute who doesn't mind killing to get his own way,' Mercy said quietly. 'I don't want you to hurt my friends. I don't want you to hurt anyone else. You want me? Fine. But you don't touch my friends.'

519

'And if I already have?'

Rafe silenced the volume on his own phone before Ephraim's words could draw more gasps from his parents. The Sokolovs could still hear Ephraim, but he wouldn't know they were listening.

Mercy shivered, suddenly cold. 'Then we're done. I'm not trading myself for dead bodies.' Rafe glared at her, but she ignored him, focusing all of her attention on the snake on the other end of the line. 'I want proof of life. Let me talk to Farrah Romero.'

'You don't get to make demands,' Ephraim snarled.

'Shut up, Ephraim,' Mercy snapped. 'You want me. I'm not sure why, but you've gone to a lot of trouble to get me. So, because of that, I do get to make demands. Let me talk to Farrah, or this conversation ends right now and whatever you're trying to accomplish by getting me ends with it.'

She held her breath, counting her own heartbeats in the silence that followed, even checking that the call was still active. It was.

The silence was abruptly shattered by Farrah's voice. 'Mercy, don't you dare. Don't you dare trade yourself.'

There was the sound of a slap and a low, furious growl from farther away. André. André was still alive, too.

'Are you hurt, Ro?' Mercy asked.

'Not too bad. We're all still breathing.' Then Farrah sneezed three times in quick succession. 'I'm not breathing well, but that's not Burton's fault. I just need my allergy meds, that's all.'

Mercy found herself smiling a little. Her best friend was smart. 'Damien? He's okay, too?'

'He's lost some blood. He's—'

'That's enough,' Ephraim said roughly, taking back the phone. 'You have your proof of life. If you want them to continue breathing, you'll come alone. No cops. No Feds. No weapons.'

'And I'm supposed to just believe you'll hand my friends over? No way. You're a bastard and you lie easier than you breathe.' And suddenly she knew what to say. 'I met your mother, you know.'

A beat of silence. 'Yes. I know. You stole from her,' he said bitterly.

Mercy laughed, surprised to hear the sound. 'Well, that's open for interpretation, I suppose. You say stole, I say I got a present from her. I have her key, the one she kept in the little treasure chest that Amos made. She gave the key to me willingly. I let her keep the chest.'

Another beat of silence. 'She wouldn't have given it to you. She's not in her right mind.'

'I don't know. She seemed pretty lucid to me. We chatted. She said such nice things about Aubrey. Not so much you. You apparently don't visit her often enough. We got along brilliantly. We even sang your song together. I was close enough to kill her myself and I know exactly where she lives.'

'You bitch,' Ephraim snarled. 'You don't talk about her. You don't even say her name.'

'Belinda,' Mercy said flatly. 'Belinda, Belinda, Belinda. You want to play games, Ephraim? I'll play. I can have your mother in FBI custody before you can end this call. She harbored a fugitive. They can arrest her for that.'

'They won't. She's old.'

'So? They'll put her in prison nursing care. They have those, you know. For the lifers who can't take care of themselves. I can't imagine it would be nearly as nice as the place you've been paying for all this time.'

'I'm not trading your friends for my mother and if you think I am, you're the fool.'

Mercy could picture his snarl perfectly and she had to lock her knees once more. 'I never thought you would. But if my friends aren't breathing when we make our little trade, your mother will suffer, and I'll make sure that she knows she's hurting because of you. Am I clear?'

He said nothing, just breathed hard. She remembered that, too.

'Am I clear, Ephraim?' she asked again.

'Yeah. You come alone. No cops. And bring the key with you.'

But . . . I don't have it anymore. He doesn't know that. 'What's it worth to you?'

He snarled again. 'Let me put it to you this way. When I get my

521

hands on you, if I find that you haven't brought that key, I'll show your friend Farrah what I do to women who cross me.'

Mercy's stomach rolled. *Oh God, oh God, oh God.*

He laughed at her silence. 'I see you remember what that means. Oh, and if I see any cops, your friends die and my mother's just gonna have to deal. Am I clear?'

She swallowed hard. 'Crystal clear,' she whispered.

'Then wait for my instructions.'

The call ended and Mercy's knees gave out. She sank to the floor, her back against the closet door. 'Oh my God,' she whispered, rocking herself. 'Oh my God.'

Sacramento, California
Wednesday, 19 April, 12.15 P.M.

Rafe blew out a breath, then, balancing on one foot, lowered himself to the floor beside her. Stretching his bad leg in front of him, he turned the volume on his phone back up and pulled Mercy close to him. She was shaking like a leaf, goddammit. 'You get all that, Dad?' he asked.

'Yes,' Karl said. 'Mercy . . . thank you. We're not letting you trade yourself, just so you know, but thank you for being willing. And for making sure Damien was still alive, too.'

'Yes, *lubimaya*,' Irina said, no longer crying, but her voice was still thick and unsteady. 'Thank you. But what did Farrah mean about her allergy medication?'

'She's allergic to trees,' Mercy said weakly. 'It was her way of telling us that she's outside.'

'He might still have that camper,' Rafe said. 'If so, he's mobile, which sucks. But if he's actually using Farrah's phone – versus spoofing her number – we can track it.'

'How long will that take, Raphael?' Irina asked, hope in her voice for the first time.

Mercy shook her had. 'No cops for now, please? He means what he says and I don't trust that Molina won't ride in with a platoon of black SUVs. Let me try something else first.'

Rafe didn't want to upset her, but he was bringing in the police. At least those in SacPD who he trusted.

'Please,' she begged, and Rafe sighed.

'What are you going to try?' he asked, without making any promises.

'Finding Farrah's phone.'

Rafe felt a spurt of hope. 'You have a Find My Friends app or something?'

She shook her head and his hope fizzled. 'I don't. The very thought of anyone tracking me makes my skin itch. Farrah and I just text each other. Was Gideon able to start a trace when I was talking to Ephraim?'

'Not sure. He hasn't gotten back to me yet. He's working on it now. I'm going to call my lieutenant. He can add our tech resources.'

'Gideon has brought in the FBI?' Irina asked, fear in her voice. 'I trust Gideon, but I don't know who he's working with, nor do I know your lieutenant. Burton might kill them, Raphael. Can't we just use Find My Phone?'

'Farrah has an Android phone, plus you need to enable those location apps, Irina. It's not something you can use without turning it on in your settings first. Just give me two minutes. I need to call Mama Romero back. She might be able to see Farrah's phone.' Mercy dialed Mrs Romero, blurting out, 'She's alive,' as soon as Farrah's mother answered. 'I talked to her.'

'She's alive?' Mrs Romero asked through her tears. 'Are you sure?'

'I'm sure. I heard her voice. But she's being held hostage. And you're on speaker,' Mercy added. 'I'm with Rafe and his parents. Their son Damien is with Farrah and André. Farrah's the smartest woman I know and André and Damien are good cops. They'll figure out how to hold on until I can get to them.'

'We,' Rafe muttered.

Mrs Romero whispered a thankful prayer. 'But . . . this is the man who killed our Quill, isn't it?'

'Yes,' Mercy said. 'And we don't know what he's going to ask me to do, but he has her phone. He called me from it.'

'*Us* to do,' Rafe said. 'Us. Not you. Dammit, Mercy.'

Mercy huffed impatiently. 'Fine. Us, not me. Now let me talk. Mama, do you still have that tracking app on your phone? The one you made us download when we went on that cruise last year?'

Rafe's eyes widened. 'Really?'

Mercy nodded. 'There were over twenty of us who went and we had a mix of iPhones, Androids, and even a few Google phones. Mama Romero didn't want to lose anyone, so she found an app that would work with everyone's phone.'

'I do!' Mrs Romero's voice was trembling. 'I'm looking now. Don't you have it?'

Mercy winced. 'No, I took it off because I'm too paranoid. But can you see if Farrah still has it?'

Mrs Romero exhaled on a soft cry. 'She's here. I can see her phone. It's blinking. She's somewhere called . . . Dunsmuir?'

'That's up near Mt. Shasta,' Rafe said, excitedly, then sighed. 'That's a lot of area to search. Mrs Romero, can you make a screenshot? Maybe zoom out so that we can get a better—'

Mrs Romero gasped, interrupting him. 'Oh no. It's gone. The blinking dot is gone. I started to take a screenshot for you, but the dot is gone!'

'It's okay, Mama.' Mercy was trying to soothe, but her voice was thin and thready. 'He's probably just turned her phone off. But we know about where he is. I'm leaving right now.'

'No, ma'am.' Rafe put his hand on Mercy's thigh when she started to stand up. 'We need a plan. I'm not letting Mercy trade herself, and she will have backup.'

'What can I do?' Mrs Romero whispered.

'Stay where you are,' Rafe said, 'and answer if you get a call from Farrah's phone. Let André's family know that he's alive and ask them if they can track his phone as well. But do not go to the press. I don't know who we'll notify here, and I don't know if you should notify your area police or not, but I don't think they can do anything that we can't do here. The more people who know, the more likely it is to leak out. We don't want that.'

Mercy was glaring at him, but when she spoke to Farrah's

mother, her voice was soft and kind. 'Keep watching that app, Mama Ro. If the blinking dot comes back, call me immediately. Text me if I don't answer. Cell coverage up there can be spotty. And do not lose hope. Farrah is smart and so are André and Damien.'

'And pray,' Irina added. 'As will we.'

'That I can do,' Mrs Romero said. 'We love you, Mercy. This is not your doing, child. I want you to listen to that man you got there. Do not give yourself up to the man who killed our Quill. She will haunt you, baby. Hand to God, she will haunt you.'

Mercy's laugh was shaky. 'Yes, ma'am.'

They ended the call with Mrs Romero, and Mercy let her head fall back against the closet door. 'What do we do, Rafe?'

Rafe kissed the side of her head. 'We get Gideon and then we all get in the car and drive to Dunsmuir. I already asked him to track Farrah's, André's, and Damien's phones. He's probably contacting the cell phone carriers as we speak. Okay?'

She nodded. 'Okay.'

'Mom, Dad. We'll call you back. Check with Jemma to see if she and Damien have anything similar to the Romeros' tracking app. Love you both.'

Rafe took a moment to breathe after ending the call, then pulled Mercy to his lap. 'Let me hold you for a minute. Just a minute.'

She nodded, winding her arms around his neck. 'I thought that would be it,' she whispered. 'The thing that made your parents tell me to go.'

'Oh, baby. That's not going to happen. Haven't you figured that out by now?'

She buried her face in his neck. 'I guess I'm starting to.'

'I need you to promise me again,' he said, his voice like gravel in his throat. 'You will not sacrifice yourself. Even to save Farrah. You promised, Mercy.'

'I know,' she whispered. 'But if he hurts her . . . how do I forgive myself for that?'

He sighed. 'I don't know.'

'At least you're honest.'

He tugged her chin until she met his eyes. 'I won't lie to you.

Ever. But I can't concentrate on helping my brother and your friends if I'm worried that you'll throw yourself in front of Burton if things get bad. You need to trust me, but I need the same. So promise me.'

Mercy closed her eyes. 'I promise.'

'No. You look me in the eyes when you promise me. Look at me.' She did and he struggled for the right words to make her understand. 'I lost the last woman I cared about and it nearly broke me. If we lose anyone today, it'll hurt both of us. I know that. But if we're focused and do this right, we can save them. Help me save them. Promise me.'

Her eyes filled with tears, but she nodded. 'I promise.'

'Okay.' That would have to be enough. 'Now I need to get up. Can you get my cane?'

Dunsmuir, California
Wednesday, 19 April, 3.55 P.M.

'This packet from the warden has a lot of information in it,' Tom Hunter said from the front passenger seat of his FBI-issued SUV. He'd been pulling into Rafe's driveway when Mercy, Rafe, Gideon, and Daisy had opened Rafe's garage door, ready to drive to Dunsmuir. Assigned to bodyguard duty today, he'd picked up Amos at the Sokolovs' so that he, Gideon, and Mercy could spend the afternoon together.

Which they were, just not the way Mercy had planned. Instead of sitting on Rafe's comfy sofa and catching up on the years they'd missed together, they'd spent the last few hours in the Feds' SUV, barreling up the interstate toward Mt. Shasta. When Amos had heard about the abduction and Ephraim's ultimatum, he'd begged to come, citing his marksmanship skills. Mercy had lent her support, because Amos had always been an amazing shot. But it was more than that.

She, Gideon, and Amos needed to be there when Ephraim was taken down. It was personal.

And tense. Mercy sat between Amos and Rafe while Daisy sat in the very back with her rifle and a helluva lot of ammo. The woman didn't mess around and Mercy was glad she was on their side. Rafe said that Daisy was the best shot he'd ever met. Mercy hoped that they wouldn't need Daisy's expertise, but she was damn glad that the woman was with them, guarding them as Gideon drove up north.

Tom Hunter also had a rifle, but he'd spent the last hour of their drive sifting through the deputy warden's report that Rafe had forwarded. 'A lot of this information about Aubrey and Harry Franklin was already available, but some of it's brand-new.'

'Are you going to be able to use any of it?' Gideon asked.

'I don't know,' Tom said. 'I think it might be more helpful to someone in the behavioral department. They might use the files to build a profile on Benton Travis, aka Herbert Hampton, aka Pastor. I'm better with computers. Well, maybe not better. I was up all night trying to trace Burton's bank account activity. So far I've been hitting brick walls, but I've broken through worse. It just takes time.'

'What does that mean?' Amos murmured in Mercy's ear.

Okay. How do I explain that? 'Ephraim has a bank account in Santa Rosa and uses it to pay for his mother's care in a nursing home,' Mercy told him quietly. 'We do a lot of banking through the computer now. You can still go into an actual bank and the money is still physically there, but all the records are kept on servers.' She sighed when he frowned. They had a lot of catching up to do, emotionally and with respect to how the world had changed. 'You remember floppy disks?'

Amos nodded cautiously. 'I take it that those aren't used anymore either, like phone booths.'

Mercy smiled at him despite the churning of fear in her gut. It helped, talking to Amos. It kept her from thinking about all the horrible things that Ephraim could be doing to his hostages this very moment. 'Right. Well, imagine billions and billions of floppy disks, all miniaturized into a small box. That's data storage. That's what a server does – it's like a file folder. So instead of billions and billions of pieces of paper kept in a bank vault somewhere that record our deposits and withdrawals, the information is kept on the servers.

You can see your own bank statements on the computer – like finding one file folder in all those billions of pieces of paper. Banks can see everyone's deposits and withdrawals and, with the proper permissions, the government can search the files, too. Tom's checking Ephraim's bank account activity, trying to find where the money came from.'

'It should trace back to Eden,' Rafe added. 'We think they keep their money in offshore accounts – those are usually banks outside the US, and they've typically been less willing to help law enforcement find dirty money.'

Amos seemed to digest this information. 'Like Swiss bank accounts?'

Mercy blinked up at him. 'You know about Swiss bank accounts?'

Amos gave her a look that was slightly chiding. 'They had those in the olden days, Mercy.'

She winced. 'Sorry.' Then she had a thought. 'How did you give all the money from the sale of your grandfather's land to Pastor when you joined Eden?'

He lifted his dark bushy brows. 'I wired it to a Swiss bank account. I had help, of course. My grandfather's attorney handled it. I was only nineteen, but I was his sole heir and the terms of his will commanded that the money go to Pastor.'

Tom spun in his seat to stare back at Amos and Daisy leaned forward to hear more. 'You wired money to Pastor? What's your attorney's name?'

Amos leaned back, eyes wide. 'That was thirty years ago. You won't be able to find that money. Can you?' he added as a stunned afterthought. 'That attorney was really old in 1989. I'm sure he's long dead by now.'

'Doesn't matter,' Tom said excitedly. 'It's another place for me to start hunting.'

Amos's frown deepened. 'I can't remember his name, though. I haven't thought about this in too many years.' But his brow remained furrowed, thinking so hard that Mercy could almost hear it. 'His name was like food.' His lip curled a little in distaste. 'Something gross that I didn't like, but that my grandfather did. It was a joke between them. Every Christmas the lawyer would send my grandfather a case of the stuff. It came in little cans and you spread it on sandwiches. Like Spam, but not. Had a . . . devil on it.'

They all stared at Amos, completely confused, then Daisy broke the silence.

'Oh, oh!' Daisy exclaimed. 'I know this one! Is it Underwood? Like the deviled ham?'

Amos snapped his fingers. 'That's it. Underwood.' He made a face. 'I hated that stuff. I had to pack deviled ham sandwiches in my lunch for months after Christmas because my grandfather never let food go to waste.'

Rafe turned to stare at Daisy. 'How did you know about that?'

Daisy made a face identical to Amos's. 'My stepmother loved it, and it keeps forever, so we always had it on hand.'

'What are you doing?' Gideon asked Tom, who was now typing frantically on his laptop.

'Starting a records search on that attorney,' Tom answered. 'This could be really important, Amos.'

'I hope so,' Amos murmured. 'It's the least I can do after everything.'

Mercy squeezed his hand. 'You've already helped. You warned us about DJ and gave us information we didn't have before, like Pastor's name. The FBI knows who murdered poor Ginger too, so stop kicking yourself.' Which was easier said than done, of course. Mercy knew that better than most, so she changed the subject. 'What about the safe-deposit box key, Tom?'

'Warrants are being signed off as we speak,' he said. 'Hopefully we'll know what's in it by the time we get back to Sacramento.'

'He'll be expecting me to have a key,' Mercy said grimly, bringing her mind back to the confrontation ahead. 'What if it comes down to that? What should I do?'

Rafe pulled out his own key ring and slid off a key. 'This opens my safe-deposit box in Sacramento. It won't look exactly like his, but it may be close enough that you can fool him momentarily. And sometimes momentarily is all you need.'

Mercy took it and put it in her pocket. 'Thank you.'

Rafe pursed his lips, then whispered, 'Promise me you won't confront him.'

But that's exactly why I'm here. To confront him. To distract him, so that the FBI could get Farrah, André, and Damien to safety. And then, hopefully, take Ephraim. *Dead or alive.* She hesitated. 'I won't sacrifice myself.'

Rafe closed his eyes. 'Dammit, Mercy.'

'Would you let him kill Damien if you could stop him?' she asked quietly.

He shook his head. 'No.'

'It's like that for me with Farrah. Don't make me promise to sit by and—' She broke off with a sharply indrawn breath when her phone buzzed in her hand. 'It's a text from Mama Romero. Her app is showing Farrah's phone as active again. Ephraim must have turned it back on. Mama Ro sent a screenshot of the blinking dot on the map. She says it's not in the same place as it was before, that it's closer to the interstate.'

She started to show Mama Romero's map to Rafe when her phone buzzed again and her heart climbed into her throat. 'It's Ephraim,' she choked out. 'He just sent me a text from Farrah's phone with map coordinates.' She swallowed, pushing her fear into the box in her mind, nailing it shut. 'And a photo of Farrah, bound with duct tape. You can see André and Damien too, but just their torsos. They're bound, too.'

'Is there a message?' Gideon asked tightly.

'Yeah.' Mercy cleared her throat and forced the words to come. 'He says, "No cops or Feds or they all die".'

'Let me see,' Rafe asked, his voice harsh with renewed fear. 'Sonofabitch. Damien's got blood all over his shirt.' He closed his eyes, drew a breath. When he opened his eyes, they were clear and focused. 'Give me the coordinates he sent.' He typed the coordinates into his map app. 'Burton's coordinates match the map in Mrs Romero's screenshot. He is closer to the highway than where he called from before by maybe ten miles. We're not far now. Another twenty minutes.'

'That's good, though, right?' Mercy asked. 'That he's closer to the highway?'

Rafe shook his head. 'I think he's just getting in position for his getaway. Gideon, take the next exit.'

'I will,' Gideon said, then glanced at Tom. 'Can you let Agent Schumacher know where we're going?'

Mercy whipped around to stare behind them, noticing, for the first time, the SUV tailing them. It was black, a carbon copy of the vehicle in which they were riding. 'Agent Schumacher is following us?'

'Yep,' Tom said. 'She caught up to us about an hour ago.'

Right about the time he'd opened his laptop. 'You knew you had backup,' she accused. 'That's why you were comfortable letting someone else keep watch.'

Tom sighed. 'Schumacher is a good agent, Mercy. Try to trust us, okay?'

Mercy blew out a breath, trying to control her temper. 'I *did* trust you. *You*, Tom. Not some agent I don't know. I guess Molina knows, too?'

Gideon put on his turn signal for the upcoming exit. 'She does. And I was the one who called her, not Tom. I trust Molina, Mercy. She's got a lot more experience with hostage situations than you do.'

Mercy saw red. 'And I have more experience with Ephraim Burton than any of you! *Goddammit*, Gideon.' Fury had tears springing to her eyes and she wiped them away. 'I thought you understood that Burton means business, but you're all caught up in the *rules*.' She spat the word. 'If he touches one fucking hair on Farrah's head—'

Rafe pressed his finger to her lips. 'Stop. Do not say things you'll have to take back later. I don't trust Molina either, but I do trust Gideon with my life. And yours.'

Mercy jerked her face away, pursing her lips. She faced forward, looking at no one and willing her tears not to fall. These weren't tears of sadness. These were tears of pure rage and she hated it. 'Did you know, Rafe?'

He exhaled quietly. 'Yes.'

That was that, then. No apologies, just a simple yes. *Goddammit.* She'd trusted them. She'd trusted Rafe. *I should have known better. I should have come alone.*

There was a rustle behind her and Daisy was sliding her arms around Mercy's shoulders. 'Rafe's right. Gideon saved you, Mercy. He broke a lot of rules to do it. So did Rafe.'

Mercy swallowed, the gentle words hitting her hard because they were true. Her rage collapsed from a raging fire to barely smoldering embers. 'I know.'

'Then trust Gideon with Farrah's and André's lives. Rafe trusts him with yours and Damien's. If there is a way to get all three of them out safely, these guys know how to do it. And Molina's not all bad. Her bark is worse than her bite.'

'I don't know about that,' Rafe said, and Daisy smacked his arm.

'You are undoing all my hard work, Rafe. Look, Mercy, I get it. I really do. But you need to understand that Gideon went through the same thing when you were taken. So cut him some slack, okay? He's a good agent. And he loves you.'

'Dammit,' Mercy muttered, shame replacing her fury. 'Now you're making sense.'

Daisy chuckled. 'I thought so. You want to hold Brutus? She's good for situations like this and you left your cats back at Rafe's.'

Mercy shook her head. 'No, I'm okay. I'm sorry, Gideon. I was out of line.'

Gideon met her eyes in the rear-view mirror. 'It's all right. And you're right. You do know Ephraim better than any of us. That's why you're here. You and Amos.'

She glanced at Amos and found him nodding reluctantly. 'We'll do our part, Mercy,' he said. 'Let the Feds do theirs.' He looked over her head to Rafe. 'Feds and detectives.'

She turned to Rafe. 'I'm sorry. You're right. Thank you for stopping me before I said something awful.'

Rafe kissed her softly. 'I'm good. Now try to relax. We need a plan of action, given that we all know this is a trap. Is Farrah's phone still active?'

Mercy texted the question to Mrs Romero, then nodded when Farrah's mother replied. 'Yes. And still in the same location.'

'Then if it doesn't move, it's a lure. He might not have Farrah and the others there. Hell, he might not even be there right now, but that's where he wants us. We can only hope we have the element of surprise. Hopefully he doesn't know that Mrs Romero could see Farrah's phone and that we were waiting for his next text.'

'He turned her phone off,' Mercy murmured. 'He might think that kept us from tracking it. He'd had it turned off before he called me, because Mama Ro's calls kept going to voice mail.'

'And Damien's and André's phones were found in Damien's car,' Rafe added. 'I'm hoping he thinks that we're just leaving Sacramento and that he has a few hours before we arrive.'

That, at least, was comforting. 'Should I reply to his text?' Mercy asked. 'Is there any way he can know where I am?'

'Doubtful, but let's make sure.' Tom reached backward. 'Give me your phone.' Mercy did and Tom pulled another phone from his pocket. 'Mine's a burner,' he said. 'I never leave home without one. I'm going to answer him from my phone, spoofing your number. It'll look like it came from you, but my phone's untraceable.' A minute later he handed her phone back. 'Done. I told him that you were on your way with an ETA of seven thirty. It'll be dark then. Burton thinks he'll have that advantage.'

Gideon met Mercy's eyes in the rear-view mirror, his expression severe. 'This is what's going to happen,' he said in a tone that brooked no argument. 'When we get to the stop, I want you and Amos to stay in the SUV. He had a rifle in Snowbush. He *will* be waiting for us again. We'll park a quarter mile away from the coordinates and Tom and I will check them out. Rafe, you and Agent Schumacher will stay with the vehicles in case Ephraim's watching and comes after Mercy.'

Rafe's jaw tensed, but he nodded. 'I'd slow you down, so yeah. Okay.'

Gideon huffed. 'Come on, Rafe, you know you'd balk if I told you to leave Mercy.'

Rafe laughed then. 'You're right about that. It's a good plan, Gid.'

Gideon shook his head. 'I keep putting my foot in it.'

'After this, I say we go out for ice cream,' Daisy said. 'You can buy me a double, Gideon, and I might even share with you.'

Gideon pretended to be scared. 'I would never even ask. Nobody who values their life gets between you and ice cream.'

'Molina's here as well,' Tom said conversationally. 'So that you aren't surprised if you see her.'

Goddammit. Mercy had figured as much, but it still pissed her off. 'With a platoon of agents?'

'SWAT,' Tom corrected. 'She and the team got up here about an hour ago. Flew in to Dunsmuir by helicopter and settled in to wait. They'll drive to the coordinates, then canvass the area, looking for Burton and the hostages.'

'And you're just telling us all this now, Tom?' Mercy asked through clenched teeth, terrified of what Ephraim would do to the hostages if he saw Molina and the SWAT team.

Tom put away his laptop, then turned in his seat to look at them. 'Yes. You would have worried unnecessarily otherwise, and don't even try claiming that I'm wrong.'

Mercy blew out a breath. 'You're not wrong.'

'I know,' Tom said, but there was no trace of condescension or smugness. 'Also, there are vests and helmets in the very back. The windows of this SUV are bullet-resistant, but we're not taking any chances. Daisy, if you could give everyone their gear?'

Daisy did as Tom asked and no words were spoken as they put on the tactical gear.

They remained silent until Rafe said, 'Pull over here. We're a quarter mile from the coordinates.'

Gideon did and Mercy suddenly felt sick. This was it. They were going to face Ephraim Burton. And she was going to trust her new family to make sure that all of them walked away alive.

Except for Ephraim. *I want to see him die. Painfully.*

Dunsmuir, California
Wednesday, 19 April, 4.25 P.M.

Sonofabitch. Ephraim backed away from the road, his heart pounding like a motherfucker. *They're here. Already. How are they here already?*

But they were, specifically Gideon and that tall blond Fed who'd visited the Sokolovs' house twice on Sunday, and they were approaching the tree stump where he'd left Farrah Romero's phone.

How *were* they here already? They'd just left Sacramento half an hour ago. Mercy had said so.

Mercy had clearly lied. Rage bubbled up and he had to breathe through it so that he didn't punch something or snarl. Because Gideon and the Fed were so close that they might hear him.

She'd lied and disobeyed, bringing the Feds. How many others were here?

Was she even here? If she'd double-crossed him . . .

Motherfucker. He was going to kill *all* of the hostages and he was going to make it hurt. He crept back to the camper, fuming. He'd parked off the road about a quarter mile away but had been about to move the camper even deeper into the forest. It was too late for that now. If he started the Escalade's engine, Gideon and the other Fed would hear it and come running. And even if they didn't, he'd be shocked if law enforcement hadn't barricaded the road.

He'd thought he'd have at least two or three hours to prepare, even if Mercy did tell the cops. Instead, he'd wasted what time he had sleeping. *Goddammit.*

He needed to find another way out. And of the three hostages, Dr Romero was the one most likely to help make that happen. The other two he'd kill now, because there'd be no controlling them. Together they might be able to overpower him.

Leaning Granny's rifle against the side of the camper, he drew Regina's gun, gave the suppressor a tightening twist, and opened the camper door. Both Damien Sokolov and André Holmes were motionless except for the deep breaths they drew. He wished he had time to let them wake up. He wanted them to suffer, not die in their sleep.

He frowned, because the bench seat of the dinette was empty. Dr Romero had been there. Where the hell was she?

Ephraim stumbled backward at the sight of the woman on the floor as she rolled to a stop at the open door. Her feet kicked out and he stumbled backward several more steps, gasping at the sudden pain in his groin. Romero lay on the camper floor, her legs halfway out the door, bound feet dangling. Breathing hard through her nose because he'd duct-taped her mouth, she lifted her head enough to glare at him.

If she'd kicked him one inch lower, she'd have had him curled on the ground in the fetal position. As it was, it hurt so bad that he was dizzy with it. But he wasn't down for the count.

I am going to enjoy killing you.

He staggered to his feet and grabbed her by the duct tape that bound her ankles, holding her feet away from his body as he pulled a knife from his pocket and sliced the tape. Once her feet were freed, he yanked her up by her shirt collar. 'You will cooperate or die,' he whispered. 'But you get to see your fiancé die first because you don't know how to behave.'

He leaned down to pick up the golden gun he'd dropped when she kicked him, but straightened to backhand her hard when she tried to twist out of his grasp. 'Bitch,' he snarled softly.

A loud thump from inside the camper made him jump. Then swear, because the camper's stereo began blaring. It was only static because the dial had been set by the honeymooners to a Nevada station, but it was loud.

The nightmare only got worse when the New Orleans cop appeared in the doorway, using the door's frame to push himself to his feet. The only saving grace was that his hands were still cuffed behind him.

I guess he wasn't asleep, Ephraim thought numbly, and then his brain kicked back into gear. He yanked Romero back to her feet, nearly stumbling when she tried using her body weight to drop out of his grasp. She did stumble, but then she paused . . .

And kicked Regina's gun under the camper.

'Fucking bitch,' he hissed, dragging her a few steps backward as her fiancé staggered down the stairs, murder in his eyes.

Fucking hell.

'Stop! FBI!'

The shout came from the direction of the clearing where Gideon and the other Fed had been nosing around. 'Fuck,' he snarled. The Feds were coming. Grabbing the rifle from where it leaned against the camper, he aimed and fired at the New Orleans cop who was charging him.

The man was built like a linebacker, so the shot should have hit. But it didn't because Romero threw herself into Ephraim, knocking his arm so that his shot went wide.

He turned to shoot again, but the cop had taken cover behind the camper and Ephraim was out of time. He shoved the barrel into Romero's back. 'Move. Now.'

She glared at him. But she walked. Actually she stomped, making way too much noise.

'Faster,' he whispered. 'And cut the noise, or I will go back to New Orleans and kill every member of your family after I kill you.'

Her jaw set and she moved faster.

Twenty-nine

Dunsmuir, California
Wednesday, 19 April, 4.30 P.M.

The silence in Agent Hunter's SUV was so oppressive that Amos wanted to shout, speak, whisper – anything to make it stop. To get some relief. He was antsy, needing to move. To do something.

'Where is Gideon?' Mercy whispered, the sound making him jump.

'He's all right,' Agent Schumacher said from the driver's seat. She'd joined them seconds after Gideon and Tom had taken off to explore the coordinates that Ephraim had given them.

The coordinates to the trap Ephraim had prepared.

'How do you know he's all right?' Mercy insisted.

'He's been in contact with me,' Schumacher replied. 'They're fine.'

But Amos didn't believe her. The woman's mouth was tight and her shoulders even tighter. Of course, that could have been disapproval that the four of them were there to begin with. Luckily Daisy had passed him one of the rifles she'd been keeping in the backseat when Schumacher had been talking to Gideon and Tom before the two had left them. If Schumacher had seen that, she really would have disapproved. Only Rafe displayed his weapon openly and Schumacher had also frowned at him.

At least I'm armed. It gave him a sense of control that was likely unwarranted. Except that he was a better shot than Ephraim. If Amos was with an Eden hunting party, they came back with something – a deer, a goose, quail . . . something. Ephraim rarely hit

538

where he aimed, but no one in the compound knew that. Only trusted members were allowed to join the hunt because hunting meant possession of a firearm, even if only for a short time. The Elders had positioned it as not wanting anyone to be inadvertently hurt by the weapons, but now Amos knew it was because they feared an uprising.

Amos wished he'd known then. *I would have shown them a damn uprising.*

'Have they found Burton?' Rafe quietly asked Schumacher.

'Not yet,' she said brusquely, and then her tone softened. 'They will be all right. Molina's SWAT team is nearby. Try not to worry, Mercy. It'll be f—'

The gunshot splintered the tension in the SUV, and everyone moved at once. Amos and Rafe both pushed Mercy to the floorboard and Daisy had her rifle aimed at the back window before Amos could draw a breath.

'Farrah,' Mercy whispered hoarsely. 'He's shot her. Or André or Damien. He's shooting them.'

'You don't know that.' Schumacher tried to soothe, but she'd also drawn her firearm. 'I'm going to check the immediate area. Stay here.'

She slipped from the driver's seat and crept around to the other side of the SUV. The forest was on the passenger side, thick and dark, despite the sun still shining overhead. Someone could hide in the trees and never be seen.

But the action wasn't happening in the forest, at least not on that side of the road. This was nearly what Mercy had dreaded, but at least her friend was still alive.

'Rafe,' Amos muttered, pointing through the SUV window to the forest across the road. 'Through there.'

Ephraim had a rifle pressed into Farrah Romero's back and she walked briskly, her hands bound in front of her with what looked like duct tape. Tape also covered her mouth, and tears streaked down her face.

I can't allow him to kill that woman. I let him kill too many already.

'What's happening?' Mercy whispered.

539

Rafe drew a breath. 'He's got Farrah, but she's alive.'

'He wants to trade,' Mercy said numbly.

'That's not going to happen,' Rafe snarled, saving Amos from having to do so. 'You promised me, Mercy.'

'I'm not going to trade myself,' she hissed back. 'I'm just saying that's what he wants to happen.'

Amos was suddenly calm. He wasn't going to sacrifice himself, either. He finally had all of his children together. But he wasn't going to allow Farrah to be harmed. 'We can take him. He might think Mercy is here, but he doesn't know that I am.'

'Or me,' Daisy added. 'He hasn't seen us yet. We still have the advantage.'

Rafe's door opened, revealing Schumacher, who was crouched below the window line. 'Reynolds and Hunter are headed back, so I'll have backup. I'm going to circle around behind Burton and get the drop on him. Don't worry, Miss Callahan. We'll get your friend out of this.'

Still sitting on the floor, Mercy gave Schumacher a stiff nod and they watched as the agent took off at a run into the woods behind them.

Amos glanced back, blinking when he saw no Ephraim. No Farrah. 'They're gone.'

'Back into the woods,' Daisy said. 'Let me out. I want a better angle.'

Rafe complied, opening his door and slowly sliding down and out, staying out of sight of the window as Schumacher had done. 'Come on,' he said to Daisy, then frowned when Mercy moved to join them. 'Not you.'

Mercy glared at him but stayed put, even when Amos followed the others out of the vehicle.

Rafe had his handgun and Daisy a rifle, which she handled like an extension of her own arm. Gideon's chosen one apparently had many skills. Daisy knelt behind the front tire of Hunter's SUV, positioning the rifle on her shoulder.

Satisfied that she knew what she was doing, Amos lifted his gaze to search for Ephraim.

'He couldn't have seen us yet,' Rafe murmured.

'Probably just the SUVs,' Daisy murmured back. 'He stole your dad's Tahoe back in Snowbush to escape. Maybe he's planning to get away using one of these Fed-mobiles.'

'There he is,' Amos said quietly. Grimly.

Because Ephraim had reemerged from the forest, the rifle now slung over his shoulder by its strap, a pistol in his right hand pressed into Farrah's temple. His left forearm was clamped over her chest and that hand held a revolver, the muzzle shoved up under Farrah's chin. He shoved the woman forward until he was ten yards from where they stood.

At least he'd removed the duct tape from her mouth. Farrah was sobbing now, a heartbreaking sight. She wasn't moving a muscle, her fear tangible. But even through her tears she showed a defiance that made Amos glad this woman was his daughter's best friend.

And made Amos determined to save her.

'I just want to get away,' Ephraim called. 'Nobody needs to get hurt. Step away from the SUVs and I'll let her go.'

'We can't shoot him now,' Daisy murmured, 'and neither can Schumacher. He's got fingers on both triggers. One wrong twitch and he'll kill her.'

'I know,' Rafe growled under his breath, then raised his voice. 'Let her go first. Then we'll talk.'

Ephraim edged closer. 'I'll tell you where to find your brother, Sokolov. You might want to get to him quickly. He's already lost a lot of blood. You know, from the crash this morning and the bullets I pumped into his gut. You can still save him, though. Every second counts. Get out of my way and you can save him.'

Dunsmuir, California
Wednesday, 19 April, 4.50 P.M.

Rafe's heart skipped a beat, fear for his brother nearly overwhelming him. In that moment, he was tempted to do as Ephraim demanded, but he knew the man was lying. Ephraim would try to kill them all.

Except for Mercy. She would be taken back to Eden and made an example. Rafe's blood ran cold at the very thought.

Of course, Ephraim couldn't succeed. He was too outnumbered. But Rafe wasn't willing to risk even one of them for this monster. They just needed to get Burton's guns away from Farrah's head. Daisy was right. One wrong twitch of Ephraim's finger and Farrah would be dead. Rafe hoped that Schumacher was fully aware of the situation. He hoped that she was somewhere behind Ephraim, ready to shoot but waiting for the right moment.

Mercy cracked the SUV door open. 'He's lying, Rafe.'

'I know,' Rafe hissed. 'He's not going to just walk away. He'll kill us all. Close the door and get down.'

'No. Look at Farrah. Watch her mouth.'

Rafe did and immediately felt a wave of relief. Farrah was mouthing over and over again, *He's okay. Your brother's okay.*

'Oh thank God,' Rafe whispered. 'Where the fuck is Gideon anyway? We need a diversion. Anything to get him to loosen his hold on Farrah.'

Mercy scrubbed her face with her palms. 'He's not going to let Farrah go. He wants me and he wants his damn safe-deposit box key. Let me open the door wider. I want to talk to him. And I won't leave the car, I promise,' she snapped before he could warn her not to do just that.

Rafe sighed and opened the door, because he had a very bad feeling that backup wasn't coming. Not only were Gideon and Hunter AWOL, the SWAT team that Molina was supposed to be bringing was not here. And they should have been. He was starting to wonder if Schumacher was really in the woods waiting for Ephraim to lower his guard. He thought she would have shown herself by this time, maybe even crept closer. Something was very wrong.

Daisy's face was pinched and drawn. She knew Gideon should be back by now as well. But she was holding it together.

'Ephraim,' Mercy shouted. 'Let her go. I know you want me. I know you want this damn key, whatever it's for. I know you don't want your mother dying alone in some prison ward, but she will if

542

you hurt any of my friends or family. So let her go and deal directly with me.'

Ephraim's answer was a gunshot through the SUV's side window.

Everyone hunkered on reflex, but the glass didn't shatter. Rafe chanced a look around the SUV, hoping that Ephraim had pulled both guns away from Farrah while he was shooting, but he still had the revolver shoved firmly under her chin.

'That window won't hold forever,' Ephraim shouted back. He pushed Farrah a little closer. 'And when it breaks, someone inside that SUV will get the next bullet and I'll aim for heads.' He shot again and the glass pebbled.

'He's right,' Rafe said, his jaw clenched. 'The glass will take two more hits, tops. If he gets much closer he'll be climbing in the damn window.'

Dammit, Gideon, where the fuck are you? This was Rafe's worst fear for how this situation would end. With him having to put Mercy directly in Ephraim's crosshairs.

'What do you want?' Rafe yelled. 'Be specific, Burton.'

'I want that SUV!'

'Take the other one.'

Ephraim had continued inching closer and now Rafe could hear him laugh. 'Fine. As long as Mercy is in it.'

Mercy crouched on the floor of Hunter's SUV, pale but determined. 'Where is Molina's SWAT team?'

'Good question,' Rafe growled. 'But a better one is what do you think you're doing?'

Because Mercy was sliding across the floor to the open door. 'I'm going to do what I did in Snowbush. Except this time I've got a vest and helmet. And this time you're going to be ready. Daisy, can you climb a tree?'

Daisy nodded. 'I've done it before. You want me to be your sniper?'

'Well, I think we're on our own,' Mercy said. 'Don't you?'

'Yes,' Rafe agreed. 'I expected the cavalry to have ridden in by now.'

'Amos,' Daisy whispered, 'how good are you with a rifle?'

'Very good,' Amos said seriously. 'Good enough to keep my son and daughter's family safe.'

Daisy gave Amos's arm a quick squeeze. 'Keep him in your sights while I'm crawling to the woods. If you see him drop those guns away from Farrah, shoot. Okay?'

Amos nodded once. 'I will.'

When Daisy was safely in the forest, Mercy leaned forward to kiss Rafe hard. 'I am not a sacrifice,' she whispered. 'I am a diversion. Watch his hands. The minute he doesn't have the muzzle of a gun on Farrah's body, shoot him. I don't care where. I want this over.' She kissed him again, softer this time. 'I trust you.'

Rafe swallowed hard. 'Dammit, Mercy.'

She gave him a sad smile. 'Let's get rid of the baggage I've been carrying all these years, okay?' Then she patted Amos's cheek. 'You were a good shot when I was little. I bet you're a lot better now. And if you're tempted to do anything stupid, remember that Abigail needs her papa. And so do I.'

Amos shuddered out a breath. 'I'll remember.'

She nodded once, then slid from the SUV to the ground. Staying bent at the waist, she walked to the front end of the vehicle and straightened to her full height.

'All right, Ephraim,' she called. 'I'm right here. Let Farrah go and we can talk.'

Dunsmuir, California
Wednesday, 19 April, 5.10 P.M.

Mercy was a lot calmer than she thought she'd be under the circumstances. Of course, she was digging her nails into her palm so hard, she'd be surprised if she wasn't drawing blood.

Ephraim had advanced another few feet and now stood in the middle of the road, less than ten feet from Hunter's SUV.

Mercy met Farrah's frightened eyes. 'Hey, Ro. You okay?'

Of course Farrah didn't answer or nod. But she blinked once. For 'yes.'

Mercy's throat was suddenly so thick that she couldn't swallow. 'I love you,' she said quietly.

Farrah's eyes narrowed. And she blinked twice. For 'no.'

Not that she didn't love Mercy back, but because she was forbidding her to do anything stupid.

'That's very sweet, *wife*,' Ephraim snarled. 'But I don't want you here. I want you in the vehicle. Now.'

'Let her go and I'll go with you.'

'You're lying,' he spat.

Mercy met his eye. 'Maybe, maybe not. But you won't know until you let her go. You can't handle both of us. We're not twelve years old.'

He sneered. 'Tell your guard dog to come out and throw his guns to me. Even his backups.'

Mercy heard the light *thump-thump* of Rafe's cane as he came up behind her and her heart sank. *Rafe, no. What are you doing?*

When Rafe stopped next to her, he tossed his gun to the side. It landed on the road, skidding until it came to a stop about ten yards away. 'I have no backups,' Rafe said. 'If you don't believe me, feel free to check for yourself.'

Ephraim snarled. 'Get down, Sokolov. On your stomach. Face to the ground. I've had enough of you.'

Mercy tensed, every fiber of her existence screaming at Rafe for leaving the shield of the SUV.

Rafe went down on one knee slowly, his hand sliding down his cane to grip it in the middle, which she hadn't seen him do before.

Ephraim's features twisted with rage. 'I said face to the ground.'

'I'm slow,' Rafe said. 'I'm on disability leave, you know. Which should humiliate you, because I took you out in the airport from a wheelchair using only my cane.'

A muscle twitched in Ephraim's taut jaw. 'Face. To. The. Ground.' Keeping the pistol pressed into Farrah's temple, he straightened the arm across her throat, aiming the revolver at Rafe. 'I am so going to love killing you.'

Panic began to swirl and Mercy had no idea what was happening.

Until Rafe offered her his cane, his expression one of broken devastation.

'Give it back to my dad, okay?' he said thickly. 'It belonged to my grandfather.'

'But . . .' *Oh.* It hadn't belonged to his grandfather. Karl had made it for him only three days ago. Rafe was faking it. He had a plan.

She drew a shuddering breath. 'Don't do this,' she whispered, not faking her fear.

Rafe continued to slowly lower himself to the ground. 'Tell Gideon that I'll always owe him for saving us that night.'

Mercy's eyes filled with tears and she bent over, trying to pull him back up. 'Please, Rafe, don't do this.' She tried to make him take back the cane, but he kept pushing it back into her hand.

'Keep it,' he finally snapped. 'You might need it someday.'

And that was when she saw movement behind Ephraim. Gideon had come out of the woods and was soundlessly approaching Ephraim. Then she understood.

With Ephraim pointing his revolver at Rafe, that was one less gun pointed at Farrah. But he still had the pistol pressed against Farrah's temple, his finger still on the trigger. *If I can make Ephraim angry enough, he might point the second gun at me.* Then Gideon could make his shot and Farrah would be free.

But goddammit. That was still one gun pointed at Rafe. Panic began to swell in her mind and she dug her nails into her palm again. *Think. Think. Be ready for whatever happens. At least Rafe's wearing tactical gear. Farrah has none.*

'Take off that damn helmet,' Ephraim ordered.

Fucking hell.

One side of Rafe's mouth lifted. 'Somehow I thought you'd say that.' Resting his weight on one knee, Rafe tugged at the strap holding the tactical helmet in place. 'Anything else?'

Gideon was two feet behind Ephraim now, weapon in one hand, his other outstretched toward Ephraim's pistol. Ephraim didn't notice, too focused on Rafe, the revolver in his hand steady. And pointed at Rafe's head. Rafe's gun was out of reach and all Mercy had was his damn cane.

Keep it. You might need it someday.

I took you out from a wheelchair, using only my cane.

Oh my God. Really? She wanted to scream. *This* was Rafe's plan? For her to hit Ephraim with the damn cane while Gideon wrested the revolver away from Farrah's head?

Apparently so.

Gripping the cane in both hands, Mercy was shaking, but chanced a glance at Farrah. Her best friend's eyes were narrowed, aware that something was going down.

'Say goodbye, Mercy,' Ephraim said, smiling. 'But make it quick.'

But his smile vanished when Gideon reached for Ephraim's wrist and bent it at an odd angle that had Ephraim howling in pain and his hand opening completely. The revolver went off as they'd feared, but it was no longer aimed at Farrah. The bullet hit the road, sending asphalt chips flying. Farrah immediately dropped to the ground and Mercy brought Rafe's cane down on Ephraim's other wrist, hearing a cry that sounded agonized and feral and . . .

And was coming from her own mouth as she swung the cane at Ephraim's head, at his face, at his chest. She kept swinging and swinging.

Dunsmuir, California
Wednesday, 19 April, 5.20 P.M.

Rafe twisted back up to his knee and yanked the revolver from Burton's now limp fingers. It had all happened in less than two seconds, but it wasn't over yet.

Mercy was screaming at the top of her lungs. Screaming and swinging Rafe's cane and striking Burton wherever she could. Again and again, with a viciousness that could only come from the sudden release of emotions damaged through horrific abuse.

Gideon stood frozen, his gaze locked on his sister, who swung the cane in a mad frenzy. Rafe shouted his friend's name, but Gideon's mind was in another place. In another time.

Oh. Oh no. Too late, Rafe realized that Gideon was coming face-to-face with the man who'd beaten him near to death the night of his

547

thirteenth birthday. The man who'd brutally raped his mother and his sister. *Oh, Gid. I'm sorry.* Gideon had thought he could handle this, but . . . *Who could?*

Part of Rafe wanted to let Mercy beat Burton to death, but he knew she would regret that later. Other people deserved to see Burton punished. The bastard needed to face his many victims, which couldn't happen if Mercy killed him.

'Mercy!' Rafe lunged for her, but couldn't reach her from his knees.

Farrah reached for Mercy's arm but she couldn't extend her hands high enough with her wrists being bound with tape. She was flung backward when Mercy swung the cane again, too deep in her rage to know whose hands were on her.

'Help me up,' Rafe gritted to Farrah. Offering her shoulder, she gave him something to grab on to as she helped heft him to his feet. Catching the cane midswing, he handed it to Farrah, who laid it on the road and backed away as if it were a live snake. Farrah sank to her knees, trembling head to toe as the reality of being safe finally sank in.

But for the moment, Rafe was focused on Mercy, turning her in his arms. Balancing on one foot, he wrapped his arms around her and rocked her slowly. He took off her helmet and stroked her hair, pressing her face into his neck and murmuring that it would be all right. That they'd done it. They'd stopped him.

That *she'd* stopped him.

But he didn't think she heard a word he said. She was sobbing uncontrollably, her legs abruptly folding, taking them both to the cold ground.

Behind him, Rafe could hear the click of handcuffs and Gideon's hoarse voice commanding Burton to his knees, then informing the man of his rights. Seeing Mercy collapse must have been the jolt he'd needed to come back to himself.

It was over. They'd done it. Turning on his ass so that he could see Gideon, Rafe pulled Mercy into his lap, unwilling to let her go. Burton was on his knees, hands cuffed behind him. His face was bleeding and . . . Rafe swallowed. His eye had fallen out under Mercy's well-deserved assault.

Burton looked ghastly. There was no other word for it.

'Is it over?' Farrah whispered. She looked up at Gideon. 'Please say it's over.'

Gideon nodded once. 'It's—'

But he didn't get to finish, because Ephraim Burton jerked, a quiet pop filling the air. The man toppled over as they watched in shock.

Farrah screamed. Then gagged.

Because half of Burton's head was gone, his brain matter spattered over all of them.

Mercy stared in shock. No, more than shock. Her expression was slack, her eyes vacant. This was the disassociation he'd seen at the airport. Helplessly Rafe squeezed her a little too hard, trying to give her that little bit of pain she needed to defuse the panic.

'Mercy. *Mercy.*' But he'd missed that little bubble of quiet space she'd spoken of, that moment it took to center herself and stop the panic attack in its tracks. So he held her. It was all he could do. 'Gideon?'

Gideon was still staring at Burton's body. 'Who . . . who shot him? I didn't.'

At that moment Amos came running from the other side of the SUV, rifle in hand, and Gideon's expression hardened. Coming to his feet, he bellowed, 'What the hell, Amos? I had him subdued.'

Amos ignored Gideon's question. 'Mercy! Get her down!' he shouted, and a second later Rafe had been knocked over, Mercy still in his arms and Amos covering them both, having mowed them down with his body. Rafe felt Amos's body jerk above his, just as Burton's had done.

What the hell? What the fuck was happening?

'Oh no. Oh no.' Gideon fell to his knees. 'Amos? Oh my God.'

Then there was a loud crack of gunfire, coming from the trees nearest the SUV. *Daisy was still out there. What the actual hell? Why had she fired her rifle?*

'Get him off me,' Rafe gasped, pushing at Amos, but the man was dead weight. 'What's happening? Who shot him? Did Daisy shoot him?' He didn't know if he meant Burton or Amos or both of them. His thoughts were beginning to fray, his head spinning from the impact with the ground.

'I don't know.' Then Gideon's numb-sounding voice hardened in urgent command. 'Farrah, get Mercy into the SUV. We have an active shooter.'

Rafe heard Daisy's voice, getting louder as she came closer. She was running and out of breath. 'That last shot was me. It was DJ who shot Burton. He was trying to shoot Mercy, but Amos . . .' She looked at Amos's still form in dismay. 'Oh God. He shot Amos?' Not waiting for a reply, she squared her shoulders, charging into action as she usually did. 'I'll get the first-aid kit. Farrah, come with me, honey. Gideon, get Amos off Mercy. I'll come back for her in a second.'

Rafe's head was still spinning from hitting it on the ground, and, coupled with Daisy's whirlwind of energy, he was unable to think clearly. 'Amos? You okay?'

'No, he's not okay,' Gideon said briskly. 'He's been shot.'

Oh right. Daisy said that. Amos was shot. Amos's weight disappeared, Gideon having rolled him off Rafe and Mercy. 'Oh no,' Rafe breathed. Amos was bleeding and it appeared to be from a neck wound.

Daisy ran back to them, a first-aid kit in her hands.

'Thank you.' Gideon took the kit. 'Can you move Schumacher's SUV? Park it between our SUV and the trees across the road. If DJ comes back, I want cover. We're sitting ducks here. I want SUVs on both sides.'

Daisy ran to do as he asked.

'DJ?' Rafe asked thickly, not sure he'd heard her correctly.

'That's what she said. Just wait until she comes back. I need to get Amos's wound packed and I'm not . . .' Gideon grimaced. 'I'm not okay right now.'

A minute later they were sheltered between the two SUVs. Daisy jumped out of the vehicle she'd moved, dropping to her knees next to Gideon, who glanced up at her, his jaw taut. 'Explain, please. *Slowly.*'

'Amos saw DJ first,' Daisy said, taking over Gideon's task,

putting pressure on Amos's wound. 'That's the name that Amos said right after Burton fell over. Then I saw him too, when he stepped out into the open. DJ was aiming for you and Mercy, Rafe. That's why Amos was running. That's why he threw himself over you. The shot you heard was me, trying to stop him. I did hit him, but it wasn't enough to take him down. He'd shot Amos by that point and I guess he decided to retreat. He got away on a dirt bike, through the forest. He's gone. For now, anyway.'

Rafe stared, his thoughts running in slow motion. 'DJ Belmont, the one who killed Mercy's mother?'

Daisy nodded grimly. 'And the one who unwittingly helped Amos escape Eden.'

'How do you know you hit him?' Gideon asked.

'Because he dropped his rifle. He picked it up and ran for the dirt bike. If he'd been able to, he would have kept firing, so I assume he's injured badly enough to keep him from shooting, but he's not dead. Unfortunately. Is Mercy hurt?'

Rafe had already checked her for injuries. 'I don't think so. This is what she calls her zombie episodes.'

Daisy lightly stroked Mercy's face. 'Honey?'

But there was no response. *Shit.*

Do something. At least for Amos. Rafe patted his pockets, searching for his phone to call 911, but Gideon was already calling, telling the operator where they were, and then he hung up. 'I have to leave my phone open. We have other issues.'

Rafe frowned. 'What other issues?'

'Hunter and I found the SWAT team about a quarter mile on the other side of the coordinates. Of the six men, four were dead. The other two are injured badly. Molina's also hurt. Tom's with them now.'

'What about Damien?' Rafe demanded. 'And André?'

'They're okay. I was running back here to you guys when I heard the shot. That was Ephraim, shooting at André, but he missed. Damien was still in the camper. André was trying to follow Burton, because he'd taken Farrah. André said that Burton ran them off the road, then drugged them. Burton was going to shoot André and

Damien right before I got there, but Farrah kicked him almost in the nuts. Enough to send him off-kilter. That's when he left with her to come here.'

Rafe shuddered, fear for his brother slowly ebbing away. 'What about Agent Schumacher?' he asked, although he thought he already knew and dreaded the answer. 'She was circling around to get to Ephraim from behind. The way you came. But she never came back.'

Gideon shook his head. 'She's dead, too. I found her body when I was running after Ephraim. I think DJ must have shot her, too. Ephraim's rifle didn't have a silencer and the golden gun he's been using got kicked under the camper by Farrah when he was dragging her away.'

Daisy looked over her shoulder at the SUV where Farrah sat, staring straight ahead. Probably in shock, Rafe thought. At least André was okay.

'Way to go, Farrah!' Daisy cheered, then frowned. 'But why did DJ kill Agent Schumacher? And Burton? And why would he try to kill Mercy?'

'Schumacher was likely in his way, like Molina and her crew,' Gideon said grimly. 'And he went after Mercy because he didn't finish the job the first time. Mercy didn't think that Ephraim knew she was still alive, and I agree. I think DJ lied and said she was dead and now he's afraid that the community will find out. If you hadn't stopped him, he probably would have kept firing. I would have been the next target, but he would have tried to silence all of us because we know the truth, that Mercy is not dead. The only person who could get that information back to Eden was Burton, because the rest of us don't know where Eden is. And now that Burton's dead, he can't tell us.'

Rafe felt Mercy shudder in his arms. She looked up, blinking like an owl. 'I did it again?'

Rafe kissed her forehead. 'Burton is dead.'

'It was DJ,' Gideon added.

Mercy closed her eyes. 'Tying up loose ends?' She sounded weary, but unsurprised.

'Seems like it,' Rafe murmured.

'Oh!' The cry came from Farrah, who was now out of the SUV and running. 'André!'

Rafe slid to the front bumper of the SUV on his ass, too tired to even crawl. But he was glad he'd made the effort, because Damien and André were crossing the road, moving like they were sleep-walkers, plodding and slow. André had one arm around Damien's waist, keeping him upright, but his other hand held a golden gun and strapped to his back was a rifle.

Damien fell to the ground beside Rafe with a groan. Dropping the golden gun, André wrapped Farrah in his arms, her happy cry like music after everything they'd experienced.

Rafe slung an arm around his brother's shoulders, immediately letting go when Damien groaned. 'Sorry, D.' He grimaced at the sight of the open wound on his brother's head. 'That happen in the wreck?'

But Damien didn't answer, because he was staring at Amos. 'What happened?'

'He was shot protecting me,' Mercy said softly. 'André, where did you get the rifle?'

'And is that the Santa Rosa madam's golden gun?' Rafe added.

Daisy glanced up briefly before returning her attention to Amos's wound. 'That looks like the rifle DJ was using.'

'Because it is,' André said, 'if DJ's the guy with the really blond hair and the rifle was the one he was using to shoot at you.'

'He is and it is,' Daisy told him.

'Well,' André said, not letting Farrah go, 'Farrah kicked the gun under the camper when Burton was about to shoot me with it. Once Gideon came along and untied Damien and me, I went under the camper for the gun. Came in handy, too. I saw the guy with the rifle on the edge of the woods. He fired twice before somebody shot him in the shoulder.'

'That was Daisy,' Rafe said.

'He rode off on his dirt bike with the rifle,' Daisy told him.

'He dropped the rifle after I shot him in the arm with the madam's gun,' André said. 'He started to come back for the rifle, but his arm was hanging at his side, like he couldn't move it. The first shot –

553

Daisy's – got him in the left shoulder, then I got his left arm. I think that's his dominant side, because he was all over the place after that, like he couldn't steer with his right arm.'

'Did you see which way he went?' Rafe asked.

André nodded. 'Should be a trail of blood. I tried to chase, but was too damn dizzy.'

Gideon redialed 911 to have a BOLO sent out on DJ Belmont and his dirt bike, then asked the ETA for the medics.

Mercy's gaze had returned to Amos, whose breathing was slow and frighteningly shallow. 'When will help be here, Gideon?' she asked when he'd ended the call.

'They're sending a helicopter,' Gideon told her. 'Should be soon. They'll airlift Amos and probably the guys from SWAT who were also shot by DJ. They'll have to send a second rescue unit for Damien and Molina.'

'I should go with Amos,' Mercy said weakly. 'He got hurt saving me. He can't die. I just got him back.'

'He's still breathing,' Daisy murmured, 'so don't lose hope.'

Sacramento, California
Wednesday, 19 April, 11.30 P.M.

Wincing at the sudden pain in her hand, Mercy looked down at the little girl gripping her hand as if her life depended on it. *Maybe it does.* Abigail was staring at the sign posted on the doors into UC Davis's ICU, her little body so tense, like she'd shatter at any moment. *Right there with you, sweetheart.*

'What does that mean?' Abigail asked, so quietly that Mercy could barely hear her question even in the deathly quiet of the ICU family waiting room.

Mercy slowly lowered to one knee, stiff and sore from where Amos had knocked her down, saving her life. *He saved my life.*

And now he fought for his own. He'd lost so much blood at the scene, lapsing into unconsciousness almost immediately after DJ's bullet had ripped through his throat. Daisy had stayed with him as he'd been airlifted to Sacramento, not leaving him until he'd been taken into surgery. In all that time he hadn't regained consciousness, and that wasn't good.

Mercy brought her and Abigail's joined hands to her lips to kiss the little girl's white knuckles. 'ICU means Intensive Care Unit. It's the part of the hospital where they put patients who need someone watching them constantly.'

And was probably not the place for a seven-year-old, but Abigail had been insistent, according to Irina, who'd driven the child to the hospital herself. Well, along with Karl, who wasn't letting his wife out of his sight after the events of the day. The man who'd been so kind and welcoming was still pale, still trembling, even though his son was mostly fine now that the effects of Ephraim's sedative had worn off. Damien had a concussion, but was home with his wife, who, according to Irina, hadn't left his side.

Mercy figured that once it all sank in, she'd be as shaky as Karl. For now she was blessedly numb, which kept her from breaking into tears in the face of Abigail's fear. The little girl's expression was anxiously trusting, as if she'd believe any word that came from Mercy's mouth but desperately hoped the words were what she needed to hear.

'Will he die?' Abigail whispered.

Mercy almost said *no*, but she wouldn't lie to Abigail. Too many people had. 'I hope not.' She tucked a stray hair behind Abigail's ear. 'Papa is a strong man.' Totally true. 'He loves you very much and will fight to stay with you, but if his body is hurt too badly . . .' She sighed and, tugging her hand free, pulled Abigail into her arms. The little girl came willingly, sliding her arms around Mercy's neck and fiercely holding on. 'If he doesn't wake up, it won't be because he didn't want to stay with you forever. Does that make sense?'

A slight nod, but Abigail was trembling. Crying. *Oh, baby.* 'I'm sorry, Abigail. I'm so sorry.'

Abigail shook her head. 'You didn't shoot him,' she said into Mercy's neck.

No, I didn't. 'There's sorry-apologize and sorry-sorrowful. I mean the second one.'

Another slight nod. 'Can we go in now?'

Mercy pulled back, wiping Abigail's wet cheeks with her thumbs. 'My mama used to dry my tears like this,' Mercy whispered. 'Then she'd kiss my forehead. Can I kiss yours?'

Abigail leaned forward, presenting her forehead, which made Mercy smile as she kissed her. 'Your papa would be so proud of you right now. You are a very brave girl.'

'You are, too. You helped save your friend. She told me.'

Farrah and André had returned to the Sokolov house to rest and be taken care of by the Sokolov horde. Farrah had texted Mercy that she felt right at home. 'Farrah is my very best friend. Of course I helped to save her. That's what you do for the people you love.'

'Like my papa saved you.'

Mercy swallowed hard. 'Yes.' And by extension, he'd saved Rafe, which guaranteed him a place at the Sokolovs' table forever. *If he wakes up. Please wake up, Amos. Abigail needs you.*

I need you.

'Will he be . . .' Abigail's body went rigid. 'Will he have blood on him?'

Mercy's heart crumbled. 'No, sweetheart. He's all cleaned up. But he has a bandage on his throat and there are machines and tubes that will look scary.'

Abigail nodded stoically. 'Miss Irina told me. She said he has a tube that helps him breathe.'

Mercy kissed Abigail's forehead again. The girl's skin had gone clammy with fear. 'That's true, and I won't lie to you, it's really scary. I . . . I was scared, Abigail. I still am.' Which was why Rafe hadn't left her side in Amos's ICU room. He was waiting for her there now, elevating his leg in the room's recliner.

'You're scared he'll die?'

Do not lie to this child. 'Yes,' Mercy whispered. 'But I have hope, so you should, too. And, Abigail, if being here at the hospital is too scary, and you want to go back to Irina and Karl's house, you can do that. No one will be upset with you. Especially your papa. I promise.'

Abigail's jaw set stubbornly. 'I want to see him.'

'Then we will.' Mercy stood, took Abigail's hand, and hit the ICU admittance buzzer with her other hand.

Poor Rafe. Mercy hurt a little, but Rafe was in serious pain. One of the doctors had checked him out when they'd arrived at UC Davis, worried that Amos's tackle had reinjured tendons that had been shredded by a bullet six weeks ago. From the expression on Rafe's face when he'd thought she wasn't looking, he was afraid of this, too. It would put him further back on his PT rehab schedule, which meant even longer before he could be a cop again.

If he ever could. Mercy had felt the anxiety coming off him in waves and it broke her heart. But it was time to shift her worry over Rafe to Abigail as a nurse opened the ICU door to take them to Amos's room. They'd had to get special permission, but Irina had worked her magic and they'd been allowed an hour. Squeezing Mercy's hand hard, Abigail walked into her papa's room, pressed close to Mercy's side.

Rafe looked up with a tired smile. 'Hi, Abigail.'

Abigail nodded, her eyes fixed on Amos in the bed, on the way his chest rose and fell, powered by the ventilator. Her lips moved, but no sound emerged and she was even paler than she'd been before.

Mercy moved closer to the bed and took Amos's hand with her free one. 'Abigail's here,' she said quietly. 'She is so brave, Amos. You've raised her well. You're a good papa.'

'Can he hear us?' Abigail whispered.

Mercy smiled down at her. 'Maybe. But in case he can, let's let him know we're here, okay?'

Abigail joined Mercy close to her father's bedside. 'Hi, Papa. I'm . . . here. I'm here, Papa. I hope you can hear me.'

'I think he can,' Rafe said softly. 'When I had my surgery and was recovering, I could hear Mercy talking to me.'

Abigail lifted her gaze to Rafe, who sat on the other side of the bed, studiously avoiding Amos's face, half-covered with the ventilator mask. 'What did she say?'

'She mostly read to me, I think.'

Mercy was surprised. 'You heard that?'

'I did. I don't remember exactly what you read, but I'd hear your voice and it gave me something to hold on to.'

'It was an astronomy book.' Mercy sat in the chair next to Amos's bed, biting back a sigh of exhaustion. 'Come, Abigail.' She patted her knee, relieved when the girl sat in her lap easily, resting her head on Mercy's shoulder. 'It was the only book that I had in my purse at the time. I'd bought it for my brother John's daughter. She wants to be an astronaut.'

Abigail looked up at her. 'What's that?'

Ignoring Rafe's stunned expression, Mercy answered levelly, because she knew exactly what Abigail hadn't been taught – and what lies she'd been fed. 'It's a person who goes into space. A few men went to the moon, but that was long before I was born. I think even before your papa was born.'

Abigail's lips pursed. 'That's not true. My teacher said it wasn't true, that it was a movie, made in Hollywood. That the government lied.'

'What else did she say was a lie?' Mercy asked patiently as Rafe gaped in astonishment.

'Phones. Oh right. They're true.' Abigail's brow scrunched, the little girl in deep thought. 'Bigfoot? One of the boys in school said Bigfoot hides in the forest.'

Mercy couldn't contain her laugh. Across the bed, Rafe was biting back a grin. 'Well,' Mercy said, brushing Abigail's hair from her face, 'I'm not so sure about Bigfoot. He's probably not true. But astronauts are totally true. I'll get you some books so you can read about it for yourself.'

Abigail resettled against her shoulder. 'Can you read to Papa now?'

Mercy toyed with the bands holding the girl's braids in place, tugging them off. She ran her fingers through the plaits, stroking the hair she'd freed. *Like Mama used to do for me.* 'How about I read to both of you?'

Abigail yawned. 'What book do you have? I read *Ramona the Pest* at the library. I started to read the next book, but then Irina came. And then the FBI.'

'Let me check.' One-handed, Mercy opened a browser window on her phone and searched for the next ebook in the series, finding it easily. 'You started this one?'

Abigail sucked in a breath, her finger hovering over Mercy's screen, afraid to touch. 'Yes. It's in your phone?'

'It will be in a few seconds.'

Abigail was staring at the phone. 'How does it fit?'

Mercy tried to think about how to explain data to a child, but she was way too tired for that. 'Can I explain it later? For now, all you need to know is that you can fit a lot of books on a phone.'

'How many?'

Mercy blinked. 'Thousands, at least. Rafe?'

'At least.' He did a search on his own phone. 'Twenty thousand books, give or take.'

Abigail's eyes were like saucers. 'Really?'

'Really.' Mercy glanced at Rafe while she purchased the book, then downloaded it, grateful that the ICU had lifted its rule against cell phones. 'You want to read or do you want me to?'

Abigail looked over at Amos. 'I want to. I want him to hear me. Can I hold your phone?'

'Of course.' Mercy showed her how to swipe, amazed at the child's ability to absorb new things so quickly. Cuddling her close, she kissed Abigail's hair and listened as she read to Amos with a strong, steady voice.

Gradually, though, Abigail's voice grew softer, sleepier, and Mercy had to rescue her phone when it slipped from the little girl's small hands. 'I need to get her back to your parents,' Mercy murmured to Rafe, before realizing that he'd fallen asleep, too.

'We're here,' Irina said from the doorway, Karl at her side. 'We were waiting for her to finish before we took her home.' She aimed an affectionate look at the sleeping Rafe before coming in to crouch by the chair. 'Abigail?' She gave the child's shoulder a light shake. 'Time to go home with me and sleep in a real bed, okay?'

Abigail murmured something unintelligible, snuggling into Karl when he lifted her into his arms.

'You can come back tomorrow,' Karl whispered, then gave Mercy an unsteady smile. 'How are you doing?'

'I'm okay. Sore, but okay.' She glanced at Amos, who was unchanged. 'I think it'll start sinking in soon, but right now, I'm okay.' She realized she'd said 'okay' three times. 'Well, maybe not so okay.'

Balancing Abigail on his hip with one hand, Karl cupped Mercy's cheek with the other. 'You did well today. You stood up to Ephraim, faced your worst fear, and you won.'

She looked over at Amos. 'At what price?'

'He will pull through,' Irina said stubbornly. 'You must have faith, *lubimaya*.'

'What does that mean?' Mercy asked. '*Lubimaya*?'

'Beloved,' Karl answered. 'It means you are loved.'

Mercy's eyes stung. *Not again.* She would not cry any more. So she forced herself to smile. '*Spasibo*,' she said, pronouncing it the way she'd found online, then stood to hug Irina. 'Thank you.'

Irina beamed. 'You said it right the first time. Now, I suppose you will stay here tonight.'

'Yes, ma'am. I don't want him to wake up and be alone.'

'Then Rafe will stay with you,' she said. 'I won't even try to wake him up. He won't leave you anyway.'

She and Karl left, taking Abigail with them, but no sooner had they left than Gideon arrived. She hadn't seen him since they'd all given their statements to Molina's second-in-command.

Five agents were dead: four SWAT members and Agent Schumacher. All shot by DJ Belmont. Who was still out there, free as a damn bird.

She hadn't really allowed herself to think about DJ yet. She didn't have the mental energy now, so she shoved thoughts of him into the box in her mind and visualized herself hammering down the lid. One thing at a time. Deal with Amos first, and then she could focus on DJ, because the bastard was still out there and he would be back. But not tonight, at least. The FBI had posted guards in the ICU, so she didn't have to worry that DJ could get to them. For now, she could just worry about the people she loved.

Poor Gideon hadn't been allowed that luxury. Molina's second-in-command had kept asking questions about DJ and had Gideon filling out paperwork for hours. He hadn't had a moment's peace.

'Hey,' she said to Gideon. 'You want to sit here?' she asked, pointing to her cushioned chair, because her brother looked just awful, his face drawn and haggard.

He pulled up a plastic chair and sank wearily into it. 'No, you sit. I can't stay long. I just wanted to see how he's doing.' He nodded toward Amos.

'The same. The doctor said that they were able to repair the damage to his artery, but they don't know if he has any nerve damage. It missed his spinal cord, thankfully. Another fraction of an inch and he'd be dead. They'll do more tests when he wakes up.'

Wake up, Amos.

Gideon blew out a breath. 'I swear, I thought he'd fired the shot that took out Ephraim. The last thing I said to him was to accuse him of shooting that SOB.'

'He'll understand,' Mercy said, confident of that, if nothing else. 'How is Molina?'

'Hurting,' Gideon murmured. 'She'll be out for at least a few months. He shot her in the leg and nicked a bone. And she's angry.' He winced. 'But not at us. Not really. She's pissed off that we took you with us to Dunsmuir, but we gave her all the information as we received it, so we'll probably just get smacks on the wrist – Tom and me, I mean. She's mostly angry because she's in pain. And that DJ got the drop on them. And wants to know where he was trained.'

'Where *was* he trained?' Mercy asked quietly. 'He took out eight federal agents, Gideon. Molina and two of the SWAT guys will live, but he incapacitated them. He killed five agents.' He'd shot them all with a sniper rifle, apparently from the trees. 'He had to have been trained by someone. He isn't a mercenary with any large organization, because he can't leave Eden, except when he makes deliveries.' *Oh.* 'He's making deliveries to drug dealers. Did he learn how to shoot like that from them?'

Gideon looked impressed. 'Nice job. I think that's exactly where he learned his skills. He knew enough to aim for the exposed area of the neck, because Molina and the SWAT team were wearing tactical armor. Same with Schumacher. And Amos.'

And me. He was aiming for me.

Nope. Not thinking about that. Shove it into the box. 'It doesn't explain how he knew we'd be there, though.'

Rafe stirred in the recliner. 'He had to have been tracking Ephraim,' he said with a yawn. 'He made sure he killed Ephraim before he started on the rest of us. Well, after he stopped Molina and the SWAT team.'

Mercy shuddered at the thought of Amos lying on the ground, bleeding. So much blood. 'Thank goodness for Daisy. If she hadn't shot him, he might have killed all of us.'

'She's upset that she didn't kill him,' Gideon said wearily. 'She's afraid he'll be back and she's right. But he's gone for today. We'll have to regroup and manage security, though. But I'm going to let the Bureau handle it for now. I'm too tired.' He rubbed his temples. 'But you're right, Rafe. DJ was tracking Ephraim. The Escalade that Ephraim was using had a tracker stuck to the under-carriage.'

'How did DJ get a tracker on Ephraim's vehicle?' Mercy asked. 'And how did he get an Escalade?'

Gideon sighed. 'The Escalade belonged to Belinda Franklin's doctor. Police found him dead in his home. Broken neck, same as Ephraim's other victims. Ephraim's prints were on a coffee cup in the doctor's house, so he was definitely there, but we don't yet know how DJ connects.'

Mercy couldn't think about how close they'd come to losing Farrah, André, and Damien, so she shoved that fear into the box, too. Hammered the lid. *Focus on facts, not fear.* 'But that means DJ knew Ephraim would be visiting the doctor at his home.'

'We recovered the doctor's cell phone,' Gideon said. 'It'll take a little time to unlock it, but we've got software to do the job. We'll figure out who called him and when.'

'What about the safe-deposit box?' Mercy asked. 'The key I got from Ephraim's mother.'

Gideon's grin was feral. 'We got the warrant and will be opening the box first thing in the morning. I'll let you know as soon as one of them tells me what's in it.' His grin became a scowl. 'I'm officially not permitted to even be in the room when they search the contents of the safe-deposit box. I'm too close to the case. Had to recuse myself. Again.'

'So what will you do?' Rafe asked. 'Go back to work and try to find someone to leak you info?'

'Yes,' Gideon said simply, then smiled when Rafe snorted. 'Seriously, someone will give me the basics on what they find. In the meantime, I'm going back to my normal job, translating chatter, but I'll keep my ears open for mentions of psilocybin sales.'

Mercy leaned forward in her chair to lightly clasp Amos's hand. 'Thanks for that tip, Amos. We owe you one for that.'

'Yeah, thank you,' Gideon said gruffly. 'And I'm sorry that I thought you killed Ephraim.' He sighed heavily. 'And thank you for saving Mercy. For that I owe you everything.'

Mercy rested her head on Gideon's upper arm. 'I owe everybody,' she said lightly, 'because all of you have saved me at least once.'

Rafe met her eyes across Amos's bed and gave her a slow wink. 'Worth it.'

Gideon hesitated, then hugged Mercy to his side, hard enough to make her wince. 'Worth it,' he whispered. 'I'm so damn glad you're here.' He cleared his throat. 'You too, Amos. I'm glad you left Eden. I'm glad you got Abigail out. I'm glad you're with us. So . . . don't go anywhere, okay? And, just so you know, we will make sure Abigail is safe and cared for until you get out of here.'

Mercy leaned up to kiss Gideon's cheek. 'That was sweet.'

Gideon tightened his hold on Mercy until she let out a little yelp, then abruptly let her go, looking a little embarrassed. 'I'm sorry. You two should get some sleep. Like in a real bed, not in hospital chairs. I'm headed out now. You should, too. Rafe's place is less than ten minutes from here. If Amos wakes up, they'll call you.'

Mercy stroked Amos's hand lightly. 'I don't want him to wake up alone.'

'But if you get sick because you're not sleeping, the ICU won't let you in at all,' Rafe commented.

Gideon gave him a less than discreet thumbs-up. 'Good point. Mercy?'

Mercy rose reluctantly. Rafe really did need to sleep in a real bed. 'All right. But if the nurses call, you have to agree to bring me back, even if you were sleeping. Unless you're okay with me taking an Uber.' Because the only car they actually had left at this point was Sasha's Mini. All of their other vehicles had been taken into evidence or destroyed by Ephraim. They'd get Rafe's Subaru and Gideon's Suburban back in a few days, but for now they were dependent on others. Considering the DJ threat, it would probably be the FBI they depended on for a little while longer at least. The Uber was really a joke.

By the way both Gideon and Rafe glared at her, they didn't think the joke was very funny.

'No Uber,' Rafe said, grabbing the aluminum cane he was using once again, his second wooden cane having been taken as evidence. 'But I will wake up to come with you, however we get here.'

Mercy leaned over the bed rail and pressed a kiss to Amos's forehead. 'Wake up soon, Papa,' she said softly. 'Abigail needs you. So do I.'

Gideon brushed a hand over Mercy's hair. 'Daisy's with Molina. I'll get her, then we can go.'

Sacramento, California
Thursday, 20 April, 1.40 A.M.

Mercy hung her coat in Rafe's closet wearily. Molina's temporary replacement had arranged protection for them, but it had taken the agent a while to arrive. Now he sat outside on the curb, keeping watch. Because of fucking DJ.

Mercy still couldn't think of DJ Belmont or she might shatter into a million little pieces. Instead she focused on the small things that she could control. 'I want to eat your mother's food. And then I want a long hot shower with soap that doesn't smell like a hospital, and then I want to sleep for two or three days.'

Rafe dropped onto the sofa, pale with exhaustion. 'I like that plan. I'll microwave the leftovers.'

'No, you stay put. I'll stick a casserole in the oven and then I need to wash my hair again.'

His grimace said that he understood. Rafe's sister Meg had been their savior, stopping by Rafe's to get them clean clothes while they'd waited in the hospital. The hospital had allowed them to shower because they'd all been wearing some of Ephraim's brain matter. Mercy was overjoyed that Ephraim was dead, she just wished that it had been less . . . nauseating.

Mercy picked a casserole from the fridge at random and put it in the oven, hoping her appetite would hold steady. It had been iffy all evening, plummeting every time she remembered the sight of Ephraim's body.

Poor Farrah. They'd had to stop the SUV several times on the way back to Sacramento so that she could throw up, a combination of the trauma of being kidnapped and held at gunpoint and, of course, witnessing Ephraim's grisly end.

And me? Mercy turned on the shower and took off her clothing. The police had taken the clothes she'd worn upstate, which was fine. She'd never wear them again. If she ever got them back, maybe she'd burn them in some kind of cleansing ritual.

Ephraim was dead. *And I'm not sorry.*

She'd nearly killed him herself. *And I'm not sorry.*

Maybe she should be. *But I'm not.*

She got under the shower spray, shivering when the warm water hit her skin. She'd been so cold. So damn cold. And tired.

And scared.

'I'm still scared,' she said quietly.

'Me too.' The shower door opened, and then Rafe was staring at her like he'd never seen her before. 'Is it too pushy to ask if I can join you?'

'No,' she whispered, then repeated it louder when he didn't hear her. 'No. The water's nice.'

Rafe's clothes went into a pile next to hers. 'The hot water helps my leg.'

'Then I'll give you the spray.' She moved out of his way, but he was having none of that.

Leaning against the shower wall, he pulled her into his arms and buried his face against her neck. 'I don't even know how to feel,' he said quietly.

She flattened her palms against the muscles of his back, sweeping up and down, just needing to touch him. That they were wet and naked and that he had the hottest body she'd ever seen was really . . . secondary. 'Me either. I'm scared. And sad. And furious.' For a moment they stood there, saying nothing, and then she sighed. 'What if Amos doesn't wake up?'

'He will,' Rafe said stubbornly. 'He'll fight to come back to Abigail. And to you and Gideon.'

'If,' she whispered. 'The doctors said "if" he woke up. If he doesn't, who will take care of Abigail?'

'My mom will,' Rafe said without hesitation.

'Or . . . I could.'

He pulled back enough to see her face, turning them around so that his back blocked the spray from hitting her face. 'You could,' he said, pushing the hair out of her eyes. 'Do you want to?'

She nodded. She'd been thinking about Abigail the entire time that Molina's replacement had been scolding them. 'I do. I mean, I know what Abigail has heard her whole life. I know what she'll be facing, relearning . . . And she's not blood, but she's still my sister.'

His lips curved. 'And you said you didn't know how to do relationships.'

She didn't smile back. 'I don't. That's why I'm scared.'

'Mom does. I do. You'll have a lot of help.' He stopped talking then, pursing his lips.

'What?'

He reached for a bottle of shampoo that Daisy had left behind and started lathering her hair, making her hum contentedly.

'This must be how Rory and Jack-Jack feel when I pet them,' she murmured. She leaned her forehead against his chest, closing her eyes to fully enjoy the feel of his hands in her hair, massaging her scalp. 'You should charge for shampoos. You'd have a line out the door.'

'Nah. Unless you're okay with other people seeing me naked.'

She jerked her gaze to his, then flinched when soap got in her eyes. Irritated, she wiped it away. 'Um, no. I find that I'm adamantly opposed to anyone seeing you naked.' She hummed again when he turned them around to rinse the shampoo from her hair, because he covered her eyes. Like her mama had done.

No one had taken care of her like this since she was a little girl, too young to truly appreciate how special it was.

She smiled up at him when he put the conditioner in her hair. 'You're good at this.'

'I've never done this for anyone before,' he admitted.

'That makes me even luckier. Going back to my question before you tried to distract me with scalp massages – what? You said I'd have a lot of help, then looked like you'd sucked a lemon.'

He sighed, shampooing his hair in about ten seconds. 'You'd have help from us. But we're *here*.'

'Oh.' Now she got it. 'The Romeros would love her, too. And they love me.'

He kissed her forehead. 'Maybe you're borrowing trouble. Amos will wake up.'

'But even then, I wouldn't see Abigail grow up.' *If I go back.* After the last few days, she wasn't so certain.

'But you have all your siblings' kids when you go back to New Orleans.' His smile was lopsided and sad. 'It'll be a hard choice.'

No, not really, she thought. Because Rafe would be here. 'I have a plan.'

He kissed her. 'What's your plan?'

'The Romeros have moved Quill's life celebration to Sunday afternoon. I'll go back to New Orleans for that and I'll pack a few things while I'm there, then I'll come back here for the rest of my leave. I have to get therapy as a condition of my return, but I could do that here, too. Let's take these seven and a half weeks and then . . .' She shrugged. 'Then we can see.'

He swallowed, his brown eyes filled with a mix of longing and hope that stole her breath. 'You're considering staying? Even after?'

'Yes. I'm not stupid, Raphael Sokolov. What you and I have here is something special. Gideon is here and now Amos. I love

567

my families in New Orleans, but Gideon, Amos, and I – and now Abigail – we have history. Shared memories. And then there's you.'

'Then there's me.' His brows lifted. 'What will you do about me?'

She laughed. '*That* is a leading question, Detective Sokolov. Give me some time, I'll make you a list. But for now? I want to go to bed with you and make you forget about this day for a little while. Is that okay?'

'More than okay.'

He kissed her again, long and sweet. 'I'll go to New Orleans with you, if you want. For Quill's celebration.'

'You'd do that for me?'

'Not much I wouldn't do for you,' he said lightly, but the intensity in his eyes spoke differently. 'I'll still be on DB for the next two months at least. We can take all the time we need to figure this out.' He hesitated, then shifted his weight so that his injured leg was in the hot spray. 'I might not be a detective anymore.'

She wanted to apologize, but bit the words back. That wasn't what he needed. She kissed his chin, then rose on her toes to kiss his mouth. 'I know. Maybe we can figure out some other options for you, just in case. You know . . . together.'

It was the right thing to say, because he sagged against the tile, his eyes closing, relief stamped on his handsome face. 'Yeah.' He swallowed hard. 'Together. I like that.' He reached behind her to turn off the water.

'Hey,' she protested. 'I wasn't done.'

'We would have been standing in ice water in about four seconds.'

'Oh. Good to know. You know, for that list I'll be making for all the things I want to do with you. Long showers probably won't be on it.' She opened the shower door and grabbed two towels from the rack. 'Dry off and get into bed. I'll get us food. And then we sleep. There will be time to start worrying about everything when we wake up.'

Sacramento, California
Thursday, 20 April, 12.15 P.M.

Reality intruded sometime after noon, with a loud knocking on the door. Rafe lifted his head from the pillow with a groan. He was already awake and contemplating waking Mercy the way she'd woken him before dawn – by kissing every inch of her body. He did not want to entertain any visitors.

Curled up against him, Mercy stirred. 'What is it?'

He scowled. 'Somebody's at the door.'

The knocking started again. 'Open up, Rafe!'

He groaned again. 'It's Sasha.'

'I brought food!' she hollered. 'Oh, hi, Gideon,' she said loudly enough for them to hear. 'I brought enough for everyone, but brother dear won't open the door. I've got a key, Rafe!'

'Don't you dare!' Rafe shouted back. 'Give me a minute.'

Mercy sat up in the bed, beautifully naked, which Rafe loved. But her hair was going every which direction. Rafe thought it was damn adorable but somehow he knew that she wouldn't agree, so he kept that thought to himself.

'I'll get it,' she said, treating him to a wonderful view when she bent over her suitcase to pull out clean clothes.

'Sasha spoils everything,' he muttered, making Mercy laugh.

'She did bring food.' In less than thirty seconds Mercy had covered all that pretty naked skin with jeans and a turtleneck sweater. 'Coming, Sasha,' she called when Sasha started knocking again. She threw Rafe a pair of sweats and pulled the silk screen so that he had some privacy.

'Hey, Mercy? You should check a mirror before you open the door.'

A muted shriek met his ears. Mercy marched back to her bag, glared at him, found a brush, and dragged it through her hair, muttering about going to bed with wet hair. Then she opened the door. 'Sasha,' she said in a singsong.

'Mercy,' Sasha sang back. 'Is he decent?'

'Not remotely,' Rafe called from the bed, struggling with the sweats. But he could smell chicken and waffles and his stomach growled. He looked at his chest and decided a shirt would be a good idea. He was pretty sure that Mercy wouldn't appreciate him showing off the line of small bruises she'd left while kissing down his chest during the night.

That had been a pleasant way to wake up and he'd had plans for more of the same. And then Sasha showed up.

He put on a T-shirt, grappled for the cane that had rolled out of reach, then rounded the silk screen to find that Gideon and Daisy had joined them. Mercy was setting the small dinette and Sasha was unpacking the food she'd brought. It was a tight fit with just the five of them.

Rafe added finding a larger place without stairs to his mental to-do list. Right after brainstorming new careers.

It should have felt really shitty, but as he watched Mercy moving around his little kitchen like she belonged there . . . She'd said that she'd consider staying. *That we're special.*

Suddenly the thought of changing careers was much less terrifying than it had been yesterday.

'How's the leg?' Gideon asked.

Rafe shrugged as he lowered himself into the dinette chair. 'Hurts. I need to make an appointment with my doctor. And I've got Cash this afternoon. I missed two appointments this week, so it was going to hurt a little anyway.'

Mercy's mouth opened and Rafe pointed to her. 'Do not say you're sorry,' he said. 'That I forgot about my appointment so that we could go to Snowbush had nothing to do with you, and there was no way I was going to go to therapy yesterday with all that happened. Now, what are you feeding me, Sasha?'

'Chicken and waffles from the Forty-niner Diner,' Sasha said.

'My favorite,' Daisy said, digging in. 'What?' she asked, when the rest of them snickered. 'I've been up since five and already had my workday while you guys were snoring.' She lifted a brow at Rafe. 'Or something.'

Gideon winced. 'Can we not go there?'

Mercy laughed. 'Fine.' She quickly checked her phone, her smile fading. Which meant either no news about Amos or bad news.

'Well?' Rafe asked.

'No news at all,' Mercy said. 'I'm going to call the hospital really quickly, just in case he's awake and they're too busy to text me.' She dropped a kiss on Rafe's cheek and went into the hall to call.

Gideon watched her go. 'Part of me doesn't want her to go near the door, with that stained glass. It's not bullet-resistant. But that's overbearing, right?'

Daisy chuckled. 'Right,' she said around a mouthful of chicken. 'Especially since there's a Fed on the curb. Where are Farrah and André?'

'At Mom's,' Rafe said. 'Mom wanted to keep an eye on them until the sedative was all out of André's system. They'll be coming back here later to pack.'

'They're here,' Mercy said, coming back into the apartment, Farrah and André on her heels. And following them was Tom Hunter, who'd apparently driven them from the Sokolovs' house.

Luckily Sasha had brought plenty of food, because they had none left by the time they'd all eaten their fill.

'That was so good,' Mercy moaned, and Rafe wished everyone were gone so he could hear her moan like that again, but kicking them out would be rude, so he gritted his teeth.

And gave Sasha the finger when she smirked at him.

Tom put his napkin down. 'So. I know some things now.'

Everyone stopped talking. 'Like?' Mercy prompted.

'Like what's in that safe-deposit box,' Tom said. 'The box held a spiral notebook, handwritten. Two different writers – Ephraim and Edward. Or Harry and Aubrey, if you prefer. It was a list of all the things they'd done – in Eden and before. But it wasn't just a detail of the brothers' activities. The sins of Pastor and Waylon were noted as well. In graphic detail.'

'Why?' Farrah asked. 'Why would they write that down?'

'It's a dead man's switch,' André said, 'or an insurance policy. If one of them gets killed mysteriously, the records will be shared, usually with the newspaper or law enforcement. It's a way to keep order among the criminals. Otherwise they would have turned on each other years ago.'

'Which is why Belinda Franklin said she hadn't used the key,' Mercy murmured. 'She said her baby was dead, but she didn't use the key. Because Aubrey wasn't killed by one of the other Founders.'

Gideon's mouth tightened and Daisy hooked her hand around his arm, pressing a kiss to his biceps. 'I'm glad he's dead,' she said fiercely, but Gideon's gaze flicked to Mercy before looking away.

'Gideon. Look at me.' Mercy leaned across the table to grab a handful of his sleeve, yanking until he met her eyes. 'Now listen to me. I'm glad you killed him. I'm glad you got away. And if I'd known the truth back then, I still would have been happy you got away.'

Gideon swallowed hard. 'But you didn't get away.'

Inclining her head, she let go of his sleeve and clasped his hand. 'Yes, I did. Eventually. And it was awful, I'm not gonna lie. But I'm also not lying when I say that had I known then what I know now, I still would have been glad. Now wrap your mind around that, because it's the truth and until we put this behind us, we can't move forward.'

Gideon's mouth twitched up at the corners. 'Yes, ma'am.'

Mercy gave him a hard nod. 'All right, then. Tom, what else did the notebooks say?'

Tom cleared his throat, his expression momentarily shaken by the exchange. Rafe knew how he felt. He loved Gideon like a brother, and Mercy . . . well, not like a sister at all. The two had suffered so much and Rafe desperately wanted to make them okay, but all he could do was be there for them.

And help them track down the assholes who'd hurt them. *One down, two to go.*

Tom squared his jaw, a determined gleam in his eyes, and Rafe had the feeling that this guy was going to be key in taking Eden down.

'All right,' Tom said, having regained his composure. 'The parts you need to know at this point are that Pastor and Waylon met at Terminal Island Federal Correctional Institution. Pastor was arrested as Benton Travis for forgery and money laundering, and that does appear to be his real name. He met Waylon in prison, just as you suspected. They were, according to Aubrey Franklin, running drugs in the prison. Aubrey came along a little later and they became friends, so when Aubrey botched the bank robbery, he reached out. Waylon and Pastor had already fled to the first Eden site. They gave Aubrey a very rudimentary map, which Ephraim re-created in the notebook, so in time, we may be able to find that first site.'

'Why would you want to?' Mercy asked. 'They aren't there any longer.'

'But Amos said that they reuse locations, so maybe they'll go back,' Gideon said, clearly excited. 'What else don't we yet know?'

'That Pastor transferred all the money he was given by his new members to offshore accounts, which, again, is something we suspected, but they've been sitting on that money for *thirty years*. The money was to be split between the "Founding Elders".'

'Who were Pastor, Waylon, Ephraim, and Edward,' Gideon said.

Tom shook his head. 'Apparently there was a fifth Founding Elder. Ephraim wrote about him in the notebook. Called him "Doc". Said he died three years after they started the community, but that he was really old, so no one suspected foul play.'

'That's news to me,' Gideon said, 'but I arrived a few years after that. I never heard him mentioned. But back to the money. How do you know that they've been sitting on it? They could have spent it.'

Tom shook his head. 'Not according to Ephraim Burton. He visited the box regularly to make updates in the notebook, using his Eustace Carmelo ID. The last time he updated his record was about six months ago. Pastor had shown them the ledger and their account had grown to more than fifty million dollars. With Waylon and Aubrey gone, the money would be split between Pastor, DJ, and Ephraim.'

Mercy gasped, and she wasn't alone. 'Fifty *million*?'

Rafe whistled quietly. 'That is one helluva motive for Ephraim and DJ to want to kill each other.'

'Especially since DJ obviously lied about my death,' Mercy said, still shaking her head in disbelief at the amount the founders had hoarded. 'Once Ephraim found out, he had leverage on DJ. All Ephraim needed was to haul me back to Eden and DJ would've been toast.'

Rafe sucked in a breath so sharp that it hurt. 'Sonofabitch.'

'And all DJ needed was for Ephraim to be dead so he couldn't tell,' Gideon said grimly.

'We would have been icing on the cake, Gideon,' Mercy said. 'Still might be. As long as I'm alive, I'm a risk to his position. I mean, it's only a big deal if Pastor finds out, I guess, but DJ has to know now that we'll be actively looking for Eden. Fifty million is a lot of reasons to keep us quiet.'

Farrah's eyes narrowed in dismay. 'Mercy Callahan. Don't talk like that.'

Rafe's blood went ice cold. 'We need a safe house for you.' He'd thought about it the night before, but he'd been too tired to articulate it to Mercy, knowing she'd be resistant. But his fear from the day before returned and he blurted it out in a rush.

Mercy reached for Farrah's hand while shaking her head sadly. 'No. I know you want us to be safe, but we could hide forever and he could wait us out. That's not living, Rafe. I've come too far to hide now. What we need is to find Eden and stop DJ and Pastor. And then set everyone in Eden free.'

She was right. He knew that she was, even as the chicken and waffles churned in his gut. He'd finally found her. He couldn't lose her now. But locking her away wasn't the answer, either. 'Then let's find Eden.'

Tom nodded once. 'That's my job.'

His dismissive tone had Rafe biting back a *Hell, no.*

Gideon sat up straighter, frowning. 'Not just your job, Tom.'

'But technically not your job, Gideon,' Mercy pointed out. 'You recused yourself, remember?'

Gideon frowned. 'I know, but . . .' He sighed. 'You're right. Why do you have to be right?'

'It doesn't happen often,' she said dryly. 'Let me have my moment.'

Gideon chuckled. 'What can we do to help you, Tom?'

Tom rose from the table, smoothing his tie. 'Stay alive. Be there when I need answers to Eden questions and *stay alive*. Be careful. Be aware. Don't take chances and don't go anywhere where you're out in the open. Like Snowbush. For now you'll have protection. But I can't guarantee how long that'll last, and the new guy isn't promising one way or the other. He's just keeping Molina's seat warm.' He lifted a brow at Gideon. 'Or so I've been told.'

Gideon coughed. 'Yes, I said that. I'd prefer that the acting special agent in charge doesn't hear that I did, though.'

Tom chuckled. 'My lips are sealed.'

'But we will get updates on the regular?' Rafe asked, annoyed to be sidelined. He'd thought Hunter was on their side. *And when did I regress to being a little kid? There are no sides. There's justice for Mercy and Gideon, and that's it.* 'You won't do the "my lips are sealed" over that, too?'

Tom smiled. 'I might get chatty if I was filled up with your mother's cooking.'

Rafe smiled back, mollified. 'Consider yourself invited every Sunday at two. Bring Liza.'

'She'll like that.' Tom pushed his chair neatly beneath the table. 'I've got to go. Text me when Amos wakes up? He's a good guy.'

Mercy walked him out, again like she belonged here, and that made Rafe smile. He was still smiling when she came back and sat beside him. 'What?' she asked.

'He's besotted,' Farrah said with a happy laugh. There were still shadows in her eyes, but that was to be expected. She'd suffered a near-death experience the day before. André looked slightly better, but Rafe knew they needed to get back to New Orleans, where family could help them heal.

'And if I am?' Rafe asked her, completely okay with being besotted.

Farrah became serious. 'Then I'm happy. I'd be happier if you lived in New Orleans, but . . .'

Mercy cleared her throat, hesitant. 'I'm going back for Quill's celebration. Rafe said he'd go with me.'

'I'll go, too,' Gideon said. 'I want to meet Farrah's family. And of course John and the others.'

'And then you're all coming back here, including Mercy,' Farrah said calmly. She squeezed Mercy's hand. 'I figured that out already. It's okay, Mercy. I understand.' She smiled then, and it was a true smile that brightened her eyes. 'You'll come back to see me, because we're having a big family. You know that you're going to be a godmother eventually.'

André's eyes widened. 'She is? I mean, we are?' His deep voice actually squeaked. 'When?'

'Not now, thank God. That would be really bad timing with that bastard causing us all this stress.' Farrah shook her head. 'But soon, okay?'

André looked at her like she was the moon and all the stars. 'More than okay.'

Mercy wiped her eyes. 'Darn it, Farrah. You had to go and make me cry.'

'But good tears,' Farrah said smugly.

Mercy laughed. 'Very good tears. Now, once Amos wakes up, everything will be perfect.'

Epilogue

Karl Sokolov tapped a spoon to his glass of sparkling cider. 'I'd like to make a toast.'

Rafe was so happy that he didn't groan – not even on the inside. His father was one for toasting and typically embarrassed whoever was unlucky enough to be the toastee, but he knew his father wouldn't embarrass Mercy. *Maybe me, but not Mercy.*

In six weeks she'd wrapped his father around her little finger, and Rafe loved it. He loved her. He hadn't said the words yet, but they battled for freedom every damn day. At first he'd resisted because he didn't want to rush her, but now he was waiting for the perfect moment. Because she deserved every bit of perfection he could muster.

'I'm going to need a chair,' Damien muttered. 'Move over, Meggie.'

Meg gave him a shove. 'Get your own chair.'

Because it was standing room only in the Sokolov kitchen this day. Karl glared at Damien and Meg and they stopped bickering. 'Sorry,' they muttered together, as if they were their kids' age and not grown-ass adults.

'We're all gathered here today,' Karl began, 'to celebrate our Mercy's birthday.' He paused to let the hoots and hollers die down, smiling down at Mercy, who was blushing beet red and looking very flustered.

And very cute, but Rafe allowed that he might be biased.

'We've waited a long time to welcome you into our family,' Karl went on, 'and we couldn't be happier that you're here. We adopted Gideon years ago, so now we have a matched set.'

Mercy laughed and half covered her face with one hand. Rafe pulled it away from her face and kissed her palm.

'Besotted,' Farrah said, rolling her eyes. She and André had arrived the evening before, surprising the hell out of Mercy when Rafe had led her into his parents' house, blindfolded. But it hadn't just been Farrah and André. Mama Romero and half the Romero clan had shown up.

So had John Benz, his family, and three more of the 'sibs'. The others hadn't been able to make the cross-country trip but were tuning in via Skype. Rafe had met them all and liked them. Gideon and Daisy had too, and for Gideon it meant being immediately engulfed in more family than he'd been able to handle. At that first reunion, Rafe had taken his friend off to the side, standing with him while Gideon watched his new family, overwhelmed and cuddling Brutus while trying not to cry.

Rafe had been so damn happy for Gideon that he'd been the one to cry. Which Mercy had thought was precious and had earned him some very hot sex when they'd returned to her apartment to pack her things.

Because she'd moved to Sacramento. She'd really done it, quitting her job with NOPD and applying for a position in the SacPD crime lab. She started work on July first and she couldn't wait.

'Not only do we welcome Mercy, though,' Karl said, 'we welcome her family as well. All the "sibs", the Romeros, and Amos and Abigail.'

Amos bobbed his head, smiling, his arm around Abigail. Amos had woken up after a few days and they'd all been thankful that there had been no permanent damage caused by DJ's bullet. Amos was still weaker than he wanted to be, but he'd put himself to work, rehabbing the fixer-upper that Rafe had bought around the corner from his Victorian.

It was a two-story and one of the first things Rafe and Amos had done was to install an elevator. Rafe continued physical therapy, but he'd come to accept that it was unlikely he'd gain back enough range of motion to return to the force. At least as a homicide detective. Some days were harder than others, but he'd signed up with Tom's old therapist and it was helping. He hadn't lost hope and was keeping busy. He and Mercy had joined Karl and Irina in a few of their fundraising ventures.

In the meantime, he and Amos had made a lot of progress in a few short weeks. The man was a master carpenter and would be able to command top prices anywhere in the city, but for now, he was fixing up a home for his daughter. For Mercy.

And in exchange for labor, Amos and Abigail had taken over the top floor of Rafe's Victorian. They'd gotten Abigail a puppy, so her life was pretty complete.

'Are you finished, Karl?' Irina asked, poised to strike a match and light the candles on Mercy's cake.

'Almost, *maya lubimaya*,' Karl said with a sweet smile. 'I can't forget Tom and Liza.'

Rafe almost laughed out loud at that. His father had a serious crush on Tom Hunter, the former basketball pro. Karl was all sports, always, so having a pro in their midst made him as giggly as Abigail with her puppy.

Tom shook his head, looking embarrassed. Liza looked . . . sad, and Rafe made a mental note to talk to her. They'd gotten to know the younger woman fairly well over the last few weeks. She almost never missed Sunday dinner and seemed to thrive on the family atmosphere.

They knew she was originally from Minneapolis, that she'd served in Afghanistan, that she was going to study nursing at UC Davis starting in July, and that she had an adoptive family of her own back in Chicago, but none of them understood the relationship between Tom and Liza. The two claimed to be 'just friends', but Rafe wasn't buying it.

'And,' Karl said dramatically, 'we also welcome Geri and Jeff.' He turned to Jeff's mother. 'Geri, you are welcome anytime.'

'Dad!' Zoya whined, but Jeff Bunker shook his head and laughed.

'You know I'm kidding, Zoya,' Karl said fondly. 'I don't think Jeff is in any danger from any of us.'

'For now,' Rafe said darkly, but it was an act. Mostly. Bunker had proven himself to be a smart guy with a truly soft heart. 'Just . . . you know.'

'Rafe,' Zoya hissed.

Jeff faked a shudder. 'I know. Touch your sister and you'll break my fingers, yada yada yada.' He held up both hands. 'I'm not touching.'

'I know,' Zoya grumbled.

Rafe laughed. 'Finish your toast, Dad. Mom's about to light herself on fire with those matches.'

Irina shot him a withering look and Rafe sank down in his chair, but he was unable to hide his grin. 'You are the one to watch yourself, *sinok rodnoy moi.*'

'Ooh.' Mercy elbowed him. 'She three-named you. With sarcasm even.'

Sasha cleared her throat loudly and pointed to Erin, who scowled back at her.

'And Erin,' Karl said. 'Although I feel like you were part of our family before, because of your friendship with Rafe. However, now we welcome you as *nashe dochke.*'

Sasha gulped audibly, turning to Erin to whisper-shout, 'Daughter.'

Erin turned four shades of purple and her eyes filled with tears, but she nodded her thanks.

Karl lifted his glass. 'Assuming I have forgotten no one . . . To us – the family we're born into, the family we make, and the family we collect along the way. And happy birthday to Mercy!'

Irina lit the candles and put the cake in front of Mercy, who looked a little alarmed. 'I can't blow that much.'

To which the entire family, except for poor Abigail and the younger grandkids, died laughing.

'Oh my God,' Farrah gasped, fanning herself. 'Merciful heavens, Mercy.'

Too late, Mercy realized what she'd said, and she closed her eyes and muttered a Russian curse that made Irina start laughing again.

'Blow out your candles, Mercy. I can see my children have been adding to your vocabulary.'

'Nope,' Mercy said cheerfully. 'I learned that one from Karl.'

'Hey,' Karl protested, then shrugged. 'Yeah, it was me.'

Mercy gripped Rafe's hand, then blew out the candles with one huge breath.

Rafe leaned in to whisper in her ear, 'You're really good at blowing things. Out.' He laughed when she elbowed him harder. 'I said *out*.'

'So who wants cake?' Mercy asked. 'Everyone but Rafe? Okay.'

Rafe had to kiss her for that, because he was so damn happy that he needed to let some of it out or he'd bust. 'Can I have cake now?' he asked when she broke the kiss to breathe.

'No,' she said, even as she cut him a slice. 'Now leave me to cut this cake in peace.'

Quitting while he was ahead, Rafe grabbed his plate and his cane and moved to the back of the room where he could watch Mercy . . . glow.

He wasn't very surprised, though, when Tom Hunter joined him. The man had been trying to ask him something all afternoon, but one of them kept getting pulled into another conversation.

'What's up?' Rafe asked. 'Is Liza okay?'

Tom shrugged. 'You'd have to ask her.'

Ouch. Okay. Rafe backed away from that little bomb. 'What did you want to talk to me about?'

Tom looked relieved. 'I was wondering if you'd considered going into the private sector.'

Rafe frowned up at him, confused. 'Like . . . what?'

'Like private investigating.'

'Sure. Of course I have. But I've been advised not to make any huge career shifts for a little while longer.' It had been his therapist's suggestion and it had felt right to Rafe. He'd regained more flexibility and balance, and thankfully the pain was less, but he had a long way to go, both physically and mentally. 'Why?'

'Because I have need of a PI.'

Rafe gave Tom his full attention. 'Is it Eden?'

Tom huffed a mirthless laugh. 'What else might it be?'

Excitement sent a shiver down Rafe's spine. 'Did you find them?'

'Not yet, but we're close. If you're interested in hearing more, we can meet tomorrow. Somewhere quiet.'

'And Mercy?'

'Don't mention it to her for now. I don't expect you'll keep it quiet forever, but for now keep it to yourself. Let her enjoy her birthday.'

And didn't that sound peachy? 'Is she in danger?'

'Not to my knowledge. Tomorrow?'

'Send me a time and place. I'll be there.'

'Thanks. Now I'm going to get some cake.'

Rafe watched Tom amble back to the table and give Mercy a kiss on the cheek. Irina took the cake knife and shooed Mercy away from the table to 'keep Raphael company'.

'I've been dismissed,' Mercy said with a chuckle. 'What was that about? You and Tom?'

'I don't know,' Rafe answered honestly. 'I asked him about Liza and he kind of blew me off.'

Her brow lifted. 'I think we're done with blowing things off and out.'

Rafe snorted. 'Off, yes. Out, yes. Other blowing? Not a chance that we're done.'

She lifted on her toes to peck his lips. 'Cake's good.'

'Did you get any?'

'I licked my fingers.' She demonstrated, sucking on all of her fingers, and he groaned.

'You're killing me here, Mercy.'

'Good. You deserve it.'

She was looking up at him with unfettered . . . something. More than fondness. More than affection. It was time.

'I love you,' he whispered.

Her mouth fell open, then curved in a smile that was both wicked and sweet. 'And I love you. I was wondering when I could tell you.'

'I kind of figured it out myself.' He set the plate on a countertop and cupped her cheek. 'I'm so glad you're here, Mercy Callahan. In this house and in my life.'

'I'm happy to be here. With you.'

They just smiled at each other, with no passionate kisses, no clawing at clothes. Just joy.

'Thank you,' he said. 'For being willing to leave everything behind for me.'

She kissed him then, slow but chaste. 'I left nothing behind. I added on, like your father said. But if it came down to either everything or you, I would have left it all behind.'

He slid his arm around her waist and pulled her close, so that they leaned against the wall watching their families merge.

Mercy rested her head on his shoulder. 'We are going to need to start Christmas cards soon.'

He looked down at her. 'It's May.'

She waved a hand at all the people. 'Look at this list. I hope you have good penmanship, because I'm not writing all those cards myself.'

He wasn't going to complain. 'Together. We'll do it together.'